THE FACULTY OF
USELESS KNOWLEDGE

Yury Dombrovsky

THE FACULTY OF
USELESS KNOWLEDGE

Translated from the Russian by Alan Myers

THE HARVILL PRESS

LONDON

First published in Russian in Paris 1978 by YMCA-Press

First published in Great Britain 1996 by
The Harvill Press
84 Thornhill Road
London N1 1RD

A CIP catalogue record for this title
is available from the British Library

This translation was published with the
financial support of the European Commission

ISBN 1 86046 054 4

Extract from Tacitus: *The Agricola* (chapter 3) on p.vii from the translation by
H. Mattingley (1948) revised by S. A. Handford (1978),
published by Penguin Books, Harmondsworth.
Translation © the Estate of H. Mattingley 1948, 1970.
© S. A. Handford 1970. Reprinted by permission.

Typeset in Linotron Ehrhardt by
Rowland Phototypesetting Ltd,
Bury St Edmunds, Suffolk
Printed and bound in Great Britain by
Butler and Tanner Ltd, Frome, Somerset

The author dedicates this book
to Anna Samoilovna Berzer
with profound gratitude
on behalf of himself and all others like him.

Now at long last our spirit revives . . . Yet our human nature is so weak that remedies take longer to work than diseases. Our bodies, which grow so slowly, perish in the twinkling of an eye; so too the mind and its pursuits can more easily be crushed than brought to life again. Idleness gradually develops a strange fascination of its own, and we end by loving the sloth that at first we loathed. Think of it. Fifteen whole years – no small part of a man's life – taken from us. Many have died by the chance happenings of fate: all the most energetic have fallen victims to the cruelty of the Leader. And the few of us that survive are no longer what we once were, since so many of our best years have been taken from us – years in which men in their prime have aged and old men have reached the extreme limit of mortality, without ever uttering a word.*

* Adapted by Dombrovsky from Tacitus: *The Agricola*, Chapter 3.

CONTENTS

And when they ask us what we're doing, you can say, We're remembering. That's where we'll win out in the long run. And some day we'll remember so much that we'll . . . dig the biggest grave of all time . . .

RAY BRADBURY

The new era differs from the old chiefly in that the lash begins to imagine itself possessed of genius.

KARL MARX

I

CHAPTER 1

THE ARCHAEOLOGISTS HAD been busily excavating, but dig as they might, they had turned up nothing. Meanwhile, August was drawing to a close: swift slanting rains came sweeping over the market stalls and gardens (it always rains in Alma-Ata at this time of year) and there could only be a month left for work at the very outside.

Nevertheless, it was still scorching during the daytime: the expedition's huge white Titan water boiler got too scalding hot to touch. If you went up the hill and spilled water out of your bucket, the pool evaporated on the spot, leaving the grey earth dry and impervious. One day a workman got genuine sunstroke and what a terrific commotion that caused! They ran to the medical centre at the collective farm and got a stretcher. It was propped up against the wall and when Zybin – the leader of the Kazakhstan Central Museum excavation – bent over it, he caught a whiff of iodoform and carbolic from the grey canvas which almost caused him to let go the handles. Out there was the orchard, the wind, the smell of herbs and apples, the glint and shimmer of leaves, their shadows sharp and black against the grass; here was a hospital and death.

Well, after that, everything proceeded apace – the patient was covered over with a shaggy green blanket and hauled off down below. There were pointless shouts from everybody: "Gently! Gently does it! Go easy with him then, he's a sick man!" They flagged down a five-tonner at the foot of the hill – all the vehicles come back empty from the rest homes at that time – lifted the stretcher carefully and placed it next to the engine, where it would get less of a shaking; at once, two young diggers leaped aboard with a flash of polished boots and seated themselves alongside. They had already contrived to clean and smarten themselves up somewhere and were well washed and combed. As for the working day of course, that was lost. They all dispersed around the orchard; some went on down to the stream and an accordion struck up in the bushes as a girl's voice began to bawl. The bawling was like it was at all the village get-togethers – a loud, shrill caterwauling.

3

"Ah, just listen to them," said Kornilov delightedly, lifting his soap-blinded head. "They're over the moon! Some workmen we've got ourselves, Georgi Nikolaevich, eh? Just the boys to dig up hidden treasure."

There were two of them. The expedition chief Zybin, and Kornilov the archaeologist. Both of them were standing over an icy mountain stream (this was the Alma-Atinka) with their white, litre jam tins, drenching themselves from head to foot.

"Oh, never mind them," said Zybin. "There's nothing left of the day anyway."

"That's right, blast it, the day's gone," Kornilov assented listlessly, subsiding into the current up to his shoulders. "But you know what that means, don't you?" he went on, scrambling out and snorting. "It means, doesn't it, that while we were worried to death over that Polikarpov, somebody had already managed to shoot over to Potapov at the office and get hold of an accordion; that, I may tell you, is a good mile and a half across the hills. I checked it on my watch once while I was walking – half an hour, a good mile and a half."

"Have you seen Potapov today?" Zybin asked swiftly.

"Yes I have. What a row they were kicking up, bastards, what a row. One of them came diving straight into my tent. I was developing a film and the swine deliberately pulled the flap wide open! 'Our mate's at death's door, and here's you laying out your . . .' His mate's slipping away, see, blast him! A fat lot he cared." He sank shoulder-deep in the torrent once again. Zybin waited for him to emerge and rub his eyes open, spluttering and swearing; then he said: "They're sick and tired of us, Volodya. They're disappointed and fed up; they've lost faith in us. ("Precisely," agreed Kornilov, "that's it exactly, they've lost faith, the rats!") Remember how it was at the beginning? Come rain or shine they would beaver away into that hill. But now after two months and nothing to show, not a pot or a horn, well it stands to reason . . . You might have dug up some more of your cattle bones at least."

Kornilov stood in mute ill temper, rubbing his belly, chest and neck red with the icy water. His movements were expansive and powerful. When Zybin mentioned the cattle bones, he paused abruptly and asked: "Nobody phoned while I was in town?"

"No, no . . ." Zybin began dully, then all of a sudden clasped his hands. "Oh, yes they did, twice in fact! Potapov answered it for you. Some woman rang. I told them to give her the museum number. Was that all right? Did she catch you?"

Kornilov's eyes suddenly took on a keen glint.

4

"A woman, eh?" He seized a shaggy towel from a large blue boulder and began cheerfully drying his back, with swift, deft sawing movements. He was a short man, tanned, muscular, swarthy and extremely lively in his movements. With him everything was involved: arms, back, muscles, lips, eyes. "You're a show-off," thought Zybin feasting his eyes on him. "What a show-off! You learned that at the Sandunovsky baths."

"It's all right, dear Georgi Nikolaevich," said Kornilov breezily. "Not only all right, it's positively splendid." He bundled the towel up and tossed it to Zybin. "Get ready then, put your new trousers on and let's make tracks. The director must have been waiting ages for us."

He always talked like that when he was excited: "make tracks", or even "when you see it, it'll rock you".

"Director?" Zybin had to sit down on a boulder (the director as well, to add to the turmoil!). "But surely he doesn't . . ."

"Well naturally," Kornilov responded, amiably cheerful as he glee-fully regarded the other's pale plump face and light, watery eyes – eyes which took on a briefly foolish expression. "And why not, dear Georgi Nikolaevich? He's fond of you, isn't he? And when he's fond of someone, he comes along himself and brings a few visitors. And what visitors! You'll be rocked when you see them. That's just what he told me: 'Wait for me, I'll be along.' Now then, let's go and meet them."

They picked their way through the underbrush and up the steep hillside. Zybin halted suddenly at one ledge and said softly to Kornilov: "Volodya, just take a look over there, over yonder towards the road."

"What about it?"

"It's just like an old print, that's all."

Dusk was drawing in by now. A fine mist came drifting down across the ledges, and everything – fiery-scarlet, pale blue, dark green, violet and simply white – the rounded leaves of the aspen grove, already suffused wine-purple; the abundant forget-me-nots on the bright marshy meadow, angry black bullrushes; the damp, intensely green field, clean and dense as a young onion (on one side azure-white cow parsley parasols swaying, on the other the tall, severe stems of willowherb, with its delicate pointed leaves and mauve flowers) – all this drowned in the evening and the mist, subsiding and becoming attenuated, distanced and fantastic.

"Like an old print under tissue paper," Zybin repeated.

"Just you mind where you're putting your feet," Kornilov suddenly shouted angrily. "You've gone and dirtied your trousers, oh calamity!"

Zybin had blundered into a patch of steppe wormwood and it had stained him with its sticky yellow pollen.

"Now why your hands, what are you doing with your hands?" Kornilov cried with mounting exasperation. "You're just rubbing it in more. As soon as we get there, we'll get a dry brush and give you a good scrub down. Let that do the job, not you. Otherwise we'll get nowhere." He shook his head waggishly. "There's the commission, O great one. They'll be here to see what's going on. The workmen are knocking back vodka. One of them's even been taken away for dead. The scientific staff are having a high old time and the Leader's sitting in his hut with no pants on. Not a pretty sight! And what about the scientific results, eh?"

"There's your old bones, Volodya," Zybin said sweetly. "Your hooves and horns. We'll put them on show. You haven't interred them again yet, have you?"

Kornilov regarded him enigmatically.

"And what would I do that for?" he asked. "Why should I cover them up again if . . ."

The story of the bones was as follows. After the initial modest successes of the expedition, there had ensued a series of complete failures. Kornilov, going by signs only he recognized, had suddenly resolved that the place where they were digging was of course useless. Now if they were to tackle that small, steep-sided hill on the apple clearing . . .

"That thing is a burial mound," he kept assuring Zybin. "A very rich one, probably, a horse-burial. We just have to try it. We just have to."

They had dug fruitlessly for ages. They changed the site repeatedly and dug up the entire area; finally they were rewarded. They uncovered a gigantic pit full of bones, evidently the remains of some epic thousand-strong feast. Cattle, sheep, goats, horses, pigs! – a pile of skeletal material the like of which had never been seen before. So then, they had dug them up and they covered them over again. What else could you do with bones? But a rumour went the rounds of the collective farm that the scientists had disinterred a cemetery of diseased animals. Then the fur began to fly! First the farm downed tools, then the ladies from the Council of People's Commissars rest home got worried; after that the alarm bells started ringing throughout the Health Ministry. An emergency enquiry team from the Epidemic Board flew in to the excavation; young scientists with the look of terrorists in their pince-nez, equipped with test tubes and retorts and cases marked with a cross. The pit was re-opened and roped off and a grim individual with a holster was put on guard. While the enquiry proceeded, two of the diggers had their heads broken at a party. "Spreading glanders, eh, you bastards! Wait till we get hold of your boss. We'll screw the heads off the lot of you!" Nobody's head got screwed off and the commission departed, having produced a report that the bones presented no danger to health, by reason of age; still, the whole affair might have been a disaster had it not been for the foreman, Potapov. He had the bright idea of hauling two buckets of carbolic up there at first light and pouring them into the pit. The stench was frightful of course, but it calmed everybody down at once. It was a whiff of 1920, railway stations, barrack blocks, assembly points, pass offices – utterly everyday things; at any rate, glanders, seeping out of a thousand-year-old grave, didn't smell like that.

The director had heard about the incident only a month later after his return from an urgent official trip to the capital. He summoned Zybin and scowled (though his eyes were twinkling): "Well, we'll pass over the fact that you've wasted government money off your own bat – blind them with science; nobody knows what it means, so no questions asked. And if those farmers crack your academic skulls, what of it? I'm not your keeper!"

So the pit gaped in the middle of the orchard, smelling of the '20s and everyone who walked past it spat and mentioned the scientists.

. . . Kornilov regarded Zybin enigmatically.

"And what would I do that for?" he asked. "Why should I cover them up again if they're being carted off to town tomorrow?"

"Why's that then?" Zybin halted. "Boiling them down for brawn are they?"

"Because," rejoined Kornilov with magnificent nonchalance, "because, my dear man, the Vetzooinstitute is buying our bone material. So, the director and Professor Dubrovsky are coming tomorrow, he'll examine it all, see to the paperwork and after that he'll post us the shekels. But, as the bone idle say, that's tomorrow-tomorrow, not today. I just told you it was today to give you a scare."

Zybin began to laugh.

"Won't wash, Volodya. The name gave it away. You should have picked somebody else. Professor Dubrovsky was arrested a month since."

"It's a different one then," Kornilov crooned sweetly. "He was a historian, dear, this one's a vet."

7

Zybin looked at Kornilov and felt like saying something sarcastic but abruptly thought better of it. He recalled that there were actually two Dubrovskys and one of them, the elder, really did have the zoological chair at the Institute.

"It's not true is it?" he asked timidly (his trouser knees were a mass of yellow).

"God's truth," responded Kornilov impressively. "We have sold the bone material of pure-bred cattle of the third to fourth centuries. You still don't believe me! All right then. Potapov's got a genuine icon of Nikola Mirlikiski. Let's go – I'll kiss it. There's vodka there as well. Come on."

Zybin stooped down and began dusting off his knees with sharp lateral blows of his palms. Kornilov stood over him and watched. The state of Zybin's trousers no longer troubled him.

"You're a genius," decided Zybin at length, raising his head from his knees, by now hopelessly covered in yellow-olive mess. "Ostap Bender the Second. To dream up a thing like . . . no, it's pure genius!"

"Not me," returned Kornilov modestly. "I am a genius, I am an Ostap Bender, but it was only the basic idea that was mine, the putting into practice . . ." He kept mysteriously silent. "Tomorrow you'll see that part of it yourself. Ah, they're already banging the rail over there. Porridge ready! Let's go and see Potapov. I told him, just be patient and I'll haul your scientist over!"

The commission turned up unexpectedly towards the end of the next day, in two vehicles. The director and the old carpenter rode in the first of these, a battered old M–1 banger that the whole town knew. Why they were bringing the old man along was a mystery. But there he sat, proudly smoking and gazing about him. Now one side, now the other. He looked as sober as could be.

"Eagle," thought Zybin.

The third occupant of the car was a tall, extremely beautiful girl, with an Indian look about her. She had a long, clean-cut, lustreless face and dark, shining hair. Clara Fazulaevna was in charge of storage. She was gazing over and beyond the car and thinking thoughts that were profoundly her own. Behind the M came another car – long, lean and yellow, eager and thrusting like a hunting hound or a borzoi (Zybin was completely ignorant of car makes). It contained only two people: a tall, gaunt old man in a tussore silk suit and a stout little bespectacled German, blond and lightly freckled, wearing a cork helmet and a camera slung across his shoulder. It was he who had been driving.

8

The museum car reached a mound, rumbled up onto it and came to rest, rocking and roaring. The old man and the director jumped out. Clara stayed inside. The director asked her something or told her something (he jabbed a finger towards the tents and snorted), but she merely twitched a shoulder by way of reply. The two archaeologists watched them from the summit of a nearby hill. The workmen stood all around, some with picks, others with spades. It was precisely this hill they were engaged on excavating. Only now it was conjectured that rather than a citadel, it was in fact the tomb of a chieftain, a burial mound.

"Another half-day gone! Best part of the day too, in the cool," sighed Zybin, gazing at the road. "Well, all right; Volodya you go and be the welcoming party while I run over to the shop. Seeing they've brought the old man along, there's no way we can get by without." He ran off down the hill.

Kornilov watched him for a moment, considering, then called out: "Just get vodka, though! We've got champagne, it's standing in the stream!"

"How do you mean?" Zybin stopped, astonished.

"What I said," snapped Kornilov, trundling downhill.

Zybin stood still for a moment in thought, then shrugged his shoulders.

"What on earth put champagne into his head?" he asked, bewildered. "He's forever up to . . ."

"She let him down," explained a nearby youth gleefully, "she didn't come. That's why he's selling you what he had put by!"

"Who? Oh, don't be silly!" Zybin brusquely waved him away and set about the descent. Just then, another of the workmen, Mitrich, middle-aged and stolid, smuggled onto the expedition by foreman Potapov (being of small use on the farm), confirmed authoritatively: "No, she did, she did come. He came with her from town. They parked the car over there by the river – she was doing the driving – and they both went over to the pit straight away. He says: 'Wait, I'll show you – there, there, see?' He took hold of her umbrella and started stirring away, she stuck her nose in her hanky: 'Stop, don't, I know what you mean.' "

Everybody started laughing. Zybin thought: "They don't like Kornilov, do they?" He couldn't decide whether the thought gave him pleasure or not; at all events, he realized in that instant that it was actually possible not to like Kornilov.

"Well, what happened after that?" he asked.

"After that, they came over to my place: 'Mitrich, some visitors for

9

you'. The wife fixed them an onion omelette, and I was sent for cognac. On my way back, I picked three apples for her, the cream of the crop, the biggest you've ever seen; she was positively scared: 'Oh, what a size, they don't grow that big, do they?'"

Zybin glanced at the workmen. They were listening and smirking.

"Well, who is she then?" asked Zybin, nonplussed. "Where did she come from?"

"As to where she comes from," said Mitrich delightedly, "Where she's from, I don't know! I didn't listen in, did I? But what I did realize was this. She seems to have met you somewhere. Either you were on holiday together or went on a trip somewhere."

"Me? Never!" said Zybin. "That's impossible."

"No, it's true, it's true, she knows you; she was very interested! She says: 'He won't recognize me now.' And he says: 'Yes he will.' Then he shot off and brought her two skulls – goats I think. The tablecloth was clean and he dumps them straight down! The wife washed it in ashes later on. After that they went over to the stream together . . ." He paused, then added: "To wash their hands!"

Everyone sniggered in unison.

"All right, Mitrich, let's go, you can give me a hand! While they're over there . . ."

"Beautiful, she was," said Mitrich, following him. "Nice and plump! Fair hair, about twenty-five, no more! Hair-do! Chain! Little wristwatch!"

The clouds had dispersed and the sun peeped out, making it very hot all of a sudden. Over all, the summer had been a dry one. The rains had started only recently, a fine, slanting drizzle – the kind they call mushroom showers if they happen anywhere near Moscow or Ryazan. Here the earth, exhausted by the heat, had accepted them thirstily, wide open with all its hills and gullies, all its acres of brown clover and white campanulas, all the withered leaves of its shrubs. White parachutes floated in the air – the dandelions had seeded. The lifeless, tender blue chicory on tall, gnarled stalks, as firm and straight as hawsers, had faded and turned porcelain-pink, white, grey, translucent. The heat quivered like the steam above a samovar. But crickets seethed everywhere. Inclement weather subdued them, but when the sun shone, they chose the very driest, sunbaked outcrops, and then everything vibrated with the sound of their chirring. That sound was so tediously steady, it seemed to Zybin that he had been surrounded all these months not just by silence, but by a deathly hush. But now all around was once again filled with tiny, sharply wounding splinters of sound. The grass sang, groaned and chirred. Zybin could even distinguish separate voices. Somebody pleading distinctly and plaintively: come here, come here, come here ... And there, hearing him out to the end, came the reply crisp and angry: no, no, no! Walking past a stem of cow parsley, Zybin caught sight of her – green, huge-eyed, as if snipped out of a greeny-white silver leaf of maize; a female. "A she?" he thought. "But female locusts don't chirp do they?"

The director and Professor Dubrovsky were standing in the midst of the clearing. Clara was standing with them.

"Flush the stomach with wine. The constellations have completed their circle. The gentle cicada, hiding from the heat, groans softly," said Zybin as he came up, and pressed Clara's hand. "A poem of Alcaeus, Veresayev's translation, collected works, volume 9. Welcome, comrades!"

"No, as to wine, we'll likely wait a bit," replied the director gaily. "You and I haven't earned enough for kvass yet. So there would seem to be no occasion to flush the stomach. Well, greetings, greetings, Keeper! We've come to see you about these bones."

He spoke, looking at him directly with his kindly, humorous eyes.

"But perhaps you and I have earned it, haven't we," said Clara softly to the director.

"But you and I," the director waved a hand, "you and I, as we all know are worth our weight in gold! We're practical folk, sticklers for the fact, no joking with us. So." He turned to the professor. "Allow me to present – Georgi Nikolaevich Zybin. You've no doubt read his article in *Kazakhstan Pravda* about the library. He raised the roof over that all right! But we call him the Keeper of Antiquities. Our overall site manager. Keeper, this is Nikolay Fyodorovich Dubrovsky, our customer from Vetzoo. Well then, shall we surrender your bones to him or not?"

"Volodya's a genius," thought Zybin, but said out loud: "What's there to surrender, though? They've been drenched in carbolic, haven't they? There's no getting near them."

"Oh, that doesn't matter, doesn't matter at all," intoned the grey professor vigorously, rather like a preacher. "We shall soak and wash them clean, dear colleague. If you only knew the sort of things we'll get out of them. Your fiasco is the greatest possible luck for us. A quantity of bone material like that, thoroughbred cattle of Central Asia in early AD just doesn't exist anywhere. For Artur Germanovich," he nodded in the direction of the pit, "it's pure treasure trove! He's a horse man after all! He just happens to be writing his master's thesis on the history of the Kirghiz and Przhevalsky's horse. Look," he pointed across the clearing, "you see?"

Zybin looked and smiled. The little German, as he had instantly dubbed him, had rolled up his trousers and crawled into the pit. Kornilov jumped in after him.

"Our idiot goes in as well," said the director, annoyed, and shouted: "Vladimir Mikhailovich, if you grope around in that filth I'm sending you to the Titan to steam your hands! You really could pick up half a ton of stone age syphilis!"

The professor laughed and placed a hand on the director's shoulder.

"No, no, that's impossible," he said pensively. "That's out of the question, my dear Stepan Mitrofanovich. You say yourself they're fifteen hundred years old. What can there possibly be! . . ." All of a sudden he took the director elegantly by the arm, professor-fashion. "Best if we go over there and take a look . . ."

. . . The bones were lying in a dense pile. On the top, they had turned black from the carbolic, but when the heap was stirred, they were white, yellow and cream-coloured. Evidently they had first been exposed to the wind, rain and snow – for centuries perhaps – and so had become light, dry and resonant. At all events, the stick had disturbed something like a heap of multicoloured lace; the florid-faced assistant sat over the pit, revolving an equine skull in his hands.

"Anyone at home?" Kornilov called to him softly.

"Look at that." The assistant abruptly raised his head. "Even the back of the skull has survived. And look there . . ." He thrust the horse's skull into the professor's hands.

The latter took it and turned it this way and that before placing it carefully on the ground.

"Yes," he said, flicking his fingertips clean. "All this is very, very interesting! Let me introduce, this is the boss Georgi Nikolaevich Zybin. And this . . ." Here he mentioned the name and patronymic of the assistant.

Artur Germanovich smiled and got to his feet.

"How do you do?" he said. "Excuse my not shaking hands. I've got a letter for you from Polina Yurevna. Only it's back there in the car. If you'll excuse me, I'll . . ."

He cast a regretful look at the horse skull, then went off. Zybin left and followed him. He was so taken aback, he asked no questions.

"My God, my God," something inside him cried out. "Lina. Good God almighty."

The letter was in a narrow, flimsy envelope, and Zybin at once recalled Lina's hand inside a glove.

Dear Georgi Nikolaevich,
I've already been here a fortnight. I've been searching and searching and still can't get you. I found out in Moscow that you were working at the museum, but when I called in there, your charming colleague couldn't tell me anything except that you were on an expedition somewhere. But there is a God in heaven! I ran into Vladimir Mikhailovich and he told me everything. So then, please find me. That will probably be a lot easier than the other way round. I've got a telephone in my room. Ring directory enquiries. It's the Alma-Ata Hotel, room 42. I'll be staying here another two weeks. I long to get out to you in the mountains. True, I did get there once with Vladimir Mikhailovich, but without you. Actually it was probably a good thing you weren't there. Now I have an absolutely precise idea of where and how you live; you'd have distracted me with your talk. But you know what really shook me? The mountains! Like the sea back in '35. Still, you've probably forgotten all that by now. But I remember.
I long for your reply, as nightingales July,
Yours, Lina.
PS Do you really remember the sea, though? I mean the sea, the Anapa museum, the crab under the bed and all the rest of it? Those were the days all right, Georgi Nikolaevich! It scares me to think! So please give me a ring. Once more, yours, Lina.

He thrust the letter into his pocket.
"Polina Yurevna very much wanted to see you," said Artur Germanovich deferentially. "She even intended coming with us; we waited half an hour for her specially, but apparently something went wrong."
"Really?" said Zybin, not fully taking in what was being said. "So, then . . . it's . . ." He didn't know what to say or what to ask.
"The way it happened was," the assistant explained stolidly, "Vladimir Mikhailovich brought these bones into the Institute with a request

to identify them and report their findings. We sent him on to the zoology department. It was there he met Polina Yurevna. She'd only just arrived and was familiarizing herself with our teaching museum. Well, she saw this bone material and had a word with Vladimir Mikhailovich. She asked him to show her the whole pile on the spot. She came and saw them, and took something or other for the laboratory. After that she submitted a report to the university administration and the Institute of Kazakhstan History: 'A large quantity of bone material has been found, belonging to domestic cattle and predating any cross-breeding. I consider it necessary to acquire the entire collection.' Professor Dubrovsky supported her. Money was allocated for the purpose. So we've come to see what we're buying."

"Right," said Zybin, having recovered himself. "Right! Now I understand it all. "Suddenly he was seized by a terrible urgency and began bustling about. "Right, I'll go and phone Polina Yurevna straight away, otherwise the office will be closing and . . . Do go over there, please. I'll join you presently. I'll just phone and dash back. It won't take a minute."

In the office there was only one tablelamp burning, and the accounts clerk was sitting, glumly flicking his abacus. Zybin came in and picked up the receiver without asking permission. All he could hear was noise and crackling. At times there even seemed to be snatches of conversation. He replaced the receiver and picked it up again several times, but there was nothing to hear apart from thunderstorms and electrical discharges. "Like a seashell," he thought vaguely. "Like a big seashell." And at once he pictured himself walking at night again by the narrow path along the precipitous shore, with nothing around him; pitch darkness, except for the lone spherical white light of a streetlamp up ahead, while the sea boiled, seethed and crashed down below. Once upon a time he had taken such a walk, carrying a crab in his cap. The crab had been huge, greeny-black, ill-tempered, and spiky as a cactus. "Yes, that crab was a character," he thought. But the noise persisted and he dropped the receiver. The accounts clerk clicked for the last time, sighed and threw the abacus onto his desk.

"Our phone's on the blink," he said, pleased. "We've had trouble with it for more than two years now. Sometimes you need an urgent connection and there's no way, not a chance!"

Zybin looked at him, then in a sudden access of fury slammed his fist down with all his strength on the cradle. Something snapped inside

14

the receiver, some membrane burst and once more the noise resumed. The sea had returned.

"Why the hell did I have to flare up like that?" he thought, suddenly sober. "Fine time to choose." He picked up the receiver, by now almost unconsciously, to hear a woman's crisp voice saying: "Second."

"Second, would you be so kind?" he shouted, leaping up. "Get me the Vet Institute! Which number? Doesn't matter, any! Enquiries, get me enquiries!"

The phone went silent, then the same voice said: "There's no number for enquiries. I'll give you personnel."

No one picked up the phone for an appreciable time. Then a woman's voice asked whom he wanted. He asked how he could reach Polina Yurevna Pototskaya. "Just a second," said the voice. Then suddenly he heard the staccato tap of hurrying heels: tuk-tuk-tuk. "They used to call her a goat in the Institute," he recalled. The receiver clattered and he heard a glad "yes". He caught his breath. It was her!

That was her "yes". That was it! They had met! And he had got another "yes" from her. Just as glad and sincere as ever. And, as ever, just as meaningless and worthless.

"Hello, Lina," he said. "It's me, Georgi. When did you get here?"

As soon as he said his name, she cried in something approaching resentment: "Well, at long last . . ." And . . . At all events, after the conversation had ended he couldn't remember how it had started. All he recalled was that it had immediately gone smoothly despite the years, the meetings, the breakings-off, the partings. Recollection only came back to him fully when her questions began.

"Well, when are you coming anyway? I very much want to see you!"

"Good lord, whenever you like," he replied. "Now if you want!" And it was true, he was ready like a little boy to run out to the highway and board any passing vehicle.

She laughed.

"And here was I afraid you'd changed. Still, no, today's out. Our people are there with you, aren't they? Are you alone at the moment?"

"Yes," he replied. "Why?"

"Well, what about the bones? Is everything all right? All in order?"

"Very much so," he answered, although he was taking in absolutely nothing – what bones? What was all right? "Everything's fine, couldn't be better," he said.

"And Volodya coped all right? Well, give him my regards. We didn't manage to give you a surprise after all. Listen, Keeper (they call you Keeper here. I laughed and laughed). I'm always free after two. So, let's say tomorrow, eh?"

"Terrific," he replied stoutly. "Where?"

At this point she began to adopt a rather different tone, like in the old days, like that time by the sea. He even felt himself go hot at the sound of her voice.

"Wherever you like, my dear, wherever you like. I could drop in on you at the museum."

"Yes," he said with a start. "Drop by the museum." Then he bethought himself. "Wait a minute", he said, "not the museum. You know the main entrance to the park, where the fountain is? Well, there. All right?" He at once thought no, it wasn't all right, altogether too many people around.

But she had already replied.

"I always loved that scene by the fountain. 'To abase myself before the proud Polish girl?' Brilliant, as Volodya says. Don't you be too late though, me standing there in full view of everybody . . ." Just then someone shouted to her in the background. "There you are, someone's just prompted me – young, beautiful and alone! All right, that's fixed, by the fountain. Now get my professor on the phone. Do hurry, though, people want the phone. Everybody hereabouts is interested in what he's buying."

They had chosen an excellent spot to celebrate the purchase in a manner befitting. They had positioned the table up on the hillside. At this point, a damp sandy slope ran down to the highway – not yellow, a rusty-orange rather, and overgrown right up to the summit itself with reeds, thorny berberis with its rounded crimson leaves, and a sort of small, finely formed burdock, neat and even like Chinese parasols. Beyond the highway began the sedge-swamps, with a dense blue scattering of forget-me-nots, and the turbulent Alma-Atinka, in which, among the foam and spray, the flash and thunder, there gleamed a huge black boulder like a wallowing hippopotamus. Altogether a marvellous spot!

Sunlight and shade, cool and fresh.

As he came up, though still some way off, Zybin caught the voice of the director. The director was thundering. That meant he was fulminating against somebody. "Who's getting it?" thought Zybin.

He approached, invisible among the apple trees. They were all sitting down and listening. Only the independent old man slept, snoring softly as he leaned his head up against a tree trunk. Several cigarette packets lay in front of Clara on the tablecloth. "But she doesn't smoke, does she?" thought Zybin vaguely. Clara was toying with her fork and saying nothing. Dasha, foreman Potapov's niece, soft, pink and freckled, sat next to her. She was in the fourth year of her theatre studio course and Potapov couldn't bring himself to forgive her for that. All of them were staring fixedly at the director.

He had concluded one tirade, however, and was sustaining a kind of pause for effect; then he sighed, speared an onion ring, chewed it zealously and continued in a different tone, light and studied: "And another thing, Professor, don't think that this is a minor matter. Telling your lecture students that 'Comrade Stalin is in error', is a real crime against the state."

"Ah, so that's why they're so quiet," thought Zybin and glanced uneasily at Kornilov – had he taken a lot on board? No, not particularly, it seemed; at all events he was sitting like the rest.

"But it wasn't like that, it wasn't like that at all," said the professor, on the verge of tears. "In answer to a student's question whether the Roman Empire fell as a result of a slave revolt, my brother replied . . ."

"That's not the point. That's not the point at all," cut in the director, imperiously waving away his objection. "The point is, he said 'no'! He said 'no' when the Leader had said 'yes'. How could it be otherwise? What do his words mean: 'I don't know what Josif Vissarionovich meant, but the fact is that after the Spartacus revolt, Rome lasted another five hundred years and became a world empire?' Didn't Comrade Stalin write perfectly plainly and simply: The barbarians and slaves brought the Roman Empire crashing down. Therefore that is the scientific truth. Is that so or not?"

"That's so of course," the professor assented miserably. "But . . ."

"That's so of course, but your brother has been arrested," resumed the director, now in full flight. "I understand, ah, how I understand it all. But it's the old old story isn't it? 'Hush, I know all that very well, but that rat is my godmother.' Meanwhile the uncle of that girl," he pointed at Dasha across the length of the table in a menacing antique gesture, "has been taken into custody. Very well then, surely his brother, the collective farmer, her father, doesn't say, 'I don't believe it, it's impossible, the security organs have made a mistake' does he? No, he says: 'If they've arrested Petya, there must have been a reason.' That's the way a plain collective farmer reasons about his very own Soviet power. But we, the intelligentsia, sly and cunning that we are . . . no offence, I'm tarred with the same brush, that's why I'm talking this way . . ."

"But Stepan Mitrofanovich, they caught Uncle Petya red-handed engaged in sabotage, but their brother . . ." said Dasha timidly and flushed crimson.

"Ai-ai-ai!" The director shook his head, beaming and swivelled bodily towards her. "Ah, you, so-and-so, you clever-clever girl, what do you think, then, that propaganda from the professor's chair isn't sabotage? It is worse than sabotage, my dear girl. It's an ideological diversion against your puppy-dog souls, and heads have got to be pulled off for tricks like that." He clenched his fist grimly. "Because there is nothing in the world we hold more dear than you, freckled and snivelling though you are."

"But, Stepan Mitrofanovich," the professor was positively pressing his hands to his chest, "surely what my brother said was just the personal gloss of a specialist historian, Stalin's teaching . . ."

"Comrade Stalin is a giant in all branches of learning," Kornilov broke in with swift harshness, flicking a glance at Zybin (he was the only one to have seen him). "Historians have no need to elucidate him."

"Well yes, yes of course." The professor looked at him helplessly and began mumbling, by now comprehending absolutely nothing. "A giant I agree! A giant in all branches of learning! No need to elucidate him! I agree, no need . . . but surely every petty little thing can't . . ."

"But there is nothing petty in Comrade Stalin's teaching," Kornilov pronounced just as grimly, with a sideways look at Dasha. "Give us an inch, sly and cunning intellectuals that we are, and we might well . . ."

At this point the professor was so flustered he dropped his spectacles on the table.

"And you'd best be quiet," the director enjoined sternly all of a sudden. "Best hold your tongue for a bit. You've got a great deal too much to say, my friend! You and that Keeper of yours will talk yourselves into a fine mess one of these days . . ." ("Well, well, that's all I needed," thought Zybin, aghast.) "And now you've misunderstood me again," he turned to the professor. "What's the real point here? The important point is the one he tried to impale me on just now. You don't catch me like that though, dear man. Yes! The teaching of the Leader is complete and indivisible! Yes! There is no pettiness in it, laugh all you like! It is not for discussion! It is to be taught! Understand, taught! Like your ABC in school."

"Good lord, good lord, what on earth's he saying," thought Zybin.

18

"He's not a stupid sort, but . . ." He emerged from behind the tree, but only Clara noticed him.

"We are on the eve of war," the director went on after a pause, in quite a different tone of voice, quiet and pensive, "the most frightful, ruthless kind of war. The enemy is only too keen to seek out any crack in our mental make-up. In their mental make-up I mean," he indicated Clara and Dasha, "because we'll be sending them, the boys and girls, our children, to die for our system. So then, are we going to let some gentleman poison their emerging minds with stuff like that? After all, if the Leader has made an error here, there could be more of them. That means he spoke without thinking, didn't he? Or spoke in ignorance? That's no better. So then how can a man be regarded as a leader if he . . . No, no, it's absolutely unthinkable. You, or I, or she can be in error, but the Leader – no! He cannot. He – is the Leader! He must lead, and it is us he leads. 'From victory to victory', as is written on the walls of your institute. He is wise and great, an omniscient genius, and if we all think of him that way we shall be victorious. Your brother has been arrested because he placed all those truths in doubt, if only in one isolated instance. But that's a crime, and he'll be tried for it. That's all about it. For the rest it's up to the security organs. Perhaps they really will take his age into consideration. And don't talk about this to anyone else. They're bound to pick you up on some word . . . But where the hell's that Keeper? He's never there when you want him!"

"I'm here," said Zybin. He came over and sat on the proffered stool.

And at once everyone stopped talking and looked at him.

He said nothing as he leaned on his elbow, staring at the tablecloth.

"And what exactly did they charge your brother with?"

The professor made to open his mouth.

"But how does he know?" The director fairly cried out, harsh and disquieted. "Enquiries are still in progress. All right, end of subject! Clarochka, show the Keeper what the old man got hold of for us, then we'll be off. It looks like they'll have the drink to themselves. They never let that go to waste!"

And Clara opened the first of the cigarette packets lying in front of her.

It was gold; fragments of something, scales of some sort, edging, platelets, pale yellow, dull, lacklustre. It was genuine dead gold, the sort that spills from the eye sockets when a brown skull is ripped from the clinging earth, the sort that glimmers between the ribs, and settles in the grave.

In short it was unmistakably archaeological gold. Zybin, oblivious of all else, silently revolved the roundels and platelets. The largest of them resembled a yellow birch leaf more than anything else. The same colour, the same fine, broad sharp point.

He carefully picked them up one after the other, then lowered them back into the cotton wool of the box. Yes, yes, it was the same material he had handled several times before. Once a driver had brought some in; on another occasion, a barmaid had given it up. But now whole heaps of it lay on the cotton wool.

"And here's an earring," said Clara, opening a matchbox. "Look what an odd subject it is – a mouse gnawing the belly of a seated man."

"Give him the magnifying glass, go on," enjoined the excited director.

"A piece of a diadem," Clara went on, opening a long cigar box. "There are three altogether. We've only got hold of one."

Zybin's hands fairly shook. The thing was so extraordinary. The piece comprised an open-work gold plate, divided into two bands. The upper band depicted a horned dragon, supple and feline in shape, on its tensed legs. It stood writhing and baring its teeth. Every fang of the beast was crisply chased. The lower band revealed a kid. A little nimble kid – a teklik as they called them in these parts. It was standing on some sort of hillock or summit, staring into the distance. Its tiny hooves were tucked up together, its little face gazing out. Then there were some swans flying by, pheasants and ducks rising, little birds fluttering here and there. Separated from these, seemingly perched on the capital of a column, was a finely moulded winged horse – but no Pegasus this. It was a plain little Przhevalsky's horse. Another similar horse was soaring through the sky. On his back was a young woman. The wind had swept her hair up into a helmet. The very crouch of the rider conveyed the headlong speed of the flight, plunging through the roaring air. The second band was taken up by something long, thin, flowing, slightly tangled – seaweed perhaps, or grass, lifted by the wind.

In all this could be discerned the hand of a master, the fingers of genius, accustomed to model, cut and chase. Zybin had never come across anything like it before.

"Analogies?" Kornilov asked. "China?"

Zybin shrugged a fraction.

"But still?"

"I don't know," Zybin responded. "That is, of course not China. Chinese dragons are reptiles, snakes. What we've got here is a horned cat, a Balkhash tiger."

"Have you looked at the holes underneath?" Clara pointed. "The diadem ended in a veil. She went about with her face covered."

He looked at her, seemingly lost in thought.

"A crown of gold with dragons and a wedding veil," he said, picturing to himself how it must have looked. "A bride. A princess of the blood and a priestess."

"Shamanka," said Kornilov. "The Siberian shamans had something of the sort."

"Yes, maybe a sorceress too," he assented. "The grave goods will tell us. And the skull of course. But if she's as young as all that," he went on after some thought, "she's hardly likely to have been a sorceress. Although . . ." He spread his arms slightly. "What do we know about them? About her? What was she? We've invented her almost."

"No, leave that possibility, leave the chance she's a sorceress too," pleaded Kornilov. "I mean, what a marvellous thing: a young bronze-age witch with dishevelled hair flashing through the evening air mounted on a dragon. Zh-zh-zh! Jackdaws and ravens scattering on all sides. 'Kra-kra-kra!' And a trail of smoke, smoke billowing in your eyes! And over the mountains – a trail of fire. And she wearing a veil and a crown of gold." He stole a glance at the director. "Marvellous, don't you think?"

"I'll give you what for!" A smiling director wagged an admonitory finger. "Just you be careful with that tongue of yours!"

"Well, have you put the place under guard?" enquired Zybin. "You've been there yourself? What is it, a burial mound, a grave or what?"

"All right, that's enough," the director sighed heavily. "Come over tomorrow and you'll see everything for yourself. Our dear little treasure-hunters will be over too. I've got their identity cards in my desk. You take two or three workmen with spades! And not a peep out of you till tomorrow. Wet your whistles tonight! Come along, Professor."

"Oh, good lord, good lord!" Zybin almost let go of the diadem fragment. "Professor, Polina Yurevna's waiting for you on the telephone. Good lord, how could I forget! Let's get over there quick, quick!"

But the professor was already getting up, frowning and putting away his spectacles.

His hands betrayed a faint tremor. He was once more in full control of himself – austere, resentful, perhaps, of course, slightly drunk too: archaeological gold, horned dragons, witches, none of it had affected him in the least – it was all outside his field.

"Artur Germanovich here is the man to run along with you quick,

quick," said he, with acid politeness. "For me, at sixty-five, quick-quick is ... Anyway, what's the point in running now?" He looked at Zybin and shook his head. "How could you do it, though, eh?" He spoke heavily. "It's business, man, business! We had to make arrangements about meeting tomorrow. Where am I going to find Polina Yurevna now? Oh, with you people everything ... That's because it's always quick, quick, quick ..."

The office was empty. The receiver was still lying on the desk as it had been. But now it was completely dead, cold, voiceless. There was no sound of the sea. No one dwelt or waited within.

When Zybin got back there were no cars either. Kornilov stood on a rise in the road, swaying and smiling as he stared at him. There was a glass in his hand. He was beyond caring.

"Hmm," he remarked to Zybin. "It's the slave revolt is it? And I've got to wait another 550 years, eh, eh? And you know where you can all go to, eh, eh, eh?"

These were days Kornilov had cause to remember very often in time to come. Everything that was grim and irreparable in his life began precisely on this day. And yet very little of it remained in his recollection: to begin with, the bright white glare of a paraffin lamp, under its dull globe. People kept turning it down, (must have been some trouble at the power station). Beneath it glinted the broad angles of the tall white samovar; on top of that, a teapot, white and round, like a curled-up kitten. Then rosy Dasha, slim, pretty and soft in her white silk dress with the red polka dots. She was humming and walking round the room. After that, he remembered something and shouted at her: "Show-off, show-off!" She had smiled and everyone else had laughed as well.

"Finally come round," grumbled Potapov.

Then at once darkness again, silence, peace. A smell of something salty, of kvass and mould. Like a barrel of gherkins standing nearby, or cabbage fermenting to make kvass. There was a washbasin behind the partition: drip, drip, drip ... One drop every minute. When he finally came to in the morning, he glimpsed a dim grey window overhead and someone laid out next to him on two benches. He raised his head and the other also stirred. That maybe meant he was on watch, not sleeping.

"Well, how do you feel?" asked the other, whom he now perceived to be Zybin. Perceived and took fright, by now in real earnest. Up to this moment his head had been vacant, something murky floating about, something fragmentary and vaguely unpleasant. But now he remembered all the talk of the previous night. Or rather, not all of it but enough to base conclusions on. And what about after that?

"Good god," he reflected. "Good lord, I've put my foot in it. I shouted, didn't I? I was being taken somewhere and I shouted out. Two witnesses. That's all the law needs, anyway."

"Give me a drink of water," he requested hoarsely. "Was I very drunk yesterday?"

"No, no, it was nothing," Zybin dismissed this carelessly. "We brought you in here straight away."

"And I shouted out?" asked Kornilov, heart sinking.

"You yelled out something or other. You want a drink. Wait a minute."

He left to return immediately with a huge enamel mug.

"Drink this now," he said, stooping over him. "Drink as much as ever you can."

"Oy, what is it?" Kornilov took a sip and thrust the mug away.

"Gherkin brine. Don't ask, just drink, drink."

He forced him to drink nearly half, then said: "That's good. Now go to sleep."

He went out taking the mug with him.

Half an hour later, when he had indeed slept and wakened to the sound of a door creaking, Potapov came in, galoshes on his bare feet and nightshirt askew, and stood over him. He remained lying stretched out with eyes closed, still snuffling in sleep; the other had stood for a while, then gone out. After that came a sort of confused delirium. He was half asleep, half slumped in feverish oblivion. When he did at last wake up properly, it was broad daylight: a bright, sunny morning, birds singing their hearts out. There came the sound of conversation and laughter from the next room. Potapov was telling Zybin off, bluntly but quietly. The latter was replying, just as quietly, but in an odd tone of voice, part persuasive, part apologetic. He realized the talk was about him, got up, went over to the door. He raised the latch slightly and pressed his ear to the crack. He caught Potapov's last words: "Now that's something I won't tolerate at all." Then Zybin began. He spoke slowly, pensively, as if musing.

"Yes, it really is hard to make sense of it."

"One of our foremen was arrested yesterday," said Potapov.

"There you are, you see, they've pulled in a foreman. And why? Nobody knows for sure. (Potapov growled something.) There you are.

23

And Vladimir was exiled from Leningrad for nothing too, of course. His father was a big shot under the Tsar. But children aren't responsible for their fathers – the Leader said that. So Kornilov's living on his nerve ends all the time. Naturally he breaks out sometimes. Then there's another thing: here we are, digging, digging and not finding anything apart from that pile of rubbish. Then there was that idiotic business with the snake. That cost us no end of bother. But everybody suffered in silence, didn't they?"

"He didn't though, did he," grinned the foreman contemptuously. "He kept following me about nagging away. 'What's the matter, Ivan Semyonovich, maybe we can help in some way?' He got on my nerves, him and his sympathy. I snapped at him once: 'Get off my back, bane of my life, it's bad enough without you hanging round.'" ("Nothing of the kind! There was never anything like that!" Kornilov thought swiftly.)

Then suddenly a female voice joined the conversation: "There, you're always like that. You never believe anybody. A man really has sympathy for you, wanted to help, but you . . ."

Something scraped, the floor or a stool.

"You know how many helpers like that turned up?" demanded Potapov in cheerful exasperation. "You help me, for instance, night and day. Going off to the hayloft with a book . . ."

"Well now, what a thing to say," Zybin laughed. "As it happens, she works in the hayloft. When she's a great actress, then you'll know."

"Hmm!" Potapov laughed grimly, shifting his seat. "I know all about her already, past, present and future. What about him – still asleep? Go and wake him, go on, we're not going to brew up a second time. What will you do, take him with you?"

"Where on earth to?" Zybin waved this away. "He'll get shaken up again on the journey, won't he? Let him sleep."

"Ah, you cunning little devil – want to see Polina before I do. You won't get away with that," thought Kornilov. He gave a cough, swore, lifted the latch and stood before them. Crumpled, dishevelled, with a sore head, but apparently stone cold sober, he stood there and saw that the table was laid and the samovar was glowing. Zybin was striding about the room as usual; Potapov was sitting on a stool over by the window, while Dasha was wiping the cups at the table.

"Greetings, comrades," said Kornilov loudly. "My, that's brutal brine you've got, Ivan Semyonovich. I felt better straight away. I was asleep as soon as my head touched the pillow."

"Our brine is world-class," conceded Potapov benignly. The lady of the house keeps it put by specially for occasions like this. Darya, drop what you're doing and pour him out some tea, strong as you can make it. As black as the ace of spades. That's the first thing he needs."

Dasha poured him out a brimming cup – bitter and blackish-red like manganese. He drank it off in two gulps and handed Dasha an empty glass; she refilled it to the top. He looked quickly at her and suddenly saw again that she was very pretty and had a lovely figure. A slender, long-legged creature in a light little dress – looking at him so tenderly, such a nice, clear smile, she fairly radiated freshness and purity. And she'd stuck up for him immediately, and with such vehement conviction. These musings gave him such a warm feeling that suddenly, out of the blue, and with no kind of hope, he asked: "Well, and what about a snifter?" – and was the first to burst into laughter, showing it was only a joke. And the incredible happened: Dasha silently got up, went over to the sideboard, took out a decanter and poured him a full thin-walled glass.

"There you are," she said.

"Darya, what on earth do you think you're doing?" Potapov was aghast, his eyes fairly popping.

She looked at him, smiling.

"You're the same, Uncle Vanya, when you've got a sore head . . ."

"Why you . . . you . . . really, what are you?" snarled Potapov, jumping up and spraying spittle as he bared his teeth at her.

At this point Zybin intervened.

"Enough, stop it!" he said. "Stop it! Sit down! Well done, mistress! Drink up, Volodya!"

Potapov glanced at Zybin and subsided. For some time now he had not contradicted him in anything.

"True enough," he said, turning away with a frown. "Drink up, then start yelling again till your eyes come out on stalks. You might come out with something worth listening to."

Kornilov glanced at him, then at her. She at once dropped her eyes, turned crimson and gave a feeble smile; he abruptly drained his glass in one gulp and banged it on the table.

"That's the boy!" jeered Potapov. "He's well stuck in."

At this Dasha flushed even more as she brought him a pilchard sandwich and said: "Eat up!"

All of this, especially Dasha and the way she had looked at him, the way she had submissively stood before him, holding the plate and smiling, had made his blood boil again. He sat down and as he did so, looked round at them all, restraining himself, gleefully malevolent, ready to explode at the first pretext. But no pretext came. A bit of small talk ensued about apples and the museum. (Somebody had taught Potapov how to grow apples on which the images of Lenin and Stalin stood out clearly . . . Five of these apples were on display in the museum. Presently Potapov was growing three more, bearing slogans and the state coat of arms, and wanted to send them.) Kornilov listened to this talk and seethed in silence, rocking in his chair. At length Potapov sighed and said, with a nod towards the cupboard: "Well now, in that case why shouldn't we have one as well?"

"No, no," answered Zybin hurriedly, waving this away. "I have to drive shortly, haven't I? You, of course . . ."

"I'll go with you as well," said Kornilov.

Zybin shot a glance at him and replied slowly, as if deliberating: "Is it worth it? Not really. I can ring them myself if need be."

"Why isn't it worth it?" asked Kornilov, spoiling for a fight. "And what if my private affairs are involved? I mean private, a matter of honour so to speak? I promised Polina Yurevna . . ."

"Well all right, have it your own way," Zybin swiftly conceded. "Just tell the workmen what to do and put somebody in charge, even if it's only Mitrich. Ivan Semyonovich," he said, turning to Potapov, "won't you tell them to get a move on? Time they were going out on the job."

"Dasha," said Potapov. "You go, darling."

She had already made for the door, taking her headsquare from the nail, when Kornilov rose suddenly and said as he reached out a hand: "Sit down, sit down, I'll go myself right away. No, no, sit down."

And ran out.

"He's not up to it," said Potapov, following him with his eyes. "Just can't take it. Why do people like that have to drink?" He glanced at Dasha and scowled again. "Look, since when have you started taking liberties like that? Proper little heroine! He's in a shocking state as it is, without you fetching him more of the stuff."

She smiled mysteriously at which he completely lost his temper.

"And there's nothing to laugh at either, trash that you are. Not even half a laugh. If another crazy fit comes over him and his eyes start popping out of his head, you'll get . . ." He looked round at Zybin and evinced real anxiety. "And make sure you're pretty sharp with him as well, he could drag you into something you can't get out of."

"What do you think you're saying?" shouted Dasha, shocked.

"What you're hearing," snarled Potapov. "The drunk finds himself

26

a defender. What's he to you that you go shooting your mouth off for him, eh? Have you no shame, girl!" He was more than angered. He was nonplussed as well.

"He's just a good man," said Dasha. "Good, honest and tells the truth wherever he is. Other people are sly and keep things to themselves; he comes straight out with it."

Potapov shot a swift glance at Zybin. He was saying nothing, eyes fixed on Dasha. Potapov couldn't interpret the expression on his face.

"Well, well, why so quiet all of a sudden?" he demanded. "What is this he's right about, eh?"

"Everything, everything." Tears were rolling down Dasha's cheeks by now as she swept them away with her arm. "He speaks out and everybody else keeps quiet. They say one thing and think another. Yesterday a man could be a hero, a people's commissar, his portraits everywhere; say anything against him and you get ten years. Today they print five lines in a newspaper and he's an enemy of the people, a fascist ... And now anyone who says anything good about him gets ten years. What sort of a way to run things is that? Where on earth's the truth in all that? Uncle Petya now ..."

At this Potapov slammed his fist on the table so hard the cups rattled. He was positively red with fury.

"Don't you dare say a word against your Uncle Petya, trash that you are ..." he whispered hoarsely. "Don't you dare let me hear any more of it ... I'll give you Uncle Petya ... I'm not your auntie ... When I'm in a fit state ... No, do you hear what she's coming out with?" He addressed Zybin, almost in tears. "You see what he's teaching her? For that the lot of us could be ... Not a hide or hair of us."

Zybin now got up from his chair.

"Don't shout," he said, annoyed. "A man could go deaf. Dasha, you're wrong. That is, you may be right – in general, humanly speaking, but at this moment factually, physically, historically, whichever way you like – no. I'm not talking about Uncle Petya, there's obviously been a mistake made there. I mean the commissars and the generals. You're settling the matter by yourself aren't you? Just like that, could he or couldn't he? You ask if somebody, a big man, dedicated to the task, sacrificing his life to it and now victorious and showered from head to foot – with money, say, honours, villas, all sorts of other privileges beyond our comprehension – can such a man be a traitor? And you answer no, that is never, under no circumstances. But everything does depend precisely on circumstances now doesn't it? Circumstances of

27

time, place and mode of action. Not on who the man is, but when? For what reason? Where? In time of peace, in a state of mental equilibrium? Absolutely not – he could not be a traitor. At a time of enormous historical change – wars, revolutions, social upheaval – alas, yes, he might! Half of history actually consists of treachery of that sort. Take Mirabeau and Danton – they turned out to be traitors. And they made the revolution, didn't they? And you must have read the story of Azef? Him, the leader of the fighting organization of the Socialist Revolutionary party, the keeper of the holy of holies, the truest of the true, the possessor of the keys of the kingdom, as they say of the Pope. "Is there in the revolution any figure more brilliant and prominent than Azef?" the court members asked Azef's accuser at the party trial of Azef. And the accuser answered the judge: 'There is no more brilliant figure in the revolution.' And added: 'If, of course, he is not a provocateur.' But all the same he turned out to be a provocateur."

Dasha listened in silence.

"So you see how complex a business it is."

There's nothing complex as far as those two are concerned," growled Potapov. "It's all as simple as can be to them. What can you do with her . . ."

"No, go on, go on," demanded Dasha and even folded her arms.

"This is what you have to understand", Zybin resumed. "The matter boils down to this: What happens to an idea when it becomes a reality? A great deal happens to it which is unexpected; things go wrong. It appears quite unlike itself. Instead of angels, sometimes the most horrible reptiles creep out, so that you feel like washing your hands of it and consigning the lot to perdition. It hasn't worked, people were talking through their hats, time to make an end of it. That's what comes into the heads of the strongest and most loyal people. They're human beings too, Dasha. That's the whole trouble! Besides which an idea in action doesn't have one or two faces, it has a good dozen. But they don't all become apparent at once. The face of the beauty comes at the beginning but after that it's the beast all the way; and when you see that you feel sometimes that life isn't worth living. And if a man doesn't want to go on living, he has no pity left; he'll stop at nothing. It is wrong for anybody anywhere to place death among the conditions of the contract – die but don't give in – he'll certainly crack, give in and sell you into the bargain."

"Go on, go on," demanded Dasha again, but he said nothing more, because he had caught the creaking of the door.

He looked round and saw Kornilov.

28

"Enough of your twaddle," said the latter coarsely. "Get yourself off to town instead, that's where the trouble is. The identity cards have gone astray."

"What identity cards?" Zybin asked, surprised.

"The ones those . . . those treasure-hunters left with the director as a guarantee. Treasure-hunters and passports have both gone. Clara rang. She asked you to get over there straightaway. Off you go. I'll stay here."

CHAPTER 2

WHAT HAD HAPPENED IN THE museum was this: just before his trip into the mountains, the director had experienced a fit of generosity, something which happened to him occasionally. He looked at the treasure-hunters as they stood, eyes downcast: they had handed over the gold, but there was no hint of any money forth-coming. He winked at them, seated himself at his desk and tore off a sheet from his pad on which he boldly inscribed:

Accounts.
 Pay to textile workers, comrades Yumashev and Suchkov,
 300 (three hundred) roub. on account of purchase of exhibits.
 Official paperwork later.

He concluded with a flourish, blotted it, looked up and held out the note, with a brisk order: "Let's have your identity cards, boys, then get yourselves off sharpish to accounts before the cashier goes home."

Yumashev, tall, middle-aged with a long, lean, very Chinese-looking yellow face – he had been the first to discover the treasure – smartly took the little book with its stiff green cover and gold lettering from his jacket pocket and placed it on the desk. He did not seem at all gladdened by the prospect of cash.

Vasya Suchkov too – an appealing youth – hastily took out his own booklet and put it down next to the other.

"There you are," he said. "I always carry it with me."

The director picked up the booklets and glanced at them as he leafed through. Right enough. Vasily Suchkov, born 1913, labourer. Yumashev, Ivan Antonovich, born 1880, registration, stamp. Yumashev was mar-ried, Suchkov a bachelor.

The director was about to ask something more, but at that moment the telephone rang. He dropped the cards and lifted the receiver. It was Miroshnikov, the deputy people's commissar. It was about the estimates. There was something Miroshnikov couldn't understand and something else he objected to. While the director was trying to grasp the problem,

Yumashev and Suchkov stood and waited. During a pause (Miroshnikov was for ever breaking off to locate something on his desk and read it out) the director turned to them in annoyance and asked: "Well, what more do you want?"

Yumashev replied tactfully: "There's a receipt, comrade director, in my card, inside the cover, for the repair of a bicycle. I've let it go five days and it's their day off again tomorrow."

But then deputy commissar Miroshnikov found his document and resumed speaking. The director shouted at Yumashev: "Take it!" To Miroshnikov: "You're looking at the wrong thing. Look at the graph – it's been scientifically worked out." He had turned away and was wholly engrossed in the phone.

The treasure-hunters retrieved the receipt and left.

That was all. Next day the identity cards were nowhere to be found. Only the covers were left. The police were contacted and given the names. The police asked the directory office; the directory office sent back around a dozen references, all of them wrong – the wrong Suchkov, the wrong Yumashev. They were simply not registered in Alma-Ata, nor Kaskelen, nor Talgar, nor in any of the other suburbs. Nor, of course, did they work in any of the factories either.

"That's the way fools learn their lesson," said the director, bringing his story to an end. "And nobody's to blame. I handed everything over myself. Now hunt them out whichever way you like – cross a gipsy's palm with silver if you want, or use that skull there for divination." He swore horribly.

"What skull do you mean exactly?" asked Zybin.

It was pink early morning. The cocks had not yet finished crowing. In the park, women in grey smocks were scraping away at the fountain. The chairs in the cafe opposite were upside down on the tables. The palms had been brought outside. Zybin laid down the report; it contained nothing of material importance. Clara's large handwriting simply stated that the museum had accepted such and such items, discovered on the Karagalinka river. But where exactly had they been discovered – and how? It was written: next to the remains of a human. What remains exactly? Where were those remains now? Why weren't they included in the report?

"Where is it then, this skull?" Zybin asked.

"Lying around in Clara's office: take a look at it," grimaced the director angrily. He was dreadfully cross, snorting away and dying to work it off on somebody. "You're supposed to be a wizard aren't you?

You must be if you read *Freemasonry*. So get busy skull-divining and find out where our gold has floated off to."

He took a final quick drag before stubbing out his papirosa against the bottom of the ashtray. His speech was rapid and to the point: "What you do is this; go along to Grandpa, question him and write it down, so that we have one genuine bit of paperwork at least. And I'm off upstairs otherwise those types will be round to get hold of me again."

"Who are they?"

"Angels! You'll see who! You won't escape them, don't worry!"

What Grandpa said was this (his little morning bottle of vodka lying under his joiner's bench).

"The Lord God himself has recourse to the rod when he's dealing with idiots like us; he keeps on teaching us, and we . . . Well, I go out like, out of the workshop in the morning. Into the park I go, like. These . . . jokers are sitting on a bench. Just perched there. Two of them, one old, one young. I come out of the workshop and stroll about the park, like. I notice straightaway they're keeping an eye on me. Who are they, I wondered? The young one was asking the older one something, then he gets up, comes over to me and says hello. 'You from the museum?' 'Certainly am.' 'We've brought a few odds and ends in.' 'That's the office over there,' say I. 'Take them in there.' And I goes off, like, round the park. Then I look and see he's catching me up again after a bit. 'Mister, would you take a look at them?' – and hands me the handkerchief, and all that mysterious stuff was in it."

"And the skull as well?"

"No, the skull wasn't there then. I saw that later on, I'm getting to that, don't hurry me! 'Well now,' I say, 'go over there and show them and you'll get paid.' 'Will they take them?' 'Well, they might throw it on the rubbish tip. That does happen sometimes.' I ask him questions, did you find it under your floorboards or what? Was it a family heirloom? 'No, no,' says he, 'we found it ourselves.' Well, so he tells me the tale. I can see the stuff is valuable, historically important and I say . . ."

"Wait, hold on a minute, Grandpa. In order, tell it in the proper order. What tale did he come out with? Go on and tell me. I'm writing it down as you can see!"

"Write then, go ahead and write; now that it's all slipped out of your hands, you keep writing. I'm giving you all the details. How much more detail do you want? They went hunting on the Karagalinka and found it all under a rock. He told me that and says again: 'Maybe you'll come along with us for a bit. We've got something that's world-class – marinka, really tender, home-smoked. Well I can see the things are valuable, historically significant, and neither you nor the director were around, so I fell in with the idea, to help things along, you understand. The other one, the old one got up straightaway and came after us. 'Who's he,' I ask. 'Is he your dad?' 'No,' he says, 'he's our foreman'. We all work at the same textile factory. We got to the chaikhana like, and there's another one of them sitting at the table with three mugs in front of him. He's the one who had the skull with him, in a bag he kept under the table. Of course, he fishes out a pint of vodka straightaway, orders three beers, doles out the vodka and says: 'Well, God grant this isn't the last! Here's health to good old us.' We drank it off. Good stuff! The grub he had was a bit of all right too – marinka, he cut it up on a newspaper then and there."

"Grandpa, leave the marinka till later! What did they say, then? They went out hunting, what happened after that?"

"Tfu!" spat Grandpa. "My old granda was right: you have to put your tongue in steep before you talk to a scholar. He went about the steppe with one like you before the Imperialist war, looking for times past: the scholar would ask my granda something, but as soon as he tried to explain, the other wouldn't let him get a word in edgeways: after every word it was the same – how could that be? And what was that then? Where did that come from then? Why on earth was that? Just like you now. What did they tell me? They told me they'd gone along the Karagalinka to hunt partridges and they found all that armour stuff under a rock. What are you looking like that for? What's the scientific way of saying that? Not armour, is that it?"

"That's not the point; what I mean is why were they going to the Karagalinka to hunt partridges? There's no partridges there! There are some on the Ili, there's partridges there all right, but on the Karagalinka . . ."

"You tell them that then," said Grandpa, losing his temper. "You find them and tell them they're going the wrong way. So they told me lies. So it was frogs they were after."

"All right, all right, what happened after that?"

"After that it came on to rain, it teemed down so he said, and they were soon wet through. Well, where could they shelter? The river bank is undermined thereabouts. They look around and see a rock over-hanging there and a cave underneath it. They went and snuggled together in there; it was a tight fit with the three of them, so they started

33

shifting about. Then they see it – something shining under their feet."

"How was the rock hanging? Hanging on what?"

"On the sky! Have you never heard of rocks hanging in the sky? There's scientists for you! Well, it was just hanging out over the river bank, that's all. The bank had just washed away, the rock jutted out and hung there and underneath it a sort of cave had formed. I'm really surprised at you, going about all day looking at the ground and seeing nothing. Round here it's all rocks and nothing but rocks. I've seen the day when a landslide here flattened the houses. A rock the size of this cathedral floor came down and rolled everything along with it, the lot. I remember when I was about ten, I went with my granda on the cart – my granda used to be a carter, taking loads over to Semipalatinsk, and it started raining! Three days and three nights! Granda said to me: 'You'll see, there'll be another day of this and . . .' "

"Oh, what's your granda got to do with this? Why the hell do you keep dragging him in? Just keep to the point!"

"Now he doesn't like my granda! Don't you dare say a word about my granda, you hear? I won't stand for it. He brought me up! He was getting on for seventy and he brought a young piece home, like yours, same eyebrows, ever so neat and quick! Flick, flick, flick! She had a screw loose as well, like yours! Stands to reason! If she pines away over you, the hero, the genius, while you're up in the mountains with that idol of yours, knocking back vodka in your underpants, she must be lacking. A bright lass wouldn't . . . a man like that . . . you know. There he's laughing himself – so it must be true!"

"True, true, Grandpa! It's all too true! A bright lass and a man like that . . ."

Zybin got up from the joiner's bench and went over to the window. The morning was high, limpid and cloudless. It hurt the eyes to look at the white walls of the cathedral. The poplars were still, motionless as if blinking in the sunlight.

"The gentle cicada, hiding from the heat, groans softly," he recalled. But the cicadas were not groaning. After all, the day had not fairly started as yet. "Ah, it's going to be a scorcher today," thought Zybin.

He sat down on the bench again and became lost in thought.

"So, they brought the gold and the skull to the museum, but left the bones. When the devil had it been? Ah, Sunday! Yes, yes it had been Sunday! And they'd also said they were all workmates. There would seem to have been no reason for them to have lied then. Indeed not. But why the textile mill then? Hell knows why, but they probably did work together. It followed that they all had the same day off to go hunting. That meant they had held onto the things for something like a week. They had probably thought the matter through and gone about asking questions. But they hadn't sold a single item – afraid to show the gold, probably. Perhaps they weren't yet convinced that it really was gold. So they had turned up all together. That was to be expected, but what had happened then though?"

"So what did they treat you to then, Grandpa?" he asked. "Marinka, was it? And you say home-smoked? You're sure it was home-smoked?"

"It was, it was," the old man looked up from his plane. "One sniff tells me what's home-made and what's factory stuff. Try it, they said, we did it in the chimney, they said . . ."

"Right." Zybin got to his feet. "A celebrated dish is smoked marinka!" he thought. "I wouldn't mind a bit now, if I knew where to get hold of it. Well, all right, I'm off to see Clara and get a look at that skull at any rate! Might lift my spirits a bit."

On the grey inventory card was printed, with handwritten additions:

1. DESIGNATION OF OBJECT. QUANTITY	2. PROVENANCE OF EXHIBIT (indicating the name of the discoverer, place and circumstances of the discovery)	3. DESCRIPTION OF EXHIBIT
Human skull.	*Found on the River Karagalinka under a large overhanging boulder, together with 300 objects of gold jewellery (see card No.–) 60 miles from the textile mill – More detailed description of site unavailable.*	*Skull.*

It was over this document that Clara was sitting.

Zybin frowned as he lifted the skull from the desk. It was small, a yellowish nut-brown – and as dry and hard as a nut as well. The jawbone lay beside it. Zybin glanced into the eye sockets, drew his finger along the lips, was about to say something, but shuddered all of a sudden and sat down.

This went on for about half a minute. He held the skull silently in front of him, staring into the sockets.

"Why are you doing that?" queried the director, with a hint of alarm.

It had been like a fainting fit or some irrational state coming over him. There had been a click, something shifted position and all of a sudden something large and soft descended and enveloped him. He was holding in his hands the skull of a beautiful woman. She had

35

probably not yet turned twenty and had large dark eyes, lofty arched eyebrows and a small mouth. She had walked with her head held high.

He revolved the skull and gazed at it in profile. The beauty had possessed a delicate, gleaming skin. She had a regal smile, was proud and taciturn; she had been accounted a sorceress, a witch, a shamanka, then they had killed her and cast her away at the ends of the earth. And as the centuries went by, a heavy rock had lain over her, hiding her from human view. And now he was holding her lifeless head in his hands.

"You've written," he said, " 'found under an overhanging boulder.' That's not a burial!"

It was a statement not a question; he knew for certain it had not been an interment, just desolate land, a boulder and her body beneath it. He didn't understand himself how *it* had come to him, but *it* had done so all the same and he knew everything about *it* now.

Clara shrugged.

He remained standing there, lost in contemplation. Here had been her lips, here her eyes, here her ears and the earrings they had borne.

"Write this," he said. "Write here in this column: 'Female skull of young individual, graceful build.' Then a bracket: 'cranial sutures incompletely closed; masticatory surfaces not abraded; milk teeth present in the upper jaw.' End of bracket. Full stop."

He turned to the director.

"That's all for the present . . ."

"Well, did the old man have anything particular to tell you?" the director hastened to enquire. The beautiful face began to flicker and melt before dissolving altogether as Zybin replied: "He told me about some home-smoked marinka. Ah, I'd love some home-smoked marinka right now, but where to get hold of it? It's not the season, is it? Still, Clara, we could go to the market for some. Shall we go and look?"

"For marinka?" asked Clara, astonished.

"Marinka, marinka," he answered, tenderly.

"Marinka?" said the director, bristling all of a sudden, but at once bursting into laughter as they all did. "All right," he said. "you can go and look for marinka later. Go upstairs and see what's going on there in my office. The angels have arrived. In full angelic uniform. They're sitting there, writing and asking for you. I told you that you wouldn't escape. Go on, don't worry. They'll keep you entertained."

*   *   *

36

There were indeed some extremely boring people sitting up above. These dull folk had arrived the previous day and taken over the research assistants' room. They had begun by expelling everybody; then they called Grandpa in, sat him down and started interrogating him. They had done this grimly and methodically, tapping their little pencils on the desk but not smiling. They asked what these plunderers of socialist property had looked like. They called them by this term, explained the senior man, because of the decree of 7 August, socproperty was sacred and inviolable. Anyone who failed to understand that got ten years in the camps and afterwards nobody would give him a residential permit. They also enquired as to what the plunderers had been wearing, what they had said about themselves and how they had addressed one another. Then, when they had written it all down, they made Grandpa sign every sheet separately. After that, they poured all the platelets and earrings into a large white packet and sealed it with sealing wax. Then they summoned Clara and ordered her to take the packet and put it away at once in the safe, because it was socproperty and socproperty was sacred and inviolable. The following day they would come and question Clara and Clara must remember and tell them everything.

And sure enough, they did arrive on the following day. They took the packet from Clara, examined the seals and said that for the moment she was at liberty. She was not to leave however; she was to sit and wait in her office until they had talked with her. After that they drew up a report in which the things were termed artefacts made of yellow metal; it was stated that the said artefacts were being removed for examination in the investigative section of the prosecutor's office.

Zybin was called in to sign as a witness.

"Wait a minute, wait a minute," he said, placing his hand on the packet. "You can't treat museum valuables like that. They're not sunflower seeds."

At this the younger one lifted his grey eyes and without raising his voice, said very gently: "You're the one who seems to have forgotten that they aren't sunflower seeds. Rest assured that what comes into our hands won't go astray. Just sign here. And you as well, young lady."

And his eyes were very clear and insolent.

"Well now," said Zybin, turning to Clara, "just you run and fetch the director. And don't you grab them, don't grab," he said abruptly, quietly furious enough for his cheekbones to stand out. "The director will be here in a minute, he's the boss here, not you and not me."

"Well, let me tell you, dear comrade . . ." began grey-eyes gleefully, but at this point the senior man interrupted him frostily: "Leave it. We have to see the director anyway."

The director arrived promptly. Doubtless Clara had caught him on the stairs.

"What's going on here?" he enquired of grey-eyes. "What is all this? Who gave authorization?" He picked up the package from the table and glanced angrily at Clara. "As for you, dear friends, I'll have you officially reprimanded," he said fiercely. "Is this the way to handle exhibits? I've never heard the like. Scandalous."

"The matter is very simple," replied grey-eyes with that same hint of veiled insolence which quivered in his every word, oozed from every pore of his bland, clean-cut face. "We're taking these things for examination. It's quite possibly gold. This gold was brought in to you by persons unknown, whom you have permitted to elude you. If you had detained them and telephoned the security organs, as was your bounden duty," he raised his voice, "the gold would still have been here. How much currency the state has been deprived of as a result of somebody's idiotic complacency (he took a particular relish in pronouncing that word – it was really terrifying at that moment: "Complacency – an idiotic disease," the Leader had said only recently), has not yet been ascertained. So we are investigating the matter. You are the director of an institution, a party man, highly esteemed and it would seem should have . . ."

"I'm a member of the Central Committee and a Supreme Soviet deputy as well, good citizen," said the director and handed the packet firmly to Zybin. "Hold on to that, Keeper. If you part with that to anybody, say goodbye to your head." He touched the senior man's shoulder lightly. "Let's go over by the revolving doors."

He returned in a couple of minutes accompanied by Grandpa and Clara. The former had a smile on his face; as a stickler for the firm hand, he was very pleased.

"Oof!" said the director, collapsing onto the sofa. "The people you come across in their line . . . Well, that one, the senior one, is still . . . still a human being, but that other one, the young one, he's precocious – wants to be one of the wolf pack, but he's not out of the puppy-dog stage yet. Still, he must have graduated from some special institute, he's well informed on all these matters. Now then Keeper, what sort of eyebrows did Alexander the Great have? Ah, you don't know. And Nero's nose? Don't know that either. Why on earth didn't you ask them? They'd have rapped it out on the spot. Grandpa, how many kinds of eyebrows are there? Well, like . . ."

"Oh, to blazes with them," Grandpa dismissed this. "I'm fair wore out – what sort of nose, eyebrows or lips one or the other of them had. All by numbers. What were they getting at me for? Eh? You'd think I'd shoved half the gold into my boot."

"You should have told them it was all the director's fault." The director fairly thumped the arm of his chair with his fist. "Answer everybody that way: I don't know anything, ask the management. No, I handed it all over with my own hands, old fool! Signed for the money, dolt!" he cried with a sort of bitter, almost masochistic elation. "It's those three hundred roubles that did the damage. They got the point straightaway. There must be kilos and kilos of that gold, mustn't there? Goblets, jugs, mirrors, harness. Eh, Keeper? Could there be another twenty kilos or so, what d'you think?"

"Grandpa, listen and I'll tell you the story." Zybin abruptly turned towards him. "So then, three hunters are walking along the bank of the Karagalinka when there's a sudden cloudburst. Where to find shelter? They start to look about them. They spot that the bank has been washed away and there's a boulder sticking out of it. Stepan Mitrofanovich, I believe you know those places pretty well? Now in that report of yours you've got that it was located some sixty miles from the textile mill, where those three are supposed to work. That means they must live near there. How comes it that they're so far from home? They've just got enough supplies for one day, haven't they? Maybe they've begged a car off their director or something, promising to bring him back a bird, eh?"

The director shook his head.

"No, you can't get through along there by car. I've been there myself. Just boulders, pits and gullies. No, it's on foot or nothing."

"Are there any partridges thereabouts?"

"Why, they weren't after partridges were they? . . . There's no partridges round there. You find them on cliffs. They never mentioned that to me. I'd have been onto them straightaway."

"There you are, but that's what they told Grandpa. Now about the gold. There couldn't possibly be a great lot of gold there, Stepan Mitrofanovich. This isn't a burial. Nobody was ever buried under stones in this area; in fact we don't know of any interments apart from tumuli here. So the rock is just a rock, but the woman wasn't buried, she was just put under the boulder. She was killed and just left there."

"What are you trying to say?" asked the director, much taken aback. "I don't quite understand," he spread his arms. "Who did it then? . . . And in that finery as well!"

Zybin said nothing.

"Hold on, hold on a minute! People don't dress up like that for no reason at all. It might be for a wedding or some formal occasion. And if so, there must be people around, guests. So how could she have been taken away and murdered, answer me that."

Zybin shrugged. Grandpa sat in his armchair and ostentatiously dozed.

"No, it just couldn't have happened like that," the director concluded.

"Clarochka, could you please bring me the archaeological map of Alma-Ata province," requested Zybin very gently. "I left it on your desk."

Clara turned and left without a word. The director followed her with his eyes.

"What's all this?" he asked quietly. "Had a row or something?"

"No, no it's nothing at all."

"Quite so, nothing at all". He shook his head. "Here's the young lass going around for three days now with her eyes puffed up. And yesterday we came out to see you and while she's there, you go running off to ring your ... You know, no restraint at all ... Bear in mind, please, I don't like that sort of thing."

"But what have I done ... ?" faltered Zybin.

"That's it exactly, you all do nothing, nothing at all, and yet things turn out pretty badly, very much so! And what did your colleague up and do yesterday? What was he yelling for all the team to hear, eh? That was nothing either was it? Wait, I want a serious word with you. You can't seem to instil a sense of discipline into your subordinate. The sniveller gets a few inside him, and then starts announcing his attitude to the Soviet system. What's happened in the past is totally forgotten is it? What good is all this supposed to do?"

Grandpa suddenly opened his eyes. He always supported the director on these occasions. The boss was supposed to make demands of his staff. Otherwise nothing would get done. What notice do we take of kindly words?

"Young and daft," he said fervently. "They can't take their liquor without telling the world. He drank a gill and imagined he was God and the Tsar. Starts showing himself to the people. My granda now, every Sunday ..."

"Just wait, I'll be down on the lot of them," vowed the director. "That joker up yonder and his protector here present. Shh! Quiet. I can hear her heels clacking. Conversation over. Let's take a look at the map."

The map was spread out on the desk and secured by drawing pins. It was like a carpet – huge, multicoloured, covering the whole desk top. Everyone except Grandpa bent over it. Zybin said: "Now then, here's the whole Karagalinka basin for you. Empty! For a hundred years there hasn't been so much as a pot or a drinking horn. A blank space! The rolling steppe for thirty miles around. Who on earth could have buried our little witch in this steppe? And why did they have to bring her corpse here? But if it wasn't a burial, what was it then?"

And once more, all three stared and pondered in silence, although it was obvious that there could be no answer. Even Grandpa gazed at the map and brooded along with the others, and like the rest, failed to come up with anything.

"A blank space!" he repeated thoughtfully.

"But perhaps," the director tentatively surmised, "it actually was a burial, just, you know, of a special kind. A sarcophagus, for instance. Maybe the hunters took shelter under the lid of the sarcophagus, not a boulder. The rest of it had crumbled, but the lid was left. Perhaps that's how it was, eh?"

As he talked, he looked at Zybin – now, in front of the map, he tacitly acknowledged his authority.

"No, actually, that's not the answer," Zybin shook his head. "In the first place, sarcophagi are dug into the ground, they're not just put up in the middle of the steppe. Secondly, if it is a sarcophagus, it must be enormous – after all, at least three men sheltered underneath it. To ferry that here and excavate a pit for an enormous thing like that, you'd need at least ten men. And that means that the gold would have disappeared. There'd have been at least one thief among the ten. After all, the steppe is bare and empty. Also it's a boulder that keeps being mentioned and a sarcophagus is built of worked slabs. Finally we come to the crucial point: we've never heard tell of any sarcophagus burial in these parts. Here, look at the 'Topographical Report on the Tumuli of the Semirechiye and Semipalatinsk Regions'. We're the Semirechiye. So, it says here: 'The Semirechiye tumuli are built in layers with stones, more rarely out of stones only.' And here: 'The layer of stones is quite often head-high, sometimes higher. This layer was covered over with earth.' And this is what it looks like: 'The tumulus is circular or oval, with a steep slope; on the top there is quite a significant area of depression.' That's it! You couldn't possibly mistake that for a boulder. The source: *Tomsk University Transactions*, Volume I, 1889, section—, page 142. Any questions?"

"Well, I'll be damned," said the director, much put out. "You're right! Still, what the devil can it be?"

Zybin shrugged his shoulders.

"What can it possibly be! We've got to find this boulder at all costs, then we can sort it all out; at least it seems certain that it isn't a burial! They simply abducted the girl, killed her and stuck her under this boulder. But you're right – what about the diadem? How could anybody have killed or abducted this young princess, or priestess out of the palace and carry her body more than sixty miles as well? And what does sixty miles mean? It means galloping for days across the steppe with a dead body across your saddlebow! Or was she still alive then? And why is the gold intact – why hasn't anyone come across it before now? It was lying right on the surface, wasn't it?" He spread his arms. "Well, who knows anything about it? Not me, for one; I can't even hazard a guess. There's only one thing for it: the place has to be found."

A pause ensued.

"No, it can happen," said Grandpa. "It can happen quite easily. They decoyed this young lass, had their way with her, suffocated her and got rid of her. That's all about it. The same thing happened in our village once. A wench was murdered. They hunted high and low and it turned out to be her next-door neighbour – the priest's son."

"Where on earth are we to find the place?" the director sighed. "Who's going to show you? This is all we've got left." He took out the green identity card covers and tossed them angrily onto the desk. "No, there's obviously not a hope in hell. That's what that senior man told me." He brooded. "So what sort of eyebrows did Alexander the Great have anyway?" he asked suddenly. "Don't know? Well what kinds of eyebrows are there? What sort have you got? Don't know? You don't know what your own eyebrows are even? Lend an ear then." He pulled out his notebook. "There are short brows, middling and long; straight, arched, broken, sinuous, bristling, tilted up or down or rigidly horizontal! Phew, ran out of breath. There's an investigator for you – and what about you? Take that ear of yours – you think it's just an ear, and that's all there is to it? Not on your life! Do you know how many distinguishing marks an ear has? Twenty. The lobe alone's got six. Now there's a science! Look at the way they put Grandpa through it!" He broke into a laugh. "So comrade scientist, you make a lot of fuss, but precious little comes of it! It seems it isn't a science yet, or rather it is, but not an exact one! Exact science is what they have over there – in the little grey house." He rose. "They ordered you to step in to see them as soon as the museum closes. You do that." He retrieved a piece of paper from his jotter. "There, comrade Zelenin, room 242. That's the old one. He's all right. When you get back, give him a ring; there's the phone. Take the acquisition report with you just in case. Ring me if need be. I'll be at home today." He got up from his chair and stretched till his bones cracked. "Well, we'll go our separate ways, comrades. You stay behind for a minute, Clara. We'll have to discuss the storage organization, otherwise something . . ."

Clara stayed behind, and Zybin deliberated before setting off for the market. An idea had occurred to him and he was very keen to check it. As a rule he always had a fear of the crush and press of crowds, enclosed spaces, congestion: "I get indigestion from the word congestion," he used to say, half-joking, half perfectly serious. And oh, how he recalled from past years the deadly boredom that reeked of carbolic! The ennui of snoring stations at night, the refuse tip depression of goods wagons which wouldn't let you sit or lie down, and the almost timeless boredom of Clear Ponds. It had been twenty years before. His first memories were of lime trees with dusty leaves, grilling heat, grey sand. Boredom and depression. The circular walk was hemmed in by baking-hot green benches. And sunflower seeds everywhere . . . The ground was totally covered in a crackling layer of sunflower seeds. The band was in the middle of the circle, soldiers sitting in a bandstand raised above the ground, blaring away. Below this circle moved another – nannies, maids, mademoiselles, governesses – all of them solemn, decently dressed, sternly smiling. Some wore cloth mobcaps or headbands. Others had on black headsquares with opulent flowers, the sort that bloom on wallpaper, dress materials, café teapots and trays. Shawls. Tippets. A bare head was seldom seen. Still lower came a third circle: wretched upper-class children gripped tightly by the hand. He was an upper-class child too and was gripped tightly by the hand and tugged along. The sun blazed down, the band thumped away. The circle moved slowly, slowly on; you couldn't escape, beg off or run away. You walked at a decorous childish pace with a tin spade in your dirty, sweaty palm, waiting for the panting trumpet's last desperate bellow. After that, the musicians would suddenly lower their instruments all together and start coughing,

43

blowing their noses, shifting about and talking. Nanny releases her pincers. The lower-class lads are everywhere, whistling, shouting, making backs for one another and altogether running riot. They're street arabs and don't give a damn for anything; they're allowed to do as they like. You aren't allowed to do anything at all. You're the son of well-bred parents. Hence boredom, sultry heat, a permanent headache, and a hand aching from nanny's pincers.

Why did those nannies circle and wheel? Why did the bandsmen blare and crack their breath? Why did they play "On the Hills of Manchuria" and "Weapons Sparkling in the Sun" to the nannies? Well, no doubt it all reminded them of upper-class conversations about high society, snapshots in *Ogonyok*, the cover of *Sun of Russia*, masked balls with prizes, strolling in the Tsar's garden, or other things of that sort. After all, a colonnaded white building stood opposite, the Coliseum cinema, which showed society films. Ever since that time, Zybin had cherished a bitter hatred for gatherings of all kinds and avoided them like the plague. But about two years later it had all flooded over him: the revolution, night trains and stations, cattle trucks and platforms! Ah, how familiar they had become over the last quarter century!

That was the reason he dreaded crowds and the Alma-Ata markets were the only such places he would willingly visit. There were a number of these: the Haymarket, the Flour market, the St Nicholas market and finally the nearest, the Green or Collective Farm Market. This market was a festive, drunken, almost crazy place. Zybin liked it better than all the others. This is where he headed from the museum.

The Green Market!

It was only at first glance that it seemed like a crush. A closer look revealed that it was an integrated, well-planned, precisely modelled organism. Everything had its place within the scheme of things. Melon sellers for example, always occupied one side of the market. On this side crowded the horses, the camels, the donkeys, carts and lorries. A vast number of lorries. They are filled with watermelons. They lie there in a jumbled pile: white, dark blue, black, striped. Husky lads in vests and check shirts stoop over them – they pick up one, then another, throw them up with ease, catch them comically, bend over the side to the buyer and thrust it to his ear: "Listen to it crackle? Ekh! Take a look, beardy, it's free!" Then with a flourish, plunge a knife into its dark-green striped flank; there comes a crunching sound and a red triangular segment quivers above the crowd on the point of the long

44

blade – the crimson living flesh, dripping with juice, all pink veins, cells, grains and crystals.

"Now then chuckle-head! You won't' find a white one these days, not for a thousand. Take this one! I'm giving it away! Go on!" shouts the vendor and flings the melon to a customer.

The same things are shouted from carts, fish boxes, trestles or just standing on the ground. Here the melon-thrusters are nimble Kazakh girls with dozens of plaits. They haul pails and huge brass kettles, singing almost in verse:

"Here's fresh cold water!"

"Who's for fresh cold water!"

"Water! Water! Two kopecks the mug. Step right up, little Ivan!"

Next to them come the small retailers – a stand selling muslin, dead slices of watermelon now lying underneath, limp, sticky, clotted with brownish watermelon sweetness. Above them drones a swarm of large metallic-purple flies (called shimpan flies locally). Touch a slice and you whip your hand away at once: in among the black and yellow lacquered seeds, three or four of the predators lie motionless, apart from the tremor of their delicate tigerish abdomen.

"H-here's your water! Who wants fresh cold water!" the pure girlish voices ring around, with a calm hexameter very occasionally breaking through: "Now here's sweet melons, they smell lovely! Who'll buy? Fragrant sweet melons. Who'll buy?"

These fragrant sweet melons have their own special row of stalls. They're a delicate commodity. They don't get poured out in heaps, they're set out in rows on matting. There are spherical melons, precisely shaped, with gentle streamlined sides – the local name is "tun", but what they most resemble is some internal organ belonging to an unknown monster – a kidney or a heart. Their flesh is orange-yellow or a suffused green, like Chartreuse. There are long, conical ones too, like mines or spaceships (in those days they used to draw them like that in the magazine *Round the World*). There are melons golden as autumn, as leaf-fall, as sunset in the tranquil waters of a pond. There are melons reminiscent of the heads of huge tropical reptiles, with their blotches, bruises, colours mingling in predatory serpentine patterns. Melons exude a barely perceptible aroma and anyone who makes his way along these rows seems to breathe it in. The vendors in this row are also somehow other, just as their customers are unlike those who flock round the watermelons on board the five-ton trucks. These vendors are old, respectable people, Uzbeks or Kazakhs – proud chieftains with grave

45

beards, brown icon-like faces, wearing black and white skullcaps. They stay calm, no rushing about or shouting; they just sing out: "Now here are sweet-smelling melons." You step up, inspect, pay your money and take your purchase away. Not everyone is allowed to taste the melons. It's a ritual in itself. To begin with, they cut it in half; then they take the thinnest possible translucent slice. Then the transparent pink flake is borne on the tip of a long knife, thin as a razor, right up to the customer's face; take it into your mouth, suck and evaluate. The customer too is his own man. Round the watermelons you find boys, old wives, seasonal workers, drivers, boozers. If they haven't a knife, they simply smash the watermelons across their knee and having done so, tear it apart with their bare hands. They eat it on the spot, champing away, suffused with sweetness, stomachs rumbling, getting their noses, eyes, their very hair almost, into the rind. The green crescents and skins lie scattered everywhere on the ground. Melons are carried home under the arm: once there upon its white porcelain dish, placed in the centre of the table, that table lights up and becomes a festive board. A melon is so richly coloured, so tender, so luminous, patterned with hot sun and gold, reminiscent of a precious majolica vase.

Next came the tomatoes and onions. Onions – are bundles of long blue-green arrows, but also tubers, laid out in rows. In the sunshine they glow Suzdal-gold. But peel away the gold leaf and a juicy, tightly packed droplet of incredible purity and brilliance rolls out, whitish-green or violet. According to Perelman, water in space takes precisely this form. Violet or green, however, they still get chewed on the spot with hot bread and grey camel-salt. They crunch as their extraordinary bitter sweetness takes the breath away, goes up your nose; still people bite into them, gnaw and crunch them. "Good and strong," they say, smiling through their tears. "Sweet onions, none like them anywhere!" But there are no tomatoes anywhere to compare with those in the Green Market either; they lie in boxes, in trays, on counters – huge, soft, filled to the brim with viscous sap, taut and glossy tropical fruit. They have all the tints of red and yellow, from amber, coral-pink, clouded and translucent like moon rock, to market-red rough matryoshki. They are purchased and borne away by the tray-load – round taut spheres, crimson cavalry caps, yellow rounded pebbles. All the same, you won't expend more than a rouble here. Near the trays of tomatoes, onions and multicoloured potatoes (yellow, white, black, pink, almost coral!) the trading area divides into two. On one side, are the rows of stalls, the other leans up against the wall. This is the post office. It is from here that the celebrated Alma-Ata Oporto goes winging to every corner of the land. Here they sell packing cases, fresh wood shavings, linen pieces to cover the boxes. They sew them up, write on them and weigh them. At the same time, swift efficient personages flit by with hammers, nail-pullers and indelible pencils behind their ears. There is a different price list for everything, one for packing and nailing up, another for writing the address handsomely, for weighing, standing in the queue for you and despatching. It is here that a certain obscure personage is to be found wandering sadly between the stalls. The habitués know he is an actor and poet-novelist. He has the dreadful blue-white face of the dipsomaniac. He's been fired from the theatre, so he wanders round the market telling fortunes. He has a thick tome underneath his arm. *How the Steel Was Tempered*, the braille edition. He places it on his knee, opens it and tells your fortune. Next to him, an old woman is trading in the denizens of the deep. It's a lively spot. There's a beer barrel standing here and hands go flying above it, with mugs and pint bottles. Shouting, laughter. Here they drink that way, half a mug of beer chased by half a mug of vodka. Seafood goes down very well with a combination like that.

Zybin loved this section best of all. But this time he didn't go as far as that; he turned off to the right to the fish stalls. Various kinds of fish were on sale here – smoked, tender-golden as if wrapped in fading palm leaves, even a metallic violet shade. Fish lay on the counter, hung in bunches, splashed about in zinc tubs and pans. Zybin's arm was tugged as he was offered Caspian herring, Aral catfish, carp from Lonely Ponds. He bought nothing and asked the price of nothing. He reached the end of the row and turned back.

"Have you got no marinka today?" he asked a lanky middle-aged vendor, who was standing with his hands tucked inside his apron, silently regarding him.

"Well, where would we get hold of that now? You won't come across marinka at the moment. Unless anybody's got some dried left. We don't deal in that."

"Dried, did you say?"

"Just the dried stuff. There's a ban at the moment on anything else. What do you expect! The plan hasn't been fulfilled. Unless they pinch some from somewhere. Come back in a month's time, there'll be a bit then."

In the ensuing silence they exchanged glances, still not trusting one another totally.

47

"What a pity, what a pity," Zybin said. "And I really do need some marinka desperately."

"Fresh?"

"Fresh or smoked, doesn't matter. Smoked would be better."

The trader looked at him, taking his measure before asking: "Need a lot?"

"I'll take as much as there is. My sister in Vyatka asked me to get her some." He fished a letter out of his pocket.

"It's called Kirov now, not Vyatka," corrected the fishmonger. "Then all you have to do is take a trip over to the Ili. They've got as much as you want there. You'll see it as you go along the bank – tons and tons of it. It's the First of May Collective. Any of the farmers will fix you up with a dozen kilos."

"Who should I apply to there, do you know?"

The trader deliberated; once more they looked at one another, before full and final comprehension dawned.

"Well, in that case, as soon as you get to the collective office, by the bridge, ask for Pavel Savelev right away. He's a driver there. Tell him Shakhvorostov, Ivan Petrovich, sent you."

"Thank you, I'll just make a note of that – right, Shakhvorostov, Ivan Petrovich, there! Tell me, you haven't heard of a Yumashev, Ivan Antonovich, have you? He used to be a mate of mine, I think he's still there."

"What was that – Yumashev? No, no, can't bring anyone to mind. I don't know many of the new people over there. Could it be Ishimov you're after? There's one called that. Works in the weigh-house"

"No, it's Yumashev right enough," said Zybin, nodding slightly. "Well, thanks, I'll go over there straightaway. Pavel Savelev! Thanks a lot."

He went off, but soon halted again. People were crowding around the fretted gates bearing the legend FOR COLLECTIVE ABUNDANCE, all smoking, sending up clouds of fumes, and cracking sunflower seeds. He squeezed through them and caught sight of an artist busy at his easel. Zybin knew this eccentric individual well. A month or so before he had submitted an explanation at the police station (the neighbours had kept complaining) and had signed himself: "Genius of the first rank, Earth and Galaxy, stage designer and performer at the Abai ballet, Sergey Ivanovich Kalmykov". As we know, only one man was accounted a genius of humanity at that time, and a prank like that could have

48

turned out very badly – who knew what a title like that might conceal? Perhaps it was sarcasm, or demonstrated a desire to challenge. Apparently doubts were expressed in certain circles, but that was as far as it went. Perhaps one of the powers that be had encountered Kalmykov in the street and decided that a scalp like that wouldn't be worth taking. But he would have been wrong! That head was worth a good deal. When the artist appeared in the street, a minor tumult took place around him. The traffic would slow to a halt. People would stop and stare. Something utterly extraordinary went floating past them: something red, yellow, green, blue – a thing of stripes fringes and ribbons. Kamykov used to design his own attire and took trouble to see that it were absolutely inimitable. He had a theory of his own in that regard.

"Just picture it to yourself," he would explain. "From the depths of the universe, millions of eyes are looking down, and what do they see? A dull, monochrome grey mass crawling and crawling over the earth, then suddenly, like a pistol shot – a bright red blob! That's me going outside."

Now too he was dressed for the galaxy, not for other people. On his head lay a beret, flat and somehow thrustful; an elaborately adorned pale-blue cloak draped his thin shoulders; under it glittered something incredibly garish and ghastly – red-yellow-lilac. The artist was working. He was flicking one dab, a second, a third onto his canvas – all of this careless, offhand, playful – then, going off to one side, he abruptly lowered his brush; the crowd shrank back; the artist would size up, select and then suddenly out would shoot an arm – got it! – and a rich black daub would fall onto the canvas. It adhered somewhere near the bottom, crooked, askew, seemingly totally out of place, but after a succession of daubs, a few prods and touches with the brush, forming splodges of colour – yellow, green, blue – and lo! – out of the colourful obscurity on the canvas, something would begin to emerge, condense, take shape. And a portion of the market would appear: dust, heat, sand, glowing white-hot and resonant, and a cart loaded with watermelons. The sun has blurred the outlines, drained the colours and eroded the forms. The cart flows, quivers, diffuses in the scorching air.

The artist creates and people watch and appraise. They jostle, laugh, rally each other, crane forward. Each wants a better view. Drunks, children, women. There are virtually no serious people. This sort of charade holds no interest for serious people! They glance and pass by: "He's a dauber," is what respectable folk say of Kalmykov – he's got an idiotic face and he dresses like poor Poll! "In the old days people like him were let out of the madhouse only on major holidays to their kin." Zybin had heard this sort of conversation himself. A cultured old boy, a veritable Chapaev in his moustaches, high boots and field jacket, came pushing his way through and stood there in front of them all; he was clearly somewhat under the influence. He stood for a while, looking and stroking his moustache, harrumphed and asked most politely: "Excuse me, are you in the Artists Union?"

"Uhuh," replied Kalmykov.

The old chap screwed up his eyes, practical-fashion, and stood there, considering.

"Forgive me, but what is it you are painting exactly?" he enquired affably.

Kalmykov nodded absently towards the square.

"Those carts over there with the watermelons."

"Where have you put them then?" said the astonished old chap. He was all merciless politeness, sternly knowledgeable and ironic.

Kalmykov walked away from his canvas for a moment, gazed at it narrowly, then suddenly seized something from the air, caught it on his brush and hurled it onto the canvas.

"Look closer!" he cried gleefully.

But the other looked no more. He shook his head and said: "They never used to paint like that in our day. If they drew you felt like taking hold of it and eating it like an apple, a watermelon, or gammon – but what sort of a thing is that? If I don't clean out the henhouse for a day that's what the floor looks like!"

Kalmykov shot a cheery sideways glance at him, then all of a sudden, bent over the canvas. The brush began to flicker. Had the old fellow's words inspired him or had he grasped the key at that very moment? At all events, he started to work and forgot all else. The cultured old boy still stood there watching, then shook his head and asked coarsely: "And what's that you're wearing? Supposed to be a joke is it? To shock people? Artist! In the old days they'd have taken an artist like you by the scruff of the neck and off to the police station with you straightaway. Nowadays, of course, it's do your own thing!"

And off he went, a picture of angry dignity, bearing a tight black scroll under his arm – Swan Lake on oilcloth.

Meanwhile Kalmykov fiercely went on painting. Nobody asked him any more questions. He had conducted the conversation very well, at ease with himself and with considerable dignity, and Zybin thought at the time: "Well, God knows what sort of an artist he is, but he knows his own worth."

He turned and left the crowd.

He was to recall this encounter many years later, when Kalmykov's notebook came into his hands. This was after the death of the artist, when the notebook was lying around on the floor of the dead man's room. Zybin picked it up unnoticed and carried it off to read. All the notes were in strict alphabetical order (the book itself was indexed). The dead man had jotted down everything he remembered or came into his head: old verses, lines from newspapers, his expenses. Under the letter "N" for example, Zybin read: "Nobody enjoys painting in the open air more than I do. That's my forte! All around, people look, yawn, stare, all according. The children are seeing it for the first time! Others are envious, or bored or heckle. I hold forth, snap at them, make witty remarks – in short I feel completely at home, in my element in fact! There's no one to touch me here! I really should be carried shoulder high for all this; I've been doing it free all my life! Doing the work of ten! Nobody cares, the fools couldn't care less, but I'll make it hot for them!"

Then again (letter "K" now): "When you talk a lot about what really matters – everybody runs away; nobody has time to listen to long conversations on serious topics. So, with the constant daily talk with one or another, you develop a constant habit of talking about everything flamboyantly and with gusto, after which the happiest formulations come into one's head! There! 'I've come back from the streets and I have a discovery in my head! I walked along in silence, talking to myself . . .' "

Yes, that was what he was – extremely sure of himself, invulnerable to jibes, beyond the reach of criticism, veiled from the world by his genius which had no desire for recognition of any kind. Certainly it was to him alone out of all the artists, poets, philosophers great and small, successful or not, that Pushkin's words could have been applied with total justification "a king then – dwell alone". That was how Kalmykov lived, aware of his uniqueness. It was only trifles which could disconcert this monarch. Something like this: "There's wax paper on sale at a rouble fifty-four, but I've only got eighty." Yes, that did upset him, but still not very much, not very much. This is abundantly clear from the alphabetical notebook. No means no, and there's no use dwelling on it. He understood that iron word "no" perfectly well.

Many years went by. Kalmykov died, and the first article about the deceased ended as follows: "A strange man used to walk the streets of Alma-Ata – dishevelled hair under an ancient beret, wide sackcloth trousers, sewn in broad stitched coloured threads, and with a huge decorated bag by his side. In the final years there is a note in his diary: 'What is a theatre or circus to me? For me the whole world is a theatre.' "

No, not just the world, the whole galaxy. However all this was very far from apparent in that year, 1937.

Something else was clear. That was the time when the periodical *Literary Kazakhstan* published a piece about the Artists Union jubilee exhibition. It said approximately the following about Kalmykov: "It is absolutely incomprehensible how and why the exhibition organizers let through the pictures by a certain Kalmykov. One of them has two citizens standing swinging suitcases. It is clear these suitcases are empty, because they couldn't swing them if they were full. An objectionable, talentless daub." And that's all. Give it what for. Objectionable, talentless daub. And it was just at this time that the artist was executing that magnificent series of drawings, to which he gave peculiar and, as always, not wholly comprehensible names: "Chevalier Spendthrift", "Lunar Jazz". It is impossible to write about these drawings – you have to see for yourself the enchantingly subtle lines, the modulations of the human body. There are many women among Kalmykov's countless sketches, and they are all beautiful; it seems likely that as an artist he was incapable of representing an ugly female face. His women are like palm trees, elongated southern fruits, they have slender arms and almond eyes (one need not shy at using such words in this context). They are very tall and slender, taller indeed than anything else. Standing or lying, they take up the whole drawing. Some of them have tiny wings – evidently fairies. Others are just women and that's all. For example, (if we take just the published drawings) there is a beautiful woman in a long, soft, heavy robe. It's not worn, merely thrown on to reveal leg, breast and waist. She carries a long-necked eastern vessel. A candelabra burns on a small table. It is like a bough in blossom and bears three little flowers. Close by is an open book, with a bookmark lying on it. Night, silence, no one there. Where is this solitary beauty going? A strange creature is running after her, not exactly a cat, nor yet a little dog; it's impossible to make out which. And that is all there is.

In this drawing, everything is musical. Everything is orchestrated in one tone, the three flowers on the candelabra, the tablecloth, blending with the softly gleaming robe, the woman's body and this strange creature with the doggy ears and the feline shape. The rhythm achieves an extreme laconic simplicity and suppleness of line.

And another drawing. It's called "Lunar Jazz". It shows a waitress with butterfly wings – the same tall, delicate, cool blonde beauty (Kalmykov evidently acknowledged only one type of feminine beauty). She is carrying a tray with a long-necked bottle and a vase with a twig in it. She has on the same light clothing which reveals her entire body. Or, put another way, her entire body is a single flowing line embraced by the oval of her garments. Night. A staircase, an outdoor stage. A servant is descending the steps wearing a weird hat and cloak. And again that is almost all there is. And once again it is impossible to describe and convey in words the fascination of this drawing.

After Kalmykov's death, a great number of such drawings remained, perhaps two or three hundred of these suites, jazzes, sketches. They are executed using a variety of techniques. Line, dotted and continuous, coloured or uncoloured outlines, pencil and watercolour. For example, there is "Chevalier Spendthrift" among others. Outwardly, the chevalier is very reminiscent of Kalmykov. The same billowing cloak, the same beret, the same crazily-coloured mantilla. And the medals, medals, medals! Orders from every non-existent state on earth. He walks along, laughing and gaily looking at us. But that was never Kalmykov, he was always serious. If asked, he was willing to answer any question, but he never spoke first. That bit about "nobody likes painting in the open air as much as I do" was perfectly true. But he allowed no one into the world where lunar jazz was played, where winged beauties floated and bold Chevalier Spendthrifts strutted along. There he was always alone.

Zybin was unaware of all this, nor could he have known of it – and to be completely frank, would not have wished to know at that point. The times were not altogether propitious for the likes of Lunar Jazz and Chevalier Spendthrift. But in any case he simply didn't know of it. That day too in the Green Market, glancing at the artist, he understood nothing and remembered nothing. The article about the empty suitcases (which incidentally he himself had edited and corrected) simply came into his head. He just thought: "That's the odd fish, then!" And how pleasant it was that the population of odd fish in Alma-Ata had increased by one. But meet Kalmykov he did, and this was how it came about. One day, some fortnight previously, the director had said to him: "What are you doing on your day off? Going anywhere special? Excellent! Right then, I'll pick you up and we'll go over to the Alma-Atinka. All right?"

53

"All right," he had replied, though somewhat surprised. It even crossed his mind that the director intended inviting him to a shashlik restaurant. That summer they had sprung up on every corner. But the director at once elucidated.

"We're building a branch near Gorky Park. 'Science and Religion'. I've had Grandpa working since yesterday morning over there with a team of carpenters. We'll drop in and see how things are going."

He shrugged his shoulders.

"What do I know about that sort of thing?"

"Carpentry?" The director registered surprise. "Absolutely nothing. From what I see, you can't knock a nail in straight. That tiger of yours is going to drop off the wall one day and smash to smithereens."

On the wall there hung "Tiger attacking a company of soldiers near the town of Verny"; it was an ancient picture, dark, dull, bad and much prized in the museum. Snapshots of it were even on sale in the entrance hall. And why not indeed? What a subject!

"As it happens, Grandpa hung that up there," said Zybin.

"Really? The old sod! Look, he's hammered the nail straight into the brick and bent it. Well, I'll let him know when I get the chance. You see, we've got an artist working locally. Kalmykov – heard of him?" Zybin shook his head. He really didn't know who he was. "Go on, yes you do. He goes round the streets in a beret and blue pants. A proper vagabond king he is! You must have seen him."

"Well, well," replied Zybin and began to laugh.

The director joined in.

"So he's remembered. Well then, he's an excellent artist all the same. And he'll do whatever we ask him to. It seems that's his line of work too. He paints sets at the opera. I said to him: 'Paint it so that the visitor stops dead and has convulsions.' He says: 'I will.' He promised to come over next day and bring the designs. So, we're going to see what he's dreamed up."

They got to the Alma-Atinka early in the morning and they could see immediately that things were humming. Grandpa and the artist Kalmykov were standing on a gigantic blue boulder. Grandpa was holding a folded sheet of Whatman and Kalmykov was explaining something to him, with quiet conviction. Grandpa listened in silence.

"Meanwhile Grandpa doesn't approve," said the director. "He doesn't approve of all those folderols of his. Grandpa likes strictness. If he was in charge he'd shave all his hair off and stick him into linen pants. Let's go over there then."

54

They approached. Kalmykov greeted them with austere dignity. He gave a slight bow, while keeping his trunk completely stiff and touched a finger to his beret; the director bowed also. All three suddenly became grave and judicious, as if they were at some official reception.

"Well then, show us the drawings."

On the large sheet of Whatman was depicted the golden sky of the astrologers. There was the circle of the zodiac, then the constellations of Virgo, Andromeda, the Great and Little Bears, and others of that kind; below there were two black sphinxes along with the enormous triumphal arch from Palace Square in Leningrad. A tractor, an ordinary CTZ, was going through the arch and heading straight as a die for the heavens and their golden constellations. All this was drawn firmly and precisely, as colourful and graphic as a school visual aid. But besides this clarity there was something else, pertaining to art. Only an artist could express such a dark-blue mysterious sky. So blue was it, it was almost black, so deep that the stars dotted about it really did seem to sparkle from infinite distance. The colours Kalmykov employed were perfectly ordinary, simple schoolroom colours, and yet all had been achieved: the infinity of the canvas, the immensity of the sky, and eternity itself symbolized in these mysterious sphinxes, somehow shot through with black light. And through the Palace arch, that scrapbook and poster image, hymned and worn smooth in editions of millions, proceeded a common or garden tractor, with a lad in a workman's jacket seated behind the wheel. All these diverse and unmatched elements, the other world and this one, were drawn together into a simple, limpid composition. In its precision, integrity and naturalness the concept of the artist was expressed.

"And what is this going to be?" asked the director, "The entrance?"

"No," replied the artist. "I've done another sketch for the entrance. This is the mural."

"I see," said the director. "Ye-es. Well, Keeper, your opinion?"

Zybin shrugged.

"It will all be very striking. But the composition itself is a bit over the top."

"How's that?" enquired the artist sweetly.

"It's supposed to be the 'Science and Religion' pavilion, isn't it?" said Zybin. "So we get the golden heavens of course, and the sphinxes too. But the tractor and that arch . . ."

"The Red Guards went through that arch when they stormed the Winter Palace," the director recalled.

"And the tractor is just like real," came praise from Grandpa. "My grandson drives one of those. It's got no little flag though."

Again they stood in silent thought. Zybin could see that the design had taken the director's fancy, but he was aware of its unconventional nature and was worried in case that got in the way of its intelligibility. Not everyone would appreciate the artist's conception.

"Come, come, out with it, Keeper," he pressed. "Let's have a discussion."

"And the space is a bit odd," said Zybin. "Not fully resolved somehow. It's not a plane and not a sphere. The objects lack perspective; they don't all seem to exist at the same time."

Kalmykov shot a sharp glance at him.

"Exactly," he said. "Exactly. You've put your finger right on it. I have annihilated time here. I . . ." He paused and spoke clearly and distinctly, as he gazed into Zybin's eyes: "I have violated the balance between angles and lines and once that happens they become extended to infinity. Can you imagine what a point is?"

Zybin pictured to himself what a point was, but shook his head just to be on the safe side.

"There," sighed the artist in profound satisfaction. "You alone out of all the people I know have admitted that you do not know what a dot is. A dot is the zero state of an infinite number of concentric circles, of which some bearing one sign spread around the circle and others bearing the opposite sign spread from the zero circle inwards. A point may be the size of the universe too."

He said this, or rather blurted it out in a single breath and glanced triumphantly at them all.

The director, however, frowned his dissatisfaction. Now he realized: no, this wouldn't get through to the masses. Too complex.

"That won't do for us," he said shortly. "Remove the tractor and the arch; you can leave the sky. But we need something else for the other walls. The trial of Galileo, say. The battle of the dinosaurs. God did not create man, man created God in his own image. Come in and see me tomorrow and we'll sort through them together and make a choice."

"I understand; it shall be done," said the artist and walked away silently to the banks of the Alma-Atinka. His easel was standing there, and a crowd of gapers and children had already gathered. A lanky individual, drunk, was solemnly explaining that he was well acquainted with this artist and he went about permanently in green trousers for religious reasons.

Zybin also approached the easel.

"May I have a peep?" he asked.

Kalmykov shrugged.

"By all means," he said indifferently. "But what's there to see? Nothing's been finished yet . . . Now if you were to drop round to my place, I could show you a thing or two." He turned to him abruptly. "Perhaps you could do that?"

"Thank you," Zybin said, "I'll certainly do that. Just let me have your address, I'll come by today."

Many years later he wrote: "It was only a quarter of a century later that I got there, however. That was because I somehow couldn't find the time that particular day, and after that he didn't invite me. Then we went our separate ways and I completely forgot about Kalmykov the artist. I only knew that he left the theatre on a pension and got a one-room flat somewhere (previously he'd lived in the old barrack blocks) and, a confirmed vegetarian, was now living by himself on milk and porridge. He was often to be seen about the streets. During my last visits, I did see him two or three times, but he ignored me as he did everyone else around, so I walked past him without a word. I noticed that he had lost weight and grown sallow; age had pinched and dried up his features and accentuated the deep straight furrows by his nose. 'A face as crumpled as a paper rouble,' Grin writes somewhere of such faces. But what he had on was absolutely inconceivable – a loose overall, wide trousers with golden stripes, and on the side something resembling a huge tambourine, embroidered with tongues of vari-coloured flame – silken threads of bright red, yellow, violet and crimson. He was standing by a newspaper kiosk buying papers. An enormous number of them, all that the stallholder had on offer. I recalled that when I entered the artist's room on the third day after he died. There was a huge quantity of newspapers. Of all the sorts of furniture that existed, he knew only pouffes, made out of bundles of newspapers. There was nothing else. A table. A teapot on the table, a couple of glasses and that was all. What more did he need after all?

"Deliriously happy, a man of purpose and integrity lived, moved and talked among these newspaper pouffes and folders stuffed with interminable novels.

"On these pouffes he dreamed colourful dreams, which he then wrote down in his indexed book (under 'E'):

E

Endless number of bears, white, Arctic, northern bore me on a black lacquered litter! Bakstian negroes headed the procession! Little capuchin monkeys followed after them!

Or (under 'I'):

I

I have seen suites of halls, sparkling with multicoloured tiles!

I have passed through chambers, speckled with signs of all kinds.

"Yes, Sergey Ivanovich Kalmykov, the quondam artist-performer of the Abai Opera, inhabited a beautiful and extraordinary world.

"And it was at this point, among truly shining tiles of lunar jazz, fairies, and chevaliers, that I glimpsed on a piece of cardboard something quite other – something troubled, overwrought, lathered, agonized, almost frightening. I glanced at the date and suddenly realized, what I held in my hands was what Kalmykov had wanted to paint a quarter of a century ago, on the very day of our one and only conversation. In broad brush strokes of whiting, ochre and Prussian blue (if that's how painters name their colours), Kalmykov had depicted the place on the Alma-Atinka where, in the director's opinion, the magical 'Science and Religion' pavilion ought to rise.

"Boulders, massive rocks, fine coloured pebbles, sharp gravel, the rough foaming torrent with its eddies and pits – spray and booming, and on the largest rocks, people in shorts lying about sun-bathing. It was the sun which epitomized it all; its direct beams penetrated and transformed everything, it emphasized volumes, moulded forms. And every object responded to its warmth with its own effulgence – a harsh, yellow, penetrating light.

"It was the sun for instance, which made the stream look like a flayed body. The bunching muscles were clearly visible, white and yellow hummocks, frozen in their convulsions, overstretched fascias. The picture is so dissonant, it dazzles the eye. The tension of it becomes wearisome. Not a view to hang on your wall. But if it was exhibited in a gallery, however many canvases hung alongside, you would be bound to stop before this one; intense, unpleasant, unlike almost anything else. Of course, you will pause, look at it, then pass on, shrugging perhaps: what a picture! Is that our Alma-Atinka, or what?

"But later on, in the street or in the evening having tea or lying in bed, you are bound to recall it without any prompting: 'That stream now! What did he mean by it? What was the idea underlying it all?' And approximately a week later that is exactly what happened to me; I suddenly realized precisely what was depicted here. Kalmykov had painted the earth. The earth as a whole. As it seemed to him that far-off morning. An alien, as yet unpeopled planet. The arena of savage unequal forces. It didn't matter that there were boys sunbathing; the stream had nothing to do with them: it had its own cosmic significance, its own goal and was fulfilling it with the calm persistence of any inert matter. That was why it resembled a naked bunch of muscles. That was why everything in it was tense, everything at the limit. And its boulders were also in keeping, because they weren't boulders at all, they were shards of the planet, pieces of a mountain chain. And their colours are savage, muted, the sort people never use. And it is quite irrelevant that the little stream is wretched and the blocks of stone aren't blocks, simply big rounded boulders. Nevertheless, it is still nature itself – *natura naturata*, as the ancients had it; nature being nature. And here on a tiny piece of cardboard, in the depiction of a dozen metres of a city stream, rages the same cosmos as that above us in the stars, galaxies, metagalaxies, and God knows where else. And let the boys skim pebbles at her feet, let them sunbathe, let them, let them! It was no concern of hers. Hence the harsh colours, the sharpness of the light and the emphasized masses – they are all inherent features of inert matter, testifying to the tempestuous forces which created them. Yes, these same stones were nothing more than the crystallized essence of her might, flung asunder and solidified. Thus had the artist pictured the Alma-Atinka the day he unrolled the first sheet of his Whatman before us with the ancient astrological heaven and the tractor progressing through the Palace arch up to the Milky Way itself. It is the Alma-Atinka, seen from the Andromeda nebula. Now that picture hangs above my bookcase and I look at it every day. It turns out that one can derive positive pleasure from it – so superb is the execution. Today Kalmykov's pictures hang in the Kazakhstan Gallery. They were piled into a heap and taken there. If they are ever put on show, I would advise you to go and look: a good deal will seem monstrous or incomprehensible, but don't condemn it and don't condemn the artist at once, out of hand. Kalmykov the artist never created anything thoughtlessly, just for the sake of it; every sketch has its meaning, its idea, even though sometimes it is not so easy to think through to it. What can one do – after all there do exist such odd, ungovernable things as dreams, imagination, or simply a personal vision of the world."

... He turned on his heel, extricated himself from the crowd and set off for the museum. The storage department door was half-open. He entered and saw Clara sitting at the desk, chin on hand, staring straight at him. Her face was calm and untroubled, but her eyes were sick. There was no trace even of that cold, sad brilliance he had noticed a couple of hours before, when they had been talking about the skull. The skull was lying close by now, and a fresh white ticket on a red thread was already dangling from the eye socket. Zybin came in and halted by the lintel. Clara did not speak. He wanted to say something to her but she was looking straight at him and he could not fathom what this portended. So they went on staring at one another in an agony of awkwardness, closeness and constraint. Then all at once he realized that she was simply oblivious of his presence.

"Clara," he called softly.

She did not stir, and remained in her strange abstracted state a few seconds longer, then gave an abrupt gentle sigh and, with perfect serenity and no transition, said: "Come in, Georgi Nikolaevich. I've already catalogued the skull. You can have it if you want it."

At this, he swiftly went on over to her, placed both hands on her shoulders, shook her gently and said with tender insistence: "Clarochka, sweetheart, now what's the matter? What is it? Has something happened?"

She sighed faintly and inclined her head, whereupon he quietly moved close to her and cuddled her to him.

"Have I hurt you in some way?" he said, and at once thought: 'Oh, you idiot, you idiot.' "

She freed herself with a lithe, barely perceptible movement of her shoulder and stood up.

"Of course not," she said calmly, putting all this from her. "So then, you don't need the skull? I'll put it away in the cupboard then. Have a look though and see if I've rewritten the card properly."

He pushed the card away without a glance.

"Yes you have, my Usuni princess," he said tenderly. "It's all perfectly all right. And, do you know who she was?"

"Who?" she asked.

He took her silently by the temples, turned her towards him and kissed her on both eyelids, firmly and carefully. Then again and again. All of a sudden, her face was bathed in perspiration and her mouth trembled like a child.

"That's your great grandmother, my dear," he said. "Your very own grandmother, sorceress of mine."

She opened the cupboard and placed the skull on a shelf, then closed the doors and stood there for a minute or so with her back to him.

"Are you going in to see the director? Best if you didn't just now," she said without turning round. "He's not in the best of moods, I don't think. I've been speaking to him and . . ."

The conversation had been as follows.

"Clarochka, the reason I asked you to stay behind was that I wanted to have a serious talk with you about our Keeper," said the director, too embarrassed to look at her. "After all, apart from you, the fool's got nobody."

He picked a folder up from the table and tossed it angrily down again.

Clara glanced at the director, who caught the look and scowled.

"Well, I don't count," he said snappishly. "I'm an old man, an administrator, so he looks at me like this." The director made a tube of his fist and brought it to his eye. "Well, maybe that's how it really is, but from the practical viewpoint . . . Well, you can't go on the way he does! You just can't! Not in times like these! And he just doesn't realize. Well, what do you think of Kornilov, for instance?"

She made a vague gesture.

"What sort of a person is he? Valuable worker, knowledgeable colleague or what?" insisted the director.

"Yes, I would say so," answered Clara.

"And self-disciplined of course? Yes? Sits over his books day and night, yes? Or what? The Keeper, now, he may take a drink but he does work. But that one – drinks and doesn't work?"

Clara considered.

"But that business with the bones – it was him who . . ." she said warily.

The director frowned.

"Yes, yes, that was him all right. But there was something else involved in all that. An old flame turned up, you see, and she . . ." He shot another glance at Clara and dried up. Clara said nothing. "So this is what I wanted to ask you," he resumed after a pause. "Have a word with the Keeper. Get him to tell Kornilov: 'Bite your blasted tongue in half.' Got that?"

"No," responded Clara, "I don't. That is, I . . . What's the trouble then?"

"Just this," the director exploded. "They'll both come crashing down like a couple of copper saucepans! And that's the last you'll see of them! With the young one it's his mouth and with the other it's stupidity; because he listens and says nothing. If he keeps quiet, he's acquiescing, and if he does that, he's an accomplice. Well of course, how else can it be? Who is not with us is against us. Know who said that? Mayakovsky!"

A pause.

Clara stood and thought.

"Forgive me, Stepan Mitrofanovich," she said at length. "There's still something I don't understand. All right, he shouts a lot. But what should Zybin do? Run off to report him?"

The director smiled painfully.

"No need, other people have already come running! A dozen times, probably. He should have yelled at him: 'Shut up, you fool! If you want to crawl down the pit, don't drag other people with you.' That's what he should have done. Is that so hard to understand? I'm surprised at you if so. Clever girl like you and doesn't see. Oh, what's the use of talking . . ." He waved a dismissive hand, paced the room angrily, then went over to the window and closed it. He approached the table, sat down in his chair, opened a drawer and closed it again, picked up the telephone and replaced it. He was greatly upset.

"Well, all right," said Clara grasping the import of all this. "Let's suppose Georgi Nikolaevich tells Kornilov to hold his tongue and Kornilov ignores him. Then what? Run and report him? Maybe he's told him already, come to that."

"Told him?" The director opened and shut his drawer with a tremendous flourish. "He hasn't said a bloody thing to him! Drank with him – oh yes! Kornilov has to be told so that he stays told. And if he still doesn't, damn him to hell and punch him one good and hard, so he stays out cold for an hour. That's what I'm begging you, tell him all that. He might take notice of you."

"What about you?"

"Well, what about me?" replied the director reluctantly. "I'm in charge. If I know something, then I have to . . . take steps, not issue warnings. The idiotic disease of complacency – do you know what that is nowadays?"

Clara considered.

"Well then, I won't issue warnings either," she said.

"What? You won't?" The director was greatly taken aback.

"No," responded Clara, painfully adamant.

"But he'll be put inside, the idiot, bound to be!" shouted the director grimly.

"That's up to him," sighed Clara. "I can't be any help at all in the matter."

"That's great," said the director, rising and moving towards Clara. "That's something I never expected. Don't you have any feeling for him at all? Friendship, at least?"

Now they were standing facing one another and staring into each other's eyes, the way people very rarely do when talking.

"Why ask that?" she answered, tormented. "You know . . ."

"So it's better for him to go inside?" blazed the director.

She sighed but did not avert her eyes. This conversation was a confusing agony for her, but she realized it was inescapable.

"Of course not, it would be worse. But only the individual can decide what's better or worse for him. Nobody else can show him what to do in things like this."

"So," repeated the director. "So." Then suddenly burst out laughing. There was compassion in his laughter, even grief, but relief at the same time. "I had no idea you were like this. Well, you know best, of course. But where do people like him come from, quiet, tiresomely persistent, and absolutely stupid? He knows very well what's going on and yet he heads on into the pit."

"I don't know," she sighed. "I don't know, Stepan Mitrofanovich, but maybe nothing's going to happen, maybe it'll all blow over."

The director shook his head.

"No."

"Then what about firing Kornilov?"

"I've already thought of that; can't be done," sighed the director. "That's the point, it can't be done now. Miroshnikov rang me two days ago. Kornilov wasn't to be sacked. He was to stay where he was, supervising the dig. That was without any prompting from me. He said

63

I ought to realize why he wasn't to be sacked. That was the whole conversation. I did realize . . ."

"Best if you didn't go in to the director," said Clara. "He's not in the best of moods, I don't think. I've been speaking to him."

"True enough," concurred Zybin. "Of course, he's not happy about anything at the moment. Did you notice the way he threw those slipcovers onto the desk? You didn't? Well, all right, it can wait! Listen, Clara, I'm going to need your help. Urgently. There's no one else I can take."

"Are we going somewhere?" asked Clara.

"Yes indeed," responded Zybin nonchalantly. "Not far, a matter of an hour and a half. Over to the Ili for a swim and a bit of a lie on the pebbles. After that, we stroll four or five miles upriver. I stay there and you come back. That's it."

Clara looked silently at him.

"Well, we'll walk a bit, have a swim, meet the fishermen, sit by the camp fire and boil up some fish soup," he elucidated. "The fishermen have got some marinka over there. It's a fish farm. First of May. Just step outside the station and there's tons and tons of the stuff. I know a driver there. Savelev. What say, shall we go?"

"Today?"

"There you go, 'today'," he said, annoyed. "Why do you say things like that?! Tomorrow, tomorrow morning, around five o'clock time. All right? I'll ring and you come out to the fountain."

"All right," Clara responded. "Tomorrow morning at five by the fountain. You ring me and I'll come out. Okay."

She looked absolutely exhausted.

After that he began at once making preparations. It was still only noon and he went the round of the shops with his holiday suitcase, stocking up. He bought a bottle of vodka for himself and one of Riesling for Clara; he bought a thermos and a kilo each of two different kinds of sausage. He had already left the shop when he suddenly remembered, or thought of something, came back and got another full litre of vodka. He went back to the museum with his bag and made his way up to the loft where he had a little something stowed under an old beam. This object was wrapped in oiled canvas; it fitted the palm of his hand, and was of gleaming blued steel – a weighty, mysterious and fearful object, not to be shown to anyone, not even Clara. He had come across it that spring, when he was examining the loft. Behind the uppermost beam, there had been a piece of canvas wired to the roof. In it was a Belgian

64

Browning and two boxes of ammunition, an officer's briefcase, complete with binoculars, compass, a two-inch map, cigarette-lighter, a naval dirk and one of Doctor Oks' "Doctor" notebooks. The notebook had turned out to be completely blank; only the first page bore some writing. Zybin left everything as it had been, apart from the Browning and the bullets, which he took down and secreted elsewhere. He didn't know himself why he hadn't taken his find to the director immediately. Nevertheless, he did not do so; he left it in the loft and it was there every month that he retrieved it, unwrapped it, inspected and oiled it and put it back again. This time he got it, looked it over and lowered it into his back trouser pocket.

"I'll need another glance at the map as well," he thought. "Although we are going along by the fisheries."

He went downstairs and traversed the rooms of the museum. "But there's the tumuli to bear in mind as well," he reflected. "Maybe I should take a pioneer's spade along. I think the director's got a couple. Still, lugging them along . . . never mind, I'll do without."

He called in at the security office and stuck his bag of provisions in the cupboard. The Kazakh security man was asleep on the trestle bed with his back to Zybin; he lay on the bare boards with just his skullcap as a pillow. "How does he manage to sleep like that?" thought Zybin. "He sleeps during the day and at night, and on his day off he comes here from home to sleep." He smiled wryly and went out onto the wide staircase of the shrine. There were still oceans of time till two o'clock, and he had no idea what to do with himself. Just then a uniformed man came up to him. It was the same man with the soft voice and gentle eyes who had arrived an hour before to collect the diadem as material evidence to add to something compiled against some person. The same man who enjoyed saying: "The decree of August 7 – public property is sacred and inviolable, ten years in the Taiga and five loss of rights." And always expanded almost physically whenever he pronounced the sacred formula.

"Georgi Nikolaevich," said this individual, "the boss has asked you to step in for a matter of ten to fifteen minutes. I've got the car here."

"And what about the Browning?" A swift pang went through Zybin. "Go in to Clara and stick it in the cupboard – what would she think? Anyway this hellhound wouldn't let me."

"Why not? Let's go," he agreed lightly. "I can spare half an hour."

He had always been something of a fatalist.

*　　　*　　　*

65

The orderly told him to wait in the corridor while he himself went into the office only to reappear almost at once.

"You'll be called," he said. "Wait here."

Zybin looked at the door. It was high, impenetrable, padded with black oilcloth.

The corridor on the other hand was without frills altogether – bare walls. Not a form, not a chair. People waited here on their feet, he realized. He only had to wait for five minutes, however. The door opened part-way and he was called in. He entered. The office turned out to be a big comfortable room with large windows opening onto an avenue of poplars. A map of the world took up the entire wall. Under the map stood a number of soft chairs under white slip covers, and a small light table, the sort you find in street cafés, was perched in the corner by the door. The writing desk nearby, however, lorded it over everything else. It was a vast monster – green baize, mighty pedestals, with heavy bronze fittings and a small horseshoe-shaped pen stand. Behind this desk was seated a military personage – stout, grizzled, pink and benign, with some highly meritorious badge on his chest. Before him was a sheet of paper with yellow roundels on it.

To one side, stood a tall swarthy man with a splendid shining hair parting. Both were regarding Zybin and smiling.

"Ah, the comrade scientist," said the military man jovially (the swarthy type was in civilian clothes), "we've been looking forward to seeing you. Well now, what do you think of our small change here. Comrade Zeleny, please show him."

The plain-clothes man moved the sheet of paper a little way across the desk.

Zybin picked up the roundels, looked at them, turned them over, tried biting them and remarked: "What are these then, did you get them from the dentist?"

The chief glanced over at the swarthy man, who grinned, revealing a poor set of patterned teeth.

"Why do you think that?" the pink military man enquired swiftly, half rising.

"No think about it! They've been prepared for melting down. See how they've been flattened out."

"Logical," swarthy smiled benevolently. "The comrade is no fool."

The colonel reseated himself.

"Oh those museum folk understand everything in the world," he grinned. "You know what they call him over there? The Keeper of

66

Antiquities. So then, comrade Keeper of Antiquities, how is it that you didn't mange to keep hold of those antiquities of yours? You kept digging up skulls and dogs' bones but as soon as they brought you in some gold, you immediately went crazy and let it slip out of your hands. Something doesn't fit there, eh?"

"May I be allowed to sit down?" requested Zybin, lowering himself onto a soft chair by the wall. "That's right, it doesn't fit at all."

"Sit at that little table there," said the military man. "It's more comfortable."

Zybin sat down and found he was sitting in the very corner of the office on a squeaky little chair, faced by the enormous desk, behind which presided someone with the power to Bind and Loose; a judge both righteous and incorruptible. "Good thinking," reflected Zybin. "First psychological point to you, by all means!"

"But it's turned out so neatly, there's no finding a culprit." The colonel spread his arms. "And there might have been forty kilos of gold there. In the Prischepinsky hoard, they found twenty-five kilos of Scythian gold alone! And fifty of silver! A whole sack of currency! And you missed it! How was that?"

"Ah, that's my boy," thought Zybin. "He knows about Scythian gold!" Without noticing it, he smiled; the colonel pounced at once.

"You think it's funny?" he enquired bitterly. "You think it funny and we're crying over it. Because you let it go and we're being asked for it. They're telling us – we don't care where you get it as long as it's on the table. Well then that's where it's going to be! We'll drive ourselves into the ground, but we'll put it there! The scientist comrades were keeping it but they failed to hold it, but the chekists will drag it out from under the ground and bring it to the state coffers. That's our duty. Comrade Lieutenant, is the carpenter here?"

"He's been sent for, comrade Colonel," replied the lieutenant.

"Fetch him to me at once!" ordered the colonel in a voice of brass. "But you too, comrade Zybin, bear a heavy moral responsibility! Yes, heavy and considerable. Not everything is clear to us in this affair, we can't believe everything we hear. Such irresponsibility in a state institution . . . yes, the lieutenant will be having a word with you about that. So be sure you tell him everything you know – everything! The truth, the whole truth! If you suspect anybody or you feel they've made a mistake, then come straight out with it. We won't bite your head off, and it'll be a great help to us and yourself. The truth is your only salvation!"

67

"So much for the fifteen minutes," thought Zybin.

"You need have no doubt," he replied from his squeaky chair, "that what I know, I will tell."

"Oh, we have no doubts whatever in that regard." The colonel shook his head. "We can see whom we are dealing with. So then, comrade Lieutenant, fill out the blank record of witness evidence. Comrade Zybin will write the rest himself. Comrade Zybin, come along over here. That's all right by you I take it? Everything in the proper order, now – no hurry, nothing to worry about, frankly, intelligibly, leaving nothing out. What you think, what you surmise and any suggestion you might wish to make. All right?"

"How the museum procedures came into being – or lack of procedures?" Swarthy intoned liltingly. "Had there been any losses of valuables previously? All this is of the greatest interest to us."

"Yes, yes of course," confirmed the colonel. "Well, I shan't say goodbye, comrade Zybin. We shall meet again. All this is for examination and conclusions," he ordered and proffered the paper with the roundels to Swarthy.

At this point Zybin almost shouted aloud. Under the heavy table glass he had caught sight of something absolutely incredible: an enormous eye, the size of his palm, a circular pupil and inside it a fist grasping a Finnish dagger. Next to it was another photo: another eye, this one containing a whole composition – a street lamp, a wall and the brutish face of a thug: brutal scowl, scar across the forehead, cap pulled forward over the brows, hank of hair.

Zybin glanced at the colonel. The colonel frowned and Swarthy touched Zybin on the shoulder.

"Oh, they're up to all the dodges, they're smart," he thought, following Swarthy over to the desk. "Oh the tricks! Digging the pit for you! Actors! Sleight-of-hand merchants! That's why gangsters gouge out the eyes of corpses because things like this turn up on police tables, tricks that would say to a hoodlum: 'Look how far our science has got! Don't be a mug. Spill it while you've got the chance. We told one of your lot: make a clean breast of it, save your stupid skull. No, he wouldn't. He got the chop. And so will you . . .' Sure enough, next thing you know, the hoodlum confesses. And if not, what does it matter? At all events he won't be complaining to the prosecutor about blackmail!

"All right, what do I care about thugs. They have to be tracked down. Catch the brute and fling him out of society. That's the main thing."

"Ah, so that's your line is it, comrade Zybin? Therefore the end justifies the means. There's no wriggling out of it, the end justifies the means. You can do it to a gangster but not to comrade Zybin. He has to be dealt with according to law. But why should that be, really?

"Look, it's going to be pretty tough for you presently. You've already sensed that and started cringing. So just remember, what they can do to a gangster they can do to you. And if there's something they can't do to you, it's only because they're not allowed to do it to the gangster either. That's the only reason! Remember that! Remember that! Do remember that and you'll conduct yourself like a man. That's your only salvation!"

"In here," said Swarthy and opened a door at the end of the corridor.

It was a very small room, almost a cubicle – a window, table and chair. Swarthy said: "Take a seat, please. Here's pen and ink." He pulled open a drawer and took out a number of interrogation forms. "Write: 'As regards the facts of the case I can testify as follows: such and such a date, such and such a month, at a certain time I learned from the director of the central museum that a hoard of gold had been brought in, comprising...' Well and so on, in order, what exactly happened. We'll fill in the routine details later. I'll drop by in half an hour. I'll write you a pass – all right?"

He left, carefully closing the door.

And Zybin reflected and began to write; at first about the circumstances of the find, then about its unique nature – nothing like it in Kazakhstan or Central Asia had ever been discovered before. That all conclusions as to the find and its value were, however, only preliminary. A proper evaluation depended on a series of analyses, the bringing in of specialist advice and particularly on finding the discovery site itself. He added that to do that would be extremely difficult, since owing to an unfortunate sequence of chance happenings – the sort that always plague archaeologists! – the eyewitnesses had disappeared. Difficult, however, did not mean hopeless. The discovery had not been made in the middle of a desert. There existed the archaeological map of Semirechiye. Perhaps something could be deduced from the analysis of the eyewitnesses' statements: for a number of reasons, it was quite possible that as regards the essential points – the method of burial and the circumstances of the find – they had spoken the truth. The rest of their account, again for a number of reasons, did not inspire confidence. One had to be extremely cautious, however. What mattered now was not to scare them. Archaeological gold emerges above ground with difficulty, but can easily slip back out of sight. There were a myriad examples of this. It ought to be said at this point that we are not dealing with anything like 25 kilos of gold or 50 of silver; we have here a secret bestowal of a dead body, not a burial. We can say nothing about the tragedy which occurred on the steppes almost two thousand years ago. Perhaps something will come to light later when written sources are adduced (Chinese chronicles for example). It may be that as our knowledge of the ancient Usuni increases, we will come to understand what this unique burial signifies (assuming it is found to be a burial at all), but for the moment everything associated with the provenance of the find is totally obscure. Therefore, to hazard any surmises as to its composition (kilos of precious metals) is an extremely risky, even pointless procedure.

He signed it, then on reflection added a postscript: Moving on to the question of personal accountability, it should be said that even putting it this way is absolutely senseless. To predict the appearance of a chance discovery was impossible. It was hardly possible to predict the criminal behaviour over the identity cards either. Indeed he wasn't present when it happened. That was all he could state.

Signed: Senior scientific assistant and head of archaeology department . . .

He put down the pen and glanced at his watch: he still had an hour. He picked up the receiver and told the operator that he wanted to speak to comrade Zeleny.

"You don't know the number?" asked the receiver. "I'll give you the operations group."

But the operations group suddenly spoke up in a lilting feminine voice: "Zeleny will be back in five minutes. Who wants him?"

He said who he was. He was then asked if the document was ready. He said it was and that he was in a considerable hurry.

"I'll be along presently to sign your pass," said the receiver.

A tall, slender young brunette with a smooth hairdo came in. She wore a police blouse.

"Well, all done?" she asked, smiling.

She had a serene smile, a sonorous voice, a calm and clean-cut face. It was very hard to believe she was from the operations group.

"This is it," said Zybin.

She took the interrogation form and began to read. As she read, she shook her head. But the expression of serenity, grace and a hint of gentle mockery never left her face. She read through to the end and put the statement down.

"Very interesting," she said. "Reads like a novel. But I know absolutely nothing about all this. Could you tell me the gist in a couple of words? You write here about the concealment of a body. What is it, a murder?"

He laughed.

"What's your name?" he asked.

"Valentina Sergeevna," she replied.

"Well then, Valentina Sergeevna, this murder took place, as I say, over two thousand years ago. So it's a matter for the archaeologists not you. The gist of it . . . And he recounted all about the find very briefly.

She listened without interrupting.

"All that's terribly interesting," she said when he had finished. "Really, just like Pushkin – Chernomor abducting Ludmila from the feast. Very interesting." She thought for a moment. "You mention the skull – is it intact. Doesn't show any marks of violence?"

He shook his head.

"None at all. But she was very beautiful. Evidently in the case of beauties, the blow is aimed at the heart."

She smiled again.

"Yes, if she was killed by a man. If it was a woman, it's a different matter. Female rivals often get mutilated. But a woman could hardly have taken the body so far. And of course the body wasn't just thrown down any old how, otherwise the birds would have pecked it to bits. That means several people were involved in the disposal of it. You mention a boulder, don't you? But there again – how did the gold survive?"

"I don't know," he answered. "Anything might have happened."

"True enough," she concurred, "but let's consider a bit further. The killer carries the body seventy miles (why, incidentally? That's possibly the most puzzling aspect of the whole thing) and conceals it there under a rock. Therefore the place was probably prepared in advance. So this murder was premeditated, right?"

He laughed.

"I just can't get used to these brisk words of yours. No, they're just not applicable in this case – the point is we know nothing about it for the moment. We'll go digging about in books, study maps and of course drive hither and yon, do a spot of clambering about and just keep on searching. If we climb all over the whole Karagalinka, we might come across something of the sort. Only there shouldn't be too much song and dance made about it, and I see you've already brought the dentists in on it."

She grinned. "We're the police!"

At that moment the telephone rang.

"Lieutenant Anikeeva here," she said into the phone. "Yes, comrade Zeleny! Yes, written and signed!" ("I haven't time," Zybin told her quickly.) "Comrade Zybin here tells me he's in a tearing hurry. Comrade Zybin, if you would . . ."

And she thrust the receiver at him.

"Georgi Nikolaevich", said Zeleny very politely at the other end of the line, "I'm very sorry but you will have to remain for a little while. We haven't finished our talk with you. You have the telephone at your disposal. Ring 01 and explain that you're being held up. But please go easy on the details. I'll be with you as soon as I'm free." Zybin heard the phone clatter down at the other end.

"Good lord," thought Zybin. "That means I won't see her again. "Good grief, good grief, how come I always make a stupid mess of things? And what can he want of me?" Then he remembered the Browning in his pocket and his stomach turned over.

"Listen," he implored. "I have to run over to the museum for five minutes at least. I have the keys, you see. People won't be able to go home. I'll come straight back."

"You won't be late?" she asked. "Otherwise the colonel might phone and you won't be here."

"Cross my heart". He even placed his hands on his chest.

"All right, let's have your pass," she decided, taking out her pen. "How do you mean, what pass? The one you came in here with."

He shrugged.

"No, there has to be a pass. Search your pockets. No?" She came over and tried the drawers of the desk. They were locked. "You couldn't have got in without a pass. The senior lieutenant must have kept it."

"What can I do then?" he asked, at a loss.

She spread her arms slightly.

"You'll just have to wait. There's the telephone. Ring whoever necessary. Dial 01 to begin with."

He made to pick up the phone but desisted.

"Oh, if you only know the trouble you've got me into," he said bitterly, "real trouble."

She made a gesture of helplessness.

He rang the director at home and was told that Stepan Mitrofanovich hadn't got back yet. He rang the director's office and no one came to the phone. He rang accounts and was told that the director had been there but had just been summoned elsewhere. He rang Petka, the electrician; he was not at his post. That left just Clara and she had probably gone by now.

"Yes it never rains but it pours," thought Zybin. For a moment he sat as he was, his lowered eyes fixed on the top of the desk, then sighed and glanced at Lieutenant Anikeev.

"Well, it never rains . . ." he began heavily.

"Was it something very important?" she asked him, with something of womanly sympathy.

This was the last straw.

"Look," he said vehemently. "What's that rubbish you've got under the glass? In the colonel's office I mean – under the glass, what have you got there? The pupil of an eye with a Finnish knife in it. The universal material proof for all of life's eventualities. Am I right?"

"Well, what of it?" she asked, smiling faintly.

"Oh, nothing, it was just interesting to see how material evidence is produced these days. Forewarned is forearmed. Do you have a lot of that sort of stuff?"

His tone was disagreeable, biting.

"Are you interrogating me, or just interested?" she asked, still smiling.

"Perish the thought, perish the thought!" He raised both palms. Everything was surging and leaping within him. By now he had forgotten about the Browning. "Who am I to have the right to interrogate you! No, it's you who are interrogating me. I'm the one whose statement has been taken, been locked up, held a prisoner – me, me, me! I'm the one who's being held – and whoever heard of a prisoner interrogating the investigator?"

"You're not being held," she cut in, "and I'm not your investigator."

"Really?" he replied in cheerful astonishment. "I'm not detained and you're not my investigator? Well, in that case no doubt I can just get up and go, is that it?"

"You take a very odd tone, very odd," she said. "And that's putting it mildly."

"You say more then," he demanded softly and hatefully. "You say more. Never mind tone, call it an outburst, slander, disparagement of the security organs. Where the worm of lies can elicit the fish of truth, as old Polonius said – anything at all can happen."

"Are you talking about the lieutenant?" she enquired. "Was he rude? Accused you of something? That's not allowed at all, here."

He lapsed abruptly into silence. She had come to his aid: she had switched the conversation from the authorities to personalities.

She came and sat opposite him.

"I understand, you're in a hurry to get somewhere, and you've been detained." she said softly. "Still, you shouldn't be so . . . edgy, so to speak. All that gibberish!" She smiled at him. "Worm, fish, Polonius, whoever he is . . ."

"Listen to me for heaven's sake," he grew heated again and leapt to his feet. "I'll get you a free ticket to the state theatre; go there with your husband or Lieutenant Zeleny or whoever, and see *Hamlet*. Do go at least once in your life!"

Now they were staring directly at one another across the desk.

"As for that," she suddenly flared up, all woman, "you know where you can go with your theatre and your free ticket! . . . If I want to go to the theatre . . ."

"And you will," he said, gloomily obdurate and seeming to bow his head. "You most certainly will. In my time, for instance, students of the law faculty knew the classics, knew who Polonius was, but you just get dragged through it: harry, break, expose, unmask. Ach, it's really sordid just talking about it . . ." He dried up and waved a dismissive hand.

"What do you mean by 'break' exactly?" she asked sternly. "It's not 'break' it's 'establish' – they're two different things."

"But how are you going to 'establish'?" he shouted. "Show these vile pictures and lie in your teeth? Yes? Is that it?"

She hesitated before suddenly deciding to give battle.

"Yes, Senior Scientific Assistant. If we discard the word 'vile' then yes. The purpose of investigation is to reveal the truth. You're a law graduate too, are you? Yes? History of law. So then, at that time your faculty was the Faculty of Useless Knowledge – a science of formalities, papers and procedures. We were taught to establish the truth."

"But how you establish it – that doesn't matter a damn?" he asked. "For example, they show me an order for the arrest of my wife. They say: 'If you don't sign admitting your guilt, your wife will be sitting next to you today.' So I sign! I'd sign anything, anything you like! Ask me to testify that I'm a murderer, a robber, a train-wrecker – I'd do it. Just leave my wife alone."

"And would you say where the proceeds of the robbery had been hidden?" she asked coolly. "And furnish material evidence? And name all your confederates. And so allow us to put an end to your criminal activities? Yes, then that fraud makes sense and that 'vile' photograph as well."

"Thank God I'm not married!" he cried. "That means I can hang onto all my gold. All twenty-five kilos plus fifty of silver! And I won't give my confederates away either." He picked up the phone and dialled 01 for the storage department. Clara at once came to the phone. She had evidently been sitting waiting for his call.

"Good afternoon, my darling," he said sweetly. "Good afternoon my dear. The fact is, I'm being detained at the police station and I have a business meeting with Polina Yurevna. All about those bones. So then, it's three o'clock now and at four someone has to be at the fountain to meet her. So . . ." He quickly glanced round at Anikeeva but she had already gone out, closing the door to behind her.

He sat there till evening. Then they both arrived together, she and Zeleny.

"Forgive me," said Zeleny, scowling. "I got held up." He sat down. "The top brass are in a bad mood," he said to Anikeeva. "The colonel sent for the director while I was there, the things they said! Shocking!" He laughed and wagged his head.

Anikeeva laughed too.

Evidently she understood what questioning the director involved.

"So then," said Zeleny, thoroughly serious again, "our bosses have placed a heavy responsibility on the museum. It has to make good the loss sustained. This involves you above all as the head of department."

"Great!" Zybin burst out. "What have I got to do with it?"

Zeleny frowned.

"Just this!" he grumbled. "The gold has gone missing and nobody's to blame. You were obliged to foresee cases like this, that's why you're the head of department. Did you warn the directorate that gold finds were possible? That someone might come in with it? And what to do in that event? You did speak about that? Why deny it now?"

"No," Zybin shook his head. "I never mentioned it. The thought never occurred to me somehow."

"Really? And yet we have evidence that you did give several warnings. How do you mean, you didn't? As soon as the first roundels began to reach you, what did you tell the management? You don't remember? Well I do. You said that people should keep their eyes peeled. Is that not so? (Zybin said nothing.) Well, all right, you let the management know at one point,"

Zeleny said more gently (it was evident that he did not really consider Zybin at all guilty – he was too efficient an operative for that. He understood guilt clearly and directly, as lying in action or inaction, not as a failure of foresight). You told him, and he paid nil attention, for which he bears no small portion of blame, but you are the specialist and once you had realized that the director was so inclined to dismiss your warnings, you should have communicated your ideas to us at once and we would have had your director in and had a little talk with him, nice and friendly. Then the gold wouldn't have gone missing. And now you're both responsible. But you're the archaeologist and more is expected of you."

"Less," said Anikeeva unexpectedly. "Archaeologist Zybin did his part; he gave his opinion in front of three witnesses, but his signal was ignored, so why is he involved?"

"Report, report, that's what he should have done!" shouted Zeleny. "And make a copy of it as well. So the document would be in his pocket. Then of course . . ."

Anikeeva shook her head but said nothing.

"Well it wasn't me thought all this up anyway," snarled Zeleny. "That's what his own pals say. The same ones he treated to drinks every day. They also say the filing system is in a hell of a state. No stocktaking. If you need an exhibit you can't find it. What have I got to do with it?" He suddenly lost his temper completely. "All right, let's get it done. If everybody's missed it, what's the point of asking one individual! Just sign this here paper and that's it. Go away and relax. Don't worry about it, it's a pure formality. Here's your pass. Good night! Off you go! And don't worry!"

City of Alma-Ata. 1 September 1937.

I, Zybin, Georgi Nikolaevich, resident in the city of Alma-Ata, Karl Marx street, No. 62, give my genuine signature to the Alma-Ata province police investigator Zeleny A. I. to the effect that until the conclusion of the preliminary investigation and court proceedings with regard to the crime committed under article 112 of the RSFSR criminal code (criminal negligence), I bind myself not to leave my place of residence without the permission of the investigator and the court and to present myself at the request of the investigative and judicial organs.

The accused

Parole taken by

It was gone eight and quite dark by the time he left police head-quarters. He stood and deliberated before rushing to the telephone kiosk on the corner. He asked for the number and the operator connected him, but there was no reply. He rang again and stood biting his lip, realizing that she wasn't at home. He still stood and waited though, until the exchange came back: "No reply, caller"; then he threw down the receiver and slammed the door making everything rattle. "Missed her again . . ." he said. "You . . ." Then walked homewards quickly, almost breaking into a run, before coming to an abrupt halt. There was a light on in the windows, bright, open, brazen. A rounded dark-green shadow was outlined on the curtains. Somebody was rummaging in his desk. He felt in his pocket. The keys were there. That meant they had simply broken down the door. There was a box of shells in the desk. They had already found them. It was all up then. He realized that instantly, that and a myriad sundry trivia, important and now utterly unimportant because there was nothing at all he could do about them now. Suddenly he banged his head painfully against something wooden; evidently he had stepped back and back, until he had crashed into the park fence. This at once brought him to his senses and he thought: "What about the parole, though? Why did they make me sign then?" But now he realized that the word "why" was neither here nor there; there was a good deal more than that going on nowadays, and anyway nobody knew what was going on and what wasn't; there was no point thinking about it, he had to decide something in a hurry. Run off to the director – he was waiting for his call in any case. Let him immediately ring round the dial and demand a halt, a postponement, a delay. Yes, yes, run to the director. He retreated from the fence, took two paces and at once sensed – sensed rather than realized – that all this was nonsensical, stupid, wild fantasy; this too was now pointless. They had a warrant, hadn't they? And a warrant was the most powerful thing in the world. He recalled that a mere month before, he had been a witness and an army man had shown him a warrant for the search and arrest of a neighbour. And how, at the sight of that abhorrent deckled warrant, with the blue facsimile signature at the bottom, he had gone numb and torpid and sat for two hours without moving a muscle. And how meek and understanding and acquiescent he had been made him want to vomit. And how he had turned away when the unfortunate individual had sought him with his eyes. Now the director would turn away as well. No, best to make an end. Why frighten people needlessly?

He discovered a gap in the fence – the children had broken a post away – and squeezing through, made his way over to the graves. There were two – General Kolpakovsky and his wife. Once there had been a flowerbed here, fencing and a hanging lamp, always lit. Now there was nothing. Just two enormous red granite boulders with a black anchor chain over them – a double bedroom in death! The chain roped off this part of the park from the world. It had its own emblematic significance too: the last mooring, no doubt, the holding strength of the marriage, their inseparable souls, the fortress of death and most likely of all, as they sing in church: "get thee hence . . ." Here was the chain, the stone, the cross – on this spot the worldly ended and the heavenly began. *Procul este, profani*, these places are holy. But the profane had not departed; and they had cleared away absolutely everything. They had even hauled off the marble bearing the inscription; only the chain hung as before over the two nameless graves in among the damp thickets, putting a scare into chance couples. The director had several times intended removing or simply blowing up the boulders, but couldn't bring himself to do it. Later on Zybin himself had intervened. He had said: "Say what you like, all this is history. Local knowledge. Times change. Now Khabarov is a great man again, and so is Kutuzov; even the Suvorov museum is open again in Leningrad. So who knows what will happen? Hold on for the moment." And the graves had survived. Zybin had a hiding place under one of the boulders. Once, a very long time ago, in early spring, he had noticed a hole beneath one of the slabs. His arm went in as far as the shoulder. God knows what it had been: some creature's lair, a real hiding place perhaps, or the earth had subsided under the rock. At that time, at any rate, there had been nothing in the hole except wet mud and he forgot about the secret spot. He recalled it suddenly a month later, when he was having to conceal a bottle of cognac from Grandpa. After that, the hole had served him faithfully and loyally on many occasions the whole year round. Now he sought it out again and slipped the Browning inside, along with his torch and hunting knife. "A good thing I wasn't searched". Anyway, what did he care about even that now?

All at once, he felt a terrible weariness – not pain, not fear, not despair, but genuine weariness. "So this is where my ruin lay in wait," he thought. And it had been this very morning he had swum in a mountain stream, scrambled up a hillside, listened to the crickets and stood beneath the fresh mountain breeze. How astonishing it was! And his final two thoughts were: "So, then I never did get to meet Lina after all," and the second: "Why not run away all the same, instead of giving in?" It was twenty-five miles to the River Ili. Empty lorries went that way. He could jump on one, and they'd never lay hands on him. Over yonder it was hot dry steppeland, baking earth, yellow river. Slopes, gulleys, ledges – black, green and blue rocks, with partridges rushing about among them, those same fat round birds, which never bred on the Karagalinka. Clambering down from the ledges, a broad clay expanse opens out, all covered in dry reeds and rocks. Emptiness, silence, just fishermens' mud huts with white reed roofs every five or six miles. Get to the Chinese frontier without meeting anyone and there, in China . . . He suddenly realized that he was going mad, sitting on a tombstone and raving. He got up, shook himself, found his lighter in his pocket and flicked at it, illuminating the dull mass of the rock. Yes indeed, the final mooring. There was nothing to add to that! General Kolpakovsky and his wife. Farewell, dear departed! I passed you every day and never noticed your excellencies before. And it was you who built this town, wasn't it? You laid out this park, conferred benefits, tamed, extirpated, cultivated, and I know nothing about you. My science never reached you, you were too young. A hundred years, no time at all for an archaeologist to work in. But you will soon be remembered after all. They will remember you, damn them, mark my words. They'll drag marble slabs here and incise your names on them in letters of bronze. They may well take away the chain however, no point in them in a country like ours, they'll say! All things pass, dear departed. Everything changes! For history has need of generals now. And you, young, beautiful, in crown, bridal veil and golden finery, killed by persons unknown for reasons unguessed, you whose head I held in my hands today . . .

And suddenly he felt deeply moved and an extraordinary feeling of affection and weakness came over him.

He sat down on the boulder again and wiped his eyes.

He sat for a while thinking, smiled unaccountably, then rose, cut across the lawn, emerged onto the asphalt and halted under a lamp. The light was feeble, yellow and unpleasant. He stood with arms and head lowered, thinking by now of nothing and nobody, just pressing his face into his fist over and over again.

Ten minutes went by, twenty, half an hour – still he stood there. He had to get used to the situation, withdraw into himself, start crediting what was about to happen to him presently, this minute, within the hour at any rate. He would go home and it would turn out that his house was no longer his but theirs, and he would be ordered to sit down and not move, they would turn out his pockets and sit him in a car between two of them and take him away. And he would no longer be himself,

79

but someone with buttons cut off and no shoelaces, who would be taken out twice for relief and once for exercise; interrogation, abuse, threats, orders to confess to avoid something worse. He had to picture all this, convince himself of it and resolve himself.

A laughing couple passed him. He was standing in the road and they had to go round him. At the end of the walk they turned round, and she said something to him; he laughed. Zybin walked away, seething. He strode along at a precise, confident, soldierly pace. One-two, hup-two! Nothing in him quailed or caused his heart to flutter now. He was calm. So calm that fear too had left him. "Well, we shall see, we shall see, good sirs." Something malevolent, resolute, even glad stirred in him. It was in this mood that he mounted the porch and kicked the door with all his might. It sprang open at once. In the lobby it was dark and quiet. The tiny corridor lamp illuminated three doors – two white and one black. The black one led to the loft, the right-hand white one to his neighbour's, the left-hand one was his. He was just bracing his leg to deliver it a mighty kick, when Vertinsky's voice began singing. "The bastards," he thought, "got no sense of shame at all." He didn't go through with the intended kick; he opened the door quietly, so that it didn't creak.

On the table, covered with a white cloth, stood a gramophone with Petka the museum electrician fussing over it. Grandpa was sitting in the armchair. "Witnesses," he realized. Then he suddenly caught sight of Lina. She appeared from the depths of the room went over to Petka and bent ardently over him. She was wearing a crimson scarf. A high comb was sticking up in her hair. Everything was soundless, like a silent film. He was so stricken, he clutched at the door which gave out a creak.

It was then that Grandpa saw him.

"Here at last," he jeered. "You should put out a bucketful of vodka for me. I had a real job holding onto your beauties, I've been on the point of going five times. You brought any vodka, I'm asking you? Otherwise I'll send somebody over to the drivers."

Everyone turned round. Zybin stood on the threshold. It was all strange and wonderful, like a dream.

"Lina," he said, crushed. "And I was on the point of running off to your hotel."

She laughed, the scarf dropped to the floor and now the light fell full on her bare shoulders.

"You, Georgi Nikolaevich, always want a lot and never do anything about it," she said with calm gladness. And he trembled at the sound of her voice, because it was all true.

80

"Lina!" he cried, rushing upon her. "Lina!"

"Greetings, greetings, my dear." She held out both hands to him, a gesture which seemed to bring them together, while at the same time maintaining distance between them. "Now then, let's take a look at you. Oh dear, thinner, darker, rougher, but never mind, never mind! Still just as good-looking."

"He's a treasure," croaked Grandpa. "Worth five hundred a month. If he didn't drink so much . . ."

"No, no, he'll never manage that," laughed Lina as she finally opened her arms and allowed herself to be embraced. "He keeps the wrong company. Clara and I had been waiting for you two hours or more already, all of us sitting on a bench near the house. Then a young man came along and brought us here. Apparently your key fits all the doors. You'll be cleaned out one of these days, dear friend."

"What's he got to steal, then?" Grandpa grimaced. "Papers? I tell him, give me half a litre and I'll cart the lot out to the dump, no messing."

"Lina, sweet Lina." He was embracing her, clutching her to him, and his eyes were wet with tears.

She stood there for a space, then softly disengaged herself, saying gently: "There, there, it's all right. Leave that till later. You just apologize to Clara, she's been ringing the director all this time."

It was then he saw Clara. It may have been that she was glowing in Lina's reflected light; perhaps the whole world had become beautiful for him in that moment, but Clara seemed most beautiful to him at that moment. Tall, willowy and slender, with her calm, lustreless face and dark-blue hair. Even the dress she was wearing was black and close-fitting.

"Like a black crucifixion," he recalled someone's line.

"So then, everything all right?" she asked softly, coming towards him.

For an instant he thought hard, because he had clean forgotten about everything else, and he had to go over it in his mind from the beginning. Then he blurted it out.

"All right, I've given an undertaking."

"What undertaking?" Lina was alarmed.

"What?" Clara seized his arm.

"So he won't run away," said Grandpa knowingly. "Otherwise he'd swipe the gold and be away to America. Such things do happen. When I was working for Shakhvorostov, the merchant, he had a cashier: a hopeless drunk. He could hardly afford a pair of pants, but what an opinion he had of himself! Well he got hold of the week's takings and . . ."

"But he's never even seen the gold," said Clara uneasily, looking round at Grandpa.

"They'll sort it out over there whether he's seen it or not," Grandpa interrupted with a wave of the hand. "They'll sort out all the whys and wherefores – who he is, where from, place of birth, date of marriage. As soon as the director was summoned, he vanished. They let him phone from over there, though: shut the office up, he says, and ask the scientist to come to me, if they haven't arrested him of course. He asked for you to drop by at eight."

"What?" Zybin leapt to his feet. "Then why on earth didn't you . . ."

At that precise moment the phone rang. Clara took it.

"Yes," she said. "Yes! I'm giving him to you," and held out the phone to Zybin.

"You still in the land of the living?" asked the director, overjoyed. "Here was I kept ringing the police, saying they were tormenting our scientific department. What do they want from you over there? The gold?"

"They got me to give an undertaking," said Zybin.

"What?!" exploded the director at once. "An undertaking? . . . And you gave it to them straightaway no doubt? You're hopeless! Why did you do that? You might have consulted me at least, but no doubt you lost your nerve and signed immediately. Hopeless, hopeless. Well all right, could be worse. Have you got Grandpa there? All boozing are you? And getting Clara drunk to celebrate are you? You be careful! I saw her lips had gone blue today. And who else have you got there?"

"Petya and Grandpa," answered Zybin.

"Is that all? You watch yourself, friend, or you'll make a hash of everything," said the director. Well all right. We'll talk later. Good night. I want you stone-cold sober at work tomorrow! All your wits about you, got that?"

When he came away from the phone, Lina was already in her raincoat.

"You'll see me off first," she commanded, "then you can take Clarochka home." She took Clara's arm. "Let's go dear, you're worn out as well and your nerves are frazzled. My, the nights you have in Alma-Ata!"

Grandpa declined to accompany them.

"You go off by yourselves, you're all young and gay, things of your

82

own to talk about. I've got to be up with the lark tomorrow. Nobody seems to want to pay me for doing nothing. So we beg leave of you."

And off he went, cap firmly fixed on his head and not even swaying.

"Mind you lock the door," ordered Lina from the threshold when they had all emerged. "How can you leave your house open at night – do your women look after you as badly as that?"

The moon was hanging over the cathedral, huge and mistily translucent like a piece of amber over a candle. It was light and silent, even the poplars made no noise. Lina halted suddenly in the middle of the street, put her head back and inhaled deeply several times.

"Can you smell the sea?" she asked, seizing Zybin's hand. "It's over there, there beyond that avenue! And the poplars are the same, except that they make no noise. Remember what you used to call them? Gypsies! Every last leaf trembles there, Clarochka. Here they just stand and don't even stir."

"They're just biding their time," Petya was annoyed on behalf of his poplars. "As soon as the wind gets up, they start rustling straightaway, like foam in a washbasin."

Lina looked at him and burst out laughing.

"No, Pyotr Nikolaevich, you're a dear," she said, grabbing his arm. "Like foam in a washbasin. The wife rinses out a blouse in the basin in the night, drying it over the primus, so it'll be dry by morning, while her husband turns over in his sleep and hears her. Are you married, Pyotr Nikolaevich?"

"No," he said gloomily.

"Quite right too," Lina advised him blithely. "There's time yet for you to get hitched. Now Georgi Nikolaevich here never will get married. Whatever his intentions are. I know him. We're old friends. Clarochka, is it far from here to some stretch of water?"

"Oh, a matter of about twenty miles," replied Zybin. "The train takes an hour and a half." He almost added: "It leaves at seven-thirty from the city platform."

And now he once more pictured that serene, clay-bedded river, gritty pebbles, dry white and yellow reeds, the rocky shores made up of blue, yellow, black, white, red and multicoloured stones. Heat, drought and a parching in the mouth that even water would only slake for a moment.

"We'll just have to get there sometime," said Lina. "Isn't that so, Clarochka?"

She had already taken Clara's arm, while the latter walked along

83

gazing at the mountains through the poplar crowns, the mountain forests, blue under the moon. She failed to hear Lina's question.

Lina turned once more to Petya.

"It's a real seaside town," she said confidently. "The sea lives in every house here, every poplar. I remembered the Black Sea avenues were just the same. Still, you have to see them. Do you remember, Georgi Nikolaevich, that park where you won a matryoshka doll at the shooting gallery? You know, Clarochka, it still stands on my sideboard. It's enormous! A presentation piece! Half a metre high! You've never been to the seaside, Clarochka?"

Clara shook her head. She kept on staring fixedly at the jagged mountain passes.

"Well that's fine, we'll all get together and go. You haven't taken your holidays yet, Keeper? Then don't! We'll take them together in April or May." They had stopped outside the hotel. "Well, friends, that's me home. Thank you. Now see Clarochka home and sleep, sleep, Georgi Nikolaevich, I'll ring you tomorrow after work, okay?"

"Okay," he responded. "A bit later, if you can though. I've got to go to a certain place tomorrow and I'll likely be held up."

"Where's that, then?"

"It's to do with work."

Lina laughed again.

"That's what I call an uncivilized man. Doesn't know the difference between work and play. Well, all right. We're going to take you and Clarochka properly in hand and drag you round the mountains. What a pity I've got to be up early tomorrow. Nights like these one ought to loaf round the streets till dawn. Well, so long, friends!"

And off she went, with a wave of the hand.

The three of them went back. He linked arms with Clara and sensed physically how eager she was to get to her bed and collapse with her face in the pillow. He was silent. "I'm a swine," he thought, then said the word aloud and at once burned with embarrassment: he shook his head, forced a smile and a grimace and started mumbling something. Petya shot a surprised sideways glance at him, while Clara enquired: "What time shall I ring you in the morning?"

"I like that," he responded. "Why should you have to wake me up? I'll wake you up!"

She sighed.

"Fine!"

84

"Is about seven too early?" he asked.

"No, earlier if you like."

She halted suddenly.

"Well, here's my house," she sighed with huge relief. "Good night."

And she vanished into the depths of the yard, without even saying goodnight.

Back in the house he put all the lights on again – the table lamp, the chandelier, the wall lights – then made his way over towards the desk and flopped into the armchair. Everything here bore traces of her presence: the chair over there, she had sat on that, the glass she hadn't finished, half a sweet, a book she had leafed through before throwing it onto the sofa. He now realized how utterly pointless it had been asking Clara to go with him. It would all have been so much simpler taking just Petka. Now he would have to spend the whole day alone with her. Even if they were in luck and caught the seven o'clock, he would be back at six! That meant phoning Lina at eight or nine. Another mess-up! Still it wasn't all that important. Not now. What mattered was that she had found him at last. She'd come on her own hadn't she? Wait a minute! Are you so sure she's on her own? He jumped up, sat down on the sofa and began riffling through the book at considerable speed. No, of course she was alone. Otherwise she would have said; she'd certainly have told Clara. Still you could expect anything from her. Perhaps she wasn't alone. Well then, they had met only to part at once. He had learned many things over these past years; he had "studied the science of parting". Probably this was the onset of old age. Everything had become easier to bear. Now Kornilov wasn't like that. He was young, hot-blooded and as Derzhavin has it, a devil for the truth. He wouldn't yield what was his though. Dasha now, she was his, apparently. How she had waded into battle on his behalf today! Potapov had fairly gasped with surprise. So what? She did right. For Kornilov, everything was clear, precise, unambiguous. He speaks as he finds. Whereas he himself was artful. Potapov snarled and quivered, and Clara said nothing and hid her eyes. And no one could explain properly what had come over people. Without that there was no living. Something utterly extraordinary was taking place in the world. Monstrous black tornadoes were whirling through the world, sweeping aside everything that lay in their path. Though if you read the speeches of the leaders, all was clear. "That is what the truth is," the director had said that day. "If we have faith in that we shall conquer." And people do have faith, in very truth.

85

And what a faith it was! The sort that can move mountains and take cities. Where can I get some? I believe, Lord. Help thou mine unbelief! Still why do you need belief? Remember Seneca's tragedy *Actaeon*: "Let me be allowed to remain silent – what freedom could be less than that?" So then, make use of this least of freedoms. But you won't make use of it will you – you'll start explaining and accommodating, like that story you peddled to Dasha today: "You have to know when and who." Admit it, that was nasty, wasn't it? There's none of that in Kornilov. That's why people like him. It won't get him anywhere with Lina, though. She's like a stone wall to people like him. She's interested in nothing in the world beyond herself. The sea, expeditions, camp-fires of resinous branches, the cone of sparks above the fire, walks along the shore till dawn – that's her. And she doesn't pretend – she really is like that. And you fall head over heels in love with that integrated, thoughtless, fearless existence. It is a truly beautiful thing. Then comes the sobering-up, of course. She leaves you at the station and you go away enchanted, in love, making a thousand vows to her and yourself; you sit in your room remembering and thinking, smiling at your thoughts. A week passes like this, then another, and then suddenly, you come back to earth. You realize that there was an incredible sort of coldness, callousness, curmudgeonly old age even, visible through her imperturbable serenity. And the thing is, she lets the cat out of the bag herself! No, no, she's not especially intelligent. Her harmony is based on instinct, habit, an unconscious sense of equilibrium, nothing rational about it at all. She could say something about herself in all innocence, that even in those blissful days would suddenly make him stop short for a moment, regain his senses, as it were, come down to earth with a bump, and look at her with new eyes. Lord what was this? But it was all over in a flash. She would catch his mood at once and could always make him forget it totally. Her intuition was unerring in that respect. However hard he tried to conceal the way he felt, she could see right through him. Even when they were talking on the telephone. Still, there had been one occasion when he exploded, and then they had quarrelled. And now . . .

He thought about that, oblivious of how he was drooping, dozing, nodding off to sleep in the armchair by the window. He hadn't thought anything through properly and had made no decision about the following morning.

He awoke suddenly and unaccountably. He raised his head and glanced through the window. Then all of a sudden he caught a soft scratching sound, then a tapping, also as soft as could be, "tap-tap, tap-tap". He thought it must be a twig, rocking in the wind. But the tapping resumed – precise, rhythmical, and then Lina's face suddenly swam out of the darkness and pressed up against the glass. She was looking in and making some kind of gesture. He leapt to his feet, flew to the window and wrenched the frame so severely that something fell down onto the sill.

"Good lord," was all he said.

He could find nothing more to add.

"Receiving visitors?" She enquired blithely. "Give me your hand then." And without touching the sill, she vaulted nimbly into the room. "There we are. Labour and Defence badge, first grade."

He stood before her, uncertain of what to say or do. He just stood and stared.

"Did you see the girl home?" she asked without turning round. "She's a splendid little thing! So serious and straightforward and crazy about you. And you prefer not to notice. What a man you are! Have you got a comb, by the way? Give it here and I'll tidy myself up a bit." She took out a compact and dabbed her cheeks once or twice with the powder puff. "I dread most of all getting sunburned. Listen, can you let me have one of those white hats with the brims – I think the shepherds round here wear them. You've got some I expect."

"Certainly, certainly," he said, rushing off into a corner.

"Wait a minute, where are you off to?" she laughed. "Come here instead," and she tossed her shawl into his hands. Her shoulders were exposed once more. He said nothing. She smiled and stroked his hair. "Tousled as ever. Heavens, it's two o'clock! Still, I can stay for half an hour. Any tea?"

While he paced about the room, fiddling with the tea things and washing the cups out, she sat on the sofa. Sat and silently watched him, her eyes shining, laughing and slightly uneasy.

When he had finished, he came over and embraced her firmly round the shoulders. She looked at him, smiling, as he took her head in his hands and kissed her several times, hard and painfully, crushing her lips. Then he began kissing her eyes and then her lips again. At this she gently rested her hand against his forehead.

"Now, now," she said. "No hurry! Sit down and let's have a talk. (He retained his grip on her.) You don't even know whether I'm here on my own or not, do you?"

"You're alone," he said confidently.

"And thinking just of you?" She freed herself lightly from his arms. "Just hold on, the artistic part of the evening is yet to come. Tell me about yourself." She got up and paced the room. She went up to the barometer. "Severe drought," she read. "So, you live, work and as our director puts it, bury government money in the ground. Buried it so fast you get hauled into the police station and have to give a signed undertaking. Now, just what happens next? (He made a vague movement.) All right, you're in the clear, let's assume. The director carries the can, but where does that leave you? Have you decided to settle down here? Stay in this room for ever?"

"Why?" he asked.

"No, I'm asking you why. Is it your life's work, gnawing away at these hills? Eh?"

He mumbled: "I don't know. What of it?"

She broke into a laugh.

"No, no, it's nothing. Just I never expected that of you, somehow." She looked at him. "I've thought of you very, very often."

He rose, went over to the teapot, felt it with his palm and set off round the room again. He needed to get his thoughts together.

"The excavations are an amateurish job," he said at length. "Hopelessly amateur. I don't know what I'm doing and Kornilov knows less than I do. We don't even know what things we're digging up. If genuine scientists turned up here, they wouldn't take us on as assistants. That's how it is."

She spread her hands, somewhat unexpectedly. He gave her a fleeting glance and went on: "Yes, we'd hardly be taken on as assistants. Actually they probably would take Kornilov. He went to some archaeological college. I'd be out on my ear. I mean I'm not even a historian; what I'd like to do is sit and pore over primary sources for the history of ancient Christianity. I'd really be in my element there. But what can I do? At least we know what we're dealing with in that area. And if there's anything we don't know, it's a problem for scholars. But here nobody knows anything, and that's all about it. Up to now the excavations have been conducted by a teacher of French, a statistician, a surveyor, a hydrotechnologist, and a specially seconded official. That's if you take Kazakhstan as a whole. Here there hasn't been anybody at all, apart from treasure-hunters. If we're as lucky in the future as those persons unknown – I'm talking about the gold – an expedition from the Hermitage will come here next year and chase us all out. And give us a good telling-off for the mess we've made, I shouldn't wonder. But the business would be taken care of. So that's not what interests me."

"What does then?" she asked. "What on earth does interest you, Keeper?"

He went over to the stove, switched it off, picked up the kettle and wrapped it in a cloth before making the tea, then again set to pacing about the room. He had the feeling that he had seen her that day, rushed towards her and recoiled because of that same old window glass standing between them and he had hurt himself badly. It was that pain which had sobered him.

"I want to get to the deserts of Asia," he said. "There the sands have engulfed castles, estates, whole cities; there are observatories there, libraries and theatres. Khorezm, Margiana, Bactria. Do you know what scorching sand is? Bury a man in it and after a month he dries out and turns to wood, though he keeps his former appearance. What are Nubia or Egypt compared to riches like that? Or ancient Otrar? The second library of the ancient world? It's never been found yet, but it's some-where there in a cave. And there's a niche with a chest containing the whole of Tacitus, all hundred plays of Sophocles, the ten books of Sappho, all the elegies of the great Gallus, of which we haven't a single line. That's where I really want to go with my spade. And that's just a beginning."

He went to the table and began pouring the tea.

She came over to him suddenly and put her arms round him.

"My dreamer of dreams," she said tenderly, pressing against him. "Baron Munchausen. How afraid I was that you might have changed! But you . . . Oh, leave that tea. Nobody wants it. Come to me." And she threw him down on the sofa.

"Well, all right," she said. "It all makes a sort of sense even if it hasn't got much logic to it. But you're not digging out there in the sand, are you? You're here in the clay, no sign of Tacitus or Euripides."

They were both lying on the sofa, her arm lightly encircling his shoulders.

"Wait a minute now, don't interrupt. I have a feeling there's some-thing happening to you. Why that girl with the chamois eyes? Grandpa, and the vodka? I think that you really got it in the neck after we last met and you started running about in a panic – am I right?" He made no reply. "All right you don't want to talk – don't then. I'll ask something else: these people working with you here, who are they? What do they think of you?"

"Who do you mean?" he asked, after a pause.

"Don't worry, not Clara. That sticks out a mile."

"Who then?"

"I don't like you being so thick with Kornilov," she said after a short pause. He stared at her in astonishment. "I mean he's a good lad, in spite of his, you know," she put a twisting finger to her temple, "crazy streak, bees in his bonnet, too much imagination – but he couldn't give a damn about your desert sands. He's sitting out there because he's got nowhere else to go. But he can drink as much as he likes there. And he's got a girl handy. What else does he need. A grand life for a man!"

"You even noticed the girl," he smiled.

"Well that didn't take much doing, dear. If you'd just been around when I first met him, and that trip into the mountains . . ."

"Then what?" he asked curiously.

"Just that! He came, he saw, he conquered. And he knew it straight-away. After I watched him take a running jump full tilt into . . . what do you call that whatsit of yours? Alma-Atinka is it? Well, he dived into the middle of a whirlpool by a boulder and brought up some pebbles; if you could have just seen the way he glanced at me. Thunder and lightning! Caesar and Cleopatra!"

And they both laughed a little.

"Still, why was it that you didn't like him?" he asked.

"On the contrary, I liked him a lot!" she replied. "A lot. It's the relationship between you that I don't care for. You get to arguing don't you? He says something, you know, and you answer him in kind. Am I right? And you shout for the whole world to hear?" He said nothing. "That's what I don't like. Not one little bit. Just for the most petty selfish reasons. You know what a callous, self-centred person I am."

He lifted his head.

"Yes," he answered seriously, unsmiling.

"Well, that's it then! I came specially to see you and if something suddenly happens to you, it would be a terrible blow to me – surely you realize that?"

"Yes," he said, pondering her words, "I do realize." And he repeated the words: "Yes, I do realize that. Stand up a minute and I'll shut the window."

He went out into the dark and stood for a moment, fiddling about and rattling with something, then came over to her but did not lie down.

He seated himself by her. She sensed that he had gone away from her somewhere again and asked tenderly: "Now what's the matter," clutching him round the waist and pulling him to her.

"I love you," she said roughly, all woman. "I love you, fool that you are. Can't you see that?"

"Have you been speaking to the director?" he asked, still from the same far distance.

"What do you mean?" she was calmly astonished. "Of course not."

"That means Clara told you." He nodded. "Nevertheless, it's very odd." He suddenly put a hand on her shoulder. "But since you started this conversation, tell me plainly what she said to you. Just give it to me straight now. Wait! You do want me to understand, don't you? Well then, explain what's what."

She was silent, thinking.

"Kornilov has already got himself a bad reputation," she said at once. "And you're always around when he gets talking. You're there, listening and saying nothing – that is, approving. You realize what that means?"

"Come on, come on," he said, when she stopped. "I'm listening. what comes next? Kornilov's got a lot to say and I keep my mouth shut. But was some specific conversation mentioned? Some phrase, a funny story, a joke? Details, details. When and where."

"Nothing concrete."

"And Clara told you all this while you were waiting for me on the bench today. I get it. That's what the director was talking to her about today."

"The director?" she said anxiously. "The director hasn't noticed something as well has he? If so, that's very, very serious. See what Kornilov has got you into. His drunken outbursts. Get rid of him, and have done!"

He smiled lazily and lay down by her side.

"Okay, it's too late now anyway. Better get some sleep."

"Just you listen to me. For the first and last time listen to what I say. I know what you think of me. You don't hide it do you? I can only say one thing: you're a rotten psychologist. You never made it as a writer. But that's not the point. If you only had some sort of goal, really wanted something or had your mind set on something. But you want absolutely nothing, do you? You just go round talking rubbish, risking your neck for a word or some funny story. You express your discontent in a way that could cost you your life. You are a source of extreme hazard as the jurists say."

He opened his eyes.

"For whom, may I ask?"

"Well, let's say for those you come in contact with. Get it into your head that people are simply scared. And you're threatening their existence. There's a great fear abroad in the world today. Everybody's scared of everything. There's only one thing that counts in anybody's mind: sit it out and wait till it's over."

"The way you're talking," he said, amazed. "And here was I thinking . . ."

"Oh yes, thinking! It's disgusting! You've never thought about me at all, and you still don't! You don't know me and that's all there is to it! You go on like a loutish schoolboy. There's one stirrer in every class. He gets up and asks sarcastic questions, so the class roars. And he beams – what a bright lad I am! He gives the class a laugh of course and puts the teacher in a sweat, but he gets expelled like a shot – the head won't put up with people like him. They don't give a damn who was right, him or the teacher. What matters to them is discipline. Just realize it's not you who's dangerous. What's dangerous is letting you have a free hand. What's dangerous is that some have started imitating you. They'll go further than you, maybe just a fraction further, but then it'll be a little bit more and then all the way. That's why even a word is regarded as something committed nowadays, and a conversation counts as activity. There are times when a word is a crime. We live in just such a time. You have to come to terms with that."

"You'll start on about war in a minute. Don't bother!" he said. "The director's given me an earful already."

"Don't worry, I won't, I'll just ask you something. Do you realize fully what you're doing? Is this Kornilov so precious to you? All these drunken pranks of his, very precious are they?"

"The bitch," thought Zybin. "I'll have to warn Kornilov for sure," and said: "Now, what on earth's Kornilov got to do with it? Why do you keep comparing us? Kornilov's had his tail stood on and so he's screeching. No, there's something else here." He rubbed the bridge of his nose. "You see," he went on slowly, reflective, picking his words, "you say I blab but I don't say anything, do I? I'm as dumb as a fish. But you're all of you right about my not being able to go on living like this. I just can't and that's all, I'll start squawking somehow at the top of my voice and then it's hang up your boots, as Grandpa puts it."

"Then why on earth squawk if you realize that?" she asked, bewildered. "What do you want? Has somebody stepped on your tail?"

"Wait, listen – for a whole hour today I shook in my shoes and said my farewells to life. God only knows what I went through standing there, staring up at my window. The terror of that light burning! That meant they'd come to get me. That's right! It was the only thing that occurred to me! Why? What for? How could I have asked questions like that? Only a fool asks what for these days. It never occurs to anyone of intelligence. They take you in and that's that. It's like a law of nature. Only I can't take that sort of humiliation any more, that damned fear squatting somewhere under my hide. What do I want? I want my own self. I'm like an old scratchy gramophone. I'm loaded up with seven or ten records and I croak them out whenever the button's pressed."

"What do you mean, records?" she asked angrily.

He grinned.

"Oh, I can count them all on my fingers. Here's a few: 'If the enemy doesn't surrender, he is destroyed', 'Under the banner of Lenin and the leadership of Stalin', 'Life is better, comrades, life is happier', 'Thank you, comrade Stalin for our happy childhood', 'The best friend of scientists, the best friend of writers, the best friend of athletes, the best friend of firemen – is comrade Stalin', 'The most precious thing on earth is – people', 'Whoever is not with us is against us', 'That idiotic disease – complacency'. All those taken together give us 'the new Soviet man' and 'the features of the new Soviet man'. Bloody hell!" He struck the sofa with his fist.

"Yes, but still, what are you getting at?" she asked. "You can't make the world over to suit yourself, but you don't want to accept it as it is. It doesn't suit you. We don't have any desert islands, and you wouldn't be given one anyway, so?"

She spread her arms.

"So!" he answered steadily. "So!" He went over to the cupboard and got out some sheets. "So, my dear, it will soon be dawn and we have to get some sleep. That's it! We've had our little talk."

She slowly shook her head.

"I do love you, fool that you are," she said pensively. "I would hate to lose you, you just don't realize."

He lay down on the sofa, stretched out and closed his eyes.

"You think I'm always in the wrong."

"Not at all, you're always right," he answered sleepily. "Always and in everything. That's the whole point."

*   *   *

93

He slept and thought: "There are two problems here. The first is that I love you too, very much so, and that always complicates matters. The second problem is that you're right. Clichés are always right. Remember me reading Pushkin to you:

> The flattering toady courtier's narrow mind
> Sees Jesus and Kuteikin as one kind.

"In fact, to anybody of common sense, Kuteikin far outweighs Christ. After all, Christ is a myth, whereas Kuteikin is – who he is. He is truth! And like all truths, he demands the whole of a man, his guts, his total belief. The quest has ended. The world awaited Christ and now here is Christ-Kuteikin and history has entered upon another phase. And do you know, he really does have something supernatural about him. But I am an unbeliever and therefore incur – not contempt, but destruction."

Lina did not reply; she merely made some vague motion towards the window with her hand. It was then that he noticed someone sitting in the armchair, leaning forward, listening intently to them both.

"You appear to be hinting at something," said the third presence, his moustaches quivering slightly as he smiled. "But my friend, whatever you may be hinting at, remember that drawing historical parallels is always a risky business. It really is a fatuous thing to do."

Zybin shot a glance at him. He felt no surprise: his presence was perfectly natural. Indeed, this wasn't the first such conversation. For the past month he had been coming here almost every night. What was astonishing and frightening was that the conversation was a satisfying heart to heart affair, and Zybin was filled with love, tenderness and respect towards this great wise being. All his perplexity, his grievances, even his jeering anger remained behind, on the other side of sleep. Here he was all tremulous adoration and pride that he could speak so easily and freely with the greatest man of the epoch, who in turn understood him. What was it – the absence of fear? "Baseness in every vein", as Pushkin said once when he was talking about his encounter with the Tsar, or was something else of that sort subconsciously involved? This he did not know and feared to guess at. But now he was resolved to speak his whole mind.

"The world has been taken over by petty individuals," he said, pressing his hands to his chest. "People who can't see past their nose end. They're mean-minded, silly, rubbish, Kuteikins, but it's because of them that the world will come to grief. Not because of their power, but because of their weakness."

94

The visitor spread his hands; he was genuinely puzzled.

"Illogical," he said. "Most illogical, once again. Kuteikins? Mr Nobodies? How on earth can they do anything against the will of the people? Why do you hold that in such contempt? Take Grumble-Rumble even: 'These things apparently do not depend on me.'"

"Ah," replied Zybin sadly. "Your Rumble didn't live in a time like this; there are periods in history when a snap of the fingers is enough to set everything swaying and tottering. And the one who snaps them can be some pigmy, like Thiers. Hitler's undersized too, isn't he, and surrounded by pygmies, and he sends real people, young people, the flower of the nation off to die! Splendid young men! And it'll be a struggle to the death. Perhaps even the final struggle."

"Excellent," said the visitor. "So you believe it will be the final one. And that we will survive it, do you believe that?"

"I do, certainly," said Zybin, fairly leaping up from the sofa. "As sure as I believe in God I do. But you, why don't you trust your own people? You say yourself they have something to defend. Why then the arrests and prisons? It's your favourite song isn't it? 'We love our homeland like a bride'? So how can you reconcile the one and the other?"

The visitor laughed. His laugh had a ring of genuine kindliness to it.

"My dear young chap," he said. "How can you argue with us old men when you know so little of life? To build a bridge requires years of work and thousands of people; to blow it up needs only an hour and a handful of men. Those are the handful we're getting after now."

"Yes, yes, I know, I've heard that," frowned Zybin. "And not just from you. Saint-Just said of his victims: 'Perhaps you're right, but the danger is great, and we do not know where to deliver the blow. When a blind man is searching for a needle in a haystack, he takes the whole pile.' At least he admitted he was blind, you see, whereas we ... All right. Now I have a question about myself. Why are you destroying me?"

"For the idiotic disease of complacency," said the visitor graciously. "Because you remain above the battle. As they say: 'Who is not with me is against me'."

Zybin joined in the laughter.

"Oho! You've already started quoting Mayakovsky! That never used to be your wont. Surely he isn't needed in the game now?"

"I'm better-educated than you imagine, my friend," said the visitor.

"That's not Mayakovsky, it's the gospel. You shouldn't try and put me to the test."

"Oh yes, I beg your pardon, the gospel: Matthew 12: 13."

"There you are, you see, you know when and by whom it's been said before," the visitor smiled grudgingly. "So why are you lashing out about Christ and Kuteikin when you shouldn't? The Christs pronounce and pass through, its us Kuteikins who have to do the building. That's the nub of the whole business. But you're a fly in the ointment, so we have to . . ."

He pressed a button.

The ring was loud and penetrating. Two men entered and one seized Zybin by the shoulder.

Still, he did manage to get out what he chiefly wanted to say.

"The whole question," he said, "consists solely in whether it is permissible to act in this way or not. If not, you have brought the world to the edge of the pit. There will be war, famine, death and destruction. The last people will crawl in from somewhere and warm their hands amid the ruins. They will not survive either. But, you know, I would bless such an ending. Why not? Mankind has lied and twisted; it has deserved destruction and has been destroyed. Finis! The slate is wiped clean! The apes can be called in to start all over again. What would terrify me is that you might be right! The world might survive and flourish. That would mean that intelligence, conscience, good will, humanity – everything, all that had been forged over the millennia and was regarded as the raison d'être of human existence, was absolutely worthless. Democracy would be nothing more nor less than a silly fairy tale about the ugly duckling. The ugly brute would never become a swan in a million years. Then the world would be saved by iron and flamethrowers, stone cellars and people with Brownings. Then you actually would be a genius, because in spite of our tricks you paid no attention, and did not allow yourself to be seduced by humanism! You are omnipresent, like the holy spirit – in every service blouse and pair of boots, I am aware of you, your personality, your style, your inflexibility and comprehension of good and evil. With what contempt the word 'good' is pronounced nowadays – and in the tone you use too. Not even 'good' but 'good-natured'. 'He's good-natured, that's all.' 'He's good-natured in a classless way.' 'He's a classless humanist.' 'He's good to everybody, fair to everyone.' Can there be a more hurtful judgment, a more scathing term of abuse? Yes, it's a dangerous word 'good', extremely dangerous. Cervantes knew what he was doing when he concluded *Don Quixote* with it! You believed in the right to march across everything and everybody and thus delivered us from the merely good-natured. But I did not have faith in you and therefore lost everything. I have indeed corrupted, enfeebled, destabilized and I have no place in your world of necessity. You did not let yourself be weakened by complacency, no matter how artfully our common enemies urged it upon you. Therefore there is nothing purer or more powerful than that truth which you brought into the world. Crush us then, us permanent students and voluntary attenders of the faculty of useless knowledge. We must fall down before the arms and military boots by which we are crushed, as before an icon. That is what I will say if you are right and victorious in the final conflict. God, how dreadful it will be if one of you, the Führer or you, Leader, do prevail. Then the world is lost. Then man is condemned. For all eternity because it is only the clenched fist he will serve, bow down only to the scourge, live at ease only in jail."

He spoke and wept, wept and beat his breast. He threw all the pillows about until someone unseen, standing close by, said severely: "Now give over! What are you bawling about? You know perfectly well that it's not one or another who will win, it's we who will win. The country! The people! You! The director! Clara! Kornilov! Grandpa! Dasha! Just you repeat that to yourself every day! I'm worried about you, you know – as soon as night comes you start these ravings! It can't go on, it can't! Get a grip on yourself!"

The ringing went on.

It was the ringing that woke him up. The entire room was flooded with thin, cool, early sunlight. The neighbour's black cat was sitting on the windowsill, looking at him in horror. He reached out a hand and it vanished instantly. A couple of hairpins were lying on a chair but of Lina herself there was no sign. The telephone rang again; he lifted the receiver and heard Clara's voice: "Georgi Nikolaevich, you're half an hour late already, are we going or not?"

"Yes, yes!" he shouted hurriedly. "I'll be there this minute . . . You're where, with the security man? Fine. He's asleep? . . . No, no, don't wake him up. In his cupboard there's . . . All right I'll get it myself."

He put the phone down and sat for a minute motionless, trying to separate dream from reality. He pictured everything with equal clarity and plausibility – the window, the conversation at the desk, on the sofa, what had come before and what had come after. "And why has he taken to visiting me so often?" he wondered. "It's a bad omen!" he said aloud and began getting ready.

Clara was waiting for him. She was dressed for a field expedition, in combat jacket and field glasses on a shoulder strap. His bag of provisions lay on the bench alongside. The guard was sitting nearby, yawning loudly and rubbing his eyes with his fists. He always woke up at dawn.

"And I was worried you'd be late," said Clara. "There's your bag, let's get going. There's a five-tonner leaving for Ili at seven-thirty from the provision warehouse. We can still catch it if we get a move on."

He lifted the bag easily, slung it across his shoulder and said: "We'll catch it all right, let's go."

The driver set them down near the collective farm office. He was a new man and consequently didn't know anyone there. "You could have asked the book-keeper for information," he said. But the book-keeper wasn't there; he was on his rounds. One of the shopkeepers was sitting there in his place but she knew nobody.

"That Savelev's been working here since the place was founded," she said in response to his question as to where he could get hold of a list of fishermen. "He's got all the records. I've not been here long. What's up, has there been a complaint about somebody?"

So Zybin got nothing out of her either. When Clara and he got outside (damp grey sand, ruts and the office on the topmost crest of the hill, overlooking the drop, a plywood box humming in the wind), Clara enquired: "Where to now?"

He sat down on the bench and undid the straps on his bag.

"Have you got anything special on? Nothing particular coming up in the museum today? (She shook her head.) In that case, let's go down below and walk along the river bank. There are fishermen's huts all over. Somebody's bound to tell us where Savelev is."

. . . A great stillness and tranquillity enfolded them as soon as they had descended to the river. Here everything was different from up on the hill. The sluggish, turbid water flowed on to some unknown destination. Mysteriously distorted trees stood above them. The narrow little path crunched underfoot and hurt their feet. The bank soared steeply up and overhung them, studded with boulders, yellow, green and blue. It was hushed, sombre and peaceful. He too grew quiet, lapsed into silence, and began thinking about Lina. Not think even, simply experiencing her over again.

* * *

98

"Open your eyes," he had told Lina, when it was all over.

She did so obediently and looked at him with a mild and somehow searching glance. She had come and knocked on her own initiative. And clambered in through the window. So proud and artful, no hand could hold her. He also remembered the distant past – how she had been then, by the sea, on the day of their separation – harsh and ill-tempered, all sharp corners, the hurtful snorts, the sneers. All so different from last night.

"Georgi Nikolaevich," Clara called out from behind.

He halted. Evidently in keeping pace with his thoughts he had been walking faster and faster and had got so far ahead that she was hurrying to keep up. She was breathing heavily, hair creeping down over her eyes. She drew a hand across her face to sweep it back.

All of a sudden, an almost hysterical feeling of tenderness and guilt swept over him.

He seized her hand.

"Clarochka," he said, "it's just that I completely . . ." And was just going to say that he had completely forgotten about her, but stopped short.

He hadn't forgotten about her. He had simply been thinking about Lina. He knew how it was with him – whenever he was lost in thought, he went at a spanking pace. The more he brooded the faster he went.

"It's all right," said Clara, shrugging off her rucksack. "It's just that's it so hot."

The heat down here by the river was dry, still, scorching like a great oven.

"That man behind us, I think he's trying to catch us up," said Clara.

Zybin glanced round. The man raised his arm and waved at them.

"Yes, he is," said Zybin.

"Maybe he's this Savelev?"

"Maybe. Let's wait for him."

"Ooh!" said the man as he came up. "I'm fair worn out. You can't half get a move on. I could hardly keep up and you carrying bags as well." He took out a handkerchief and mopped his face.

He was a young lad, fresh-faced and chubby-cheeked, blue-eyed, rather like Koltsov.

"Was it you who came to the management office?"

"Yes," replied Zybin, gazing at him. "It was us."

"You'd just gone when the accounts man arrived. He's waiting for you."

Zybin glanced at Clara.

"Well, let's walk back shall we?" he asked in an undertone.

"Why walk when you can ride?" the lad smiled. "He told me to leg it after you, but he's sitting in the car."

Zybin looked at the steep slope.

"How on earth do we get up there?"

"Bit further on. There's steps up by the dead tree," the lad explained. "Give us your bags."

He got hold of both bags and smiled.

"Oh!" he said respectfully. "Something in there's gurgling."

"We've got refreshments in there too," answered Zybin.

"That's nice," the lad laughed. "And our shop's been shut for two days – stocktaking."

"It's quiet round here, isn't it," said Zybin.

Now he was walking unhurriedly, again aware of the peace and quiet, the extraordinary sense of space.

"They wanted to transfer the town here, Clarochka," he said, "to this steppe-country here. That was after the earthquake of '99. A good job Zenkov dug his heels in. Zenkov's the one who built the cathedral," he explained to the newcomer.

"Great man," the youth assented readily. "They say there isn't a single nail in that cathedral. It all just stands up by itself."

"Well, let's just say they're fibbing," said Zybin. Then abruptly came to a halt.

In front of him, as they negotiated a turning, appeared a group of stunted trees with pointed green leaves, unusually soft and brittle; gigantic matt-white flowers climbed up into the crowns, and hung down from the boughs in bunches, luxuriant, vast and brilliant, like Christmas-tree decorations. Each blossom taken by itself was not huge, it was tiny, but the whole crown of the tree was huge, like a theatre chandelier. And the colour of the crown was like boiled milk: a lustreless shade of yellow-white. Zybin had never seen anything like it anywhere.

"What sort of trees are those?" he asked.

"Oh, they're dead," the youth answered. "Strangled."

"But they've got leaves and flowers," said Zybin.

"Just go up close," said the youth.

It was indeed a dead grove, made up of the corpses of trees. Even the wood of these corpses was non-living, a deathly grey, silver-green,

100

with peeling bark; and the bark had also flaked, shrivelling and simply sloughing off like dead skin. And arching along all the dead twigs, crawled a supple, clutching, lashing, bold convolvulus-serpent. It was her leaves which glowed a cheerful green on the dead branches, on all their agonizing bifurcations; it was her flowers which hung on the branches from clusters of tiny suckers and tentacles, astonishingly tender and serene. They were so alien to that austere and honest deathly sterility that they seemed almost dazzling. It was like an explosion of something splendid, like the sombre and magical secret of that dead river and its dry valley. There was something about that copse reminiscent of the hut on chickens' legs, or Koschei's hoard, or the field sown with dead men's bones.

"It's awful," said Zybin. "You realize, Clarochka, they're actually dead. Strangled by the convolvulus."

Clara made no reply, simply shaking her head slightly.

"It'll die as well," said Zybin, "it doesn't know that though. It's as mortal as they are. It'll suck them dry and perish."

Suddenly he spoke: "Look, there's two of them and they're waving to us. They're coming down!"

Sure enough, two men were descending the declivity. One, tall with a raincoat over his shoulder, the other short, wearing a raincoat and hat, coming along behind. He was bandy-legged like a dachshund.

Zybin slipped his hands into his pockets and stood motionless, awaiting their arrival. Clara came over and leaned against a dead tree. The lad was silent. Two men! Two men! The two came on in silence, without pause or conversation. Their gait was heavy and measured.

"Good thing I left the Browning behind," thought Zybin suddenly. "I should have . . ." But the thought flickered and faded.

"I should have made sure of seeing Lina," he thought, almost inanely. "God almighty, the way I make a mess of everything! And how wonderful it was that time by the sea!"

At once he pictured the white wall of the town museum right on the sea's edge, the ancient rusty cannon on the stones by the entrance, the little man with the pointer in his hand – this suddenly came into his mind for an instant, warming him and causing him to smile.

Clara was standing motionless by the tree, staring intently at the approaching pair. He addressed a remark to her; she made no reply.

The bow-legged one in the rear was the first to come up to Zybin; the tall one stopped further off and eyed Clara curiously. Comprehensively, from head to toe. The bow-legged one had curly dark hair, thick eyebrows meeting across the bridge of his nose, a small pointed chin, quick penetrating mouse-like eyes. Altogether a weak, insignificant little face.

"Greetings," he said.

"Greetings to you," responded Zybin.

"Warm isn't it?" said the small one and unfastened his coat (revealing red tabs). "Comrade Zybin? Shall we go over to the car? We need to have a little talk."

"Are you from the management then?" Zybin asked, as if continuing some sort of game. He glanced at Clara. She was standing immobile by the tree, staring at them.

"From the management," smiled Bow-legs pointedly, as he turned to look at the tall individual. He was silently surveying Clara as before.

"Well, then, go it is," said Zybin.

He pulled a tenner from his pocket and held it out to Clara.

"When you get to the management office, you'll find a lorry going your way. There won't be a train till evening," he said matter-of-factly.

"Now why make a beautiful girl go hunting about in heat like this," said bow-legs seriously. "We'll give her a lift. You can do it yourself in fact. We only want you for a couple of words."

"I'll go straight to the director, Georgi Nikolaevich," she said. "Will they let us say goodbye?"

"Ai-ai-ai!" smiled Bow-legs (the tall one stood silent and unmoving as before). "You see how much they trust us."

"Never mind," said the tall one indulgently, "we'll try to earn their trust."

Clara suddenly took Zybin by the shoulder.

"Listen! Make them show their papers, listen to me!" she cried. "Otherwise we go nowhere."

Bow-legs was smiling ever more sweetly. This made all his small, predatory, insignificant facial features merge together, and his face turned almost black.

"If it comes to papers, let's start with you," said the tall one coming up to them. "Have you got your identity card on you?"

"But you will be sure to give her a lift home?" asked Zybin.

"Well of course," the tall one assured him indifferently. "We've got two cars."

"You've got the warrant?" Zybin asked the diminutive one and took out his identity card. The tall one took it, opened it, closed it and stuck it in his pocket.

"Well naturally!" marvelled the short one. "We, Georgi Nikolaevich, behave strictly according to the law. If we overstep the mark, you'll go hauling us in front of the prosecutor. We know all about that! No, everything's in order."

The tall one extracted a fresh gleaming form from his bag. It was headed by the word "warrant". The facsimile signature was blue. His surname had been written in a rounded, almost schoolgirl hand by some young secretary, some mother's loving daughter.

Zybin glanced at it, nodded, returned the warrant and turned to Clara.

"Well, then, let's say goodbye in the proper manner. Clarochka! Is it all right?" he asked the tall one.

"Yes, certainly, certainly," said Bow-legs, flustered.

"Yes, by all means," said the tall one indifferently.

And they both went off a little way into the dead thicket.

II

CHAPTER 1

AH, CLIO, MUSE OF HISTORY!
Zybin slept soundly, and he dreamed. The Black Sea and that little town where, three years before, he had spent all of two months.

The town had been small, grubby, with back streets and side turnings, uphill and down, shops and stalls, gardens and plots, and finally a little resort-town market above the sea, right above the very sea itself.

Up until midday the market was a sleepy sort of spot, but in the afternoon it suddenly became the noisiest and most animated place in the town. Two oaken casks used to be rolled out into the middle and hoisted up on trestles; then a moustachioed Greek in a white apron, with jokes and witticisms invited one and all to partake of genuine port wine and Madeira. A couple of glasses cost 50 kopecks, a rouble bought you five glasses and for two roubles, you could drink till the cows came home.

The wine was muddy and warm, with a whiff of burnt sugar, a touch nauseating no doubt, but nevertheless, towards evening, the little mule would bear away two empty barrels.

Next to the barrels, mats of souvenirs were laid out: dried sea horses, rather like everlasting flowers; bunches of white and yellow seashells; beads made of flat lilac stones – with pictures of the sea, seagulls, palms and finally crabs. There were more crabs there than anything else, probably hundreds of them – all sorts: yellow, red, pink and purple, almost black; people would bring them from home on trays and carefully place them on mats ... There they stood on spiny legs, shiny with varnish, resembling toilet cases or patent-leather shoes or huge circular powder compacts; they were constantly surrounded by a seething crowd of holiday-makers. Zybin was less than interested in them, but he still used to go to the market – he was desperately keen to get a crab too, but not one like these. What he wanted was a real crab, black and spiny, with barbs and growths and savagely serrated claws and green submarine stains on its knobbly limestone carapace. Just the kind that never found its way to the market in fact. Probably they weren't a saleable item; you could hardly stick one of them on a white open-work cloth on your chest of drawers, between the circular mirror and the aforementioned toilet case.

Back in the Krupskaya sanatorium – where Zybin occupied one of the five bunks in a corner room – he had leafed through the brochures and prospectus and established that there were three things worth seeing in this little town. Firstly, a major port had existed here in ancient times, from which grain had been exported to Italy. An extensive dedicatory inscription to Poseidon had been discovered, and the remains of an amphitheatre had been excavated. There was a municipal museum. Secondly, virtually the only children's beach on the Black Sea was located close by. There was a children's park, a roundabout and a hospital to treat tuberculosis of the bone. There was also the Central Children's Theatre in summer, artistic director Natalya Satz. This beach, however, was not an unalloyed pleasure for Zybin. He would wake up early every morning around five, get dressed, pick up a book and binoculars and slip out, unnoticed, down to the sea. It was quiet, bright and windless. Everyone was still asleep – the doorkeeper in the doorway, the yard-porter in the yard and the gatekeeper in the gateway, so no one observed either his going or his coming back. He used to return at about seven, and immediately collapse into sleep on the bed. True, everybody got woken up at nine in time for breakfast, but he slept on. Still, he had to get up an hour later whether he wanted to or not. The corner windows gave onto the children's beach, a specially fenced-off section of it, and in the mornings, the windowpanes fairly rattled with childish shrieks. While the children amused themselves and were free to fall down or choke themselves, their mums sat on sheets and suffered loudly on their behalf: "Rudik where do you think you're going! What did I tell you? Rudik, this morning?! Only up to your chest, up to your chest, you horrid boy! Ah, you would, would you!" After which a strident shriek invariably rang out. Of course, sleep was out of the question now and he got up, put on his pyjamas and sat himself down by the window with a book in his hand. Rather than reading, however, he stared at the sea. After a while, the children would be taken away and peace and quiet would supervene. The mums would get up from the sheets, and talk among themselves before dispersing, gently kneading their stomachs and haunches with the palms of their hands. After that they ventured into the sea, but since they were special mothers, they did this in dignified fashion, without the least noise or splashing, and not for too long. Within half an hour, stunned by sun and sea, they were already scrambling ashore and climbing up under the awning. There they drank hot cocoa from green thermos flasks, rather reminiscent of civil defence gas masks, and dissected oranges with their crimson fingernails. At length, having eaten and drunk their fill, they rolled over onto one side and gently fell asleep. And so did everyone on the beach. The wind strayed along the sand, billowing up skirts and blouses, before reaching the parasols and scratching the sand with their ribs, rocking the huge blue globular beach balls, and then, finding nothing of consuming interest, little by little left the beach.

Another hour later came the lunch bell in the sanatorium. Zybin would get to his feet, toss his book onto the night-table, get changed and make his way to the dining room. And everything went as prescribed after that – lunch, bathing, a walk, a film or something of that kind, then supper, an evening walk, then bed. But sometimes, before lunch, the extraordinary did occur: on the beach, always at exactly the same time, there would appear the slender figure of a woman; black one-piece, tanned legs, fair, close-cropped mane. She walked along, arms swinging, laughing and kicking at a stray ball to send it the length of the beach. She would drop a cheery word to someone and vanish as suddenly as she had appeared.

That had been the second notable thing the town had to offer.

The third required little by way of explanation. The town was the site of the only Institute of Viniculture and Wine-making in the Soviet Union.

And the sea splashed away near the little town, a quiet dull-green, affectionate as a cat dozing in the noonday heat. Heaven knows what it had been like two thousand years before, when the red-maned sea horses and dragons from Athens and Naples had sailed up to these sinuous shores, but nowadays one could go out half a mile or more and it would still only come up to your waist, or chest, or neck and only far out where the cormorants slid into the water, was it above hand height.

Zybin had picked out a certain spot and used to come here every day before sun-up. The sky was still dark and streaked with green at this hour, the stars were limpid, as were the shadows; the sea and the beach were both deserted. There was nothing in the heavens, on the waters, or on the dry land. On the beach itself, there were only the empty bathing huts, brightly painted and patterned; disturbed sand; the awnings and the shadows they cast.

He gazed silently from the high shore down to the beach and beyond, to the sea, and still further, at the rapidly brightening horizon. And all that was in him was silent. A faint haze lay upon all the objects of the world, and the waves rolled in slow and soundless. It was peaceful and serene, with a hint of despair, a hint of eeriness like when you arrive at a deserted suburban station at night, with a single bulb glowing near the ceiling and no one about. Or a night chemist, with its sleepy dispenser, or when wandering through a shuttered market. Except, of course, that everything here was loftier, vaster, more solemn and mournful.

"As before the face of eternity," he would have said, if he had pretended to eloquence, but he did not, and so simply stood there and gazed. A great deal stole upon his mind at these moments, but it was all vague and confused; there was nothing he could seize upon and retain within himself, except perhaps for this silence, this height and distance.

After standing there for a minute or two, he went up to the wooden staircase, placed his hand on the rail and slithered down.

Here his mood altered again. Just here perhaps, he mused, on this very spot, where the staircase stood with the ice-cream kiosk below, ship owners had jostled among the sailors, slaves and relatives, awaiting ships, messengers, news of Alexander's campaign in India. There would be much speculation, astonishment, wagging of heads and rumour-mongering, with each no doubt adding his own embroidery. He had cut across Syria, hurtled across all of Asia, passed the fearful fire-breathing steppes, the abode of cannibals and Amazons, whose horses fed on human flesh and moved on towards the uttermost limits of the world. He had reached the Indus. Crossed it. Pitched camp and proclaimed universal empire, the homeland of a new race of Perso-Greeks. Change was in the air. The terrestrial globe had fallen into his hands, and he was playing with it like an apple. Now it would come to pass! All wars would cease, all conflicts; frontiers would automatically disappear and there would be a single earth and a single heaven and in that heaven would be God, and on that earth a divine youth, a superman, its master; happy is the time we live in, happy are our children.

Not a damned bit of all that nonsense actually came to anything of course. The world isn't an apple or a ball for the catching – oh no! And you can't squeeze it in your fist.

The master of the universe gave up the ghost unaccountably quickly (perhaps helped on his way by a suitable admixture), and his subordinates immediately became kings and gods too. They fought among themselves, murdered one another and began to issue proclamations. They proclaimed and proclaimed until there was nothing left to proclaim. Then they destroyed everything, put cities and libraries to the torch, stuck out their tongues and disavowed everything. And it all came to an end with the world's hopeless and terrible weariness. The waves of that weariness reached as far as here of course but would hardly have been felt severely. At that time the arms of history were not long enough to reach this far.

Then came the Roman empire. Wars, crises, killings and despair – Augustus, Tiberius, Nero, Christ and Christianity – the city had become a Roman colony. Now ships began to leave its bays with cargoes of grain (once having become Great, empires for some reason always start to starve), and in the other direction came vessels laden with bronze, marble, statues of emperors, linen and silk fabrics, debased coinage, which people used to haul about with them in sacks at that time. Then the empire started splitting along all its seams – it had turned from Great into Universal after all – some were killed, some places burned, they tried to prove certain things and of course, failed. But poets and singers went on creating; emperors went to war; jurists codified and philosophers devised a basis for all this. The city meanwhile hugged the earth and waited and waited and waited for all this to come to an end. Oh did it indeed? It did nothing of the kind; it simply went on living as it had for a thousand years, that's all! Catching and salting fish, sowing wheat and pressing grapes, celebrating weddings and having no thought beyond these things. "That's how it was," he reflected, kicking off his shoes and heading into the water. "That's exactly how it was. They lived, loved, had children, and took no thought beyond these matters. We think up things on their behalf, but they just lived and that's all about it. That's what I'm doing as well now, aren't I? Perhaps people will start thinking up things about me a thousand years from now, ascribe some extraordinary notions to me – prophetic insight, tragic stature, a sense of history, because I won't be a man any longer, I'll be a monument – and not just any monument, a monument to something. Exactly what, they'll dream up themselves."

That was his *idée fixe*; he thought about it every day, sometimes in irritation, sadness or indifference, but never cheerfully, because he knew it was a kind of delirium and that his mind was starting to wander.

At these times he occasionally encountered others like himself, idly strolling about. They were few in number, these amateurs of solitary morning walks, two or three at most. But they were all rather special individuals, quite unlike those he met during the day. Still, what of that? He wasn't exactly a diurnal creature himself.

There was one man who particularly struck him. He had been walking once along the beach when he saw a man standing in the sea, a long way out. Or rather a head sticking out of the water. "Now there's a weird type," smiled Zybin and halted. Five minutes passed, seven, ten. Zybin was beginning to get bored and still the head did not move. "What's he doing there," he thought, irritated by now, "staring at the sea, is he?" The man was indeed staring at the horizon – at the broad, bright, almost green ribbon of the dawn. Above, hung the dark, heavy sky; below lay the dark waters, while in the heart of the ribbon something seemed to be taking place, coming to a head, breaking out and shooting forth sparks. And Zybin began staring too, but soon became bored and moved on.

And met a second individual.

This one was sitting on a rock skimming pebbles into the sea. He was a short, tubby man, full-faced and sporting a bald patch. As Zybin came up, he announced without turning round: "When you throw stones into water, watch the rings, otherwise your activity will be pointless. So said Kozma Prutkov."

"Words of wisdom," sighed Zybin.

"Yes indeed!" The stout man took aim and hurled a flat pebble. "Oh dear, a failure. I used to be able to manage six." He glanced at Zybin. "Listen, where on earth have I seen you before? You're not from the Dzerzhinsky Sanatorium?"

"No."

"Blast. Where have I seen you before then?" he stared intently at Zybin. "Not at the Artfund?"

"No, not Artfund. I'm not an artist at all," smiled Zybin.

"Hm! Pity! Still, I suppose at this hour we're all artists. Yes indeed! But you haven't a sketchbook. So you can't be an artist, that's certain. So where from, eh? . . . Ah, I've got it! It was at the market I saw you! You were looking for some sort of special crab! Right? Well of course. How did you get on – find one?"

"No," Zybin replied. "Not the one I was after."

"And what sort might that be?" grinned the other.

"Natural."

"What do you mean, natural?" said the stout man in cheerful astonishment. There's none made of papier-mâché."

"I wanted a real one, black, fresh from the sea," Zybin explained.

"Ah, one like that! You won't find them there. You'll have to ask the fishermen. No, though, they don't catch crabs either; they've got a co-operative, a plan. I don't know, I just don't know where you'd find a crab like that. Listen, I've just remembered. This is the second time I've come across you here – it was you sitting on the bench near the steps yesterday wasn't it? Right? Well now, well now, can't sleep, is that it?"

Zybin smiled. He'd taken an instant fancy to the fat man for some reason. He was so completely his own man, soft, rounded, good-natured in his baggy suit and barefoot inside his shoes.

"No, no, it's not that I can't sleep," he said. "It's just that it would be a sin to sleep through something as beautiful as this."

"True," the fat man fairly leapt from his seat. "You've said a very true thing there: a sin. This is the only time you'll see it too. As soon as the mothers arrive with their kiddies and our boozers come marching in, it won't be the sea any more, it'll be a park of culture and rest, or park of rest from culture, as they say nowadays. And that's a fact! That's an absolute fact! You see, what I do, I come here while it's still dark and sit down on that boulder there – I rolled it down from the cliffside specially. And I just sit and sit, staring across at the Turkish shore. That's where the sun comes up. The sunrises here, let me tell you, are magnificent, quite different from what the books tell you. They talk about 'the interplay of colours', the struggle of light against the darkness, fire and whatever, no, no, there's nothing like that here. It's all different here – it's peace. So you sit and stare, stare until you lose all conception of time. Then they blow the bugle in the pioneer camp. That means you've been sitting like a tree stump on this spot for all of three hours. Just now when you came down the slope, did you notice a man standing in the sea – or did you? Standing there? And do you know who it is? Ah now, that's a celebrity – a Romanian communist. He was held in solitary confinement for five years. And for those five years he could see no further than that bench – that was the sort of cell he had. Walls here and here and here, slop bucket in the corner, little window up there and that was all. And a lamp inside a grille. He even started going blind. They brought him here just a week ago on a plane and wanted to put him in hospital – he wouldn't hear of it. Take me to the sea! So they did and got him a place in the Central Committee sanatorium and now the director doesn't know what to do with him. His treatment is already prescribed: lie down and get up at such and such a time, don't overbathe, overheat, get overtired. He ignores it! Goes out at night, comes back at night – what's to be done? Tie him up or something? I understand how he feels, you know. It's space isn't it? look at it! Just sea, sea, sea for a hundred miles. Look at it!" He threw his head back, threw his arms wide and inhaled deeply. "Space!"

Behind them a bugle began to sound.

"Ah!" said the fat man. " 'Get your spoon and get your bre-ead, sit you down and you'll get fe-ed.' That's what my nephew sings. That means it's nine already. Time's up! Are you going to the lighthouse? Terrific, it's on my way. Let's go. So then, if you're not an artist, what are you if it isn't a secret?"

"I'm a historian," explained Zybin. "Rome."

"Ah." The fat man grew serious at once. "Well, well. And there's a good deal to see here. You've been to the museum of course? No? How can that be? You must go. The director has got quite a collection – vases, coins, three statues. I myself . . ." He halted and declaimed: 'Quousque tandem abutere Catilina patientia nostra.' There! Ingrained for life. I graduated from the First Classical gymnasium in Minsk in 1916. Klinger, Max Adolfovich – you've never come across the name? He used to teach us ancient languages. He certainly knew his stuff. After all, he came from a very cultivated family. Most cultivated people. He was the conductor of the school choir. I remember once we were learning 'How glorious'. Well the lads at that time were always up to something! Revolution in the air! Some sang and some just opened their mouths. And I opened my mouth too. Then he bends over me and sings in my ear: 'Yi-i-id! Why don't you si-ing?' Well at that I really raised my voice." The fat man burst into laughter and Zybin laughed too.

"So then, you studied the classics?" Zybin enquired. "But I thought . . ."

"That all Jews went to commercial and modern schools," the fat man cut in. "Quite right, that's what happened. But my dad was determined I should become a lawyer. Or a notary's assistant at least. They weren't keen to let Jews into their class at that time. But my ancestor heard Oscar Gruzenberg in Kiev once and after that he seemed to go a little bit crazy. He hung his portrait up in his study, bought his speeches and had them specially bound. But I went and let my father down, I didn't become a lawyer. Just didn't happen!" And the tubby man seemed rather saddened by this.

"Yes!" sighed Zybin. "Yes!" And was about to ask the other what on earth he was, in that case, when he said: "You must certainly call in at the museum. Get to know the director. He's the sort of man, you'll see – he regards any real expert as if he were the Lord God himself.

114

There's a lot he can tell you. About the crab, now, he can give you some useful advice. He's got all the sixth-formers at his beck and call."

"I will, I will," Zybin assured him. He really did feel awkward about it: been here ten days and not visited the museum yet.

"Yes, do call in," counselled the tubby man earnestly. "Well, we're here; with that, allow me to wish you all the very best. They call me Roman Lvovich, I live here next to you in the Tsurupa sanatorium. Very nice to make your acquaintance . . . You might consider dropping by for a game of chess." He made a slight bow and went off swiftly.

But a sudden thought went through Zybin: "How on earth does he know where I live seeing as we've only just met?"

Another encounter took place – also at a very early hour – but not at this spot. It was much further on, where the shore grew wilder and there were no beaches and seats. That was where he encountered her – the one in the black one-piece and the mane. He feared to recall that, however. And he certainly didn't dream about her.

The door slammed. Zybin started up. A prison bulb glowed dimly. The glass behind the grille was violet in colour. A tall, gaunt old man with a heavy growth of stubble was sitting on the bunk opposite, regarding him.

"My, you have had a long sleep," said the old man.

Zybin sighed and sat up on the bed.

"What's the time now?"

The old man shrugged slightly.

"Looks like they've just brought supper round; there, you can hear the clanging of the containers along the floor. That means it's six o'clock already. You're not supposed to sleep here during the day, you know. They made an exception for you today for some reason." He half rose and proffered a hand. "Well then, let's get acquainted. Buddo, Alexander Ivanovich, delivered to this humble abode from the town colony. They're pinning a new charge on me. And what would you prefer to be called?"

Zybin told him his name.

"From the museum?" Buddo was glad and astonished.

"Ye-es! How do you . . . ?"

"Lord! I'm from the colony, aren't I? We read *Kazakhstan Pravda* every day there from cover to cover. You've often had articles in there: about the bible, the museum, the excavations. 'G. Zybin.' That's you?"

"Yes."

"There you are. Well, I'm terribly pleased! That is, I mean of course I shouldn't be glad but ... I spent five inconspicuous years in that colony, Georgi Nikolaevich. You might say I had a cushy time of it. I was the fuel store manager there. I gave out the saksaul. All the supervisors used to go on their knees to me! Stands to reason. I could give them seven-fifty instead of half a tonne if I wanted, or they might not even get their five hundred. It was up to me. My scales were well-trained, weren't they! Anyway I was well set up. Newspapers, books, a radio. The pictures on my day off! That was the life!"

"What happened then?"

"Then I was arrested. Now they're drawing up a new indictment."

"Talk?"

"Yes, it started off with that, but now they're sticking something a bit more serious onto it. Fifty-eight: six to seventeen. That mean anything to you?"

"No."

"Terrorism by complicity. I showed sympathy for the murderers of Sergey Mironovich Kirov. That's the picture!"

"And the witnesses are prisoners?"

"Who else could they be, the dear sweet things! The weigh-house man and an auxiliary worker. I was the one who looked after him. A really nice boy: good-looking, well-mannered, decent family – music scholar. His uncle's an academician, agro-chemist. He did me a real good turn, the bastard. Wrote a little note, testifying that I had praised Nikolaev to the skies. We'd talked about Nikolaev of course, but not in that sense."

"What sense, then?"

Zybin was aware that in jail it wasn't done to ask questions but after all Buddo had started this conversation of his own accord.

"Oh, I just said that I thought there was something funny about the business, I don't mean funny that Kirov was killed – some maniac up and did it, things like that had happened before and always would. No, I meant it was funny how things developed after that."

"In what way?"

"Well, that Stalin arrived and the two chief OGPU men went off to visit the polar bears. They say he tore their epaulettes off right there on the station platform and smacked them across the chops. Well, all right, they'd deserved it. But afterwards something queer happened."

"What was queer?"

"That they suddenly started on the aristocrats. Started grabbing them and sending them away. Why them, I ask you! They were most likely too scared even to walk past that Smolny! A party man had done the shooting, after all! A party man! With a Smolny pass and permission to carry a Browning! That was the category involved in the murder – but they arrested Pushkin's great grandson and exiled him inside twenty-four hours. 'Well, isn't Pushkin a nobleman?' That was the supervisory prosecutor's answer to a certain Pushkin scholar. I just can't make head nor tail of it, really! And then this slipped out in the reports: 'On being searched, the murderer was found to be in possession of a diary in which he attempted to adduce a personal motive for the murder.' What exactly was that, then? Let's have the whole story! Maybe he was jealous on account of his woman. Maybe Kirov had kicked the husband out and kept the woman. So he turned savage. Could be that, couldn't it? Of course it could! That's what happened with Kotovsky. Well, that's what I said and they arrested me. Complicity through compassion! That is, moral complicity in the murder. In a terrorist act! What could I do? I confessed."

"What's going to happen to you, then?"

"Happen? Nothing much! I'll get another fiver and that'll be that. And because the terms don't fit, they'll renew the old tenner and send me a long way away. All right! Let's get going! They won't chase me out to Kolyma, though. I'm sixty. You have to dig up the ground out there, haul timber, wheel your wheelbarrow. How old are you, now, thirty? Ah, that's just the age for them! They just love that age. That's the real MPL or even HPL – you know what that is? Suitable for medium or heavy physical labour. The first and second categories: the mines, the dam, the wheelbarrows! What have they got you on?"

"Don't know."

"Not even an educated guess?"

"No."

"Well, that means anti-Soviet agitation. If you don't know yourself, that means it's sure to be agitation. Article 58, point 10. An all-embracing article! Fits everybody. Half an hour's chat, the informer notes it down, a word added or subtracted – and that's it; send the black maria and pick him up. But you don't get more than five for that these days. Eight if there's really something to it. If it's just talk they've got you for, take my advice and go along with it. Otherwise they'll dream up something else. They've got a fertile imagination too! What are you smiling at? You don't believe me?"

"No, no, I believe you," Zybin answered gently, continuing to smile (it was good not to be on his own in the cell, good that he'd got an old camp veteran, rather than some youth he'd have had to reassure and talk to. On the other hand, there was surely something very distasteful about this Buddo – probably that: 'what can you do, though? All right, let's get going.' If there was anybody Zybin couldn't abide it was defeatists of this sort). "No, no, I believe you about adding and subtracting words and sending the black maria, but that's not the way it'll be with me."

Buddo smiled cheerlessly.

"Really? Let's hope so, let's hope so. I wish you all the best, but that's no consolation to me. I know they don't arrest people so as to let them go. They hang on to a man for good and all."

"How do you mean for good and all?" Zybin showed his astonishment. "If you've finished your sentence . . ."

"But I haven't finished my sentence, I haven't finished it, have I?" Buddo smiled a sickly smile. "I've been arrested, haven't I? A trifle early of course. Usually they extend it in the final year; they've been in rather a hurry with me."

"You mean nobody from your camp's been released yet?" exclaimed Zybin.

"Why shouldn't they be?" smiled Buddo, giving a slight nod in the direction of the door. "Just don't shout, otherwise he'll be knocking at the door. If your sentence is over, you won't be held another half hour, but just how long are you going to stay free? You've got to have your head screwed on as regards that as well, otherwise you won't last a month. If you get a job as a cashier, or, say, a night watchman, and keep yourself to yourself and especially don't get married – wives are great ones for getting you sent down! – just do your stint, then home to bed, then you might last a couple of years, three, maybe three and a half."

"And then?"

"Then you'll be pulled in just the same."

"But what on earth for?"

"What for. For . . . Oh, I nearly used a camp word there! They'll get you for the same agitation. They don't like thinking up new offences. Why should they? The old ones will last a lifetime."

"That's even if I keep my trap shut?"

"Even if you do. But you won't, will you, you won't! Oh maybe you'll keep quiet for a year, maybe two. But then you'll blurt something out.

No? You're a card all right! Look, let's say you've been reading a book while on night duty. Your relief asks you what sort of a book it was and you said: Oh, not bad, it's an interesting read. You enjoyed it. Or you go to the pictures, someone sees you and asks how you enjoyed the film; and you said it was boring. And six months later the author of the book gets arrested and put in jail; and the director of the film is summoned to the Kremlin to get his hand shaken and be presented with a gramophone. It's all up with you then. On the one hand praising an enemy and enemy literature, on the other slander against Soviet party art. That's a good start for you. After that, you fall out with your neighbour. You think she doesn't know where to get redress against you? Lord, the things she writes about you! Two witnesses. That's enough. In you go!"

"But look here, don't they need any more proof than that?"

"What proof? Who needs it, Georgi Nikolaevich? What more proof do they want? It's all been proved already! Have you been in jail? You have. What for? Anti-Soviet activity. All right. There's nothing against this patriotic woman, bar the sobering-up station. Is the case proved? It is. That's the end of the matter. It's all clear to the security organs. Sign to show you've read the warrant."

"Well, what if I've recanted during that time? Admitted my guilt?"

Buddo laughed and wagged an admonitory finger.

"Ah, you cunning devil! That won't wash. He's confessed, he's recanted! You must be joking. Who, may I ask, has given permission for you to recant? Ramzin, oh yes – him! He made a clean breast of everything. They let him do that. Or did you read the news about the Trotskyist–Bukharin gang, how the plotters killed the engineer Boyarschinov in case he gave the game away? And that he wasn't just a plain engineer – he'd previously been convicted of sabotage? You read about that? Well he recanted, didn't he? He was allowed to recant posthumously. For the look of the thing. But you and me – fooey! Once an enemy always an enemy. That's the way it is, old pal."

"So, according to you, it's the mark of Cain is it or what?" Zybin shouted, genuinely enraged by this talk.

"According to me!" Buddo smiled derisively. "We'll gloss over that, but according to comrades Yezhov and Vyshinsky that's the way it is. And it isn't even a hot iron brand that heals up eventually. It's a disease of the blood, a tainted inheritance, genes passed on from father to son, son to grandson. That's why it's not just aristocrats, it's their distant relatives who get expelled from Leningrad. That's the class approach for you. I didn't realize that, fool that I was, and shot my mouth off. Why? What for? I should have known all about it, idiot! That's why I've landed in it."

"So you think you've been arrested for something you've done?"

"Naturally! Of course! Innocent people don't go to jail in this country, Georgi Nikolaevich. Whether it's word, thought or deed – all guilty. Just as you will be."

"No I won't," Zybin responded and turned away.

Buddo gazed at him compassionately and shook his head.

"You won't hold out, you know, Georgi Nikolaevich, you just won't," he said dolefully. "You'll be worn down. They hold all the cards and you've got nothing. But the point is, it's wasted effort. Whatever they've decided to do, they'll do. Nothing on earth is going to stop them. The country is at their disposal and you'll only make things worse for yourself."

"How do you mean exactly?"

"What I say! They've got these camps, haven't they? A town fuel depot or farm work is one thing; you've got your tea allowance, and the zeks can go bathing of an evening in the river, water the horses. Kolyma's a different matter. Kolyma, Kolyma, the wonderful planet – they keep their quilted jackets on day and night there, because in the winter they sleep in tents. You live and you rot. Shaking your head again? Ah, Georgi Nikolaevich, you are as yet unacquainted with grief, and still . . ."

The door opened with silent abruptness – the supreme art, mastered by very few in jails. The guard stood on the threshold.

"Who's the initial 'Z' here?" he asked. "Get yourself ready for questioning."

He was conducted along a cramped prison corridor, seemingly entirely made up of metal doors. Opposite the open food-slot of one of these stood a warder talking to the prisoner inside; when they drew level, he turned round and covered the food slot with his back. Then came another corridor, where there were only two doors, but they were huge and close-fitting, like the gates in church; they were locked and barred. They emerged at length onto a narrow stone flight of steps, rather like a servants' staircase. On the landing, there was a soldier sitting at a little table with a large ledger-like book. The guard held out the receipt, the soldier took it, glanced at it and entered something in the book. They went up another floor and emerged onto a totally different staircase; this one was of marble, spacious, carpeted and railed, with broad landings and glass doors. It led to another corridor. This one was quiet and glacially empty. Fluorescent lighting. The sterile walls gave off a clinical cleanliness and chill. A large, high door, covered in black leather closed off the corridor.

"Hands behind back!" whispered the guard as he knocked.

"Try it," responded a rich, complacent voice.

A large comfortable office came into view, with tubs of greenery. A map of the Soviet Union took up the whole of one wall. Undulating cream curtains hung at the windows. There was a horned hat stand in the corner.

The owner of the office, broad-shouldered and brawny, with full lips and curly hair, half rose from behind his desk.

"Greetings, Georgi Nikolaevich, take a seat," he invited. "That one, over by the wall." He nodded dismissal at the guard. "Well, now, let's get acquainted. Head of the Second SPD, Yakov Abramovich Neiman. First of all, how are you feeling?"

"All right, thank you." Zybin answered, seating himself at a diminutive table in the corner of the office.

"Splendid, splendid! I was a bit worried at you looking a little bit peaky – the heat, the travelling and nervous stress of course. So then, let's have a little chat, shall we? Actually someone else will be working with you, but . . . Smoke? Very sensible, better to be a hard drinker than poison yourself with this filthy stuff. So now, I have one question for you, nothing to do with the investigation, just interested to know. Does the name Starkov ring a bell? It does! Then tell me how you were involved in his case."

Zybin smiled and shrugged his shoulders.

"I wasn't involved at all."

"Not at all? Splendid!" Yakov Abramovich pulled out a drawer and picked up a neatly stitched folder. "So then, how do you explain that in August 1930, the Moscow GPU summoned you in connection with the case, and you were questioned by Comrade Razumni? Here's the record of the interrogation. Shall I read it out?"

"It was just a misunderstanding. I was questioned and released immediately."

"But on parole wasn't it? Ah, what idealistic times they were! You wouldn't get away like that nowadays! Yes, you were released. Here's the order along with the resolution. But the fact of release implies that you were arrested all the same, right? Listen while I read the record of the interrogation: 'You are accused of having, on 14 August of the current year, wrecked a meeting of the staff-student council of your institute, who were discussing an *Izvestiya* article about the brutal gang-rape of a second year university student, Veronika Kravtsova.'

"What have you got to say about that business? You see the form of the charge? Gang-rape."

Neiman reclined and regarded Zybin derisively. (It was then that Zybin caught the expression of deep-seated dread in his eyes.)

"Very well. We read on. Your reply: 'I did not break up the assembly. I simply gave my view on the matter.'

"Investigator's question: 'And what was that?'

"Answer: 'That we could not discuss, let alone put to the vote, the party committee's resolution demanding that the guilty person be shot.'

"Question: 'Explain why.'

"Answer: 'Firstly, because it plainly states in the code of criminal procedure: "The courts are independent and subordinate only to the law." And that would have been direct pressure on the court.' "

Neiman grinned and shook his head.

"Well you're the legalist and no mistake, aren't you?" he said. " 'Secondly, because until the trial, we know nothing in any case. All three of the accused are our comrades; they deny their guilt absolutely. There are no witnesses; the charges are based entirely on Kravtsova's suicide note to Starkov. That is all we know. There is nothing concrete other than that.'

"Question: 'The investigation shows you this note: "I have cursed you a hundred times for getting me drunk yesterday and allowing me to be humiliated. Oh, I wish nobody ill as I do you!" Surely that's specific enough?'

"Answer: 'No. The only specific thing here is malice. What is getting somebody drunk? What does letting me be humiliated mean? How could that be, really? Kravtsova isn't a little girl. She's the wife of a prominent man, former territory leader. Why did she have to go to a hotel room and drink herself insensible? The trial must answer all these questions and there's been no trial yet. So let's wait at least till the first sittings. That was what I said. Several people spoke after that and the matter didn't go to a vote.'

"Question: 'So, you don't deny that the meeting didn't vote after your speech?'

"Answer: 'No.'

"Question: 'What was your relationship to the deceased?'

"Answer: 'We said hello when we met.'

"Question: 'Where and when was the last time that happened?'

"Answer: 'Two days before her suicide, at that same meeting where this whole business began.'

"Question: 'Explain what sort of meeting that was.'

"Answer: 'It was a meeting of the student's literary circle. I was sitting near Kravtsova and saw notes being passed to her. Afterwards, I found out that the get-together in the Grenada Hotel near the Pushkin monument was arranged precisely at this time and via these notes.'

"Question: 'From whom did you find this out?'

"Answer: 'From the prosecutor's investigator, who sent for me at the time. Besides which, since the notes to Kravtsova had passed through my hands, I recognized the handwriting when I was shown them.' "

Yakov Abramovich raised his head and laughed.

"There's a dog's breakfast for you! Call him an investigator! Every secret out in the open! If I had one like him . . ."

"You'd throw him out?" enquired Zybin.

"And blacklist him!" snarled Yakov Abramovich. "All right. Let's go on.

"Question: 'And couldn't your comrades have invited you to join them as well, using these same notes?'

"Answer: 'No.'

"Question: 'Why not, then?'

"Answer: 'They weren't my comrades.'

"Question: 'But haven't you just called them comrades?'

"Answer: 'I called you comrade as well.' "

Yakov Abramovich threw down the file and roared with laughter.

"Oh, the donkey, the donkey," he said in high good humour. "And the thing of it is, he writes it all down! Collects material! This isn't an interrogation record, it's a comedy of manners! No! You can't catch Zybin with your bare hands! He's too fly. Am I right? So then! 'The record has been taken down from my own words and has been read by me . . .' " He slapped the folder shut. "Right! Well, Georgi Nikolaevich, now all the convicted men have been released long ago. They spent no more than two years inside. The rape story was thrown out by the Supreme Court, so you were formally proved right! And yet, there's something about your involvement in the affair that's not altogether clear. So then, would you not care to say something in addition to these records?"

He sat and regarded Zybin, smiling, but his eyes held that habitual, long-ingrained dread . . . Everyone noticed it – apart from himself, that is. He genuinely thought of himself as a most jovial individual.

Zybin reflected, then began to speak. ("Well, what have I got to lose? Everybody's known about it for ages. Starkov actually is free, after all.")

"It was a petty, grubby, drunken affair and all the circumstances were in keeping," he said. "Swinish: that is, they had hired the hotel room on somebody else's identity card. They met on the avenue – two birds, three lads – and the drinking party began. The court was interested in whether the girls left under their own steam or whether they had a helping hand, how many empties were found, whether there was vomit in the toilet or not. Altogether like a scene from *Resurrection*, and the witnesses were the same – the doorman, the boots, the barman and the maids."

"Yes but the suicide was real enough for all that," Yakov Abramovich reminded him sternly.

"The suicide was cheap as well. Probably drunk. That morning she'd told her neighbour: 'Don't come in for a bit, I'll be getting washed.' She went out, according to the neighbour, and then there was a sound like a fanlight being slammed shut. And that was that. When her husband broke the door down, she was lying in a pool of blood, with a Browning close by, and that note on the table. Just the sort of thing Breshko-Breshkovsky or somebody would write."

Yakov Abramovich smiled faintly.

"He used to be all the rage at the gymnasium," he said. "Listen, was she beautiful?"

"Beautiful?" Zybin pondered. Nothing he had said and heard up to now had evoked any image at all, but now he suddenly saw a woman's face of an almost deathly pallor, with firm, precise features, short dark glossy hair and cruel lips. "Yes, she was very beautiful," he replied with conviction. "But in an unusual, disturbing kind of way. Doomed perhaps. Once seen never forgotten."

"In other words, she struck you as an uncommon individual?" asked Yakov Abramnovich swiftly, making a brief movement as if trying to catch at these words. "Outwardly at least? So how could it have happened the way you said? Like Breshko-Breshkovsky, as you put it?" Zybin shrugged. "Yes, but still, why was it? Why? Haven't you asked yourself questions like that?"

124

"God moves in a mysterious way when it comes to the human soul, Yakov Abramovich," Zybin sighed, "and the paths of the Devil are even more obscure."

"That Starkov was a devil, was he?" snorted Yakov Abramovich.

"Devil my foot!" Zybin dismissed this. "Just an ordinary lad, hard worker. Not the least bit bohemian. He was lucky, that's true. We thought of him as a genius. He even published a little book. Quite a thing to us then, you know?"

"All right, but the second, Mischenko, you knew him? He was published as well, I believe?"

"He most certainly was! He had some poems in *Young Guard* even. And that's a heavyweight magazine."

"Right. And the third?"

"Oh, the third was just a decent lad. Straight from the plough. He wrote a bit, got into print, but nobody was quite sure what or where. Probably for publishers like *Millstone*, *Peasants' Gazette* or *Soviet Land*. We were on good terms and that's about it. Nobody ever called him a genius."

"And the husband? Did you see him?"

"Naturally! He was responsible for the entire festivities. He sat in the first row of seats. For a whole week the dummy listened to everything that was said about him and his wife."

"And what else was there left for him to do?" Yakov Abramovich halted abruptly in front of Zybin.

"Well exactly!" Zybin exclaimed. "What could he do? Once you stick your snout in the slop barrel, there's nothing else you can do. Gulp your fill. It was him who insisted that the boys be prosecuted for raping his wife. That's precisely how the suicide note was interpreted; the defence on the other hand, was that nobody had raped her – she'd organized the whole thing herself, gone to the hotel room of her own accord, got drunk and lain down under somebody. What else could have happened? The prosecution hung on like grim death; she hadn't got drunk, she'd been made drunk. Remember the three famous Japanese virtues? I see nothing, I hear nothing and I say nothing. That's how the judges behaved. Lord, was there anybody who didn't pass before the court? Writers, near-writers, editors, detectives, men of affairs, students, professors . . . They were questioned unfairly, mocked, put off, threatened and tripped up. I can imagine what it is to be plucked from the street and stand in front of a tribunal like that. And then two witnesses stay in my mind . . . A man and a woman . . . Still, that's irrelevant."

"No, no, go on by all means," Yakov Abramovich requested. "Who was she, then?"

"Kravtsova's best friend, Magevich her name was. Lovely dark girl with a matt complexion, rather Turkish. Veronika had invited her to the hotel and brought her along with her. There'll be writers there, it'll be fun, let's go. Well so she did, but after a while she sensed something not right about it, or rather realized it was something other than a drinking party and left. God, what she had to go through! They practically spat in her face: now it was why she went, then why she left. They put the old questions, you know, the way prosecuting counsel are so good at. Putting on the sneer? They interrupted her, yelling and shouting. The prosecutor downed glass after glass of water, and his fingers were shaking. It finished up with her virtually being sat next to Starkov in the dock, but somebody probably came to his senses in time. How on earth could they pin complicity in rape on a woman? Still, in that chaotic atmosphere anything was possible. So, I was bowled over by this Magevich. The way she sat and listened! The way she answered! She didn't weep, she didn't shout, just sat and listened. And all around her the shrieks, the laughter, the general hubbub and the prosecution's hysterics. A regular witches' sabbath! And to her it was nothing. Obviously the lawyers had told her: 'Say nothing. They can do anything nowadays. There's no restraint placed upon them.' And she did what she was told. That was the first defence witness that stayed in my mind."

"You said there were two."

"No, no, there were a lot, twenty or so. But it was these two who stuck in my mind. The second one was a man. Nazim Hikmet. I know him. He was always around our place, in the snack bars, in the corridors or during change-over of classes. The defence called him and asked him to describe how well he knew Kravtsova. And so he did. Once, he said, he was standing on the rear platform of a tram late at night, and a good-looking older woman comes up to him. She introduces herself and says she would very much like to get to know him. Well, then! He was just the man! 'Pleased to meet you,' says Hikmet. Then, without any preamble, she immediately invites him back to her place: I'm on my own, she says, my husband's in the Crimea, let's go and have a drink and a chat. Hikmet stated all this plainly, calmly, no hurry, with a pleasant hint of accent. His story made a powerful impression. Even the husband started twittering something. And then the prosecutor, to save the situation of course, asks him: 'Well, how did she strike you? A student, reading literature and wanting to get to know a prominent revolutionary poet or just a brazen prostitute?' Hikmet gave a slight shrug and in his light lilting voice replied simply: 'Brazen – no, but a prostitute – yes.' The whole court roared."

"Unpleasant!" Yakov Abramovich frowned severely. "You enjoyed that too of course."

"No, no I was ecstatic!" cried Zybin. "For the first time in all that chaos of yelling and official mumbo jumbo, I had heard a human voice. After all, Hikmet had only said what literally everyone, including the prosecution, the judges and the husband knew for a fact. Yes, she was a whore. A bitter, unsatisfied miserable whore, who didn't give tuppence for her own life and couldn't give a damn about anyone else's. And now in a public assembly in the Polytechnic museum hall her canonization was taking place. She was turning into a saint. The appalling word 'bohemian' had been uttered. A girl student done to death by bohemia. The state has need of such victims, therefore three gifted young men, healthy and fit, in no way bohemian or alcoholic – had to lay down their lives. But they were putting up a fight, the rascals, and the prosecution was intent on grinding them to extinction. I should think so too, the effrontery! They were trying to exculpate themselves! Before a proletarian court one can only confess, lay down one's arms and plead for mercy: 'I swear that if the state considers it possible to preserve my life, I will . . .' That's the way to talk, and here they are deluging the deceased with filth, questioning the charge and hiring lawyers! Pitiful worms! They think they can prove something, when everything's been proved and signed long ago! The proletariat must see the bestial face of bohemianism! Your duty to society is to assist that process, and here you are floundering about like blind kittens, trying to save your hide, insisting that you're right. What use is that to anybody. That's how it had been in that court, you follow me?"

"No," sighed Yakov Abramovich, "I don't. Explain what you mean."

He returned to the desk, sat down and placed his two fists firmly in front of him.

All of a sudden, Zybin's inclination to talk deserted him entirely. He felt positively ashamed that he had blurted all that stuff out just now. Obviously they hadn't pulled him in and brought him to this office – hands behind you! No looking back! No looking round! – just to understand and elucidate something, get some point sorted out! God, what use was that to anybody here? He grunted something and turned away.

"What? Don't want to?" He realized at once that Zybin would be saying nothing more, but that was unimportant now. By now, he had got everything finally clear, including who to transfer the case to. That over, Yakov Abramovich leaned back in his chair and lit a cigarette.

"So, Kravtsova was beautiful," he mused, not looking at Zybin. "Even provokingly so, but that fool of an investigator was right, Zybin could have gone along to the Grenada; could have done."

"Could have," Zybin responded defiantly. "Well, what of it?"

"No, no, it's all right; but could have done! Then he would have been the fourth and got the same sentence as the other three. And then you and I would probably not be having this talk today. The political articles of the code don't apply to anyone convicted of rape, for some reason."

He winked and burst into good-natured laughter.

"Yes, but now another matter arises," he said. "If it hadn't been for that business, you wouldn't have made that speech of yours, or anything else that followed, including our talk today. After all, you did tell someone that it was precisely the Starkov case which opened your eyes to it all."

"All what?" Zybin queried.

"Well, us at least, our activity. You do regard that trial as being the work of the security organs, don't you? Very well! I fully admit it! We fight as strenuously against sexual counter-revolution as against any other. We don't go along with slogans like 'our life is a kiss – then extinction', and that's a fact. The difficulty of course is that it's hard to sort out while it's only poetry and vodka – and the sort of poetry you find on sale in any OGIZ shop at that. But what's the upshot, then? People seemingly do nothing illegal, just drink and read poetry, and we go on losing recruit after recruit. After reading poetry like that you get to feeling there's no point in anything. How does it go? 'Greetings, my death, old wolf, I'm coming out to meet you,' that's it, isn't it? There you are, this time there was a booze-up as well, they read poetry and one of the participants ran off and another committed suicide. And not just did away with herself, she left a note . . . 'I curse you a hundred times . . .' The struggle against bohemianism had been our main ideological task. That meant the case had to be dealt with in such a way that the full face of bohemian behaviour was exposed. That was why it was held in public, in one of the biggest halls in the country. The strongest judicial and prosecution forces were deployed. That's right, isn't it? The papers printed accounts every day. The best defence lawyers were in action, Braude, Rubinstein, Sinaisky! What more could one want, it seemed? But you were not satisfied even then. Here, in our institute, where the dead girl had been a student, her comrades gathered and demanded the extreme penalty. Perfectly understandable. All right, so it wasn't according to the book, it wasn't legally sound. All right! Of course the court in sentencing would ignore that resolution; it has its own way of proceeding. Nor does anybody seriously demand that it should be otherwise. But public, comradely concern found expression in that resolution. Am I right? And then you raise your head, the lover of truth! And in supposedly sticking up for the law, the code of criminal procedure and hell knows what else besides, you break up the meeting. We must remember the judges are independent and subject only to the law! Well, who's arguing? Who? Who? Did you think you'd discovered something new? Prevented some illegality? Corrected someone's negligence? You just cut short the discussion, that's all. And by what right, if I may enquire? Why did you feel like wiping out the entire political significance of the trial? Everything that hundreds of our people had toiled over – prosecutors, journalists, district committee members, legal people? And now you say you don't understand why you were arrested then taken to the GPU? Don't understand? There's only one incomprehensible thing about it – why they let you go."

"Yes," replied Zybin, "that really is incomprehensible! Back then, I thought that could be the only outcome, but now I'm amazed it happened. Just think – arrested and released! What nonsense! But you know it takes time to produce the sort of investigator you would prefer, Yakov Abramovich!"

It was at this point that Zybin remembered Edinov. As he was coming back from the interrogation, he thought: "No, I should have told him about Edinov all the same. Just let him know. Because with me it didn't all start with the students' meeting, but with the president of the pupils' committee of the seventh model school, Georgi Edinov, Zhora as we called him."

He got back to the cell and lay down. Buddo was asleep and snoring. Zybin lay quietly, stretching out, arms and legs together and smiling grimly.

"Ah, Zhora, Zhora, how could I ever forget you? You're one of the most memorable people in my life. I even intended writing a novel about you, Zhora. I sat down to it once or twice too, picked up my pen and wrote a few sides, but nothing sensible emerged.

"It would now, though! You've crystallized altogether for me now! This is how I would start. Listen."

*   *   *

In one of the winding streets of the Arbat, there stands to this day a large red-brick building. When I was first taken there it had become an ordinary Soviet school, named after some professor, once renowned but now totally forgotten. Seven years before this, a gymnasium had stood here, also belonging to a professor, also eminent. The professor had constructed the gymnasium according to the very latest pedagogical principles of the time – a high bright front entrance with doors that folded back, a triumphal staircase, carpeted in red. Recreation halls with two tiers of windows and horizontal bars ("A healthy mind in a healthy body!" The professor taught Roman law). Classrooms, laboratories. The school museum. And up above on the fourth floor, one floor above the teachers' quarters, was the holy of holies – the director's study. There hung Repin's own copy of Derzhavin listening to the young Pushkin; there stood an empire-style desk with brass fittings and Napoleonic nicknacks. At right angles to it was another desk, set about with sugar bowls and elongated leaf-shaped porcelain dishes. This was where the staff meetings were held. Next door was another room – the servants' room or whatever they called it in those days. On the shelves stood a little parade of self-important samovars, one of immense size; there was a sideboard full of crockery, German silver, small champagne buckets and trays. It was from here that the professor's side-whiskered personal servant would emerge, majestically decorous, during the meeting and together with his gaunt, placid old wife would dispense tea. (I remember them well; they lived somewhere close by and often dropped round to the entrance hall to talk over times past). According to the old servants, no pupil dared come up to this floor without summons. Even the air was different here; of a morning, the study was sprayed with pine-scented water from an atomizer. So that when I came to the school, the most terrifying room wasn't the study itself – the deputy head sat there – but this servants' room with its hand-written note, PUPILS' COMMITTEE: KOMSOMOL CELL. You were the president of the pupils' committee. The deputy head entrusted our feeble souls to you and wouldn't intervene in anything. She also sent the teachers to you; you alone could punish and pardon. And soon, by means of some deft manoeuvre, you shifted the deputy head to the servants' room and took over the director's study yourself. The deputy head was an old lady, two-faced and deceitful; she wore a velvet ribbon round her neck and a black medallion with a little diamond heart. She liked it when they read Balmont and "The White Blanket" at school parties, but she was very good at seeing where the land lay, that is, she was as much afraid of you as she was of her immediate superiors. Still, what were you if not her immediate superior? You, Georgi Edinov, president of the pupils' committee, secretary of the Komsomol cell, in charge of the drama club among other things – tall, hefty, tough, high cheek-boned; face a bloodless cream (I had a hood that colour), sporting leather gaiters and a leather jacket! Nobody knew where you had sprung from or who had helped in the process. Officially, of course, you had been elected, but everyone knew you had never been any such thing. You had simply appeared and that was that. You appeared and started walking about the school, all five floors of it, noting everything, taking everything in and getting a finger into every pie. You used to say as you passed one of us: "Drop by and see me during the lunch break," and we were immediately terror-stricken. But what did we really have to be afraid of? After all, this wasn't the Tsarist gymnasium with its black lists, room servants, telltales, their Belikovs and Peredonovs, it was in an honest Soviet working man's school. And it wasn't the class inspector sending for us; it was a comrade, our comrade. That was the first and most wicked lie. All the rest of the lies, large and small, flowed from that – until that supreme lie, in whose name you appeared, Edinov. That's why I couldn't put together the material to write about you – I couldn't comprehend who on earth you really were. Just, as Dostoevsky puts it, "an urchin, precocious and depraved" (I understood that type perfectly) or some monstrous cross between a future Master of Pedagogic studies and Pavlik Morozov, also not yet born into the world (the writers of the '20s were not as worldly-wise as their belaurelled colleagues of the '30s and '50s). At all events, you were totally committed to the future. And you didn't resemble Pavlik directly; your route was an extremely tortuous one. Who was that poor, brutally murdered lad really? Was it not of such that Goethe wrote: *Du armes Kind, was hat man dir gethan?* Just think, I don't know to this day. All I see is how it all ended. It started off in all innocence. Take the health monitors. At first they were three little girls with well-washed pink fingers. At break-time they would catch us and examine our nails and collars. Still, who were little girls, after all? Who paid any attention to them? People turned their backs on them, bought them off with promises or stuck their tongues out and ran away. You quickly put a stop to this sort of amateurish approach: "The first thing to do," you instructed, "is to compile a report and submit it to the pupils' committee," secondly, behind the little girl now walked a lanky tough – he used to grab me by the collar and haul me off to the staff room. That was the mark of your genius. You introduced order and realized who should be your monitoring troikas. Instead of the best and law-abiding pupils, you began selecting the most extreme elements – the hooligans, the twisters, the thicks. Less in the way of schoolboy honour and more in the way of fisticuffs. And everything was changed. Those thugs were devoted to you, like a gang of young thieves to their adroit chieftain and so, naturally, changed from being the last to being the first. And all the hopeless cases disappeared, success rates leapt by almost one hundred per cent (our poor teachers were more afraid of you than we were). And so you demonstrated for all to see the harsh weight of the power of communal action, of the collective and the talent of the leader. And what were the old demons and imps of the old gymnasium really in comparison to you, all those room servants, inspectors, directors, useless Belikovs, paranoid Peredonovs! They weren't worth a light. Telltales and informers! – They were just stupid and powerless! They were lied to with genuinely rapturous inspiration.

But no one lied to you. You put a quick stop to all such amateurishness. Any monitor would answer any question you asked: he would tell you anything you wanted to know. He would have told you about his own brother. And just let the latter try to lay a finger on him! Oho! You put an instant stop to that as well. True, the most senior old men who had heard tell from their fathers of certain former traditions of comradeship – not those you succeeded in instilling – but those antediluvian ones, when a person was just that and not a "friend", was indeed sometimes an enemy, and friends banded together in their own mutual interest, able to avoid answering – or even tell lies. But the kids were honest and brought everything to the pupils' committee and its president in the leather jacket and squeaky leggings . . . God knows where you passed all this information on to, Georgi Edinov. But at all events you held all our feeble souls firmly in your fist. Or rather in an oilcloth exercise book, a veritable record of our existence. I was also fated to see it once. A crime had occurred in our classroom and I had to tell you about it. It was the first face to face conversation of my life between myself and the state, in a bare official room on an official matter. True, the story was an extremely unpleasant one. A revolver had turned up in our classroom after the last lesson and went the rounds. It had no ammunition of course, and the butt was worn, but the cylinder went whizzing round. Everybody took turns to give it a twirl. To hold a genuine Belgian Colt in your hands – oho! That was really something! Afterwards, someone ran over with the Colt to a stuck-up flock of girls in a corner and took aim at them. They of course fled in all directions, and then quickly recovered themselves and twirled the cylinder along with us, taking aim at one another. After that, the Colt disappeared. Who had brought it in remained a mystery. But a week later, someone blabbed and the panic started. A military weapon! Loaded! The Whites had left it behind! With a full magazine! Engraved "For the faith, the Tsar and mankind"! With a double-headed eagle! (of course neither eagle nor inscription existed but that's what the whispers were about; you really were a great talent, Edinov)! It had to be found at once and its ownership clarified. First, just the monitors were assembled, then the troikas. Then both together. Then the teachers' committee convened along with the pupils. Once, after school, a PE teacher came into the class to talk to us. He was a tall languid fair-haired chap with ginger eyebrows and a permanently dripping nose. We treated him as one of our own. Useless. Nobody knew anything. (Fortunately, our monitor was away ill.) After three days, something extraordinary was announced – a general assembly of both school shifts. Attendance compulsory. We turned up. A table covered in a red cloth stood on the stage and behind it, under the palms, sat a bony individual of about forty, wearing a combat shirt and a pair of piercing Trotsky-style pince-nez. Some member of the pupils' committee declared the meeting open and handed over to you. You rose modestly from one of the middle rows and went up onto the stage. Just the same sort of pupil as the rest of us. "Now boys and girls, one of the leading members of the party district committee has come to visit our school. He would like to speak to you." The comrade from the committee got to his feet and began to speak. His voice was soft and pleasantly modulated, but with a certain steel. "What surprises me most in this unpleasant story of the Colt?" he asked directly. "Not the gun itself, no. What surprises me most is your attitude to your own pals, your own comrades. They ask you about it and you either keep quiet or tell them lies. Why tell lies to your comrades? That I can't understand at all! Deceive Zhora Edinov! Pull the wool over Blagushin's eyes! (We had a ruffian called that. Formerly he had been one of the real rogues, but was now one of the most responsible pupils). You sit with them at the same desk, play football with them during breaks, go home with them, share your sandwiches with them – and yet you tell them lies! Why? Don't you trust them or what? I just can't take that in, lads! And there's another thing that absolutely beats me – I find that there's been talk among you of sneaks, denunciations, informers and slanderers. What sneaks? What slanderers? Those are long-dead concepts from our accursed past and I can't understand who would resurrect them and why. We've driven a stake through their heart long long ago. There can't be informers among you – you can't inform on yourself, can you? Isn't that so, lads?" Here he laughed shortly. "But," now instantly stern, "you have to be conscientious friends, and if a friend of yours, wittingly or not, has behaved in a manner unbecoming to our socialist society (were those words about our socialist society actually uttered? Now I have my doubts. Perhaps it's just an historic aberration, an aural illusion, and I heard what was actually spoken much later), you are obliged on his behalf to bring it to the attention of your senior comrades, your senior comrades!" He addressed this theme for another hour. So then, after that meeting you sent for me, Edinov. There was nobody in the pupils' committee room. The electric light was already on. You sat at the desk; I was some distance away. "Well now, what do you say?" you asked. What could I say? – I held my tongue, that's all! Then you said: "You know who brought the gun in. Be careful – you are doing badly in maths and your conduct is execrable. And the school is the best in Moscow. This is just the time for you to bear that in mind!" I said nothing. "Right?" you asked. I still said nothing, because it was no more than the truth. You sat there, looking mysteriously at me and saying that you had called me in only because you wanted me to understand all the implications. I had just heard a fine speech from a responsible comrade. That comrade had explained everything, surely I wasn't going to persist in digging my heels in? And ruin myself? In our country there are no such things as incorrigible cases. Could I not remember what Nikolay Blagushin had been as recently as last year? Good! And now? He had acknowledged his deficiencies and had genuinely reformed. As for me? No, Soviet students didn't comport themselves as I did. At any rate, Soviet students in an exemplary school, bearing the fair name of the great scholar Mikhail Kovalevsky (honestly, that was what you said, perhaps tongue in cheek) did not conduct themselves like that. So you spoke with tender severity, looking straight into my prevaricating eyes. The fifteen year-old captain – you could scarcely have been older – of our wallowing school ship. Meanwhile, I wriggled and hinted and didn't know where to put myself. I fairly burned with embarrassment and rage. I hated myself, you and all those who had placed you in authority over us. And you pointed the finger at me at every turn, never pressing but never retreating – you simply followed in my tracks. At length I grew so fed up with your constant "You must . . ." (consider, decide, tell?) that I snapped out: "There's no must about it, just get the hell away from me . . ." It was then that you pulled out the drawer, took out the book of life and stroked it lovingly. "Now why say that?" you asked with gentle insolence. "You're going to tell me anyway, there's nowhere for you to hide. Here's where I've got you. Shall I read it out?" "Yes!" I shouted. "Yes, indeed I will read it," you said with that same smile of loving hatred, "but in that case you'll be expelled from the school at the next meeting of the pedagogical council. What'll happen when you tell them at home? You'll get a thrashing, won't you? With a strap. I know they beat you at home. They do, don't they?" You winked at me. You were right, I did get beaten at home, but if I'd had that Colt, and if it could have fired, I'd have emptied the whole magazine into that insolently smirking face. But I didn't have it, so I said nothing. I had reached such a pitch of despair and humiliation that I could go no further. I was past caring. By now I was simply unable to help myself. Then all of a sudden, Edinov, you gave me a hug! "Well, little idiot that you are," you said simply and affectionately, "you're cracked and there's no help for you. Take a look at that." He took the Colt out of the drawer and tossed it onto the desk. "Pick it up! Have a look at it! Hero! It hasn't even got a trigger! We got hold of it the same day, but the important thing for us was the owning up. Whereas what we have is a vicious circle. How can we tolerate that in a Soviet school? Smoke?" He took out his leather cigarette case and proffered it.

That was an act of supreme trust. You got suspended for three days for smoking, sometimes a week, or even for good. Rumours were rife that Edinov smoked, but no one had ever seen him doing it. Maybe only the reformed Kolya Blagushin . . . So we parted, having smoked as he put it, "the pipe of peace" and you never summoned me before the pupils' committee again, just smiled conspiratorially when we encountered one another. After all, we had a secret in common; your whole life was bound up with these secrets – responsible, in the know, understanding everything from the loftiest point of view, mysterious . . . Where are you now? Are you alive? Are you snaring souls as before, or has someone managed to do the same for you? That could easily be. Trotsky's portrait used to hang over your desk, didn't it? And the fellow you brought in to us, he had a high-sounding party name, but about ten years afterwards I came across it with the suffix: "now unmasked as an enemy of the people". I believe you worked with him later on, so that anything's possible when all comes to all.

He was asleep by now, and saw all this in a dream. Meanwhile, the day had fully dawned. The band of sky beyond the bars had turned through white and blue to pink. The bushes near the window were already chirring with a jaunty daytime intensity. Bright female voices could be heard from the corridor – the medical orderly and the nurse, going from cell to cell.

Buddo was sitting on his bed and leafing through an English grammar of 1913.

"Congratulations on your baptism of fire, Georgi Nikolaevich," he said when Zybin raised his head. "Your supper's been left there since yesterday. Eat it up. Buckwheat porridge."

Zybin got up silently, went over to the table and sat down. He did not start eating, however.

"What's the matter with you, then?" Buddo reproached him. "Too upset, is that it? Never mind, go on eat it, or you'll turn your toes up. Although no, during the investigation they don't allow you to do that. Afterwards – that's up to you. Go on, eat your fill. Buckwheat porridge and meat! You know what they call it in here?" He glanced at the peephole, " 'Stalin shrapnel'!"

"Clever," smiled Zybin and began spooning it up.

"Well, it'll do you good," applauded Buddo. "Zeks are like that, Georgi Nikolaevich, quick-witted and sharp. Only the investigators are that much more so! One too many, as they say in camp. So then, they've pinned one on you? What, not charged you yet? What the devil have you been doing then? You've been working through the questionnaire. Oh, they love that, that's just their thing! They're psychologists here. You're all of a tremble, turning over inside and they just say: Where were you born? School? When married? They bleed you drop by drop. Who's your investigator, then? Don't know? Who've you just been with? What, Neiman himself?" Buddo went so far as to put his textbook down. "What does he look like then? Yes, that's right, short, curly-haired, thick lips. Oh-h, man, that means they're taking a serious interest in you. What on earth was he asking you about?"

Zybin smiled and spread his arms.

"Meaning?"

"Oh just rubbish. Things of days long gone. And nothing to do with me either."

"Still, what . . ."

"Well, you see . . ." Zybin considered and began to talk.

He told him what he had told Neiman, adding a bit more on his own account. So he said that Kravtsova's suicide made perfect sense to him. She had been a strident woman, generally disillusioned. She'd been a personal secretary before becoming a wife. Nurtured an almost physical revulsion towards her husband. She was openly and brazenly unfaithful to him, out of a kind of positive despair. This had been fully brought to light in court. There was no knowing whether she had loved Starkov or not; but the fact of being jilted she had taken badly. As to why he had thrown her over, that was clear too; his wife and child had arrived and something had to be decided. If he had broken everything off straight away, nothing would have happened of course, but he spun things out, told lies, planned and calculated; in short he tried to keep both of them in play. He avoided talking to her directly. That's when she dreamed up that ill-fated party. It was there, in the hotel-room lobby, that their crucial discussion took place. Pinned against the wall, Starkov unburdened himself to her, without sparing his words, no doubt. Anyway, they had a mortal quarrel. Kravtsova was a resolute woman, the vodka was there too and there you are . . . 'Well now Volodya, come here.' Volodya did. The light went out, then went on again. Starkov, looked, spat, swore and left. But again everything might have blown over if Volodya had thought to ring her in the morning. That was when 'the fanlight slammed'. It's a loathsome, drunken, filthy story; disgusting even to talk about."

While Zybin talked, Buddo silently riffled through his book before raising his head to ask: "Right, but how were you involved?"

Zybin told him of the meeting and his own speech.

"Clear enough! So then, you know how the indictment against you is going to start?" He closed his eyes for a moment and thought.

"This is the way of it: 'It has been established in the course of the investigation, that while still a student of such and such an institute, Zybin, G. N., in attempting to rescue his drinking companions, arrested for thuggish behaviour, wrecked a students' meeting devoted to discussing and branding their criminal activity. Arrested and questioned by the GPU at the time, he gave testimony incriminating himself. The investigation, however, in an attempt to be as objective as possible towards him, did not consider it necessary to involve him in criminal responsibility at that time. Taking advantage of this and mistaking magnanimity for weakness, he . . .' and so on and so on. Yes, the omens were bad for you from the first; Neiman, that's really something! That's really, really grim! Although . . ."

He suddenly flung the book aside, gasped and positively clasped his hands.

"Listen, man! A brilliant idea! Yes, yes! That's what I'd do, reduce it all just to that! Yes, yes!" He broke into a laugh. "Exactly. Ah, hell's bells! No there's something in the old noddle after all! That would be terrific! Take advantage of it! You must take advantage of it!"

"What's terrific? Reduce it to what?" Zybin asked, still in the dark.

"God almighty!" Buddo cried. "How can you not understand? They've held an olive branch out to you. Listen, in that business, apart from depraved conduct and being drunk and disorderly, they aren't accusing you of anything! Isn't that so? Well, what more do you want? Confess, and be done with it! Just say: 'I confess that I spoke out at the meeting because I wanted to get my drinking partners off the hook. We used to drink a lot together. I'm the same way now, I go out on the town, boozing, bringing women home, neglecting my duties, but politics, no – I never touch politics! I don't need them. It's just that I'm a bohemian, an amoral personality!' That's all there is to it. You know nothing more about anything. They're sure to get off your back."

"How do you mean, get off my back?" Zybin was astonished. "That's a specific charge! Neglect of duties. A fine lookout!"

"What charge!" Buddo cried recklessly. "What charge? There is no article in the criminal code covering bohemianism, Georgi Nikolaevich; there is a letter code SDE – socially dangerous element. For that, through the Special Board, you're supposed to get three years without loss of rights or confiscation! And you won't end up in Kolyma; you'll go to a local penal colony. You'll get remission there and after eighteen months you'll be let out with clean papers. Beautiful! You listen to me, times are rough nowadays; you'll sit it out behind a high fence. Blame it all on the booze and that's the end of it."

"What about the three years, then?"

"What a man you are, honestly!" Buddo lost his temper. "Were you born yesterday or something? You want to be let out of here and go free right away? Not guilty of anything! Mistaken arrest again! Isn't that right? That would mean that you'd get out and the investigator would take over your bunk. Is anybody going to do that? Why can't you get it into your head that it's simply impossible for them to let you go now?"

"And why is that?" Zybin asked vehemently.

"There's saintly simplicity for you. Because you're already inside, that's why! Wait, wait a minute, you consider yourself innocent don't you? Right? Well now, seven years ago they released you; what of it? Were you contrite over that? Did you feel any gratitude towards the security organs? Not on your life! No doubt you went about everywhere yelling: 'The swine! The bastards! They kept me in the cells for a night!

What for? Provocateurs!' Right? Correct me if I'm wrong!" He laughed.
" 'Kept me in for a night!' That's why you can't be let out. The guilty
can be released, the innocent never. The guilty fall on their knees, the
innocent make with the knife! So, it follows that they're going to stick
a charge on you. The question now is, which one? If you're going to
kick against it and rile them – they'll choose a right one for you . . .
and send you off to a right place . . . They're good at doing that. You
know there are camps where the zeks don't last above six months. So
you pay heed to what I say, Georgi Nikolaevich, get an SDE out of
them and that'll be the end of it. That's where your salvation lies. They'll
dig their heels in and shout a bit at you, but they'll come round."

"Damn and blast this madman," thought Zybin. "And he's not even
putting it on, he's serious. That's the hell of it!"

"God knows what you're talking about, Alexander Ivanovich. You'd
have to be crazy to . . ." he began angrily, but abruptly faltered, recalling
that even Neiman had said: "And then, most likely I wouldn't be here
talking to you. A man convicted for something like that can't have
political charges pinned on him."

"Yes, oh yes," he reflected. "Yes indeed. That's how it is for sure.
It may be madness but there's method in it. They all know and they all
pretend, the investigators and those under investigation, they're all playing the same game."

He sighed soundlessly, picked up his spoon and started eating his
Stalin shrapnel.

"For God's sake let me not go mad, that's what I think," he said.
"That's from Pushkin. But I'll thrash about a bit! I'll see what comes
of all this. Yes, I'll wait and see!"

Buddo only sighed by way of reply. Neither of them spoke for the
rest of the evening.

Once again he dreamed, tossing and turning as he saw his prison in his
sleep. "God, what a ridiculous mess this is, I really should have made
sure of seeing Lina. She'd still be waiting, wouldn't she! God almighty,
how stupid. And how lovely it was, the two of us there by the sea."

And all at once he saw the white walls of the municipal museum, the
ancient rusty cannon on the stones by the entrance and the little man
with the pointer in his hand.

Talking together, they moved away from the window. The director
was a gaunt, sallow man with a small moustache. His whole life story
could be read in his face. He had probably started off by teaching history

or geography in secondary school. Then he had been put in charge of local studies – beginning with the butterfly collection, birds' nests and the herbarium and ending up with the shards of black-figure vases and fragments of marble inscriptions. And when the time came to open a museum, he naturally became its guide and director. In the evenings he wrote reports for the centre and planned exhibitions. During the day, he led tourist parties. He could hardly complain of being overworked – now, for example, he was just conducting through the rooms a single indifferent holiday-maker, indifferent to the whole world. To every explanation, the visitor either nods agreement or murmurs. What's the town with its centuries of history to him, or museums either! And in fact Zybin wasn't interested in the town at all, so mundane and dull did it look, as if someone had, without looking, taken an axe to a piece of old Moscow; after chopping out a number of old alleys, they had been banged down here on the sands. And so, the sea came lapping close by the cul-de-sacs and mansions of Bolshaya Meschanskaya Street!

Now that sea was affecting Zybin with a fearful, languid power; it was entering and sinking into him ever more deeply, penetrating all his pores, splashing and moaning in his every thought and dream. Yes! It was filling him to the brim, this "pale lilac sea, in its dull azure vessel", unconscious as he might be.

The director, having said his say, moved away from the final display case. The working day over, it was time to close the museum.

"You're not from these parts, are you?" he enquired. "Ah, you're from the Krupskaya sanatorium? Well, well, I know it. I live next door. Let's go."

They left. The day was high, sunny and limpid, seagulls crying. The sea lifted and fell back, echoing gently and hissing down below, under the high shoreline. They walked along in silence and Zybin suddenly began to feel awkward.

"You know," he said, "Latyshev in *Archaeological Commission Proceedings* for, I think, 1910 published a Greek inscription from this area concerning a society of shipowners. It follows that somewhere about here there was a statue of Poseidon erected in a newly built shrine. It would be a good thing to find out where it stood."

"What – what was that you said?"

The director stopped and taking out his notebook, asked him to repeat his words.

"*Proceedings* of 1910? You don't recall the number?" Yes, that information hadn't come his way for some reason. They didn't hold copies of the *Proceedings* in the museum. He would have to ask for it through the inter-library system.

"Hasn't the library really got . . . ?" Zybin asked.

"Have we got a library? You know what we've got? This is what we've got . . ."

The director had become animated all of a sudden and thrusting the notebook back in his pocket, started telling Zybin about the questionnaire he had received from the provincial authority. He unfastened his leatherette briefcase and took out the paper to show him.

"There, feast your eyes on that – 'Planned finds for the current year'. You know what they're asking about?"

"Yes! It's *Crocodile* material" Zybin laughed. "How are you going to answer?"

"Yes, that's it, *Crocodile*," the director snorted resentfully, stowing the questionnaire in his briefcase. "But there's nothing you can do, is there? You have to answer them."

And he resumed talking about the museum and the idiot sitting there somewhere up above, at provincial level, who does nothing, knows nothing, and has no interest in anything. He simply sends round this sort of blanket instruction to all his subordinates. They spoke of him, the dummy, the bungler, then not just about him, but about other dummies and bunglers, then yet others and finally about those it's not done to talk about. But they did so all the same.

And now between them, like a kind of salvation, like something implied, a certain person appears – a covert individual, without bodily presence. He is spawned by the very air of this year, 1937 – dense, pregnant with terrors – and walks along as the third member of the group, listening in to their every word, remembering all and saying absolutely nothing. But he does not merely remember. He also misinterprets what he has heard. Misinterprets it after his own fashion, that is, the most fearful fashion, one not compatible with life. Because of all those heading here by ship, car or aeroplane, he is the most fearful man to walk along this shore. He is inscrutable, insensate and as deadly as a delayed-action mine.

Later on it transpires that he is also terminally wretched.

He is locked inside himself for ever. Because these two carry him within, always – the third.

He was laughing and chatting as he walked with Buddo along the seashore, gay, carefree, ready to embrace the whole world. A warm wind blew. The day was as quiet as could be and the water darkly limpid, like smoky topaz; in it could be seen the glimmering interplay of multi-coloured pebbles, lank seaweed, and shoals of tiny fish.

"Just here, under the rocks," said Zybin, halting, "live the most enormous crabs. You have to have at least one of them for the museum."

"I've thought of that myself, actually," replied Buddo. In this dream he was also the museum director. "I've got one, but the claw's snapped off."

"It's wonderful to have got away!" Zybin thought elatedly and his heart gave a positive skip, so filled was it to the brim with space – the sky, the sun, the sea – so mellow and content with all around him. "And what a good thing he listened to me! Alexander Ivanovich! Old son! As soon as I arrived, I realized what was what straight away. So we're free."

They were on their way to catch crabs. They bred close to the high shoreline, with its dark flat slabs and boulders. There were a good many such boulders hereabouts, white, black, red and green in colour, so slippery it was as if someone had rubbed them with liquid soap, one step and you'd fly straight in. Whole families of crabs lived beneath them: very small, a little larger, then larger still and finally giants the size of a saucer. Only the very largest of all were lacking. They no doubt inhabited submarine grottoes or lived out in the open sea.

"I must have the biggest crab there is," said Zybin. "Not the sort you see at the market; they boil and varnish them there. I wouldn't have one if they were giving them away. What I need, Alexander Ivanovich, is a real black one from the sea bottom."

Then they set out into the water and began lifting stones. One rounded boulder was enormous and had sunk half-way into the sand as well. They were soaked from head to foot; they were bruised and had broken nails. At length they managed to overturn it. Beneath was a large, circular pit, completely dry. In the centre sat the crab of crabs, a Tsar-crab, the monarch of all crabs on these coasts, a huge spiny monster with green reptilian eyes. The water did not rush into the pit, and he stayed sitting there, but when Buddo bent down, the devilish thing suddenly leapt up almost with a hiss, and threw out a hideous knobbly claw. Now he resembled a many-armed Indian idol – Shiva, was it? Black, ancient and terrible.

"Just look at its eyes," said Buddo, recoiling. "It's a special kind of crab, poisonous. One nip and you're dead."

Zybin meant to reply, but just then the water began to seethe and bubble, foaming like a copper as a whirlpool began to form. At once, they both found themselves up to their knees in water and starting to spin.

"Shout for help," croaked Buddo, alarmed. "Go on, shout, otherwise we'll be submerged."

He wanted to shout but he couldn't; his voice was gone.

And the water drew nearer and nearer, brown, angry, swirling flotsam and foam. It was already up to their chest, their shoulders, their neck. At this point he tensed his whole body and shouted at the top of his voice. A pitifully puny sound, but he knew at once that he was saved.

A yellow light glowed. A soldier was bending over him, shaking him by the shoulder.

"You haven't to shout," said the startled soldier. "You get the punishment cell for that." Then suddenly he asked in a kindly voice.

"What's the matter? Heart, is it?"

The soldier's nice country boy's face had a sort of whitish bloom, a youthful down, and round nut-brown eyes.

"No, no, just something..." Zybin mumbled, unable to recover himself for the moment. In his mind's eye, the sun was still shining, the sea slapping, and Buddo, tall, strong, young-looking stood close by him. He glanced round. No Buddo. The English self-tutor lay on the empty bed.

"The doctor, maybe?" asked the soldier.

Zybin shook his head.

"Well, go to sleep, then," ordered the soldier, stern once more, and went out.

Zybin stretched out and closed his eyes.

It had all happened! It had! the sea and the director, and that walk along the wet pebbles after crabs, and the waves tumbling forward and racing back at their very feet. The crab had a story to itself. Special and not altogether straightforward. He had realized that at the time. One of the girl students in his year had asked him to bring her a crab like the one he had described to the director – huge, black, covered in thorns, limestone incrustations, dark blue algae. But the girl had a story of her own, also rather special. He had fallen in love with her as early as their third year; she was aware of this, but her attitude was difficult to fathom. At all events, he couldn't make it out. This order for the crab was part of it.

"Make sure you have a really good look," she had demanded. "I want the biggest there is. Something I can put on my writing desk. It will be a lifelong reminder of you. All right? You'll fetch me one?"

"All right," he had replied. "I'll fetch you one."

"Not from the market, though," she admonished. "They sell them boiled and red, like bar prawns. I don't want anything like that. Catch it yourself."

"All right, all right," he had smiled. "What a fuss over nothing. I'll catch one! You don't have to go on about it. I'll bring you one."

But it turned out to be quite a job. No matter how often he looked in at the market he never saw any crabs other than those revolting ones looking like women's patent-leather shoes or little boxes made of seashells. It proved impossible to find out where they were caught. "Over there, over there, on the spit! Yonder by the high shoreline. Yonder by the lighthouse! From a boat out at sea!" that was the sum of what he learned from the fishmonger.

So on and on he walked, searching all the time. Ten days passed and he had found nothing. At this point he said: Well, to hell with them all! I'll catch one on my own.

Having resolved upon this, he turned up at the museum and said to the director: "Well, I've come to catch crabs. Like this! He held a javelin, with a botanizing pouch at his side.

"Hmm, catch crabs!" The director smiled. "No easy matter, you know. Don't the market ones suit you, then? Not natural, are they? Oh well, wait a moment."

He went into the store and there were bangs and thumps before he carefully brought out a piece of cardboard. On it there was something clumsy and spiky, sticking out in all directions, dark-grey with dust.

"You see there's a claw missing," he said regretfully. "It was lying next to it all this time and now it's got lost somewhere."

"That's not a crab, is it?" Zybin was reluctant to credit his eyes.

The director blew and both of them started coughing at the dust that arose.

"It's been standing on the cupboard for two years," replied the director crossly. "The Young Naturalists here used to photograph it and they broke it, probably." He placed the cardboard on the table and dusted his hands. "Well then, a claw missing's no good to you?"

"Where on earth do crabs like these breed?" Zybin asked in amazement, gazing at the little monster from all angles. It bore a strong resemblance to some sort of strange machine with pistons, toothed gears and a cut-off switch. "I've never seen any like that before. They don't have any like that in the market."

"You won't see any there," replied the director. "It's a particular species. The zoologists don't know what it is yet. They only breed in one place. So, you really want one like that? There's a certain individual you can go and see."

"Oh, you'd be saving my life!" Zybin exclaimed. "When could we do that?"

The director glanced at his wristwatch.

"Well, it's closing time now. Let's go now, shall we, it's not far along the shore. He's most likely at home."

"Who is?"

"Oh, a certain old man here. A Greek. He catches them. Our veteran – I wrote down his memoirs of the Civil War as well. Let's go."

So they made their way along the very edge of the beach, along the damp and glistening strip where little wavelets splashed against their feet. Zybin listened while the director talked. A warm breeze stirred. The evening was fine and sunny, and the pebbles underfoot – Zybin had kicked off his sandals – were warm and moist. Ever afterwards he recalled with his skin how pleasant that had been.

"Look there, what's that?" Zybin asked, halting.

Close to the shore, a strange-looking marble boulder projected from the water. The director went over to inspect it and shook his head.

"Probably of considerable artistic value," he said, suddenly angry. "Somebody at one time laid out a great deal of money for that tombstone. And now it's lying around under our feet and nobody cares."

Zybin leaned over and picked at the stone with his nail.

"There's something written on it," he said.

The director looked up at the steep shore.

"It fell down from there, do you see? Every year three or four metres crumble away from the cemetery and collapse into the sea. He bent over the stone. What's written here is: 'Lord, I believe; help thou mine unbelief.' "

"Interesting!" Zybin exclaimed.

"Very. Terribly interesting even. So interesting, the priest wanted to throw that stone out of the cemetery altogether. He used to nag away at the widow. 'He should have thought earlier about this believe-don't believe business, dear Anna Ivanovna. Whichever way you look at it, the matter is settled now. Now he just has to lie there!' Yes. And he's been lying here thirty years. Baron Von Drizden, infantry general. You may have heard of him?"

"No." Zybin shook his head. "I've never heard the name. Not my field."

"Well, I remember him. He died just before the 1914 war, you know. Just a little chap and a beard like Chernomor, down both sides, or a silver fox's tail; he would always present us with mint lozenges, if we had a cough." The director bent over the monument again. "See what it's got here? A reading desk and an open book. The gilding on the letters is peeling already. Another two years lying like this and that'll be the finish. It could be of great value – some noted Italian did the cutting, but I can't find out his name."

"An Italian, really?" Zybin said doubtfully. "What would an Italian be doing in these parts? Some stonemason from Novorossisk probably."

"Just bend down, bend down and take a good look," said the director, annoyed. "See how it's been done – page on page! And the ribbon in the middle, look, look, see, watered silk! And the bookmark; you can see every twist in the thread! No, there's no getting away from it, it's the work of a great craftsman, a great craftsman. He lived with the general for a year. He cut his daughter's headstone. After that, the general began . . . I mean, after his daughter died, he started thinking. You've seen her monument? What, you've not even been to the cemetery? You're missing something. You really should go! They don't have that sort of thing even in Moscow. You see it's so . . ." He glanced about, braced himself and stood up, sighing and making a sort of circular gesture, as if wanting to outline it all at once, then at once subsided, turned to Zybin and started talking normally again. "It's like this: on a marble boulder, you know there's a kind of marble that sparkles with lilac spangles – a girl stands, light she is, light as air, just on the point of floating away . . . No, there's no way I can explain it to you. But really, another second and she would be off into the blue yonder! But her garments draw her back to the earth, to the slab, the tomb – the garments are long, a floating voile, is that it? While the girl herself is ever so slender, with arms like wings. In this direction, towards the sea! And there's a poem on the stone."

"From the scriptures?"

"No! Not from there! It seemed she wasn't a great believer. The usual poetry, Nadson, Pushkin, Lermontov – like an album, you know. She wrote verse herself too, so they say. After she died, her father even published a book of them: *Tanya's Poems*. That was her name, Tanya. She didn't reach twenty."

"Died?"

"Threw herself off the lighthouse. Straight onto the rocks. Dashed to pieces"

"Was it love?"

"Yes, seemingly, but who knows really? People give different versions. She was supposedly in love with a fisherman, so they say. You get some very handsome Greek fishermen round here, real Apollos, but her dad wouldn't hear of it. A very self-willed old man he was! They say he cursed his daughter, or said he would, or something of that nature, but she was a chip off the old block; she would have her way. It was diamond cut diamond. I'm going to get married, and that's all about it. So that's what happened . . ."

He fell silent, wiped his hands and made his way to the shore.

"Well how did she meet her end, then?"

"This is it," said the director abruptly. "This is what has to be done: we need to petition to have it preserved as a monument. As being an object of value. Yes, yes! I know it can be done. In Feodosia there's an Armenian church and nobody touches it. On the Turkish gates, there's a sign saying PRESERVED BY ORDER OF THE STATE. It's possible. How did she die? Accounts differ. They say he went to sea with the fishermen and a storm blew up during the night, waterspouts. She stood all night by the great beam on the lighthouse. She watched and watched, and in the morning saw wreckage on the shore and the planks and tackle from his little boat. So she hurled herself from the lighthouse onto the rocks; that's what they say. You've seen the lighthouse? Well, that was the end of it. Smithereens!"

"Could it have been like that?"

The director considered for a moment, then laughed.

"No, of course not. You can't see a vessel go down in the night from the lighthouse. It might have been something of the sort. But that she threw herself off the lighthouse – that's a fact. That's how she's depicted probably. In flight. Ascension."

Zybin closed his eyes and in the pink glow of his eyelids, he imagined something white, misty, swan-like – slender arms, dishevelled hair, lifted by the wind. All in the evening sun.

"And it's a fine monument, you say?"

The director looked at him.

"There's a rise a bit further on. We'll climb up and have a look. And

147

you can read the poem. She loved one poem especially; it's not there actually, but a local read it to me:

An easy life we ask of the Almighty,
An easy death is what we should implore.

"You don't know who wrote that, do you? She used to repeat it all night, so they say. When we get back we'll go up and take a look."

CHAPTER 2

THE GUARD CAME ALONG, TAPPED with his key on the peephole and repeated: "Lights out! Lights out!" All the cells awaited this blissful moment (after lights out, no one was summoned to interrogation), but Zybin was asleep in any case. Unaccountably, in gross contravention of all the rules, he was being allowed to sleep as much as he wished. This knocking by the guard however, penetrated even his slumbers.

He suddenly saw himself climbing up a narrow spiral staircase; each step made a thunderous clang that echoed through the room. And the staircase was frightful – the metal was slippery with filth; there were scales beneath his feet, fish bladders, potato peelings, sodden newspapers, matchboxes – all crunching and slithering under his shoes. And yet he kept climbing on and on, although by now he realized perfectly well that what he ought to do was slide into his cell, dive beneath the blankets and pretend to be asleep. Though he was aware of this, he continued to climb. He reached the final tread and rested his forehead against the ceiling. This was covered in rusty stains and cobwebs: yellow planking projected. He stood, staring at it, not knowing what to do next. But something was bound to happen at any moment. And sure enough, it did; a little door sprang back and he saw Lina in the rectangular opening. Just her face, in sharp cut out – the square of her brows, eyes, cheeks and chin. All baleful, glum and scowling.

"Ah, it's you," he said helplessly.

"Yes, it's me," was her cold response. "Why did you try to deceive me? You thought I didn't know the woman you were looking for, and where you were hiding from me?"

As soon as she said this, he realized he had been tricked. They had contrived to blacken him and she had believed them.

"Good god," he implored her. "Why listen to them? I can explain everything."

"Oh, you and your explanations!" She dismissed this angrily. "Right, show him, let him be convinced."

At this point, Neiman suddenly appeared. Now they were no longer standing on the staircase; they were back in that office with the potted palms and leather chairs. Neiman was smiling his sweetly venomous smile, his eyes fixed on Zybin's face, when he suddenly drew his hand along the chair back. An abominable, piercing shriek rang out. He started, and Neiman smiled even more broadly and affectionately, saying: "Well, take a look, take a look."

On the floor stood a stretcher under a black tarpaulin. A hand stuck out from under it. "It can't be," he thought, going cold. "Take a look, take a look," Neiman insists and kicks the tarpaulin aside. On the stretcher lay the marble girl. She is exactly as she had been on the mountain, her arms spread in just the same way, prepared for flight. But the eyes, they were not marble. They were human: light, limpid with pin-sharp pupils – living eyes in marble. Was she looking at us all the time like that, and we didn't notice? he wondered.

"And you wanted to deceive me," says Lina. "Pretend that one was this one? I realized immediately why you had run off to the Ili away from me! You were running after this marble witch, not the one they found on the Karagalinka."

"I wasn't running away, I really wasn't!" he says, on the verge of tears. "The whole trouble was I got arrested over there. A bit more time and I'd have discovered her, proved everything – they just stopped me doing it!"

Lina stands looking at him, her face registers suffering and contempt.

"Oh, Lina," he rushed towards her. "Why on earth can't you see? This isn't her at all, not the Karagalinka one. This is the one we went to see up on the high shore. You remember the old grave digger?"

Lina turned and went away. He would have darted after her had not Neiman thrust out a timely boot; he fell and crashed his head heavily on the floor. The pain was sufficient to make him see stars; he felt he had split his skull open.

He had indeed rammed the bars of the bed head with all his strength. Buddo was standing in front of him, holding him by the shoulder.

"Now then, they have been putting you through it," he said pensively. "You've been mumbling and thrashing about since last night. I was just coming over to wake you up when you gave a jump. Why, look, it's bleeding. Don't feel sick do you?"

"No, no, I'm all right," Zybin mumbled. He felt unaccountably awkward towards Buddo.

"All right, he says! Now then, lie down and be quiet!"

He got up suddenly, went over to the door and gave several sharp knocks on the eyehole with a bent finger.

"What are you doing? Why?"

"Because it has to be done," snapped Buddo.

The feed slot clicked and opened – an oblong face appeared in the small, lengthwise slot in the door.

"Citizen guard," Buddo reported crisply, coming to attention. "The prisoner Zybin has injured himself in his sleep."

The opening slammed shut; the bolt rattled and the guard came into the cell.

"How do you mean, injured?" he enquired suspiciously. "What on?"

"Here, the bed head," Zybin answered sheepishly. "I was dreaming!"

The guard went over to the bed and felt the metal bars.

"On these?" he asked, businesslike.

"Yes."

The guard ran his finger along the bars.

"Your whole eyebrow's cut open. I'll put you down for sick parade tomorrow," he said, raising his voice. "You should be asleep at night not thrashing about!"

"I was sleeping."

"You were sleeping badly, a bump like that! I don't know what the doctor's going to say . . ."

He left and Zybin said grumpily to Buddo: "Now I have to see the doctor! Why did you have to do that, honestly?"

"Because, dear Georgi Nikolaevich," responded Buddo genially, "all bumps are strictly accounted for here. Nobody allows you to acquire one without due cause. It's five days here for illegal bruising."

"That's interesting! Which ones are legal then?"

"The ones you bring back from upstairs. The investigation block. You can have as many of them as you like, nobody's going to bother. But self-inflicted ones, then calling in the prosecutor and announcing a hunger strike: 'I demand a change of investigator, this one's thrashing me' – no, that won't wash here. They take a poor view of that. Then again you might have been in a fight! That's a major infringement – they can prosecute for that."

"So then they beat you up there, is that it?" Zybin almost yelled.

"No, they serve tea and cheese fritters," Buddo grinned at him. "And you're not allowed to cry either. If you do, it's the punishment cell."

"What about the prosecutor, then? You said just now that you could call the prosecutor, start a hunger strike or reject your investigator."

"You're quick off the mark, aren't you? Wants to reject his investigator. Again, that's only when the bruises are illegal. If there has been no order to use force and the investigator has gone ahead anyway, to get the case over with or because he fancied a few embellishments and let you have more than he ought. But against legal bruising, the prosecutor's no defence. If the order to use force has gone out, that's the end of it. They'll beat you until they thrash everything they want out of you. But that decision is up to them – he pointed a finger at the ceiling."

"In the interrogation block?"

"Further up still. Seventh heaven, with the citizen commissar. A while ago the radio went off the air in the courtyard. That means it's getting on for one. If you're awake in two or three hours, you'll hear it yourself."

"What?"

"People coming back from interrogation. Some walking, some being dragged by the armpits. If you wake up, have a listen. It's interesting. All right now, let's go to sleep."

Buddo moved away, lay down on his bed and stretched out. He pulled his horrible army blanket up to his neck and was snoring almost at once. His face was now serene and content. It appeared that for his part he had resolved all questions long ago. Seventh heaven held no terrors for him.

Zybin lay there thinking. What Buddo had been talking about was absolutely impossible. They could no more beat people up here than they could devour human flesh. The supreme judicial organ, the official state body where the spirit of the October knight, Iron Felix, still resided, could not, simply could not have been transformed into a court of torture. Every biography of Dzerzhinsky told of how he had been on the point of shooting an investigator who had lost his self-control and struck a prisoner. And when had that been? Why, during the years of the Civil War and White Guard conspiracies. The books were on sale today at all newspaper kiosks. No, no, for all his poor opinion of them, they couldn't strike him. Of that he was certain. However, this was only the way one half of his brain thought, the logical, healthy half; with the other, the reckless unchecked half, he knew something else with equal certainty: no, they did beat people, beat them horribly. This notion had occurred to him for the first time when he had read the prosecution

152

speech at one of the Moscow trials ("Talk of torture," Vyshinsky had said, with magnificent airiness, "we will dismiss as frivolous.") and especially of course when he saw the fearful evidence the accused had given against themselves. He was not a lawyer, had never taken any interest in the law and never attended the open sessions of the court. He wasn't even a great fan of western detective novels. But that the accused should vie with one another in damning themselves, that witnesses at these solemn, almost ritualistic sessions should be fetched and taken away under guard, and that there should be no other evidence offered – all of this seemed to him so absurd, so fantastic, that he felt the only explanation could be the use of physical coercion, not excluding torture. What kind of torture was better not to imagine.

A conversation had once taken place between him and the director, and the latter too had not been altogether direct and candid, but on that occasion they had pursued the undiscussable topic to the very end. That morning the director had been sitting in his office reading *Izvestiya*. When Zybin came in, he tossed it aside lightly. It slid off the glass and landed on the floor. He got up and paced about the room.

"What swine!" he said warmly. "What scum they are, makes you sick just to read about it! I mean there's no shame or conscience left. Everything flaunted. Read it?"

Zybin shook his head.

"There, read it! You'll enjoy it. The swine! The damned dogs! They weep, they fall on their knees, they beg for things to be taken into account, they swear they can still be of use."

"And will they be taken into account?"

"That they will!" snarled the director. "They'll be slapped about like dogs, and that'll be all."

Zybin merely shrugged. He said nothing.

"What are you looking surprised about?" the director said, angered. "You're for leniency in such cases, are you?"

"No, I don't mean that, but why on earth are they confessing, then?"

"Hmm! Why confess? They're confessing because, man, they want to live. Very much so! The crematorium doesn't seem all that attractive from a seaside resort or a villa in the Crimea."

"So – that's why they have to incriminate themselves?"

"I suppose you wouldn't?" sneered the director. "After being interrogated like that, you'd just get up and act the goat would you? Is that it?"

"But if there's no proof."

"No? There is, though! They've got the best proof there is. When they present you with it, you'll tell all you know!"

A silence ensued.

"What do you mean?" Zybin asked.

"What I mean is that you needn't go pretending to be a simpleton," said the director angrily. "You think they're visiting their mother-in-law in there? Lolling about in bed with their lovers? No, friend, you'd sing right enough in there! What happened and what didn't, you'd remember it all!"

"Even what didn't happen?"

"Don't go saying things like that. You know what'll happen. They remember what took place. And they confess because the trial has to be a showpiece, a national event. The eyes of the world are on our Hall of Columns – therefore the facts must be convincing, clear and simple."

"And true?"

"And true! And above all, true, naturally. Why, do you have any reason for doubting that Kamenev, say, or Zinoviev are not enemies of the people? Or that Rykov didn't oppose total collectivization or that Jew-boy Trotsky isn't using fascist money to wage war from abroad against our Leninist Central Committee and against comrade Stalin personally? Have you got factual information showing none of this happened? Well, nothing to say? Have you or not, that's what I'm asking? Well, if all that is true, the rest is trivial. Went to such and such a place or not, said such and such or didn't, met a certain person or not – that's all needed to increase the visual impact. Now you're interested in everything – are they incriminating themselves voluntarily or not. Well firstly, what can be voluntary where spying and sabotage are concerned? It's never been that way and it isn't now! Secondly, you are an educated man, you listen to the radio and read the papers. I'm asking you, have you not read there what the bourgeoisie are doing in their torture chambers to those that fight for the rights of the working class? What Franco's doing to the republicans, you know that? How Hitler tortures German communists? What he did to comrade Thälmann? Have you ever considered that? So then, they can slice our brothers into little pieces while we in our Soviet state can't lay a finger on these swine and gangsters? What will the working class say to us then? Won't it damn us to hell for being as humane as that? Well, what are you looking at me like that for? So then am I right or not?"

"Well, let's accept that, but . . ."

"That's it then, if so. And no buts! And such people have no place on our Soviet territory – do you acknowledge that or not? Now, further. Why a trial, you ask? If they'd been ordinary spies or criminal riffraff, nothing could be simpler – press the fingernail on them and they'd pop like lice. And no public statements necessary. But who are these people? The president of the Comintern executive committee, the president of the Soviet People's Commissariat, members of the politburo, people's commissars – you can't get rid of them on the quiet. The people have to hear from them personally, who they are and what they've done. And so that our people understand something else. Any deviation from the party line means death or treachery. People in their position slipped into the bog of oppositionism; they strayed from the right road and look where they ended up! What about us then, the Soviet person will say. Where on earth will we wander off to if we start wavering and being clever-clever, questioning the Stalinist line? That's why these trials and confessions are necessary. Well, what more have you got to say?"

Zybin shrugged.

"Nothing."

"Well, if so you've no business playing at this classless humanism! Don't give me this intelligentsia crap – he doesn't understand, won't allow it! Well Lenin did. He said: 'We have beaten the enemy, are doing so now and will continue to do so.' And he was perhaps a purer humanist than your Lev Tolstoy."

"Why my Tolstoy?"

"Who else's then? Mine? I wouldn't have him if he was going free! Don't give me that non-resistance to evil in 1937. It was possible for them. Not for us. When you get home, look and you'll see a poster by the entrance. A very graphic little poster."

Zybin had already seen the poster. Every wall was covered in them. An iron glove, studded with spikes, was throttling a snake. The snake was writhing and spurting crimson blood. Human blood, not reptilian. And the metal spikes were also bloody. The whole poster resembled a blood-soaked handkerchief. The caption was: THE YEZHOV GAUNTLET.

It was after this conversation that Zybin's mind seemed to split in two. He didn't take the director's arguments completely seriously – who cared what notions came into his head – but a dark, chill, almost supernatural horror suddenly took root in his soul. He was afraid to pick up newspapers, but nevertheless did so and read them more than he had ever done before. He feared to talk of the arrests, but nevertheless did so. He was afraid to let the things that lurked in the hidden depths enter his conscious mind, but nevertheless that chilly murk lived and grew within his soul, and was now present in every encounter, in each and every fleeting inane conversation. His reason, however, was still securely protected by that "impossible". That was why he really did not know why the accused at the trials were so frank, so voluble and looked so well and why they were moving in such a friendly, jolly crowd towards certain death. What was prompting them to do it? Surely not conscience?

That same night, but probably close to morning, Buddo gently touched him on the shoulder. He awoke and at once screwed up his eyes. The light, even more brazen, naked and revealing, was fairly beating into them. In its radiance all objects seemed as if they had been sliced out cleanly by an axe. He was about to ask something, but Buddo was digging two painful fingers into his shoulder and saying "ssh!"

Somewhere very close at hand, a woman was crying – a muffled, bitter weeping, her face pressed into a handkerchief or a pillow, most likely.

"Who is it?" Zybin asked, but Buddo again said "ssh!" and placed a finger against his lips.

The guard walked past, lifted the eyehole and asked the woman something. She gave a strange sob as she answered and commenced weeping and wailing once more. At this, Zybin almost started to his feet. He recognized Lina's voice. It was she who was crying and lamenting there beyond the wall. In fact he would have leaped up had not Buddo pinned him to his bunk.

"Shut up!" he commanded fiercely, almost soundlessly.

The conversation proceeded. Now the woman was no longer crying; she was listening and answering questions. Suddenly she uttered his name clearly. At this point he shot up and Buddo gave up his attempt at restraint. Pain and an appalling misery seared him almost instantly and he became oblivious of all around him. He wanted to run, smash everything, grab the stool and slam it against the door. Just so that the duty guard would yell at him and mention his name, just so that she realized that he was there next to her, hearing and knowing everything. And at the same time some force, limit, ban, power, impossibility constricted his throat, so that instead of shouting at the top of his voice, he merely began mumbling something rapid and incoherent: "I . . . hunger strike . . . A fast to the death to them! I . . . the Prosecutor General . . . To the people's commissar! The seventh floor this minute!"

"Will you shut up! Shut up!" hissed an alarmed Buddo, clamping a hand over his mouth. "What are you getting so worked up about? Well? It's nothing at all. Just your imagination. That's all it is." At length he managed somehow to bend Zybin at the waist and sit him back on his bunk. "Hysterics indeed," he said with pitying contempt. "It's nothing but an emotional illusion, delusion. I kept hearing my wife's voice the first week. Here, have a drink of water."

As soon as he moved away, the woman on the other side of the wall burst into loud laughter; he realized it was not Lina. The voices were quite different in fact.

"Lord," he said, relieved, as if all his strength had drained away at once. "Lord." He collapsed sideways, his head on the pillow.

Meanwhile the woman said something, by now quite loudly and went off along the corridor, clattering and crooning to herself.

"There's a storeroom next door," elucidated Buddo. "Buckets and containers. That's why you imagined it."

"But why on earth did you . . ." Zybin began, loudly indignant, but at once drooped and did not go on. He really didn't care any more.

He felt his brow automatically. The bruise – an object of strict prison account – hung down like a plum, making ready to cover his entire eye by morning.

He was summoned for questioning in the morning. "Not to Neiman again, surely?" he thought. He realized at once that this was not to be. He was conducted down, not up. The office too was totally unlike Neiman's. It was small and rather dim, the poplars stood close up against the windows and there were no sofa or chairs. The investigator's name was Khripushin (Zybin read his name while he was signing the interrogation form). This Khripushin was a well set-up man of about forty, with a stolidly military bearing, a broad smooth forehead and formidable eyebrows, like the horns of a stag beetle. The eyes beneath those brows were a light pewter in colour. In addition, he had a parting of thread-like accuracy, a field shirt and shiny boots. All in all, he was just the man for the job, of course. The snarers of men's souls are fond of the likes of him. "Keep an eye on such and such a student," they report. "I've chatted with him a couple of times; he seems to be one of us." Khripushin of course was in all particulars, one of us.

"Good morning," he said sternly, dismissing the guard with a curt nod. "Sit down over here," he went on, indicating a chair by the door. "What's the matter with your eye?"

Zybin replied that he had knocked it in his sleep.

157

"Why such a restless sleeper then?" enquired Khripushin, with mocking severity. "You've been to the doctor? Good, then we'll check . . . So, first name, patronymic, surname; year and place of birth. Everything accurately and in full."

Zybin answered, Khripushin noted it down, and then ensued two hours of concentrated work for both of them. Who were his parents? Mother's maiden name? Education? Where worked? Any black marks against? Places of residence prior to arrest? Addresses? Any brothers or sisters? Address! Any other relatives? Addresses! Foreign languages known? Ever been abroad? Ever been subject of judicial process or investigation? Detail, details, details! No hurry. Nowhere to get to.

But Zybin had no thought of hurrying. His voice even took on certain especially broad notes – when he was explaining what the Dokuchaev phytopathological station was, where his sister worked, that Dokuchaev was spelt with an "o", phytopathological with a "y", an "a" and two "o"s. Khripushin copied it all down meticulously, with the occasional glance of searching menace from those pewter eyes. Could the enemy be making mock of him? The enemy, however, was perfectly serious and composed. He well remembered Buddo's words: the investigators were perspicacious these days, not like before. He would see right through you from the first interrogation. You'd be sat down by the wall and he'd start to squeeze the soul out of you: how, what, where – while you are all on edge wanting to understand the point of it all as quickly as possible, and he goes on grinding and grinding away . . .

No, no, you won't catch me with that, dear comrades. Neiman was enough on his own – I've got loads of patience and a small cart. Uncle? Before the revolution, my uncle on my father's side Sergey Terentievich worked in Mariupol as a conciliator – with an "o" – and during the Imperialist war served in the Union of Cities. I think that's got a capital.

So on they wrote in perfect harmony till evening. They finished one form and started another. The light was switched on. Finally Khripushin laid aside his pen and said: "Now tell me the names of everyone you know."

At this, Zybin was actually on the point of dissolving into laughter at the way everything had gone exactly as he expected. Two months previously, Kornilov, after taking on board a considerable quantity, had told him the tale of his own first interrogation. After a most punctilious and leisurely questionnaire conversation, the investigator had, in exactly this fashion, laid aside his pen and leaned back in his chair, saying: "And now tell me the names of everyone you know." I ask him: "How do you mean, all of them?" "What I say, everyone. Why, do you have such a lot?" So I began to go through them; the people at work, that was a piece of cake; then my neighbours, no problems there either, then came my classmates. Here I began to consider: there were the people in my year and those who were real friends – and with my friends the doings and the talk had been frank. So should I name them all or not? I didn't name them all. Then the women – I was absolutely stuck there. If I named them, they'd be dragged in as witnesses; if I didn't they'd be dragged in even quicker maybe – so should I name them or not? What would you have done?

At the time, Zybin had shrugged and said that it was difficult for him to answer straight off ("Aha! And you think I found it easy?" said a gleeful Kornilov), but still, surely you couldn't conceal some of the most obvious friendships. "So you would have named them, would you?" Kornilov pursued. "And the questions would have started straight away. Where did you first meet? Did you see her often? Where? When? Who else was present? Did you go to restaurants? When? Which ones? In company? Maybe in the office? Then they'd call her in and show her your statement. Not all of it, of course, a dozen lines or so, where you mentioned the restaurants. And that's all. And the girl is firmly on the hook as well. As I pictured all this to myself, I found I couldn't breathe. I looked at the investigator and said nothing. He does the same. He's waiting. He's in no hurry. His pay's coming to him in any event. At that point I started howling. From the ludicrous helplessness of my situation, from not knowing how to answer! Ah, that first interrogation. I remember it so well. After that things went much better – we got onto matters of substance. And although I wasn't guilty – I've told you how it all came about, haven't I – this was something totally different! Once somebody had implicated me, as the joke goes, 'don't waste your strength struggling dearie, just sink quietly to the bottom!' So that's what I did, I spilled the beans and scrawled my signature! Without looking! What was there to see? But that first, quiet – note that word, absolutely quiet – interrogation, has stayed with me for my entire life. Well, later on it transpired that they didn't know a damned thing. They were just trying to scare me into it. They use tactics like that on the highly strung!"

Zybin had memorized that conversation. He even remembered the words "implicated" and "spilled the beans". Neiman's psychological assault had also taught him something. So now, when Khripushin put the self-same question to him – name your acquaintances – it was with huge relief that he replied carelessly: "Oh, I don't have any."

"What?" Khripushin seemed to choke on his words from sheer amazement. "You mean to state that . . ." And at once, not letting Zybin recollect himself and add anything, seized his pen and wrote it down. "There. I have no acquaintances," he said, proffering the record to Zybin. "Read and sign. So then, very well! You've been living in Alma-Ata for three years and know nobody here? Excellent! That we'll bear in mind!"

He picked up the telephone and summoned the guard. He was very pleased. Put to the test, this Zybin had turned out a complete idiot.

An hour later, however, Khripushin was summoned upstairs, where he was made aware that he was the idiot. Gulyaev, the department chief, a prim and proper, coldly gracious shrimp of a man, sat him down in an armchair, opened his cigarette case and moved it towards him, then enquired about his application for a trip to Sochi. Could he finish with Zybin before then? Khripushin merely harrumphed and proffered the interrogation form.

"I'll have done with him in two weeks!" he said.

"Really?" Gulyaev was somewhat surprised. "He struck you that way, did he? Interesting. What, admits it does he?"

"No, no, the opposite. He's twisting and turning but in a muddled sort of way. And he told a whopping lie straight off. Right over the top."

"The blue ball twists and turns!" sang Gulyaev, reading. He had a pure, ringing treble. Evil tongues said that he used to sing in a church choir till he was seventeen. "He's a good liar of course. Look into this, here!" He tapped his finger along one line. "His father died in Samara in 1919. Why should he go and die in Samara all of a sudden? He was a Muscovite born and bred. Maybe he was shot? The Czechs had been there previously, hadn't they. Maybe he'd gone over to them, eh?"

"Yes sir, look into that!" replied Khripushin, smartly and cheerfully, army-style.

"Yes, look into it. That would be relevant to his overall character profile. Yes, yes, yes. Ah, the rogue. Not implicated in an investigation, eh? The night he was in a cell in Lubyanka doesn't count, I suppose. In spite of the talk we had with him. He's a sharp lad!"

"Do read on," smirked Khripushin. "The end!"

"We're reading the end. Yes, yes, yes. Good, go-od!" Then abruptly Gulyaev threw the record onto the desk in annoyance. "What's the meaning of this 'I have no acquaintances'?"

"You see what an idiot he is," Khripushin went on readily. 'I have no acquaintances,' now I can catch him out at every turn."

Gulyaev shot him a look, was about to say something, but instead took a papirosa out of the case, twisted the holder, clicked his lighter, lit up, then shook the lighter to dowse the flame; only then did he speak: "You will catch him out at every turn; you mean mention the names. That's just what he wants. He'll find out straight away who's linked with the case and who isn't. He won't be naming names to us, you notice, we'll be telling him. That's the point."

"The swine! On the next interrogation, I'll . . ." Khripushin had leapt to his feet. He had got the whole picture at once.

"Sit you down!" Gulyaev smiled. "Don't take it so hard. You'll be starting your questioning with the story about the white bullock. You'll say: 'You're lying.' He'll answer: 'No, I'm not.' 'You have got acquaintances.' 'No, I haven't got any . . .' – 'Oh yes, you have' – 'Oh no, I haven't.' How long can you keep it up, for heaven's sake? Naturally, you'll be in a hurry. You've got a holiday coming up! And of course you'll name him some names. And that will be that. We've let slip the initiative. But he's crafty! He's a crafty devil! No, if you didn't get him at the first attempt, you won't get him now."

He took another draw on his papirosa and pondered. Yes. This time Neiman had been right. Khripushin wasn't the man at all for this job. A subtle, carefully thought-out approach was what was required. It was no small matter that was involved here. A public Alma-Ata trial along the lines of those in Moscow, no less. A professor, former exiles, writers, Troskyists, military men discharged from the army – espionage, terrorism, sabotage, wrecking on construction sites. Pyatakov had been on a visit and left his agents; there were links with Japan through Sinkiang. Zybin had also been about to make off there with the gold. But if he could not be forced to name names and write them down, then everything could fall through. Every month was important here, the situation altered with lightning speed at times; so what mattered was to contrive not to let the thing slip! Neiman had warned that foul language and the fist would get them nowhere. But then he reflected: if after the initial strictly legal interrogation, some Cerberus could be let off the leash – a baying hellhound with slavering jaws – he might yet be taken. At all events there was the punishment cell! If that was no help, truss him up swallow-fashion. Followed again by legality, correctness, low-key conversation, tea and chocolate biscuits. The latest books. Besides, this Zybin was such an unstable character, weak and unworldly. Here he'd been at his wit's end, talking all kinds of rubbish. So indeed he could be taken. Of course, Khripushin was good only for the first five or ten interrogations. After that, they would take over, Neiman and himself. But Khripushin was useful as the primer. So he had thought – but now he'd misfired. But had he though? Perhaps it was just an accident. After all, the active interrogation had not yet started. They had to wait. He took another drag, then laid his papirosa aside and held out the record to Khripushin.

"Take it, then! Well now! Nothing's happened that can't be mended; we all learn by our mistakes. But now I will ask you in future to write out the report in rough and bring it to me. Give it to him to sign the following morning. That would perhaps be better."

"You can count on me," Khripushin implored him hotly. "He can't get away, I'll . . ."

"Now, now." Gulyaev rose, went over to Khripushin and clapped him lightly on the shoulder. "It's all right, it's all right. These things happen. From now on, just bear it in mind, that's all."

When the door had closed, Gulyaev went over to the desk and pulled the telephone towards him. He had intended ringing Neiman via the operator, but as soon as he heard his sharp, crisp voice, he at once replaced the receiver.

"The important thing is not to rush matters," he half thought, half spoke aloud. "What's called for here is restraint!"

CHAPTER 3

WHEN ZYBIN GOT BACK to the cell, Buddo wasn't there. On the table stood two bowls, one of porridge and one of small fish. He sat down on the bed and began to eat. "Well, today it seems we played a draw, but that can't go on. It's going to be a bloody battle from now on. A mental struggle? To hell then, so be it. And what can I be charged with specifically? Some involvement with the gold? On the whole that couldn't be ruled out, of course, but it could hardly be that, otherwise the director would be here – though indeed he might well be. Then there were a few conversations, funny stories. That was more likely. Jokes carried a high value nowadays; the most banal and unfunny would get you five years, and if comrade Stalin was mentioned, you wouldn't get away with less than eight. Yes, but actually he hadn't told any funny stories; he had a bad memory for them. Kornilov used to tell them (again, how did he know he wasn't here on the other side of the cell wall)? The workmen used to go in for it a bit. Grandpa used to sing a Civil War snatch ("Trotsky sitting on the grass, gnaws the hind leg of an ass. Ugh, he says, it's really rotten. Soviet beef is misbegotten"). He didn't though. He laughed, yes. And he didn't break up the talk before it got going. Nor had he given the appropriate reprimand! Nor had he made any indication to the authorities! These days that counted for something as well! All that was true, but it could hardly be that. He sensed something else here, far more serious. Did they know anything about Lina or not? And if they did, and sent for her, then . . . ?" This idea roused him at once; he leapt to his feet and began pacing his cell. "Say they did bring Lina in, what could they get out of her? What do you think? Anyway, what do you know about her? Honestly, now, honestly! 'Yes I know a lot, everything, especially after that night.' Idiot! After that night, nothing is exactly what you know about her. Surely you must realize that? Just hold on a minute, hold on, why don't I know anything? She did tell me then that she loved me and that was precisely why she had come, because she loved me . . . 'It will be a bitter day for me if you're arrested.' That's what she said at the time. Yes, and she said something else as well:

163

'Why do you talk so much rubbish? It's deadly dangerous. You are the source of increased danger.'

"That's it! Start from there! The danger!

"She's afraid of you! And they'll send for her and say: 'Polina Yurevna, you have only the very highest references from your work. You are a young, rising specialist. We know you're submitting your thesis this year. But dear me, the people you've got mixed up with!' And do you really think she'll snap out with: 'That's the man I love. I know nothing to his discredit?' Might she answer Neiman like that? Honestly now, honestly, you know how you like fooling yourself."

He paced about the cell, picked up his earthenware jug, drained it in one breath and replaced it. The whole trouble was that she might indeed answer in that way, not "I love him", of course not, she wouldn't say that. But that she knew nothing bad of him, she would tell them that. How could she actually say otherwise? It stands to reason that if you know somebody is worthless then why the hell get mixed up with him? But then they'll start saying: "Ah, so you know nothing to his discredit? What about this then, or this!" And pile up God knows what in front of her. He is – why bother to hide the fact! – not a particularly good man; he's lazy, an incorrigible windbag; he drinks a lot, besides which he's cowardly, lecherous and ungrateful. Grandpa had said as much to him once: "It's all because you don't honour your parents, you know that? Honour thy father and thy mother, and what do you do?" I don't honour my mother, that's true. But let's say they don't give a hang about all that, and they say something else to Lina. "You must have noticed, surely, that he wasn't one of us, not a Soviet person?" Here he is walking our soil, living in our wonderful era and just goes round looking for something bad, seeing nothing but failings, muckraking, disseminating unhealthy attitudes . . ." She couldn't very well quarrel with that, could she? She would say: "You know I sort of didn't pay much attention to that. I thought it was trivial." "A-a, no," they would tell her, "far from it. Let's go over a few things." Would you blame her if she did recall something of that kind? How could she be a hundred per cent sure of you? You talked too much to her that time, why couldn't you have said the same thing to someone else, Kornilov, say? You remember what you told her, don't you? "I just can't help myself and croak away like a raven at the top of my voice, then it's hang up my boots." She's going to recall those words after your arrest, isn't she? Well, that's that then! As for helping you – she can't. But she can damn herself in a second. Then again, her thesis is coming up, how in the world can you blame her?

"I'm not blaming her," he said loudly. "No, no, I'm not blaming her in the least, let her say what she wants."

But he felt extremely grim about it all. If only Buddo were here, perhaps?

Buddo arrived an hour later and sat down on his bunk, swearing. He was greatly upset over something.

"What's up?" Zybin asked.

Buddo took the jug of cold tea from the table and began to drink.

"This," came the angry response. "They held me for five hours. Some new chap with bulging eyes turned up. I've never even seen him before. Eyes like a sheep. 'Who else did you have anti-Soviet talk with? Why didn't you name so and so, Petrov, Ivanon, Sidorov? We know you shared your anti-Soviet plans with them.' What bloody plans, I asked. That I wanted to blow up the camp or gallop off to America on a camp mare! What plans were these then? And the bastard mentions only those due for release this year, wouldn't you know. I started to say something and he jumps up and smashes his damned great fist down. It's the size of a kettle. 'Ah, still hoping, are you! Not laid down your arms yet, swine! You're not on your knees! Well we'll take you, you swine, before the military tribunal. Nine grams of lead! Write everything down immediately!' How could I write? If I did it would mean a fresh sentence for them and off to the logging camps. They're students, brawny chaps. Just the sort they want out there. But I'll have to write, what else can you do?"

"You mean you intend . . ." Zybin shouted.

"If only you wouldn't shout." Buddo grimaced painfully and touched his temples. "My head's splitting as it is. No, no, I'm holding out for the moment. But what's the point. If I don't sign they'll just send them to the SB. It'll be the same five or eight years. If you go through the Special Board that's the very last stage. You hope for the best and you get the worst. Ach!" He waved a hand, lay down, stretched out and closed his eyes.

A minute of heavy silence ensued. Zybin asked tentatively: "And what's the SB?"

"What? You don't know that either?" Buddo raised his head. "What sort of a scholar are you? SB! Special Board! It's such a clever little

165

machine that we can sit here and it stamps out our destiny over there in Moscow. And that's it – five, eight, ten years! And you sign to say you've read it."

"What do you mean, stamp? Without even a look at me?"

"Hmm! What do they want to see you for?" grinned Buddo. "Some oil painting you are. They've got ballerinas there for that sort of thing, don't worry! As for them being there and you here, don't worry your head. All they need is the case! Your case will be brought to them, placed in front of them, reported on, proposed decision read out, they vote on it and that's that! The secretary will make a note, the typist type it out and off you fly to the mountains where they mine the gold. There you'll be given an SB machine – two handles, one wheel, and you push it for the complete victory of socialism in one country. What are you looking at me like that for. What more do you need to know?"

"Wait a minute, wait a minute," Zybin passed a hand across his face. "You say they'll take the decision in Moscow, but in the Criminal Code it states plainly that the verdict is delivered by the court according to the evidence of the preliminary investigation, examined in a hall of judicial assembly. I've read it myself. Myself! So how on earth can they examine it without me?"

"You don't understand?" Buddo grinned. "What I don't understand is something else: how is it that you, a scientific staff employee, hear one thing and ask about another? I'm talking about the Board and you ask me about a court. What the hell's a court got to do with it. There is no court. Only the Special Board. The Special Board of the People's Commissariat in Moscow. There, a man is convicted without judges, charges, witnesses, investigation; no verdict and no appeal. They've listened and they've decided! Throw a letter at him, and that's all!"

"They send them off with a warrant? Not to the camps, then, is that it?"

Buddo smiled painfully and shook his head.

"Oh, you'll be the death of me! Travel warrant, he says. Not a warrant, a letter, that is, according to the letter; and the letters differ. If it's ASP, say, or ASA, or CRP or CRA, then you've got a chance. But if they stick a CRTA on you – counter-revolutionary Trotskyist activity – or SE – suspected espionage – it's all up. Hang yourself straight away. You won't be allowed to live in any case! You get the picture now?"

"No," Zybin said in despair. "I don't. I don't get it at all," he repeated hopelessly. "No code articles, no judges, no verdict? . . ." Then he suddenly implored Buddo: "Alexander Ivanovich, don't go having fun with me, a man could go mad pretty soon that way! Explain to me what this Special Board is? What are these letters? All right, all right, I'm an idiot, a cretin, a lousy intellectual! I haven't had a roast chicken stuck up my backside yet! I've lived like a dummy, blind to everything. All that's true. Of course it is. But in the name of everything that's holy, what in the world does it all mean? And where are we living? Not in some enchanted kingdom, not in some cannibal giant's castle! In fact there's a war just around the corner; the people have got to be prepared for it, but meanwhile we . . ." He choked on his words. "Or . . ." His lips began quivering; he wanted to go on but nothing came. He turned to face the wall.

Buddo glanced at him and became serious at once. He rose and brought the water jug over.

"Now, now," he said soothingly clapping him lightly on the shoulder. "Don't go on so! Don't! Here, drink this! It's a bad job! It is a bad job right enough. Where's it all landed from on top of us? Ivan the Terrible maybe left it with us, or those damned Mongols brought it in? there's just no explaining or telling!"

And he began to explain.

This strange monster came into being in 1934. It was then that the all-union executive committee decree "On the formation of a public NKVD" (i.e. as a permanent constitutional body) in place of the abolished GPU (a temporary emergency body) stated the following:

5. The judicial college of the OGPU is to be abolished.

6. The NKVD of the USSR and its local organs are, at the conclusion of the enquiry, to send criminal cases investigated by them to the competent judicial bodies in accordance with (which?) established procedure. . . .

8. A Special Board is to be set up, attached to the NKVD, to which is granted, on the basis of the relevant statute (which one? Lord, which one?) the right to implement by administrative order, imprisonment in corrective labour

167

camps up to a term of five years and expulsion from the
USSR.*

KALININ AND YENUKIDZE,
Moscow, Kremlin, 10 July 1934

That was the way the first and, it seems, virtually the only information
about the Special Board, appeared in print. It was mentioned officially
(apart from Vyshinsky's speeches) only once, apparently, in the statement
concerning the murder of S. M. Kirov. At that time, the procurator's
office was sending the cases of some of the accused to the military
college (this meant shooting within 24 hours without appeal or pardon)
and others, "by reason of the absence of corpus delicti" to this same
Special Board. These bills of indictment were signed by A. Vyshinsky
and compiled by Lev Romanovich Sheinin.

That seems to be the sum total of the printed references to the Special Board.

All in all, it seemed positively not to have existed at all. The people
constituting that fearful, omnipotent and completely irresponsible troika
(it appears certain that there were three of them), had neither surname,
rank nor post. They were the SB. Not a single condemned person ever
saw their signature on a sentence. None ever reserved sentence pending
appeal. Because there was no sentence and no appeal. There was a neat
form about the size of a postcard. For example:

COPY OF SPECIAL BOARD REPORT
From
Heard:	*Resolved*:
Concerning the anti-Soviet activity of Ivanov Pyotr Sidorovich (year, place of birth). Certified exact copy – (flourish).	Sentence for anti-Soviet activity Ivanov Pyotr Sidorovich (year, place of birth) to five years deprivation of liberty to be served in Svitlag.

* In the collection of materials on the history of socialist criminal legislation, Yurizdat
M. 1938, there is the following more precise definition: "It is to comprise a) The deputy
peoples' commissar of the USSR NKVD b) the authorized representative of the RSFSR
NKVD c) the head of the Chief Police Authority d) The peoples' commissar of the
republic on whose territory occurred ... The USSR chief prosecutor or his deputy
must attend ... in all eight or nine persons not counting technical staff." [Yu. D.]

"Sign on the reverse that you have read this," the officer used to say kindly, proffering this standard form, "and again here on the copy . . . Thank you!" and stow the paper away in the folder. The condemned man was led away and from that moment the camp wheelbarrow began for him.

But this childish term, five years in the Svitlag, lasted only a very short time. After that the SB machine* began to get up speed, the wheel began to turn, the terms started to jump: eight years, ten, fifteen, twenty, twenty-five! Then terms disappeared altogether and the shootings started (true, this was during the war). But the form stayed the same, "heard" – "resolved" and "sign on the reverse". That was it.†

But if, for this mysterious trinity of the SB, there existed neither proof, forensic investigation, questioning of the accused, article of law, nor indeed the law itself – in a word, everything that makes a court a court, and murder murder, and if, further, in its gravest actions, the SB feared neither prosecutor, supervision, law, nor state, nor its own conscience, since it subsumed all of these – law, prosecutor, court, state conscience and state, there was nevertheless, a small particular, a certain semblance of legality, to which the SB did have regard, since without it, its own existence would end. This particular was called by different names at different times: from the material standpoint it was "the special note" and "the memorandum", while from the political it was "isolation" and "strengthening the moral-political unity of the Soviet people".

And it was not Ivan the Terrible who bequeathed it to us, nor did the Mongols infect us with it. We ourselves devised and nurtured it. The name itself, SB, is certainly a legacy of Alexander III's police state. It was precisely through this Special Board "constituted according to article 34 of the statute on state security" under the Internal Affairs ministry, that one Josif Djugashvili was condemned to exile, a man who, as it later transpired, was endowed with a short memory for all that was good but an excellent, truly creative one for what was savage and frightful. True, in those years, to deport even this same Djugashvili, required no more nor less than the personal signature of the emperor himself – "Agreed". Nowadays, nothing at all was required, apart from a stout,

---

* "The SB machine – two handles and one wheel," the zeks used to say. And it applied to the SB as well as the wheelbarrow. [Yu. D.]

† The only thing stated in the statute relating to the SB: "The basis for the imposition of these measures must be indicated." [Yu. D.]

sealed package of thick paper. But this package was not part of the case, it was merely enclosed with it. What was in the package, nobody knew, not the prisoner, not even the military judge advocate, who had sanctioned its despatch to Moscow. He was simply informed in general terms of the contents. The accused was told nothing – it wasn't anything to do with him.

There is the game "Odd Man Out". Something of the sort was involved here. Two played and the third took no part. He was the third party, the superfluous one, the one under investigation.*

The stout sealed package contained the memorandum or special note. This note was compiled from an array of materials. Among them were included:

a) Agents' reports and the evidence of informers. That is, material which was even forbidden by law to be regarded as proof. These however formed the basis of the entire case. Without informers the memorandum could simply not have been compiled ("secret workers" was the name given by Soviet people to those they detested, the tribe of informers working for the GPU, NKVD, MGB and so on).

b) Anonymous letters.

c) Denunciations. (Denouncers included wives, husbands, lovers, neighbours, fathers, children, those who had their eyes on more living space or a legacy, a young man, a good-looking woman, schizophrenics who denounced people because they really thought it was true; sometimes people denounced themselves, afraid of their disconcerting nocturnal thoughts and criminal doubts. Sometimes, and not all that rarely, people didn't wait for the night visitors and made an end themselves. Taken together, this also made up an extensive section of the material).

d) Character profile. (These references are usually compiled by the operations staff, signed by the head of the operations section, and confirmed by the deputy people's commissar. There were as many falsifications here as anywhere else. Anybody with the name of Gagarin was

* Letters such as SE (suspected espionage), AFI (agent of foreign intelligence) and so forth, played a considerable part in the work of the SB. *This* had not formerly been the case. "The Special Board is competent to deal only with representations concerning exile, subject to the Ministry of the Interior; as a civilian department, it cannot control the actions of the military authorities. But here it was just the other way around. Only the military judge advocate, who himself only knew the letters, but absolutely in the dark as to the actual case, sent off these cases to the SB (generally on this V. Lemke "250 days on the Tsarist staff", pp. 282–83. The attitude of General Bonch-Bruevich to Beletsky). [Yu. D.]

always referred to as a prince. Ivanov, Pyotr Sidorovich, was considered to be a scion of princely stock if his mother had been a Gagarina. Everybody who had been born in Riga or Libau in 1900 passed as a citizen who "had resided for a prolonged period on the territory of a hostile state maintaining friendly and familial ties with it".)

In addition, if it came to light, even in the most remote branch of the family tree, that there existed some person who had been repressed (and who didn't have such a person in all honesty at that time?) he was invariably referred to in the memorandum as "a close relative of one now unmasked as an enemy of the people" ... The memorandum would conclude: On the basis of the foregoing statement...

IT IS PROPOSED

that Ivanov, Pyotr Sidorovich, scion of a hostile class, be condemned for anti-Soviet activity, to eight years deprivation of liberty, to be served in the camps of Siberia or the Far East.

The head of the special department would sign this paper. It would be confirmed by the deputy people's commissar and the case flew off to Moscow with an adviser from the people's commissariat.

Then it would be examined on one of the dates specially set aside for the given republic, at a session of the SB.

The folders lay on the desk, the members of the SB would pick them up for a moment, flick through the pages, glance at the memoranda, talk among themselves, washing it all down with Narzan mineral water. They laughed. Cracked jokes. The republic representative reported to them on the case and read out the proposed decision. Then the president would ask the opinion of the adviser and carried out thecross-questioning ("Well then, comrades, are we agreed?") and in the morning, the typist was already typing on the form "heard-resolved" ...

That, at any rate, was how Alexander Ivanovich Buddo pictured the business to himself, and it seems it was so in actuality too.

This monstrous thing went on existing for twenty years until September 1953 – (see the progressive journal *Soviet State and Law* 1959, No. 1).

"So that's the long and short of it, my dear Georgi Nikolaevich," said Buddo. "The accused isn't at all interested in proving his innocence.

Well, let's say the court turns the case over for further enquiries. Well, so what? They'll hold him for another couple of months and send his case off to the Special Board. The court would have given him five or six years in a local colony, picking melons, but on the memorandum they'll give him the full ten and chase him out to 'Kolyma, Kolyma, the wonderful planet' – and there's an end of it. You know, next to us, in the other corridor, there's a cell full of people cleared by the courts. They're sitting and waiting for the SB to slam a tenner on them. And they will, God knows they will!"

"Why?" asked Zybin. His head was buzzing and his mind was functioning poorly. He was willing now to believe in anything. Here he was, having fallen into a machine; the wheel had started to turn and it was humming and stirring into action. There was no way either in or out. And nothing had significance any more. Lies, truth, fortitude, courage – nothing at all! And absurd chance had marked him and the rest had been left to specially appointed people to carry the process to its conclusion. And it was pointless blaming either chance or the people.

He felt limp and feeble, rather like being immersed in stringy cotton wool. More than anything, he wanted to lie down and stretch his limbs. He lay down and stretched out.

"Why? you ask," said Buddo, shifting over to give him room. "Because, dear Georgi Nikolaevich, anyone condemned through the SB is like Lieutenant Kizhe, a secret arrestee with no bodily presence. All decent zeks have an article of the code, he has letters. Every criminal has in his hands a sentence, where it can be seen why he's suffering, and – by all means! – he can show it, but this one just has a copy of a bit of paper. All decent people – thieves, murderers, rapists, profiteers, scribble out appeals in their spare time, but he's got nothing to write about and nowhere to write. All criminals are let out on the dot, but with him, it's in the lap of the gods. A paper will arrive from Moscow 'heard-resolved'. Stay there another five years. I know one chap who's already done fifteen years and now it's coming to an end, he's waiting for his new sentence. He's forgotten even to think about freedom; talk about it to him and he'll just wave you away. The authorities understand that a criminal is just a criminal, but this individual's a sort of fiend in human shape. You may not know what he's guilty of, but he's a lifelong danger and the sooner he kicks the bucket the better for the human race. So they drive him into the taiga, deep underground or to the tip of Chukhotka, to fell trees, push wheelbarrows, dig for gold. They chivvy him like that for about three years and that's the end of him. Put an identity tag on him and it's into the permafrost. In a nutshell, God forbid you get yourself cleared altogether! Opt for the bohemianism! Take it while the nice man offers it. I advise you to do that, honestly I do, honest!"

CHAPTER 4

...THAT DAY I GOT MY CRAB all the same. The director had not misled me, the Greek did indeed exist. He lived by the sea in a tumbledown shack and caught all manner of things: he used to bring in starfish, sea urchins, snakes, scorpions and crabs for the pleasure of the holiday-makers. When we approached his shanty, he chanced to be returning from a trip out to sea. He had a fish spear in one hand and a tin pail in the other. On catching sight of us, he put down his bucket, straightened up and saluted with the spear. He was a tall, sharp-featured, moustachioed Greek, burned almost black by the sun.

"Good health I wish you, kind gentlemen," he said with crisp mockery. "Or do they not say that nowadays? Oh yes, citizens, citizens it is now." He'd obviously had a rich catch and regarded us with humorous liquid eyes. "Good day, citizens, how can I be of service?"

I glanced at the director.

"It's like this, Satiriadi . . ." he began uncertainly.

"Ah, it's you, comrade director," Satiriradi said, as if only now recognizing him. "Good day, good day, good day, please, Ivan Nikanorovich. I didn't get anything in your line, I'm afraid. Maybe a few crocks, not worth anything. Come in and have a look?"

"No, no, a crab is what we want," the director said coaxingly.

"A cra-ab!" The old man seemed positively surprised. "What then, surely they're not short of them in the market? There's lots there, get any good one you like, red or yellow."

"It's not that sort we're after."

"Well, what sort do you mean, then? Like these?" He placed the bucket on the ground.

I looked. There was only yellowish water in the bucket above the dark, convex bottom. Lying on the bottom were two red pebbles and that was all.

"Where's the crab, then?" I asked.

"There, look," the director said and poked the pail with the point of his shoe; thereupon something stirred as the sand billowed up, and I saw that it was not the bottom that was black. It was a crab. It was

174

frighteningly large and flat, and as I leaned over it, I could make out bumps and spikes, seams marking out the edges of the carapace, serrated crests.

The director lightly shook the pail and the crab moved; in one place, apparently close to the feelers, the sand-grains began to eddy, as if a whirlpool was starting up.

"He is a big one, isn't he," the director shook his head, seemingly overwhelmed. "He's probably bigger than the one I've got."

"No contest!" Satiriadi shook his own head. "There hasn't been one like this for something like five years! See where he bit my finger! Right through! I won't be able to do a thing for a week now." His thumb was indeed swathed in a grey rag. "What do you want it for, just yourselves or somewhere else?"

"Oh, not for me. It's for this young man here." The director nodded in my direction. "He wants to take it away to Moscow. For scientific purposes. If you don't charge too much, of course."

"Now why should I do that? Just enough to cover the price of vodka. I need a lot of that now. I'll be putting spirit compresses on my thumb. Might get blood poisoning – then I'll be in trouble!" He hoisted the pail. "Well then, let's go in the hut if that's the case, can't stand bargaining on the doorstep."

He took quite a lot for it all the same. I gave him all I had, and begged an additional fifty kopecks from the director. Still, we reckoned we had done well out of it, and going back we walked on air.

"Five years or not," said the director genially, "it's certainly not every year you find one of those. He was telling no lie there! Fine, but what are you really going to do with it? I mean, I can help you shell him, but how will you kill him? Ether won't do the job, he's too tough a nut for that, He'll have to be chloroformed, but where can we get hold of that? Have your doctors got any, perhaps?"

"Never mind," I replied (now that the crab was sitting in my bucket, it all seemed as easy as pie). "I'll just put him under my bed and he'll have keeled over by morning. They can't live without water, after all."

"Indeed," assented the director.

And as soon as we had climbed up the steep shore, you immediately bumped into us, Lina. You were wearing a white dress and dark glasses, remember? What a sight you were, eh? Ah, Lina, Lina!

He wagged an admonitory finger at her, guffawed and turned over onto his side. At this, the fearful white sterile light beat against his face.

Towards morning, that light intensified and became so penetrating that it pierced through everything: eyelids, palm, pillow – anything at all! Zybin hated it. Sleep meant freedom, light meant prison and that prison was present in all his dreams. Just now, they had stood on the high shore above the sea, happy, gay, free, chatting and laughing. Now the white, ghastly light, piercing through from the waking world, burned above him and he was still in jail.

That was how his nightmare always began; the two things inter-mingled, sleep and wakefulness interrupting one another, tearing him to pieces. And he would thrash about, rave and jerk upright. But this time he did not plunge into delirium, this time he simply stood there looking at Lina. And Lina took him by the hand and said: "Now then, Ivan Nikanorovich, take a look at this gallant knight! In days of yore, the knight used to save the maiden from the robbers and carry her off to his castle. This one saved her from robbers and vanished! Listen now, saviour, that's a wicked thing to do, eh?"

She talked away, holding his hand, smiling and gazing into his eyes. It was so pleasant, he started quietly chuckling again into his pillow.

... Her leg had evidently given way, Alexander Ivanovich; she lay on the shore as if she was dead, on her side; this is how she was lying, look, Alexander Ivanovich, I'll show you. This is how she lay, with her arms flung out, you see? Across her head somehow. A kind of unnatural waxwork curve. That's the way dead people lie too. That's why I took her for dead. But only for a minute – no, less, less! Nothing like a minute, a few seconds just! She suddenly lifted her head and yelled at somebody: "Take it and go! Take it and go! Otherwise our people will be here directly."

And as soon as he had shouted this, the white light flooded over him, like an overturned bucket.

"Quiet!" Buddo hissed. "Come on now, wake up! You'll be giving yourself another bruise! Now then, lie down properly! Come on!"

Zybin opened his eyes and saw right in front of him Buddo's smoke-dried face, streaked with a kind of yellow soot, and at once shrank back in repulsion: "The SB machine, two handles and one wheel", the grey-brown stubble, the tobacco-coloured adam's apple, a neck like a hundred-year-old tortoise and the ingrained smell of dog meat and rough shag.

"What's the matter with you?" Buddo asked, angered. "Having your

176

dreams again? It's all because you don't lie like a normal person. It's obvious you've never done any physical work. You should lie loose and relaxed. You lie curled up like a hook and naturally your lungs get squashed, your heart misses a beat and you start dreaming all sorts of rubbish."

"Yes, yes, I'm sorry! I know!" Zybin mumbled hastily. "Presently . . ." And closed his eyes again.

But the sea had vanished. There was no more sea, sun or seagulls. There was only a pinky-yellow darkness under his eyelids and that damned light. Then he stretched out, closed his eyes and began counting to a thousand. And after ten minutes, probably, the light went away and they were together again.

Together they went up the hill where the monument stood. And she had some slight doubts as to whether they should go at that moment and kept asking: "Isn't it late to be going there? It gets dark very quickly here, and I'm such a coward, you know."

And she did limp slightly, she really did.

. . . You realize, Alexander Ivanovich, why she was limping: she'd twisted her knee in the water. It's a very easy thing to do. There are these boulders everywhere; they're flat and slippery, your foot just shoots away. So she had stood up, slipped and put her knee out. A good thing it was so shallow, otherwise she might have drowned. That has happened on the beach there before now. So then, it was shallow and she crawled out of the water and over to her clothes. Her bits of things were lying on her headsquare – woman's gold watch, Leica camera, mother-of-pearl opera glasses, purse. If it had happened on the beach and not so early, it wouldn't have been much of a problem; help would have been at hand. But picture it to yourself: a wild high stony shore, nobody walking along it, bathing not allowed, about six in the morning. She just had to lie there and wait! So this young lion rolls up – there's plenty of them about at that time. Comes up, takes a look and says straightaway: "What's the matter, madam, can I help in any way?" She was overjoyed to think a genuine person had come her way and asks him: "Call at such and such a sanatorium and ask somebody to come. As you see, I've twisted my knee, I can't walk." "Say no more, madam, straightaway!" Comes up, snatches the watch and purse and runs off!

Well, Alexander Ivanovich, if he'd just walked away and hadn't started running, I wouldn't have twigged what was happening. I'd have rushed over to her to begin with and he'd have got away with it, but since he started running, I set off after him immediately. And he ran on about another hundred metres, sees he's not getting away, that I'm catching him up, and flings everything onto the sand. Well, of course, I didn't bother chasing after him. I came back and went to her. She's lying there. Full length and white as white can be, face wet with tears and sweat, bitten her lip – there she's lying. "What's the matter?" "It's my leg!" That was all. You know, Alexander Ivanovich, I wonder to this day: why did I act like I did? Where did it come from? I'd never had anything to do with such things before. Well, I'd read something similar in Jack London or Mayne Reid, but I don't remember all that clearly what I read where. "Wait here," I said. I sat down on the sand and took hold of her leg, looked at it and felt the kneecap – she's lying there, just gritting her teeth and groaning a bit – I raised the leg and gave it a big twist. Then again. And again! Something clicked and I felt everything go back into place. I looked at her, and she was unconscious, head digging into the sand. The pain, of course, had been fearful. She'd bitten her lip and her whole face was damp with perspiration. I lowered her leg and sat down next to her, Alexander Ivanovich, took her leg and laid it across my knees . . .

He chuckled and shook his head slightly. Of all his fond memories, this one was by far the fondest. He cherished it like a treasure, and kept on and on returning to it, turning it this way and that, examining everything down to the most insignificant detail, adding yet others which had never happened.

After that she came to herself again, and he began raising her from the sand. At first they couldn't get this right at all. Then he said: "Stand up then, and we'll try it that way." He clasped her round the waist, sat her down and then supported her back. She sat up, caught her breath, licked her lips, tidied her hair at the sides and said: "I've got a flask of cold water there, give it to me, please." He did so – it was a plain aluminium water bottle. She unscrewed it, and began to drink. She drank and drank, then placed it on the sand, glanced smilingly at him and said: "What a performance, eh? You couldn't think of anything sillier." "It's all right," he had replied. "Such things happen. How are we going to get along though? You can't walk and I'm not leaving you here alone." He was terribly serious, grimly serious. Somehow he wasn't up to joking. "You can get up, can't you, holding onto me, eh?" She gave him a smile of martyrdom. "I'll try as long as you keep a tight hold round my waist." That didn't work either. She tried several times to stand up, but could only half rise before flopping heavily back again. "No, that isn't going to work. You know what, grab hold of me lower down and give me a good shove. This way's no good." He understood and held her round the waist with one arm while pushing her upwards with the other. Then again. And once more. Then several more times. And she came upright and stood on one leg, swaying a little, with one arm round his neck. She was scarcely touching the ground with her injured leg. "How's that then?" he asked. "Just getting used to it," she responded. "You know what, let me down again and I'll get dressed." He lowered her gingerly and handed her the dress. She twirled it in her hands for a moment, considering, then said: "No, I'll never get it on like this. Let's get up again." They got to their feet once more. She gathered the dress up in folds, hoisted it above her head, saying: "Hold me round the waist please. Careful though, I'm scared of making any sudden movement."

And so she got dressed, but again somehow made an incautious movement, disturbed the leg and let out a groan. Thereupon he lowered her to the sand and she donned her slippers. After that she said: "Now let me rest for five minutes or so, then we'll make a start." She lay down and stretched out, while he sat next to her gazing out to sea. She lay with her eyes closed, breathing gently, she was so . . . so . . . At length he said: "There you see how steep it is. I'll have to carry you as far as the road. Then you can continue under your own steam." "All right," she said submissively. "Only let's rest for a couple of minutes first." After about five minutes, he said: "Come on now, take hold of my neck. Got a tight hold? Right, hold on then! Up we go!" He raised her from the ground and carried her in his arms. (Again this was his very fondest memory).

". . . Well after that she started walking. She was limping heavily, but I couldn't nerve myself to carry her all the same – we were in the town now after all! Picture the sight! There was no one about yet, but I still couldn't bring myself to do it. She was an absolute brick, moving along without so much as a groan, just crying out a bit when the leg bent. My shoulder ached for three days afterwards though. I didn't notice anything at the time. 'Does it hurt,' I kept asking. 'It's all right, it's fine, keep going.' 'How about a rest? There's a bench over there.' 'No, keep going, keep going, it's not far now. Just round the corner.' As soon as we got round the corner, a whole crowd of boys and girls with life belts and beachballs came rushing out and made for her at once. 'Lina, what's the matter, what's happened?' They surrounded her, supporting her back and sat her down on a bench. Somebody ran to fetch her sister. I fled, naturally. That's the whole story, Alexander Ivanovich, you can see what sort of a saviour I am."

"Yes," responded Alexander Ivanovich. "I can – and feel it too. But why did you go up the hill with her? Was there something particular there?"

They climbed the hill towards evening. There had once been proper access here; first, a short flight of stairs, then some kind of metalled road – now there was nothing: there remained only a treacherous path, forever giving way underfoot. You had to be careful as you went, holding onto the bushes and selecting a suitable place to put your weight, otherwise you would crash knee-deep into clumps of tall weeds and the omnipresent nettles. The nettles here were uncrushable: as high as a man, black, with tender yellow catkins, powdered with grey pollen, they gave off a mysterious fragrance. Everything which lay on the hillside below the level of the path was in fact mysterious: rounded black spiky bushes, whitish-yellow stones, spotted with rust, goat bones, a dog's skeleton, the delicate tracery of the ribcage open to the sky. A merlin perches in a slender aspen, watching with yellow, feline eye. A sweep of the arm or a shout would merely elicit a slight crouch for the sake of appearances, but he would keep his position. You make your way along, thinking: I wonder what goes on in these thickets? Down in the prickly bushes, the yellow reed-beds, those mighty burdocks, the thistles and the nettle clumps – what's in there? Who walks here, who lives here, and why is there a grey tarpaulin cap, soaked with grease, hanging like a pancake on that hollow reed over yonder. Who had hung it there? When and what for?

"Hold on a minute, saviour," said Lina, relinquishing his arm. "I'll slip my shoes off, otherwise my feet keep slipping. Wait for me up above there."

She fussed about for a long time, taking off and putting on and when she eventually came up to him, the sun suddenly went behind a cloud and it abruptly grew dark. The sky immediately above them did stay bright, and the sea still dazzled the eyes as they glimpsed it through gaps in the hillside, but a limpid twilight was already lying across the lower slopes. The pancake on the reed now seemed quite brown. Close by here was a real precipice. Zybin missed his footing somehow and there was a crumbling as the stone broke away beneath his feet and bounded softly down the grassy slope, before it reached the burdocks and came to rest.

"Come on, just a dozen steps," he said cheerfully, "one more turn and we're there."

He spoke merely to put heart into her but it actually did turn out as he said. They went up a few more steps and at once found themselves on a broad straight road and immediately in front of them, green and tranquil as in some fairy tale, there was a level glade, covered in short grass, and beyond it the white cemetery wall.

"There you are, we've arrived," he said. "Shall we have a rest?"

The wall was low, no higher than a man's chest. Beyond it could be glimpsed crosses and burial vaults – strange cubes and rectangles of yellow limestone. Such things are only built for the dead. But dark cypresses stood close by and the effect was beautiful nevertheless. He gazed at all this, shadowed by the light limpid twilight, which gave an effect of smoked glass, and mused: "Why the hell did I have to drag her here now? In twenty minutes or so it's going be completely dark. Should have waited till tomorrow and come up the other side."

"Sit down, we'll have a rest," he said perching himself on a roadside stone. It was lying here right by the road – a large rectangular marble block.

She also sat down, sighing heavily, and closed her eyes. He looked at the block: on one side it had been squared off. Clearly it had been hauled up here, but only as far as the cemetery wall before being abandoned. Why? Perhaps the revolution had drawn near and the living had little time for the dead?

He pulled out her flat flask from his pocket and said: "I'd offer you some vodka, but ..." She frowned slightly.

"Water would be nice ..."

"All right, we'll go and look for some, then," he said briskly. "There's a pipe of sorts sticking out here. We can go over there if you like."

"In a minute," she pleaded, but remained sitting for a long time until it was completely dark before getting up. "Let's go."

They had only proceeded a few steps when the white wall stopped short; through the gap they glimpsed the night. All its elements merged together; the dark of the earth and the dense undergrowth, the mauve tint of the marble and the angels, the tops of the trees and the sea, as if strung out between them, and far above, the sky with its huge dark-blue stars and swift purplish flashes lighting up the heavens. He fished out his torch and the lilac beam flitted across the grass and dissipated before it reached the wall.

"Come on," he said.

They got up and went on, but after a few paces, stumbling against the first grave, something hooted and began to moan. She pressed his hand. He laughed quietly and clapped her on the arm.

"There, there," he said, "nothing to worry about, just an owl. There must be thousands on this estate. Look at the flats over there."

He shone the light on a traceried window with multicoloured panes and bronze palm trees in place of mullions. Then all at once, his hand shook: a tall, gaunt old man in a dark-blue boiler suit had appeared out of the ground before them and stood motionless, regarding them. "Good night," said Zybin somewhat taken aback.

"Good evening, good evening," responded the old man benignly. "Night indeed! It's evening! And what do I see – you've come up from this side?"

"Yes. Why do you ask?"

"What do you mean why? How did you come to risk it? There's obstacles put up. You're not supposed to walk that way at all. If you fell, you'd be smashed to smithereens. Two people were fatally injured last year. The police have warned us most strongly! The whole thing here's crumbling."

He seemed to be smiling as he talked, however.

"Well we didn't see any obstacles, grandad." Lina pressed close to Zybin, lightly brushing his shoulder with her chin.

"Now how can there not be when I put them up myself?" The old man wagged his head. "No, they're there all right; you ignored them that's all. That's it! Well, if they've fallen down onto the road, it doesn't matter. There's a notice in black and white there: 'No Entry'."

"There was nothing there at all!" Zybin exclaimed.

"Somebody hasn't pulled it down again, have they?" the old man said in calm surprise. "That must be what's happened. That's the third barrier of mine that's been overturned! Yobs! Louts! They can't leave a thing alone! There's a monument here. Stood here a hundred years, maybe. The Whites didn't touch it, nor did the Reds or the Greens; then along comes one of your heroes, a scholar in a white suit, sits down under it, takes out a bottle, has a drink or two – and that's it! He stretches out, gets up two hours later and stares round like some sheep; what he sees is an angel with a cross. Looks and sees whether he can knock it down with his shoe – no good. He tries putting his back against it. Still standing! Then he braces his backside against it, puffs and pants till he's blue in the face, this drunk's a tough swine. The angel stays upright. That made him so miserable, so miserable! He turns away from

182

the monument and doesn't know what to do. And there's nothing to drink for love nor money. He catches sight of me. 'Grandad, get me a half-litre!' 'No,' says I. 'We haven't any vodka. We don't serve drinks to the dead and we don't drink ourselves. I'm wondering why you've given up trying. You've heaved at it with your back, you've pushed it with your backside, why not try your forehead – that's a terrific one you've got there. Maybe that'll bring it down.' 'Ah,' says he, 'all this is due to be pulled down in any case!' That's the sort of scholar you come across. And what are you doing about so late? You should come here when the sun's high in the sky. Have you been out walking and got lost, or have you come to have a look?"

He was an odd old man. He posed his questions and told his tale in exactly the same tone of voice – light, humorous, mellow-old-man fashion, and it was evident that he didn't care a rap about anything, including the fact that somebody might walk along this path and be smashed to pieces. Zybin replied that no, they hadn't been walking and lost their way, but had come specially to have a look at the cemetery.

"Well, well," the old man seemed genuinely pleased. "There are certainly things to see here. I should say so! There's one outstanding monument here they want to put in the museum . . ."

Zybin said it was precisely because of this monument that they had come here.

"You're going the wrong way then! You'll get completely lost. Stay where you are. I'll show you the way directly."

He moved away from the wall and was at once lost to view. One moment he was there, the next – gone. He had either melted into the wall or sunk into the ground. Lina pressed Zybin's hand, but the old man had already emerged from somewhere underground. He held a large soot-begrimed lantern. "Well, off we go," he said. He carried the lantern like a bucket, swinging it so that the shadows flickered in all directions. It showed up only what lay beneath their feet, the grass and the earth: up ahead was as dark as before.

They passed several crosses and angels, before drawing level with a vault, large, long, looking like a warehouse. One window was lit up from below with a yellow paraffin light.

"But someone lives here!" Lina was astonished.

"Certainly they do!" he replied glancing pleasurably at her face. "That's where we live. I've got my toolshed over there and this is our habitation. There's two of us; me and Mitri Mitrich the gardener, an old fellow like me. He's well into his eighties now."

"Gardener?" said Lina, surprised.

"Gardener, citizeness, gardener. Mitri Mitrich was a celebrity in his day. At one time he used to work for Count Poliustrov on the islands and supply flowers for all the great banquets. They tried to lure him to Tsarskoe but he wouldn't go. My grandad laid his bones here, he would say, and my father too, and I'll be here with them. And you see it didn't work out like that. He got stranded here during the Civil War and here he's stayed. So we live here together."

And again the old man's voice was light, jocular, almost mocking, as if he was telling a story and inviting his auditors to laugh at his words.

"You're not frightened?" Lina asked.

This so took the old man's fancy that he halted on the spot.

"Who's there to be afraid of here?" he asked cheerfully, his eyes twinkling with good humour. "There's nothing for evil-minded people to do here, citizeness. There's no profit to be made here. Some alcoholic might come blundering in blind drunk. You do get incidents like that. But otherwise it's mostly couples." He flashed the torch briefly on them both.

Lina squeezed Zybin's fingers and asked hesitantly.

"What about vampires?"

"Wha-a-t?" The old man frowned. "Vampires? So that's what you're on about! Those things that leave their graves and suck people's blood?" He gave an abrupt laugh and shook his head. "No, citizeness, nobody gets out of there. Everything's well battened down! The grave's dug, the stone's put on top and that's it. Safer than when he was alive! A dead person is the most harmless kind. It's the living who keep dashing about, grabbing things for themselves. It's always 'not enough, not enough, give us a bit more, give me that as well!' A dead one gives out everything he's got. And when there's just the skeleton left – that means he's distributed all his wealth. He's just left himself with the basics. That's his own, what he got from his mother! That's how it is, young people!"

He regarded them both cheerfully as he spoke. Zybin noticed that Lina had suddenly winced, and her face looked thin and pinched. The old man was evidently well-versed in this sort of talk, and enjoyed it.

"I'm still frightened," said Lina and pressed close to Zybin. He held his arm round her back. She clung still closer.

"Frightened! The idea! Goodness gracious!" The old man sounded almost genteel. "It's nature! The law! The law of nature, sirs! Created

184

from the earth, to the earth you return! What's there to be frightened of in that? I'm surprised at you. Especially at you scientists, I really am! Teach you nature study, syntax, but when it comes to the push, you're worse than the most ignorant muzhik. Honestly, you're worse. There's that grandson of mine going into the sixth form this winter. He reads the papers and says: 'Mama, you're behind the times; they don't say it that way nowadays.' The scholar speaks! He was with me here once, getting late – I was fixing up a running noose for him – and he spent the night. In the morning he ran off about his business, then I see him come chasing in with an awful look on his face. What's the matter! 'Granda, granda, a dead man's just crawled out of the grave!' 'Where is he? What's he up to? Come on, let's go and take a look.' 'No, no, I'm not going.' A fine scientist, I must say!" The old man laughed once more. "I went out and someone really was scrabbling and rocking the railings on the grave. I came up and he'd already vomited all over the place and was climbing up onto the monument. He was horrible and filthy and all covered in soil! A real vampire! He'd been banging and banging against the railings and only managed to hurt his noddle. So then he thought of climbing up the monument and throwing himself clear of the fencing, you see. That's where boozing can get you! You do get things like that happening here, yes. But what you're saying . . ." He smiled as he looked at Lina and made a slight dismissive gesture with his arm. "Well, here we are. There's the monument, look at it!"

. . . You realize, Alexander Ivanovich, that statue was really magnificent. When we shone the torch on it, it fairly took off before our very eyes – a terrifying lightness! The pedestal was of dark granite, but you couldn't see that. And down below, Alexander Ivanovich, there were all those inscriptions. Granite is invisible in the dark of course, but just a flash of the torch and it flares up and gives off blue sparks. And so, when we were looking at it from all sides, and this old woman appeared . . .

Not an old woman of course, she'd probably not have been fifty. They didn't notice her at first. They had just climbed up to the monument, when suddenly out of the darkness came a placid, deep, sonorous voice.

"Hello, Mikheich. Who've you got with you?"

And the old man suddenly started fussing about.

"Ah, it's you, Dora Semyonova," he bleated. "Why didn't you let me know? Where's Rostislav Mstislavich? Is he with you? You see, these young people wanted to pay Yulia Grigorevna a visit and got mixed up among the graves. I decided to guide them, seeing as it's dark."

"I imagine you can get mixed up here during the day as well," said the woman equably out of the darkness. "I've been walking about here for ages. It's a mess. You don't look after it, not you nor that shard of empire!"

"Now how can we keep everything in control here, Dora Semyonova?" The old man waved his lantern about. "Heavens, it's all crumbling into the sea. The road over there has collapsed, you can't walk along it. There was a policeman here yesterday and announced that this was our last summer; they're stopping us living here."

"The sooner they chase you out the better, maybe! There's no point in it in any case!" The woman heaved a sigh and came up to the fence. She was tall and strongly built, with a colourful shawl about her shoulders."

"Good evening," Zybin bowed slightly. "We didn't keep track of the time as we went and got caught by the dark. This is our first time here – it's tough going!"

"If you come the right way, it's not hard," responded the old woman. "You should have come up that way, then it would have been easy. It's best to come here of a morning or when there's a full moon. If you've just got a lantern, what can you see? Well, go ahead and look!"

She came out of the enclosure and stood revealed as a tall, powerfully built brunette, not yet old, with large features, a coarse yet handsome face, with very straight black eyebrows and a velvety glance. When she lifted her arm to brush away some dark threads of hair from her brow and temples, there came a flash of bracelet.

"It would be better if they closed the place down," she said. "Nobody needs us nowadays! Up till this summer there was a photograph here, but the glass got smashed and the rain blurred it. The railing on that side's been pulled down and dragged over there? What for? Why should anybody want to do that? And there's nobody to complain to. Never mind about the railing, but it's a shame about the monument. Cost a lot of money. It's a museum exhibit. Ought to be in the Hermitage!"

"That's forbidden, Dora Semyonovna," sighed the old man. "There seems to be some special decree – it seems there's a cult grown up around it!"

"I know there's a cult. But look, young people, look closely! Otherwise you'll come here again and see nothing – they'll have used it as limestone. It can easily happen nowadays! Cult. My father put it up, thinking

186

it would stand three hundred years and it won't have lasted twenty-five! If the dead could only rise and see the work of his hands! He lies right next to it here, you know. Family plot."

"Tell me, you knew her? That girl?" Zybin enquired circumspectly.

"Of course I did! Yulenka was my cousin. I'm two years older. We've scrambled all over these hills. In those days, there was a Georgian kursaal, with music. Shashliks and red wine. And there were benches over here. She used to like coming here in the mornings before there were many people about. She would sit there and always be drawing the sea in her album – she drew very well in coloured pencils."

"And how did she die?" Lina asked cautiously.

The woman did not reply at once. She seemed to reflect for a while.

"Death came and so she died," she said indifferently, then suddenly began speaking with a brusque rapidity. "Not because of love! No! That's all just resort talk. Fisherman, lighthouse! That's all rubbish. Nothing of the kind. She didn't properly understand what love was then. She had a crush on our cadet cousin, that was all. The verses on the stone here, she wrote them down in a special album. She intended to present them to him later. Making out that she loved him, but he didn't return it – she was ready to die for him, and he just found it funny. That was the sort of love she imagined for herself. And wrote letters like that to him. After she died, they found them all in her box. But she died in an ordinary way. Stupidly, I mean. Streptococcal angina. Clambered about the hills and caught a chill. Then the infection set in and that was the finish. She was burned up in a week."

She drew the shawl more securely round her shoulders and approached them. A very well-preserved forty-five-year-old woman, heavy features, sensuous lips and a deep, penetrating glance, somehow ample and calm, a glance which caused Zybin a distinct qualm. A strange feeling came over him. "Presently she'll go away and we'll never find out who she is and where she sprang from," he thought with a pang, peering into the lilac shadows near her mascara-laden eyes and the merciless arch of her brows. "We'll come back tomorrow and find there's nobody here, no Mikheich, that is, there was once but he died forty years back, the vault in ruins and nothing left but a pit, a few bones and the monument." Thus he mused and felt himself stiffen with fright. Where had she come from? There was no sign of her here and then she just appeared all of a sudden. And the old man had crawled out from under the earth to bring them here to this old woman.

He looked at Lina. She was staring fixedly at the woman.

187

"You know I've seen you somewhere before," she said abruptly.

"And I you," responded the woman readily, with a faint smile. "On the beach. We even went bathing together once." She stretched out a hand. "Allow me to introduce myself, artiste of the Moscow Philharmonia Dora Istomina-Dulskaya. You may have seen the poster with my picture? We always tour for two months in this area. I think we go the same way? Let's go then. Light the way for us, Mikheich."

"Old grave digger, old grave digger, wherever have you gone, old grave digger? Bury me in the earth old grave digger, so that I see no more, old grave digger . . ." he mumbled, tossing from side to side, while a soldier stood over him, shaking his shoulder and repeating: "Get up, get up! To the interrogation, the interrogation . . ." At length he jumped up. The yellow light was on, that meant it wasn't all that late. Buddo's bunk was vacant. He got to his feet, smoothed his hair down, took a drink of water, got dressed and asked the soldier: "It's lights out isn't it?" "Let's go," the soldier replied.

And so they went. He was probably running a temperature. As he passed along the corridor, he clutched at the walls, swaying. At length they came to a halt in front of the door familiar from yesterday. "Stand up straight," said the soldier. "Why are you so scruffy?"

The door opened of itself. Khripushin was standing in the middle of the room. He looked at Zybin and smiled ironically. No doubt Zybin was indeed a sorry sight: dishevelled, unbuttoned, shoes without laces. Khripushin took the receipt, went over to the window and signed without reading it; the soldier went out. "How are you feeling?" Khripushin enquired. "Quite well, thanks," Zybin responded, seating himself on his corner chair. Khripushin also moved over to the desk and sat down ponderously, placing his fists on the desk in front of him. He was well-shaved, pressed, cleaned and turned out. "Well, can we dispense with the thanks?" he asked. "Yes," replied Zybin, passing a hand across his face: he certainly had a temperature, it seemed, and he ached all over. That was all he needed, to fall apart here. It had really shot up though. Pity there was no mirror. "You haven't got a mirror, have you?" he asked. At this, something wholly incomprehensible occurred. Khripushin suddenly started bellowing like a bull. He smashed a fist down on the desk. The ink shot out of the inkwell, pencils scattered, something tinkled.

"Well, stand up!" Khripushin roared, leaping to his feet. "I'll give you . . . Stand up when you're told!"

But Zybin remained seated. He was perfectly certain now that he was feverish. His brain was functioning extremely sluggishly. He didn't fully take in what had happened. Then Khripushin at once appeared next to him somehow (had he leaped the desk, perhaps?).

"On your feet, prostitute!" he croaked in Zybin's ear, shaking him to the point of suffocation. "Stand up when you're told! . . . Want a mirror! Ask your whore for one!"

This had all happened so suddenly and ludicrously that Zybin actually did rise to his feet. At this, Khripushin released him.

"Oh dear," he resumed with a hint of sorrow. "Really cheeky about it, aren't we, enemy sod! Give him a mirror! Just where do you think you are? Think you're visiting your whores do you? Bastard, swine, enemy! Forgotten where you are, have you?"

Zybin regarded him mutely. "This is the end," he thought. "Now he's going to hit me and I'll hit him in the face and smash him in the jaw and go in with my foot when he falls. Now, this very second."

He knew this was certain to happen. After that, a gang of alarm clocks would burst in, well-fed young stallions who would grab him, throw him to the floor and stamp on him till he was just a sack of bones. At least they were good at that. But there was nothing he could do about it, it wasn't up to him. It was a pity, though, that investigators, as Buddo had informed him, no longer carried Brownings, otherwise he might have had the last laugh and escaped painlessly. Still if this was the situation, so be it. He eyed Khripushin with a smile.

"But why prostitute, for heaven's sake? Aren't you going to charge me with Trotskyism then? Why prostitute?"

Khripushin caught his breath and relaxed his fists. He had realized something at least by this time. That is, he understood nothing of course; he was still in that heady flight of anger, which couldn't survive interruptions. The way he had come roaring out from his chair, banging his fist on the desk was how he should have continued: bawling, thumping and cursing – in short, turning a man into a piece of shit. Seconds were crucial here. If the enemy yielded and began to talk, even if only to register a protest – he would go on to tell everything. But this time something was holding Khripushin back from using his voice and his fists. Not any kind of calculation or understanding, but something more keen and subtle, something akin to feel or intuition. Besides which, he didn't have permission to use violence. Permission is not always given for this and not in connection with all charges. Here the rule was: if the zek puts pen to paper – good man! The victors are never called to account. But if a row blew up about it, you'd get your knuckles rapped for infringing the rules!

So they stood and gazed at one another. Khripushin in bovine fury, with perhaps an admixture of uncertainty. Zybin simply standing upright because this was probably his last day, the end towards which his whole complex, absurd life had been leading.

He did not feel a hint of anger towards this husky brute. He felt, rather, a sensation of nightmare, the terrifying absurdity of things taking place in a dream which he was powerless to prevent. "How grand it was back then, by the sea," came the sudden swift pang. "And now this ... and what good is it to anyone? None at all."

Finally, Khripushin turned sharply on his heel, strode away behind his desk and sat down. Zybin also sat. Both men at once sensed that they were at a loss over how to proceed. They sat and tried to avoid one another's eyes. Suddenly the phone rang. "Major Khripushin here!" he shouted in relief. He replied "not yet" to some question, then said "yes". Evidently he was summoned to attend elsewhere. He barked "sir!" and immediately dialled a number (he had not glanced at Zybin). "Good man!" he said after a moment. "What are you doing? Get the file and drop it into such and such an office." He replaced the receiver and looked at Zybin.

"Well now," he said reluctantly. "You be careful you don't take liberties. Jumps up, indeed! We've seen worse than that here. Sit there, think it over. You'll still have to write in any case."

There came a knock at the door.

"Yes," said Khripushin.

An extremely youthful fair-haired lad entered with a folder. He had a perfectly boyish face and a blond moustache. He looked like a hussar out of some historical-revolutionary film.

"Permission to enter?" he requested, halting close to where Zybin sat.

"Yes, yes, come in," said Khripushin, rising. "I'll be back directly."

CHAPTER 5

THE BOY SAT DOWN at the desk and opened up the folder. He sat there for a moment, leafing through it, making a note on a sheet of paper. Then he raised his impassive eyes to Zybin and asked gently: "Why keep on refusing to confess? That's bad!" His tone was weighty but perfectly amicable.

All of a sudden Zybin began to shiver. His insides were turning over and jangling. His back was starting to ache. He was realizing only now what it meant to be unnerved.

"Well, what's there to confess?" he half snapped, half complained. "They don't ask me anything, they just bawl."

"You see you shouldn't be anonymous, you should tell everything truthfully, then you'll be treated with courtesy," said the boy didactically. Then he abruptly asked in quite a different tone: "What do you confess to then?"

"So this must be the alarm clock," it suddenly dawned on Zybin and cheered him up to such an extent that he almost laughed out loud. Buddo had told him about these alarm clocks. They were students at the NKVD higher law school. They did their practical work here, their chief function being to sit on the conveyor. The investigation was supposed to go on for several days without a break, otherwise there was no point. The investigator, let's say has finished his shift, snarled out his allotted number of hours – God knows how many he's supposed to do, whether it's eight or all twelve – and has gone off to his wife and family. Then the alarm clock takes over and starts muttering: "Confess, confess! When are you going to confess? You must confess, you must! Go on and write, write. Here's a pen and paper, sit down and write." And so on till morning, till the owner of the office arrives having had his beauty sleep. This is regarded as part of his practical work. So these future jurists, prosecutors and judges not only learn the subtleties of Soviet law, but also prepare for their exams at the same time. They all have a textbook in front of them or *Questions of Leninism.*

In front of this alarm clock lay, not books, but some sort of fit-up case – clearly he was sitting his exam in investigator's clerical work.

"Marvellous!" Zybin said. "So that's what you are then!"

"What do you mean – what are we?" The boy was startled.

"Those alarm clocks! You're what, twenty years old? Well, you know what the scientific name for you is? 'Veglia'. You can make a note of that. 'Veglia', that is to say 'conveyor' in Russian, or vigil, wasn't invented by you. The term belongs to a sixteenth-century Bologna jurist, Hippolytus of Marseilles. In Russia it was first applied in 1864, I believe in the Karakozov case, and produced excellent results."

"What are you trying to say?" the boy asked, aghast.

"Me? Nothing. Nothing at all! True, they operated rather differently in those days. They placed the prisoner on a high bench and two gents jogged him from either side so that he got no sleep. And so the learned jurist Hippolytus writes: 'I became convinced that this apparently frivolous experiment, almost reminiscent of a children's game, was in practice so effective, that even the most hardened heretics could not hold out against it.' Listen, young man, hardened was what they called us prisoners."

"What is all this about? I don't understand!" the young man cried, almost in a panic.

Khripushin came in quietly, signalled to the boy with his eyes and stayed by the door, listening.

"It's about this," Zybin pursued, trembling all over in his despair, his utmost readiness to follow wherever this was leading – a fight to the death with this alarm clock; at all events what he had lacked all these past days now had descended upon him – the mighty liberating power of contempt! All his apprehension instantly left him and everything became easy. Surely he hadn't really been afraid of these pipsqueaks?

"About this," he repeated, now with relish. "About what the gendarmes did to Karakozov long before you. Do you know that name? No, of course, how could you, that's not what they teach you, is it? Well, they sat him between two alarm clocks like you – only they were gendarmes, not student informers like you – and they didn't let Karakozov get any sleep. Whenever he dropped off, they gave him a jolt. Later, one of them told the tale: he sits between us and swings his foot, the bastard. So we watch and when he stops swinging it, that's when we bump him . . ."

"That's enough rubbish!" said Khripushin harshly, walking through and sitting down at his desk.

The boy got up as Khripushin dismissed him with a nod, but stopped to listen as he reached the door.

"So this alarm clock tells how the prisoner craftily contrived to sleep, the sod, and swings his foot even when he's not awake, so we . . ."

"Get to the end," Khripushin gestured.

"So we started jogging him every five minutes, whether he's swinging or not. That's what!"

"And did he talk?" Khripushin asked.

"He did."

"Well and so will you, mister scientific secretary," grinned Khripushin. "And bear in mind you're going to tell it all, every word, every little name! Because you're with the Soviet Chekists not the Tsarist secret police. And we'll teach you to respect the investigation. So there, good citizen! Thank you, Igor. Off you go."

The alarm clock left, bestowing on Zybin a fleeting and, as it seemed to him, a somewhat humorous glance. "A good lad," thought Zybin. "Maybe he'll sit here a few months and understand everything. Although he understands it all now and still stays. Yes, the devil is strong! Very strong!" The jangling within him had passed off completely. Now he was completely calm and had himself well in hand. It was once more with a smile that he looked at Khripushin. But the other was smiling too.

"Still waging guerrilla warfare?" he enquired. "Indulging in anti-Soviet agitation here as well? Never mind, carry on, carry on, you can say anything you like here. Soviet people can take it."

He took a sheet of paper from the folder, stood up and brought it over to Zybin.

"Read and sign that," he said.

The sheet stated that he, G. N. Zybin, date of birth, employment, according to materials in the possession of the Kazakhstan SSR NKVD, is proven to have penetrated the Central Museum of Kazakhstan, circulated defeatist rumours, disseminated anti-Soviet propaganda, slandered measures taken by the party and government; later to have concealed currency valuables belonging to the state and to have attempted to flee abroad with them. In addition he has been caught organizing exhibitions with wrecking intent, dragging in photographs of those now exposed as enemies of the people alongside portraits of heroes of labour, that is, committed offences provided for in articles 58.1 and 58.10, part two, 58.7 of the RSFSR criminal code, and the decree of 7 August. Therefore, in order to prevent concealment and the obstruction of the investigation, he is liable to arrest and search. Signed Belousov, head of 1st operations department, sanctioned by the deputy republic special prosecutor Dubrovsky.

"Sign it," Khripushin repeated, handing him a pen. "Go over to the desk and sign."

Zybin dashed off his signature, returned to his place and sat down. Khripushin did the same. Both said nothing for a minute or so.

"Well then, what's it to be." asked Khripushin. "Are we going to confess or not?"

"To what?"

"To what's written down here, in due order. That you, while still a student, conducted corrupting work in your institute – we've been sent some very pretty materials on that – how you deceived the security organs and evaded responsibility, then how and with whose assistance, you wormed your way into the museum – we are aware of all your sponsors as well and we'll talk about them separately. The sort of wrecking activity you carried on in the museum, who supported you in it – that sort of thing, frankly, frankly, concealing nothing! Who you recruited, how in the end, growing bolder you proceeded to direct action. Then about that story involving the gold. Go on like that to the end."

"Terrific!" Zybin said, roaring with laughter. "That's rich! You've drawn me a picture of the investigator's dream, haven't you just? Come on then, let's talk about the facts!"

"That's just what we have here!" Khripushin said with steadfast obtuse conviction. "You're arrested – fact! You have been accused – fact! That means something, doesn't it? Or do we pull innocent people in?" (Zybin shrugged.) "No, no, answer: what do you think we do, arrest innocent people? Is that it? Aha, nothing to say? There are the preliminary facts for you."

"You mean there are others?"

"There are plenty of facts relating to you," Khripushin assured him. "Here, in this desk there are three folders full of facts." He took them out and laid them out one after the other. "Over there in the cupboard there are another five like these, so we've got plenty."

"Then show me them," said Zybin.

"I just have," Khripushin again evinced a surprise that was perhaps even genuine.

"What sort of facts do you call them? They're the articles I'm charged with."

"What a man," Khripushin shook his head and almost smiled in the consciousness of his unshakeable rectitude. "And how can you be charged other than on a factual basis? This is all stuff which you've signed and they are the facts of the accusation. You aren't being accused of terrorist activity or espionage, are you? And why is that? Because there are no such facts at the disposal of the investigation. It has at its disposal quite other facts. You have slandered the organs of the NKVD – is that a fact? It is. Spread anti-Soviet fabrications – again fact? It is. Organized museum exhibitions with wrecking intent – another fact? Not just one either! For a start tell the investigation about these facts. The gold question we'll take up later."

Zybin merely shrugged, grinning.

"So then, we're going to sit in silence together," Khripushin asked. "All right, let's do that, we've got plenty of time."

"I'm just waiting for you to ask me about something specific."

"Ha! Am I not asking you about something specific? Here's something then. Tell us about your anti-Soviet activity in the museum. About the subversive organization of the display cases. Now what's there to laugh at? Be kind enough to tell me why are you laughing, eh?"

There came a knock on the door and Khripushin called crisply: "Yes, come in!"

And a woman entered. She was very young and beautiful, tall, with dark hair, somewhat reminiscent of a certain American film star of the silent screen. She came in, halted by the door and asked, smiling: "May I come in?"

In those days there were quite a few women like that around. The time was coming when no magazine cover, or cinema or resort poster would be complete without one.

Those same years when, according to the most conservative estimates, the number of political prisoners exceeded ten million.

When the concept of "active investigation" appeared for the first time in law studies, and a coded instruction was sent out to the special public prosecutors not to believe stories of torture and not to accept complaints along those lines.

A time when a wave of mass shootings without trial swept through the camps of East and West. So many of the condemned were crammed into a cell that some, without waiting for an easy death, died standing up and the corpses also stayed upright.

During these same years there was a particularly splendid blossoming of cultural parks; firework displays were especially frequent, and there was a plethora of roundabouts, sideshows and dance floors. Never was there so much dancing and singing as during those years. Never had shop windows been so beautiful, prices so stable, earning a living so easy.

> I know of no other land,
> Where man breathes so freely –

sang the young pioneers as they set off on their marches. "Everyone is young now in our youthful, beautiful land," boomed the orchestra at public merry-making. And many people actually did believe this. The slogan "Life is better, comrades, life is happier" became a state truth, the basis, the axiom of our existence. Because that was precisely how "the most humane man on earth" perceived the reality he had created for us.

After writing that line, Fadeev had shot himself.

So these women had appeared at that time – wondrous, enigmatic flowers of the West, from which we had taken everything – its humanism, science, progressive art and literature and finally even the beauty of its women. But these were our own socialist beauties, and therefore everything: eyes, hairdo, hair colour, smile, walk, were dependent upon a certain harsh canon of permissibility. And the suits were tailored appropriately in light tweed – nothing overloud (the China Railway had just been sold to the Japanese), emphasizing the height and shoulders, with vague hints of a bosom. No décolleté, no short skirts, no bare knees or trousers. A simpler version of such women was spawned in typing pools, management offices, secretariats, hairdressers, but the most elegant élite settled in the central boards and people's commissariats. To have a secretary like that became a matter of honour for any people's commissar.

They perched on severe armchairs, upholstered in black puffy lea-therette. In front of them was a bureau and a little desk set about with telephones.

Everything about these beauties was extraordinary. They carried handbags of incredible chic. In these bags lay powder compacts the size of a bun. They wore golden, transparent stockings with arrows, mascu-line Zenith watches made out of alloyed steel, and the most chic of them used to lead about spiteful little dogs with visceral snarls, eyes like telescopes and toad-like muzzles. These ladies did not eat in canteens. The cleaning ladies brought them breakfast and tea. They carelessly lifted the starched napkins, instantly selected a sandwich or cake with long cool fingers and a passing farm worker would be dazzled by the flash of mother-of-pearl nails – sharp, pink darts. The visitor would be stunned and go away crushed ("Where do you think you're going, comrade, can't you see it's break time?"); when he came back an hour later, flustered and apologizing for his existence, timidly awkward – trousers drooping, boots pinching – he accepts without argument whatever he is presented with: the polite rebuff, the kindly advice to apply to the third deputy (who will consign you to the devil!) and even the order to collect up your papers and clear off – those matters are not dealt with here! But there were also other visitors – mysterious; either supple undulating eels or jovial bears. They either slid quietly into the office or noisily crashed into it, thudding into armchairs so that the springs twanged, unbuttoning and discarding this and that, putting their bulging briefcases on their knees and now extracting something, to be spread open and solemnly placed on the desk. An ecstatic cry rang out and then the keeper of the gates began to sing like an oriole. "You shouldn't have, Ernest Gendrikhovich . . ." she would sing. "You are a one, really you are, Mikhail Potapovich, I've told you before. You must have gone to such trouble . . . They're beautiful! And how much . . . ?"

"Take them, take them, my dear," the Ernest Gendrikhoviches or Mikhail Potapoviches would say, and elbow the bags away from them. "They are all trial specimens you know. They're going into production from the end of the quarter. But that wouldn't be the same . . ."

"Oh, naturally that isn't the same thing at all," gushed the Keeper of the Gates.

And then the office door would seem to open by itself. The people's commissar awaited.

They were Mary Mays and Gloria Swansons for the masses . . . And there were a great many varieties and ranks – from almost authentic Hollywood stars with languorous mouths, from tall long-faced blondes to simply pretty curly-haired girls, for whom everything still lay ahead. But these were, so to speak, the daytime stars – wives, lovers, girls looking for a mooring. There existed another kind, purely nocturnal divas; these built their nests in quite other places – in the gloomy buildings of the public prosecutor, in the secret departments, in the reception offices of emergency authorities, in hush-hush establishments, tribunals and prosecutors' offices.

This was one such valkyrie of the night – a secretary or a secretary-typist – and had fluttered into the lamplight of investigator Khripushin's office.

"Come through, come through, please," Khripushin fussed and

fidgeted. "Over here, look, here." His head kept jerking in little bows.

The woman, retaining her everlasting smile, went through to the desk and placed a paper on it.

"Ah-h," said Khripushin, "yes-yes! But . . ."

He glanced round, seeking a chair. There was no chair. There were chairs, five or six in fact, on the last of which sat Zybin, but they were all solidly strapped to each other (in case of some serious talk between investigator and prisoner).

"One moment!" cried Khripushin, and fairly whisked out.

At this, the secretary (and Zybin knew for certain she was not some typist, but a real secretary of god knew which high-ranking official), turned and looked at him. Just for an instant. She turned away again at once and began sorting out something on the desk. He was just a prisoner after all – there was no shortage of disoriented and absurd folk like him, lacking shoelaces and belts, trousers sagging (nothing metallic was permitted inside prisons, so trouser buttons were cut off too). She was obliged to see sights like this every night, plenty of them. But Khripushin flew in at this point with a chair and at once began talking to her. Then she sat down and so did he. He read what she had fetched him; it took some time, scowling, then he swiftly raised his head and asked in surprise: "But where?" He did not go on, seeming to swallow what he was going to say; he snatched the desk-jotter, wrote something down and pushed it over to her.

"He's here," she replied and added: "You go and I'll stay here." And since he said nothing, but continued to gaze at her, waiting for something more, this time she repeated sharply: "Go!"

At this he rose and swiftly quitted the room.

The secretary sat on for a while, then raised her head and took another look at Zybin. But this time it was a direct, unconcealed masterful look. Zybin did not see this one.

He was far, far away . . . By the sea again. It had been coming closer for a long time, sounding and pounding in his temples, penetrating the green varnish of the walls, the portraits of Stalin and Yezhov – and now it had broken through that murky veil to seethe, froth and inundate everything. He was standing above it on a rocky outcrop under a hot, clear sky without shade or cloud, and shouting something downwards.

From below, from the strip of sea and sand, an answer came. And now Lina was running towards him, saying: "There, I only just got away from my people. I promised to go back in a minute. Quick, let's go. Is it still under your bed?" "Yes," he answered, and so they made their way, racing down the stony path. She was clinging to his shoulder and laughing at something all the way. "What's up with you?" he asked her. "Nothing. It's lovely isn't it?"

"It certainly is," he responded, inhaling a deep breath of the sea.

They walked along the sand, waving their arms about and laughing . . . Now Zybin too smiled at them, young and handsome as they were, as he sat on the edge of his chair and peered at them past the portraits of Yezhov and Stalin.

"What's that drifting in from the sea?" she asked, halting. "What a peculiar smell! Can you smell it?"

"Yes," he answered, inhaling the salty tang of the air. "It smells of the sea and dried-out fish. See all the seagulls? They've dragged it along here."

Just then a large white bird with a black cap and leaden grey wings flew directly over them.

"It's their canteen here on the shoals," he said. "Look at them splashing. And the row they make! As if they were rinsing out their washing! That's where the smell comes from."

"Sea and fish?" she asked.

"Sea and fish," he replied.

"No, but how marvellous it is here!" she cried, stopping. "Look, never mind your crab, just let's wander along the shore."

He meant to say something in reply, but just then from somewhere outside, from beyond the looking glass, from the dark depths of another existence, where there was no sea or sky, just a desk, chairs, and portraits on the naked walls, a cool, sharp voice rang out: "What's this? Came here to sleep? Why's that then? Let's have no more of it." The secretary was sitting at the desk staring fixedly at him.

Khripushin was coming through the door.

CHAPTER 6

F ROM THAT DAY FORWARD, the conveyor entered fully into Zybin's existence; that same infallible method which the celebrated jurist, Hippolytus of Marseilles had discovered in 1550, and which had later been deftly put into practice by Alexander's gendarmes in the 1860s. A directive covering the application of this and similar methods had been issued by the Leader and they had been given an ideological basis by the Prosecutor General and the secretary of the Central Committee, Yezhov. They had been elaborated upon by modest practical men, republic people's commissars, investigators in the state security directorate, law philosophy professors, heads of departments and doctors. Except that at this time nobody yet called these doctors "killers in white coats"; that title still awaited them.

The whole day, from eight in the morning (the office was filled with sunlight at these times; the old poplars beneath the window hissing like sea foam; birds flitting everywhere in the neighbouring children's park, orioles calling, a gentle breeze ruffling the papers), the investigator and himself, with an hour's break for lunch, sat opposite one another in silence. But keeping silent all the time wasn't allowed either, and so about four times a day, Khripushin fairly hurled himself out of his chair; he jumped up, went red, then purple, thumped his fist on the desk and swore savagely – for the people next door to hear. The prisoner responded in kind, though more quietly, so the people next door wouldn't hear. Thus they cursed one another for twenty minutes or so and cordially hated one another for that period. After that, as if at a signal, they lapsed wearily into silence from then on. Both of them were heartily sick of all this, but there was nothing they could do – such were the implacable rules of the game they had entered upon. So matters proceeded till evening, and when the windows turned mother of pearl, and different, nocturnal birds began singing in the park, a cheerful Khripushin would switch on his lamp and call in the alarm clock. "Now this time, make sure you write something! Otherwise we shall have to have a little talk!" he would say breezily to Zybin, then smile at the alarm clock and depart. These nocturnal watches also passed peacefully.

It could well have been different; in the adjoining offices the yelling went on, with intervals, all night long, and although Zybin got lots of different young lads, they conducted themselves, on the whole, in identical fashion. Apart from a few "confess, confess, when are you going to confess?" "Come on, let's stop messing about, here's the paper – get writing!" – apart from these perfectly peaceable and obligatory refrains, the lads undertook no other investigatory talk. On the other hand, they were vastly interested in non-investigatory questions. ("Is it true our scientists have discovered a wild woman in the Taiga? Is it true that Alexander the Great's tomb has been dug up in the valley of the Syr-Darya and they found forty lorryloads of gold in there? How are people executed in the electric chair? Does hypnotism really exist or is it just a myth? Who was Mata Hari? The man in the iron mask? Azef?). True, some of them began by attempting to din some political sense into the layman Zybin, why people like him simply could not be tolerated in a developed socialist society, why it was called socialist legality and what would happen in five years time when capitalism would remain perhaps, only across the ocean (that was when he, Zybin, would be released), but after five minutes, the conversation had got into such a hopeless dead end that the alarm clock either resorted to frantic newspaper demagoguery and lapsed into an angry silence or admitted that they hadn't got to this bit in their course. There had been one disagreeable episode, nevertheless.

That evening, when Khripushin summoned the alarm clock, there arrived a gaunt middle-aged man, with a sallow, pinched face and swiftly darting eyes. He wore a tightly buttoned black field shirt and leggings. He came in without any books, but with a large typed list of telephone numbers. Glancing at him, Zybin thought, no, he's nothing like an alarm clock – probably an investigator, or maybe even a duty man on the investigative block. When Khripushin went out (which he seemed to do very swiftly, without his usual parting thrust) the alarm clock went behind the desk, put the telephone list in front of him, rang somewhere to advise them that he was in place, then looked at Zybin and asked simply: "Well, aren't you fed up with this?"

Zybin said he was, very much so.

"Well, let's have done with it," cried the alarm clock or investigator peevishly. "Here's the paper and pen, sit up to the desk and write."

Zybin said he would be glad to write, but there was nothing to write.

"How do you mean, nothing? Why are you sitting here then? For vile anti-Soviet activity that's why? So that's what you write about! Run through the organizations you've been a member of! Well?"

Zybin shrugged and went through them – he had joined the pioneers organization, then the education workers trade union, and OSOV-IAKHIM.

"My, my, we've got a clever one here!" the alarm clock broke into a laugh. He got up, put his hands in his pockets and came over to Zybin. "No, those are all our organizations. You tell me about yours, the coun-ter-revolutionary ones." (Zybin shrugged mutely.) "Now why go hunch-ing yourself up like that. This isn't the place for doing that, it's the place for talking." He moved up very close and hung over him, face to face – "Well? Come on. How long may I ask are we going to play dumb here? Don't turn away, don't you turn away!" he snarled suddenly. "Look people in the face when you're spoken to, damned contra! Why are you hiding your eyes? When you were selling your own Soviet Union to the Japanese, you didn't hide them then, I don't suppose? You looked them right in the eye!" He braced his knee against Zybin's and bared his teeth like a maddened cur. "And why've you spread your legs like an old whore? Now then on your feet! Up you get when you're told!"

"Look," Zybin straightened his legs and began peaceably, in a patient formal-sounding voice. "I would ask you all the same . . ."

"On your fe-e-t! I'll ask you! I'll ask you all right, bastard!" Then suddenly he lost control, swung back his leg and crashed a boot straight into Zybin's knee.

At once a searing, fiery pain ran right through Zybin. He probably lost consciousness for a moment. The blow had fallen full on an old scar, a bone-swelling so painful that since childhood Zybin had been unable to kneel on it. For a minute he sat motionless, awash with the pain, then gathered his breath, wiped away the tears with his fingers, bent forward and rolled up his trousers. The boot had ripped off the skin. The scar had swollen up and resembled a black caterpillar. Zybin pressed it and drew blood. He sighed and shook his head.

"Don't you dare talk to me like that," bawled the alarm clock, losing his head completely, and drawing his leg back again. "Get up!"

Zybin rose submissively, looked at the alarm clock and suddenly with a lightning gesture, took him by the throat "by the Adam's apple, go for the Adam's apple" as they had shouted in one historical-revolutionary film. Holding him for a second, he drove his knee into his stomach, shook him like a puny rag doll this way and that before catching him underneath the chin and flinging him towards the door. All this took five seconds – precisely and efficiently as he had been taught on the self-defence courses. The alarm clock flew towards the door, struck the frame, and sat down on the floor with a grunt.

Zybin also sat down and wiped the blood away with his palm. For some time both of them said nothing.

"My, my," the alarm clock said from the floor, astonished. He was going to shout something, but was overtaken by a paroxysm of coughing.

"Drink some water," advised Zybin, and half rose to get the decanter.

"Sit down!" barked the alarm clock, getting unsteadily to his feet. Zybin wiped his palm on his trousers and bent over his knee once more.

"If you've damaged my kneecap," he said, his voice suddenly rising to a shout: "Blood! You've drawn blood! See what you've done, degenerate! See the blood! Ah you miserable little shit!"

The alarm clock hissed apprehensively, leapt to his feet and braced his back against the door. But it was already being pushed.

He stepped away.

"What's happened, captain?" came a calm, deep voice, and a handsome, grizzled old man with a white quiff appeared, wearing military uniform. He was portly and resembled one of Catherine the Great's grandees – it was Major Puikan, head of department. Zybin came to attention, his knee was bare and bloody.

"It's just he took it into his head to act the goat," replied the investigator bad-temperedly, recovering himself immediately. "He worked himself into a fit. I'll call the doctor, he'll be all right shortly! I'll have him in the straitjacket! He's hurt his knee, just fancy . . . !"

"Is this the same one?" the old man asked, scrutinizing Zybin.

"Yes the same one! Scholar! You won't get away with this! You won't play the guerrilla with me! With me here, you'll heal up like a dog! It's all right, what's a knee! It's all right!"

"Yes, we've heard about his exploits, indeed we have," said the old man significantly and went out.

The captain waited until the door had closed, then returned to the desk. He sat down and asked: "Do you know what'll happen to you for that?" (Zybin said nothing). "Roll your trousers down. You'll go straight to the punishment cell from here." ("Good God," thought Zybin, "they won't do that will they? Wish I'd got my sleep out!") "Roll your pants down when you're told!"

"Just one word: if you hit me again . . . ," said Zybin gently.

"Then I'll hit you," the investigator cut in recklessly, "I'll do it a hundred times. And smash your face in, what will you do about it? Eh? Eh?" However he did not stir from his chair.

"It will turn out badly," promised Zybin, quietly intense. "Very badly. I'll land you with the reputation of somebody who gets thrashed! They'll chase you out of here tomorrow with a club! Thrashed!"

"Swineface! Talk, but spare me the crap!" shouted the investigator.

"No need to yell, you old goat, I'm not deaf!" shouted Zybin. The investigator at once deflated.

"All right," he promised ominously. "I'll show you something tomorrow. Roll them down, your pants, down," he said suddenly in quite a different tone. "Women pass through here you know, it's embarrassing! Started scrapping, a scholar! Let them down!"

It was true, during these night shifts a woman had appeared in the office a number of times. It was always the same secretary. And each time she came, beautiful, slender, smartly dressed, smiling discreetly as she asked the alarm clock something, Zybin always caught her glance. Now she stared at him directly, intently, without dissembling. And he felt embarrassed and fidgeted; he was a real eyesore at this moment – grubby, unshaven, cut about. He couldn't make out what the glance betokened at all: sympathy? An unspoken question? Or just feminine curiosity – what sort of beast are you?

Later, in the sleepless nights, sitting on that chair, he mused: "Have I come not come across her somewhere in the city? But it seems not; I've never met her."

CHAPTER 7

BUT NEITHER THE PUNISHMENT cell nor the straitjacket followed. Indeed nothing else followed at all. Khripushin turned up in the morning as usual – fresh, showered, mellowed overnight – and the captain departed. Khripushin kept repeating something to himself, laughing briefly, then doffed his short waterproof and hung it on the metal stand. Someone correctly wrote recently that the short topcoat served almost as a uniform for the security organs at that time. He made for his chair and sat down, then, levering himself erect, he asked quickly: "Well, hero, thought up anything overnight? No, you've got a bright head on you, but it got landed with an idiot's body, that's right isn't it?"

Then, once again, the long, hot, senseless day dragged on. They sat opposite one another, exchanging listless abuse, conversing fleetingly, and sometimes lost sight of each other for ten or fifteen minutes at a stretch – one dozing off while the other pretended to write or read something.

In the evening, a fresh alarm clock appeared, and another the next night – and they weren't captains, not duty officers, just lads of twenty, twenty-three – ill-tempered and kindly, taciturn and talkative, obtuse and keen-witted.

So another three nights passed.

Sleeplessness, soft and sinuous, shrouded the zek's brain. Everything became unreal, trance-like – everything began to slide away in layers, like a pack of cards, noiselessly spilling along glass. He moved and had his being in a strange kind of space – slightly displaced and skewed, as if through a crystal. The air seemed dense and had a dark-blue tinge, like the interior of a smoky log cabin. Everything became edged with sleep and reached him through cotton wool. That was a help – nothing roused him to bristling fury; on the whole, he felt a total indifference. It was only when Khripushin assailed him with foul language that his response mechanisms seemed to switch on automatically: probably it was the ancient cave bear of instinct that bristled and roared. The beast had realized that he was not to be assaulted here. If they struck him once, they would do it again, and a thousand times more, until they killed him. Because now it was not even a matter of a blow, it was the question: "Look, what if we try this on you?" Then came the answering roar: "Just try it!"

The pain in his knee grew and grew. It was hard to sit, but when Khripushin asked him what was the matter with his knee, Zybin simply answered that he had hurt himself.

"How come you're always hurting yourself?" Khripushin shook his head and despatched Zybin to the sick room under guard.

The sick room was a cool white cell. Spirit lamps glowed and there was a smell of valerian; it was quiet and peaceful. The orderly who bandaged Zybin was a small woman, still young but already hopelessly dried up and constantly besieged by golden flies. Then, from behind a screen emerged a handsome young man, with long hair on both sides of his face. His fingers were firm, cold and methodical. All in all, he so much resembled Stankevich or the young Khomyakov, that in response to being asked how he on earth had come to hurt himself in such a way, Zybin was on the point of blurting out the truth. The young man prodded his groin, asking whether it hurt, then said: "Sit and lie down more. I'm excusing you from walking."

"I sit for days on end as it is," Zybin responded, but the young Khomyakov appeared not to understand and went off to the washbasin. Then Zybin was taken back to Khripushin's office, and the same childish game resumed.

This was how it went. (Both sit there, weary, sweating, sick to death of the whole business).

"Well now, whenever are we going to talk?" the investigator asks the zek.

The zek replies: "What about then?"

"About your foul anti-Soviet activities," says the investigator.

"I don't engage in foul activities," answers the zek.

"Then you really think," comes the bored, habitual drawl of the investigator, "that we just go picking up Soviet citizens for no reason at all! Is that it? That doesn't happen with us." A yawn.

"Perhaps," the zek replies with a yawn, "perhaps that doesn't happen with you, but with me that's just the way it's turned out."

"So you really think . . ." and in dull, habitual fashion, the investigator starts again.

That goes on for another hour or so. Then both of them are finally worn out and lapse into silence. At this point, Khripushin rings for the guard. But still, there was the occasional surprise. Sometimes the investigator was careless and started on the favourite argument of these places: "Nobody gets out of here."

But at this the zek asks swiftly.

"So you mean the Soviet courts never find anybody innocent?"

At once an acute tactical situation is created: there's no saying either "yes" or "no". And the investigator starts yelling . . .

"Don't you dare disparage the proletarian court!" he splutters, "What do you mean, no one is released? Whoever should be released, is released!"

There was once when the investigator referred to the fiery sword. "You have been struck down by the fiery sword!" And this damned zek cut in straight away. "Oho, you be careful about that fiery sword! You know whose it was? It belonged to the Archangel Michael! You've heard of the Union of the Archangel Michael? A coalition of the gendarmes and the dregs of society. 'Smash the Jews and Save Russia'! So watch what you're doing with that sword, won't you?"

But there could be worse.

"Look, stop yelling will you?" the zek requests.

"Decent folk don't get shouted at," thunders the investigator, carried away.

"And speak politely, please."

"It's decent folk that get spoken politely to," the investigator rolls on ecstatically.

"And charge me with something specific for heaven's sake, or let me have a personal confrontation."

"It's decent folk that get personal confrontations," rumbles the investigator. But at this point the zek guffaws, and the investigator falters and shuts up.

Why the questioning went round in absurd circles like this, Zybin was at a loss to understand for quite some time. It was Buddo who explained matters to him. It happened about two hours after the sick room. The telephone rang, Khripushin listened, hung up the receiver and said: "All right, get away and have a rest! After that you're certainly going to talk, you're not dealing with the police, you know."

After the sick room, his leg started paining him in real earnest, and Zybin was limping as he returned to his cell. He entered, sat down on the bed and bared the leg to inspect his knee; its dry heat could be sensed through the dressing. "Well, the sod," he thought, "the miserable bastard, God forbid I should ever run across you again. I'll spill your blood for you in front of everybody, parasite! Perhaps I really should tell them – look, the investigator has used violence on me." He dismissed the notion at once. If he was to start on that, then it should be with the firm intention of pursuing it – hunger strike, calling in the prosecutor, give battle if need be (he realized now that you wouldn't be killed during interrogations – that would mean allowing you to escape). So then, once you started, you had to go on to the bitter end. Apparently it would come to that. But was it worth anticipating events?

An hour later Buddo came back, and was extremely glad to see him. They hadn't seen each other for almost a week.

"Oh yes, you're a real hero!" he shouted, giving him a hug. "After so many days and nights . . . but you signed what they wanted in the end, didn't you?" Zybin shook his head "What? Nothing at all? So why did they let you go, then? Why are you holding your knee?"

"Well, it's . . ." Zybin exposed the knee.

"Great!" Buddo shook his head. "Your baptism of fire! That's a legal bruise all right – wear it with pride, nobody will say a word! How did he do it? The boot, I expect! They enjoy that! How did it happen – did you say something to him or was it, you know, just in the course of active interrogation?"

"Active interrogation," grunted Zybin and offered no further explanations.

Buddo stared at him and sighed heavily.

"Ah, Georgi Nikolaevich, Georgi Nikolaevich!" he said. "That certainly means that they've set about you properly! They've put you on the conveyor, and that's your reward. Things are bad, mate, eh? Really bad. Why force them to it? What's the point?"

"Thanks very much! So it's me forcing them is it?" Zybin grinned derisively.

Buddo pulled an unpleasant face.

"Ah, friend, you'd do better to leave off your silly arrogance and look the plain truth in the eyes. Honestly, that wouldn't do any harm! Arrogance, stubbornness 'don't touch me' – that's all very well when it's legal tender. It's the wrong bank here. It's interrogation here, And not just questioning either – active interrogation. That means that when they ask you, you have to answer – and not any old how, but properly."

"What can I answer? What?" Zybin jumped to his feet. "Let them ask questions and I'll answer. But they don't ask questions, do they? They just rack your soul. 'Confess, confess, confess.' Confess what? Bloody hell, what? You say it and maybe I will confess. But they don't say, the bastards, they just bleed your soul drop by drop."

"Huh!" Buddo sneered. "And just what do you want the bastards to say? You have to tell them because you're a zek. That's what you haven't understood up to now, man. That I can see. It's time you did! Really it is. You listen to me now, and I'll tell you. Our security organs are noted for three things . . . Can I ask you to hear me out without interrupting?"

"Go on, go on," said Zybin, lying down.

"Only if you really don't interrupt. So then, first: they have no doubts as regards the arrested man. There might have been over whether to pull you in or not, but they ended the day before your arrest. Now it's all up. Now you're not only arrested, you're convicted – don't be a donkey, wise up to what's going on and everything will go smoothly for you and for the investigator. And don't snarl at him, why do that? It wasn't him who brought you here, and it won't be him who lets you go. He's just a dogsbody – he prepares your case and passes you on . . . ! But filling out documents is no easy matter either. There are lots of forms and every one has its own shade of meaning. Let's suppose everybody here is a counter-revolutionary – all right! But the propagandist has his own distinctive features, the spy another, the wrecker a third sort. Here everything has to accord with the directives – acquaintances, things said, nationality, who he drinks with, lives with, all of it, all of it!

"In a nutshell," sneered Zybin, "I'm not an individual, I'm a criminal, defined in advance, like a beetle in a reference book – such and such feelers, wings, wing-cases, mandibles. Defined and pinned down, right?"

"It may be in your language, scientifically speaking, I don't know. But as regards being a criminal, you're wrong again. You're not a criminal, you're a person, is-o-lated from society. Because, man – and this is the second principle – you are harmful, doubtful, non-Soviet."

"Whose am I then?"

"The lord knows who you are, and whose; well, probably those gentlemen who sit there abroad and jeer at us. Chamberlain, Lord Curzon, Mister Ford – the capitalist sharks."

"And where did you get the idea that I was like them?"

"I didn't, they did – from your whole attitude. Your whole manner: you're not straightforward, you make game of people, crack jokes, play with words. But what's there to laugh at, though? There's nothing to laugh at at this moment! We live in a serious time. They can laugh out there, walking about in the parks, and you no doubt are given to laughing behind closed doors. With company! That's not done – suspicious! And altogether . . . Now tell me straight: do you acknowledge that our leaders

– are the absolutely genuine power of the people? And that no other either has been or will be? Do you admit that or not? Straight, now, straight . . ."

"Let's organize a vote and ask the people, after all, who am I to talk?"

"There's your demagogue! Ask the people! He isn't the people. Yes, yes, it's true, you're not the people; the people trusts its authorities, but you're a sceptic, a grumbler; you go about, winking and sniggering. And if you don't believe, you could lead others astray – even worse if, God forbid, there was a war on. It was written somewhere years and years ago: 'Woe unto him who shall offend one of these little ones'. There! And the Leader has remembered those words from that time. That means you're a dangerous individual. Leaving you in society would be risky – you have to be isolated. So they isolate you. Via the judge advocate to the SB. Is that just? According to classical jurisprudence, no; but according to revolutionary notions of legality – absolutely. Is it humane? In the highest degree! The aim after all is easily stated! The felicity of future generations!! For that nothing is too high a price to pay!"

"For who to pay? You?"

"Not for me! Not for me! I'm as much an enemy as you are! For the best minds, the conscience of mankind, Romain Rolland, Feuchtwanger, Maxim Gorky, Shaw, Aragon, they are ready to pay! They are men of fortitude, they're not frightened of blood. Why are you grinning like that?"

"It's all right! You have an original way of putting it!"

"No, no, dear man, for us, the old intelligentsia, it's not original at all. It was promised to us long ago, though we didn't repose all that much faith in it. 'He who is not with us is our enemy, he must fall.' They used to sing that little song to us back in 1905! Yes, and who sang it? Nadson's friend! The Symbolist poet Minsky! And a proletarian writer of genius, Gorky, added in our own day: 'If the enemy does not yield, he is to be destroyed.' Well, you aren't yielding! You kick up a row, you work on that bruise of yours! Only an inveterate enemy behaves like that, so therefore . . ."

"No, no, I agree," Zybin laughed and waved this away. "If it can all really be boiled down to that, I agree with you."

"But you still doubt that it has all been boiled down precisely to that long ago? You're wrong! No, that's not correct, of course. That's where the essence of your hostility lies, therefore you have to be destroyed, or, more gently – we are humane after all, the only true humanitarians!

– isolated! Good; if you've got that so far, we proceed. What can possibly be the point of interrogation at all in that case? Well, one reason I've already mentioned – bureaucracy, the clerical work. The case must have a completely finished look to it. So that it can be shown to anybody, even the highest authorities. You've seen what's written on the cover of our files? 'Keep permanently!' Oh! Permanently! That word! For ever! So Pushkin may be forgotten, Shakespeare, Byron, all those Shelley-melleys will be forgotten but not us! The finger will be pointed at us enemies for ever! Look, children, that's what enemies were like! . . ."

"But those bastards who made us enemies are going to snuff it as well," Zybin roared at length. "Maybe a bit sooner than us! Skulking rats!"

"Ah, enemy, enemy! – That's what he's thinking about," Buddo laughed. "Posterity! It's our descendants, brother, who'll be pointing their little fingers at us. 'Posterity is a stern judge!' As you once wrote about Derzhavin, or rather Derzhavin wrote it, but you quoted him approvingly. And it's a very apposite quotation. Yes, a stern, severe judge is posterity. And a just one! So then, that stern and righteous judge will pick up your case, ages from now and say: 'They were right to crush my ancestor! Communism couldn't be built out of rubble like that. They got off lightly, even! They wanted to steal our happiness, the mystical, idealist swine!' And the bourgeoisie of the world would also have to shut up if your little folder gets into their clutches by any chance. Everything there has been proved and signed, all legal safeguards satis-fied, presumption of innocence – there at the very beginning. The criminal confessed under the weight of overwhelming proof! Great investigative and operational skill is displayed on every page. We are true humanists, nice gentlemen. Man is the most precious thing on earth to us. We don't simply grab people. We are people experts, as the great Gorky put it. One hundred per cent quality. And so we may picture," – he glanced round and lowered his voice to a superstitious whisper – "what if Comrade Stalin himself should want to look at your case, to check it personally, so to speak – how should it look, eh? That's the thing, isn't it?" He sighed, and after a pause, said judiciously: "That's one side of the business, but there is another."

Buddo got up and began pacing about the cell. The eyehole in the door kept blinking, but he ignored it. He obviously liked the sound of his own voice. In his own trade union circles, he was most likely the life and soul. Now he flowed on like a violin.

"The second side of the question, my dear, sweet and clever Georgi

Nikolaevich, is this: nobody knows your affairs better than you do, right? So reveal them down to the last detail. Why should this Khripushin of yours curtail the investigation? He simply has to get out of you all there is. So that's what he's doing. Who gave you support? Who were the yes-men? Who came up with something himself? Let's have them, then."

"And they do?" asked Zybin. He was sitting on his bed, alert and attentive. All the cotton wool had vanished to be replaced by a razor-sharp apprehension of reality. And he groped after something else, slippery and artful, eluding the fingers – but what it was he could not for the moment identify. He merely sensed it.

"You think they don't? If your head's been chopped off you aren't worried about your hair-parting. Someone who's let himself in for a tenner isn't worried about anybody else they hand over – straight away too, can't be too quick about it. A husband hands over his wife, a son his mother (less often the other way round), brothers do it to brothers, friends to friends – that's quite usual. They destroy each other in personal confrontations. And after that, you know, when they are allowed to meet in the presence of the investigator, oh, the embraces, the weeping! Good grief! They're both doomed, they've both just perished! The informer won't see freedom again either! Sometimes a whole family sits in the same corridor – what's going on? Article 58.11, anti-Soviet organization. Two talked, one listened and said nothing. Two go to the camps, one upstairs to Neiman. And it's precisely this that the third thing stems from. Now, you're asking why the investigator doesn't charge you with anything concrete and just keeps on: 'Talk, talk, tell us!' It's because, friend, a man brought you here, not the holy ghost. A man that you know! More than that – your best friend and brother; he can't be given the third degree, can he? He's as necessary to the country as air – he's noble, trustworthy, tried and tested, effective and oh so welcome anywhere. He should keep working away, cleansing the country of rats and traitors – and you would destroy him in a second. Whisper to a visitor at a meeting, say, 'special greetings to so and so' and a meaningful look and that's that! Nowadays people pick up that kind of thing in a flash. Or a note gets passed out of a camp via a released prisoner – and the game's up again!"

"Yes, yes, that's it!" Zybin got to his feet and paced the cell (the eyehole in the door was flesh-pink, someone was standing behind it).

"Yes, yes, Alexander Ivanovich! You've explained it all very well! Very well! . . . I think I'll turn in for a bit. My head isn't quite . . . My friend and brother! And my brother is Cain!: 'Cain! Cain! Where is thy brother Abel?' And Cain answered the Lord: 'Am I my brother's keeper?' "

He came awake to a sharp metallic click. The knock of a key against the metal cladding of the metal door. He jerked upright. Buddo was standing over him and shaking him. The eyehole was drawn back. The face of the guard stood behind it.

"Now if you lie down again," he said, "you'll go to the punishment cell."

"What for?" asked Zybin.

"For contravening the rules and regulations. There's the directive hanging on the wall. Read it!" And the soldier slammed the window-slot.

They said nothing for some time after that.

"Yes," Buddo wagged his head, "they drive you to the limit! Ah, Georgi Nikolaevich! Why wage your guerrilla warfare, why stick your neck out for nothing? What for – I just don't understand!"

Zybin sat down on his bunk and felt his knee.

"Why am I sticking my neck out? Well, by all means, I'll explain it to you," he said thoughtfully. "You see a historian told me a curious thing. After the February revolution he was working for the commission looking into the affairs of the Tsarist secret police. They were chiefly interested in the list of agents of course. For every agent a personal file had been opened. So these folders were almost full, but one of them was empty, except for a scrap of paper, a letter. A certain young man was putting himself forward as an agent, salary negotiable. This letter had arrived the day before the uprising. All right: the members of the commission read it, had a laugh and didn't proceed to arrest him solely for an intention – but they did publish it! And then for about two years until the historian lost sight of him, this wretched little student walked about with the newspaper trying to justify himself: 'I'm not really a provocateur, I never did anything, I was just thinking about it . . .' And everybody laughed. Tfu! Better if they really had put him in jail! See what I mean?"

"No, not altogether," Buddo shook his head. "Could you clarify it please: you say the letter was sent the day before . . . So you think . . ."

"There you are, already jumping to conclusions! No, no, I don't think anything. Don't compare things! This is something quite different. This young man wrote a dirty little bit of paper against himself and lost his peace of mind permanently. That's like me – what I fear most is losing my peace of mind. I'll survive everything else one way or another, but

213

for me that really would be absolute death and destruction. I'm not at all sure whether I'll ever get out of here, but if I do, I won't give a damn for anything I've seen or been through here; and I'll forget these damned people for ever and a day – because I'll be able to live at peace with myself, not frightened that I've left something in their hands that could at any moment catch me in a steel trap like a rat. Well, and if I don't get out . . . So what? 'Posterity is a stern judge!' And it's that judge I really fear! See what I mean now?"

Buddo made no reply to this. He went over and sat down on his bunk. Zybin did the same, falling into a pensive doze. And as soon as he closed his eyes, there came a knock.

He raised his head. The little window was drawn back, and someone's face was swaying behind it. Then the door opened and two people entered the cell – the duty man and the chief. Zybin jumped up.

"I'm warning you: on your next violation you'll go straight to the punishment cell," said the chief, in measured tones, not angry. "For five days! Second infraction in one day!"

"But I haven't slept for a week!"

"I don't know anything about that," said the chief severely. "But here you're not allowed to sleep during the day. Talk to the investigator."

"You know they don't pay any attention to us."

"I know nothing about that. My business is following the directive. Here it is. One is not allowed to sleep during the day. Write to the prosecutor." He turned towards the door.

"Wait!" Zybin rushed over to him. "I'll write to him, let me have some paper."

"You'll get it next Tuesday," said the chief steadily.

"No, now! This minute!" Zybin began shouting. "I'll write to the prosecutor. I'll declare a hunger strike! A fast to the death, no water! You hear me?"

"I hear you," frowned the chief evincing faint annoyance, and turned to the duty man. "Five days in the punishment cell for him, after that give him paper and pencil."

So Zybin landed up in the punishment cell. And there for the first time in seven days, he fell asleep on the cement floor.

And the sea once more came to him.

. . . I was terribly clever then, you know. I was so clever. I thought if I put him under my bed he'd keel over and that would be that. Now I can't understand how I could ever have done such a thing. Pain and suffering I understood well. I got thrashed a lot when I was a boy. With a clothesline, till I came up in welts and the blood started flowing. My mother was an extremely cultivated woman, a Bestuzhev Institute graduate. She taught at the gymnasium. She used to attend all sorts of poetry-concert things there; she doted on Severyanin and Balmont. We had Böcklin's "Elysian Fields" hanging in our dining room. I was given zoological atlases and Brehme as presents ("he's certainly going to be a zoologist"). And she thrashed me horribly. Father didn't intervene and used to pretend not to notice anything. And then he died and my stepfather turned up. He gave instructions for me not to be fed – he was even more cultivated, wasn't he?"

"How did you get by then?" she asked softly. They both started at the use of the intimate "thou".

"Oh, if you can imagine it, I didn't get on too badly actually. I had my friends, wrote poetry, very badly of course; at first I imitated Yesenin, then Antokolsky. I liked everything that was high-sounding and lofty. I was permanently on fire with love for some girl in my year. Then I applied for the literature faculty, passed all the exams pretty easily and got in. I hoped they would give me a grant. They didn't. I was from a well-off family: my stepfather was a professor and my mother an assistant professor."

"Did you drink?"

"No, I didn't drink at all in those days. I never touched a drop. I started drinking a lot later. When I had almost graduated. Those were terrible troubled times, you know. The Yesenin mania, bohemianism, the suicide league – oh, yes, even that existed! Three lads from our faculty started the league. They hanged themselves according to lots. Two did it, the third one didn't. You know how they hanged themselves? They didn't hang up anywhere. They throttled themselves with straps lying on their bunks. Ahh!" He suddenly gave a shout of surprise and stopped his narration. "That's it! Now I realize why his face is familiar. He questioned me about those suicides. But that was before the Kravtsova business! Yes, yes! But how could he have forgotten me? Or . . ."

"You're talking about . . ."

"Well, about him, him! He's an investigator, but why on earth didn't he tell me so at once?"

"You know," she took him by the shoulder, "he proposed to me yesterday."

"What!?" he exclaimed, clutching at her shoulder in turn. "To you . . . ? Hell's flames!"

"Yes, last night, after your neighbours took you away from here."

"Marvellous! And what was your answer?"

"I asked him to wait. I said I had to think. I would think about it and give him an answer. Well I have thought."

"And?"

"I'll thank him and say I'm sorry but I can't."

"You can't?"

"No, I can't. I've fallen in love with you! I've just this minute realized I love you! But don't you go thinking you've made me sorry for you! No, no! In fact, you shouldn't have started on all that nasty stuff to me. Now I'll have it on my mind all the time! But there is something in you . . . A kind of poison, maybe. I'm not one of your susceptible types – no, no, not at all! And I'm not a sucker for any of that lyric stuff or confessions. But you fell in love with me so wonderfully easily, you didn't notice it yourself. And now you don't know what in the world to do with me."

"No, I don't," he laughed.

"No, and you're so impossibly frank as well! That's something really horrid about you. Good. Tomorrow we'll think up something together. Don't start thinking yet."

They walked on a few paces in silence.

"Listen," he said suddenly, coming to a halt. "Now you've just said you love me. I love you too. So then what? Hugs and kisses? I don't feel like doing that. Not in the mood for that at all!"

She laughed very quietly, hugged him, planted a kiss on his cheek and said: "No, no, everything's all right. And there's the sea. Let's get the crab!"

The crab had been sitting under the bed for a week – he sat in exactly the same place, near one of the legs and whenever anyone bent over him, he would thrust out a serrated pincer in impotent menace. On the third day, a white foam appeared near his feelers, but when Zybin touched him, he nipped his finger extremely painfully and drew blood. At this, Zybin shifted the crab with his foot. There he sat, and later on, lay. On day five, white patches developed on his eyes, but as soon as Zybin laid a finger on him, he threw forward the same terrifying, helpless pincer (ah, if he had only been able to nip!). Something akin to mould appeared on the carapace. On the morning of day seven, Zybin said to Lina: "I can't go on – I'm going to release him tonight." She replied: "I want to be there." They arranged to meet on the shore close to a little café, where the three of them had sat the day before, before his neighbours had dragged him away to sort out some kind of argument in the block. When she arrived that evening, he was already sitting waiting for her. The crab was in his hat. It was getting dark by now and the lighthouse was switched on, as were the green and white lights on the boats. They set off. He said: "You know I never thought I had such a brute inside me! To condemn something to a slow and agonizing death. I never dreamed I could be capable of such a thing. But they take fish from the water and they die. They suffocate as well, of course, but I thought the crab would do the same. What a brute! And what for? All for some stupid female whim!"

"And is she very beautiful, that whim?" Lina asked, linking arms with him.

"Yes, not bad. But you're much better."

"Heavens," she actually stopped, "you aren't capable of noticing that are you?"

"Rest assured! I most certainly am! But that's not the point. She may be the most beautiful of women, Mary Pickford, the Queen of Holland, what of it? The point is that I'm a brute. Probably Mama was right when she said: 'I'm going to teach you what humanism is, you little sadist!' as she reached for the rope. There you are!" He laughed and shook his head.

"I'd never have thought anyone could have called you that."

"You didn't! No I was called that about ten years ago, and I kept thinking they were wrong. They were preparing me to become a zoologist and what sort of zoologist can't dissect a frog? But that doesn't matter, childish, but now . . . I was ever so clever when I bought the crab. How clever I was. I thought: He'll sit for a while then die like fish do. I should have been able to understand pain. You know how that feels, a rope taken to your arms and legs?"

He had rolled his trousers up to the knees and walked into the water. The crab lay in his hat. Lina held the torch on shore.

"Don't you want to come down here?" he asked.

"Yes! In a minute."

She quickly threw her dress over her head and was revealed to be wearing a black one-piece swimsuit.

"Listen," she said, leaning over the hat. "One more day and he would have been done for."

"Yes," he said, "of course! But I couldn't go on any more. Every brutality has a kind of natural limit. And I've crossed that too. Stop, I'm tipping him out."

He bent down and turned the hat over. The waves under the light of the torch were translucent, gentle, almost green, while their light writhing shadows fled away across the white sandy bottom. The crab fell on its back and stayed like that."

"Dead," said Lina.

"Yes," he agreed heavily. "Too late, yesterday . . ."

"Look, look!"

First the legs began working – not all of them, just one or two, then the movement spread to all of them. The crab turned itself over slowly, then stood up, relaxing and recovering himself. He stood there, huge and clumsy, gathering his strength, the water stirring his feelers. Somehow all the white patches had vanished at once.

"He's going to live," said Zybin firmly.

A tiny fry swam in, flashed like a blue spark, was consumed in the light of the torch and vanished.

Then the crab moved. He went off ponderous and squat, like a tank. He swayed slightly as he made his way along for a time, then halted.

"He'll live."

"He will."

Just then the crab with an imperceptible, lateral, purely crab-like movement, shuffled sideways to where lay a large, flat, greenish-white rock. He stood next to it, moved his pincers and at once vanished. There was only the ribbed sand, the motley-coloured pebbles and some threads of slender dark-green seaweed waving to and fro – that and the light of the torch over the water and the bright circles on the sea-bed, the shadows of the ripples on the sand and the rock, slippery with blue algae, under which the crab had gone.

"Well that's it," said Zybin. "Let's go!"

"Let's go," she said, and in a womanly fashion all her own, half-expectant, half mocking, turned to look at him. At that, he suddenly seized hold of her and carried her to the shore. He lifted her clear and carefully set her down. "Well, and have you decided yet what you're going to do with me?" Lina asked, laughing. He joined in the laughter. Then suddenly clutched her and began kissing her thrown-back face, neck, chin, the soft pit by the throat. A kind of brake was released, a kind of pause broken and he was himself again.

He was laughing now, dirty and unshaven, lying on the damp cement floor under the dazzling white light. The light here was so strong it penetrated even through his hands. But the walls, covered in white varnish, shone like a mirror, so that in ten minutes, matt rainbows began to rise.

But he was not looking at them. He was looking somewhere inside himself. He knew everything now. And was serene.

"And keep in mind, whatever else you may dream up in there," he said loudly to the soldier who peeped in at the eyehole, "whatever damned tricks you come up with, bastards! . . . Not you, of course, not you!" he hastily assured the soldier – "What are you? You're just as much a prisoner as I am! We'll get out together too! And we'll show them a thing or two! Have faith in me – I'm lucky! You and I are certainly going to show them!"

He winked at the soldier and began to laugh.

III

"A nail from the cross"

CHAPTER 1

He died and at once opened his eyes. But he was
already a dead man and saw as a dead man.

GOGOL

KORNILOV WAS LATER TO recall these days very frequently. All that was irreparable, grim, terrifying and shameful in his life started at precisely this point.

It was a Saturday; he let the workmen off early, ran down the hillside and plunged several times into the icy water of the Alma-Atinka, snorting and snuffling; after rubbing himself red with a shaggy towel, he ran back up the slope in his underpants and burst into the tent, fresh and full of spirits; he got dressed, put the kettle on and opened the latest issue of *Foreign Literature*. In the story he was reading, the people were ordinary, just like everybody else and very unlike anybody at all; ordinary words were uttered, prosaic actions performed. And yet, all this everyday and mundane activity sounded absolutely extraordinary here and Kornilov couldn't make head or tail of what was going on.

And so, seated in front of his stove, he read one page, then the next and became lost in thought. All of a sudden, it felt as if someone had pushed him. He jerked his head up and saw Dasha. She was standing looking at him, her headsquare skewed to one side.

"Uncle Petya wants to see you," she said.

"What's up, then?" he asked, leaping to his feet. Long afterwards, he realized that throughout those days, a presentiment of impending disaster had dwelt inside him, and the sight of Dasha made him aware that it was now at hand.

"I don't know, somebody rang him from town." Dasha replied. "He came back from the office and said: 'Run'. There was no sign of you during all this."

Kornilov stood there for another second, mulling over the possibilities, then carefully placed the book on the camp bed, and turned the stove off. "Let's go," he said.

223

He ran all the way. As soon as he went in to see Potapov, however, he recovered himself. Everything here was as usual. The "lightning" lamp glowed. On the glossy oilcloth near the self-important samovar, stood bottles and small glasses. Next to the host, by now somewhat animated, two men were sitting – a forester with a woodsprite's beard and a bandaged throat (he'd got a dose of shotgun pellets from behind some bushes). The other was a dashing, moustachioed building-site foreman, covered in bits of hemp. They had all had a few and looked like young eagles. "Tak-taki-tak," went the ancient tin clock with the fiery view of Borodino, "tak-taki-tak". It was this chirring which Kornilov found most reassuring of all.

"And now our scientific department has arrived," said the host, looking as if the scientific department had been the only thing lacking to complete the party. "Sit down, sit down, scientist, we'll deal you in directly." He lifted the bottle, inspected it against the light and waggled it slightly. "Young mistress," he shouted genially, "why don't you take care of your loved ones, eh? You can see there's only a bit left in the bottom. Her heart and soul's in those bits of pot," he turned to his guests, "we don't hear about theatres now: the pots have it. That's right isn't it, Dashutka?"

The visitors buzzed in high good humour as a decanter and glasses appeared on the table.

"Now that's more like it," Potapov was appeased. "See, for you it's in a decanter." He poured out a brimming glassful and lifted it carefully with two brown horny fingers and carried it towards Kornilov. "Try that Vladimir Mikhailovich," he said deferentially. "My special lemon peel brew. Smell it? Drink it for your health. Medicinal purposes!"

Potapov was talking amiably enough and looking at Kornilov with an easy, good-natured little grin, and yet a puzzling note kept edging into his voice. Kornilov said that he didn't feel like a drink: he'd just eaten.

"Now, now, turning down my bounty?" The host was quietly surprised. "No, that sort of thing isn't done here. Please, don't cause offence." (Kornilov looked at him and drank.) "That's the way, now, and good health," approved Potapov. "And now a bite to go with it. Here's a little herring! Melt in your mouth! With a bit of onion. Like in the Metropole. You've got a restaurant in Moscow called that? You have, I know! When we were ordered back from the front in '18, we had herring and millet there. We really tucked in! See, they were talking about the metro as early as that."

"You sent for me?" Kornilov asked him.

"I did, I did," Potapov replied good-naturedly. "I sent Darya over. I just don't know what kept her so long. Firstly – now, another drink and a bit of herring! . . . That's the way. Good man! Yes, first off I wanted to bring it over, but the second thing is, I want a couple of words with you, dear friend. Are you what, on your own, no higher-ups. Are they in Alma-Ata?"

"Yes, what of it?"

"They've made a discovery on their own. Ilya Muromets' sword. It was raining, the hillside was washed away and it stuck up out of the clay. Tell him," he nodded to the forester.

Sprite-beard touched his throat and said huskily: "A very remarkable sword. The point's a little bit bent but the guard's intact. Got palm trees on it!"

"Have you got it with you?" Kornilov enquired.

"No. The warden took it away. He's promised to fetch it back before dinner tomorrow. His son's at teacher training college; going to be a historian. I'll tell you what it's like! . . ." He was about to turn to Kornilov, but Potapov gestured at him.

"Now why go into the details," he said, annoyed. "When he brings it back, then there'll be some point in talking." He extracted an ancient monogrammed watch from his pocket, opened it and said: "Well dear comrades of mine, let's have one for the road . . . and you stay here now," he instructed Kornilov quietly.

Everyone quickly drank up and went out into the passage. There they carried on talking of their own concerns, lit up cigarettes and cursed someone roundly. Suddenly a horse neighed, the gates slammed and the forester galloped off. Potapov stood out in the yard for some time then came back into the room, walked straight to the table, sat down and glanced at Kornilov.

"The thing is," he said, "Georgi Nikolaevich has been arrested."

"Wha-at?" Kornilov jumped up, realizing that this was precisely what he had been expecting.

"Quiet, don't shout! Get sat down! Yes, they've arrested him. He turned up on the Ili for some reason; whether he was intending to run away or not I don't know. That's where they picked him up. They've sealed up his flat in his absence and carted away a whole sackful of papers. That's it." He had said his piece and now clammed up.

"Why is he telling me all this? Provocation? Threat? Trying to scare me? Warn me?" All of this somehow rushed through Kornilov's mind simultaneously.

"How do you . . . ?"

Potapov wrinkled up his face unpleasantly.

"If I say it, I know it," he answered reluctantly. "Clara Fazulaevna rang in on her own. They were picked up together on the Ili. They dropped her off in town and took him on to the jail. That's the way it is."

"A threat? A provocation?" But a glance at Potapov's disconsolate and somehow extinguished face was enough to make Kornilov realize it was neither one nor the other. He was simply at a loss; he was afraid and didn't know what to do.

"Good God almighty!" he said despondently. "Real trouble."

Potapov's eyes gave a sudden flash of their former wicked glint. He even grinned.

"There now," he said with a certain grim satisfaction. "You've started praying, like we all do when the knot reaches the arse. Until then, of course, we don't need anybody, God, Tsar or hero. We can handle everything on our own. But God, it seems, is just a wee bit cleverer than we are. Bit more of a head on him. Ju-ust flicks us a pebble in the forehead and we go belly up." He paused and sighed. "So then our Keeper has come a cropper, so he has. He's disappeared! Just you wait, you'll be called in soon."

"What for?"

"What do you mean what for?" Potapov said, surprised. "For questioning! They'll start asking you what he said, how he said it and what he was trying to put across." He looked at Kornilov and abruptly put a suspicious question. "And what about you? Sure you know nothing about it? You haven't been called in anywhere, have you? Wait a minute! You went to town on your own; said you'd stayed in the museum. But Zybin came and said: 'I don't know about him staying in the museum. Probably hunting skirt, I never saw him there!' "

"Surely you don't seriously think if I knew something I wouldn't have told Georgi Nikolaevich?" said Kornilov in astonished indignation.

"Well, if you had told him, you know where you'd be now?" Potapov interrupted him harshly. "How could you have told him? What right would you have had? What about your signing the state secrets form? And ten years for divulging them? Pull the other one, you'd have told him indeed!" He sat for some time before concluding: "Well, if they haven't pulled you in yet, just wait. They will."

"Yes," Kornilov nodded cheerlessly. "They certainly will now. Look, Ivan Semyonovich, pour me a drop more will you?"

226

"Here! But eat something with it. There's some fat bacon, cut yourself a bit. And if they do want you, don't worry about it. There's nothing to be afraid of. It's not that fascist Gestapo, they're our Soviet security organs! Lenin's Cheka! Tell the truth and nothing will happen to you, see: the truth, and that's it!" And he repeated the word several times insistently.

"I understand," sighed Kornilov. "The truth, the whole truth and nothing but the truth. Not deviating from the truth. They'll knock nothing but the truth out of me now, Ivan Semyonovich. However much they bawl and bang their fists, or use them."

"What are you on about?" Potapov was slightly stunned at this. "You're mad ... no, don't go inventing things you're not asked to! What do you mean, bawl and bang their fists? Nobody can yell at you there. They're our Soviet organs. Well of course if you distort the truth ..."

"No, I don't intend to bend the truth any more!" Kornilov grinned. "I did it once and that's enough!"

"When was that?" Potapov said anxiously.

"Don't worry: a long time ago. Not all that long ago actually, but before Alma-Ata anyway. Now – enough of that."

He sat quiet and resolute in front of Potapov. He really was unafraid. There was simply nothing that could frighten him by now.

"The things I said about myself!" he grinned. "Fair frightens me to think of it! I just scrawled my name on everything he put in front of me. He says: 'This is what your mates have testified against you: listen and I'll read it out.' And he did, the sod! All the unsolved abominations that had piled up in our district over the summer, he put them all down to my account. Whatever daftness a drunk had got up to, it was all down to me. And not just done it, there'd been agitation behind it. I'd pulled down the flag, drawn horns on somebody, smashed the party activists' window, it was all me, me, me! He was sympathetic: 'Now you see how your best mates have testified against you. Buried you good and proper, the bastards. So listen to some good advice from me, mug, lay down your arms! Get down on your knees before it's too late, and confess. Write: I am guilty of it all but I have confessed and I swear that there will be no repetition. That way you'll see freedom again. The Soviet system has pardoned worse crimes. If not, all right, nine grams of lead won't bankrupt the republic. If the enemy does not yield, he must be destroyed. Know whose words they are?' So, mostly because of those words, I signed everything."

"And you hadn't . . ." Potapov asked, bewildered.

"Heavens! I'd never been near those places. I hadn't been in Moscow at all that summer."

"But how come you believed all that? You knew your mates . . ."

"How could I not believe him?" Kornilov laughed. "I couldn't disbelieve him, could I? He was the investigator after all, and I was a prisoner, a criminal. So how can an investigator lie to a prisoner? It's the prisoner who lies to the investigator, who catches him, accuses him and pins him to the wall, that's the way I thought of it. If everything got turned upside down, what would happen? There'd be nothing left of the state! And how can an investigator act like a ruffian in broad daylight – in front of everybody, the prosecutor, the typists, his colleagues? They're forever in and out; they see and hear everything. No, no, nothing of the sort could have occurred to me. I thought of it this way: they really have blackened my character and I'm done for. The only decent man in all this was – the investigator. I had to do what he told me. It was understandable that he should shout at me: he didn't believe me either, there was too much against me." He sighed. "My trouble is, Ivan Semyonovich, that my father was a lawyer, and he left two cupboards full of law books; I like a fool read through them all. Never mind! I don't resent that sod of an interrogator! He taught me a lesson for life. I'm grateful to him."

"Yes," said Potapov thoughtfully. "Yes, he did! And that: 'If the enemy doesn't yield . . .' Maxim Gorky said that?"

"Yes."

Potapov sighed.

"Strong words. When Agafya, Pyotr's wife went to the investigator, that was the first thing he came out with. And in school those were the words they accused Dashutka with at the Komsomol meeting. Yes, yes, Gorky! So he knew what he was talking about didn't he?"

"Of course he did."

"Yes, yes he did!"

Potapov remained sitting, lost in thought, then suddenly rose to his feet.

"Wait a minute, sounds like somebody walking about." He went outside. "It's you, is it?" Kornilov heard him say. "What are you up to? I'll put a hen house up for you! And a few layers! Get to bed!"

He marched about a bit more, shut the gates, stamped about in the passage, came back in and sat down to the table, unhurried and grave.

He extracted his pipe, knocked it out against his palm, filled it and lit up.

"So the upshot was that you got confused and confused your investigator as well," he said, firm and harsh, in the tone of a man who has at last seen the light. "For that, of course, you were bound to be punished with all due severity; you got what you deserved, but now we don't have an enemy of the people like Yagoda in charge; we have the Stalinist people's commissar Nikolay Ivanovich Yezhov. He wouldn't injure an innocent person. So you can drop all that!"

"Oh, I already have." Kornilov sighed and stood up. "Well, I'm off, Ivan Semyonovich. I've to be up early tomorrow. Thanks for the hospitality."

Potapov gave him an uncertain look.

"Hold on a minute," he said, scowling. "Just sit down, sit down. Now Dashka used to go running over to your place and there were plenty of names named. You shot your mouth off all over the place, and she's a daffy young thing in any case. No wonder the Komsomol used to tell her off. She goes mentioning Uncle Petya and what did we know about him? They came and picked him up and who's going to explain the whys and wherefores, eh?"

"That's the holy truth of it, Ivan Semyonovich," Kornilov confirmed. "No, Dasha never said anything when she was with us. That's what I'll say and they'll all back me up. Well, so long."

He was already beyond the gates when Potapov caught him up again.

"Your director's going to ask you," he said as he came up, "so just, you know, till the proper time, this tittle-tattle of ours today . . ."

"Right," Kornilov answered. "Got it."

"And you watch what you say now . . ."

"Got that as well; since we've been discussing it for nearly an hour, we're both candidates for – that place! Unless of course," he grinned, "one of us is smart enough to think of running over to the highway and hitching a lift into town."

"Still making a joke of it?" Potapov grinned mirthlessly and sighed.

"Joking, Ivan Semyonovich. Just joking, man. No point in running anywhere now. It's too late."

On his return, he attempted to resume reading, but after a few lines he threw the magazine down again. The story was only getting on his nerves. He lay down on the camp bed, drew a blanket over him and closed his eyes. "I wish I had your problems," he thought balefully. "Caribbean pirates, I ask you. Pity there's no booze of course." Was that really the case, though? What time was it? Twelve. Things would be in full swing over at Volchikha's. He turned down the lamp and went out. It was a clear and moonlit night. All around was chirring and ringing. Every creature was working away that night on his own particular wavelength. A bat passed right in front of his face, like a soft cloth. He was passing an old oak-tree where a whole nest of the chamois-leather horrors was keeping up a constant squeaking. Volchikha's large red-curtained window was illuminated. He knocked the stipulated three times and entered. The lady of the house was sitting at a table sewing. He said his hellos and crossed himself in the front right-hand corner of the room. In this hut, as in dozens like it, this never failed to work. On the table stood a bottle, carefully wrapped in newspaper.

"That's not for me by any chance?" Kornilov enquired.

She lifted her head from her sewing and smiled, she was wearing an off-the-shoulder sarafan and looked very youthful indeed (she'd just turned twenty-nine). The picture of a sturdy dark-haired Ukrainian girl.

"We can always find something for you as well," she said affably, biting off her thread with a twang, "but that there is for Andrey Ernestovich." She nodded towards the corner.

Kornilov swivelled round. On a bench by the wall, where two green samovars had stood since time immemorial next to some plywood-covered buckets, sat an old man. Tall, spare and wiry, with a neat, little pointed beard. He wore gold spectacles and had a blanket round his shoulders.

"Oh, I'm sorry, Father Andrey," Kornilov said respectfully, somewhat startled. "I didn't notice you there. How are you?"

"Good evening", responded Father Andrey, raising his frosty sky-blue eyes to Kornilov.

Father Andrey was working on the inventories at the museum. Up till now, however, Kornilov had not had occasion to speak to him. A couple of months previously, the director had taken it into his head to catalogue the museum collections. This was no easy task: a fearful muddle reigned. Exhibits had been deposited in strata, like fossilized species, a picture of successive historical epochs.

The first was the calmest, most peaceful layer.

The Semirechiye Province exhibition of 1907.

Photographs of the zemstva; old eighteenth-century plans of the town of Verny; treaties with the Mongol Hordes, written in ornate Arabic script, with black, white and red seals on the cords; models of fruit and vegetables.

The second layer.

The Provincial museum 1913.

Boots produced by the local factory; postcards of the World Postal Union "Commercial Street, in Verny"; examples of useful minerals; a set of test tubes containing oil.

The third layer.

The Orenburg Territory museum.

Here was the revolution in real earnest: a confused, heterogeneous, explosive stratum – ROSTA window placards, DOWN WITH WRANGEL; bayonets; garish posters with dragons; advertisements, rather like cinema posters – red, green, blue paper, and below, instead of the name of the star the word "Shot" in a playful, curlicued script. Newspaper files. Here too there was peeling, gilded furniture with swan-neck arms, a collection of fans, gilded porcelain, a stuffed bear with a salver for visiting cards in its paws.

The fourth layer.

The devil himself would break a leg in this lot: nobody could sort out what things were there and why, and what was the connection between them. Up in the loft for example there was a wooden case holding Allah alone knew what: it might be insects, it might be icons. In one corner of the galleries, fossils, in another, ancient metal; where these had come from no one knew. But it was a peaceful layer relating to the '20s and '30s. It had been deposited imperceptibly – in boxes, parcels, acquisition lists. So – four layers, and try sorting them all out. Then the director, a swift, decisive, peppery individual took it into his head to establish order army-style, at one fell swoop. He indented for special funds, hired ten inventory clerks, attached Zybin to them as consultant and documentation photographer, and made them write out cards. This was the way those astonishing people, the inventory clerks made their appearance in the cathedral.

During the first days, all the sections went along to have a look at them. The youngest of them had recently turned sixty and had renounced the cloth the previous week in the paper. The director, an old professional atheist, cherished a peculiar kind of fondness for persons of this class, despised and ridiculed as they were by all the posters and wall newspapers. He treated the fathers with respect and deference and constant benevolence. Of them all, this Father Andrey now swathed in the blanket, was his special favourite. "You must get to know him better, comrades," he had advised Zybin and Kornilov. "You won't set eyes on a priest like that again. An academician. Brainbox! Our propaganda brigades will never show you a priest like him! Where could they find one!"

"And what has brought you here, Father Andrey?" Kornilov asked awkwardly, with a sideways glance at his shoulders.

"You mean why am I sitting in this garment?" Father Andrey laughed. "It's turned out rather awkwardly, you see. I caught against a tree in the dark and nearly tore the whole sleeve off. I'm grateful to Maria Grigorievna. She, kind soul, has come to my assistance, as you see."

"I'll sew all your buttons on properly as well," said Volchikha. "As it is they're hanging by a thread."

"I would be extremely obliged," Father Andrey bowed slightly. "I live with my daughter here, comrade Kornilov. In her dacha as it were. She's an agronomist. Today the director sent me with a note to foreman Potapov. Some report he had to submit, and I was supposed to help him to compile it. The trouble is, I've been going round the farm all day but I can't get hold of him. They tell me he's somewhere, then somebody else says he's left. You work in his sector don't you? You haven't seen him?"

"Did you see if he was at home?" asked Kornilov, evading the question.

Father Andrey frowned.

"I went there towards evening. But I must admit I couldn't make up my mind to go in."

"But what . . ."

"He had company."

"So he could have heard what we said," thought Kornilov. He asked: "Did you come across Georgi Nikolaevich on your travels?"

"No, why?"

"I can't think where he's got to . . . Drove into town yesterday, promised to be back by noon today, but there's no sign of him. Of course, a certain lady did come to see him here . . ." This last came blurting out spontaneously somehow; it sounded nastily playful, with a hint of leer. He almost choked from surprise.

"It's high time he did," said Father Andrey. "At his age, I had a large family already – three souls. Of course, it was the rule. In those days the clergy married early."

"Before taking holy orders," suggested Kornilov for some reason.

"Absolutely right. Before consecration. You know about it, then. Still, times have changed of course."

"Yes, times have changed, indeed they have," Kornilov assented stupidly.

The lady of the house laid her sewing on the table, went out into the passage and returned at once with a bottle of vodka.

"Are you paying now?" she asked, picking up the field shirt again and surveying the cuffs.

"I'll drop by tomorrow and settle up. For everything." Kornilov answered.

"Don't make it morning in that case. I'm going into town in the morning," she said. "Your daughter's not looking after you very well, Father Andrey. All your buttons are hanging on by a thread."

"She's a wonderful daughter, Maria Grigorievna," said Father Andrey with quiet feeling. "A real worker. She's been earning for the family since she was fifteen. I wasn't a provider even then. Her husband's a fine chap too. Easy-going, but thoughtful and reserved. Reads a lot. He's doing winter duty on Wrangel Island at the moment, so he's taken a whole library along with him. We're waiting for him to come home on leave this month."

"Then you two will have a real . . ." said Kornilov, smiling obscurely, (it was as if some imp kept on tugging at his tongue).

Father Andrey also smiled.

"Oh, bound to. But he knows his limit. Once he's had enough, that's it. And my daughter won't even touch beer. Wasn't brought up to it."

"What about you?"

"Oh, I'm a sinful man – I learned the way of it in the north. I used to go out on the open sea with the fishermen. You can't get by without it there. You get frozen, wet through, chilled, so hard liquor is the first aid. A good rub down inside as well."

"You didn't drink at all when you were young then?" Kornilov asked sceptically.

"Vodka you mean? Heavens above, no!" Father Andrey shook his head very seriously. "I did drink up what warmth was left in the chalice. Warmth is our priest-talk for the sacramental wine we use in the communion. Well, I used to finish off what was left in the chalice; otherwise – no, God forbid! But nowadays, after the north, I sin, ah how I sin! You can't get the stuff round here – so I came to Maria Grigorievna. Thankfully, she's a kindly soul and doesn't turn me out."

"Why, aren't I a human being too?" asked the lady of the house earnestly. "I'm always glad to see decent people. It's only from you,

Father Andrey that I hear anything worthwhile. From you and his mate. He drops in to see me as well."

"So this is where Zybin used to get himself to," thought Kornilov. "Still, I'll have to go and get my sleep out. The director's bound to call me in tomorrow. He can't stand the sight of me. Well, so what? I'll just tell him I know nothing, I never heard anything, I was working during the day and drinking at night with Father Andrey."

"Dear lady," he said, "how would it be if me and Father Andrey here were to tip back a little glass?"

"I've already said I'm always pleased to see decent people," replied Volchikha, very serious once again. "I'll bring some salted gherkins from the bin. There, that's your clothes, Father Andrey." She went over to a cupboard and took out glasses and a plate. She put the glasses on the table and went out into the passage with the plate. Father Andrey put the shirt on and went over to the mirror and straightened himself up.

And he turned out to be a lean, trim, spruce, almost soldierly old man. He glanced at Kornilov and winked. And suddenly something utterly incomprehensible happened to Kornilov. For an instant, everything went fuzzy, dream-like. He even gave a start. "Good lord," he thought, "why, it's all like that story I was reading. Both truth and lie. It is and it isn't. What on earth's the matter with me? And what am I doing here? At this precise moment? With a priest? And this tavern keeper? Or have I really gone crazy?"

It even occurred to him that all of this – the table, the bottles, one in its newspaper the other not, the fat-faced tavern keeper, the priest in his field shirt – that all this would waver and dissolve like a pack of cards. That sort of thing happened to him when he had malaria and was in delirium. And along with it, as used to happen to him before a good shock to the system like a booze-up or bath-house session, he experienced a lift, a slight giddiness, a kind of swooning, soaring sensation. And an access of almost febrile inspiration. He got up and went over to the mirror. No, all was as usual; he was, as ever, dull, everyday and uninteresting. Nothing in the world had altered. He'd be arrested and nothing would change then either. This priest would go on making love with this tavern mistress and knocking back her vodka.

He unstoppered the bottle and poured out a glass for both of them.

"Well, Father," he said rather roughly, "to everything good and bad. Hurrah!"

"For those at sea, travelling and pent in dungeons," Father Andrey half spoke, half sang, church fashion, with grave fluency. "Maria

Grigorievna, get yourself a glass now. Everyone should drink to a toast like that."

After that, they started discussing life. All three were convinced that success had eluded them, but the attitude of each was different. Kornilov was peevish, Volchikha uncomplaining, while Father Andrey was positively glad at the way things had turned out.

"Yes, yes tell us fairy tales, do," grinned Kornilov rudely. "The old old story. I used to have a nanny," he addressed himself to Volchikha, "and if you asked her: 'Nan, do you like pastries?' 'No,' she would answer, 'nanny only likes black bread crusts.' "

"Yet you know," responded a smiling Father Andrey, "she was right. I prefer black bread to cakes as well. Ah, dear comrade, or whatever the form of address is now, you don't know yet what black bread is, the heel of the loaf – there's nothing tastier in the world. You haven't been taught that yet."

"They taught you a long time ago, did they?" Kornilov grimaced.

"Long long ago, Lord preserve them. I'll tell you in all honesty: it was a good thing they did, I'm grateful. This way I wander about the earth meeting all sorts of people, earning that same crust of black bread, wretchedly, truly in the sweat of my brow! My job with you came as a sort of lottery prize. It finishes in a month and I'm glad! From the bottom of my heart I rejoice! It's wonderful to be alive. Truly wonderful. It has been wisely ordained that each man's joy is precisely fitted to his capacity. It can neither be stolen nor conferred: it simply would not fit anyone else."

"And when you were the governor's confessor, did you also think that way?"

"No, not like that, not at that time. But at that time I did not yet know the taste of black bread."

"And how did you feel? Worse?"

"Not worse exactly; how should I put it, more foredoomed. In the priestly sense. No grief, no joy. The river rolls on. Everything in its place. Source, upper reaches, lower reaches – then the end: it flows into the sea and vanishes."

"You sang the liturgy every day, I suppose?"

"I sometimes delegated that to others, sinner that I am."

"Did you grant absolution?"

"I did. I absolved a good deal. Everything in fact! Robbery, murder, corruption and the fact that my spiritual son had given the order to fire on the crowd – I absolved everything, everything: 'Go and sin no more.' " He raised his calm, grave eyes to Kornilov. "And it's good that you are being ironic now. It is certainly worthy of ridicule and insult."

"How could that be, Father?" Volchikha evinced surprise. She had already stealthily contrived to shed a tear over the workings of fate (two dabs at the eyes to wipe the tears away) and was now sitting looking like a puffed-up bullfinch, quiet, mournful and comely.

"It was like this, my dear," replied Father Andrey graciously – "I didn't dare to. What sort of paragon of goodness and benevolence was I to be dispensing absolution? How could I forgive a bandit for killing a child, I ask you? Killing my child? Would I not be held to account for any such forgiveness? No, I forgive because I'm a priest. And priests speak a language of their own. Nobody takes his absolution seriously. The lord's mercy is limitless, therefore pour it forth without stint. His mercy is limitless of course, but where do I come in? I don't give orders to my God. Our hostess-shopkeeper here spent three years in jail for someone else's crime. The book-keeper came sneaking up to her: help me out for a couple of days, please. So she did. Then he disappeared. But I know him! He's a devout man! Went to church regularly and twice came to my secret confession. He's bound to turn up again for a third time. 'Father, forgive my sins.' Well, how can I do that? She's been in prison and I'm to forgive him? And in exchange for that absolution, he slips me a fiver out of the money he stole, I shouldn't wonder. What sort of absolution is that? All nonsense. Ludicrous."

Volchikha abruptly got up and left the room.

"What about Christ?" asked Kornilov, pouring out another half-glass for himself and Father Andrey. "How did Christ forgive everybody, then?"

"Thank you," said Father Andrey, taking up his glass. "Well, this will have to be the last. Christ, you say? Vladimir – Mikhailovich, I think your father's name is? Christ could forgive sin. It's not for nothing we call him the redeemer. He is God, after all. The same that is one in three persons, so then why can't he, being God, that is, omnipotent, forgive sin without descending from heaven? Not forgive even, simply absolve the sinner, as we priests do, without stirring? Why that suffering, that death, why? Have we thought of that? No, of course we haven't: for you, Christ, the Trinity, and the Lord God the Father, allowing his son to be put to death, and the Son praying to his Father before his execution, 'Father, let this cup pass from me' – all those things are myths, but do these myths have a meaning or not? What moral do these fables teach?"

"Christ isn't a fable," said Kornilov. "I believe there was such a man. He lived, walked the earth, preached; he was crucified for that."

"Well, now that makes things easier. You believe in Christ-man, therefore. And I believe in the Christ as well! In God the Word. As John has it: 'In the beginning was the Word, and the Word was God'. And if all that is so, the moral of this fable is a simple one: even God did not dare, you hear, did not dare, forgive people from heaven. Because such forgiveness would have been worthless. No, you step down from Mount Sinai, don the hide of a vile slave, live and work for thirty-three years as a carpenter in a dirty little town, endure all that a man can from other people: and when they have mocked you to their heart's content, they chastise you with whips and scorpions – you know what they used as whips? Chains with little balls on the end! They whipped people till their innards were exposed. So when they rip you up like that with whips, drag you on a rope and nail you, stark naked, mind you! – to the cross to be exposed to shame and mockery, then ask yourself from that accursed tree, ask yourself: do you love people as you did before or not? And if you can say : 'Yes I love them as before! Just as they are! I love them for all that!' Then you can forgive sins! Then indeed that terrible power will dwell in your forgiveness, that any who believes that he can be forgiven by you, will be forgiven. Because it is not God in heaven who has forgiven the sin, it is the crucified slave who has forgiven you from the cross. And not on behalf of someone unknown, but on his own behalf. That is the meaning of the fable of redemption."

"So now, therefore," asked Kornilov, "you can forgive but not absolve?"

"Yes, now perhaps I can forgive! The trouble is, now that I've earned that right, it turns out that nobody has need of it."

Kornilov sat, swaying a little, and gazed at Father Andrey. A great many thoughts were taking shape in his mind, but he was unable to articulate them.

"What, you can forgive any sins?" he asked. "Or just those you've had committed against yourself. No doubt you've been sold more than once, can you forgive Judas?"

Father Andrey looked at him and smiled.

"And why not? After all, Judas was a man who grossly over-estimated his own powers. He took too much upon himself and collapsed under the strain. That is a permanent lesson for us all, weak and feeble that we are. Don't bite off more than you can chew. Don't try and play the hero to no purpose. Three quarters of all traitors are failed martyrs."

"What, you mean Christ didn't know who he was recruiting as martyrs?" Kornilov grinned unpleasantly. "Well, you know, in that case he fell a long way short of our methods of personnel selection. They aren't perfect, but his way . . ." he shook his head. "Just think of the crew he got together. Peter denied him, Thomas was a doubter and Judas betrayed him. Three out of twelve! Twenty-five per cent failure rate. Any personnel manager would get the sack for recruitment like that. And be blacklisted too. Take Peter; it was only chance that stopped him being a traitor. Well, aren't I right? A damsel from the governor's palace: 'You're one of them?' And how did he answer her? 'I know not the man and I have nothing to do with him.' And so three times: 'No, no and no.' Well, what if one of the powers that be had been present and overheard what the girl said? He would have pounced straight away: 'What's that you say? This one? The one with the beard? Now then, come here, sir. So who are you exactly? Birds of a feather, eh? Ah, no? Not heard or seen him? What's she talking about then? Slander is it? Ah, the rascally woman! He's lying too? And so is this one? All slanderers! The swine! Just wait, I'll see to them all! Grab him! This innocent one! Into the cooler with him! Strip him to his underthings! He thinks he's visiting his mother-in-law! You're a liar! You'll sing all right! It'll all come back to you, and how!'" Kornilov acted out the scene with a good deal of expression. "Well that would be the end of your Peter. You recall what Christ said of him: 'Thou art Peter and upon this rock I will build my church.' A fine rock, I must say! And your church incidentally hasn't fared much better! Never mind, those two are clear enough but where are you going to put Pilate? The handwashing judge? Who condemned to death but is somehow guiltless. Because if the populace has howled 'crucify him, crucify him!' what is there left for the judge to do but crucify him? So what are we to do with our president of the military tribunal? Forgive him too? Because his hands are clean? He didn't just crucify, he washed his hands beforehand? He didn't want to, you see, but he gave in to the populace. Ah, a mitigating circumstance indeed! So will he ascend into the kingdom of heaven or not?"

"Without the slightest doubt," replied Father Andrey. "If the judge suddenly sensed the blood of an innocent man on his hands, he had already begun to reflect. And once he had started he would think the matter through to the end. Remember what Marmeladov says to Raskol-nikov: 'Crucify me, crucify me, righteous judge, but pity me as you crucify, and I will kiss your hand . . .' Still what do we know for certain about Pontius Pilate, proconsul of Judaea?"

They were considerably drunk as they walked back. Father Andrey was flailing his arms about, saying: "Yes, Christ's teaching 'Neither Jew nor Greek' wasn't original! It had all been said before. One has to admit that. But in what sense, dear comrade Kornilov! Just one! That's the tricky thing about truths of that kind. They are always with us and to utter them takes no great store of wisdom, but to die for them . . . there you are, the philosophers were not too keen on dying . . ."

They swayed along, shouting, and even the odd farm dog ceased barking at them. A profound, black southern night floated over mountain and orchard. Clouds covered the sky. It was sultry, as if a storm was due. It was as quiet as could be: the cicadas had ceased their chirring, the crickets no longer sang; the speckled marsh warblers no longer chirped among the tall damp grasses. The only thing audible was the rumbling of the Alma-Atinka down below, like the sound of a distant railway crossing. The icy torrent had become swollen by nightfall (all day the snowcaps had been melting) and was at work breaking through the hills and rolling boulders along its bed.

Before leaving the house, Maria Grigorievna – soft, warm, yielding – had thrown a black rose-covered shawl over her bare shoulders, but when Kornilov made to embrace her, he encountered the rough wiry arm of the priest. "Damned priest," he thought. "Over sixty as well."

"I have a book at the moment," said Father Andrey. "Your director gave it to me to read. *The Correspondence of the Apostle Paul and the Philosopher Seneca the Precursor.* Have you heard of him – Lucius Annaeus Seneca? With Pre-cur-sor added?"

"Well, what's special about him?"

"What's special about him, my dear comrade Kornilov, is that the gentleman was no Christian precursor. It's all a fraud. He'd never heard of Christ. Nor of Paul, of course. And if he had, he'd have hoisted both onto the cross without turning a hair. But he understood the behest of the age correctly. That's why he's a precursor. It was impossible at that time to hear the footsteps of the Commendatore and not become so."

"Hear the footsteps of the Commendatore," thought Kornilov. "The hound probably writes poetry like the priest Iona Brikhnichev." And said: "Could you simplify it a bit? I'm not at all sure what you're talking about."

"What I am talking about is this. The republic had died during Seneca's time. Or rather, whether it was already dead or merely in the process of dying, no one knew for certain, because no one was interested. Vampires and monsters had emerged into the world. And they were called emperors, that is, leaders of the people. There was nothing to look back to. There was nothing to look forward to. The present did not exist. There were graves behind them and graves before them. 'A third generation is now being born amid the flames of civil war.' That is Horace on Rome's past. 'Wolves will sleep in the squares and howl with hunger in the empty halls.' Ovid on Rome's future. But that was still the golden age. Augustus. The principate. The flowering of the arts. Later on, the darkness and hopelessness really did descend. And the lawyer Ulpian explained the reason as follows: 'What pleases the sovereign has the force of law, because the people has transferred to him all its rights and power.' And Seneca realized: if that was the case, one couldn't rely on the people; it didn't exist. Nor the state – that was only a concept – but only on the person, those closest to you, because there he is, and he is always by your side: a plebeian, a manumitted slave, a slave, the wife of a slave. Not a poet, not a hero, but the naked man on the naked earth. You understand?"

"Well, I'm listening, I'm still listening," responded Kornilov.

"Because a man, if you look at him that way, is not only the most precious thing on earth, he's the most reliable. The latter is something comrade Stalin is far from fully understanding."

"Now he's coming out with it," Kornilov thought. "Why mention that? In front of her too." He surprised himself by saying, however: "I am hearing the speech of a man, not a boy. It reconciles me to you, father."

"Thank you! I won't waste words, just thank you!" Father Andrey gravely replied. "Yes, Seneca realized that and because of it was given the sobriquet 'precursor' by the later fathers of the church. But not Christ! Now, about Christ. Some thirty years previously, a carpenter or builder had been roaming the sandy roads of Judaea, at the other end of the empire. It was said also that he made ploughs. A beggarly preacher with a crowd of vagrants like himself. They neither sowed nor reaped, but they gathered in the harvest – that is, they simply went round cadging from people. They ate on what they collected and where darkness found them, there they spent the night. They all obeyed their leader implicitly – he had an irascible temperament, fierce but easily appeased. Altogether he had a plain and simple nature. He was not an educated man but he

240

did know Greek (how otherwise could he have talked with Pilate?). He certainly knew how to preach, and delighted his hearers. His speech, though rather dry, was picturesque, simple and precise, with a great warmth of conviction. He was most cautious and it was impossible to make him say anything injudicious. And although everyone realized that he denied everything – the emperor, the emperor's power, the emperor's gods and morals, it was impossible to catch him out. News from Rome trickled through very slowly and no one knew what was going on in the empire. In any case, what was high politics to these fishermen and artisans? Philosophical and historical works, the books of the age, so to speak, did penetrate of course even to this benighted spot, but this carpenter or builder never unrolled them. For all that, there was one thing he understood more clearly than all the poets, philosophers, orators and political thinkers – the world was weary unto death and had lost its faith. It didn't have the strength to live. There was only one way out – man had to be restored to his rights. But he knew one more thing – the thing of paramount importance! He had to die for that! And not the way Socrates had done, amid his weeping disciples; not do away with himself like a Roman magistrate in his suburban villa, now opening, now binding up his veins. His was to be a naked and brazen death. Do you realize what death on the cross involved?" asked Father Andrey, suddenly halting. " 'Masmera min hazluv' – the long nails of the cross, eh? You do realize?"

"What, is it very painful?" Maria Grigorievna fairly sobbed. Kornilov sensed that she had clung to Father Andrey while he crushed her to him, deliberately hurting her.

"Now why did you have to bring that up?" asked Kornilov, annoyed.

"Death on the cross meant this, young man," Father Andrey resumed. "The legionaries have reached the spot with the condemned men. The crosses are already erected. 'Halt!' The condemned men's clothes are torn from them. They have been given something to fuddle them along the way and they are like drowsy flies, forever on the verge of dozing off from sheer weariness. Ropes are thrown round the condemned and they are raised up and sat on a sharp beam that projects in the middle of the post. They haul up the arms and stretch the palms out. They fasten them and nail them. They work above and below. On their knees and on ladders. The crosses are not high. High crosses are reserved for celebrated criminals. All around are the crowd – gapers, execution habitués, relatives. Town criers. Coarse laughter, grinning, hubbub and shouting. The women wail, eastern fashion and tear their faces with their nails. The soldiers bawl at the condemned. One of the nailing detail snaps at the condemned. Hold your arms straighter. It's no easy matter after all, nailing up a living man, you can't help yelling. At last they have finished the nailing. The crowd melts away, the interesting part being over. Only the crosses and the soldiers remain. Both waiting for death. But here she is a capricious visitor, she picks and chooses. She keeps them waiting. The soul, as Seneca puts it, is squeezed out drop by drop. You don't die from loss of blood on the cross, for the wounds are not open. The body is wrenched unnaturally and any movement causes unbearable pain – the condemned man has been torn by the whips, remember. After about two hours, the wounds become inflamed and the man feels he is on fire. The blood strains the pulse and flows towards the head, bringing on appalling bouts of dizziness. The working of the heart is disrupted – the man is succumbing to heart failure and terror. He raves, mumbles, jerks his head about on the crossbeam. Because of the body's weight, the nails would have torn the hands long ago, were it not for the projection half way down – those far-sighted executioners! The condemned man half hangs, half sits. Consciousness comes and goes, now flares up, now dims. Death spreads from the extremities to the centre, along the nerves, arteries and muscles. Meanwhile above the earth it is day, night, morning. Day, evening, night, morning – one shift goes off as another comes on; sometimes it goes on for ten days. Guard duty here is voluntary; the soldiers gamble at dice, drink, light fires – the nights are icy cold. Women come to visit them. There they sit embracing, drinking, bawling out songs. A picture indeed."

"Yes, a picture," said Kornilov disapprovingly. "And you seem to be adept at painting such pictures."

"Christ was lucky. He died before sunset. He suffered greatly, however. He lost faith in everything, writhed and raved in delirium: 'My God, my God, why hast thou forsaken me?'

"Then came: 'I thirst.' One of the bystanders dipped a sponge in an earthenware pot and put it on a long reed and wiped his lips with it. Evidently the pot contained the usual Roman concoction – a mixture of water, vinegar and eggs: the soldiers used to drink it on the march. He had probably lost consciousness by then. One of the soldiers pierced his chest with his spear. Blood and water flowed out – that was the lymph from the auricle. That happens when the heart ruptures, especially in the heat of sunstroke. That is how Christ died. Or, rather that is how Christianity came into being."

He came to a halt, took a deep breath and said: "What I mean is, that is how redemption took place, my friends. Man was once more restored to his rights."

"So that our beloved Leader could say two thousand years later: 'The most precious thing in the world – is man'," responded Kornilov.

"Ah, how indiscreetly he said that," Father Andrey shook his head. "Ah, how indiscreetly. And so untimely!"

Kornilov remembered little of what they talked about after that, or indeed where they went. Apparently they both saw Maria Grigorievna home. Then afterwards she did the same for them. Later, Father Andrey evidently walked along with him, explaining something. He sobered up abruptly. Ahead of them, a green torch beam flashed, dazzling him as it lit up a tall, slender female figure on the path. A voice from behind the beam called out: "Vladimir Mikhailovich . . ."

"Dasha!" he cried, rushing forward: then suddenly all went dark again. Whether Father Andrey vanished at this point or was with them the whole time, standing in the darkness, he could not recall at the time and couldn't find out with complete certainty later on either. At all events, he said nothing more.

"They took uncle away today," said Dasha from the darkness.

"What? How?" cried Kornilov, pressing her hand.

From that moment, everything he said to her and heard her say, he recalled in fragments, as if in the leaping light of the torch-beam. First light, then dark. He remembered very clearly that she said: "An army man knocked at the door. Very polite. Said good afternoon. Asked uncle to go with him for an hour. He said he would fetch him back later. I waited and waited, then I came to you."

"I didn't know anything," he replied quickly for some reason, before adding. "It's probably to do with Zybin. He's been . . ."

She clutched at his arm.

"What?"

"Just that."

Then they stood in silence, crushed by all this; suddenly he hugged her shoulders and said: "Never mind, never mind, it'll all come out in the wash!" And at that moment it really did seem so to him. That it was so unimportant as not to be worth thinking about. Then Dasha abruptly burst into tears. Just pushed her head into his chest and wept quietly and bitterly, like a child. He stroked her hair, like a strong, older man, repeating: "It's all right. It's all right."

And asked: "Did he show any sort of document?"

It seemed he hadn't done so. The soldier had simply said: "I am requesting you to come along for an hour and afterwards I'll fetch you home myself . . ." And her uncle had merely sighed imperceptibly and replied: "All right then, let's go!" And glanced at her, as if intending to say something, but thought better of it. He simply took off his jacket, got dressed and followed the army man out. Out on the road, beneath the hill stood a car, ablaze with purple headlights and with a driver at the wheel. That was what had happened.

"Yes," said Kornilov. "Happened already. Well then, you'd better come along to my place."

Once again he felt absolutely serene.

When they came in, Kornilov flicked the switch and the light came on.

"Just look at that, they've repaired the power station, after all!" he marvelled, and although it was the merest trifle, it made him feel unaccountably glad. He went up to the table, pulled a chair out and said to Dasha in a plain and everyday fashion: "Please sit down! The place is a mess, of course, filth everywhere . . ."

"Never mind, never mind that!" she replied in the same commonplace tone, schoolgirl-fashion, and oddest of all – smiled!

He smiled too.

Despair and recklessness went to his head like strong wine.

"It's all right. They took him away and they'll bring him back," he said briskly and firmly. "As to what's going to happen to us . . ."

"To you?!"

"To us," he nodded. "Zybin and me."

"They won't . . ." She sat poker-backed, staring at him with large eyes, shining with tears (it was very bright in the room).

"No," he replied. "No, they won't let him out, he's not your uncle is he? No, no, if they pull us in, then it's for good. They'll turn up with a warrant, take us in and then it's hang up your boots, as they say!"

Acknowledging this and saying it aloud afforded him a kind of cruel pleasure.

"What was that again?" she asked. "Hang up . . ."

"Your boots, your boots," he reiterated, smiling. "That's what the old man carpenter says. That old man who was with the director when they visited your place that time."

Dasha was still looking at him.

"But what for?" she asked.

He burst out laughing.

"Sweetheart, you'll have to ask them. And you know what their answer will be?"

"What?"

He smiled again and waved a hand.

"Dasha, Dasha," he said with an air of long-suffering tenderness, "what a little girl you are still."

He had such a gentle, fine voice, when he said "little", that against her will, she smiled through her tears. He came over and squeezed her shoulders.

"Now listen to what I'm telling you," he said, bending over her. "Your uncle may be home already. When you get there, don't tell him you've been with me."

"Why not?"

"Just don't that's all. They'll fetch him back and he'll probably pace the room for an hour or so, saying nothing. Then he'll drink some vodka. A lot. Maybe a glass and a half. Then he'll call for you and tell you that you're not to say a word to anybody about him being taken away anywhere. 'There'll be needless talk. Why stir it up? No need for it,' he'll say. You must answer: 'Very well, uncle Petya.' 'And not a word to Kornilov, God forbid,' he'll say. And you must answer again: 'All right.' That's all. And you'll see how your uncle will be a changed man after tonight. For the better, for the better, Dashenka! He'll be affectionate, gentle, sociable; the only thing is that when you're alone together, he'll perhaps get onto you a bit more that your tongue shouldn't wag. You'll start getting visitors, each more cheerful than the last."

"Uncle always enjoyed having visitors," said Dasha, as if defending herself against something. She was now looking at him almost in alarm.

"Not that kind, not that kind!" Kornilov waved this away. "It wasn't this sort of visitor he liked. You'll see a completely different sort now. The sort he wouldn't allow near him, the ones he used to call bastards, blabbermouths, elements."

"I don't understand you," complained Dasha. "I don't understand what you're saying at all. Explain it to me please."

But he kept pacing the floor, the gleeful malice surging ever more strongly within him.

"On the other hand, he might be completely different – in which case he won't see any visitors at all. He'll get all morose and taciturn. He won't want to know about anything apart from work. You'll never get him into company. 'Damn them,' he'll say, 'I'm sick of them.' But that's unlikely. Probably it will all go the way I first described."

"How?"

"Very cheerful and noisy."

"You say dreadful things," said Dasha plaintively.

"Dreadful, yes. But after all, everything that's going on now is dreadful, and incomprehensible too, which is the main point. I mean I don't understand it; other people understand everything. Take Georgi Nikolaevich, for instance. You like him a lot, don't you? That one understands it all, everything. Not only that, he can explain it all too. In his own words! He's got as many of his own words as you like, all of them good ones, choice in fact."

"Why do you talk like that?"

"Because I heard him telling you the tale about traitors and betrayal. I was lying next door in the storeroom and heard him. Very contemporary ideas the comrade was putting out. Very! Oh, I'd give a lot to be able to listen to him talking to them in there! He'll put them through it."

"You really think so?" Dasha asked.

"I swear by the last day of creation! The investigator can only yell and swear at him. But now they'll be singing in unison. Which one can outdo the other! You know how the wolf and the fox quarrelled over who loved the bear the most?"

"Now why talk like that?" Dasha said, upset. "He's such a nice man."

"What about us, are we so bad then? We're all right too, aren't we? The only trouble is – there's a lot we don't understand. Now Zybin's been arrested and you don't know how, what for and why; now if you were to be arrested, or me, he would understand immediately why and what for. He knows the entire history of the French revolution by heart! He'll come out with so many fine, clever words about why you can't trust anyone in the world – apart from him of course. He is truth itself. And now you see, somebody has upped and doubted it."

"And you're glad?"

Kornilov stopped in full flight and looked at her.

"Glad?" he repeated, as if sadly considering the point, then suddenly concurred and nodded. "Yes, perhaps I am glad. In a bitter sort of way: after all the same thing is waiting for me! They'll pick me up, haul me off you know where and ask me: 'And why don't you love the bear?' And there's nothing I can do – I don't love him! Ah, how I don't love the shaggy beast! And that's a mortal sin, not to love the bear! Now Zybin does love him. Only now, other people, with as much gift of the gab as he are explaining to him that he doesn't love him enough yet.

He doesn't love him ideologically, pedagogically enough. Loving the bear the wrong way is a dreadful sin. You have to love the bear not because he's shaggy and has mauled and eaten so many people – no! God forbid! But because he rips them up and roars: 'Remember, the most precious thing on earth is man!' and Kornilov laughed loud and long, jeeringly, insultingly.

"Why, isn't that true?" Dasha asked.

"Rubbish! Dog's delirium! 'All men are loathsome trash,' said Gogol and he had the right of it! That's how it is. A cloth rag's worth more than a man. Dung is manure and doesn't come amiss. But I was taken by the scruff of the neck one night and thrown out of the house where I was born. They didn't even give me time to get my things together properly. Three days to settle my affairs and fly away, little sparrow. What for, why, how? Nobody explained. 'Banishment without charge'— we have that legal formula. They don't talk to you, they don't ask you anything, they don't explain anything to you, because there's nothing to explain. It's just that someone who's never laid eyes on you, decides according to his book of regulations that you're a dangerous person. So they take you by the scruff of the neck and throw you out. Hang out in some regional centre and don't dare to raise your eyes. People will glance at you and you'd better avert your eyes and keep your head down and turned sideways as you pass. And the most important thing is, don't dare tell anyone you don't know why you've been flung out here. You must know! You're obliged to know! Just as you're obliged to expiate your guilt. Above all you must repent. And go round sighing. Otherwise you haven't demonstrated contrition. I didn't understand a thing. Do you know how they interrogate people nowadays? The first question is: 'Well then, tell us.' 'Tell you what?' 'What do you mean what? Tell us why we've arrested you.' 'I was waiting for you to tell me that.' 'What, me tell you? What do you mean, have you really lost your marbles? Why, you enemy swine! Prostitute! Up on your feet! What are you standing like? What are you standing like, prostitute?' They're very fond of that word in there. 'Why are you standing with clenched fists, prostitute? You asking for the punishment cell? You'll get it soon enough! Come on now, tell us!' 'Tell you what then?' 'What – bloody hell, man! About your foul anti-Soviet activities. How you betrayed your own Soviet system, that's what you have to talk about!' And foul language, and fists, once on the desk once across the face! That's what the conversation amounts to."

"No, you're joking!" said Dasha.

He grinned.

"You know what you get for jokes like that nowadays? . . . Joking? No, I'm not joking. No, it's someone else who's having a joke with us and hell knows how it will all end. But he's got something of his own in mind, that's for sure. He'll kill himself laughing. That's my belief! Well, that's enough about that. I'm just curious as to how Zybin answers questions like that. Something about the French revolution again? He's a master at that! As for what I'm going to sing about . . . Dasha!" he exclaimed suddenly. "What's the matter, dear? I've told you he's coming back, haven't I? Your uncle's coming back. He's no use to them at all. We're the ones they want, Zybin and me."

She got up suddenly and came towards him.

"If they take you, Vladimir Mikhailovich," she said steadily, "I don't know what will become of me. So now you know."

And hugged him round the neck.

CHAPTER 2

H E EXPECTED SOMETHING fearful to happen immediately: a search, perhaps, arrest or a summons from the security organs. But it was as if he had been forgotten. Dasha did not reappear. The director had been called to military region headquarters by cable and hadn't come back. Nobody phoned from the museum. Only the cashier had turned up to hand out the men's wages. At length, Kornilov could no longer contain himself; he went over to the forester and got the sword of Ilya Muromets from him (it had turned out to be an ordinary stage weapon). Potapov, scowling and ironically squeamish, gave him a lift on the farm Gazik as far as the museum. "Well, enjoy yourself while you can," he said on parting, and that was the only joke Kornilov had heard for a week (Potapov appeared to know nothing of his conversation with Dasha).

The scientific secretary was sitting in the director's office: a smooth young man who had recently been moved to the museum from political enlightenment. As Kornilov entered the office, the young man's face at once hardened and went as taut as a football. Kornilov, however, gave no sign of noticing this; he said hello and handed over the find. The young man pounced on it.

"What? Dug it up? Well now, at last we've got some tangible scientific results! Have you prepared a report?"

He had previously taught junior history, and had then headed the museums section at the people's commissariat; his knowledge of either history or excavation was, however, minimal.

Kornilov patiently explained everything to him but declined to write a report.

"After all, I'm not an expert on ancient Russian weaponry," he said. "When comrade Zybin gets back . . ."

At this, the scientific secretary, fairly leapt off his chair.

"What on earth do you mean, when he gets back?" he asked, scandalized. "Zybin has been arrested by the security organs."

"Wha-at?" It sounded almost sincere.

"You must have known, surely?" the scientific secretary marvelled. "You mean you knew absolutely nothing?"

"Well how could I?" Kornilov muttered. "How? I was in the mountains, wasn't I? He said the director had called him in and he might be away several days. I thought he must be going on some official trip."

"What? What?" The secretary became animated. "Away? Official trip? That's the way he put it to you? You've got to tell the investigation that."

Kornilov spread his arms ingenuously.

"Nobody's asked me about him."

The secretary made up his mind after a pause: "Right, you go back straight away. You've got nothing else to do here?"

"No actual business, but I wanted . . ."

The scientific secretary frowned, then spoke with abrupt clarity: "Let me strongly advise you not to want anything at the moment, nor see anyone. Go back. What about this sword – it was found independently of him? Excellent! All the best."

Kornilov went, but paused at the door.

"And what was Zybin arrested for? Anybody know?"

"What do you mean?" The secretary shot back the question, icily harsh. "He was arrested as an enemy of the people."

The tone was hard and final.

"Ah-h," said Kornilov, and left.

An hour later, bouncing about in the little blue bus that served the suburban area, he remembered: Zybin had been a friend of this type. They'd gone out drinking together, frequented dives together, once even landed up at the police station together.

The bus made its cautious way up the mountain road. The morning mountains rose calm and clear in the dull silver and blue-grey of the magpie's plumage. "How he loved them!" Kornilov thought, and for the first time realized that he was sorry for Zybin after all. "Yes, hang up your boots. What about dropping everything and heading off for the back of beyond? He had money in his pocket, hadn't he? No, really, get off and head back! And Dasha? What's Dasha to me? . . ."

"Mountain Giant Collective farm, end of the line," said the driver loudly and climbed out of his cab.

"Ah well," thought Kornilov, "if you've got to go, you've got to go! As the parrot said when the cat dragged her out of the cage by the tail. We'll wait and see."

In the event, he did not have to wait. The very next day, he was summoned to the office telephone. It was a call from there. Lieutenant

Smotryaev introduced himself and asked whether he was free the following day. If he was, could he possibly drop in to the Internal Affairs PC, room 205, at about this time, or a little either way. A pass would be waiting for him. The lieutenant's voice conveyed the impression that he attached little significance to the call, and was bothering Kornilov only as a matter of routine. For some reason, this was what struck Kornilov most unpleasantly of all. He had spent the evening with a doleful Volchi-kha (Father Andrey had not put in an appearance since going off that last time), and in the morning he was knocking at room 205 on the dot. He was feeling very grim. The very building on the square had always depressed him with its monotony, and its deathly, inexorable grip. It was narrow, grey, flat and balefully oppressed the entire area. Inside, however, everything resembled an expensive hotel: well-lit red-carpeted staircases, windows open wide, halls and even potted palms. In room 205, two splendid young chaps were idling. Smotryaev turned out to be a lieutenant, young but already putting on a fair amount of weight, with rather languishing blue cow-like eyes. A vest of dazzling whiteness peeped out from beneath his open collar. He was extremely florid, with very blond hair and white teeth. His uniform seemed to have been moulded on. His companion on the other hand was not wearing uniform, merely a blue silk sports shirt. They were both delighted to see Kornilov. And why not indeed, a fresh face! An archaeologist! In from the mountains! If he, the mountain man, only realized what a bore it was sitting under a load of paperwork on such a beautiful sunny morning. How the pine trees tugged at one – the window opened directly onto the children's park. Here was the sun flooding the whole room! And the noise! The kids squealing, the creak of seesaws. The band playing. The organizers bellowing through their megaphones. And they had to sit here! Nothing they could do about it, all part of the job. Then both abruptly adopted an air of seriousness and began asking Kornilov questions about the excavations. Then about the museum. Then about the gold. Then Smotryaev, à propos, told a good story about an enormous hoard of gold buried near his home town some three hundred years before.

"But there is a cossack captain still living," he said, "and they say he definitely knows where the gold is buried. The son went on his knees, begging him to reveal the place, but the old man pretended to be gaga, and that was that. And our tutor was practically besotted with that gold as well. He used to get us together and then he'd start: 'Four tons of gold, lads, reckon up how many tractors and locomotives that could buy!' And every year we were dragged out to dig. We dug and dug and never found anything but one old sabre. But the old man was stubborn! A fanatic! 'It wouldn't run away, would it, he used to say. I'll track it down!' He peppered every institution with copied letters. After everybody else had gone home, he'd stay behind after school typing away in the office."

"Well, it's true that he was, you know . . ." said the silk shirt.

"So it seems! Well, towards the end he went completely off his head. Last year I was at my parents' and dropped by to see him. He lives right on the outskirts with some shopkeeper. He's got no children of his own, so he goes playing skittles with them. He's got three beehives in the garden. Messes around with them all day. I mentioned the gold to him, but he just waved his hand: 'A-ah! Stupidity! There's nothing there!' 'But why did you go on looking?' He didn't answer. I started talking about politics. 'Not interested.' 'How can that be? You used to teach history, didn't you?' 'What's history to me? I exist, I draw my pension, and if anybody in authority finds my existence superfluous – they'll wipe me out straight away.' That's all he said. And he had been a revolutionary. Done time. He only got out because of the February revolution."

'No doubt you rolled up in that uniform," thought Kornilov.

"Little Menshevik I expect," responded the one in the shirt. "When they get old they go completely round the bend. They read the papers and think it's all about them."

"No, he doesn't even read the papers. He subscribes to the *Palaeontology Herald*, that's all."

"Palaeontology, palaeontology . . . wait a minute, that's . . ."

The telephone rang.

"Second lieutenant Surovtsev here," barked the one in the shirt cheerfully. "Certainly, comrade captain." He pulled a folder out of the desk drawer, locked it after him, tugged at it, stowed the key in his pocket and said to Smotryaev: "Well, that's it again till evening. I'll drop by then. Au revoir, comrade Kornilov. I also wanted to tell you something. I've got a very old book entitled *Featr of History*, with the old round "F". What is that – Featr or theatre?"

"Theatre."

"It certainly doesn't look like a theatrical one. It's all about these kings and caesars."

He went out. Smotryaev sighed and said reflectively and with feeling.

"Yes, Ivan Petrovich Shilo was my tutor. He was a good teacher, I'll say that for him. We're all indebted to him. A man of the old school. You know, 'Sow what is great and good and everlasting.' Well, Ivan Petrovich was like that." He offered a packet of Kazbek to Kornilov. "Smoke? No? Lucky man! I can't give it up! Well now, I wanted to have a little talk with you, or rather an exchange of views. But first I wanted to . . ." he bent over the desk, took out a folder from a drawer and opened it.

But at that moment the phone rang again. Smotryaev picked it up, listened for a moment, then said: "Yes! Yes! Yes! No! Certainly comrade major! I'm on my way." He touched Kornilov lightly on the shoulder. "Let's go through to the major."

And picked up the folder.

Major Khripushin was sitting at a desk, clasping his big square fingers on the glass top and staring at them without moving.

"Good morning," he said, then paused, looked at Kornilov and added: "Take a seat."

They sat down, each in his own place. Smotryaev walked over to a writing desk at the side. The major, keeping his eyes fixed on Kornilov, took out his cigarette case, extracted a papirosa, clicked the lighter noisily and lit up.

"I want to put a number of questions to you," he said. "What is your opinion of Zybin?"

Kornilov pondered conscientiously.

"I really only know him from a work point of view."

"And what do you know from the work point of view?"

"Well, he's my boss. The director used to praise him," Kornilov replied.

"What was that for, then?"

"Well for his erudition, his capacity for work, his discipline."

"But he drinks like a fish!" exclaimed Khripushin flashing an indignant glance at the blue-eyed Smotryaev.

"He laps it up, the man does, laps it up no end," Smotryaev confirmed indulgently.

"And when he's had a few he'll say hell knows what!"

The other said nothing.

"Well, does he?"

"I don't know."

"What do you mean, you don't know?"

"I've never drunk with him so I don't know."

"What are you then, a teetotaller?" Khripushin sneered.

"No."

"So what do you mean, then?"

"I've just never had occasion to drink with Zybin."

"Why not? Explain yourself! Didn't he trust you? Kept his distance, did he?"

"No, no, I don't think so . . ."

"Then why not?"

"It just didn't happen somehow . . ."

"Somehow! And he never once asked you to have a drink with him?"

"No."

"And never invited you to join his company?"

"No."

"Hmm!" Khripushin took out his case again and opened it. "You smoke?"

"No."

"You don't smoke, you don't drink; don't go much on women either, eh? Right enough, what's the point of asking a man like that anything? But you've just said, haven't you: he didn't invite me to join his company. So Zybin had some sort of circle that you know about, right?"

"No, no, not like that, comrade major," Kornilov replied sincerely. "I simply answered your question whether Zybin used to invite me to join his company – no, he didn't."

"Well where did he invite you, then?"

"He didn't invite me anywhere. We did once sit at the same table, it's true. But there were a lot of outsiders there. So you couldn't call it company. That was when we were selling the bone material to the Vetzooinstitute."

"We'll talk about the Vetzooinstitute later on," Khripushin said with a mean glance. "So then, you sat at the same table, drinking mineral water as silent as statues, is that right?"

"No, why should we do that? We talked a lot about work, but that wouldn't interest you, would it?"

"And what does interest us?"

"Well, evidently you're interested in his states of mind, but I know absolutely nothing about that."

"And you never heard him utter a single anti-Soviet remark, you, his closest colleague, working side by side with a confirmed enemy?"

"Of course not. Why should he take me into his confidence? We weren't close."

"You think people who are close hold anti-Soviet conversations?"

It was a totally pointless conversation – flogging a dead horse. Not a bald devil could emerge from it. All three of them were aware of that. Kornilov looked at Khripushin and saw clean through him. The man sitting opposite was a dull, incompetent brute, who had most likely been dragging himself listlessly from course to course in the lower reaches of some college, when the snarers of human souls had fished him out. He had been earmarked and picked out for his complete openness of soul and because of his penchant for frank conversations and confessions in the trade union committee office; for his ability to understand everything and regard it as right and proper; because among the students he had masses of drinking partners but not a single friend. In addition he was brawny, loud-mouthed and unscrupulous to a degree. If someone had also called him apolitical, he would have been genuinely offended but he really was profoundly apolitical in the very make-up of his soul, in the heart of his mental existence. That is, of course, he was apolitical in that special Hottentot sense of the word, where the only system a man regards as correct is one which has need of men like him, which marks them out, cherishes them and rewards them well. Everything else that system proclaims is accepted by such men automatically, but they actually are devoted to it through conscience as well as fear, so that foes of the existing order of things are their foes as well. In this regard, Khripushin was certainly not lying. He detested and feared enemies. This particular characteristic was, of course, taken into account and prized most of all. But besides that, he doubtless possessed certain other qualities which rendered him suitable for a form of work which devours a man body and soul and gives nothing very much in return; a higher salary, earlier pension, comfortable flat, special rest home – but chiefly a blank and mute fear around him, a fear which in some mysterious fashion mingled common or garden fear, philistine respect and normal human squeamishness.

"So then," said Khripushin, rising from his chair and walking back and forth about the office. "So then! That's interesting! It follows that close friends conduct anti-Soviet conversations with each other. Right!" He brought his face close to Kornilov. "Why don't we stop playing the fool here? You're a Soviet man, aren't you? That's what we all think here. What's past is past and done with, and your present we see before us. You are a Soviet man, Vladimir Mikhailovich?"

"Thank you," responded Kornilov, touched to the heart, "you're absolutely right! I am a citizen of the Soviet Union and I . . ."

"There you see!" Khripushin cried jubilantly. "You see! Do help us, Vladimir Mikhailovich; you know the times we live in, do you not? An enemy has been working close by our side for months on end. A thorough-going, intelligent, vigorous and well-camouflaged enemy. He has conducted his subversive activity extremely skilfully."

"Yes," Kornilov nodded, crushed. "In that case, he certainly has been extremely clever and well-camouflaged."

"There you are, you see! But you were able to see through him and understand his game, right?"

"Yes, yes! Now I understand what he was playing at. The rogue used to say the same thing to me as you have."

"What was that?" Khripushin gleefully clutched his shoulder. "What did he use to say?"

"He used to say: 'Volodya, you know the times we live in, don't you? You have to be on the alert.'"

"Really? Is that so, now?" Khripushin stepped back. "I'd be interested to hear the context of that remark."

There came a soft knock at the door and a man in a close-buttoned army uniform came in without waiting for an answer. He was stocky and broad-shouldered, with curly hair and fleshy African lips. His eyes, however, unlike Khripushin's, were mouse-like, swift and sharp; they bored into you intently. He bowed slightly to Kornilov, smiled at Smotryaev, and enquired of Khripushin, with deliberate deference: 'Would you allow me to be present?' He waited for permission before walking over to the desk and taking up position by the wall.

"Well, there were lots of contexts," replied Kornilov. "Events in the West, the Leader's speech, the arrest of our stores manager."

"So what did he actually say on the subject of the arrests?" Khripushin asked.

"He used to say that the whole trouble was our idiotic disease of complacency. That's why the criminal had been overlooked. One had to be vigilant."

"Just who did he say that to?" asked the thick-lipped one keenly, as he picked up the case file from the desk and began leafing through it. It was a thick file, with bookmarks in it, greasy red marks and ticks in the margins.

"To me, the director, foreman Potapov, lots of people."

"Well and what else did he say?" asked thick-lips, still looking through the file.

"He used to talk about the French revolution."

"Really? The French?" said thick-lips in humorous surprise, as he came across one mark and showed it to Khripushin with an indulgent smile. Khripushin also read it, nodded and fixed a piercing stare on Kornilov. "Your account doesn't sound altogether natural," said thick-lips, tearing himself away from the file. "Zybin reads an article in the paper about enemies of the people, says 'You have to be vigilant' and then starts talking straight away about the French revolution. That's all very well, but what did he say about the enemies of the people, though?"

"He talked about how hard it was to recognize enemies. Take Azef, he said, he was the head of the operations organization – the holy of holies in the SR movement, but he turned out to be a traitor. That's the sort of thing he used to say."

"And is that all?" Khripushin asked. Thick-lips found something else in the file and showed it to him; Khripushin read it and frowned, then his eyes bored into Kornilov: why are you clouding the issue, they seemed to say, the business is clear enough.

"The boneheads," thought Kornilov in turn. "Fancy trying that on. That's as old as the hills."

"That's all there was to it," he responded with a hint of asperity. "We didn't have any other conversations."

"Right then . . ." Khripushin tapped his finger on the desk and was about to get slowly to his feet, when Thick-lips asked gently: "And he never gave any hint of wanting to cross the Chinese border?"

Khripushin resumed his seat.

"Why would he talk to me about that?" Kornilov was genuinely astonished. "How could I have helped him?"

At this, Thick-lips swiftly took a notebook from his pocket, wrote something on it and passed it to Khripushin. He read it, nodded, and for a time both of them leafed intently through the case file. Then Khripushin stubbornly reverted to Kornilov and said, after a pause: "Well, all right. We won't take a note of your evidence today. It's hardly evidence, anyway. We'll have you in again in a few days time and have a discussion. Try to be a bit more prepared for that conversation, for now . . . Comrade lieutenant! . . ." and he gestured vaguely in the direction of Kornilov.

"Yes, yes," Smotryaev rose. "We would like to have a couple of words with comrade Kornilov as well. Let's go, comrade Kornilov, and have a chat."

*   *   *

257

"Now this is the situation", said the blond, light-eyed Lieutenant Smotryaev, seating Kornilov opposite him. "You've just been talking to the major, but I want you to know that it was we who invited you, not the major. He simply wanted to chat with you in passing about this Zybin. But our business with you is of quite a different order ... I spoke to you about my old teacher, now then ..."

The office they were sitting in was only large enough to hold a desk and two chairs. It was a cubicle rather than an office; such cubicles abounded on people's commissariat premises, courts, prosecutors' offices, investigation blocks. The window, on the other hand, opening wide onto the poplars, seemed enormous. There were a great many poplars, a whole avenue of them. The entire inner courtyard, as well as the prison which was situated in that yard, were set about with similar avenues.

"I wonder," thought Kornilov, "whether it's the same window. That one was the very end one. We used to come up to the fence and it was directly opposite us. When the walks were in the daytime, there used to be a tall blonde sitting there. We thought she was beautiful. Still we thought that of all women then. A typist or a secretary. Yes, it was the same window. What on earth was she doing here?"

He took a stealthy glance outside, but the cubicle was on the fifth floor and the yard was out of view. "Whenever she appeared, we used to cough loudly and sigh and hem and haw – and laugh. The guard used to shout 'No talking!' and then she would look at us and give us a secret smile."

"Now then," said Smotryaev, shutting the window. "I didn't recall that old man today just by chance. We've had material on another old man lying here for a month now. Can you guess who I'm referring to?"

Kornilov shrugged.

"No."

"Your fellow employee, Andrey Ernestovich Kutorga. Well? Surely you know him?"

"Now that's worked out just fine," passed through Kornilov's mind. "When they picked up Zybin during the day I was working and at night I was at Volchikha's with the priest as witness."

"Not only know him," he said, "I spent an entire evening with him just lately."

Smotryaev's eyes narrowed.

"Drinking no doubt?"

"For my sins," sighed Kornilov.

Smotryaev guffawed.

"Well, well! And I probably saw him the same place that you did. You were at the beautiful Ukrainian's? Well, well! That was precisely where I got to know him. I'd come over to see a friend, but we'd run out of petrol. 'Hang on,' he says, 'let's drop in and restore the spirits.' So we barged in. And what do we see? The priest sitting at the table drinking and nibbling mushrooms. I took a real fancy to him then. I really did! Such a calm, dignified face, beard like an icon. We got on talking. He told me straight away, 'I am a minister of religion – a priest.' 'You remind me of a certain writer,' I said. 'I am a writer; I, comrade lieutenant, have been cogitating over one book for ten years.' 'What book is that, then?' 'On the sufferings of Christ.' 'Well, nowadays the publishing houses won't pay for books like that.' 'I don't need their money,' he says, 'I always pay my own way. I'm a lumberjack, I'm a fisherman, I'm a navvy. If need be I'll repair a roof and install a stove.' I really took a fancy to him. And then a month later, this pretty little pile of material comes to me. Take a look."

He opened the folder, took out a double exercise-book page and handed it to Kornilov.

"Evidently two people involved. One writing and the other typing. It's typed by a literate person."

"Up until the revolution, the museum was a cathedral," read Kornilov, "and a cathedral it remains. There are more priests in it now than before. They've been collected up from all over town and a sacristy has been provided for them – they sit there idling and drinking to their heart's content and say: 'This is the life'. They have such trust reposed in them that if an exhibit doesn't meet with their approval, it is at once destroyed. And no record is kept of it. Isn't the director aware of this, then? On the contrary, he's very well aware of it all, but keeps quiet and lets it go on."

"What rubbish!" exclaimed Kornilov.

"Read on, read on," smiled Smotryaev. "Leave that bit out, read this here."

"The most inveterate and malicious of all this holy company is the former provincial archbishop Kutorga. He engages in anti-Soviet activity for all to see. He slanders our Soviet life and our collective farm system. 'They've been building and building it and there's still nothing to eat, grain is distributed in grams.' He tells stories about comrade Stalin and his glorious comrades in arms. As to himself, he announces: 'When I ate and drank at the governor's, it was like a fairy tale. And I've lost that life to these yids and bums. I'll come back from the next world to take my revenge. Every night I sing the liturgy to myself and consign them all to anathema.'"

"Lord, it's the other way around, precisely the opposite. He denounces his former way of life; he's satisfied with this one!" Kornilov exclaimed.

"Right," said Smotryaev, satisfied, taking the paper from Kornilov, "that's just what we expected you to say. That's why we bothered you. You see the way it is: every letter we get like that is strictly noted. When we get one, we have to give our response and either investigate or close the file. But to close it we must have another document. After getting this letter and discussing it, that's exactly what we have done. We summoned Zybin, took his evidence about Kutorga, then sent it all to records with a clear conscience. In other words we quashed the affair. So matters rested until last week, but now Zybin's been arrested himself. What had been a justification was now an accusation. You understand now why we called you in?"

"No," Kornilov shook his head. He really didn't understand.

"It stands to reason," the blond, light-eyed Lieutenant Smotryaev reproved him gently. "If we put enquiries in hand, then the authorship of the letter will be established immediately. That's no problem. He'll be called in as a witness, his evidence will be taken and an anonymous letter will turn into material evidence. Then the old man is done for. Comrade Khripushin and his deputy, comrade Neiman will take over the case; you saw them both today. They can always turn up a couple of necessary witnesses. But we feel that Kutorga is a good and decent old man, and doesn't engage in any criminal activity. He just sits writing his gospel, and that's it. Now you understand why we had recourse to you? We needed the honest, perfectly impartial testimony of a trustworthy individual. Wait a minute, though, we want no lies! If the old man is guilty of letting his tongue wag – what of it? Nothing to be done about it. Murder will out, as the saying goes. You'll just write 'guilty' for us. In any event, some Soviet man will be found to inform the organs about it, nowadays everybody tells what he knows. If not, on the other hand, if the old man is all right, we are relying on you. Your evidence will be sufficient."

He paused, then asked abruptly: "What did you talk about? Did you touch on politics?"

"Not on your life. We discussed the earthly existence of Christ." Kornilov smiled.

"And the lady of the house heard you?"

"Yes, she did. As regards the Soviet system, he spoke very positively as it happens. He was grateful that it delivered him from a lie."

Smotryaev laughed with pleasure and fairly rubbed his hands.

"There now, you see what a good thing it was that we asked you to come in? You're willing to sign your testimony? Excellent! Thank you! But not now, of course. We won't write anything down for the moment. That was a chance meeting you had, after all. He was seeing you for the first time and might not have opened up. Besides, we're asking the lady to come in and so we'll have two sets of testimony. This is what we're going to ask you to do: meet this holy father again. Have a drink and a sit down and get talking about what matters – he's a sociable old fellow and likes talking. Start the conversation going, say, about the same our lord Jesus Christ. Afterwards we'll call you in and we'll put together a report. We'll write in this today's testimony of yours as well. Okay?"

Lieutenant Smotryaev looked at Kornilov with his clear blue eyes. He was smiling and spoke simply and sincerely. It could be sensed that there was no sort of trap in this offer of his. He was inclined to save the priest for some reason, no more than that. "Who on earth could have cooked up that filth?" Kornilov wondered. "Could it be the Massovichka? Yes, most likely it was. And her literacy! Ah, the bitch. And this, of course, wasn't her only victim. I dare say she had her finger in Zybin's arrest as well."

"Okay," he said. "I agree. What number shall I ring?" He took out his notebook.

Several totally blank days ensued. One week ended, another began, and a fearful silence enshrouded Kornilov. The world he inhabited – these orchards and foothills – were so deserted and unpeopled that it sometimes seemed to him that Zybin had no earthly existence at all. And the people he was attached to, or was used to, had also disappeared. The director was somewhere far away. Dasha remained out of sight; the foreman failed to drop in on him. The workmen dug away in silence. Had Kornilov been a touch more experienced, he would have known that this always happened after arrests. Only the doleful Volchikha and Father Andrey remained as before. The latter suddenly appeared at Volchikha's, pleased and glowing, with a huge briefcase under his arm. It seemed that some friend had loaned him a typewriter for several evenings and so he had been sitting in town typing away and had just finished the previous day.

"Won't you let me read it?" requested Kornilov. He was sure that Father Andrey would find some excuse for not doing so, but on the contrary he was positively glad.

"Take it by all means," he said. "Here, I'll give you the second copy, the amended one. And do keep an eye on the style incidentally. I write in the old, ponderous sort of fashion, giving chapter and verse; nowadays, they tell me, you have to keep it light."

"Well, here's something I can talk to Smotryaev about," thought Kornilov, as he returned home with the manuscript. "I don't need anything else." But time passed and he was still not sent for. Kornilov didn't know whether this was a good or a bad sign. In the museum, everything was calm and subdued as well. The responsible young man sat as before in the director's office. Once a week, Kornilov took the works and scientific reports in to him. He would take them, flick through them and ask with a fleeting smile: "Haven't they found Ilya Muromets' horse yet?" and put the papers in a desk drawer. One day however, he asked Kornilov to stay behind as the office was crowded. When everyone had gone, he said: "You've been asked to phone in. No later than tomorrow."

He held out a sheet of notepaper.

Kornilov looked at it, said "If I may," and went over to the phone.

"Of course, of course," said the responsible young man, all of a flutter; he rose very quietly and locked the door.

It was not Smotryaev who picked up the phone, however, it was his office companion, Lieutenant Surovtsev. Kornilov greeted him and said that as he chanced to be in town, he could drop by that very minute.

"Have you got the book with you?" asked Surovtsev.

"Yes," returned Kornilov.

"I'll organize a pass for you," said Surovtsev.

Kornilov replaced the receiver thoughtfully, stood for a moment before nodding to the responsible young man, still frozen in his demure pose of understanding and non-interference, and went out.

On the way, however, a poignant thought struck him: "Isn't this playing with fire, though? This guy here is certain I'm working for them. Is that a good thing?" But Father Andrey's work lay in his briefcase, the pass had been ordered and the only thing left for him to do now was to get a move on.

Lieutenant Surovtsev was sitting at Smotryaev's desk. He was wearing a grey tweed suit and a loud tie.

(Ah, those tweed suits, oh those garish ties. They're a miniature cross section of a an entire epoch. The China-Eastern Railway had just been ceded to the Japanese and unheard-of goods had begun appearing in the shops. Tinned soya and fine, high quality fabrics – tricot and tweed. People crammed the shops for them. On the counter they dispensed a soft, gentle glow. They were refined and beautiful like Copenhagen porcelain. Two months later, they had split and turned into rags.)

As Kornilov entered, Surovtsev got to his feet, greeted him and showed him to a chair.

"Now then," he said. "Lieutenant Smotryaev's been dealing with you but he's on an official trip just now. So for the moment you'll have to talk to me. No objection? The matter involves this same diocesan father as I understand it? Yes? Excellent! So you've been talking to him? What about?"

"About the trial of our Lord Jesus Christ."

"What? What?" the lieutenant's eyebrows lifted and his eyes began fairly darting about like a playful cat.

Kornilov repeated what he had said.

"Now that's really something!" Surovtsev laughed. "And what does he have to say then? I read the story at one time, you know! Is that the bit about the traitor?"

"As it happens Kutorga's written a whole book about him."

"Now then! Now then!" Surovtsev took the manuscript and began to read.

"As it is written!" He exclaimed suddenly. " 'When a judge delivers an unjust sentence, God turns his face from him, but if he is just, even for one hour, the whole world draws strength from it.' That's really terrific! What is it, a quote from the law-givers of that time?"

"Yes," replied Kornilov. "The bit in the inverted commas is a quotation."

"Aha, aha!" Surovtsev nodded. "Yes, yes, it's a quotation! No, I've not heard of these things. We did do the history of law but briefly, just glanced at it!" He bent over the manuscript again and read to the end of the chapter, then lit a cigarette and said: "Yes . . ." and began walking about the office. "But still, you know what I liked best?" he remarked, seating himself at the desk. "This maxim here: 'A court sentencing to death once in seven years – is a slaughter-house. And its members are called members of THE BLOODY SANHEDRIN.' Yes, this needs thinking over before we decide anything. You know what I'm going to ask you? Leave this with me two or three days. He didn't give it to you just for the day, did he?"

"Yes, of course, take it," said Kornilov, "but I have to give it back sometime. He gave me it so that I could correct the style."

"Of course I'll return it, why not?" Surovtsev assured him. "Well, what else did you talk about?"

"Well, about Judas."

"Oh! Now that really is interesting! All I know is that he was a traitor and people use the expression, 'Judas kiss'. What was that, then – he gave that sign during the search and arrest?"

"Absolutely correct. According to Matthew, he told the soldiers: 'Whomsoever I shall kiss, that one is he: hold him fast.' Judas was very faint-hearted and hasty; he had nothing prepared to say apart from the absolutely senseless: 'Hail, master.' 'Yes, it is indeed I,' Christ answered him, and then they seized him."

"So then," said Surovtsev. "But that's all plain and straightforward, there's nothing there to write a whole book about."

"What Kutorga writes is this: as it happens there's a great confusion behind the whole story. After all, Christ didn't hide himself away, he spoke in public. He could have been seized perfectly easily any day even without the help of Judas. 'Why these swords and staves,' he said when he was arrested. 'You've seen me every day, and I preached among you. Why didn't you take me then?' "

"Logical," smiled Surovtsev. "I mean, logical only for Christ. People who are arrested often ask that question. They are ignorant of the operational considerations involved. What was the problem in the story of Christ?"

"Well, operational considerations played a role there as well," smiled Kornilov. "As ever. The point was that Christ had been very cautious. They hadn't managed to catch him out by anything he said. He had repulsed the most provocative questions. He was sharp-witted and resourceful. In general he stuck to the principle in these cases: 'Render unto Caesar that which is Caesar's, unto God that which is God's' – that is, this is the earth and yonder is heaven. You take the earth and leave heaven to me, let's settle on that. But of course, in the family of disciples, with his closest people, he spoke of the earth too in rather different terms. So then, one of the disciples was needed in order to take note of any such talk. And not just one disciple; there had to be at least two. And since there were no such things as state prosecutions at the time, there could be no accusation, let alone trial, without these two witnesses. The criminal was brought in to the court by the accuser, the plaintiff. So Judas was that plaintiff and it's clear why he was paid thirty pieces of silver. And the circumstances were chosen as being suitable too, a secluded spot out of town, a deserted place, dead of night, a knot of conspirators, a vague aura of mystery surrounding the arrest. But in that case there had to be one more witness, who did no seizing, no revealing, didn't summon the guard; he simply maintained a silent presence. And afterwards gave evidence. And there was such a man in Christ's case, he only appeared once later at the sanhedrin in secret. They listened to him, wrote down his words and released him. Therefore, we do not know who he was. But it was someone very close to Christ; so close, that when the master was arrested, and later dragged to the judgment seat, he walked along and wept with all the rest. One can imagine Christ's feelings when he saw him there and he spoke. But the secret remains behind closed doors. Christ wasn't able to pass it on to his disciples."

"And Judas himself?"

"He didn't want to pass on the name either, though he could have done. His role was different. His job was to fetch the crowd, that is, do his betraying openly and publicly. That is what his masters demanded of him. Why he went to his own destruction isn't clear. He must have got himself too deeply compromised. After all he was the treasurer, that is, the most practical of Christ's entourage. No doubt he carried out other commissions too. He was their intermediary or something of the sort and he was caught. At all events, to swap Christ's money-chest for the sanhedrin's thirty pieces of silver, or twenty-two gold roubles in old money, made no sense at all in his case. And the sanhedrin demanded for their thirty pieces of silver, not only Christ's head from him but his own body and soul to boot. Such courts occasionally needed witnesses who would publicly betray others even at the cost of their own destruction – that is, across their own dead bodies."

"Yes, yes," Surovtsev shot Kornilov a swift oblique glance, and resumed pacing the floor. He walked about, stood for a moment, then resumed his seat. He took his cigarettes from a drawer but did not light up, they hung forgotten in his hand. "Tell me, Christ never guessed who that second man was? Or perhaps . . ." he asked.

"No, one can be certain he didn't. Only in the case of Judas did he know in advance, and that last night, the last supper, that is, was very painful for him. According to Kutorga, it was a typical night before an arrest. Christ at that time went through everything typical of such circumstances: despair, loneliness, exhaustion, hopelessness, hope, 'perhaps it will all blow over somehow', although it was perfectly obvious that it would do no such thing. And finally, that almost invariable: 'Well come on, hurry up! What are you hanging about for! Go on, go on, go on!' And in an access of deathly exhaustion he says to Judas himself: 'That which you are minded to do – do quickly.' And Judas goes."

"And the other one?"

"The other one sits and waits. He doesn't have to do anything or go anywhere. They'll call him in their own good time, and he will testify, and with that his role will be over. But that night he was very nervous of course, what if Christ had found out something? And only when the teacher said: 'Today one of you will betray me,' did he relax. As long as it was one, not two, not him and Judas, but Judas alone, it mean that everything was all right."

"Listen," exclaimed Surovtsev suddenly, genuinely roused, "mightn't the second man be just an outsider, not one of the disciples, just somebody . . . Mightn't Judas have just taken him up into the loft and hidden him, or stood him by the door or concealed him behind a curtain somewhere . . . He was the treasurer, after all, you say, so he was in charge of the administrative arrangements, while they wandered round the courtyards. And he was the one who found them their accommodation, so he could have hidden anybody. There's any amount of cases like that. So couldn't he have been an outsider?"

Kornilov seemed to hear something almost beseeching in the investigator's words, but he shook his head: "Alas, that can hardly be. The old book where the second man is written of – the Jerusalem Talmud, published in Amsterdam in 1645, plainly states: 'Two disciples testified against him, brought him before the court and accused him.' Disciples! But we know only one, don't we – Judas. Where on earth is the second?"

"Yes," said Surovtsev. "Yes, you're right, where on earth's the second? A sad story." He sat thinking, then smiled. "So enquiries into cases involving agitation were known even in those days. Even then!" He sat for a while, half-grinning. "Yes, a good clean job! Can't be overturned! They really put their minds to it! And you see how all the legal safeguards seemed to obtain; the court a fair one, the witnesses impartial, but if they want to get somebody, they get him, in spite of all the laws! You hear everybody talking about 'Trial by jury, trial by jury'. But who jailed Katyusha Maslova? A jury. Who sent Dmitri Karamazov to forced labour? A jury. Who sat Sacco and Vanzetti in the electric chair? A jury. A class court! However you hedge it round and restrict it, a court like that won't let its own power come to grief. Nor do we – so what's all the fuss?" Saying this, he at once started bustling about: he took out a clean sheet of paper, placed it on the desk and began: "Well now, Vladimir Mikhailovich, shall we place it on record?"

"What?" Kornilov was alarmed. "This?"

"No, no, not what we've just been talking about of course," the investigator smiled. "Something along these lines now: 'I consider it my duty to bring to your attention that at such and such a time, date, month I talked with citizen Kutorga at your behest. The conversation took place in the presence of (her name here) who can confirm all my testimony. Citizen Kutorga spoke of his scholarly researches into church history; he touched on no other questions and did not speak of political matters. He uttered nothing ideologically harmful . . .'" That's it! Signature. You can add, if true: 'He is satisfied with his life and said of the Soviet system: "I am grateful to it for delivering me from a lie" ' You did say that last time, agreed?"

"Yes, of course," returned Kornilov, "but couldn't we dispense with this: 'I consider it my duty to bring to your attention . . .' and 'at your behest . . .'?"

"What do you find embarrassing?" Surovtsev smiled faintly. "It's the truth isn't it?"

"It's the truth certainly," Kornilov faltered, "but . . ."

"No buts, Vladimir Mikhailovich," Surovtsev cut in with stern benevolence. "The only value your testimony has lies in the fact that we ourselves asked you to assist us. That's why we trust your replies and evidence. Otherwise all this is a waste of time. Surely you realize that?"

"Yes, but . . ."

Surovtsev gave him a stern glance, then abruptly burst into laughter.

"Well, you're a strange character, Vladimir Mikhailovich, no offence. Very strange. More buts . . . Now what are you afraid of, really? 'But' indeed. After all, you're not the first known witness, nor the second unknown one. You're not a disciple and not a plaintiff. You are establishing the innocence of a man, no more nor less. You're refuting a denunciation! No reason to feel awkward about that, eh?"

"No, no, of course not. Thank you."

"Well, so then we write, 'I consider it my duty . . .'" Surovtsev bent over the paper.

When the report was completed and signed, he rose, and placing a hand on Kornilov's shoulder, said: "You have nothing to thank me for, of course. But I am really grateful to you. A very interesting talk we've had here. Food for thought."

Another week passed. The orchard was now sad, damp and empty. The apples had been picked and the foreman transferred elsewhere. Kornilov was waiting for the order to stop the dig, but there was no one to issue it. "As soon as the chief arrives, he'll see to the arrangements," the political enlightenment man would say, smiling mysteriously. You must be in the know, he seemed to say. You're not a silly innocent, are you? But what actually was there to know? He did in fact behave like an innocent. He phoned Surovtsev without fail on every trip to town, and was received at once. And there they sat in the bright, spacious office, with a map of the world on the wall, overlooking the children's park, drinking mineral water and talking away. They chatted about everything under the sun: treasure trove, how some play by the Tur brothers, or Sheinin's *Confrontation* was brilliant, a penetrating slice-of-life play on a very relevant subject ("Have you read Vyshinsky's article in *Izvestiya*, incidentally? You really must! Some curious facts there!"). About Zybin, the excavations ("You mean you haven't been sent a new man yet? How can you work then?"). After that, they passed on to the old man. ("How's the old man? He's lived his span. There's no altering him. He can just sit and write away."). At length they would put together the same paper. It started: "I consider it my duty to inform you . . ." and ended up with: ". . . he said positive things about the Soviet system."

This went on for a week, then something happened. They were just finishing off, when Khripushin entered the office with a folder in his hand. He gave Surovtsev a curt nod before coming over to the desk and leaning over Kornilov.

"Well that's fine!" he said, smirking. "We'll soon be welcoming the little father into the party. That's the way things are going."

"Well, why not?" Surovtsev smiled briefly. "If he deserves it, we'll accept him."

"He will, he will! I can see from your papers that he will!" Khripushin assured him warmly. He undid the file and took out *The Trial of Christ*, brandishing it in front of Kornilov. "This is some work! Nothing to add to that: great!"

"What's great?" asked Surovtsev.

"The way the priest has kept on fighting his corner!"

Surovtsev mumbled something, as Kornilov looked at the major in astonishment, a calculated astonishment of course.

"What corner, you mean?" the major answered. "Just this: whatever Marx, Engels, Lenin or Stalin might have written about it, Christ did exist!"

"That is, there existed a man called Jesus, on whom the evangelists bestowed the appellation Christ?" Kornilov ventured.

"That's not important, not important at all," Khripushin waved a gigantic paw at him. "People can read what they like into it. What matters is – he existed! Secondly, you can see how humanely trials were conducted in those days. We chekists have rejected that priestly humaneness." He suddenly exploded and began roaring. "So, what the priest wants will never be. What will be is: 'You will get what you deserve – and in full measure!' And thirdly – and most importantly. It was the godless who crucified him! Our Lord God! And on the third day, having overcome death by his own, was resurrected and ascended into heaven."

"Look, as it happens, that isn't in the manuscript!" Kornilov shouted. He was genuinely aghast.

"What do you mean, isn't in?" Khripushin turned wrathfully towards him. "What do you mean it isn't, when it's down here in black and white. Are you trying to pull my leg?" He tossed the manuscript onto the desk. "Take your holy gospel! Surovtsev, get a receipt from him that the material has been returned."

"What?" Kornilov jumped to his feet. "I just gave him all that without a receipt. Why on earth . . . ?"

"What's that?" Khripushin turned his grim face towards him and looked him with pewter eyes. "So you came here to play games with us, did you?"

"I . . ." Kornilov began.

"You what? Was it material evidence you submitted to the organs or *The Empress in Love*? Lieutenant Surovtsev!"

"Yes, yes," Surovtsev began hastily rummaging through the papers. "We'll do it, we'll do it! Vladimir Mikhailovich it's just part of enquiry procedure."

"Why bother explaining things to him, no need to explain!" Khripushin had completely lost his temper. "You'd better ask him who he is! USA or Soviet citizen? Is he obliged to assist the organs or not? Why you . . . !" He clenched his fists and his cheeks flushed. "And let's have no more of these detective stories! All I've got here is a hundred pages of divinity! I'm not having it! And don't try and pull the wool over my eyes. Watch it, Surovtsev! Just watch it if you please! I hold you fully responsible!" And with that he banged out of the office.

Both said nothing for several seconds. It must be said that if Khripushin had wanted to create an impression, he had certainly done so. The six-foot tough with the tensed fists and flunkey's hairline parting had created an impression all right! Still, it was possible he had intended nothing of the kind. Simply by overstepping a certain threshold, he had absolutely automatically, actor-like, assumed the appropriate mood. Towards the end, he had screwed up his nerves – and he was constantly prone to hysteria. He was hysterical when he was interrogating a prisoner, hysterical when he was harrying a witness, hysterical when he began bawling, and when he stopped, realizing that this time it was useless.

And there was one more thing which had come to him over the past few months. Never before had he been so conscious of having both feet firmly on the ground. He knew it was not for nothing that he had been hauled here from the back of beyond and given the rank of major; a great deal had changed in the world. The long-awaited hour was at hand, when the Leader would at last arm his glorious chekists with the investigative methods which he himself had perfected – all of which stemmed from a profoundly creative understanding of the idea of Marxism and the Stalinist analysis of international worker solidarity. An unshakeable base had already been laid down by the Leader for these new methods, or rather, new forms of the class struggle. Then these bureaucrats, who now looked down on him would hold their tongues for evermore, because what was required now was not just book-learning and piddling matters of form, but something else, something living, not dead. That was something he possessed, and he was straining at the leash, whereas they were still humming and hawing. That was why he had existed all these months in a heightened state of tension, in constant expectation of something great and resoundingly glorious coming to pass. It was precisely for this reason that he would get overwrought and take to bawling more often than usual.

"Ah, that turned out badly," frowned Surovtsev uselessly when Khripushin had gone. "And you just had to say . . . Well, never mind, never mind. Here's the paper, write . . ." He pondered. "Write it this way: 'From the enquiries concerning A. E. Kutorga, the 224-page manuscript *The Trial of Christ* has been received back by me Vladimir Mikhailovich Kornilov, as being of no value to the investigation.' Signatures. Date. That's it! Give me it! Phew, damnation, that was a proper mess. Want some water? (Kornilov shook his head.) It's all right, it's all right! Worse things happen. I'll tell you why the major is in a foul temper: he's had a rocket himself."

"Who from?"

"His chief. As it happens, the lieutenant-colonel called me in with the case. I reported to him that everything was going fine. He kept leafing through the case, picked up *The Trial* and read a couple of pages, then he says: 'A cracked old man, that's all! We'll probably close the matter, but you know what? It won't look so watertight from our side. Here we've got five reports, all of them saying the same thing: He doesn't say what he shouldn't. And what did he say? Discuss the holy liturgy did he? Did they talk at all or just drink vodka? What if he's just keeping it back? We close the case and then he goes round squawking at the top of his voice – what do we do then?' I said nothing, there being nothing to say. Then he had another think, and decides: 'All right! We'll give it another week – it can't hurt, and we'll have more to go on . . .' Then he puts pressure on the major. And the major on us. That's all about it."

"I had to stick my oar in with that manuscript," said Kornilov bitterly. "Who asked me to bring it in to you. Who dragged me in by the tongue, idiot that I am? Why you . . ." And he struck himself on the forehead.

"Come on now, come on!" said Surovtsev in pained agitation. "This is excellent justificatory material! We've already had a response on it! You've done marvellously! As for the conversation just now . . ." he gave a sudden laugh and an airy gesture. "Don't give it a thought, honestly, ignore it. We get it here a thousand times a day! Honestly." However, as he wrote out the pass, he suddenly grew grave and said, this time without the smile: "Only now, I have something to ask of you. The matter really is getting to the end. Play a more active role. Start the ball rolling about politics yourself."

All that week, Kornilov's state of mind was grim in the extreme. The weather over the mountains had finally broken. It was rain, rain, rain. The Alma-Atinka swelled and roared, rolling stones along in the torrent. A grey, rusty sleet drove over the excavation sites. The tent leaked, forcing him to move his bunk and put a pan to catch the water. And then a dog had got into the habit of howling in the night. He would get up half-asleep and hurl something at it. It would leap back a little distance then squat down and howl on and on, the wretched animal.

And the rains went drearily on and on too, day and night, night and day – fine, grey, slanting rain; life wasn't worth living. Against that background, anything might happen. All the same, the worst thing of all was his encounter with Lina. He called in at the institute to see her, half opened the office door and called out; she shot out immediately, dazzling, bright and joyful. He almost cried out: what a sight she was. On seeing him, she at once subsided. Nothing remained for him apart from: "Oh, it's you, Vladimir Mikhailovich." So, they talked in the corridor outside the half-opened door – about the excavations, the mountains, the rain, the apples. Did she need any help in getting some? He could do it! No, thank you, I don't need anything! Then he dropped a hint about Zybin and she swiftly replied: "I know – they told me. Well, what about it? He's innocent, they'll sort it out and let him go . . ." That was how it was. And that was all. He went away, and the way he felt after that he might as well have walked straight into the Alma-Atinka.

Father Andrey too he only saw once, and that for just three minutes. The farm Gazik was standing close by under the hill, and in it sat his daughter and somebody from the management. Father Andrey rushed in for the manuscript. As he took it, he asked: "Read it? Did you like it? No? Well, later, later!" and stumbled off down the hill, an old foolish priest in his broad priest's hat, his cape, resembling a monk's cassock, and his boots with the deep galoshes.

It was all this petty, oppressive absurdity, gnawing at him like an aching tooth, that was totally unnerving Kornilov, and making him positively ill. It was simply bundling him out of the world. And he realized: there was no running away from this, no hiding place; it was always with you, because it was – you. And his conscience tormented him as well – why oh why had he stuck his oar in? Who had dragged him by the tongue? He felt like saving the reverend father? So, saviour, save thyself first. And now they were calling him in, ordering him to write things, adding to them, correcting, shouting, threatening, and he had to wriggle and justify himself. Why? In hell's name why? And what was he really worth, for all his vows, and what in the world did he understand anyway? The important thing was, what was he going to do with himself now? Get drunk? He'd already done that. He'd got drunk at Volchikha's once, then he repeated the process. Some lads with an accordion had come in for vodka; he'd played a bit on the instrument and they'd started inviting him to a wedding but he refused. After that, he'd got into such a fight with the workmen that he'd been vomiting for two days and couldn't lift his head from the pillow; everything was spinning or aching; he didn't feel like doing anything and he didn't give a damn. It had taken him till the third day to get up. He threw up in the doorway of the tent – and at once felt better: he lifted his head and wiped his mouth with his hand. It was trembling, as was his whole body as he set off. He swayed as he went, but he made it to the Blue Danube nevertheless. It was packed to the rafters. A plump pink barmaid presided over the barrel – a prize specimen, fit to crown a teapot in a souvenir shop. He made his way blindly towards her through the crowd and ordered six pints of beer at once. Somebody fetched them to a free table. He sat and drank without pausing. One glass, a second, then a third – they all stood side by side on the table. People stared at him and sympathized. Nobody rallied him because they all understood. Then he got up and went on his way. At the halfway point the clouds suddenly broke and sunshine flooded through. At once, everything around him began to brighten, to glitter, chirr and chirrup. It grew light and warm, there was a sense of life and space. He lowered himself under a bush. He sat and thought for a while, relieved himself and felt at peace with the world. And the sun warmed him, shining, dazzling him and tumbling him to the grass – of how he fell down and slept, he could remember nothing.

It was evening when he woke and he jumped to his feet at once. He was as light as air, half here and half nowhere at all. Everything now seemed stunningly easy. He went lightly up the hill, stuck his head airily into the tent and stiffened. A bespectacled Father Andrey was sitting at the table, writing.

"Andrey Ernestovich," he exclaimed, overjoyed. "But I was ..."

Father Andrey turned and looked at him. His glance was, as the fine writers have it, moist. That meant he was already ...

"I was just writing you a note," he said. "I came, saw you weren't here, everything strewn all over the place. How could you do such a thing? You've got a new suit here, a gramophone and a Leica. Everything just lying about. Your bicycle's outside. These days you get a lot of people in the mountains; they'll pinch your things and you can whistle for them. So I decided to wait till you came back. What are you doing with yourself, eh?"

Kornilov bounded over to him, seized him by the shoulders and hugged him, sobbing even, so much affection did he feel at this moment towards this old man, how splendid it was that he had come.

"Now, now," said Father Andrey, smiling. "What's the matter? Had one too many again, I expect. At Volchikha's?"

"No, not at Volchikha's," said Kornilov, surveying with affection that gaunt, icon-like face, that pointed beard, those endearing fine tiny wrinkles. "No, not at Volchikha's, Andrey Ernestovich, with my lads. I paid them off and ..."

"And they were overjoyed! I hope they didn't blow the lot! Left something to live on? Well, that's all right then. Headache, I suppose? Let's go and I'll set you to rights."

"To Volchikha's, Father Andrey?"

"No, not to Volchikha's, dear comrade Kornilov," pronounced Father Andrey proudly, with a slight lift of the head. "To my own residence. Yes, sir! I'm a bachelor now. My daughter's gone away to see her husband in Sochi. So I'm my own master. Well then, let's go to my place. I'll show you my cell in the dell. Take your Leica with you, don't forget. Nothing comes amiss to the good thief."

The cell in the dell was what Father Andrey called his glassed-in winter balcony. It was very long and projected like an opened matchbox. God knows when and why villas like this had been erected. The first things that caught Kornilov's eye were the bookshelves. They stretched from end to end and from floor to ceiling. He studied them: sets of *Novy Mir* and *Krasnaya Nov*, tied up with string. The collected works of Chekhov (a supplement to *Ogonyok*), the complete works of Lenin, various fat tomes of Marx and Engels and a lot of translated '20s belles-lettres – colourful paper covers with sketchy drawings in indian ink and carmine.

"And where are the religious books?" Kornilov enquired.

"This is my religion," said Father Andrey, leading him over to a small shelf above the writing desk. They were all medical works, among them several textbooks on midwifery.

He looked at Kutorga in bewilderment.

"That came in useful as well!", Kutorga nodded. "They all came in useful! That's the north for you! The Golden Kolyma as they called it there. I passed special medical orderly courses in the camps. That was nothing, of course, I already knew how to mend dislocations, do cupping and bandage peoples' hands. But the fact that I worked for five years with a famous, one might say world famous luminary, passing him his lancets and tweezers – now that is something! I did abdominal operations, if you want to know! Once in a fishing village, I cut out someone's appendix right there on the table. I got them to steam the table and scrape it white and do all the disinfection."

"No anaesthetic?" Kornilov marvelled.

"Well, I did have something of the sort, but it was, you know, more or less symbolic. In those days I used to rely mostly on spirit. I'd give him a tin mug full of spirit and say: 'Drink it in one go, now!' Then straight on the table. Well of course I didn't open up the stomach or anything, but I did sometimes have to lance fingers. You don't believe me, is that it? Ah, I wouldn't wish you there, but if you had been and got out alive, oho! You'd understand a great deal about life. All right, I'll get busy round the house and you have a look at the books in the meantime. My daughter's brought all of them in. Mine are just this shelf; there's things worth reading there."

When he came back Kornilov was standing by the writing desk, twirling a small bronze bust in his hand.

"What's this, Andrey Ernestovich?" he asked. "Where did it come from?"

Father Andrey looked at it.

"It's part of the writing-table fittings," he replied. "It used to fix onto the inkwell. Now what interesting fact are you going to tell me about it, eh?"

It was a bust of Don Quixote. On the whole, it hardly differed from the image created by Doré, and subsequently imitated by hundreds of artists, caricaturists, sculptors, and operatic and dramatic actors. The same modelling of the gaunt, noble features, the same moustaches and little beard, the same headgear. But this Don Quixote was laughing: he was poking out his tongue and teasing. He was full of venom and malice. He was triumphant. He was enjoying a satanic triumph over somebody. He was no longer the knight of the doleful countenance, but an imp, a devil, Satan himself. It was Don Quixote being transformed as you watched into Mephistopheles. It then became clear that he wasn't wearing a helmet at all, it was a hood – and there were horns beneath it; that he had a pointed impish chin, and moustaches like the hound of hell.

"Well, what do you say to that?" asked Father Andrey.

Kornilov was still looking at the bust.

"Well now, that could be a solution," he said at length. "There would be nothing to contradict it."

"What solution?" asked Father Andrey.

"Just this: the poor knight, Jan Huss, Don Quixote, Francis of Assisi . . ." he gulped back one name, "and one or two others. Did they bring good or evil into the world? Who on earth can tell? Does not their goodness and pity torment the world? After that good of theirs, there follow killings, madness; after Saint Francis comes the Holy Inquisition. After Huss, the Hussite wars, beggary. In short, after the martyrs, the executioners infallibly arrive. So how did you come by this thing?"

Father Andrey came over and sat down by him.

"My father left it to me! That father of mine was a wonderful man; one might call him the history of Russian social thought! A journalist, an 1860s poet. And an egregious sinner! I'm most probably expiating his sins. He used to write for *Fatherland Notes*. He used to write letters to Herzen. He travelled to Astrakhan to see Chernyshevsky. He kept wanting to ask him what he had hatched out in the prison at Viluisk. What truth was revealed to you there? Fearful questions! But he didn't ask them, he didn't ask them at all! And apart from a conversation with Olga Socratovna he achieved nothing at all. He came back home and started drinking. He was a terrible man for the drink! He would get a skinful and roar his head off. Roar, mark you, not weep. He died of it while still comparatively young. I barely remember him. He was a fervent atheist. Though perhaps not so much an atheist as a theomachist; there were such people as well in those days. As soon as he died, my mother threw that devil up into the loft, and after the revolution I was raking the cabbage patch and turned it up. He's been standing by me ever since; he's a part of the furniture, he's made himself at home."

"Yes," said Kornilov. "Yes!"

He sighed and replaced the bust.

"I'm not feeling too good these days, Andrey Ernestovich."

"Why, what's the matter?"

"I don't know . . ."

"You haven't got . . . What do they call it? Toothache in the heart?"

"The sort Heine says lead fillings and Berthold Schwartz's tooth powder can cure? No, not that?"

"What is it then?"

"I don't know. That is, I do know. When I get drunk, I'll tell you, perhaps. In any case it's an anachronism, isn't it? These bullets, I mean, an anachronism! Where would I get hold of them? They might suit the noble Werther, but not us. For us, it's arsenic, the fourth floor, the loft and the noose. That's just the thing for the likes of us. What do you think, Father?"

Father Andrey frowned.

"What do I think? I think the only sin that God does not forgive a Christian is suicide. Suicides are cast out for ever and ever from the Lord's mercy. They cannot have a funeral service or be buried in consecrated ground. To the animal cemetery, all right, haul them off, dig a pit and throw them in. Cover them over and let them lie!"

"Really?" Kornilov sighed. "That's a cruel God of yours, then, very cruel. And no forgiveness? Terrific! Give me that devil again. He's laughing, the wretch. Did he laugh in the face of your atheist father? Incidentally, how did he die?"

Father Andrey lifted the bottle and filled their glasses.

"He hanged himself. In the loft."

They drained one glass and poured another. Father Andrey began talking about the North. He was an accomplished raconteur and pronounced the broad "a" with an actor's skill. Kornilov was in stitches throughout. He was especially tickled by the story of the co-operative cook – Baroness Serafima Bark. Her arms were as rough as bark too, but some days she wore bracelets and a signet ring. Once in his presence, with a fisherman's oath she had seen off a brawny tough who had come in for vodka; she at once turned to Father Andrey and explained in French: "It's awful the way one has to talk to these people but alas (hélas, hélas), it's the only language they understand. Now he realizes that it's a definite refusal, he'll turn round and take himself off." And so he did.

"Incidentally this Fimka woman caused a real mix-up," said Father Andrey. "Some Institute organized a folklore expedition about five years ago. They were looking for old storytellers all along the coast. But where could they find them? There weren't any! Anyway, somebody, whether out of stupidity or mischief, sent them along to Fimka. She sang them a couple of dozen songs. Cribbed them straight out of Avenarius, the one who wrote the children's book about the Kievan heroes. Their eyes fairly stood out on stalks. What material! They sat there day and night. They did reams of writing and saw off a bucket of vodka. The old woman was making a profit out of them! So they went away. Then they came back again. So she told them fairy tales from Sakharov, served up the naughtiest ones there are. In the North, there's no shortage of that kind of thing! Again they covered page after page with this stuff. Then on the very last day, as they were leaving, after the champagne and the toasts, she told them who she was, and where she came from – she was a wicked woman, may God forgive her. The leader of the expedition nearly took a fit! He clucked like a broody hen! 'But-but how can that be? What, what? The Smolny Institute. But that's government money! But that's . . . but that's . . .' What do you think of that?" Father Andrey roared with laughter, flapping an arm.

"But what if he knew where I've been with his manuscript," thought Kornilov and abruptly blurted: "You see, I've been called in." He was instantly stricken and thrown into confusion. Not knowing what to say, he repeated urgently: "There! There! In there!" and followed the example of the scientific secretary in pointing to the ceiling.

Father Andrey glanced at him, tipped the glass down his throat and shook his head.

"D-damnation!" He whispered. "It's blasted strong! Seventy degrees shouldn't wonder." He caught his breath and got to his feet. "Well, what of it, Vladimir Mikhailovich, we'll all be there! 'To this favour we must come.' Wait a minute, I'll pop and get the gherkins."

It was odd, but the almost raw spirit had no apparent effect on Kornilov. An extraordinary sobriety and clarity had descended upon him. He sat and mused.

"This is all very well, of course, both the priest and his cherry brandy; and what I said, it's all right – but what happens next? The director will be back soon. I'll settle up and get away, head off somewhere and leave them looking silly. What about Dasha? Lina? Zybin? Well, to blazes with Lina, but there is Dasha."

At this he began to consider seeing Dasha again and what he would say to her. It was pleasant to think about. He even smiled.

Father Andrey came out with a plate of gherkins.

"Just try these," he said. "All my own work! They call everybody in. They called me in."

"What?" Kornilov was stunned. "You too!"

"Me too. Go on, eat up, eat up, please! Yes, they called me in. But what could I possibly know? Georgi Nikolaevich in the museum is up there," he pointed to the ceiling. "And I'm down here." He pointed to the floor. "Who am I, a priest! Flogger of dead horses. Georgi Nikolaevich is persona grata. He gave us an instructional talk once on how to fill a card in and that was the only time I saw him. That's what I said and they didn't even bother writing it down."

"Who was it interrogated you?"

"Interrogated!" Father Andrey smiled, shaking his head and sighing. "Lord, such words! They didn't interrogate me. They interrogate accused persons. They ta-alked to me. It was a Lieutenant Golikov who did the talking. It wasn't him who asked for you?"

"No, not him."

"Well, naturally, there's lots of them there. The size of the place. Well, what of it? I get one, you get another; they ask me about one, they ask you about another – then perhaps the truth will emerge."

"What truth is that, pray," Kornilov scowled. "Why do you think they arrested Zybin?"

Father Andrey smiled and shrugged his shoulders.

"Still, come on, why?"

"I don't know, Vladimir Mikhailovich, and I'm not even interested. Earthly powers – they're tricky things. People like your boss are usually arrested not for something they've done, but for some reason."

"What was that again?"

"Or in the name of something. So they don't get in the way of things, I mean. The authorities think up something and he doesn't agree and obstructs it. Or has the capacity to do so. Therefore they pick him up in good time, on the principle: 'It is better for us that one man should die for the people, rather than the whole people should perish.' They arrest him on that principle."

"What's that from?"

"Oh, it's the gospels again. The celebrated John, chapter eleven. Well, from the point of view of the earthly powers it's perfectly logical."

"Terrific," Kornilov looked at him and suddenly felt roused to fury. " 'Better for us'. And who are 'You'? I'd love to get a look at your bright, shining face just for one minute! Just to find out in the name of whom or what you're acting like bloody gangsters! Benefactors indeed! Although, yes, yes!" He brandished an arm. " 'There is no power but of God.' You've got a quotation for every occasion! Oh you priests!" He smiled obscurely and paused and shook his head. "But you are right about one thing. If a man is dangerous, they eliminate him. Click – and that's the end of him. So, someone has demonstrated to someone else that Zybin was dangerous; that's the long and short of it. But it's something else that I don't get – take you. You're a dangerous individual too, one of the former – pre-revolutionary folk, and yet here you are sitting drinking vodka with me, writing an obscurantist work, and they don't touch you. Why? There's a reason for that, is there?"

"Hmm!" Father Andrey smiled wryly. "Since when have I been a dangerous character? It's true I'm a priest, an obscurantist, a harmful element. Harmful, though, not dangerous! I would ask you to mark that! I am in no way a threat to anybody. I've been suppressed, that's all. And nowadays I'm useful, not harmful at all. Because I work for a living. I chop down trees, I go to sea, I break my back for my father and grandfather's sake. What on earth am I to do? I have to eat. Now, don't go frowning, I can see my priestly lack of principle annoys you. I won't harp on about it. Anyway, why have we got onto this? Tell me what you thought about my book, then."

279

Kornilov gripped his cut-glass tumbler till his fingers started going numb.

"I enjoyed it," he said softly, though his eyes still flickered. "I enjoyed it very much. And not only me; comrade Surovtsev did too."

"Who is this comrade Surovtsev?" asked Father Andrey, slicing the gherkins.

Kornilov had been rising higher and higher; he was now soaring above creation. It was from this altitude that he felt bound to disgorge everything that was struggling to be free. He was really exhausted by now.

"I don't know who he is," he said, smiling ironically. "An investigator or an operative; well, anyway, he sits in the big house and takes a special interest in you."

"And he asked you for the manuscript?" enquired Father Andrey peaceably.

"He didn't have to. I brought it to him myself. As soon as I got it from you, I took it along. He's called me in and asked me: 'Who is this Kutorga?' I answered: 'A priest.' 'What's he doing these days?' 'He's working on a book about Christ.' 'What sort of a book is it?' 'I can bring it along if you like.' 'Do that.' So I took it. He put it in his drawer and a week later rang me: 'Come and collect your gospel.' I went there and got it. That's all."

He blurted all this at once, in cold bitterness, but in an almost feverish haste, afraid to stop for a second in case he cooled down and then he would say nothing more. Now he talked and talked, unable to call a halt. He didn't just want to talk about this, he wanted to go on talking. Talking about himself and his absurd, ludicrous existence; where he had been born, how and from whom he had learned things; how he had been married off unsuccessfully at the age of twenty-one. And all the rest of it too, about his father and mother, his elder sister and her husband, a prominent military man; how much they loved him, looked after his interests, sent him packages and parcels; how he didn't need anything just so long as he was left in peace, so long as he was left alone! Yes, in peace, in peace. That was why he was bursting to talk, simply had to talk about his first investigator and how the swine had tricked him back then. He would have started talking about it even if Father Andrey had been short with him and cut him off, saying that decent folk don't do such things – who had given him permission to take his manuscript along to that building? Ah, then he would have simply overwhelmed him with words! Positively awash with indignation!

Ah, Andrey Ernestovich, Andrey Ernestovich! Governor's confessor! Hell, what sort of a spiritual father are you if you can't even make sense of that?

But Father Andrey was looking at him in a perfectly commonplace fashion, and Kornilov couldn't read anything in that direct gaze. He simply ran up against it and subsided.

"Earthly powers!" said Father Andrey pensively. "What can you say about them? But put us in their place and in a couple of months we'd send the whole enterprise to the bottom. Yet you see the little ship's still afloat, still afloat . . ." He thought for a moment, tapping his fingers on the table. "As for showing them my manuscript, that was the right thing to do. They'll feel easy now. A priest's a priest, what else can you expect! They'll turn me out of the museum no doubt, but let that pass."

"What do you mean, Andrey Ernestovich!" Kornilov was outraged. "Why talk like that? Our director would never agree to that!"

"He will, that director of yours, he will," said Father Andrey with the suspicion of a smile. "Why, you ask? It stands to reason: to keep obscurantism out of cultural enlightenment. Well, well, it's not the first time and it won't be the last! I'm used to things turning out this way. It's all right. I'm not afraid of work. Take a look at my palm here. No, feel it, feel it! Like wood, isn't it? Another month and it'll be just my time of year – I'll go and get a job with the forestry. I'm not a priest in that field, I'm a professor! Now then, where's your glass, let's drink to that profession of mine. Still, why stick to tots? Wait a minute and I'll fetch proper glasses."

"Earthly powers", said Father Andrey, as he snorted and pushed away the empty glass. "They're very tricky things. You can't make head or tail of them. They're governed by a thousand and one considerations. In that context, the story of Pontius Pilate is very instructive. There's no fathoming what his attitude to Christ was, even now, is there? Opinions have divided diametrically, one might say. Take you: 'President of the military tribunal! – condemned him and washed his hands of it! What does that mean? Although he crucified a man, he is blameless?' And, I, mark you, wouldn't laugh. I would have understood that such things also happen. Because they are tricky, very tricky, these earthly powers! Spiritual powers now, they're much more straightforward. In the Christ story it was all only too straightforward in that regard. They didn't like Christ, he was seized, judged, condemned, and put to death, that's all there was to it. Although it was no easy task condemning him."

"Not easy?"

"At first it was not at all easy. Later on, things went more smoothly, but at first the thing almost fell through altogether. You don't resort to false witness straight away, do you, there have to be some promptings of despair. During investigations too, they don't start bawling at you straight off; an interval has to elapse while they get used to the prisoner, as it were, look their fill at him. In those times it was all a thousand times more difficult. Listen to the way the presiding judge spoke to the witnesses." Father Andrey went across to the writing desk, opened a folder and took out a sheet of paper. "Perhaps what you say is based on supposition or on rumours, the words of others, and you do not realize that before we can accept your testimony, we will test you by way of question and answer. Remember that if the case concerns money, restitution can be made in money, but in this case, the blood of an innocent man, and all his unborn descendants for ever and ever will lie upon the false witness, for it was not in vain that the Lord God said of Cain: 'The bloods of your brother Abel cry out unto me.' (Mark that, 'bloods', not 'blood'! 'The bloods of the unborn posterity of Abel.') This is why Adam was created unique, in order to teach you that he who destroys one soul, destroys the whole world, and he who saves an inno- cent man, saves all mankind. For if a man makes a thousand impressions from his signet ring, they will all be identical, whereas God took the image of all people from Adam, so that although they are equal, no one is like unto another. This, therefore, is what you have to decide; whether the whole world was created only for the sake of the man who now stands before you and whose life depends on your word.' Those were his final remarks. After that begins the questioning of the witnesses; they come in one at a time. The circumstances are as follows: dead of night (the cock crew a second time, so the whole business took place between two and three o'clock), seven-branched candlesticks burning; the hall is vast, stone-built and empty, half of it always in darkness; seventy-two judges on cushions on the floor, in two semi-circles, facing one another, so that everyone can see the others' eyes. Three secretaries in the centre – one to note down the words of the accused, two others the testimony of the witnesses. One for the prosecution witnesses, the other for the defence. Well it's obvious that false witnesses in circum- stances like that will tend to lose their way and get confused: 'For many bare false witness against him . . . but their witness agreed not together,' says Mark's gospel – that is, not one of the witnesses could wholly confirm the words of any other. And now two witnesses spoke individually whose testimony seemed to coincide."

"Judas and this other?"

"I don't know, perhaps it was them. After all, everything concerning this nocturnal court is obscure. Who could know what took place there? The court was secret, with no outsiders present – and the accused isn't here now either, having been executed. So, two witnesses spoke, both testifying that Christ had reviled the temple. A more heinous crime could not have been imagined but this evidence too was rejected. According to Mark, Jesus is supposed to have said: 'I will destroy this temple that is made with hands, and within three days I will build another made without hands.' In Matthew, it has a different sound: 'I am able to destroy the temple of God and to build it in three days.' Ah! You see the contradiction there!"

"No, I don't," said Kornilov. "It's the same thing in my opinion."

"Ha! In your opinion! You're a poor lawyer, then. There's an enormous divergence. Just think now: 'I will destroy this temple.' This one! Terribly precise – that is, the one we are talking about at this moment! The definite article is there. The one in which is preserved the tabernacle of the Lord, the holy of holies for the people of Israel – the temple of Solomon. And I will build another not made with hands. Which is that then, may one ask? Your own? The temple of Jesus? The son of Joseph and Mary? The one who has brothers called Jacob, Joseph, Judas and Simon, as well as several sisters? What sort of temple are you promising, prophet, to build for us in your name in place of this one of Solomon's – that was the meaning of the testimony of the first witness."

"Well, what about the second?"

"The second testified thus: 'I can destroy a temple of God and build it in three days.' Meaning of course, not that I can, but that I could – the subjunctive mood there, but never mind. As if to say: 'This is how strong I am.' What temple? There is no definite article, so then, any temple! And of course there was an abundance of them. All temples were sacred after all! So in three days, you can build us a synagogue? You are a braggart of a builder indeed! Got a lot of money out of fools probably. They would have a good laugh and walk away. And that was it. So the two testimonies could not be combined. The accusations petered out and Jesus had to be released."

"Where to? Back to His beloved disciples? To Peter? Thomas and Judas?" Kornilov could not understand why, but the fact that his confession had apparently made not the slightest impression on Father Andrey, who had simply heard him out, then upped and talked about something else, had been a severe shock to his nerves. Better if he had abused him or struck him, or thrown him out; otherwise it made it look as though nothing else could have been expected of Kornilov.

"Why have you taken against Peter?" Father Andrey grinned. "After all, say what you like, he was the only one who did not abandon his teacher. The others, as Mark tells us, 'all forsook him and fled'. Do you know why that whole sad story strikes me as thoroughly authentic? Everything about it is so bitterly and unattractively human. Could these really be apostles? Or martyrs? More than that, could they really be Christians? A Christian is supposed to

> March to death singing hymns,
> Into the jaws of ravening beasts
> Look without flinching.

"Or as Saint Ignatius said: 'I am Godly wheat and let me be ground by the teeth of beasts and become the bread of the Lord.' Or again. 'Even a robber chief, the leader of a band of villains, even he is never betrayed by his swinish followers, unless he has first betrayed them.' So says Porphyry, a bitter foe of Christ and Christianity, about the apostles. You're not the first to be ironic about Peter. 'How could he be the foundation of the church if on hearing the word "Jesus" from the mouth of some wretched rabbi, he was so terrified that he broke his vow three times?' That was Porphyry again. What of Christ himself? Remember: 'My soul is exceeding sorrowful, even unto death: tarry ye here and watch with me.' And again: 'Father, all things are possible unto Thee; take away this cup from me.'

"And on the cross: 'Eli, Eli, lama sabachthani. My God, My God why hast thou forsaken me?' and in some manuscripts, even more harshly: 'Why dost thou humiliate me?' And then that prayer: 'I thirst!' And the kind-hearted executioners offer him the sponge of vinegar. Where will you find anything like it in the lives of the saints? No wonder that other hater of Christianity, Celsus, is maliciously direct: 'If he has himself decided to accept execution, in obedience to his father, why call on him for help and pray to be released: "Father, let this cup pass from me"? Why didn't he endure his thirst on the cross, as any one of us often has to?' And Porphyry also adds: 'All these speeches are unworthy, not only of the son of God, but even of a sage who despises death.' Alas, all this is so. And there is only one answer: 'Ecce homo!'

And the evangelists could do nothing with this man. They didn't dare!"

"But they wanted to?"

"Well of course they did! 'Three and four times over,' writes Celsus, 'they re-wrote the first copy of the gospel, to avoid revealing it!' Yes, the most terrible revelation of all, that of the truth. And yet they didn't dare wipe out this weak, panicking, aching, utterly human element. And God, feeble and weak as he was, remained God. The God of men. You understand? No, no, how could you?"

"Yes, yes, I do understand," Kornilov assured him earnestly. "And you know what I've just remembered? Lessing wrote somewhere that a martyr is the most undramatic figure in the world. You can't write a tragedy about him. He performs no feats, he does not hesitate or suffer – he simply endures. He is tortured and he endures, he is tempted and he prays. Tfu! How depressing! But let's return to our muttons. So the witnesses got themselves mixed up?"

"So much so that the prisoner had to be released. But as the saying goes, they don't pull you in just to let you go again. The presiding judge addresses Jesus: 'I adjure thee by the living God,' he says, 'that thou tell us whether thou be the Christ, the Son of God?' Oh! This is a gross violation of the law! He should only have addressed the witnesses in that way. If Christ had now disavowed it or had answered in a vague or ambiguous fashion, they would have had to release him. But he honoured his life's work above life itself, above mother, sisters and brothers, the law and the temple, and in that most dreadful moment of his life, he did not dare – you hear? He simply did not dare! – to betray it. If he had just said: 'No, I am certainly not the man you take me to be,' that would have ended the matter. He would have beaten the sanhedrin. The seventy-two judges, followed by the guards, witnesses, secretaries, lay-brothers, altogether about a hundred of them, the whole crowd, would solemnly lead him out onto the square. And on that same square where he had preached, place him before the crowd and his disciples, and proclaim: 'We have judged this man and found him inno-cent. He never gave himself out to be the Christ, and he did not promise you the kingdom of heaven in his name. He merely preached the prophets to you according to his lights and understanding and you did not comprehend him.' And that is all. And Christ would vanish from our sight. The world remain unchanged. History would pass by. But he knew that this temptation would one day come and he would have to overcome it by death – but dying consciously and of his own free will, not like Seneca, the precursor, but like the son of man."

285

"You mean you don't think Seneca died of his own free will?"

"Perhaps he did, but not in that way. He fled rather than died. For Seneca, death was a release from compromise. And oh, Seneca was guilty of that! Acknowledging it fully, he once wrote this. Very finely. He could write beautifully. 'Wherever you look – you see the end of your torments everywhere. You see that ravine? In its depths lies your freedom. That crooked tree – stunted and twisted? Your freedom hangs from it. You see that river, the sea, that well? At the bottom of them is your freedom.' But Jesus felt himself to be perfectly free all his life in any case, free as the wind, like God. The gospels have brought to us that feeling. 'Here is a man who liked to eat and drink wine,' others wrote of him. 'I am come that they might have life, and that they might have it more abundantly,' he said of himself. Life for him was joyous, an exploit not a torment. That was precisely why he did not deign to answer 'no' to the presiding judge's question; he said 'yes'. The evangelists convey his answer in different ways, but at all events he answered very simply, monosyllabically – anything to have done with it all. Porphyry reproaches him for that. It seems to him that at such a decisive moment a man should grow to be as granite, break out in thunder and lightnings and with his tongue sear the judges' hearts. 'The same way,' he says, 'that Apollonius of Tyana accused the emperor Domitian! The fur flew!' But Christ was not Apollonius; he was worn out and weary unto death; he was sickened by all that had been happening. At that moment he wanted just one thing – let it be over quickly, quickly! Perhaps he was afraid that he wouldn't be able to stand it and collapse. But the judges were also in a hurry. 'Thou hast said.' The presiding judge ripped his garments open to the waist. This was equivalent to breaking his judges rod. 'Guilty of death,' he said. 'Guilty of death,' confirm the seventy-one. The end. 'And the whole multitude rose and led him to Pilate.' Rome now enters the case – the proconsul of Judaea, Pontius Pilate."

"He came of a rich Samnite family and therefore was never accounted a man out of the top drawer. The Samnites after all, were so-called allies, not Romans. They even had different emblems: the Romans had a wolf, but they had a bull. If you remember, there had even been three Social wars, when the bulls had gone for the wolves as a herd. But all that was over and done with. Now Pontius Pilate, at any rate in Judaea, felt himself to be a Roman patrician, a white man in a savage eastern

286

land. By nature he was a vigorous and active individual. Such people were known in Rome at that time as "homo novus", "new man". There's something untranslatable in that sobriquet – a hint of scorn, a light flip on the nose. Nouveau riche, upstart, *le bourgeois gentilhomme*, rags to riches, that sort of thing. Eusebius writes that Pilate was sent to Judaea by Sejanus – there was a cruel villain of that name at Tiberius' court. Later on, naturally, he also was executed. So, Sejanus is supposed to have appointed Pontius Pilate as proconsul precisely because of his detestation of the Jews. Very possibly. At all events, Judaea had never before experienced such a tyrant. 'Bribery, violence, execution without trial, endless horrible cruelties,' – so, according to Philo, wrote Herod Agrippa to Tiberius. Very well, that was probably no more than the truth. But all the same, he did not want to execute Christ. Why? This is where the confusion arises. The Christian writers have complicated the issue dreadfully. I recall here a conversation I had with an academician long ago. He said to me: 'But what do you find inscrutable about him, father? There really is no mystery about it. In our education work for instance, we're up to our ears in people like Pilate. He's a typical middle-ranking official of the imperial era. Harsh but not cruel, shrewd and worldly-wise. In minor and uncontroversial matters – just, even principled; in more important matters, evasive and indecisive. In every other regard he was extremely crafty in his dealings. Therefore, although he realized where the truth lay, he would start squirming at the slightest hint of complexity, wash his hands of it, so to speak. In the incident with Christ, this was demonstrated especially clearly. That was all there was to it.' But in this, as I now realize, the academician was not altogether correct. Special factors were at work."

"What were they then?"

"Well, I've already mentioned the first of them. He couldn't stand these filthy Jews. And since they reciprocated the feeling, everything got inextricably tangled up. And in these stratagems, Pilate at times positively lost his head. The shrewd, sober man was so on edge all the time that occasionally he would forget all about constraints. And at such moments he could be recklessly foolish. A bull beset by jackals! He dealt out humiliation where he could – and annihilation too. Luke describes in one place: Christ was told of some Galileans whose blood Pilate mingled with that of their sacrifices during divine service. And Christ answered calmly: 'Do you think those Galileans were more sinful than others?' You see the terseness, the simplicity of it! No point at all in enquiring about why these innocents were slaughtered; they had been killed, that was the point. A run of the mill incident. So commonplace in fact that it wasn't worth talking about. But the grateful populace, while allowing themselves to be killed, had taken due note of this and had sent 'lamentations' to Rome. And when they came to the eyes of the emperor, Pilate received a telling-off. Explanations were demanded of him. Tiberius was an experienced administrator and couldn't stand a lot of fuss being made over nothing. Yes 'O, race of slaves!' Yes, the people were flatterers, slaves, cowards and traitors, but one had to be able to deal with them. With me they don't shout even when I suffocate them. Why do they shout with you, proconsul?"

"It was him who brought in penalties and punishments for every word of opposition, I believe?"

"It was, it was him. The law of AD 15. 'Criticism of the actions of the emperor is tantamount to insulting the majesty of the Roman people.' For that you lost your head at once."

"Some experienced administrator!"

"What was wrong with it? Tiberius, unfortunately, was far from being the only idealist in history. They haven't diminished much over two thousand years. However that might be, Pilate came to a bad end. Some sources say he took his own life under Caligula. Others say he was put to death by Nero; still others that he was banished to Switzerland where he drowned in Lake Lucerne. There is a mountain in the Alps called Pilatus. On Good Friday, the day of the court hearing, a great shadow appears on it and everyone washes their hands over and over. It was in Switzerland, in 1912, that I saw a mystery play – an enactment of our Lord's passion. There were around ten thousand spectators. It all took place under the open sky in an alpine valley. A meadow amid dazzling snowy heights. And below them moves the procession: legionaries, the brigands and a large white figure – Christ. Then I recalled Shakespeare. His chronicles. He's the one who could have written a tragedy about Christ! And you know, he would hardly have needed to invent anything. It's all there in the gospels. Images, characters, circumstances, deathless dialogue, where one line says it all. Borrowing something from the apocryphal writers, it might go like this:

PILATE: Art thou the King of the Jews?
JESUS: Askest thou this thyself or art thou repeating what others have told thee?
PILATE   (smiling derisively and shrugging his shoulders): Am I a Jew then? That is thy people. Thy high priests

288

	have brought thee here to me. What hast thou done then? Art thou a king?"
JESUS:	If my kingdom was of this world, my subjects would surely not have allowed me to be seized and brought before thee?
PILATE	(*insistent*): But art thou then a king?
JESUS:	Thou sayest it. What I say is: I came to the world to establish the truth.
PILATE	(*grinning peevishly*): Truth, truth! And what is truth?
JESUS:	It is that which is from heaven.
PILATE	(*grins*): So then it does not exist on earth?
JESUS:	Thou hast seen what is done on earth to people who speak the truth! They are delivered unto such as thou.
PILATE:	Whence art thou? (*Christ does not reply.*) Why dost thou not reply then? I can either crucify thee or release thee.
JESUS:	Thou seest – thou canst, and thou wouldst not have that power if it had not been sent to thee from on high! But then thou art not to blame, judge! The sin is upon those who have brought me before thee.
PILATE	(*deliberates and comes to a decision*): Let us go! (*He goes out of the hall into a yard filled with people and takes his place on the judgment seat – the judge's raised marble chair. The soldiers bring Jesus in after him.* (*Hubbub*).)
PILATE:	Here is your king. (*A thunder of shouting:* "Death to him, death! Crucify him, crucify!")
PILATE	(*impatiently*): Quiet! Listen! You have delivered him to me as an agitator of the people. I questioned him in your presence, investigated all the circumstances and did not find him guilty. I sent him to Herod and he also found him not guilty. So therefore I will punish him and let him go. (*Indignant cries.*) Wait! Easter is upon us. Your custom is that I should release a prisoner of your choice. At the moment I have Barabbas. He has been convicted of murder during a revolt. Whom

	then should I release unto you. The brigand or Jesus, called the Christ?
SHOUTS:	Barabbas! Barabbas! Crucify him! Death to him!
PILATE	(*shouting in rage*): I see! I'm to crucify your king am I, wretches? (*One of the high priests approaches, saying quietly, insidiously and insistently*: "We have no king but Caesar. Anyone calling himself king is an enemy of Caesar, proconsul.")
SHOUTS:	Crucify him, crucify! Barabbas! Barabbas!
PILATE	(*beside himself, almost hopeless*): But what evil has he done you?
SHOUTS:	Crucify him, crucify! (*Pilate surveys the crowd in silence. He then makes a sign and brings a vessel and towel.*)
PILATE	(*washes his hands*): I am not guilty of the blood of this just person: see ye to it. (*Howling of the crowd. The soldiers take Jesus away. At this moment a high priest approaches him.*)
HIGH PRIEST:	Eh! Destroyer of temples and builder of them in three days! Now save thyself, come down from the cross! (*Laughter from the crowd and shouts*: "Let him be crucified! Let him be crucified! Let his blood be upon our heads! On ours and those of our children!")

"That's approximately how it would sound if you were to set out the gospel story dramatically. I've only put in the stage directions and filled out the very obscure place about what is truth, from the apocryphal gospel according to Peter. And so, the Jews disliked Pilate. They kept writing and writing to Rome and their constant lamentation and complaining finally had its effect. Pilate was recalled. One can imagine the exasperation that had developed on both sides. Hence Pilate's initial hesitation. He simply didn't want to execute anyone for the benefit of the Jews. But there was a second consideration. Reasons of state this time. The fact of the matter was that Christ, or someone like him, suited Pilate's book very well. Surprised? It's quite simple really. He had thoroughly assimilated two aspects of Christ's teaching. In the first place, this wandering preacher did not believe either in war or revolutionary upheaval; no, man must refashion himself from within, and then everything would happen by itself. Therefore he was against rebellion. That was the first point. Second: the only thing that Jesus sought to destroy and actually was undermining all the time, were the authorities. The authority of the sanhedrin, the Sadducees and the Pharisees, and so, perhaps unwittingly, the authority of Moses and the temple. And it was in the monolithic and unquestionable nature of these that the greatest danger to the empire resided. Clearly Rome needed precisely the sort of subversion that Jesus represented. And this was an intelligent subverter too. He knew perfectly well that if you wish to destroy something ancient and cherished, you never say, I have come to destroy this. No, say you have come to support this sacred edifice, renew it, replace the decayed elements in it; then, when you are trusted, you may wreak your will, and drive the people as hard as you want, and no dawdling! Crush and smash! Take the well-known beginning of the Sermon on the Mount: 'I am not come to destroy the laws but to fulfil' and then the ending: 'Ye have heard that it was said by men of old time: "hate thine enemy", but I say unto you, love your enemies, bless them that curse you, do good to them that hate you and persecute you.' Grand? And all this taken together comes under 'till heaven and earth pass, one jot or one tittle shall in no wise pass from the law'. An iota? The whole thing was shaken to pieces. Now imagine the state of the world at that time and ask yourself whether or not such utterances in the mouth of the Galilean did not suit Pilate? Didn't it mean a prescription to pray for and love him, the occupier? Surely Pilate, a state official who knew the East and the land he was attempting to pacify, realized that this was the very force on which he ought to rely? That Christ was indeed a force – this he did sense. He also had a vague intuition of something else: any kind of meekness was immensely powerful. You don't recall who said that?"

"Tolstoy I expect?"

"No. Dostoevsky. In his last years he thought a great deal about Christ: he didn't know quite how to treat him, and so essayed various experiments with him. In one of these he left him with meekness and love, and took away his sword and scourge as being superogatory. The result was Lev Nikolaevich, Prince Myshkin – a personality not only lacking vitality, but destructive of all who love him. After that he returned the sword to him and threw out all the rest. The result of that was the Grand Inquisitor, that is, Christ putting Christ to death. But in that regard Pilate was much more realistic than Dostoevsky and his Inquisitor: he understood Christ as he was, and that Christ suited him well."

"You mean he didn't even suspect the revolutionary destructive power of Christ's preaching?"

"Who could have suspected it then? Even long afterwards, nobody could see their way clearly in that regard. A hundred years later, the younger Pliny made an attempt to comprehend what it was, but apart from 'a savage superstition taken to absurd lengths', he could see nothing in it. This is what he wrote to the emperor Trajan. Tacitus was even more to the point than that: 'people hated for their nastiness and evil deeds, whom the mob called "Christians".' And further (speaking about the burning of Rome): 'they were accused not so much for having started the fire, as for the hatred they bore towards the human race.' I am quoting from memory, so I can't be quite exact. That is the way the most refined, intelligent, enlightened human minds thought and wrote about Christianity many years after Christ's execution. But Pilate didn't think like that. He knew: this wandering preacher was very necessary to Rome. He was listened to, people believed in him and followed him. He was capable of founding a new cosmopolitan religion, acceptable to the authorities. Whether he was mistaken in this view, is still unclear. Opinions have differed sharply on the point. So much for the second reason, but there was still a third: why the devil should they be trying to frighten and blackmail him? Why should he play the role of synagogue executioner? They had been deprived of the *jus gladii*, the right of the sword, so now they wanted to cut off an inconvenient head using his hands. The hands of a Roman patrician! To Beelzebub with them! The dirty tricks they had played on him too! Hadn't they disrupted work on the aqueduct? Indeed they were pigs, they had no use for clean water. They used to wash in ponds and here was he wanting to bring in water from the Jordan! They wouldn't let him. Just think, Caesar's image, the Roman military banners – they wouldn't allow them into Jerusalem! Wouldn't allow it and that was flat. Even the shields had to be removed from Herod's palace – they bore the emperor's portrait, you see. And they got away with everything – he was the one who got the blame – didn't know how to approach them. And who the devil were they? Liars and traitors! Filthy eastern dogs. And now he – the representative of the emperor, the first man in the land, had to put this wretch to death at their whim and behest, simply because he, Pilate, had need of him and he was therefore hateful to them. And there was nothing for it – he had to do it. Ah, if he had only been Gallio! Do you know who he was? Seneca's own brother. Proconsul of Achaia. His residence was in Corinth, and this is what had taken place there on one occasion. I remember this place by heart: 'The Jews made insurrection with one accord against Paul and brought him to the judgment seat, saying: this fellow persuadeth men to worship God contrary to the law.' You see, just as it was with Christ. But this was Gallio, and this was the upshot. 'If it were a matter of wrong or wicked lewdness, O ye Jews, reason would that I should bear with you: but if it be a question of words and names, and of your law, look ye to it; for I will be no judge of such matters.' And he drove them from the judgment seat. And all the Greeks took the chief ruler of the synagogue and beat him before the judgment seat. And Gallio cared for none of those things.' A grand scene and a grand patrician. 'Look ye to it,' but that was something Pilate couldn't say; he simply didn't dare. Palestine wasn't Greece, Jerusalem wasn't many-columned Corinth, and he wasn't Gallio, just Pontius Pilate 'homo novus'. So that when he heard the dreaded: 'If you release him you are Caesar's enemy', he caved in, washed his hands and carried out the execution. Just like you and I! My dear friend," Father Andrey seized Kornilov by the shoulder, "You say: they summoned you and took my manuscript from you. They took it, you say, because they don't want to crucify me. That means you were talking to people just like Pilate, wretched people like Pilate on whom absolutely nothing depends. With murderers and cut-throats in the name of an alien god! With poor Judas, whom it is impossible even to forgive, because there is nothing to forgive! For it is not they who are guilty, but rather those nonentities who sit behind seven walls and send them coded messages: 'Seize, judge, kill!' "

"Oh," Kornilov grimaced, wincing from nausea and a ringing pain in his temples. "Whom do you mean?" Father Andrey loomed over him, tall, angular, with his gaunt sallow face and weird, absolutely circular all-engulfing eyes.

And once more it seemed to Kornilov that this was all a dream, that any minute there would be a tremor, a shift in the delicate rainbow veil on which all this was being depicted; it would split asunder and he would wake up in his own bed. All he had to do was want it to happen.

"Whom do I mean?!" asked Father Andrey with quiet menace. "You understand whom! Those two. The florid dwarf and the half-witted Moses. The two vampires I'm talking about."

"Yes, a dream," thought Kornilov. "A horrible, drunken dream; it'll burst in a minute and I'll wake up."

And mumbled: "What are you talking about Father Andrey? What dwarf is this? What Moses? Better just pour me out a drop more."

Here Father Andrey suddenly began to weep. He sat down, dropped his head on his hands and, ever so quietly, began crying like a child. This brought Kornilov round completely. "It's all right," he thought. "The dacha's empty. Nobody to hear anything. It's all right."

"Father Andrey," he called softly.

The priest sighed, slowly raised his head and all of a sudden fixed Kornilov with a piercing stare. His eyes were normal again, old man's eyes, glinting with tears.

"Oh, my dear chap," he said with simple bitterness. "No matter how many times I tell that story, no one ever understands what it means at all. And nor have you. But really, it's quite simple. Very simple. Yet people die or betray because of it!" For a minute more he regarded Kornilov with a smile of ineffable bitterness, then sighed lightly, slid the decanter over and said: "Very well then, yes! Let's have one more! For the road!"

The following day Kornilov came joltingly awake. He sat up and looked about him. Hell! Sure enough, he was lolling on top of the blanket with his boots on. The ignominy of it. Zybin had sometimes collapsed onto his bunk like that ("bones and all") and he had ticked him off for it: "That's pigging it, can't even be bothered to take your things off!" Yes but still, Zybin used to leap out of bed wide awake and run over to the diggings to spend all day on his feet. And here was he, slumped on his bunk with his head splitting, wanting nothing in the world but to be left alone. His watch had stopped of course, but he wondered what time it actually was. A feeble yellowish dawn, like boiled milk, seeped through the scratched celluloid window. He raised himself, wrinkling his nose and groaning a little, then crawled as far as the zinc water tank. He greedily drained two mugs one after the other and wiped the stickiness from his parched lips. He felt slightly better. He sat down on the stool and suddenly felt a fearful pang! God! He was done for! He'd fallen right into the very thing he had feared. What had all that been yesterday? That damned priest had cracked and blurted out every-thing he'd been storing up inside! And now the priest's goose was cooked. And so was his, if he shielded the priest. All of a sudden, Kornilov wanted to finish with the business at one fell swoop. Wipe the slate clean. Go in there and say: There's my testimony – the last! There's my signature for you – the last! And for the Lord God's sake leave me in peace! "There was no talk of politics!" That's it, there wasn't any!

"I just had to," he said loudly, "I just had to didn't I, bloody idiot!"

He got to his feet, had a wash and cleaned his trousers then went out onto the road and raised his arm on the verge.

One five-tonner went by without stopping. A light van went by without stopping either; a third was about to slow down but suddenly a cheery pair of frontier-guards looked out and he lowered his arm at once.

"Must be fate," he reflected and scrambled back up the hill. "Well to hell with it. If they want me they can come and get me. They won't let the grass grow."

It was a week before they came to get him however. One fine bracing morning, a messenger galloped up, leapt from his horse, saluted smartly and handed him a summons in an open delivery book (it chanced to be his lunch break and he had been somewhat late leaving his tent). "Here," said the messenger, proffering a pencil.

He perused it:

> Citizen Kornilov, V. M. You are ordered to present yourself tomorrow . . . . to comrade Smotryaev, in connection with case . . . .
> Room No. . . . .
> in the capacity of . . . .
> In the event of non-compliance, you will be brought in by force.

The paper was thick, the seal large and it looked more like an invitation to the saluting-stand at the May Day parade than a summons.

"Day, hour and minute. It's now eleven," said the messenger.

"Right," responded Kornilov, signing. "Right, dear comrade! I'm all for avoiding misunderstandings." He returned the book. "Tell them I'll be there."

"You can tell them that yourself," smiled the messenger, touched his cap and left the tent.

In the mountains, autumn was really setting in. The rains had abruptly ceased and an extraordinary precision and clarity had manifested itself in nature. The trees, the hilltops, the snow-capped peaks stood out sharply, as if engraved on the air. But this freshness only remained high up above the stands of trees. Down below, everything was withered, yellow and drooping. The garden mallows, grey and bristly, rustled as they rubbed against one another; it was chilling to look at them. Kornilov crumpled the summons in his hand and shoved it into the pocket of his field shirt. He walked off, away across the hills and his mood was again

295

one of elation. Tomorrow he would have done with all this, then go to the museum to settle up. After that they could all go to blazes – the diggings, the drunken priest, Zybin, the lot of them. He felt some regret for Dasha, it was true. But he kept conjuring up a picture of himself, turning up one morning all unexpected in his sister's fourth-floor flat. "Will you welcome a deportee, citizeness. What? Wouldn't have recognized me?" And his sister would be stunned and shout: "Oh, what do you look like?" and hang round his neck. And he would grin with hard-bitten courage: "Not as bad as all that am I, sister? Ask me how I got away." And go straight over to the phone and ring round his friends. He was walking along, thinking of this and smiling, when suddenly someone called his name. He looked round. Dasha was standing by a poplar looking at him. He cried out for joy and ran towards her, as she stretched out her arms to him. They were standing near the fence of the Potapov house. That was how far he had been striding over the hills without noticing.

"Dashenka, Dashenka," he kept repeating, panting from a kind of soaring, ecstatic tenderness; he suddenly seized her hands and twirled her round: "Come on now, do let's have a good look at you. What a beauty, a real beauty. And what's she wearing?" (Dasha was indeed wearing a tweed coat, a light blue semi-stole and carried a handbag which shone like a black mirror.) She was embarrassed, and he suddenly took hold of her, crushed and rumpled her then kissed her resoundingly on both cheeks.

"There you are!"

"I was coming over to see you this evening," she said, carefully freeing herself.

"Why wait, let's go now, this minute!" he cried. "I've such a lot to say to you!"

"So have I," she smiled.

"Really? What a coincidence. Well then, let's go, let's go!"

"No, I can't just now. Later, after eight when uncle's gone to town."

"You won't let me down?" he asked, again catching her hand.

"No. No, I won't let you down." She smiled in a way he had not seen before. "You know they're sending me to Moscow."

"Really?" He was delighted and astonished. "Well, that really is marvellous. I'm going to Moscow as well. We can live together. I'll show you all the galleries and we can go to the theatre! Wonderful!"

"Oh yes! And I've still got my practical entrance exams to do," she looked at him with a long-suffering air.

"They're nothing! You'll sail through." At this moment, everything really did seem to him of small consequence. "Now this evening I'll give you one of Laurencia's monologues from *Fuente Ovejuna*; it'll rock the lot of them."

"No, really?"

"By the true holy cross," he intoned gravely and crossed himself.

She was about to say something to him, but suddenly hissed: "Uncle!" and leapt away.

Foreman Potapov, grave and frowning in his black quilted jacket, bore more than a passing resemblance to a sturdy dung beetle. He approached from the direction of the wicket gate and began to open it. He had a sack on his back, containing boxes of some sort.

"He's sending apples off to Moscow today," whispered Dasha.

"Smart devil," thought Kornilov and asked: "How is he these days?"

"Let's go, let's go, he'll be out again in a minute," whispered Dasha and tugged him behind the bushes. "You shouldn't have done that, Vladimir Mikhailovich," she said, suddenly serious.

"Done what?"

"All of it! What you came out with that time? Remember? And none of it was true."

"What wasn't true? What, grief of my heart?"

"Well, that somebody had called uncle in and made certain suggestions to him; none of that's true."

"Wonderful!" he exclaimed, flabbergasted. "It was him who told you that?"

"Yes. And he also said: 'What's he doing, going to Volchikha's? There's nothing to interest him there. Just rotgut vodka.' That Volchikha would have been put out of the collective farm long ago if it hadn't been for uncle. And now she goes . . ."

This Potapov-type note in Dasha's voice was something totally new. She didn't look at him.

"Well, and what else does your uncle say?"

"He says you were wrong to get mixed up with that priest. He's a hardened drinker. He drank away his pectoral cross. He tells everybody he lost it in the sea. But that's a lie – he drank it away! His own daughter has turned her back on him ("Once they'd forced her," he rejoined). Nobody forced her and if he was a father like that, what of it? She did right! He's done time in prison and felled timber in Siberia. Last year, the divisional police inspector used to come out to him every day on a motorbike. He's here today and gone tomorrow. Surely he's not a pal of yours?"

"Well, who is then, Dashenka?" he enquired peaceably. "Zybin? They've put him in jail as well."

She said nothing. He took her hand.

"Dashenka, my sweet clever girl! What's all this you're coming out with? Do you really believe it yourself? Surely not? In the name of all that's holy, don't believe it. None of that's so, none of it. Never in the world! Somebody's just dreamed it up; it's like some dark pall, an eclipse, an evil spell, a black dog, as my old nanny used to say. It's reached you – your uncle's brought it back with him from in there, and now you're talking its language. And it's not you, not you at all! There's nothing to be done about it, probably there are always periods like this in history. Our planet's under a curse maybe, going in the wrong direction, or the sun's shining a different way, the beams are the wrong kind – so people go out of their minds, and that's all there is to it!"

She said nothing for a long time, then spoke: "And that you should get away from here quick."

He grinned.

"Well then, let's go, let's go to Moscow!"

"No, not to Moscow", she answered stubbornly. "You should go somewhere far away, not Moscow, somewhere where nobody knows you."

He looked at her.

"Now that's brilliant! Is that your uncle again? You go to Moscow, and I go away from it. Great! Well, tell him not to worry. I shan't bother you there. Tell him that."

He turned to leave but she suddenly clutched his arm, seemingly wanting to say something, but unable to find the words, or indeed breath; she simply fell with her face pressed against him.

"Dasha?" he said, astonished.

She said nothing.

"Dasha."

She abruptly straightened up, kissed him awkwardly (it landed on his nose) and ran off.

"Dasha!" (She kept running). "Now, Dasha! You might at least turn round!"

She turned round.

"I'll come, I will come today, Vladimir Mikhailovich. Wait for me. I'll be there!" She spoke almost in a whisper but he heard every word distinctly.

She didn't come. He lay till dawn with open eyes, then got up and trudged down to the highway to hitch a lift. He had no sooner got down from the hills when he caught sight of Volchikha.

She was standing by the roadside, head down, apparently waiting for somebody. He came up and touched her on the shoulder. She lifted her head, looked at him and smiled tautly.

"I've just been seeing Andrey Ernestovich off," she said. "I helped him to carry his bits of things."

"Where's he gone, then?" asked Kornilov ("another new case file").

"To the North. Fishing in the White Sea. The lads have been writing letters. Come back soon, they say. Well, let him go, let him. He likes it there. Let him go. I'm glad." And turned away so as not to cry.

This time both masters were present in the office. Surovtsev was standing by the open window, looking down at the yard. Smotryaev was in a fluster as he riffled through a folder, looking for something. As Kornilov entered, Smotryaev put the folder to one side and exclaiming something like: "Well, here he is," "Well, talk of the devil," advanced to meet him. All in all, it was like a meeting of old acquaintances. Kornilov asked him about his holiday in the Crimea, Smotryaev waved a dismissive hand and said never mind the damned Crimea. He hadn't been in the Crimea, he was just out of hospital. How was that then? Very simple, he'd been sunbathing two days and had contracted catarrhal inflammation of the lungs, no more no less. He'd been lolling about for a month, and now his temperature in the morning was all right but it was well up by five. That's why his lips were sore.

"You're still under treatment?" Surovtsev expressed concern. "You ought to be lying down, not walking about."

"Can't," sighed Smotryaev briefly. "Work to be done." He nodded in the direction of the folder. "Take a seat, please, Vladimir Mikhailo-vich, and let's have a talk." He opened the file. "Well now, we are on the point of reporting to the higher-ups and closing the case. We were only waiting for you. Have you brought us anything new? Excellent! Let's have it."

"Bear in mind though, that this is the last," Kornilov said, taking out an exercise book. "He's gone away."

"Gone away?" Smotryaev was astounded. "How do you mean?"

"Just that. He upped and went."

Smotryaev looked at him in silence.

"That's certain is it?"

Kornilov shrugged.

"That's what they say, anyway. I went to see him twice and the door's got a lock on it."

"Well, that's marvellous!" Smotryaev slammed the file down in exasperation.

"Oh, to hell with him! Let him depart from sin as far as possible," said Surovtsev from the window. "He's always going off to the North, to Siberia. Well, nobody's keeping him. Folk have got their hands full there. No time for anonymous letters! Isn't that so?" He turned to Smotryaev.

"Yes, from one point of view, that's so," he said with a dissatisfied frown. "But from another . . . well, did you have at least one heart to heart with him this last time?"

"I was at his dacha even."

"Oh, so you met his daughter."

"She's in Sochi at the moment."

"Ah, while the cat's away . . ." Smotryaev laughed. "I see, I se-e! So you had a few, then talked about the Lord God Jesus Christ as he goeth upon his way neither weeping nor repining, was that how it was?"

"We talked of this and that," Kornilov replied coldly; he was fretting to get away. "He talked about the North, for instance, about being a surgeon there, cutting up fingers and bellies."

"Oh, there's a priest now! Eh, Alyosha?" Smotryaev turned to Surovtsev in high good humour. "The age of enlightenment is upon us. Our village reverend nearly drowned me. He didn't close the nostrils when he dunked me head first in the font. I was blowing bubbles by the time they hauled me out. The old woman brought me round with vodka."

"No doubt the priest was, you know . . ." He clicked a finger against his throat.

"Of course he was, the priest, the godfather, the aunt and uncle, and this sage of ours as well. He liked his drink."

"Now there I completely disagree," said Surovtsev. "He's a learned man! Academe! Look at the thesis he rattled out."

"So Christ existed?" Smotryaev suddenly asked Kornilov point blank.

"Yes!" Kornilov returned.

"Excellent! Alexey Dimitrievich," he turned to Surovtsev. "We have to close this case."

"Absolutely", Surovtsev nodded briefly.

"Close it. But see what we're left with: in this folder here there are five reports, and they all end the same way. 'In the course of the entire conversation, he did not voice any anti-Soviet utterances.' What does 'voice' mean here? Was he just avoiding the subject? Perhaps he didn't voice anything because he didn't trust you, realized he was being pumped – that's a question that might be raised."

"Quite legitimately," Surovtsev put in.

"Yes, legitimate even. These days things are . . . acute. So why should we believe that this priest who's been through the mill, passed through fire and water, the brazen trumpets and the wolf's jaws, is going to – oh, by all means sir! – turn himself inside out for you? He's nobody's fool! He knows the cost of a wagging tongue by now. So he keeps a tight rein on it. He likes a drink of course, but his mind stays clear. Maybe some doubts will be raised about that and how can we answer them?"

"I've spoken to Vladimir Mikhailovich about that," Surovtsev inclined his head.

"Well then? What did you say in answer to that, Vladimir Mikhailovich? The facts, where are the facts?"

Kornilov opened his briefcase and extracted an exercise book.

"I've jotted everything down here very roughly," he said. "It will have to be copied out again anyway. You've got special forms for that."

"It's content we're interested in, not forms," Smotryaev interrupted harshly, giving Kornilov a stern look. "What have you got there? Let's have a look."

"I consider it my duty to advise you that on 25 September of this year, at your behest, I paid a visit to Andrey Ernestovich Kutorga. Kutorga lives with his daughter Mariya Andreevna Shakhrostova, an agronomist at the Mountain Giant, in a cottage on land belonging to one of the farm brigades. On the aforesaid day, 25 September, Kutorga dropped in to say that since his sister had gone to Sochi to meet her husband, he was in full charge and therefore desired to invite me over. Mindful of your commission to me, I hastened to fall in with this. We set off. The cottage allotted by the farm to agronomist Shakhrostova has three rooms. Kutorga occupies one of these, together with the adjoining winter terrace. While he was setting the table, I acquainted myself with the room's furnishings. My attention was drawn to the bookcase. Apart from fiction, it held the collected works of Lenin, Marx's *Capital* and comrade Stalin's *Questions of Leninism*. There were also some medical books. As com. Kutorga explained to me, these represented his private property which he had come by in the North, where he had worked for a time as a surgeon's assistant in a fisheries co-operative. Kutorga was very willing to talk about this period of his life. He also recalled working with prominent specialists and scientists."

"But you didn't ask their names, did you?" Smotryaev shook his head reproachfully. "Why ever not? The materials should be absolutely precise and be checkable against the relevant document at any point."

"After this, Kutorga told me about his father, whom he called 'an old '70s man'. He told me he had travelled to see Chernyshevsky in search of the truth. After that, Kutorga proposed a toast to the Soviet system and comrade Stalin personally. He called comrade Stalin 'a great helmsman, leading us from victory to victory, to the final triumph of communism'. In accordance with the commission which you had entrusted to me, I expressed doubt and put several questions to him, which he answered with vehement sincerity; he called me one of little faith, unworthy of the great age in which we live."

"Went as far as that, did he?" Smotryaev glanced sharply at Kornilov. "What a priest, eh!"

"After that, the talk passed to Kutorga's scholarly writings and all the rest of the time we discussed Christ. As far as I understood him, Kutorga regards his story from a purely realistic viewpoint and rejects any kind of mysticism. I never once heard him call Christ God, or God-man. On this occasion I stayed with Kutorga about six hours, after which he saw me home by torchlight. I vouch for the accuracy of the foregoing. V. Kornilov."

"And why V. Kornilov? Haven't you got a pseudonym?" marvelled Smotryaev.

"What do you mean, pseudonym?" Kornilov turned to Smotryaev in astonishment, but the latter merely grimaced and brushed this aside.

"Well, all right!" Smotryaev took the file from the desk and stood up. "Very well! That's probably enough. Let's go through to the colonel."

"Just take a seat here. I'll be back directly."

For a fraction of a second, Kornilov had a glimpse of a window under a billowing cream-coloured curtain, a secretary's desk, dotted about with all kinds of items – folders, flowers, pencils, and above them something youthful, sparkling, colourful – a sky-blue cardigan, golden hair, fresh face, noble, refined features. Like a film star. Then the door closed with a soft swish and Kornilov was left alone in the corridor. The corridor was cramped and dark, with dimly gleaming green walls. All in all, it was a horribly official corridor, a true symbol of depression and apprehension. But her appearance had overshadowed it all. And he recalled that back then too, when he had sat it out before his tumble into disgrace, signing everything that was put in front of him, a similar woman had also been present. She had come in lightly and gone out the same way, come in again, asked the investigator about something, he had given a cheery reply and they had laughed. Once she had brought him tickets for some sort of celebrity concert, and his first thought had been to refuse – "I'm pushed for time" – but she had said: "Shame on you! Where will you ever hear this again?" and he had at once pulled out his wallet. All in all, things went on between them as if the prisoner Kornilov didn't exist, and the investigator – not the investigator, simply that good fellow Boris Yefimovich and his colleague Sofa or Moura, had got him tickets from the local party committee. You sat and listened until it seemed that there was no special investigative block, secret and extraordinary at all, just a sort of benevolent civilian organization, with secretaries, cleaning ladies, tea, numbered in–out discs, the same business going on there as everywhere else; the office writing things; the local committee distributing tickets. Otherwise on what basis, in the name of what human or divine right had that woman turned up here? What business did she have here? Who was working with her here (working?) – her husband? Brother? Fiancé? Ah, how he wanted to talk to her, but that was impossible, even in the physical sense – they simply wouldn't have been able to hear him. And so, he would not be able to resolve this incredible immoral marvel of her presence here. After that, a good deal happened and he completely forgot about her. Only now had it all come back to him. A woman like that here! After all it wasn't just simply accidental; it meant that everything was in order – you people can't just shake us off! There's the local committee, the trade union committee, the wall newspaper – here it's just like where you work.

Good! And what about the forgeries? What about your offices where you're not allowed to sleep for five days and nights? The punishment cells – those damned pencil cases with the sparkling walls, where day and night, day and night, huge lamps the size of children's heads give out an inhuman light that eventually makes white horses start coming out of the corners – what about them?

Come now, citizens, come now! You should be ashamed to believe such things. Don't be such philistines! We're peaceable people and after work we go to the concert hall with our families to listen to a famous violinist. Let me introduce Valya who works in our section, the wife of my colleague. Surely there isn't anything here of the sort you mention? Valya, eh Valya? There you see, she's laughing! Come now, come now, citizens!

The door opened and Smotryaev's head poked out.

"The colonel will see you now," he said affably.

The office was huge, clean and light with tall windows overlooking the children's park. Out there, music was playing and someone was joyously shouting out: "A-one! A-two! Two stamps and three claps!"

The colonel, a puny little fellow with a knobbly, muddy-looking face was sitting at the other end of the office behind a massive desk. Another desk, very long and narrow was placed at right angles to it. This was set with crockery along its entire length, ashtrays, sugar bowls, finger bowls, vases, large oval dishes; there were a great many chairs drawn up to it too. The table could have seated fifteen to twenty people. "So they have production conferences here as well," mused Kornilov.

"I'll send for you," said the little colonel softly to Smotryaev, who inclined his head and left the room.

The colonel waited until the door had closed before rising, taking the familiar green folder from the desk and coming over to Kornilov.

"These are all your statements?"

"Yes."

"And these?"

"Those as well."

"Excellent! And finally your statement of today, yes?" The colonel swiftly extracted a sheet and ran his eyes over it. "So, you maintain that this Kutorga is one of us, a Soviet?"

Kornilov shrugged his shoulders.

"Judging by his remarks, it would seem so."

"Seem!" The colonel smiled. "Seem! That doesn't count for a great deal of course, but at least you've reported all his remarks on that subject correctly. Not missed anything out, or twisted it? No? Excellent! Then I will ask you to read this one here. Recognize the handwriting? Who wrote that?"

"Kutorga?"

"Kutorga! Read it!"

Kornilov began to read and after the first few lines exclaimed: "Has he gone off his head or what?"

"Read it!" repeated the colonel, placing a small dry hand on Kornilov's shoulder. "Read it!"

"Further to my previous statement I can add the following. On 15 September on your advice, I called on cit. V. M. Kornilov and invited him to my place. As on the previous occasion, Kornilov got drunk and began reviling the Soviet system and the Leader in particular. Thus, regarding the Leader's celebrated speech: 'The most precious thing on earth is – man' he laughed insultingly, remarking ironically: 'That's all rubbish! In this country a man is valued at less than a floor cloth. They just took me and threw me out. They didn't even explain anything.' Desiring to probe his state of mind fully, I permitted myself a number of slanderous utterances. Cit. Kornilov heard them out with complete approval, was keen to second them and encouraged me to go on. From this I was able to conclude that . . ." Kornilov was about to turn the page, but the colonel placed his hand on it and asked, almost sympathetically: "Well, is that enough? Poor you! He's done for you properly, the swine, hasn't he? Up and off with your head! We're not letting you out of here now!"

"But that's a pack of lies!" Kornilov leapt to his feet.

"Sit down, sit down," the colonel waved a fastidious hand, as he gathered up the folder. "What do you mean, lies? You listened, echoed what you heard and said plenty yourself."

"But . . ." Kornilov jumped up again.

"All right! If we confronted you with this character, what would come of it? Well? Nothing at all, because it's all true, isn't it? Well, why should he do the dirty on you, tell me that? Did you have a drunken fight? Or wouldn't share that old woman? Why should he lie – explain that."

"Very simply. He thought I had shopped him, and so . . ." He stopped short.

"Well then, well then," the colonel softly urged him on. "That's a reasonable point. So he was in a hurry to get in first? Right? Very possibly, very possibly. But it follows that there was something for you to shop him for? Yes? Well is it yes or no?" Kornilov said nothing. "Yes! Yes! Yes there was, Vladimir Mikhailovich, there was, man! And you were pulling the wool over our eyes. Yes indeed! Khripushin had the right of it when he said that from the way you described him, that priest should be welcomed into the party straight away! We trusted you and you lied to us! It's people like you, dishonourable and cowardly, who go about sowing distrust between Soviet society and the security organs. You teach them to trust nobody. Well, what's the use of talking. It's a bad business, a very bad business!" The colonel gestured and took the folder back with him to the desk. He took out a pen and made a note on his calendar, then dialled a number and gave an order. They both sat in silence. "I trusted you and you lied to me all your life," went through Kornilov's mind like a gust of wind. What was that? Where was it from? Who wrote it? An iron fist seized and clawed his heart before releasing it and squeezing again. He was filled to the brim with rusted metal and despair. And that despair was also metallic, dull, stony. Not despair even, a terrible heaviness. This was the end. Now they would take him in. That was how freedom would end for him – without a search, without a warrant, without even an arrest. He fumbled in his pocket, came upon some sunflower seeds, clicked them together and almost wept. Only an hour ago he had bought those seeds from an old woman on the bridge, but how sweet and far away that was now, another world. Dasha, the apple orchard, the dig, these seeds. My God! My God!

There was a knock on the door. "Yes!" said the colonel. Smotryaev and Khripushin entered.

"Kornilov, go into the corridor," the colonel ordered quietly and waited for the door to close.

He sat there for an hour, a second, a third. Then the doors opened and people came pouring out into the corridor: army types, some just as they were, some in their leather belts; blondes with manes of hair; young misses in bright cardigans. Three workmen went by in a din of metal, one carrying a ladder on his shoulder. Then a stern, distinguished old woman rustled by with her chicken gait; she would have graced either the presidium or the church of God. It occurred to Kornilov that yes, women here were as numerous as men. But this no longer surprised or affected him. The employees streamed past and he felt awkwardly in the way, as he sat by the wall; all of them seemed to be walking through him. He got up and went over to the window. Outside were the pine trees of the park, music playing, children shouting, the roundabout creaking. After five minutes or so, the corridor emptied and he returned to his place (this was a hard flat seat, built into the wall, so that he had to pull it down to sit on: if he got up, it snapped back noisily). Meanwhile the three of them went past him, the sickly colonel and the two investigators. The colonel was saying something rather mysterious.

"No, no!" he was saying, brandishing his pen. "The rapids are nothing to me! I'll drag her over twenty times if I have to. Mosquitoes, now, that's a different matter!" They whooshed through the glass doors at

306

the end of the corridor and all became still once more (beyond the glass doors there was a staircase, with a sentry on the landing). About an hour later, the corridor once more filled with the noise of people, then again emptied and silence returned. Only occasionally did an employee pass swiftly from office to office, clutching papers to their bosom. He sat and stared out of the window. It was the single living thing in this expanse of wall. He watched it grow dim: from white and golden, it turned to blue, then ultramarine and violet. When it had become completely dark, a deliberate grey-haired lady, looking like Catherine the Great, came through the glass doors, opened something in the wall and turned a switch. Blue forget-me-nots came on, and the slippery green walls turned a dull shade of lilac. An hour later, as if on command, the offices opened up again and disgorged a fresh wave of employees. But this time it was raincoats, tweed and leather. In the other direction came a rustling counterflow – also decked out in waterproofs, tweed and leather. Offices once more opened and closed. The dark window suddenly erupted in bright green light and Kornilov glimpsed the shining prism of a streetlamp and the delicately pointed blue-black leaves of a poplar. Somewhere it struck ten, then eleven. Then a blank supervened. then suddenly it struck one. He made to jump to his feet, but pain took him in the chest; he cried out as the seat beneath him clattered and he slumped down on the floor. His whole body ached. Breathing itself was painful. After all, he had been sitting hunched up for around twelve hours. He braced an arm against the floor, got to his feet, stretched, pressed against the wall, threw his head back and spread his arms wide. He stood like that for about ten minutes and felt better. He went over to the window and sat on the sill. The sentry watched him silently through the glass door. It wasn't the same sentry; that one had been relieved long ago. Soon the sentry, the corridor and the glass door vanished. Something grand, burning, festive possessed Kornilov. He was standing on stage, spotlights all around him, someone was waving their arms and chorusing exultantly: "Musicians, music! Music and music! Musicians, music!"

And then sleep was abruptly whipped away from him like a blanket. He saw people. They were coming down the corridor again, some one way, some another. Khripushin was standing over him, shaking him by the shoulder.

He was so sleepy he could barely walk. As he went along, he shook his head to dispel the weight; his body ached anew. Khripushin led him into the office and sat him down on the sofa. He looked at him and shook his head: "A pretty sight, I must say!" He rang somewhere and ordered strong tea to be brought.

"What's up then?" he asked, in seeming bluff, man-to-man fashion. "Aren't you well, or what?"

"No, it's all right."

"What do you mean all right, you can hardly sit up straight! I've got eyes in my head!"

A waitress in a cap came in, white, neat and demure, like Gretchen in an old German book, placed a tray on the edge of the desk and began setting out the glasses.

"You can leave them," said Khripushin. "I'll give you a ring later." The waitress nodded and went out. "Have a drink of tea, go on, go on, it's hot. You're done in." He paced about the office. "That sharp brain of yours has got landed with a fool for an owner! Well, isn't that so?" Kornilov whimpered something. "Now you see what sort of a character you wanted to shield. Eh? The good father! Well here he's shielded you like a good boar covers a lousy sow. You wanted to demonstrate your high-mindedness and it turns out he doesn't give that for it. Spit and rub it out. What did you want to prove by all this, tell me that. Well?"

"I don't know, I . . ."

"Shut up, shut up, it's a pain to listen to you. You won't say anything sensible in any case. Have a sandwich, drink your tea and fill up. Dear, dear now you're in line for eight years in Kolyma, where the law of the taiga rules and the prosecutor is a bear. You've heard of that? You'd have heard of it in the logging camps. Come on now, eat up, eat up. We've got some writing to do yet."

"What's there to write, then?"

"What do you mean – what?" Khripushin was astonished. "What's there to write? The withdrawal of all your previous statements. And a confession. Forgive me, say, for being a fool. I'm guilty all round. It won't happen again. Well now, if you try being artful after that, you son of a bitch, if you try it on, you'd be better off dead! The organs have let you off once, now twice, but the third time – it's off with your head! That's the situation! Now, why aren't you drinking your tea? Drink up!"

Kornilov put down his glass.

"I'll drink it later. Tell me what to write."

Khripushin eyed him mistrustfully.

"You're in no fit state to make a proper job of that, are you? You

308

can come in tomorrow and write it. Meanwhile here's a sheet of paper, sit up to the desk and write." He pondered. "Right! Do it this way: 'I hereby undertake to preserve as a state secret all conversations which the employees of the NKVD have conducted with me. I have been warned as to my responsibility.' Now sign it. Date. Remember, this is the last time you'll sign with your own name. From now on you're going to have a pseudonym. You know what it is? 'Gadfly'. See what a pseudonym we've chosen for you. One fit for a hero, a people's pseudonym. The name of a great revolutionary, like Spartacus. You have to earn a pseudonym like that. It's also an act of faith after all! Give me your pass to sign. Now sign again on that summons. Make it 'Kornilov' as well. Get a night's sleep somewhere and come back tomorrow at eleven on the dot. Straight in to the colonel. You'll see what sort of man he is. If you do your work conscientiously, there'll be a lot in it for you. He's got a soft spot for scientists. Well, good night. Away you go."

But as Kornilov touched the door handle, he stopped him again.

"Just bear in mind," he said earnestly as he came over. "You really mustn't think of messing us about again. You don't know who the colonel is sending you to, do you? And he won't leave you on your own without checking you. He'll check you a dozen times, understand?"

"I understand," replied Kornilov.

"Right you are then, no more slips, so we don't have to go through all this again. There'll be no more lettings off! Go on now. Good night to you."

"Gadfly," thought Kornilov as he descended the staircase. "What made me remember that today? What was it? It came back to me – oh, yes, yes: 'I trusted in you as in God, but you lied to me all your life.' Yes, yes. That was it, I trusted in you, but you lied to me.

He lay face down on his pillow. He didn't care any more and was indifferent to everything in the world. He had sat hunched up in a corner of the bus, thinking: if he could only reach the mountains, his tent, his bunk and flop his bones down. He still had a bottle of vodka left there. And for no one to come near him, say anything to him, ask him anything, not today, not tomorrow or ever again. He wasn't sorry for anybody or anything, he had no regrets and no desires. Just peace and quiet! It was as if oblivion had already lapped round him in cold, tranquil waves. It was right that the Styx wasn't an abyss, a grave or a pit, but simply a leaden-grey flowing river. He was sure that he had damned Zybin for good and all. He had written a paper to that effect, and later on, after it had been corrected by the colonel, had rewritten it and added it to the evidence in the case. But he didn't even care about that. He also realized that his own end was now on the horizon, but this too affected him not at all. Perhaps it was because his capacity for suffering had been exhausted, perhaps because it was as inexorable as death – and who thinks about that?

It stopped raining, then started again – a fine, lashing drizzle. He fell asleep to the sound of it. He woke up during the night and saw someone standing near the door, but he had no wish to see anyone – he closed his eyes again, breathing quietly and evenly, as if in sleep. And indeed, he did sleep. And again it was peaceful and dreamless. It was morning before he awoke. The sun was blazing through the yellow celluloid panel. Dasha was standing in front of the piled-up expedition cases, looking in his shaving mirror and pinning up her hair. Her mouth was full of hairpins. A neatly folded overcoat lay beside her on a box. She saw he was awake and said without turning round: "Good morning!"

He jumped out of bed and at once collapsed back onto it. He was lost: What was Dasha doing here? Where had she sprung from? He was inexplicably alarmed.

"How did you get here, Dasha?" he asked.

She turned to him.

"I spent the night here," she said imperturbably. "I slept over there – she nodded towards the mat in the corner."

"Ah," he said fatuously. "Ah!"

At that moment, she looked so young and pretty that she fairly hurt his eyes.

"I came in, saw you were asleep, and intended going away; but you started rambling and groaning, so I came and touched your forehead. You were all wet. I thought, if there's anything the matter, there'll be no one to even give him a drink of water."

"Oh," he said. "Oh."

He looked at her and still couldn't work out what he should say or do at this point. He didn't even know if he was glad she was there or not.

"And how's your uncle?"

She knit her brows.

"He's gone," she replied, after a pause.

"Right," he said. "So I was rambling last night was I? What did I say, do you remember?"

"You were shouting at somebody and it was 'I feel terrible' all the time. You mentioned uncle twice. Towards morning you quietened down altogether. I fell asleep myself then." He made as if to move. "No, no, stay there, stay there. I'll run and get the doctor in a minute."

He stretched out again submissively. "What shall I do now?" he wondered.

"And where's your uncle gone?" She shook her head. "What, you don't know? How could you be going to him then that time?"

"I came to see you," she said, glancing directly into his eyes, "to say goodbye. I've already got my ticket."

It was as if an enormous weight had slipped from him. And at the same time he felt utterly wretched. "Well, it's all over now," he thought. "She'll go away and I won't have to tell her anything."

"Oh, that's really terrific!" he said with counterfeit enthusiasm. "You've got away from all these Uncle Petyas and Volchikhas. You'll see Moscow. You'll study and become an actress. Ah, that's grand!"

She looked narrowly at him; her eyes were filled with tears.

"You really think that?" she asked softly.

"Well of course!" he exclaimed mirthlessly.

"And what about you?" she asked, then said with sudden resolution: "I love you, Vladimir Mikhailovich."

"Well, well, the hour of reckoning has arrived," he thought. "And quickly enough too, within twenty-four hours. No point in wriggling and guessing this way or that. This is it."

"Come here now, Dasha," he said. He wanted to sit up, but as soon as he took his head from the pillow, an appalling headache felled him. Everything around him began to shimmer and objects lost their equilibrium and began flowing like water, as a sour aching throbbed in his temples. He was instantly soaked in sweat. He even lost consciousness for an instant, and was recalled to himself by Dasha's voice. She was wiping his brow with a towel, on the verge of tears.

"Good God, what have they done to you, then?" she kept saying. "How on earth can I leave you? . . . I must get the doctor!"

"No need to do anything," he said, wincing with nausea. "Don't you go anywhere. I have something to say to you too. Sit down here."

She did so.

"Now then, now then, go on," prodded the grimly sober man inside him. "Tell her everything, everything this minute. If you don't tell her now, you never will. You know how gutless you are." He looked at her

311

and hastily averted his eyes. He couldn't do it. He looked at her – so fine, so submissive, wholly his, and he couldn't say anything.

"Well, all right," he thought. "Let's say you keep quiet. And a couple of days from now they call you in and ask you about her; how will you wriggle out of it then? Tell her everything this minute! Go on, go on!"

"You mustn't love me," he said stiffly. "I'm not the right man."

"That's not true," she said. "You are, you are, you are. It's me who isn't the right one; you remember those bad things I said? And let you down by not coming! But you are, you are! And all that," she nodded at the empty vodka bottle, "is because of your unsettled state. You've been hurt, badly and undeservedly, so you . . . But with me you won't drink. You'll see, you won't because you won't want to."

She blurted all this out at once, without pausing and he realized that it was with this, these exact words that she had been coming to him.

"Dasha, sweetheart, I don't mean that," he said, wincing.

"What then?"

He sighed but maintained his silence.

"That's it then," he thought, "the end! I shan't say anything more to her. I've let the moment pass."

"There's one thing that interests me," he said reflectively. "Where does fear come from? Not being afraid for your skin, the other sort? It doesn't depend on anything does it? Not reason, not character – not anything. For instance, when a man holds something dear and people threaten to come and take it away, it's understandable. But if he holds nothing dear, what then? Then why should he be afraid? And of what?"

She got up suddenly and threw on her headsquare.

"I'm going for the doctor," she said. "Just lie there, Vladimir Mikhailovich, I'll be back in a flash. Please don't try to get up."

She tried to rise but he took her arm and sat her down again.

"Why didn't you come that time?" he asked harshly.

"I . . ."

She paused, then said softly: "It's all right. It was my fault. Let it go."

"Let what go?" he asked, astonished.

"Let everything be as it was before. It doesn't matter."

"Let what go, Dasha. How was it before? What are you talking about?"

"I know that evening you went to Volchikha's and she got you drunk," she said quietly.

"Oh, that's what you're on about," he smiled sadly. "Yes, yes, yes,

I was at Volchikha's. And she got me drunk. And not only then, that's the trouble. I met Father Andrey Kutorga there too. Former holy father. You didn't know him?"

"Yes, I did."

"So I got to know him. Didn't I just! All his lectures about Christ. About Christ and the two disciples. One betrayed him openly, the other secretly and arranged it so neatly, the bastard, that even now no one knows his name. The first one, the open one – Judas – hanged himself, but what happened to the other one, nobody knows and nobody knows who he was either. Ah, how much I'd give to know that!"

He was smiling as he talked and his face was calm and pensive.

"Why do you want to know?" asked Dasha, dismayed.

"I'm just interested. Oh, if I only knew how he lived afterwards. Pretty well probably! A devout life, respectable, got married and forgot all about his master. Probably blamed him for everything. Used to say, no doubt: 'He nearly did for me. He got what he deserved!' Or perhaps it was the other way, nearly joined the ranks of the martyrs; called his teacher 'Rabbi' or 'Father'. 'When we went through Galilee once with the Rabbi . . .' and 'The Father said to me once . . .' Probably talked like that. He didn't have to hang himself because he was the secret one, wasn't he? It's the open ones who hang themselves; the secret ones, no, they go on living. So tomorrow they'll call me in and ask about Zybin – ask what I know about him. And I'll reply: 'I know nothing but bad about him. He nearly did for me.' 'Excellent. Write it down and sign it.' And I'll write it down and sign it."

"Oh, what are you saying!" shrieked Dasha. "How could you?"

"What?"

"But he's . . ."

"It's what he deserves. Yes, yes, he almost cooked my goose. Anyway, it's all nonsense. Him today, me tomorrow. What difference does it make? So then, what were you saying to me just now?"

She lowered her eyes and was silent.

"Oh, it doesn't matter."

"I love you, Vladimir Mikhailovich," she said, embracing him. "Love you, love you!" She kept repeating the words deliriously. Evidently his madness was contagious.

"Really? That's marvellous," he guffawed coarsely, a kind of gay reckless devilment was at work within him, and he felt wholly at ease and carefree. "So then you love me, do you? Terrific! And you know, they say that the second traitor, not the open one, had a loving wife.

313

Probably that's the way it was. But what interests me is whether he told her anything or not? What do you think, Dasha? He probably did and she said: 'Look, forget about it! You mustn't be so sensitive and go torturing yourself with that sort of nonsense!' That's what she said, most likely, that loving wife. Because love, Dasha, if you look at it from that point of view, is the vilest thing!"

He died and at once opened his eyes. But he was already a dead man and saw as a dead man.

IV

". . . he is like unto a man beholding his natural face in a glass: for he beholdeth himself, and goeth his way, and straightway forgetteth what manner of man he was."

(JAMES I: 24)

CHAPTER 1

"COMRADE STALIN HAS NOW AWOKEN. Good morning to you, comrade Stalin! What a lovely sunny day, comrade Stalin, eh?"

The soldier grinned, dropped the iron lid of the eyehole and went away. It was a special cell. It was not done to knock or shout near it because it wasn't a cell at all in fact, it was a punishment cell, and not simply a punishment cell; it was a special one for those on hunger strike. This zek had been sitting here for more than four days. Every morning they brought him bread and a mug of hot water. He took the water but returned the bread. That morning he did not even take the water which meant that he had gone from a straightforward hunger strike to a decisive fast "to the death". The corridor guard had to inform the block overseer at once of any such fasts. This is what he had done that morning. The overseer arrived straight away; lifting the round eyehole he had looked long and hard at the zek.

The zek continued to lie there.

He lay agreeably somehow, and very much at ease; his knees were drawn up and his head drawn in; he had adopted a sort of croissant position and might have been on a feather bed. In ordinary punishment cells, wooden blocks are the norm at night; just three or four slabs fastened together. These are fetched to the cell at eleven and are collected during reveille at six; they are bare, damp and knotty – very difficult to lie on. In this cell, even they were lacking. The zek simply lay on the cement. Lying down wasn't allowed during the day and the overseer gave a couple of knocks with his key for form's sake, shouting: "Hey! No lying down! Get up! You hear, zek? Get up this minute!" And departed. The zek had not budged.

"Is he calling for the prosecutor?" he asked the corridor guard. "Well, it looks like he's getting him. Stay here, don't go away. I'm going off to report."

"Why the kid glove treatment for him?" The deputy prison governor made a sickly grimace as he heard all this. "Right! I'm on my way."

The block overseer was going to tell him that the zek greeted comrade

Stalin every morning, as well as addressing him several times during the day, but bethought himself and held his tongue. As he left his superior's office however, he did step into the corridor and announce to the guard: "Ah, to hell with him, let him lie – but make sure his head's towards the door! And watch he doesn't yank his shirt off!"

Discarded shirts were a cause of apprehension. The previous year, a zek had contrived to fashion a noose after tearing his jacket into strips; he had then lain down and fastened it to the bedhead, strangling himself very neatly and swiftly while still in that position. But that had happened in an ordinary cell. In a punishment cell there was nothing to loop a noose round. It was bare. All the same, the guard would knock several times with his key on the metal cladding: "Prisoner, turn your head towards me! Prisoner, you hear me?"

The prisoner of course did hear, the swine, but failed to budge an inch. Nor did the soldier put his heart into it; he knew that his power, and not his alone, that of the whole system, ended here. Because now it couldn't devise anything more terrible for this zek. The soldier therefore contented himself with a threat: "Well, just you wait!" And walked away from the peephole.

And almost collided with the prosecutor.

The prosecutor entered the cell along with the prison governor, a stout and seemingly good-natured Kazakh. Zybin knew him. In the previous summer of 1936 a number of new cafés and meeting places had opened up in the city, all of them extremely lively spots. The governor was easy-going and genial by nature, greatly at odds with his grim official position (of course he wasn't really, otherwise how could he have held the job? But the correspondence evidently ran along lines invisible to the innocent eye). However that might be, they had come across one another quite frequently, on one occasion going so far as to spend an exceptionally agreeable evening together in a restaurant. They had eaten shashlyk, drunk cognac, requested music and swapped humorous stories. Now, as they came into the cell and saw the zek on the floor with his face to the wall, backside towards them, the governor abruptly turned crimson and barked out: "Get up!" But the zek didn't so much as stir. The governor ground his teeth, bent over him and grabbed his shoulder. The prosecutor, however, made some barely discernible gesture and the governor quietly straightened up at once.

"Good morning, Georgi Nikolaevich," said the prosecutor respectfully. "My name is Myachin. I have come in answer to your application. Can you talk?"

The zek turned over, and raised himself to a sitting position.

Special prosecutor Myachin was a well-nourished, smartly turned-out, florid-cheeked, fragrant-smelling comrade. His hair was combed back and he wore horn-rimmed spectacles.

"How gentlemanly they all are!" Zybin thought fleetingly, before scowling: "I've been waiting five days for you."

"I only got back from a business trip yesterday," said Myachin, quietly acid, even bowing slightly. "It's not altogether comfortable talking here, could we pass along into the office?"

Hunger strikers were not supposed to be taken out of their cells. The prison didn't release them even for interrogation (therefore the investigation stagnated, the investigators themselves took time off – the authorities couldn't stand cases like this and experienced zeks made wide use of the system). Zybin could easily have refused, but he levered himself to his feet. At this, he rocked and swayed so much that he slumped painfully against the doorpost.

"Gently does it," the governor exclaimed, lunging forward, arms extended; the zek, however, held his ground. He stayed for several seconds leaning against the wall. Then he sighed, opened his eyes and walked through the open door.

"Give him a hand, then!" the prosecutor hissed to the corridor guard, as he walked on ahead without a backward glance. This business was beginning to have a powerful effect on his nerves. Why the hell were they getting mixed up with Zybin? It was obvious they'd end up back at square one. The investigation had barely got under way, and here he was in the punishment cell on hunger strike. As from this morning, a fast to the death. What more could they do? Beat him up? Tether him? Whether you thrashed him or tied him up swallow-fashion, he would keep up his hunger strike just the same. And you'd spend six weeks doing nothing and get a severe reprimand into the bargain. Followed by the boot. Then it would be the college of defending counsel for you, or directing some Eastern epic like *Amangelda*. What you had to do was use your imagination, not imagine things! Neiman shouldn't give himself airs. He wanted to outdo his brother! The head of the investigation division of the Union Prosecutor's office! He wanted to put on trials in Alma-Ata the way his brother did in Moscow! Idiot! He wasn't fit to lace his shoes! He had been delighted to get the people's commissariat directive with regard to active interrogation methods. Bonehead! That directive applied to real people – Trotskyites, German and Japanese spies, railway bosses, Central Committee secretaries. And who was this? A shithouse! A drunk! A blabbermouth! It's only this year they've started picking out people like him, and you want to turn him into a leading light!

The prosecutor stepped into the governor's office, gestured him to remain seated, then spoke: "We've got to put an end to this Zybin business! I looked through his case yesterday. I'm going to have a word with Neiman. What they've started, honestly. You can't even invoke point 11 here. Nobody can be involved, so it's SB, eight years in Kolyma, and that's it."

The prosecutor was a decent fellow; he didn't try to make himself out to be a Vyshinsky or try to show that he was from some different, superior level of the security apparatus. He just came in, sat down at his desk, and if you were drinking tea, he would do the same. Over tea, he would deliver himself of notions of this kind. The prison employees thought highly of this and likewise did not allow themselves to take his simplicity of manner altogether seriously, put questions to him or presume to offer advice. People here were disciplined; each one was well aware of his place in the scheme of things and stuck to it. Therefore the deputy governor merely spread his hands.

The prosecutor seated himself comfortably, stretched his legs and picked up the paper.

"*Modern Times*," he read. "Charlie Chaplin! So then, are they going to show us Charlie Chaplin at long last or not? We look like being the last; the whole town's seen it before us."

"They were going to show it tomorrow night," replied the deputy governor, "but the women started making a fuss. We want to bring the children, they said, and how can we do that if it's at night? Of course it's odd – is there only one print for the whole city?" He shrugged his shoulders.

"The plan, the plan!" grumbled the prosecutor. "It's a matter of economics, my dear chap. Currency! That's why we don't buy them. And our cultural education has a low priority. Thank God, it's the twentieth anniversary of the revolution! We ought to be teaching others by now!"

He grinned to demonstrate that although this was no more than the truth, he was not altogether in earnest all the same, rather laying it on thick, or taking a simplistic view of reality, as he would certainly have qualified these words ("remarks") if someone else had uttered them coming out of a cinema, say, rather than in the governor's office.

"Yes, that's absolutely right," assented the deputy governor, smiling as if to show that he was perfectly well aware of all these nuances. "Yes, indeed."

He adored going to the special closed previews. They took place in the actual people's commissariat building after working hours – sometimes during the night in fact. Then everybody gathered in the preview hall – from the commissar himself down to the typists and prison staff. The hall was spacious and brightly lit with white fluorescent tubes – very cosy in demure shades of green cloth. The people seated themselves unhurriedly, smiling and greeting one another as at a family function, giving way to one another. Everyone tried to behave in as friendly and self-effacing a manner as possible. Out in the long narrow foyer there hung pictures of impeccably civilian content: "The Rooks' Arrival", "The Ninth Wave", "Alyonushka", "Bruins at the Timber-felling", (for that particular jest somebody actually had gone to the logging site to see the bruins), "The Leader reading *Pravda*", "The Great Construction". And near the bar, where stood little tables full of pastries and beer, it was quiet, unassuming and cosy. Everyone knew his place of course, but they all had a respect for one another and behaved as one family. Here the deputy people's commissar for example could simply flop down next to a corridor guard and strike up a conversation about the Spartak-Dynamo match, or inform himself as to where the latter intended spending his leave. He might even recommend something worth knowing from his own experience – go to Gelendzhik rather than Sochi, for instance: not so crowded. Or tell a simple man-to-man story of how a friend and he had raced one another at swimming and got as far as the forbidden zone before the coastguard motorboat had shot after them: "Who are you? Where from? Show your papers?" At this, both would laugh good-naturedly: vigilance being shown! It was this togetherness, this entrée into a higher sphere that the deputy governor prized above all. And perhaps it wasn't just this sense of togetherness, but also because along with that, he acquired an extra set of feelings, which were absolutely essential to him in his work. Here he had the feeling of camaraderie, the fellowship of the collective, in a word, genuine democracy. Everyone he met, from the people's commissar down to minor administrators like himself, were civil, respectable and straightforward. He couldn't help recalling something else, which had been going on recently. When his wife had been working in a children's kitchen and used to get home late, worn-out and upset: and all those conversations about squabbles, intrigues, denunciations, anonymous letters, toadyism, rudeness and petty opportunism that she fetched home every day. There couldn't be anything like that here! Certainly not! Nothing sordid here! But there was something else too. Mysterious and unsettling. In the outside world, all these heads of this and that, deputies, managers, or simple employees had been falling like ninepins – noisily, easily, stupidly. They went about complaining, scandal-mongering, writing statements hither and yon, making excuses, blaming others, and sometimes succeeding.

Here people just disappeared. Here one minute, gone the next. And no one remembered them. And there was something wholly mystical, ultimately inexplicable, but inexorable, like fate, like sudden death in the foyer over a glass of beer (he had witnessed that once). The individual was at once erased from the memory. Even a chance mention of him was considered to be tactless or in poor taste. A zone of universal silence existed here as it did everywhere else. But here, it was completely other – profoundly acknowledged and hence almost natural and free (it was one of the Marxist classics who said that freedom consisted in the recognition of necessity).

Only once had Gulyaev, a specially prominent big shot, violated this usage. At that session, their places chanced to be next to one another and while the lights were still on, Gulyaev asked him: "You didn't know your new chief at all previously?"

What he was referring to was that the previous prison governor had been summoned to a conference in Moscow and at once disappeared. The only trace of him had been a telegram: "Arrived safely. Kisses."

On the very same day, a new man from the bodyguard of the first secretary of the Central Committee had turned up in his office. A month previously, the first secretary had been summoned to Moscow in exactly the same way and had made incriminating statements from there. Arrests followed in their wake also. That was how the head of his villa security came to be prison governor. At one time they had both been duty commandants at the so-called "shooting gallery" (that sort of shooting gallery!) and it had fallen out that they had both been awarded identical scrolls and inscribed watches at the people's commissariat revolver competition.

He told Gulyaev about it. For some reason the latter had been unaware of this detail and was greatly tickled.

"Ah, I see, that's where he came from!" he exclaimed. He then asked suddenly: "You got on all right with Nazarov (the one who had disappeared), I believe?"

The question had been put in a light indifferent tone, so he replied in similar vein: "Why not? He did like a drink, it's true. But otherwise . . ." he said and then recollected himself: had he not said too much? But Gulyaev merely smiled and nodded briefly to him. At that point the lights went out. And so there remained with the deputy prison governor the impression of a light intimacy, a fleeting frankness which bound the two of them together, Gulyaev and himself.

No, the deputy prison governor really did enjoy these closed film previews, inaccessible to ordinary mortals.

"There should be fixed days for previews," said prosecutor Myachin matter-of-factly. "And why must it always be at night? I've got my daughter coming from Moscow on holiday."

Then he immediately took on an air of gravity.

"I'll be talking to Zybin presently," he said grimacing. "He keeps falling down after starving himself – so can we use your office so he doesn't have to go up to the first floor?"

"Certainly, by all means," said the deputy governor, flustered, and set about collecting his papers together.

"No, no, stay where you are, you may be of assistance," the prosecutor stopped him. "Does he lie down like that all the time then?"

"What can we do with him?" The deputy governor shrugged. "He's delirious by now."

"Delirious?" The prosecutor evinced surprise.

"Yes. I went up to his door and he was lying there talking to comrade Stalin."

"What do you mean?" The prosecutor gave a start, much taken aback. "To comrade . . . ?" Neither could help turning towards the door. "Abuse, is it?"

"No! He just says: 'Comrade Stalin is going to have dinner. Comrade Stalin has sat down at the table. There are guests there. "Let's see what we are going to get to eat," says comrade Stalin to the guests.' Like that."

"Hell knows what that's all about!" the prosecutor swore. "Have you told the investigator?"

"No, no, just you this minute," said the deputy governor and gave the prosecutor a candid look.

The latter gazed silently out of the window for a moment, deliberating.

323

"Right," he resolved at length. "You show him to the psychiatrist. I'll make the arrangements. Not via the investigative department, do it yourself, as a prison matter. He may simply be mad. I've heard he was a bit . . . you know . . . when he was outside. Maybe it's just a matter of sending him off to Kazan to the special isolator; let him kick the bucket there."

Just then there came a knock at the door and the zek was brought in.

The zek walked firmly and steadily. On the way, he had asked to visit the lavatory; there he had rubbed his face vigorously several times with the palms of his hands. He had begun to refuse water and as early as the second day, the dry mouth becomes inflamed, the lips crack and bleed, and one begins to smell like a corpse. Zybin knew this, and was therefore concerned to rinse his mouth out thoroughly, and clean his teeth with his finger. He no longer felt like drinking, however.

The prison governor and the block guard came in with him.

"Over here, please," said the prosecutor gently, and pointed Zybin towards a chess table by the window.

Zybin sat down and almost cried out. The window was large, filled with sun, and it looked out on the prison yard and an avenue of poplars. These poplars had been planted at the very founding of the city. When there had been no prison here, only a broad road heading up into the mountains; these poplars had rustled along its verges.

And Zybin went to pieces, bewildered by the sight of this measureless abundance. Branches, twigs, shoots. They were all rustling, criss-crossing, living every moment, every second, with every leaf, every sprout, every vein. They were gay, free, alive. And for him, who for so many days had seen nothing but a grey cement floor, a white light in a black cage, and a smooth wall the colour of bog slime, which gave the eye no purchase, all this fabulous tender prodigality seemed nothing short of a miracle. He had forgotten that such a thing existed. And yet it was what really mattered.

He stared, unable to take his eyes away. A light breeze was causing the leaves to rise, sink and quiver – the tree was breathing, green blood flowed along its veins to its millions of tiny beating hearts. And these poplars seemed so real, so cordially affectionate, so alive. He was sublimely indifferent at that moment to any authority, indifferent too to prison, prosecutors or operatives!

And this was probably reflected in his face, because the prosecutor looked at him and said nothing either. At length the zek heaved a sigh, tore himself away from the window and turned to the prosecutor. It was all over. He was back in prison, fasting to the death in his cell.

"Well, I got your application," said the prosecutor in honeyed tones, "but I don't quite understand what it is you want."

"Investigation," replied Zybin.

"And this isn't an investigation?"

Zybin shrugged.

"Well what is it – is the investigator shouting at you, twisting your statements? You say one thing and he writes another? What specifically are you unhappy about? Specifically, please, specifically!"

Zybin considered.

"The investigator wants me to think up the case myself, and that doesn't suit me; I didn't contract to do that. If he wants to earn his pay, let him work for it. He's not just turning a steering wheel!"

"What steering wheel?" The prosecutor was both taken aback and amused.

"He used to be a driver, you know. He drove bosses around, and now he's one himself."

"Ai-ai-ai! Rags to riches! Is that it? That's bad, undemocratic." Myachin said this with a hint of reproach. "So then, as you see it, the whole problem is the investigator. This investigator is bad because he detains you. Another would have pulled you in and then let you go. Why can't you realize that if he and I, Major Neiman and yourself were to get round this table and think up a way of setting you at liberty, even then nothing would come of it!"

"Well, perhaps," Zybin acquiesced. "It's like the labyrinth. You can get in all right, but you haven't a snowball's chance in hell of getting out."

"Exactly," cried Myachin. "Crime is always a labyrinth! That's why I'm looking at you and wondering – an intelligent man, driving yourself to god knows what lengths. What can't be done, can't be done. There's the wall, beat your head against it and what do you get?"

"One man got something." Zybin grinned.

"What?"

"He snuffed it!"

The prosecutor broke into a laugh.

"And you believe that crap? No, Georgi Nikolaevich, nothing can come of this situation. You can raise a bump on your skull, that's true, but we won't let you snuff it! The labyrinth! So all this business is stupid," he spread his arms. ". . . And your punishment stints are stupid, and so is your hunger strike, and your refusing water, all of it, stupid."

"Yes," Zybin agreed, "obviously you're right about that – it is stupid. All the same, I'm not going to work for your employee. Let him rack his own brains."

"Well, and will you tell the truth, then?"

"That's what I'm doing. Nobody wants it here though."

"Well, it's what I want. Let's have a little talk. Off the record. Something might become clearer for you as well. Tell me, were you satisfied with your work at the museum? Were you pleased with the way you were working?"

Zybin thought for a while. The work had gone badly and he replied shortly: "No."

"Splendid," Myachin nodded. "What do you put that down to, then? Yourself? Your colleagues? The management?"

"In the first place, of course, myself. The worst thing was getting involved with that expedition. We should simply have written to Moscow and requested specialist help. But we decided that as it was just a test dig, we would go ahead, turn up something of value, then write off. But we didn't know how to conduct a proper dig. I'm not an archaeologist. Kornilov is, but he's never been in the field. Things went wrong."

"And the director was aware of all this?"

Zybin paused for a moment to consider.

"Yes, of course. But what conclusion do you draw from that?"

"There you are," laughed Myachin. "Now I realize what goes on between you and your investigator. Where you're supposed to answer him, you ask him questions. No, Georgi Nikolaevich, I ask the questions here. And you answer me. And in this way we both arrive at the truth. What conclusions I draw from it are nothing to do with you. Is that clear? Let's go on. About this expedition now. What took you to that fruit farm? You fancied an apple? Or was it nearer to the town? Mornings there, evenings here?"

"It was very simple. We were brought the handles of some large vessels decorated with Sogdian motifs, so we decided . . ."

"Ah, forgive me, who are 'we'? Just you, Georgi Nikolaevich? Kornilov? The director? The director didn't decide anything, did he? He could only trust your word and provide the resources. That's what he did. And you used them to go round the farm shops and start digging up an old cattle cemetery. Which gave rise to sundry rumours about glanders and other disagreeable things. Meanwhile the gold, genuine natural gold which had never previously been found in these parts, quietly slipped away. Straight out of the museum. Under your nose, so to speak. You follow me?"

"I wasn't there at the time."

"That's right, you weren't; but you were duty bound to be there. You've been talking and writing all the time, haven't you, that gold was circulating. Why on earth, when the director had shown you this gold, didn't you drop those sheep bones, get into his car and head into town? Then the gold would still have been intact! Well?" Zybin said nothing. "Well now, Georgi Nikolaevich, what are we supposed to make of that?"

"Carelessness?"

"More precisely?"

"Negligence?"

"Still more precisely?"

"Criminal negligence?"

"Not that, not that, Georgi Nikolaevich, the wrong words in the wrong language."

"Abuse of official position?"

"Getting warmer, but still not right. You keep using everyday language, newspaper language; if you move on to political language, we'll get there. Say 'wrecking' and that will cover it."

"Wonderful!"

"No, no, not wonderful yet. Let us proceed. You were excavating near the city; the diadem was also found near the city on the other side, on the Karagalinka river. But you were arrested on the Ili, weren't you, thirty-five miles away. After the loss of the gold, you tore off there straightaway. What were you after over there? You didn't say anything to anybody. You got ready in a hurry, bought a load of provisions, took your female colleague with you and disappeared. You told her you were going for a swim, forsooth! Odd? Very Odd! We go on. It emerged that in the museum you had asked for all the maps – all large-scale and detailed. I've seen them. And those places lie flush against the frontier."

"They're archaeological maps! They've been around donkey's years!"

"I don't care if they're pornographic! With naked ladies on them! Doesn't matter what they're called. What matters is the area and the scale. They might be out of date, but the relief features are basically the same. Tell me how you explain that? I don't know, tell me."

"Very well! You say I took my colleague with me. What role do you assign to her?"

"There you go, asking me questions again. I really pity your investigator. So then, Georgi Nikolaevich, for the moment I'm not assigning any role to anyone, I'm just asking you to explain. After all, what was the course of events? The museum gets wind that somewhere there's been a find of archaeological gold. You quickly cobble together a so-called team and you go off excavating on the Mountain Giant collective farm, that is, where it's known that no gold could possibly be. The director comes out to you there and informs you that a large hoard has been discovered somewhere near the Karagalinka. He shows you this and that and says that next day these people are coming to see him and that he is going with them to the site of the discovery. You're very pleased about this, but for some reason don't go back to town with him; it's as if you're waiting for something. What was it? The following day, you are informed that a theft has taken place at the museum. The treasure-hunters have purloined their documents and made themselves scarce. Then you come haring into town and get hold of the old maps from the archive. But you go about studying them in a rather curious fashion. With the director you look at the maps of the Karagalinka region, but in your office you look through the Ili maps, that is, the frontier area. You even make a sketch on your notepad. It has no connection whatever with the missing gold. Next, you lay in a great deal of vodka and piles of eatables of all kinds, arrange to meet the very colleague who was the last person to see the missing treasure-seekers. You set off for Ili on the very earliest train. I emphasize once again, Georgi Nikolaevich, to the Ili, not the Karagalinka. Why? Who was it you had to meet there? Who was the vodka intended for? It was an awful lot just for you, even with your unique capacity; the girl doesn't drink at all – so then, were you really going bathing, or were you intending to meet someone to share it with? Explanation, please."

Zybin said nothing.

"You see, despite all your resourcefulness, you can't answer these questions. All right, this isn't an interrogation. You have a think and tell the investigator. Next. You complain about Khripushin? Very well. We'll appoint someone else. But let's get something straight here and now with the comrade governor present: you won't ask questions, you'll answer them and talk. And tell everything. Tell about that strange journey, about what's been happening in the museum lately and about your general attitude, well and so on."

Zybin raised his head. Up to now he had simply sat and listened.

"If you're interested in my state of mind I can tell you that now if you like."

The prosecutor laughed.

"Your attitude is what interests us, not your mood, Georgi Nikolaevich," he said. "Frame of mind is something else; it changes from one hour to the next. That's all right for novels but not for the investigative process." He turned to the deputy governor.

"So then, Georgi Nikolaevich calls off his hunger strike. Transfer him to a decent cell, give him bread and water and let him rest up for a bit. After three days or so, put him back where he was before. Well," he rose, "I trust, Georgi Nikolaevich, that our misunderstandings have now been resolved. We shall work together."

He had said that comrade Stalin was awake. He had been wrong to say that. It was still ten in the morning and comrade Stalin was asleep. He was sleeping on his back, a measured, deep, peaceful sleep; a heavy sleep as always, without once waking up. The previous day he had got back late to Moscow, gathered a few people together and sat at table till about two. As the conversation flowed, little by little, tot by tot, he drank down probably half a bottle of red wine. This wine was one of his favourites – red, harsh, very dry – it was produced in only one locality in Georgia. Round about 1908 or 1909, in circumstances now forgotten but extremely important for him at the time, he had spent an entire summer in that spot and developed a taste for this wine. There had been an Uncle Shalva there, who always placed a full earthenware jug on the table in front of him. An eternity had gone by since then and he had forgotten both the place and uncle Shalva, and the long, planed table in the chilly, half-darkened cellar, where they used to sit and talk while sipping their wine. Then suddenly, quite recently in Tbilisi, exactly the same sturdy red earthenware jug had appeared on the table in front of him, and none other than Uncle Shalva had entered, accompanied by the first secretary – the same moustaches, the darting eyes, the same air of the crook about him as in those bygone years, and his age was about the same. It transpired that Uncle Shalva's nephew was the deputy head of the NKVD. This came in very handy; Beria's touch was faultless in these matters. No sooner had they got sat down and he had sunk his first glass, than along with the tartness, the acid tang and hint of damp and freshness, back came all the circumstances of that summer and he remembered every detail.

The body's memory, taste, smell, muscular sensation, had always been very strong and deep-rooted in him. Any little thing – a scent, a breeze, a song, a twig catching his face – could bring back things long forgotten. His other memory had been getting worse in recent years. Some things he would forget completely or recall inaccurately. But now, with this wine, quite a different story was taking shape in his mind. Yesterday Beria had passed him a letter from a certain prisoner. He had read it through and laughed; he had been in a good mood for the rest of the day. It was a nice, sad, cheerful story. It could be told round the dinner table and even perhaps released to the people.

At breakfast, and afterwards looking through the papers, the recollection was still with him and he smiled inwardly until he came across *Bolshevik* with Molotov's article in it. At this point he remembered that the previous day there had been talk about this piece, among other things; that specialists on their own, no matter how eminent, could not be entrusted with the technical investigation of industrial enterprises, should there be wind of anything untoward. Saboteurs, diversionaries and Trotskyists had been well schooled by the party, just like all the old Bolsheviks had, and could always twist the most perspicacious expert round their little finger. This was what Molotov had spoken of and, as always when something had touched him on the raw, he had spoken in an agitated manner, blushing and stammering more than was his wont. He himself, the head of the table, had wondered what had lain behind that conversation. Evidently somebody had deftly and gently placed something on his desk, or pointed it out forcibly. Lavrenti Beria knew how to do that with inexorable politeness. He, Stalin, had never been fond of Molotov as a human being, but he placed a very high value on him. You could never force Molotov to lose control. He was dull, obdurate, utterly consistent and like some ponderous iron would singe and flatten one strip after another. Indeed, this was so much an inherent, primordial quality of his, that even if he had lately become brusque, impatient and quick-tempered, capable of interrupting a speaker in midsentence at some managerial meeting (always of minor importance, incidentally), or even putting him out of the hall – that quality remained unimpaired. On these minor occasions, he simply allowed himself to get things off his chest. And that was all right too. Beria, on the other hand, might come up with just about anything. Leafing through the magazine, Stalin found yesterday's point at issue. It was a Central Committee directive so to speak, the entire press was obliged to print it. He read: "Shaliko Okudzhava, party secretary at Ural Wagon Construction was a Trotskyist wrecker. The wreckers were exposed several months ago. In February of this year, at the behest of the people's commissariat for heavy industry, a special commission was sent out to look into the incidence of sabotage at Ural Wagon Construction. This commission was led by comrades including head of Central Building Industries, comrade Ginzburg and Central Committee candidate member Pavlunsky. This commission did not bring to light a single fact concerning sabotage at the plant. That means that the hardened saboteur Maryasin, along with fellow-wrecker Okudzhava were simply slandering themselves. Meanwhile, as the commission was on its way to the Urals, Maryasin offered fresh evidence, giving specific details as to his sabotage at the plant. He indicated a whole series of facts which eluded the eyes of the respected commission."

He read this passage again and frowned: people's commissariat for heavy industry again! Sergo Ordzhonikidze had really let that crowd get completely out of hand! He had been an invaluable man at one time, a fighter, a hero, but it seemed he'd not been up to the job for a long time. He'd had reason to put a bullet in himself in a bitter hour of doubt and remorse!

Thinking about Sergo had made him feel sad. But it was a pleasant, noble sadness. He liked and respected himself at such moments. He got up and went over to the door. It led out onto the terrace, stone-built, ample, open. On the small lawn in front grew a clump of young birches, all white and shot through with light, illumined with a kind of inner glow.

He descended from the terrace and went towards it. His guilt in the affair was of course nothing to do with that crazy Zinaida's accusations. When they had all got to Sergo's flat, she had been lying insensible on the sofa. After hearing the shot and running into the office, she had found her husband on the floor near the writing-desk with a Browning close by. She had collapsed on the spot. Then they had carried her to the sofa, and when she had come to and seen them all – himself, Molotov, Kaganovich, Mikoyan, Yezhov and Beria she had leapt to her feet, shouting: "You couldn't protect him either for my sake or your own!" At that, he had let go himself, being stricken and distressed. Besides he couldn't stand women's hysterics, it was beginning to turn him over inside. He stepped forward and told her quietly and earnestly: "Zina, hold your tongue! You know what I'm liable to do! Hold your tongue!" At which she burst into loud weeping and wailing and he left the room. Yes, he was a fine man, Sergo, a very fine man.

Then suddenly a voice asked him very distinctly: "And was Abel Yenukidze, your wife's godfather, such a bad man? Or this Okudzhava. And . . . ? And . . . ? And . . . ?" He suppressed a whole string of names.

331

Yes, that was the whole trouble: words like good and bad had no relevance here. Nothing had relevance here, no human feeling, no dictate of the heart. That was why he had been victorious: he had known this since his youth. He had divested himself once and for all of any vestige of doubt or hesitation. Anything in the world might happen, one simply couldn't prejudge or take anything on trust where people were concerned. Everyone was weak, sinful and susceptible. Of no one could it be said: "He is incapable of that." If you thought that of anyone, they would sell you down the river when the time came, starting with one's wife and ending with Sergo – and how many people and attachments had lain between them!

He was walking through the birch grove, inhaling the smell of grass, earth and tree, thinking (the previous day's talk had evidently given his reflections an appropriate direction) that after the governmental commission had reached their favourable conclusions about Maryasin and Okudzhava and gone back home, Maryasin had been summoned to the investigator and, as *Bolshevik* wrote, provided fresh incriminating evidence. And by so doing of course, he had signed his own and Okudzhava's death warrant. Okudzhava had given nothing in the way of evidence at that time, neither against himself nor against Maryasin. And it was obvious he'd said nothing previously either. A real Georgian for you! If he stands by you, it's to the death! That's how Abel had been too, not a hope in hell of getting anything out of him. Ordzhonikidze! Died without confessing. Stubborn people, so stubborn! Maryasin had given evidence but Shaliko Okudzhava hadn't. And yet they'd been interrogated in exactly same fashion. Maryasin, yes; Okudzhava, no.

These words kept echoing and re-echoing in his mind until he reached his favourite spot, a wooden stage with an armchair of woven osiers, where he sat down. He was fond of rough, unpretentious furniture, just as he liked everything that was simple, durable and comfortable. That was why armchairs like this were dotted all over the garden.

CHAPTER 2

To the special prosecutor from ZK (forename, surname, routine details, i.e. where arrested, where being held, for what period, what article charged under (article 58.10, anti-Soviet agitation)):

I wish to clarify matters between us once and for all. I am not a member of the suicide league and will not acquiesce in my own destruction. I am giving you advance notice of this. I am not a spy, nor a currency speculator, nor a traitor: I am an extremely loyal and faithful citizen of the Soviet Union – an ordinary man in the street if you like. I have a dread of politics. It is not for me. All the foregoing I have laid before Khripushin and he has answered me as follows: "If to sign you're not inclined, then this fist will change your mind." I could hardly fail to understand that, could I? That's something I realized long ago; but let Khripushin realize something in his turn: I've got a fist as well and maybe I can punch a bit harder than he can. And since in matters of this kind, "an extreme lack of scruple is allied to extraordinary attention to legal detail" (A. V. Lunacharsky), then Khripushin will end up with damn-all and I will spill a bucketful of his blood. No extra charges are going to be pinned on me – let that be borne in mind by all the great inquisitors, who, in Khripushin's words, are thick on the ground hereabouts.

By this hand, Zybin.

To the governor of the NKVD internal prison
from ZK (same details)
Explanation
In answer to your question "Against whom specifically among the security organ staff do you direct your offensive anti-Soviet attacks," I would reply: Against no one specifically, I was making a general point. If, like you, they were to inform me that nobody was trying to frame me for anything,

but merely conducting an investigation, then obviously I threatened no one with anything and cast aspersions on no one.

In response to your second question "What made you describe Soviet justice as a great inquisition?" I would reply: Not what, but who – my investigator Khripushin. He swore he would make mincemeat of me and said that patriots would help him do it: "We're not short of them." If you doubt my word, arrange a confrontation between us.

As for comrade Lunacharsky, there's no need to arrange one for me. He's long gone to his rest in "the damp earth", or rather in the Kremlin wall. The anti-Soviet remark you specified as interesting you can be found in Anatole France's *History of Joan of Arc* (preface).

To the question "Give a frank account of the anti-Soviet terrorist organization known as the 'suicide league' and your involvement in it", I would reply: This league could not possibly have been an anti-Soviet organization since it existed before the Soviets. I could not possibly have been a member of it by reason of my age at that time. In any case it seems not to have existed. Some contemporary comrade Khripushin no doubt invented it, with the help of some golden-handed Sonya of the day.

To the question "Explain the specific terrorist acts with which you are threatening the investigation", I would answer: I make no such threats, but if someone strikes me I will return it with interest. And I will not leave my cell again. You will have to haul me by main force. And I will declare a hunger strike immediately. And I will ask to see the Republic prosecutor. However, since you have said that "measures" were only applied to "those worth bothering with", the "real" people, and it wasn't worth spoiling your hands on shits like me, the matter ends there.

I should like to submit an earnest request to see the librarian: *How the Steel Was Tempered* and L. Charskaya's *Princess Dzhavakha* have been lying about in the cell for a month – and I managed to study these works thoroughly before being in prison. I ask you not to reject this request.

By this hand, ZK G. Zybin

"It's not the tone, man! That's normal, they often write like that! It's this "by this hand" business. It's this insolent, sarcastic "By this hand, G. Zybin"! I'd give you hand, G. Zybin! You'd find out sharpish whose hand it was! The nobleman writes to his yard porter! Why the . . . !'" Neiman flung both statements across the desk in exasperation, took out his pipe and began to fill it. This process was far from simple: it aped the example of one higher: he would extract two Flowers of Herzegovina papirosi, rip off the cardboard holders, tear the cigarette paper and tamp the tobacco down into the bowl with an extended yellow thumb. At length he struck a flame from his lighter, lit up and inhaled with every evidence of enjoyment. "Ah-h, that's good," he would say.

Prosecutor Myachin regarded him wordlessly. He didn't care for Neiman. To be more precise, he simply couldn't stand the chubby, rosy-cheeked, buoyant, bright-eyed little man and his veiled enigmatic gaze.

"Then show him!" he said amiably.

Neiman glanced at him, releasing a long trickle of smoke.

"Why did the bit about Lunacharsky interest you?" he asked abruptly.

The prosecutor half rose, picked up the statements and secreted them in his briefcase. He locked it before replying. "He was actually seconded to his secretariat for some time."

"Aha! Yes, yes. So he was, so he was! When he was still a student," Neiman nodded. "And you thought that the people's commissar might have opened his mind to his student at some juncture?" He suddenly gave a mellow laugh. "No, no, dear Arkady Alfredovich, that's out of the question. You're right, Lunacharsky was very fond of philosophizing. And he did talk to his students in a wide-ranging, free and easy fashion. When I was in the history faculty I heard about him expanding on this and that, but anything of that sort . . . no, no, never!"

"Well, all right, but just the same, what are we going to decide about this specimen? Eh? Obviously we can't do anything with him now – we'll have to send it to the SB. What do you think?"

Neiman went on smoking. Myachin had stung him to the quick. As a rule, only lost causes were sent to the SB, ones even the courts wouldn't accept. "Where there's no crime, there's no court, but there is the SB," as the zeks used to joke, and the investigators had slowly picked it up too. Jokes of this nature did not appeal to the higher-ups. With them, ideals were paramount and therefore they had no love for cynics.

"Be very wary, be extremely wary as regards the SB," we were

335

exhorted at the people's commissariat general assembly by Roman Lvovich Shtern, a highly-placed visitor from Moscow, a cousin of this same Neiman. "Never lose your sense of style. Everyone should receive what he has deserved! Yes! It's true! The Trotskyist, the diversionary, the foreign agent – they're all so many Lieutenant Kizhes, 'secret prisoners, having no bodily presence'. These dark shadows must disappear silently and without trace. Your people's commissariat must be a burial vault for these enemies of the people. But, I repeat ENEMIES! Take this example, some lover of political talk and jokes is arrested. Let's say a cashier, Ivan Ivanovich Ivanov. And along with him Marya, Darya and Auntie Agatha and the whole crowd disappear without court or sentence. That's a gross miscalculation, comrades! For what can a piece of paper mean to the ordinary man in the street: 'Your relative has been condemned at such and such a date by order of the SB to eight years in the camps for counter-revolutionary activity?' They're all at sea, comrades! What is this board? What's special about it? Where is it? Why does it exist when there are courts? And why are there letters on this paper when the criminal code has figures? I can't imagine how you can explain all that! The courts are quite a different matter. There you have a presiding judge, an assessor, a defence counsel, a prosecutor. The witness gives evidence, the defence counsel defends, the prosecutor accuses, the judge sentences. He's been indicted, convicted, put in the 'black maria' and away. Lodge an appeal! The address so and so. Time limit for appeal such and such! Everything clear, in the open, simple. Alas, it is very far from always being like that. One comes across cases, not so infrequently, where the investigative staff try to shuffle off any case they don't like the look of onto the SB. Why to them precisely? I'll tell you: for a court, you need witnesses and there aren't any! Well you know, when I hear that sort of thing from one of your staff, I say to him very gently: 'Dear comrade. Have you been appointed to this most demanding of jobs too soon?' Because a prisoner always feels like falling on his knees before a real investigator and no witnesses are needed. Comrades, steer clear of the SB! It is the keenest weapon in the struggle for the ideological purity and solidarity of our society. It is simply impossible for any one of us to use it to excuse his own poor, sloppy work! That would mean that mistakes are possible, wouldn't it? Come to that I stopped using that word long ago. I say 'crime'! 'Objective or subjective – it makes no difference,' as our Leader has said. And finally. Be humane and just. There is no return from that place. There are no reviews or amnesties there! Whoever is condemned by you is condemned for ever!

You are his last resort and we prosecutors, without looking – I tell you that – without looking, sign your decisions! Because we do not have the right to look into them! No one has ever been entrusted with so much. Only you. Only you. Think deeply on this, comrades!' "

After this speech of Roman Lvovich's the number of cases referred to the SB from the people's commissariat of the Kazakhstan SSR declined sharply. Moscow began to evaluate the work of the investigator in relation to the number of cases passing through the courts. This did not affect Neiman. He always knew how to get hold of witnesses.

"Very well then," he said, "if we can't dig anything up, we'll send it to the SB. We aren't going to let him go, are we?" And he added, "He's gone and put a spoke in the wheel, damn fool!"

"Are you referring to Belousov?" Myachin smiled.

"Yes, him, the idiot! The shithouse Sherlock Holmes himself! 'Must strike now, must strike now! There's a woman come to see him! If we catch him red-handed, he'll crack straightaway! He's a nutter, isn't he!' So he picked him up. And he's turned out a really hot handful. There's nothing to charge him with!"

"Point ten?"

"That's it, that's it!" Neiman seemed positively gleeful. "That crap is all I need! He went about blabbing for ten years – he might have been given another year or so at least! He might have got himself into more trouble in that time. Point ten! Do me a favour and forget it. I'm up to my neck in terrorists and spies, and you talk to me of point ten!" He grabbed his pipe, sucked at it, then snatched it out again. "I haven't got the trained staff. Staff! They're overwhelmed! You now, day before yesterday, didn't accept my investigator's bill of indictment. Well and good, but who've I got working for me, do you know that? Probationers, third year students! I'm getting my own niece in to help. She's just graduated with honours; the poor girl needs a holiday and I'm bringing her here! Here! Have you been to the city deportation camp? Well, did you enjoy it?" Neiman lit up again.

"Ye-s," drawled the prosecutor. "Yes, deportation camp; as they say, a picture worthy of Aivazovsky's brush." He had, in actual fact, been shaken to the depths of his soul. It wasn't a prison he had seen, it was a merry Gipsy encampment, a rest home, a flea market, a Moscow river beach! The administration had filled up the vast square of the courtyard with tents, huts, wigwams and eating-houses of a sort. When the prosecutor had passed through the yard with the governor, all this rabble had come spilling out. Somebody made a comment and drew a general roar of laughter. "Now let's have a bit of order here! Otherwise the humorists go to the punishment cell!" shouted the senior warder for decency's sake, but he went unheard. Glancing at the zeks, the prosecutor realized something else. These ragamuffins and "goners" were the happiest people in the world. They were afraid of nothing now. They hadn't been shot. They hadn't been beaten up. All the terrors, the glazed cubicles, the cement isolation units, the icy punishment cells, the hours of standing, the lack of sleep – all that lay behind them. They trod the grass once more, got wet in the rain, baked in the sun. And what more does a man need in all honesty? Noise, hubbub, laughter hung above the detestable spot. That old facetious prison saying: "All singing and all dancing there" was being borne out. Yes, they were dancing and singing all right, in addition to playing dominoes, fortune-telling with beans, swapping bread for clothing, clothing for sugar, sugar for tobacco and all those for an envelope, stamp and a sheet of paper; a letter could be thrown out somewhere along the way to the station, or even from a carriage window. Barrack-room lawyers sat around everywhere scribbling out complaints. They were writing to Stalin, Kaganovich, Yezhov. Meanwhile, news items trickled in from outside, each one more optimistic than the last. The prison governor had been put inside; a draft for the reform of the criminal code was on the Leader's desk – there was to be no shooting, the longest term was to be five years; at a reception for a delegation of foreign workers, the Leader had said: "We are able to declare an amnesty such as the world has never witnessed"; a government review commission had been working in the Kolyma for over a month now. Let's get there quick and . . . and they swapped addresses, invited one another to visit, and arranged to meet. "In a year's time, at home," they would say.

The deportation supervisor, an old jail rat who had been working in the prisons since the beginning of the century knew, and told the prosecutor, that in a year's time only half of them would be left and in two years, a quarter; perhaps one in ten would last out to freedom.

(Four out of a hundred survived and were amazed when they met that so many were left! "No, there is a God, there is a God after all," they would say.)

"Precisely," said Neiman. "Precisely; a scene worthy of Aivazovsky. So then, Arkady Alfredovich, with the evidence we have, I would never have pulled Zybin in. I would have waited. He's a figure with considerable potential, there's a lot hanging on him. To let him go with a tenner, especially by way of the SB would simply be a crime. I'm not used to working like that. But you see, my hand is forced. Yes indeed, the operations department have let me down."

"What about the gold?" The prosecutor taunted him.

"What? Go-old?" Neiman feigned surprise. "First you have to have the gold, dear Arkady Alfredovich! That's not a matter of your blabbermouths, it's a noble metal! If he were to send me a full confession now, I'd tear it up and throw it in the wastepaper basket. And I'd send him to the punishment cell, because it would mean the bastard was up to something again! No, we're not going to make anything out of that! The SB it is! Of course, if I were allowed to employ sanctions . . . But you wouldn't let me would you?" He put it to him point-blank.

Myachin's shoulders twitched slightly.

"Me? No! I simply don't have that right. You know the directive. Ask your chief, he can authorize it. Here . . ." He fiddled in his briefcase for something.

"Don't bother," Neiman waved this away in disgust. "With responsibility! As an exceptional measure! In justifiable circumstances! In appropriate cases! In the case of rabid agents of the bourgeoisie! Mortal enemies!" After each exclamation he jerked up a palm. "But Zybin is going through as having too much to say, not for being a mad dog!"

"What if it's done, you know, on the side? Turn a blind eye to the whole thing," smiled the prosecutor. "Call in a couple of brawny probationers to have a chat with him at two in the morning, eh?" It was far from clear whether he was being serious or merely teasing again.

"Yes," Neiman grinned coarsely, "that would be the ticket all right! And he'd go on a hunger strike and keep it up for a fortnight. And the doctors would feed him through his backside and send in a report about me. And you would write: 'Without any reasonable cause, Major Neiman has complicated the investigation. The major's professional incompetence has led to . . .' That would be just like you, wouldn't it? And I'll get the father and mother of a telling-off courtesy of you. And if he kicks the bucket, what then?"

The prosecutor laughed.

"What's that to you!" He said. "With your . . ." He stopped short deliberately.

"That's it, that's it!" Neiman pounced recklessly. "That's it! That's just what you all hate me for . . ."

"Come now! Me hate you?" the prosecutor smiled again and made to rise. No, of course he didn't hate Neiman. That wasn't the word. It was just that he found Neiman, this butcher with a cherub's face, physically repellent. But at this moment he was also puzzled: for the first time he had witnessed Neiman drawing back from his victim. And such a stupid excuse! The idiot would declare a hunger strike! They'd have to feed him! And what if he did conk out! Neiman was certainly looking for things to worry about! Let them all drop dead! As if it was the first time Major Neiman had rammed a man into his coffin! Suddenly light burst in upon him. Gazing into Neiman's blue enigmatic eyes, Shtern's little brother, he thought scathingly: "There's likely more in this than meets the eye. Something must have happened in Moscow that nobody knows yet. Maybe new regulations have been issued. Had the Leader spoken perhaps? Or one of the leading lights made a slip? That had happened once already!"

He got to his feet, looking uncertainly at Neiman, not knowing what to say or do. Then the telephone rang. Neiman picked it up, frowning; after listening for a moment, he began to beam.

"Ah, good morning, good morning, my dear," he said very affectionately. "I mean those who work for a living have had their lunch long ago, whereas various layabouts and mummy's little girls . . . Yes, just imagine, it's two o'clock already. How's the leg, then? Who's seen it? That's what he said? Well, thank heavens for that. And now think what would have happened if you'd landed on your head instead of your knee. Yes, of course you don't care, but what would I have said to my dearest sister? That's the thing, isn't it? Now get a pencil and write this down: Anatole France. *Life of Joan of Arc.* I know you haven't. Ring the library. If they haven't got it, get them to order it at the public in my name. Yes, urgent! Look, don't you try being too bright! We used to have one who was too bright and now his relatives send him parcels. Yes, that's it. I'll be back at the usual time. Lie still and don't invite anybody round. Splendid! Now do what I say!"

He hung up and looked at the prosecutor. His face was now all gentle innocence. The eyes, like those of any middle-aged man harassed by life, were tired and yellowish.

"That's the way my girl is," he bragged, "fire and ice!"

"What's up with her leg, then?" Myachin evinced concern.

"She's a mad thing, silly!" rasped Neiman, with fond delight. "She went off on my bike to see a girlfriend of hers home and rode straight into a tree in the dark. When the girlfriend rang me and I rushed over there, her knee was a mass of unset jelly; I felt positively sick, I can't stand the sight of blood! Can't stand it! And there she was laughing!

340

Must be in the blood, her father's a Georgian. Tamara Georgievna Dolidze – what d'you think? Got a ring to it?"

"It certainly has," smiled Myachin, glancing in astonishment at a Neiman he had never seen before.

"But our blood's in the little girl as well! My grandfather was a soldier's son and my father . . ."

The phone rang again, this time an internal call. Neiman picked up the receiver and at once subsided, lumpish and careworn.

"Yes," he said in a dreary voice, "this is Major Neiman. Yes, Pyotr Ilich! Arkady Alfredovich is here with me already. Oh, just sitting discussing life. Right. We'll be waiting." He replaced the phone. "The colonel will be here presently, he wants to ask you a few questions."

He settled himself firmly in his chair, took out his pipe, filled the bowl and lit it.

"Ah, that's good!" he said.

CHAPTER 3

"H AIL, TITANS," SAID GULYAEV as he entered. "Greetings, greetings!"

He was a short, puny, rather boyish sort of individual (people used to tease him by calling him polecat), and wore huge horn-rimmed spectacles. Whenever he took them off, his surprisingly small eyes would swim into view, reddish and constantly blinking. At such moments, his face would lose its ominously mysterious air of significance. A man like any other man.

"Where do you get yourself to, prosecutor?" he went on, approaching the desk. "I ring the prosecutor's office and they tell me he's gone to the peoples' commissariat, I ring his room and they tell he's been there but he's left. Where do you keep going off to, eh?"

"Well you can see where," Myachin grinned mirthlessly. "We've been sitting here for an hour, airing our views on this Zybin of yours."

"Why's that?"

"He's sent us a note," explained Neiman.

"A note? Well, that's his style," assented Gulyaev with indifference, waiting for Neiman to get up and surrender his chair. "That's something we've taught him!" He sat down, took out his notepad and placed it in front of him. "Polina Yurevna Pototskaya," he read, "works at the Vetzooinstitute, does that tell you anything?"

"It tells me a lot," grinned Neiman. "She's Khripushin's star witness. She nearly gave him a heart attack. Well naturally. He sent a subpoena to her house – and she didn't turn up! It seems she was away from home and her girlfriend took it. Then it was delivered personally to her at work – and she didn't turn up then either! She's not at the institute or at home. They only found out after three days that she was in hospital. She had some sort of recurring dislocation, and got a touch of frostbite in the mountains as well."

"So what happened, she wasn't questioned then?" Gulyaev was astonished.

"Why ever not?" Neiman's voice took on an ironic tinge. "She most certainly was. She and Khripushin produced ten sheets, both sides.

Then another five. He brought them to me. I read them and told him: 'Well now, have all this typed out nice and clean, staple it and send it off to *Ogonyok*, so they can print it with pictures. We'll go halves on the money.' "

"What, there wasn't a single relevant word in the whole lot?" Myachin laughed.

"What do you mean! There's fifteen pages of relevant words. A whole novel! The sea. The night. The moon. Him. Her. Some incredible monument. A crab of amazing size. She and Zybin stuck it under his bed, then took it out and let it go in the sea. There's a grand little report for you! I told him if he didn't want to send it to a magazine, he could take it to the toilet. In line with its primary function, so to speak. Well, what do you remember about her?"

"Well, she rings me up. Asks to see me." Gulyaev considered for a moment. "So then, shall we send her to Khripushin? Or will you talk to her yourselves?" He shot a glance at Neiman.

"Oh no! She can go to her grandmother's for all I care," said Neiman earnestly. "Perhaps Arkady Alfredovich would like to see her. Look at this then!" He walked across to the desk, pulled a file out of it and retrieved a black envelope with photographs; he selected one and handed it to Myachin. "Take a look at that! What about that?"

"Y-es," said Myachin, sighing as he turned the photograph in his hands. "Ye-es," he held out the picture to Gulyaev. "Have a look!"

"I love you dear with all my heart, this picture means we'll never part," read Gulyaev. "What's she up to? Such a lady and now . . ."

"They have a special sense of humour all their own," Neiman smirked grimly. He was irritated and on edge, though he strove not to show it. "To us fools, that is, of course. He's the same to her – 'In the first lines of my letter, our gracious Polina, I hasten to inform you . . .' or 'by this hand, Zybin.' Do-it-yourself wit, damn them."

"The hairdo, though, the hairdo," said Gulyaev.

"The very latest style! Just like the stars! That hairdo's got a special name – Putti? Mutti? Lili? Puti? Arkady Alfredovich, have you heard of it?"

"No, I haven't," said the prosecutor gravely, taking the picture from Gulyaev. "Lilian Putti hasn't got a hairdo, it's close-cropped. And very low, something like our Polish style. She's like Gloria Swanson here. Hairdos like that were very fashionable about three years ago."

"Really?" Gulyaev stole a glance at the prosecutor, who was still examining the photo, then picked up the phone. "Milya," he said, "if

Pototskaya rings again, I'm with Yakov Abramovich in 350. Bring her here. Otherwise I'm not here," he replaced the receiver and made a face. "Arkady Alfredovich," he said, businesslike, "we celebrated your name day last year. How old are you now?"

"Firty-free," responded the prosecutor peevishly, handing the picture back to Neiman.

"Exactly, exactly! Thirty-three plus fifteen! And you're still thinking about trutti-nutti? What it is to have a barrister as a father. And just look at the major! He's not the slightest bit interested. Us old fogeys are no match for him – young, fit, colour in his cheeks! But have you ever seen him with a woman? How do they put it in poetry – he's an anchorite!"

"I could be having orgies at home," Neiman grimaced unpleasantly.

"It's obvious that's what you're doing. While your mind's on those putti, cuty, footy, prosecutor, you know whose heart he's conquered? Marya Savishna, comrade Kashirina! The one who looks after our houses. You know her – Catherine the Great! The one with the curls! Tough as old boots. She got her daughter divorced and the husband arrested. But when she talks about Yakov Abramovich, her voice is like a little quail – ever so re-fi-ned. 'It's so clean, so tidy, a real pleasure to look at! You'd like to go in and never come out. And the air so fresh, all the windows open. And so neat and tidy! Like a lady's room! Not a thing out of place! You can lay your hands on everything straightaway!' That's what the working class thinks of our Yakov Abramovich. Do they think of us like that? Not on your life! What was the word? Anchorite!"

"Yes," said the prosecutor absently. "It's very, very . . ."

"But you know what really won her, Yakov Abramovich," said Gulyaev, turning to Neiman. "Your coins! So beautiful, says she, so scholarly! All the coins in a special glass case, just like watches in a Jew's workshop. And all matched – silver with silver, copper with copper. As for the gold, well those of course are in a separate box inside the trunk. They're not on show, but they are there, they are there! I've never seen anything so beautiful even at the Yukhovy merchants house, when I used to go round the fairs with them."

A remarkable character actor had indeed gone to waste in Colonel Gulyaev. No wonder they said that he'd been a boy chorister in the bishop's choir. Up until the previous year he'd even been an active participant in the drama group, which was run by a merited artist of the republic, a good-natured chubby individual, always well-oiled, but for ever after the last dribs and drabs of the vodka bottle. Gulyaev was friendly with him, first getting him onto the secret service strength, then fixing his artistic title for him. Neiman knew about this, because after the last glass, when he was being taken home, the merited one had suddenly sat down on a stone, commenced weeping and said that he was a lost man, totally and indisputably, because ... And told why in most dramatic fashion. He carried out his obligations properly for all that and was highly thought of – even being pressed for promotion. Neiman was still holding this story in reserve.

"Wait a minute," queried Myachin, shaken, "are you a numismatist or what?"

He was genuinely taken aback, indeed positively aggrieved. They collected all kinds of things in their houses: postcards, pebbles from Yalta and Koktebel, porcelain from the Arbat, furniture from sundry sales. His predecessor had even had a case of African butterflies hanging above his bed, while on a special table in the dining room, a display stand of hummingbirds had glittered with the interplay of blue and pink mother of pearl (may your owner rest in peace, little birds!) All that was perfectly normal, but for some investigator to go in for coin-collecting! And especially an investigator like this, a fat, small-town vulgarian opportunist! To the son of a metropolitan lawyer, an old Moscow intellectual, there was something almost insulting about it. But still, if you thought about it, that was only to be expected too! Quite a few archaeologists and historians had dropped into the earth through the floors of quiet fourth-storey offices. The result was as plain as could be: beginning with "and confiscation of all personal effects", then "so many kilos of white and yellow metal at so much".

"And have you got many coins?" asked the prosecutor.

"Know what he's got?" Gulyaev exclaimed. "A rouble of Alexander the Great! His profile on one side and the cavalry on the other. No, just fancy, Alexander the Blessed holding this very rouble or double in his hands two thousand years ago. Any museum in the world would give ten thousand in gold for it."

"And have you been collecting long?" Myachin enquired.

"Oh, I used to dabble in it once," Neiman dismissed this.

His hand was plump, with chubby fingers, wound round at the wrist with a red thread (he understood the prosecutor's feelings perfectly well and was merely amused by them).

"If you wish to know," he went on, "I even used to attend Professor Masson's seminars," he grinned! "Events of days long past."

"So now we're going to make you show them to us," cried Gulyaev gleefully. "Really, Yakov Abramovich, why not invite us round to your place? You've got a lady of the house now, haven't you? Prosecutor, you know Yakov Abramovich's niece? Well now, you'll forget all your putti-cutie straightaway. He's hiding her away from us, though. Well, never mind, when she starts work for us, then we'll . . ."

"No, no, comrades, perish the thought!" Neiman raised a protest. "I've been thinking of how to introduce her to our exclusive circle, but you see the trouble, she's laid up!"

"Has the doctor been?" Gulyaev asked. "Maybe she should be hospitalized?"

All three winced. That was a most fearful word. Somebody had to be hospitalized practically every day; yesterday it happened to the director of an elevator who had a collapsed lung; the day before there had been two: one with crushed fingers and the other with internal bleeding. That often happens after a kick from a boot.

"No, no, nothing like that," frowned Neiman. "She hates all hospitals, she's a crazy lass."

"Now, now," smiled Gulyaev, "no need to call her names! She's a grand little girl, bright as a button and such a sensitive soul! She'll make a real investigator. It's probably hereditary, Yakov Abramovich! You know what she said to me after she'd been present at the interrogation of this Zybin of yours? 'In my opinion, you'll get nowhere with Khripushin, comrade Colonel, another way needs to be tried. *Cherchez la femme*!' You understand what she meant? No? I got it right off. It needs a woman investigator. Eh? What do you say? At all events there's a creative notion there? Maybe we should give it a try?"

A short silence ensued.

"Do you know, that's right!" the prosecutor exclaimed all of a sudden, thumping his fist on the chair-back. "As a rule I don't trust these young women investigators, twenty-five-year-old prosecutors and operatives. Old women now, that's a different matter," he guffawed. "You know what Purishkevich came out with in 1912? Some ladies' magazine sent him a questionnaire about women's work, and he wrote in big letters across it: 'They do their best work on their backs.' Eh? He had a head on him, the swine. But seriously, they're no good at the job. First they complicate things needlessly, then they go over the top, also without rhyme or reason. It's off to the punishment cell, once, twice, three times! There he sits and time ticks by. The investigation is at a standstill of course, and the thing turns into a charade. They have to be replaced. And when they are, it's tears. But in the present case, I am actually in agreement. A woman investigator might have been tried. Might have been! But a question occurs to me here, the one I came to you with," he turned to Neiman. "What are we going to get out of him, really? Three days ago I talked to him in the presence of the deputy prison governor and I formed a very distinct impression. Of course he's lying, wriggling, holding something back, hiding something. Altogether a slimy character, a blabbermouth, boozer, anti-Soviet, all that's true. But that's all there is, comrades. There's nothing more. So is it worth complicating matters? Especially since you have told me yourself, Yakov Abramovich, that you wouldn't have got mixed up with him over a point ten matter. So why should we change the investigator? It'll be the same sort of chatter, point ten, I mean. Not via the SB, that's true, but via the courts. Of course that's a more desirable outcome, but really, Yakov Abramovich, is it worth it for just . . ."

"No, no, Arkady Alfredovich." Neiman shook his head vigorously. "It's not just for that at all. I keep telling you all the time: it's not on account of that. Zybin is a big fish. He's not a blabbermouth, he's an activist. He might shoot his mouth off, but that's probably just to cover up all the rest of it. And he began his active career early. That business of the raped student . . ."

"I'm sorry, what did you say?" The prosecutor roused himself. "I don't know anything about that."

"But we can't charge him on that, we just can't," growled Gulyaev. He couldn't stand talk like this or feeble attempts to drag in red herrings. "He was just a makeweight in the affair anyway; stuck up for his friend, that's all. They let him go at the time, didn't they? And we haven't got the file of that case, just extracts."

"Permit me to disagree, comrade colonel." Neiman inclined his head with diffident obduracy. "Of course, now he can't be charged with anything, that's absolutely correct, but in my opinion it was precisely that business which marked the beginning of his career. There was a meeting; Zybin spoke and very skilfully brought the entire collective round to his way of thinking. The upshot was that a resolution prepared by the party regional committee was thrown out. That was not at all fortuitous, in my submission. There was a whole group at work. One spoke and the rest backed him up. But even that's not the point. The point lies in the question: What brought him here? After all, Alma-Ata is the land of exile. Half of his friends have ended up either in Siberia or here. Which one of them was he looking for here then? And if he was looking for him, he must have found him, right? There's no answer

347

to that question either is there? But take a look at this." He picked up an envelope and shook it out over the desk. Several photographs fell out. He selected a couple of them. "Now here's an interesting detail. He's standing in front of some building, pressing a book to his chest. Just an ordinary photograph, but do you know what house that is? It's Krasin Street, number 74. The state archive."

The prosecutor took the photo, bestowed a fleeting glance upon it and put it down.

"Well, what of it?"

"This: that house is known all over the world as the residence of Lev Davidovich Trotsky. He lived there during his exile in 1929; he had his staff here, his agents used to convene here and it was from this house that he was sent packing abroad. So we have Zybin standing near the former residence of an enemy of the people, hugging a book to his chest. The book's format appears identical with one of the collected works of Lev Trotsky. I have made enquiries: the set came out in 1923. Just look at him standing there, the apostle and the gospel!"

"Curious," said the prosecutor, with another sideways glance at Gulyaev. The latter, however, went on smoking and staring out of the window in bored fashion. "Very good, very good indeed! But you couldn't present that photograph to the provincial court – it wouldn't be accepted!" He replaced the photo and picked up Pototskaya's picture again. "The provincial court wouldn't regard this as material evidence," he went on, examining the picture. "The man worked in the archive and had his photo taken next to it. It's not the only archive in the building either, I know the place. There's the Writers' Union there too, so any amount of people have had their picture taken there."

"What about the book?" asked Neiman.

"What about it? He'll say: 'It's the complete works of Pushkin, volume three, I don't remember the year of publication.' And that will be that."

"But the SB will certainly not ask any questions," said Gulyaev firmly, turning from the window. Haven't you found anything in his papers, then? He wrote a lot of stuff. And there are the letters. Of course the handwriting . . . looks like chicken tracks. So, nothing there then?"

"How can I put it?" Neiman shrugged. "Again nothing obvious, but a lot that's curious. Here for example, excerpts from Karl Marx's *Eighteenth Brumaire*. Not from the work itself, from the preface."

"Aha," Gulyaev came to life. "Whose preface?"

"No, no, it's Engels," Neiman frowned. "So we won't find anything . . . but the extracts are interesting though. Chosen for a purpose.

There's the bit where Engels rejects revolutionary methods of struggle. Why go to the barricades when we can simply vote and collect a majority? In which case, let the bourgeoisie go to the barricades. The idea of yellow trade unions anyway."

"Let's assume it isn't the idea of yellow trade unions," Gulyaev regarded him severely, "but Friederich Engels' idea, so don't mix up God's gift and an omelette."

"Yes, yes, that's it, that's it!" Neiman snorted. "He interrupted me in just about the same way. He had been preparing for his politics exam and had written out the extracts."

"Logical, most logical," smiled Myachin.

"Logical my foot! I'm telling you, he's a big fish. And he had something in mind, maybe even a mission. Definitely there was! Now you asked him, Arkady Alfredovich, why he'd gone to the Ili. What was his reply? He didn't have a reply! But he did go, didn't he? He did. And how did he go? As if he'd been suddenly stung. On Sunday morning he all of a sudden gets ready, lays in vodka, eatables, makes arrangements with the girl and travels by goods train. Why?"

"It's obvious isn't it, I'd guess," Gulyaev smiled. "Vodka, a picnic, a bird, Sunday! You can see why!"

"Well that's the line he takes. I like my vodka chilled. River flowing by, nobody about, girlie to hand; I had a drink, a bite to eat, and hid 'my iron clangour in something soft and feminine', just the job."

They all laughed.

"Knows a bit of psychology, at that," said the prosecutor.

"I beg your pardon," Neiman shook his head, "but it's just the psychological aspect that lets him down. Now if he'd done it a week previously, even three days previously, there'd be no questions asked. But what do we have here? This Polina arrives, the long-time love of his life, he's on hot bricks: waits for her, prepares himself, dying in case they don't manage to meet. Even in the cell he raves about her all the time. Either they're bathing together or going up a mountain, or under a mountain or he's carrying her somewhere in his arms. Right. They make a date for Sunday evening, and here he is on the Sunday morning picking up his secretary and shooting off hell knows where – to the Ili, the First of May collective farm. Why? Not known."

"Yes," said the prosecutor thoughtfully. "Yes, I asked him and he didn't say anything."

"He doesn't say anything!" Neiman exclaimed excitedly. "And he'll keep saying nothing – he's got his head screwed on! Do you know that

349

part at all? Two hours out of town. Bleak and empty steppeland, rocks and the river. Not a soul anywhere. All the way to China. Fishermen's huts for about thirty miles along the river. They catch marinka there. Hell knows who's a fisherman and who isn't. There's no identity cards, no registration, no policeman, nothing. But information gets through to us: there are ex-kulaks there, runaways and even maybe refugees from China, and hell alone knows who else."

"Caught anybody?" asked the prosecutor.

"Oh, just riffraff; the big fish got away immediately of course. You can't get close without being noticed, you know, it's empty steppe. You can see a man for five miles or more. And at night they've got their sentries posted of course. So why did he go poking about over there? And with vodka? And a bird? If his light of love had found out about the girl what then? Eh?"

"Yes," said the prosecutor, "you're right, there's something fishy about this. And you've said nothing to this Polina? Female jealousy can be a great help in our business. If one knows how to exploit it."

"Oh yes," Neiman shook his head, "they just won't see reason. I instructed Khripushin to tell him: 'If you won't talk, we'll put her in jail.' A decent individual would have given that some thought of course: then out would come the truth! But this bastard practically hugs Khripushin: 'That's right! Put her inside! Let her sit there and wait for me. Otherwise I'm here and she's having fun with somebody else. Where's the justice in that?' "

Gulyaev looked at the prosecutor and they both burst out laughing again.

"He's a tough nut," said the prosecutor, gratified.

"And she says the same: I told her about the Ili and who he'd taken along, and she said: 'There you see, comrade investigator, I told you straight off we were just friends, no more than that. He used to introduce me to his girlfriends.' That was the sum total of her reply."

"Right! So when will your niece be back on her feet again?" Gulyaev asked suddenly. "Another week yet? Well, when she's up and about, we'll give her this case; what do you think Arkady Alfredovich?"

"Is she not liable to make a mess of the first one?" asked the prosecutor warily. "Although it's true we haven't put together anything here beyond a point ten yet, I'm now in agreement with Yakov Abramovich: we're onto big game. A special approach is required. Delicate handling. A new graduate might not cope."

"Hmm, new graduate!" Gulyaev grinned. "Your notions of our young people are antediluvian, prosecutor. Yakov Abramovich, give us a brief run down on that Krasnodar business. When Tamara Georgievna was officially thanked by the head of the directorate. What she did, prosecutor, was uncover an excellently planned anti-Soviet organization. You must have heard? Come on, Yakov Abramovich, enlighten the prosecutor."

"You've probably heard," frowned Neiman. "To begin with, they arrested an old woman who ran a drinking den in her village. Illicit liquor of course, they're all at it over there. She was 68 and hadn't a tooth in her head, bent and crooked with a squint, deaf and hardly able to walk; they were about to kick her out but thought better of it. How was it she made illicit vodka and ran a drinking den, but lived on bread and milk without two kopecks to rub together? Where did it go? They questioned her, she just howled. 'My sons! My sweet little children! I haven't got anything. Look where you like. I've just saved a bit for my funeral.' 'Where is it? Show us, we won't take it, we just want to have a look at it.' 'Oh my sons, I haven't got it, no! My son came and I gave it to him for safekeeping.' Her son's a winter seasonal worker somewhere. A long, long way off! 'I had a bit of paper saying how much I gave him, but I've gone and lost it, I think; it was all lying behind the icon.' Well they'd really decided to throw her out. And they gave it to my niece to formalize the closure of the case. So she had the old girl in, and from morning to midnight she sat with her and exposed every last bit of it. It seems that an organization calling itself Widow's Mite had been working under the very noses of the authorities. Not only the village elders, but their children, fiancées, and their grandsons had been allotting five per cent of their income to condemned priests and religious folk. The set-up was a pleasure to see. The old bat had become an agent, but there was a treasurer too, forwarding agents, even an accountant! They sent parcels, or arranged to hand them over; they called relatives to fixed meetings and paid their travelling expenses. They hired defence counsel to submit appeals. But the main thing was that in several cases they got the indictment changed and reduced the sentence to practically nothing. Such are the wonders that take place behind our backs. So much for our vigilance!"

"Really, who'd have thought it!" said the prosecutor, outraged. "And what happened in the end?"

"A very happy ending," exclaimed Neiman proudly. "Three got tenners, four got five years, twelve persons exiled. The dear little lawyers all got five years in Kolyma. One never made it there, the criminals

351

throttled him on the way. That's what the little girl did! While we sat twiddling our thumbs."

"Yes, impressive, impressive," assented the prosecutor. "The lass did well. What happened to the old woman?"

"Oh, the day after the interrogation the old girl had to be hospitalized. No, no, nothing like that, just her heart, terminal seemingly: she doesn't figure among those sentenced. Actually she was no longer needed by then."

"Yes, very good indeed, can't be denied, the lass did well. She did well," repeated the prosecutor. "Well then," he addressed Gulyaev, "in my opinion we should give it a try."

There came a knock at the door.

"Aha, she's arrived," Gulyaev rose. "Right. I'll start off, then hand her over to you as the procurator's representative. Comrade Neiman will assist us."

He gathered the photos from the desk, slid them into the envelope and called out: "Come in!"

The secretary entered, and behind her the woman whose photograph all three had just been examining and criticizing.

There was a whiff of perfume.

She wasn't like a film star, however, and her hairdo did not resemble Gloria Swanson's; her eyelashes were not long, and she wasn't wearing lipstick. So she wasn't Gloria Swanson of course, might even have been the heroine of a film about Soviet women. She entered and halted on the threshold.

"Good morning," she said.

"Good morning, good morning, Polina Yurevna," Gulyaev responded with an affable simplicity. "Come through, please, and sit down. In this chair here. And so, what brings you here to us?"

"I have come to talk."

"Aha! Splendid! Let us talk. What about?"

"I've been summoned in connection with the Zybin case."

"Aha, so you know Yakov Abramovich. I am the head of the department, my name is Gulyaev, Pyotr Ilich; this is the provincial special prosecutor. All present. So then, if there are any questions or queries ... What's that you have? A statement? Do give it here!"

He took the paper and was soon absorbed in reading it. He read intently, taking his red pencil and underlining a long section in the text.

"So," he said. "I see!" And held the paper out to Neiman. "Certificates like this, Polina Yurevna, we do not hand out personally. If we are officially requested, we will answer. Did someone direct you here, is that it?"

"No, I came of my own accord," she replied.

"Of your own accord! Then it's quite incomprehensible why you had need of a certificate of this kind. You're a specialist, a Soviet citizen, you lecture to students. So who could demand such a thing of you? I don't understand that at all."

Neiman read the statement and handed it to Gulyaev without comment.

"May I be permitted an interest?" The prosecutor intercepted his hand. He quickly glanced down the sheet and laughed.

"That's where the real do-it-yourself wits are," he said to Neiman. "To blazes with them all, Polina Yurevna, and all their doubts and questions! They're nothing but a pack of Philistines!"

"No, no, they're not the point," said Pototskaya. "It's just that when your man came to the chancellor's office and started making enquiries about me, all sorts of rumours began circulating round the institute. It's understandable, after all. When your organs take an interest in someone, things tend to get very complicated."

"When our organs take an interest in somebody, Polina Yurevna," Neiman explained, "they act in a very straightforward manner: they ask them to come for a talk at a certain time. And then it is best and simplest of all for that person to do so and to appear at the appointed hour. You, Polina Yurevna, are of course a very interesting woman, but if you will forgive me, the investigation is not concerned with that: in the given instance, we are not interested in you, but in your close acquaintance, Zybin. That is why we were so insistent in summoning you. We sent two summonses. Actually, you were right; during that first conversation, it became clear that you might perfectly well not have been bothered."

"Why was that?" Gulyaev said, surprised.

"Oh, Polina Yurevna did not want to assist us, not in any way," sighed Neiman.

"Come now, why take that attitude, Polina Yurevna," Gulyaev shook his head reproachfully. "One should assist an investigation in every way possible. Why on earth hide anything? The sooner we elicit the truth, the better it is for everybody."

"I said everything I could say," responded the visitor.

"If so, it follows that there is still a lot you cannot tell us, Polina Yurevna," Neiman smiled a grimly gentle smile.

"So what happened, was something explained or not?" Gulyaev frowned.

"Well, by all means, I can demonstrate. Everything's to hand." Neiman stood up, took a folder of documents from his drawer and began picking through them, still standing. "Here's the first meeting. Here's the second. Walks one, two and three. Conversations about painting. He is indifferent towards modern monumental sculpture, she isn't. Here they went bathing. Here they made up a threesome in a restaurant. Again the threesome – the other one is some holiday-maker – out on the town all night with a crowd of students. Lighting bonfires. Here they climbed a hill together to the old deserted cemetery. There's some incredible marble angel there – all this is in their own handwriting. Listen to this: 'The monument was beautiful in the moonlight. When we were going back, the stones kept dropping away from under our feet, and if it hadn't been for the watchman with a broken lantern . . .' A page about him. 'He lived in a burial vault.' and so on. We climbed down and went home. The end. There's fifteen pages here and they're all like that. In short, it could have been written by any chance acquaintance. And he certainly did have them . . . ! There were plenty of them . . ."

"But that's just what I am, a chance acquaintance," she said with a winning smile. "I'm also one of those there were plenty of!"

She was sitting perfectly at ease, resting on the chair-arms and talking as if she had just dropped into her dean's office for a minute and been sat down to fill in a questionnaire, rather than talking in office 350 on Dzerzhinsky Square. The prosecutor regarded her, not bothering to hide his smile. People like this were his meat. Gulyaev was simply bored as he drifted in and out of the conversation. And suddenly Neiman sensed the first stirrings of approaching fury. At such moments he would become vehement: objects began to leap obliquely before his eyes; his voice would take on a tremulous purring. He piqued himself on these moments of frenzied anger because they – at least! – were genuine, but for the moment, all that was beside the point. He suppressed it, choked back the fit and said: "Now, why so modest? You, a chance holiday acquaintance? Now you know yourself that's not true! Try to remember!"

"Well of course, not chance," the prosecutor endorsed this coaxingly, almost going as far as a surreptitious wink.

"Well, if you mean that Zybin helped me to extricate myself from a very unpleasant situation," she said, "of course you're probably right. But he'd have done the same for anybody else."

"And if it isn't a secret, what was the story of that?" asked the prosecutor, hastily qualifying the remark: "If there's nothing of an intimate nature . . ."

"Nothing of the sort," said Pototskaya, frowning slightly. "I was bathing, slipped and dislocated my ankle. It was very painful . . ."

"Ah, I see," nodded the prosecutor with respectful understanding.

"Yes. And it happened very early. Around six in the morning. The beach is absolutely deserted at that time – there was nobody to call out to. I lay there groaning probably, and then this young chap appeared. He came up to me. There were some odds and ends lying on my headsquare, watch, mother-of-pearl opera glasses, handbag. He grabbed them and set off running. I started shouting. And then, from out of nowhere, Zybin rushed to cut him off. He caught up with him and took the stuff from him. That's how we got to know each other."

"Well, I keep telling you it's a novel in instalments from the *Ogonyok* picture magazine," grinned Neiman, "nothing more to be said. You know how to tell a story, Polina Yurevna, you certainly do. What really happened was this. When this beach bum stole the bag, Polina Yurevna of course started shouting, and somewhere nearby, lolling about and waiting to sober up after a night on the booze was Zybin, the gallant knight. When he heard the shouting, he too barked out 'Put that back!' at the top of his voice. And he has a throat like a cast iron pipe. The bum took fright, threw the bag away and made off. Zybin picked it up and handed it back to Polina Yurevna with all due ceremony. That's how they got acquainted. I am speaking in his words and his language. It's a wonderful story of course but not altogether relevant to us. That's why I instructed Khripushin to set it out in as short a version as possible."

"No, but that really did happen?" asked Myachin, all admiration.

"More or less," Pototskaya nodded. "Leaving out a few details. But you also know how to tell a story, comrade major!"

"Rest assured on that score! In my small way!" returned Neiman with a hint of insolence.

"But there was a bit more to it?" the prosecutor evinced a diffident interest.

"Yes, there was," Pototskaya nodded.

"And it's just that 'there was' that concerns us most," said Neiman, "but it's precisely what you haven't revealed to us."

"Well now, perhaps there are certain delicate feminine intimacies involved," the prosecutor put on a jocular frown of concern. "They can't be revealed in front of you, oh no!"

"Feminine details are of no interest to us in any shape or form, comrade prosecutor," Neiman brusquely interrupted, sensing that the suffocating fit was taking a deeper hold. During interrogations he used to deal with it at once: a bellow, a stamp of the foot, then a thump on the desk and one across the zek's cheek, bang! And the oppressive bubble inside his throat and chest would burst and the interrogation could proceed normally without any further nonsense. "We are not interested at all in any sort of feminine details," he resumed in quiet fury. "We were simply asking Polina Yurevna to tell us about Zybin's political attitudes. All right; they met, went bathing, went for walks, so then, all done in silence was it? There were things said! Of course there were!"

She made no reply, merely giving him a peculiar look. That glance stirred him up again – he went over to the desk with the decanter on it, poured himself a brimming glass and downed it equally noiselessly. But the suffocating feeling, unique in its way – that at any moment, everything would break loose and fly to pieces – that any minute now he would start yelling, banging his fist, using foul language and the talk would be at an end – never quitted him. But at the same time, he realized perfectly well that absolutely nothing of the sort would in fact happen. Whether this feeling of instantaneous lashing fury was genuine, or whether he had invented and nurtured it – i.e. whether it was a feeling at all, or some sort of professional adaptation, essential to him in his work – Neiman had never considered, and consequently did not know one way or the other.

"And don't bother telling us that there were no such conversations," he said, putting down the glass. "In our time every farmer's wife, every grandad tucked up on the stove talks about politics. Will there be a war or not? What about the bread situation? Will the price come down?"

"That's a grandad on the stove, not Zybin."

He hated her in real earnest at that moment. For everything: that she was sitting too comfortably, that she had at once taken advantage of permission to smoke and did so in a way no one had probably ever done in this office before – elbow sharply bent, gently tapping the ash into the tortoise shell which the prosecutor had provided for her – for the glance she had flung at him, for her blatant and open incompatibility with this room.

"Yes, of course, Zybin talked differently from a grandad on the stove," assented Neiman, pronouncing the words slowly, "and therefore, let's say, whether there would be a war or not must have been of interest to him."

"That did interest him, of course," she agreed casually, and, as it seemed to him, with a sneer. "I actually recall one such conversation. Some pioneers passed us on the road, singing 'If war comes tomorrow, if we're off on campaign,' and he listened and said. 'Exactly! Here's you and I making plans but if war really does come, and it's off on campaign? Then what?'"

"And what then?" Neiman asked.

"Don't know. We started talking about something else. Look," she suddenly implored him, "don't you think we had other things to talk about? Haven't you walked with an attractive woman, at least in Gorky Park? And did you talk about war to her then?"

"No, I beg you, leave me out of this, but you said yourself," Neiman proceeded, somewhat put off by the prosecutor's quiet snorting, "you said yourself that questions like that interested him . . ."

"That's right," she agreed, already smiling at him as if at a little child, "they did! But I interested him still more. And he already had someone to talk to about the war."

"He had?"

"Yes, he had, he had! He had someone he talked to very readily about war, politics and all that . . ."

"And do you recall his name?"

"I certainly do. Roman Lvovich Shtern."

It has to be said that the blow was masterly. He was genuinely rocked. For a while he was put out of action altogether; he simply sat and stared at her.

"And who is that?" he asked at length.

"A holiday-maker," she answered very simply.

"So what did they talk about then?"

He took a long time to gather his wits, but managed it all the same.

"How could I possibly know? Ask him."

It was quiet in the office. Even the prosecutor had lapsed into silence.

"How can I ask him? You don't know his address do you?"

"Why not? By all means. The All-Union Prosecutor's office. Investigation department. He's the head."

"But . . ." Myachin made as if to move but Gulyaev's calm voice interrupted him.

"And what else is he, do you know? This beach acquaintance of

357

yours. Who is he? He's Zybin's conversation partner, he talked to him about politics, he's the head of a department of the prosecutor's office; what else is he?"

"A writer?" she asked hesitantly.

"Correct! A writer. A member of the Writers' Union of the USSR. And what else, do you know? Then I'll tell you: he's also the brother of Yakov Abramovich Neiman, in whose office we are now sitting and who is conducting the case of your acquaintance."

His tone was firm and cold; for a moment or two, Pototskaya blushed in confusion.

"All of which you knew perfectly well, Polina Yurevna. That's why you rang yesterday and today, because you knew. That was the only thing that interested you. Not some certificate or other. And if we had not been forewarned by Roman Lvovich himself, then we really might have been caught off guard at first and behaved in a manner unbefitting; but we all knew perfectly well. So you did not shake us, Polina Yurevna, no, not at all."

"I didn't intend to shake you," Potoskaya faltered.

She sat, pale and tense.

"Really?" Gulyaev was good-naturedly sceptical. "There's no need to try and shock us in any way whatever! No point! Besides we hate it when someone does it! We are the masters of that game! Where's your pass?" He signed it swiftly. "There! I would ask you though, if you intend travelling anywhere, do please let us know."

But at this point the prosecutor intervened. When Shtern's name had been mentioned, he had started, sat up and gone quite still – simply taking up a genuine hunting stance, then started sniffing, fidgeting and rummaging in his pockets for some reason; in a word, trying to show that he was fearfully taken aback and agog.

"Forgive me," he said almost ingratiatingly, looking at Pototskaya, "but tell me why you were so certain you were not being deceived? There are all sorts of fakers in rest-homes. You didn't look at his credentials did you? Right? So how on earth did you . . . ?"

"No, I did see them." Pototskaya nodded briefly.

"That's odd!" Myachin shrugged his shoulders (deliberately, of course deliberately – nothing could surprise him). "His work identification is a document that . . . You didn't get it mixed up with anything else, Polina Yurevna?"

"No, I didn't. He proposed to me."

"Wha-a-t?" the prosecutor almost squawked, and for a second was certainly at a loss for words. "Why, he's a married man! We know his wife! No, no!"

"Take your pass," said Gulyaev, "here! Good day!"

Pototskaya stretched out her hand, took the pass, stood up and went towards the door.

"One second," the prosecutor rushed over to her. "What did you reply to him, then? No, no, we must know that," he explained to Gulyaev and Neiman. "What did you say?" They both stood in the doorway.

"I thanked him and said I couldn't."

"Because at the time . . ." the prosecutor brought out in exultation.

"Yes, because at that time I was fond of another man and I was intending to tell him so that very day."

"And that man was . . ."

"Yes, that was Zybin."

Gulyaev got up, went over to the door and opened it.

"Please," he said graciously, but with insistence, "I'm very glad to have seen you. You have certainly made a great many things clear to us. I'll make you out a certificate this very day and send it. And you know, if you have to, you can travel wherever you like! Good day. I wish you all the very best, Polina Yurevna!"

CHAPTER 4

NEIMAN LIVED NEAR THE people's commissariat building and always returned home on foot. True, in the mornings he was still obliged to clamber onto the blue duty bus. This bus always rolled up promptly to the block at eight in the morning and stood there roaring, while virtually the entire population of the building gradually gathered inside. The building belonged to the people's commissariat; it had been built by the administration directorate of the NKVD (and was therefore one of the best in town). The first deputy occupied the upper storey. This time, however, Neiman did not take his usual route along the avenue, that astonishingly straight and direct road, traced out some eighty years before by the sweep of an impetuous general's arm. He wandered instead through the wide connecting yards with their adobe huts, through opulent crimson gardens, ablaze with twinkling aspens and berberis; across the square with its wearily drooping maples and sweet limes, then on further, past clay dams and wattle fences, lines of railings and the booths where the irrigation controllers sat. At this hour they turned from white, through light to dark blue, then from dark blue to black. It was about ten o'clock. The corner streetlamps came on and almost at once, red, green and blue curtains shone out in unison. People were sitting on benches by the gates, cracking sunflower seeds, laughing and peaceably gossiping, evening-fashion. Someone swift and unseen slid by and quietly greeted him; he slightly inclined his head by way of reply. Since the time he had deputized for one of the heads of the operations departments, such encounters were no rare thing for him. He reached the main irrigation ditch and halted. "So then," he said under his breath. "That's the way it is." He loved these quiet hours, this place and its stony, glacial coolness. Here, by the little concrete bridge, the town came to an end: the first out-of-town lamp lit up the last town bench. Down below, in their rounded cement channel, the meltwater came silently rushing down from the mountains. In these hushed evening hours, he would shrug from his shoulders, like a heavy departmental overcoat, all that long grey building with its Dzerzhinsky Square, all its sentries, its secret holes and corners, its offices, fireproof safes, prison cells, naked corridors and unsleeping lamps – and just be his simple, uncomplicated self. That's what he really was, in his limited desires and demands, in the very core of his drab, impoverished existence. Even the flashes of rage he was experiencing more and more often these days, even those made no essential difference. They were like rockets over a snow-bound camp in the taiga. He'd seen that once. They exploded, flew apart and scattered into dozens of stars and fiery feathers, releasing long, panicking shadows across the violet snow – everything racing, blazing, falling, then after a moment, nothing – just the noiseless flight of blackened cardboard tubes down from the sky into the snowdrifts.

"I'm as poor as nature," he had read once in some confiscated and therefore obviously criminal verses, and had burst out laughing. Blasted scribbler! Martyr and crank! Poor as nature! Where does everything come from then? The rubbish they write. Still, it probably wasn't rubbish at that, it was part of a kind of truth; or perhaps the point didn't lie in that truth, but in the fact that these lines had some special, much wider significance. Anyway, however it might be, he always repeated that line to himself at times of reflection. And now, when he had to go home and write to his brother about everything, as if to exhort himself, he repeated several times: "I'm simply poor. Poor and that's all about it" – because he felt no desire at all to go home.

In these peaceful, sombre hours he often used to calculate what would happen if he were suddenly to crack, get up from his desk during working hours, put his coat on and softly-softly, telling no one, leave and head straight as a die for the last town bench. There were buses actually standing there; he could get on any one of them: they all went up into the mountains. Across one bridge, then another; then the suburb ended and the mountains came close to the highway. The air got fresher, there was a smell of snow, pine resin and earth. Stations with strange caressing names would flash by: Verigin Mountain, Forest Arboretum, Kamensky Plateau, Birch Grove, Hotbank and finally – stop! The end of the line, Shaggy Hill, the Medeo Rest Home. Here there were always crowds of skiers, sports instructors, students and schoolchildren; it was always noisy, and mindlessly cheerful. When the bus drew up, they would make a rush for it, with noise and shouting; rattling their mess tins, they would all squeeze on at once. Meanwhile, he would jump off and walk across the bridge to the café. There he would see his long-time acquaintance, Marietta Ivanovna. She would catch sight of him and at once break into a smile. She was voluptuous, fair-skinned, rosy-cheeked, like that autumn dahlia that always stood in a crystal vase above her boxes, jars and bottles. And he would smile at her in his turn, because he has missed all this and is pleased to have made his way here. He knows everything there is to know about Marietta: that she lives with her five year-old daughter and she's been working in the cafeteria for more than two years; there's no husband – he's either fled or been arrested. And Marietta knows everything about him too: that he's a geologist, specializing in some abstruse area; that he worked at one time in his directorate and has now transferred to the security organs, with responsibility for mining; hence he is often sent on official trips. During one of these trips his wife left him, not a terribly beloved wife but still ... still ... The annoying thing was, he hadn't deserved anything like that. And so he's disoriented, aggrieved, at times positively depressed, and then he comes out here. He's a quiet, harmless fellow and if he's a Jew, so what? There are yids and there are Jews. In the Medeo he drinks only beer. He goes out onto the balcony, selects a table and sits there, quietly drinking, nibbling a roll and gazing at the mountains. They talk to one another through the cafeteria serving-hatch. She keeps inviting him home but he laughs this off. This time, however, he would have gone. He would have ordered, say, champagne rather than beer, a box of "Moscow" chocolates and gone with her. "Well then," he would have said, pouring a couple of glasses, "what can one do, Marietta Ivanovna? Considering the life we lead. It's my birthday today. Express your condolences and let us raise our glasses." And they would have drunk one for the stake, two for the falcon and three for the little bird.   Beyond that, his imagination did not carry him, because he knew perfectly well that even this was unrealizable. Just try getting away! The secretary would come in and see the papers on the desk and no raincoat. She would ring one telephone, then the other; from that end they'd start ringing too and all hell would be let loose. They'd summon the four probationers, sit them on motorcycles in pairs; one pair would fly round the town, the other into the mountains. They'd find him and whizz off to Gulyaev. And Gulyaev would say later: "Well, it doesn't matter! Now if it was me who'd buzzed off into the mountains ..." But neither Gulyaev nor Neiman would ever take off anywhere. Apart from anything else, he was the department party organizer, a tough experienced operator and a genuine expert at his job. Vyshinsky had said at some conference: "I always prefer a confession in the accused's own handwriting, however evasive and partial, to one written by the investigator, however complete." And so, every confession submitted by

Yakov Abramovich to the prosecutor and his superiors, was in the accused's own hand. And his brother always praised him for that. And he valued this fraternal praise above all else. Altogether he was fond of remembering and thinking about his brother: his words, his jokes, his stories, his casual good fortune, his cheerful invigorating cynicism; but for some time now a new element had begun to crop up – one that puzzled and worried him. They had had a certain conversation alone together, when his brother, as a rule reserved and guarded – which went excellently with his simplicity and ease of manner – had told him of a holiday encounter. He did not tell him the name nor the place where it had occurred, but today while he was questioning Pototskaya, that insincere and dishonest witness, Yakov Abramovich pictured to himself approximately how it had been. Deliberately playing on his own nerves, he recalled again how she had sat in the armchair and smoked, leaving her elbow well out, smiling, leading Myachin on – that mooncalf – keeping things to herself, dodging the question, and when she was tired of doing that, flinging them his brother's head just to get clear of them, so to speak. And then all too ready to answer the prosecutor's questions. And hell knows how far things would have gone if it hadn't been for Gulyaev's smart work. He had got them back on an even keel immediately.

Ah, brother, brother! Alas, my dear Roman Lvovich – extraordinary and plenipotentiary figure – however did you get yourself into this foul mess! Rumours are bound to circulate, jokes and witticisms, words whispered in ears in ever so strict confidence! Ah brother, brother! And of course it would have to happen in front of that lousy sod Myachin! Do you remember him once amusing the public? You had mentioned something out of your practice and he came up to you afterwards, took you by the elbow and started rolling his eyes and cooing like a dove: "Here you've been telling us this story and I sat and thought, why don't they write about these things! Where have our Soviet Chekhovs gone? As soon as I see my go-ahead friend Alexander Alexandrovich, I'll tell him straight out, no beating about the bush: 'Sasha! Put your venerable bunch on bread and water, let them stir their backsides and bethink themselves; at the moment they're writing heaven knows what. And he'll do it, I know him.' (Myachin had apparently been a school friend of Fadeev's and was a guest at his dacha every summer. "Did we knock it back! Wonderful man! So open and straightforward! I really love the man!") And you laughed as well, brother, didn't you? The coming man!

The great authority! A second Chekhov! That's what he served you up; as much as to say that Chekhov and you were the only people in Russian literature to write well about investigators, and in all honesty, I prefer yours! Chekhov wrote from hearsay, whereas you write from lived experience, that's why everything you write is so lifelike, so bold, so striking. And you listened and smiled, brother. Now have a good laugh at yourself! And you remember that turd, that smooth type in the yellow patterned pumps, bloody writer! "There is a great deal of naïveté and untapped native humour in our Romasha! I don't know how he has managed to retain his freshness, considering his grim, demanding job, but when he laughs, as Pushkin puts it, you can see his insides!" So why don't you show the bastards your insides! Consign that spindly-legged trash with his little papirosa to the knacker's yard, where he belongs! And put the wind up that prosecutor in the yellow pumps so he sticks his blasted tongue in as far as it'll go. Ah, you won't do it, though, will you – you can't, you've taken the bait!

Ah, brother, brother! Though actually you're not my brother, but . . . Yes, they were rather dubious brothers – third or even fourth cousins, although they did live in the same house. Only brother Roman lived on the belle étage, as the deferential term then was, whereas brother Yakov huddled in a semi-basement, and that surprised nobody: Roman's father was the owner of the biggest mill in the district, while Yakov's worked on the page make-up of the local paper, and had a mortal dread of his third cousin! "Oh, that's a Yiddisher kopf," he would say, with an almost superstitious dread, placing his finger, deformed by the press into a twisted root, against his temple, "that's a head for you!" When cousin Roman reached fourteen, he joined the boy scouts and had a bicycle bought for him. Thenceforth, he wore a khaki uniform, went on marches, sang various special songs, spent nights out with his patrol in a wigwam they constructed themselves and took pride in being able to light a fire with a single match. Soon he acquired a Kodak camera and a Monte-Cristo pistol. From the gymnasium he brought home novels like *Sanin, The Pit* and the *Notes of Wanda Sacher-Masoch* and showed them to his sisters on the quiet. He used to read these works and say that a modern man needed to know about all such things because they contained the nerve of the age. When he reached fifteen, it was discovered that he was a genius. He had written a drama in five acts, *The Tornado*. He typed it out, tied it up in pink ribbon and sent it off to Vera Kholodnaya (he carried the paper tube around town for a long time, with "Saint Petersburg, Honzhenkov Cinematograph Institution" on it). Among the writers, Angelo Kalyari, the columnist for *Native Land* read the manuscript and said that the author had talent but it was as yet too early to think of publication: he must study life more deeply in all its beauty and variety. All of this, however, proceeded up above and reached Yakov rather indirectly. In his semi-basement there were no adult novels or dreams about Vera Kholodnaya; a perpetual subterranean twilight reigned there and rather than Wanda Sacher-Masoch, he read Nick Carter and Nat Pinkerton, skimpy little penny booklets in garish covers, while the printers' devils constituted the company he kept. On the whole they weren't a bad set of lads, and when they took part in raiding the orchards or played at cossacks and bandits, you couldn't ask for better; it was a different matter if you played pitch and toss with them on tick however. When anybody lost to him, they got annoyed and started calling him "Abram" or even worse "Abkhram" with a repulsive guttural "r", though everyone knew perfectly well he was Yakov, "Yasha, Yasha, buckle-flasher", and it was his father who was Abram – the quiet secret drinker, "golden hands", the kindest and meekest person in the world, always immeasurably depressed over something, forever quietly excusing himself for the sense of guilt he felt. The print apprentices also teased him about his "orready, orready": "Where have you got to orready, eh?" And sang out as they fled (he had formidable fists): "Yiddikin, who let him in – crucify him on a pin." Let anybody try singing anything like that in his brother's presence, gymnast, boy scout, writer, smart heavy-featured young man, with a black Kodak across his shoulder and a yellow holster at his waist. Imagine them calling out that half-crazed holy man's "orready, orready" to Roman Lvovich Shtern; he was not called Roman for nothing, it was in honour of the Romanov family; he was the son of the respected trustee of the jail, whose name in bold print adorned the advertising section of the paper every other day – and the whole town read that paper. The father, Lev Yakovlevich, for his part, revered his son's adroitness, his talent and social graces; he didn't press him to anything, but dreamed of his becoming a metropolitan solicitor and moving to Petersburg. "There he can write as much as he sees fit," his father said airily and slipped his son a copy of Plevako's speeches. His son however, confided to his cronies: "I felt like spitting on his speeches! Fancy, a case involving the murder of the actress Vasnovskaya in Warsaw! Who cares? When I'm a writer, I shan't write about stuff like that!"

When the February revolution occurred, Roman was eighteen and Yakov fourteen. While Yakov was finishing school, Roman was president of the students' committee, involved in the pedagogical council and evidently engaged upon his first delicate commissions (at any rate his air suggested that). When, a few years later, Yakov yielded to entreaties and transferred from the history department to a certain special law school, Roman already occupied a special office in the prosecution service with a sign on the door saying KNOCK.

Yes, so they had never been real brothers and the distance between the basement level and the belle étage persisted. Nonetheless, they felt genuinely drawn to one another and talked about all kinds of things perfectly freely. But one conversation, the one Yakov was recalling now, had been extraordinarily, overwhelmingly significant. Yakov was coming back from the seaside and stopped off in Moscow. His brother had also just returned from the seaside and was living with his wife at their dacha. It was there one evening that this extraordinary conversation took place. Roman began a long way off the point. He started by praising Yakov for not having got married so far, because, said his brother, he had been married in actual fact three times, once officially, and, looking back, he was simply horrified that it had really been him. "You know," he said taking Yakov by the arm, "no vile profession, an executioner, say, or an informer, no government, even one as foul as Hitler's, could squeeze the soul out of a man drop by drop as a vile woman can. I know from experience, brother. You should see what goes on in this Sunny Hills of ours, our little dacha community! The normal family: mother (not obligatory!), husband, wife and child. The husband and wife are so fed up, they can't bear to look at one another. It's like two cell mates who've been together for a year. And you know, in the theatre, I've noticed that during the action, the husband will suddenly turn away from the stage and give his wife such a hateful look. Up there, so to speak, is music, beautiful women, freedom – and next to me I have you, you . . . And she realizes that, drops her eyes and also turns away. And all this without a word being spoken, not a word! They don't quarrel all that often, because there's nothing for them to quarrel about, but when it comes to humiliation, interrupting or making mock, oh yes! That's a real pleasure. It raises the spirits at once. He vents his temper on her and then goes round wreathed in smiles: 'Oho, bitch! Cat got your tongue? That's right, oh yes!' "

"What about the child?" asked Yakov.

Roman frowned.

"The child has seen through them long ago: cheap shits, cowards, no breeding, all mouth! When he grows up he'll leave and forget, if he's got anything in him; if he's the same sort of bastard what does it matter? It's even simpler then. Now you tell me. We say 'wife', 'nearest and dearest', 'the mother of my children', well, things of that sort. And it's all true, very true. Well, given all that, can a husband share a confidence with this nearest and dearest? Of course not! Never! And not because it's impossible, sometimes it's perfectly possible, it's simply – well, why? She would only be frightened to death. That vile fear gets stored up all her life; however dumb she is, she can see very well, that what was once a man is no more. Burnt out and left not a wrack behind. She goes round, tail like a peacock, boasting: 'Look what we've got! And this as well! And this and this, when she knows perfectly well she's got sod all! All that doesn't belong to her." (His brother did not express himself more forcefully it seemed, even during interrogations).

"And whose is it, then?" enquired Yakov, his shoulders fairly twitching.

The overwhelmingly intense nature of the conversation was affecting him almost physically; he felt a genuine chill.

"How do I know? Hell knows whose it is!" Roman swore expansively. "Uncle's! She knows it's uncle's and whines and sniffles and sobs. Her nose is red and swollen, her lips are loose and womanish. Who needs that? No, brother, when things are bad for you, that's the time to keep quiet! Damned quiet! Find some tumbledown shack or an old henhouse in a field, crawl in there, so nobody knows where you are. Cry in there or hang yourself, decide which in the light of circumstances. After all, your life isn't your own, it's the lord's, but sorrow, that's yours all right and nobody else's. You can't off-load that onto anybody else, because it's death to you and a laugh for everybody else! A giggle for all and sundry! 'Got what he deserved, the bastard?' 'He had it coming to him!' That's how it is, brother," – he stopped and gave Yakov a pitifully helpless glance.

Yakov's head was reeling. He didn't know how to take all this. Surely something hadn't happened to his brother and he was to be the first to know?

But then Roman looked at him and smiled.

"Wait a minute, let's sit down on this bench for a bit. No, I wasn't talking about myself yet, or at least not just about myself. I've no reason to go crawling into empty henhouses either for the moment. It's something else. I've started taking a look at life. How have I been beguiling myself all this while? That I've got it all to come, and this is, you know, temporary ... I've still time to show them what I'm made of. I'm a writer aren't I, dammit! A creative artist! I don't just have an investigation block full of condemned men, I've got my creativity as well. I'm not just 'Romka-Fomka, gentle death' as my walking dead call me here; I'm more than that. I go out from these drab walls, walk two blocks and I'm among friends, admirers, female admirers, actresses, each better than the one before. They're all gifted people, people with brains or beauty. But you know, I look at these writer-friends of mine, intellectual giants, and I think: Which of them would I like to be? None! I look at my beautiful women and I think, which of these bitches would I like to have as a wife? Not one! And there's a thought that's been going through my head for a while now. What if a nice young girl were to fall in love with me? One with bouncing curls? One I could be sure of and know wouldn't desert me. But chiefly, if anything happened, would remember me! Not recall me, remember me. Ah, what a mighty great thing it is, brother, if you're remembered. That's all that counts! One incident here really shook me. And it was just a trifling thing really. The organs had arrested a journalist, one of the very young ones – flared trousers. Nothing out of the way – I've seen umpteen like that: Freud, Joyce, Modigliani, Kabuki theatre and all the rest of it. And he knows he should hold his tongue, but the idiot goes blabbing. Well it was the usual thing, best friend gave him away, and the organs didn't stint themselves either and gave him a tenner; his dad was something he shouldn't be as well, so that didn't help. He was sent to Kolyma, TA – Trotskyist activity – know what that means? And so when his wife came to me, a blonde slip of a thing, curly hair, probably a cheery sort of girl, life and soul of the party – I looked at her and said – no, no, not in my official capacity, it wasn't my case, but you know, nice and friendly – 'Get married, my dear. We can help with the divorce.' You know what she answered: 'And what will you do with my second husband?' And walked out! Just walked out!"

He lapsed into silence.

"That's it?"

"That's all there was to it, brother. But a couple of days later, early in the morning I got a phone call . . ."

He again fell silent, and stayed that way so long that Yakov asked him: "Well what was it?"

"Nothing! They had found her early that morning at the forty-mile mark, somewhere near Valakherinskaya under the rail embankment. The body was smashed and lacerated, but the head had been thrown into the bushes. They brought me a photograph. The head was on a

368

sort of stand, clean, white, not a drop of blood, just standing there winking at me. Then it dawned on me. "That's the sort of girl I want! Her! With her laughter and her curls! But where on earth could I find someone like that? You don't find them in our dachas. So I got to thinking, brother, and wound up extremely depressed."

"But you said yourself you had your writing," Yakov reminded him diffidently, "and that you had company, friends, women. Surely they aren't . . ."

"Ah, the man of understanding," smiled Roman ruefully. "Yes, you've put your finger right on it, haven't you! I write! I write and you collect coins!" he shouted suddenly. "How many have you got piled up over there? You wanted to become a scholar, eh? So why didn't you then? Eh? What prevented you? Why aren't you a whatsit . . . a numismatist, eh? What stopped you?"

"Hold on, hold on a minute, where is all this leading?" Yakov was genuinely lost. "When I was studying history I collected coins, but later on . . ."

"But later on you saw them as pointless. Right? For a historian they had some point of course, but what good are they to an investigator? Am I right? Well, am I?" His questioning was so furiously insistent, that Yakov was reluctant to reply: "Well, let's suppose so, but what do you draw from . . ." "Aha, they were of no use, so you stopped collecting, and you did right! And I did the right thing in dropping my real writing! Now I describe cases from my practice, 'An Investigator's Notes', and everybody's in raptures. So human! So humane! So subtle! And the hard cash rolls in! 'An Investigator's Notes' indeed! That's tantamount to Baba-Yaga's memoirs. Everybody wants to know how our cast-iron pots are boiling. So it sells. And it gets published and re-issued! And reviewed in all the papers!"

"So is that bad?" asked Yakov.

"No, no, on the contrary, it's very good! Excellent! Everybody here's writing, taking their cue from me. We're the most literary people's commissariat in the Soviet Union. No – the world! We're all masters of the psychological sketch. We're psychologists, by hell we are! Our top brass write five-act dramas for the Moscow Art Theatre. The higher the level, the more psychological it gets!" He laughed. "What do you think? 'Weak, not fully worked out, here read this review, have a think about it and we'll talk later.' No, that's not for us! To hell with all that! That sort of talk cuts no ice. Who gives a damn about the review and why the hell should I read it? You sit down, edit the thing and finish it off – that's why you're an editor or a director, that's why the state pays you, oaf! My business is to provide the material and push it through where needful, that's all! And it's a full house at the theatre. A fight for tickets, all special passes cancelled. Sitting in the aisles. That's how it is. You mean you haven't seen it yourself, or what? Surely it's the same in Alma-Ata?"

"Oh yes, it's the same here, of course," Yakov laughed. "It's just I'm surprised why it should be. After all, these dramas, in all honesty . . ."

"There you are, in all honesty," Roman smiled sarcastically. "Is it literature you're after? Read Fadeev and Fedin then! No, you look at the other end – the lights have gone down, the curtain goes up, and there stands revealed the secret of secrets, the holy of holies, the office of the head of the NKVD investigation department. A colonel sits at the desk as they bring in a spy. The clock on the Spassky tower strikes midnight. The interrogation begins. 'When and by whom were you recruited for the Gestapo? Well?' That alone brings the spectators' hearts into their mouths. After all, not a single soul has ever seen or heard this, any soul now living, that is. Therefore this isn't literature, it's an act of government faith in Soviet man. Psychologists call it the effect of presence. This effect makes the spectators' teeth freeze. Watch them leave the theatre, softly, softly! And the bar does twice the trade in cognac than when *The Inspector General* is playing. Our psychologists have taken due note of the bar! So I can live without that effect. Because I'm a real writer. So there! When I used to run around our yard playing pitch and toss with you (Roman had never run round the yard, nor played pitch and toss with him) I felt this fire within myself.

"That was when you were sending *Tornado* in?" Yakov couldn't resist saying.

"Don't remind me. That was silly," frowned Roman. "So then, it was in this frame of mind that I went away on holiday. And I met a certain non-party lady. And, as our socially close friends the criminals say, I fell for her. Because I liked her so terribly much."

"And who is she?" asked Yakov.

"Absolutely nobody! Just a woman! Nice, good-looking, intelligent – you don't think that's much? That's a terrible great deal, brother! So I tossed and turned, longing for her. To tell the honest truth, I realize now that it was altogether like being hypnotized. 'Amok' – you've heard the word? It's when you go off your head. That's what happened to me, then, 'amok'. But when I got turned down, I recovered myself; I collapsed onto the bed and began to think soberly and rationally again: there it is, she'd said 'no' and if she'd said 'yes' what then? How could I have taken her to me, with me? With her acuteness, her coolness, her freedom, that clarity and feminine tartness of hers? As one of them said, her 'formic acid'. How could I have made all that my own? Her and me – it's patently absurd! Pure fantasy, and that's all about it. First of all, we'd develop a mortal hatred for one another, not the way I hate Faina – I hate her in a calm, indifferent sort of way, even lovingly at times. No, it would have been sickeningly intense, hysterical! Then she would have tried to wring my neck. Because reforming me would be a lost cause, I'm not that sort. So – disaster. And she would be destroyed, not me. You understand?"

"No," responded Yakov honestly, "absolutely not. I mean if you know all this and can see what's coming perfectly well, why on earth . . ."

"And do you always act on what you can see coming? My foot! Anyway, as I say – 'amok' it was." Roman frowned in exasperation. "Amok, that's all. Or else sunstroke as we would say. Bunin has a story called that. Or rather, the whole business was a product of my state of mind. God, how utterly miserable I was! I was sick to my soul! Then I met her and everything cleared: the world became a pleasant place, the people in it nice, and even I wasn't too bad."

"And how did you meet her, if it isn't a secret, of course?" enquired Yakov.

"Well how do people meet at seaside resorts? I was strolling along the beach and I met her. She was walking along with some foppish individual, you know one of these freelance artist types? I'd chanced to make his acquaintance some ten days before this; I mean we'd met by chance, but I recognized him at once, as soon as he spoke to me. I'd summoned him as a witness seven years before in connection with a certain scandalous affair. He's one of those people with mannerisms as well. That was how I recognized him; but he didn't remember me. He was drunk and called out to me first on the beach: 'Ah, my midnight friend, my importunate conversationalist! On your own? Come on then and I'll introduce you to an attractive woman!' Well, we spent the whole day loafing about; we went into some shack and drank some wine. I downed a whole pitcher on my own. And the wine! Oh, that wine. I'll die before I forget it. It still sets my teeth on edge when I think about it. You know I'm not a great wine man . . . and to come across stuff like that in the baking heat after three hours walking!"

"So it was after that you fell for her?" Yakov burst into a laugh. "Oh, brother, brother! That was no sort of amok. It was a fuddled noddle, heat and exhaustion. That's all. Not worth talking about!"

"Oh, but it is, brother, it is!" Roman rocked his head earnestly. "I didn't really want to drink at all. I only did it, you know, because she was looking at me. I somehow chanced to raise my eyes, looked and almost collapsed: the way she was sitting in front of me. And all of a sudden I felt, how can I explain it, a soaring sense of release! Release from all that was mine! From my coarseness, my weight, my mistrust-fulness and I don't know what all. She was so free, easy, straightforward, unfettered, as the actors say, that I almost let out a howl. It's true, it's true! And I suddenly remembered my Faina, how she walks about the room in her dressing gown, then stands yawning in front of the mirror, yawning and picking her teeth and then suddenly the telephone rings and it's some girlfriend on the line. She talks to her and laughs, a hint or two, now and again a half question, a half answer, sentences left unfinished, 'snort, snort! Wha-at? Really? Ah-a!' One sound and every-thing's understood. She puts the receiver down, then starts her manipu-lations, feeling out what sort of a mood I'm in; that is, what she is or isn't allowed to do today. So I pictured all that to myself and felt such nausea in my heart, I positively groaned. No, no, I thought. It's all over! Take your little playthings and go to hell. I can't take any more. So I sit there, mooing away and she reaches out and touches my hand across the table, saying: 'You've just remembered something unpleasant, about home, probably?' Now how could she have realized that, how? Eh?"

"Ah, brother, brother," Yakov said again, lightly tousling his hair. "Ah my famous little brother! Now, now. Is your life so terrible, then? Are you so short of freedom? If your home life's so unbearable, well then, why not have a bit on the side? Get her a flat. Short of cash? I'll chip in if you're so poverty-stricken! You'll see, you'll be laughing! Fate's like that! If you annoy fate, it'll be the worse for you! I've been a firm believer in that for some time."

His brother said nothing, merely taking his hand and pressing it wordlessly.

"I'm perfectly well aware it's all silly," he said gloomily. "Yes, yes! Evidently I haven't very often felt well in my life. That's true enough." He lapsed into silence and stayed quiet so long that Yakov enquired: "Well what happened after that?"

"This happened after that. I got home at two in the morning and didn't see her for a long time, around ten days. She'd gone off some-where. As soon as she got back, she rang: 'You know, I positively missed you.' So again the three of us wandered along the shore. Then we swam in the sea, you know what that's like in the evening? It's caressing, so warm and milky, oars or arms leave blue swirls behind them. You've never once been to the sea, have you, but you're mistaken. Those mountains of yours are no substitute. You breathe differently, think differently, feel quite differently."

"That's precisely why you . . ."

"Yes, yes, maybe because of that! Partly due to the sea, maybe. But however many times I've been by the sea, I've never experienced anything like that. I don't know, brother, I don't know or understand any of this. So we went bathing and looked at the moon through naval binoculars, and towards morning we joined a bunch of students and things got lively! We climbed up the mountain with them, gathering brushwood; I lit the bonfire and got a round of applause. Then vodka and wine was brought in from somewhere. There were just two glasses, so the women drank out of them and we drank by turns out of a tin. Terrific!" He twisted his head a little and laughed. "They struck up some incredible rude ditty and I sang along. And then this happened. It had got cool and this fop took off his jacket and draped it round her shoulders; she took him by the arm. At this, one of the girl students asks me: 'Is that his wife? Isn't she beautiful!' And then something seemed to nudge me. 'No,' I answered, 'it's my wife; and she is beautiful.' And I said it so coolly, even harshly, as if it were really so and don't ask silly questions. And it came upon me immediately: 'Well, that's right! Wife! You've met her, don't let her go! Your happiness has found you, idiot! She'll go along with it. She likes you, and that's all she cares about.' No, but you see how awful it was? So what was I searching for, mooncalf that I was? And what had I found in her? If she didn't care? Absurd isn't it? Just as you rightly said, drunken ramblings, after taking too much on board. In a state like that people are capable of anything."

"Wait a minute," frowned Yakov. "What do they do then? Kill somebody? Shoot themselves? Sign the marriage register under the influence? What? What? Finish what you were saying. I really want to understand."

"No, no," Roman wrinkled his nose, "you're way off the point again. How can I explain it so that you understand." He considered.

"Start by explaining it to yourself, and I'll pick it up somehow," Yakov smiled at him.

"Yes, true enough," Roman smoothed his hair down and sighed. "That's the trouble, of course; even I can't really . . . I'll probably have to resort to analogy as my chief says." He deliberated. "Well, when I got back from there, I was given the case of some Feodosians, that's a Caucasian sect. What had happened there was this. These reverend gentlemen one Saturday dressed up in white knee-length shirts, sleeves this long and this wide, went out into a farm field, started singing some weird thing of theirs, lay face down, spread out their sleeves and every last one of them had a lighted candle in their fist. They lie there, singing and waiting. Any minute, angels would fly down to them and raise them up to the kingdom of heaven. Well naturally, people ran to see this, to stand and watch: there they lay, singing their dirge, candles burning, peasant women wailing. The people fell to their knees; one had a seizure. Creepy of course! Living corpses, weren't they? It lasted about three hours before it occurred to anybody to telephone. Well, things moved quickly after that. In ten minutes, the angels and archangels in red caps had flown in on motor cycles; they picked them up, threw them into five-tonners and drove full pelt into town. The rank and file were remanded and the ringleaders went off to Moscow. I came back to find their case on my desk. The investigator had dealt with them all in a week, because it was an open and shut business; nobody denied anything. It was sent in to the chief. Well, the chief looked through the file and ordered it to be sent to me for my verdict, for me to determine the degree of criminality and interpret their lying down in white shirts according to the appropriate criminal code article. After all, I'd been regarded as the specialist on all kinds of spiritual matters from as early as 1928. Remember those Schultz brothers who were shot? One was an engineer, one taught foreign languages. Well, ever since then, all the little Jesus freaks come to me. I had a look; the case was clear enough: a straightforward 58.10, part two, 'anti-Soviet agitation, exploiting religious prejudices, leading to popular unrest' – a tenner or the death penalty. But do you know what struck me most of all? In their cells, they believed that a miracle had taken place! The very thing which had not occurred, you understand? Angels – had flown down to them!"

"No," Yakov replied, "I don't understand that. What was it, a hallucination? Mass hypnosis?"

"What in blazes are you talking about, hypnosis? You should have talked with one of them: 'So you didn't fly, did you? You lay there and stayed that way till you were picked up. Well, is that so or not?' 'Just so! That's certainly true: they picked us up and we got our faces dusted for us.' 'So what about these angels, then, eh?' Silence. 'So then, there were no angels at all?' 'Just so, no angels'. 'No angels?' 'For you, no'.

'But for you?' 'What am I? I'm just an ignorant peasant lout, a fool; for me there is a God, there are angels and there are powers, for me everything exists.' That's the sum total of your conversation. Bear in mind these aren't religious cranks, one's a blacksmith, there's a tractor driver, a farrier, a lorry driver! On one occasion they got me so worked up I couldn't help telling their leader: 'When you get a bullet, then you'll see your angels!' He said to me: 'Just so, citizen chief, I will see angels and heavenly life – that's all true, citizen chief, all as it is written: without suffering, there is no salvation. We have long understood that, however much they tried to keep that from us."

"Were they shot?" asked Yakov.

"Oh, they were probably shot in the camp for sabotage; they wouldn't work, they just sing. We didn't soil our hands on them, just slipped them a tenner and sent them off; out there of course . . . Let's go, let's walk, it's getting a bit chilly."

And as they walked about the garden, golden light came cascading out from the third floor windows, as two women sang to a rumbling piano.

"Hear that?" Roman grinned. " 'Nightingale, nightingale, little birdie, the canary sings her song of woe.' My canary sings away, withering us with her disdain."

For a second, the piano fell silent, then suddenly broke into a neighing screech and splintered into a hundred angular shards. The women shrieked too, and something light, bobbing and winking began to leap and dance. The piano too began to bounce from leg to leg.

"French chansonette; that's the girlfriend she's found," commented Roman, wholly serious, "the daughter of an opponent of mine, one of the very top lawyers. Husband number three is chasing her out, the bitch, so that's her practising to hook number four. It drives you mad the way that woman of mine loves such people!" He sighed and took Yakov's arm. "As I picture it, Faina's been bending her dad's ear about me and that's where they got to know each other. I don't know what he could have advised her. The day before that encounter I was telling you about, she was intending to write to the Central Committee about me. Moral depravity of course, they can't get me for anything beyond. And not just the CC either, to the Boss as well, listen how she pronounces it! With a capital letter and this gurgle in her throat: 'Boo-oss! I shan't write to your friends, I'll write to the Boo-oss. He's a family man, a perfect husband! He'll understand me straightaway.' And she looks at me like a fakir at a cobra: on the alert for me to crack all of a sudden and blurt out something about that faithful husband, and how his wife . . ."

"Why on earth would she want to do that?" Yakov marvelled.

"Because! Her woman's reasoning tells her that then I would be where she wants me, right in her bloody pocket straightaway. I keep telling you, she's brainless!" he got up from the bench. "Let's go and have supper. Otherwise we won't get a chance at the cognac. Faina doesn't drink a lot, but that lawyer's daughter swills like a horse!"

He was already dropping off when Roman came to him.

"Tsk, tsk," he wagged an admonitory finger. "Quiet!" He was carrying a tray, bearing a bottle of cognac and two glasses. From my secret reserves, but quietly does it. She's in the next room! I'm supposed to be working in my study and sleeping on the sofa in there. Now then, to the future. Sweet dreams!"

"Isn't this a drop too much? And nothing to eat with it!"

"What are you, some lawyer's daughter? Fancy truffles do you? What do you want to be eating? Hold on, though, wait a minute, I believe I've . . . aha, got it!" He dug out a handful of sweets from his pocket. "I give them to the zeks during tea breaks. Look what sort they are, 'Bruins in the North'. Go on take one. So, all the best!" They softly clinked glasses and Yakov bit into the sweet.

"You live in style," he said.

"Well, what did you imagine? Moscow!" Roman smiled. "In France it's even better, they give them a drink of rum before the guillotine, we haven't got that far yet."

"Perhaps Zinoviev and Kamenev . . ."

"Don't know, wasn't present," Roman frowned slightly. "I turned that down flat. The nerves wouldn't take it. Anyway of course not! Rum indeed! Listen, what if we bowled down to the Sandunovsky baths with this stuff? The special room section, I've got a marvellous Georgian there; the way he massages you, you either get a heart attack or feel ten years younger. Shall we?"

"Let's see after we finish this."

"Well that's fine. And now I'm going to set you a puzzle. It's this, have I got a good life? Plenty of scope? All this," he described a circle in the air, "this isn't government issue, it's acquired, so to speak. So where's the income from? I don't work for the American secret service, I don't take bribes, I live on my salary, plus bonuses and travelling expenses. I don't get under-the-counter payments. All that wouldn't pay for one room and I've got eight! And my own car! So where does it come from then?"

"Present from the government?" hazarded Yakov.

"Who do you think I am, Papanin – or some academician?" Roman burst out laughing. "No, brother, we don't get given things like that. Well, I'll tell you. All this is the price of one special article in *Izvestiya*, four hundred lines."

"They surely don't pay that much?" Yakov was stunned.

"Yes, one article, that's all. It was only later I turned that article into a story, then the story into a libretto, that into a scenario, a play, a radio programme – I piled it all into a heap, stuck it all together and what do I see? A dacha! Only a dacha at the moment, but it still keeps trickling in. Of course I have to share it round, but while I'm still second man in the prosecutor's office, I can . . . put up with that – they take it, but politely you know, embarrassed. I'll get skinned later on."

"While you're still . . . !" Yakov exclaimed.

"Quiet, now," Roman frowned. "So then, let's repeat the dose." He poured another glass each. "Have another couple of truffles. Sometime I'm going to take her little lawyer's mouth and . . . She actually sticks her lips out. The bitch has a sweet tooth all right . . ." He choked back an oath. "Yes, brother, I'm thinking about it, so I am. In the first place I'd earn ten times more than I do at work, and secondly the motor's running down. The old nerves have been playing up. I keep remembering *Hamlet* you know. Mikhail Chekhov used to do that bit well at the Moscow Art Theatre: "I could be bounded in a nutshell, and count myself a king of infinite space, were it not that I have bad dreams." Actually, not long back I had a dream that had me jumping up in a cold sweat. Only dreams scare you as much as that. I jump up and what do I see: wife lying alongside, snoring away, has she got polyps or something? Tremendous snoozing, like a big samovar before a disaster – remember our samovar humming in 1917? I remember. My nanny kept walking about terrified: trouble coming, trouble in store. That's the way the wife was humming away. I put the light on: she's lying there on her side, with her nightie ridden up, and her flank was rearing up, damp, like a horse's, glossy like a pony. Oh god! I felt a great wave of depression come over me. So deathly I started moaning into my pillow."

"Have you had a word with the doctor?" asked Yakov cautiously.

"Not yet, I'm in no hurry. When I've spoken to people and got everything sorted out, I'll go and see what he says. Now then, let's have

377

a nightcap and off to bye-byes; you can hear something buzzing on the other side of the wall."

"Are you going to tell me your dream?"

"Some other time, I can't now, otherwise I might dream it again for all I know."

However, he did recount his dream about twenty minutes later. By that time, the bottle had been emptied, while Roman himself was riding the chair, clinging to the back as he swayed. Meanwhile Yakov was regarding him and thinking: "It's terrible, absolutely terrible! That's what our job amounts to. Early retirement and a pension. My brother's obviously all played out." But there was nothing out of the ordinary about the dream. A normal sort of dream for an overtired investigation man – there were no surprises. His brother had dreamed of his Black Sea charmer. It seemed she'd been arrested and he was questioning her. Well, what of that? That does happen sometimes and nobody gets driven up the wall by it. Again, it's all part of the job. She was standing before Roman, staring fixedly at him and saying nothing. And he was perfectly well aware that she was concealing a dreadful secret of some kind, and as soon as that secret was revealed – and it only needed her to open her mouth for it to be all up with him then and there. And so he sat at his desk, looking at her and not knowing what to say or do to prevent her speaking. And she stood there, hands behind back, buttons cut off, staring silently at him.

"You even noticed the missing buttons, you mean?" asked Yakov.

"Those clearest of all," Roman replied. "I also noted the black threads hanging down. And I was terrified, absolutely terrified! As if the door were about to open and they'd come in and grab me. And it made me feel so feeble, so faint. As if any moment – aaah! – and I would fall to the floor. And the thing was I couldn't say a word, I'd lost my voice; and I couldn't look at her either, that's how it was."

"And had anything like that happened to you?" asked Yakov. "I mean when you had to question someone you knew?"

"Yes," Roman scowled. "Even worse than that."

"And?"

"Oh, nothing much. When I'm behind the desk in my office, my head is perfectly clear; I am the power, the state, the Law! And how do you think my chief got on with Nikolay Ivanovich, his benefactor, so to speak, his wedding sponsor, "the mind of the age", not long ago in the same office? And the other being brought in without shoelaces or buttons. I'll tell you about that sometime."

"And was it all right?" asked Yakov.

"It most certainly was! On the very highest level too! Aa-h! You mean how can I write about trust between people – that vigilance and suspicion have nothing in common and all that? That's what you mean, is it? Well that's the way I write. With an easy mind. Stories and tragedies about it. I actually intend to send in a psychological play on that very subject. After Strindberg; it'll go round all the theatres. Official drama. See it and cry your eyes out!"

"What's it about then?"

"About the spiritual regeneration of a saboteur under the influence of the humane methods of the Soviet investigator. A monodrama. No, that's not it. There are only two people in it. Official drama. That's it. And there's no contradiction involved. On stage, it's the ideal, here it's reality. There is how it should be; here is what exists. There you have the artistic imagination, here this harsh Soviet reality of ours. Well, does that form satisfy you?"

"Absolutely," smiled Yakov. "Did you think of it yourself?"

"Of course not, where would I get it? A prisoner thought it up for me. Well, what are you looking at me like that for? It's true, it's true! The prisoners write all my dramas: they sit there on their own and . . . scribble away. And in exchange I regale them with Bruin sweets. And if they get a tear out of me and I'm really pleased with their efforts, I fetch them cognac. Not rum, no, we don't make that, but three-star or Starka. You still don't believe me? You should. I've got an American resident with me now; I'm thinking of sitting him down to a three-volume epic – based on capitalist espionage. Don't believe that either? Ah, my doubting Thomas!"

But at this point, Faina came in, wearing a Japanese gown with sky-blue flowers and cranes; behind her could be glimpsed the smiling goat face of the lawyer's daughter. Faina laughed, was horrified, waved her fluttering scented sleeves at them and driving her husband aloft, put out the light. All became dark and peaceful.

He lay for a long time in that warm darkness and silence, remembering and reflecting. Roman was in a pretty complicated situation: their maternal grandmother, as they used to say in those days, had lost her wits aged thirty-five and had spent as many years again in a private home for the deranged. As for his own father, Abram Noevich, they used to say he was, of course a fine, honest, compassionate man, a master of his craft, a hard slogger, who could work the clock round when necessary, without emerging from the typesetting room, but was just not up to his brother: a bit touched, dropped on his head when a baby, a hard drinker and fond of arguing when drunk; his wife had died early, leaving a son; this son was no consolation either, running wild round the back yards all day, chasing pigeons and playing for money with the apprentices, nobody to see to him. Would he ever amount to anything? Oh dear, that was doubtful!

I did, father, I did. If you could only see, Abram Noevich, the uniform I wear, the tabs, trimmings and badges, the office I sit in, the work I do! No doubt you'd be upset, wave your arms about and weep: "Oh dear, Yasha, why do you have to do it? It can't be true!" It can, old man, it can! Now I am not guilty in the sight of other people, they are in mine. Irretrievably guilty, for life, without mercy or redemption. Their time has gone, ours has dawned. Whether for better or worse, I don't know myself. Never mind, there's no hurry; we'll wait and see. It will all be clear soon. Everything! It's very close to the end now. I feel it, Dad, I feel it!

Zybin awoke suddenly in the middle of the night, as if he had been jogged, and saw that the bed opposite was occupied. On it lay someone lanky, lean and old. Yellow-brown skin, sunken dark temples, a sharp-pointed bristly chin.

"Damn," said Zybin, aghast. "They haven't dumped another one from the penal colony in here, have they?"

He raised himself cautiously to avoid jangling anything, and sat up. Yes, this was most likely another one from the camp – an Uzbek or a Tadjik. Could be from the Caucasus though. He'd seen an entire column of them once. They were being led to prison down the middle of the road. The guard waddled alongside, getting up onto the pavement, gazing about him and smiling at the oncoming people. The prisoners felt fairly unconstrained too, chatting among themselves, laughing, smoking and gesticulating. Prisoners being transferred didn't normally behave like that. There were many passers-by and they paused to watch.

"What is it?" Zybin had asked a mustachioed old boy next to him.
He gestured.

"Oh, deserters," he answered, with some unpleasantly mysterious implication. "From Sinkiang. See, they're taking them off to jail! Loads and loads of them."

"What'll happen to them?" enquired Zybin.

"We know that – two years," smiled the old boy scornfully. "Once they've chased them from Dzerzhinsky to the jail, it's definitely two years."

"They might give them the chop," said a scowling young lad nearby.

"No-o," the old boy shook his head. "Those that stay behind get that; if they've taken them out, it's two years."

So then, it seemed that it was one of these deserters who was presently lying before Zybin. He wasn't young, very far from it, but wiry and still tough. He was very tall, the feet in their woolly socks were pressing into the wall. A set of overalls lay squared up on the table, and a thick grey railwayman's jacket hung on the hooks. Under the table, stood a tourist bag with carrying straps, tightly packed and laced – tourist, not army issue! Shoes beside it. All according to some uncomplicated, but strict camp ideal. He too, evidently, was an ideal camp resident. Just like Buddo. So then, had they also brought him here for re-investigation? Perhaps, but he wasn't like Buddo. He did resemble someone of that sort though, but who? Who could it be? He carefully got to his feet and came round the other side. The newcomer was deep in a gentle, even slumber. A proprietorial sleep which proclaimed that he was well used to all this: prison, camp, transit – it was his element. Ah well, let him sleep on. They would see in the morning.

When morning came, he got a proper look at him. Yes, he was an old man, tall, very lean – collarbones sharply prominent – with rough, shaggy black eyebrows. The eyes beneath these bandit's brows, however, were quiet and somehow watchful.

"Allow me to introduce myself," announced the old man with a touch of courtliness, and got up from his bunk. "Georgi Matveevich Kalandarashvili. I got eight years from the Special Board. I was delivered here yesterday by plane. For a new investigation, I suppose."

"Not bad," thought Zybin, amused. "New investigation for this one as well, eh! Brilliant, I must say!"

He gave his name, and without anything in the way of detail, asked whether the other had any knowledge of a certain Alexander Ivanovich Buddo; he had also been sent here from the camp for a new investigation and had been in the same cell.

"Buddo was that?" The old man knit his brows. "No, there was no such in our camp. Are you sure he was from Karlag? Ah, the town penal colony! Well, that's quite a different manner. What was his charge?"

Zybin said: 58.8 to 17. The old man smiled indulgently.

"Windbag! Sympathized with the wrong man. No, I couldn't possibly have encountered him. People like me aren't kept in town colonies. I've got SE! Karaganda, Balkhash, Sukho-Bezvodnoye – they're our home territories. How long have you had the honour of bloating here?"

"What was that you said? Bloating?" Zybin was astonished.

"Bloating, bloating," smiled the old man. "Surely you've heard the word? How was it your cell mate didn't enlighten you? Thing is, for us camp inmates, there are only three states: we can graft (or "stick our horns in", which means the same) i.e. work, or loll it, i.e. not work, or bloat, i.e. wait for a fair wind. So at the moment you and I are bloating. Good! And now, do you happen to know which end they start the toilet break from? This end? Well, that means at least a half hour to wait; the corridors are long here. In which case, excuse me."

He went over to the slop bucket in the corner.

"And you know your way around," was Zybin's hostile thought. Then he asked: "And what's SE?"

"Oho, that's a serious matter," replied Kalandarashvili. "No fun in letters like that – it's suspected espionage. I got it because I lived in Georgia uninterruptedly till 1930, so being present at the founding and fall of the so-called sweetcorn republic. Well naturally I knew one or two of the Georgians who eventually emigrated. And they, according to the papers, are all spies. So it's all quite logical; but why I'm here now has nothing to do with the sweetcorn republic or SE; it's something I acquired, or earned in the camp."

"All just like Buddo," Zybin made a mental note. "Good god! All right, all right, I won't go rushing on ahead, I'll let him make the running." He said unexpectedly: "Well, they'll renew your existing term, that's all."

"Term!" The old man shook his head. "Ah, I'd grab the old term with my eyes closed. But they wouldn't have bothered fetching me here on a plane just for that. They'd give it to me on the spot and have done. No it's a different matter now, a lot more serious."

"What is it?" Zybin couldn't help himself.

Kalandarashvili threw him an amused glance.

"It's like this," he said, stretching a bony finger to the bridge of his nose. "Like this," he repeated, lightly tapping his temple.

"Heavens, what on earth's that?" Zybin cried involuntarily. "Excuse me for asking of course . . ."

"It's all right, it's all right, ask away. No, no, I didn't do anything special. I didn't kill anybody, cut anybody's throat or rob them. Just one fine day I wrote a personal, purely business letter to Moscow and sent it off. It asked the recipient to repay a loan from before the revolution. That's all there was to it. And it said nothing out of the way, nothing emotional, no reproaches – nothing!"

"And what – they stopped the letter? And you think that it's because of that . . ." Zybin's voice held a derisive tremor.

"No, no, if they've pulled me in, it means the letter got where it was sent." The old man was oblivious to his tone. "Well of course I had acted dreadfully, asking as they say for an iron wafer from a stone priest; and this priest really is made of stone, no sentiment in him. He regarded the letter from the state point of view."

"What's going to happen now, then?"

"Something bad. The chief hinted it would be pretty bad when they were taking me out of the camp. Of course, he got a hefty rocket himself. The most likely upshot is that I'll get nine kopecks in kind out of the whole sum. And that's all!"

"What's that supposed to mean?" asked Zybin (A game? Provocation? Just talking rubbish?)

"It's easy to see you've never been in a camp," laughed Kalandarash-vili. "They say that's what one defence lawyer said in a speech. 'My client, citizen judges, isn't even worth the nine kopecks our country is going to waste on him.' Investigators are very fond of that story. Although it can hardly just be a story. Lawyers are clever nowadays. They've learned how to talk to judges in language they can understand. So!" He abruptly became totally serious. "Now if you'll excuse me, I'll attend to my belongings." He hoisted the bag and placed it on the table. "You see, they hauled me out so fast last night," he went on, undoing the fastenings, "they didn't even search me. They brought this little ruck-sack out to the car straight from the store. So that I couldn't even leave my friends anything. And it so happens I got a parcel recently. And there's a bit left from the previous one." He bent over the bag. "You smoke, Georgi Nikolaevich? Oh, a pity, what a pity. In jail or the camp, it's a great support, especially when you're nervous. Is it all right, can you put up with smokers?"

"Yes, for goodness sake," Zybin was flustered. "I actually prefer a smoky atmosphere."

"I'm much obliged! But don't worry, I don't smoke much these days, the toilet breaks morning and evening are quite enough for me." He took a number of boxes from the rucksack and placed them on the table. "Just look at the papirosi they've sent me! Flowers of Herzegovina.

383

They never sent me them before, so it might be a hint! You know who smokes them? No? Look!" He quickly indicated moustaches with two fingers.

"You mean you . . ." Exclaimed Zybin, leaping to his feet.

"Sh-sh, sit down; later on, if they don't haul me out. For now we'll drink some tea." He bent once more over the bag. "Yes, today we have something to wash down. Amazing, they haven't taken anything, not even looked! Ah, I fear these kindly Danaeans! You never get gifts without strings from them. So, tea! Real, high-quality tea in packets with flowers on them. We'll brew up shortly. The mug's here, they haven't even taken that: miracles will never cease. Bruins, a whole packet. Try one, please, go on, do. And here's some of our Caucasian cheese. That's nice with young wine in the open air. Really nice that is. But not everybody realizes that or likes it, so here it is – a lump of Roquefort. It needs to be finished off quickly, see it's going hard. Sugar. Butter. Caviare. Look how clever my people at home are; they've packed everything in pink plastic toilet boxes. They don't take them off you. Well then, let's tuck in! And sceptics say that life isn't beautiful! No, that's just what it is; existence now, that's often unbearable – that's true. But that's another thing."

The key rattled, the door opened slightly and a large copper kettle entered through the crack, swaying halfway across the threshold; a plump white woman held out two neatly cut crusts with four sugar lumps. The day had begun.

They drank tea in silent concentration, that is, he drank it in that fashion, while Kalandarashvili sat breaking up his small pieces of bread and neatly spreading them with butter. For this purpose, he had a whittled and polished splinter, something like a wooden knife. Once he caught Zybin's gaze upon him and smiled.

"Go on and eat, please do, Georgi Nikolaevich. Don't pay any attention to me. I never eat much in the morning and this lot has to be finished off soon, in this heat."

And Zybin ate and ate, before pushing the mug from him with a certain effort and settling back against the wall.

"Oof!" he said. "Thanks. I'd forgotten all this existed. And now . . ." He lay down, stretched out, closed his eyes and seemed to fall down a well. It was like a fainting fit. When he raised his head again, the table was empty and Kalandarashvili was sitting reading a substantial book in a white cover, rather like a pocket prayer book.

"Terrific!" said Zybin, amazed, "I fell asleep. That's never happened to me before."

"Well, congratulations," said Kalandarashvili warmly, putting down his book. "What does surprise me is – do they let you sleep when you feel like it? Has your investigation finished, then?"

"No, I don't think so," Zybin shook his head. "Although hell knows, maybe they have finished. I haven't been called out for about three weeks. The thing is, I was on hunger strike and called it off only a week ago."

"Ah, so that's it," Kalandarashvili nodded. "And did this Buddo stay with you until the hunger strike or during it? They're crafty, you know; the first three days they leave you in the same cell and it doesn't get counted in."

"No, no, we used to meet during the interrogations, pretty active interrogations too."

"I see," Kalandarashvili considered for a moment. "And did he ask you about anything? Why you'd been arrested, what the charge was, who the investigator was and how the investigation was going?"

"Actually he didn't. Anyway, what could I have told him? Not about the investigation, about my own case. I don't know anything about that. Absolutely nothing. What I'm guilty of either."

"Mm-mm," the old man nodded. "That's what happens when there's been a denunciation and they don't want to give away who it was. Listen to me in that case and I'll give you some really useful advice: keep the three prison rules firmly in mind – don't be afraid of anything, don't believe anything, don't ask for anything! If you follow them, it'll all come right in the end."

"You mean they'll let me go?" Zybin smiled ironically.

"Now? No, hardly. Later on of course, they will. Then there's another thing – people do live in the camps you know, and they come out of the camps as people. And they don't live or come out too badly at that. They have real friends, they read good books, study things, but you have to start preparing yourself for that now – get yourself together, harden yourself to it, picture it all, go through everything in your mind, be ready for anything, but above all, remember the three rules – that of course is the hardest thing of all."

"Not hard to remember them, is it?" Zybin grinned.

"It's hard keeping to them, ah, that's the hard bit, Georgi Nikolaevich! They've got all the cards, you've got sweet nothing, just 'no!'. And no is just that, no – an empty space. However long you hold out, they'll trip you up on something or other; all you have to do is see that it's not the main thing, that they don't turn black into white. Hmm," he grinned over something, "as regards black and white, I remember something rather good. Once I was being questioned by a colleague of mine. We graduated together, even in the group photograph, our roundels were next to each other, I under 'K' and him under 'M'. We met up once or twice later on too. Whenever he was on business in the Caucasus, he would drop in to consult me. I helped him to come out on top; besides which he used to write a bit. People didn't fall over themselves to publish him, that's true, mostly it was unpaid miscellanies, but it was the fact that was important – he was a writer! That meant a great deal at the time. Well, after October, he went straight into the security organs and became a big shot! Certainly was. Higher education, experience, a sharp operator, well read, good talker. They've got nobody at all like him today. You've seen the people questioning you? Peasants! So, when I was arrested the second time in Moscow, he summoned me himself. The jail was overcrowded and I had a bad cough, so they stuck me in solitary confinement – a stone lumber room with no windows: the light was on all the time. When I was taken to him, his chandelier was on too. There were heavy blinds at the windows. We met amicably: he sat me down and offered me tea and biscuits. We smoked. We recalled various people we knew. Of course, some no longer with us, and others a long way off. Then we began to argue. Not about my case, because in reality there was no case, it was just a matter of my affiliations. So we argued on a higher level, about historiosophy rather than politics."

"There really was such a time?" marvelled Zybin.

"Yes, at the beginning. When this dear institution had real people in it instead of Vanka-Vstankas with big fists. I said to him at the end: The trouble is, dear so-and-so, that our argument can't be concluded. It's a question as old as the world – what is truth? Christ did not answer Pilate on that point, you will recall. Then he said to me: 'Well, Georgi Matveevich, would you have answered? Are you clear on that score, in all honesty?' 'Yes, in all honesty, I'm clear about that.' 'Meaning . . .' 'White is white and black is black.' 'Very well! Now how would you decide what was white and what black?' 'Very easily: you just have to look.' 'Yes, then it's all very easy in that case. Well, all right.' He went over to the window. 'Just here, between our two buildings there's an exercise yard. I've seen you walking there once. So then, do you remember what colour the walls of these buildings are, black or white?' 'White, stucco.' 'You're certain?' 'Certain!' 'Look!' He pulled back the curtain, and it was night outside, night! 'Now how can they be white, when you can see they're black?' 'Well of course they're black at night . . .' 'How can they be black if they're white? There's the lamp shining, come over and have a look – are they white?' 'They're white over there,' I say. 'So are they black or white. You see, it transpires that it isn't so easy to answer; a thing might be white in itself, but at this moment of its existence, it's black. You liberals worked in daylight, and then were out of the game; we came at dead of night, our colours are different. That's how it is.' So, would you say that was silly?"

"Well, not all that clever," returned Zybin. "Playing with words. Trickiness."

"Yes, I'm with you; not clever, but at the same time absolutely incontrovertible. And the trouble is, it's these silly but incontrovertible things and regulations you're going to be faced with every day now."

He picked up his book again and started to read.

"What's that you have?" asked Zybin. "A Latin prayer book?"

"No, no, not a prayer book, have a look, have a look," smiled Kalandarashvili. "It's a curious little book. In prison especially. Tacitus. Amsterdam 1672. I've been dragging it round with me for a quarter of a century now."

"And they haven't taken it from you?" Zybin was astonished.

He took the book and began leafing through it. The geometrically precise lay out of the pages, the margins, the lettering, like tiny crystals – calmed the spirit, like a glass of icy water. For him, books like that were like eternity itself. In nothing else did the seventeenth century speak so independently, on equal terms, to all subsequent centuries from the eighteenth onwards. And they also contained a kind of higher exactitude of truth, that was timeless and would never age.

"They say these letters were cast in silver," Zybin said.

"Perhaps, although I don't know why that would have been necessary," smiled Kalandarashvili. "Yes, that little book has passed through all my prisons and exiles along with me. My father presented it to me when I got my master's degree. See it has the retention permit on the first page. Old but still valid. Do you read Latin?"

"At one time I used to read it pretty fluently. But not Tacitus. I found Tacitus hard to read. Too compressed and capricious."

"Yes, there is that. I like him very much. No other historian interests me so much. I keep thinking and thinking and I just can't figure out what sort of man he really was, an embittered and disillusioned party to evil-doing or a surviving witness to it. I can't work it out at all."

"It would be interesting to talk about it," said Zybin, looking at the old man. He was sitting at ease and unconstrained, elbows on the table, erect, slender, smiling pensively.

"Well, there'll be time enough to talk about everything," he promised. "But they're hardly likely to keep me here for long. They don't like digging into cases like mine."

"What cases?"

"Absolutely open and shut. There's nothing to look into, you see. The letter was written in my hand. I don't repudiate it. Well, that's it! Look, what if I follow your example and turn in for a bit? How would that be?"

"Yes of course, lie down. Nobody will bother you."

"They could put me in the punishment cell. Well all right, I'll give it a try."

He took his boots off and lay down. He lay for a minute with his eyes shut, but laughed suddenly and sat up.

"No, I can't drop off. Not used to it. I was lying there thinking. Since I was a boy, I've had this dream of flying. I even bought tickets for a round trip over the city. Once at the gymnasium, and once at the university. It didn't come off either time. The first time, the inspector saw me and gave me a telling-off and brought me back to my father. The second time there was a cloudburst. In 1926 I had fully intended to fly to Konigsberg to see my cousin, when I was arrested! And when I'd lost all hope – eight years camp and me an old man, they pull me in yesterday and straight onto a plane. I was flying and I thought: now I'm not afraid of dying – I've seen everything now. What the earth looks like from above the clouds – I've seen that too. Man is not meant to see more than that, probably. I was glued to the window, staring, and the guard looked at me and smiled – have a good look, grandad, have a good look. He of course already knew what he was taking me to. They tip them the wink about that. You've never flown?"

"No."

"You must, you really must fly! It's a real thrill. When you're flying above the clouds, you think you've arrived on another planet – Uranus or Saturn, and it's covered in snow and ice, like icebergs. There's nothing left alive, everything's frozen solid, nothing but boulders of frozen carbon dioxide. Then suddenly there flashes into view a pure, clean window, with multicoloured translucent panes: yellows, blues, greens! It was our earth – its cities, fields, deserts, forests. And in them, birds sing, children gather mushrooms and berries. How wonderful it is! Yes! My own story is simple, very straightforward – listen and I'll tell you."

The story did indeed turn out to be very simple, but absolutely extraordinary at the same time.

The early spring of 1937 was a very grim and sinister one for the zeks of the drought-stricken steppe camp where Kalandarashvili was. Sinister in every regard. To begin with there was the wave of absolutely unaccountable transfers out. In the morning, the trusty would come into the hut with the overseer. He carried the usual plywood board (all camp lists are written on plywood – it doesn't warp or split, it can easily be scraped clean with glass and is therefore always clean and fresh). The trusty consulted it and called out five or six individuals with their belongings. The overseer hastily searched them, took them beyond the gates and handed them over to the special military guard. At this point all their names were called out again – the senior man had a list. Then they were counted and loaded into a van (facing backwards) and taken to the station. That was all, really. Normal transit. Five were taken from one hut, three from another, ten from a third. In general they took the best workers, but on a couple of occasions they went into the invalid huts. Once they called out an old grandad, so ancient and paralysed that he had to be carried on a stretcher. This derailed all speculation. Up to now, the talk had been of a new camp and special construction duties; now they began to discuss re-investigations. There is never any shortage of that sort of talk in the camps. Everybody writes in camp. They write to the Prosecutor General, the Supreme Court, the party Central Committee – and receive in reply identical narrow slips of paper beautifully typed: "Your application regarding a review of your case has been received, looked into, and turned down as being without foundation." And there's a signature beneath it – a sort of burst of violet, green or black lightning. True, all these rejections didn't count for much – subsequently, people sometimes got one like this: "Your case has been sent for to be checked." And the lightning again. Only there were rather too many of these aniline lightnings striking camp heads. But perhaps, so the argument went, some new wave was in progress? Maybe a new people's commissar had been appointed? But the same frail, polecat features with the piercing little eyes went on hanging above the desk in the chief's office.

And the transfers continued. Another month of confusion went by, and at last the first truly reliable news arrived. One man had been sent back. It seems they'd taken the wrong Prokofiev. He came back deeply subdued, scowling and irritable; he slept for three days. Then rumours began creeping about. It transpired that everyone was being taken to the same SCS (separate camp site). This SCS stood by the side of a railway out in the steppe; there were no other installations near it, so there was nowhere to work. According to the carpenters who had built it, it was a vast empty compound and fifteen empty new huts smelling of resin. And that was all. Then one of the builders remembered that metal grilles had been brought there one night and off-loaded at the stores depot. All this was, of course, naught for anyone's comfort. The returnee recounted that every hut held two hundred men, sleeping on the floor. The windows were barred and the doors locked. No exercise periods. It was baking hot and stifling. The food regime was as follows: five hundred grams of bread and a mug of hot water in the morning; for dinner, a ladle of "Baikal" (some fishy muck, as clear as water) and half a ladle of runny millet gruel; supper – more Baikal. No sugar, no going out to work. They just sat and waited for something; but what exactly? Nobody knew. Prokofiev didn't know either. After three days his legs swelled up and he developed uncontrollable camp diarrhoea, for which there is no cure. He was sent to hospital and the guard, escorting him to the gate, said: "And here was I thinking that he was bound to live for a hundred years after that." And again everybody was in the dark because Prokofiev hadn't spoken about the matter that most concerned them. It was a week before the whole business was clarified.

In the morning, everyone was assembled on parade. Near the club and the notice board, there was a table with a red calico cloth. An extra edition of the wall newspaper *Reforging* had been pinned up and several guards were pacing up and down. Two thousand men stood at attention for a good hour in the sweltering heat in front of that empty table (the guards paced about, shouting: "Is that the way to stand? Stomach in! No talking!"). Then came a cry of "attention"; the door of the club opened, and several persons tumbled out together: a sergeant, a lieutenant, a senior lieutenant, a captain and finally someone very stout and clumsy with no badges of rank. He had square shoulders and a huge grey pock-marked face, rather like an unbaked brick. He was holding a rolled-up notice. A chair was fetched for him. He sat down and barked: "Greetings prisoners!"

He received a hearty reply. He unrolled the notice and got to his feet.

"Now then, Gulag order, number 500 is to be read out. Gulag order, number 500. For malicious sabotage and wrecking, as well as attempted escapes with the object of causing loss to Gulag, that is, for the commission of crimes, provided for in article fifty-eight of the RSFSR Criminal Code, points seven (wrecking), eight (terrorism), nine (diversion), the assize meeting of the military tribunal, having considered in closed session, without the presence of the parties, the cases of prisoners (here followed forty surnames, with their forename and patronymic), has sentenced (rapturously, with a menacing glance at the columns of men) the prisoners (there followed the same forty names; he skimmed through them, muttering) to the supreme penalty. To be shot!" (A hammering fist). The sentence has been carried out," he declared with satisfaction and sat down.

A sigh ran along the columns, as if the crowd had groaned in unison. He too caught his breath.

"So, prisoners," he said, nodding at the guards who at once pinned the notice to the *Reforging* board. "So, prisoners, I have read Gulag order number 500. Makes you think, prisoners, doesn't it? That's how it will be with anybody who thinks he can continue his wrecking activities. And quite right! You've been given ample opportunity to reform, yes? Living quarters, bedclothes, three hot meals, a club, a wall newspaper, all that given, right? That means you work! It means recognizing your guilt! You haven't? Well that's it! The Soviet people aren't going to mollycoddle you or anything of that sort. You'll get what you deserve. Any questions? Dismiss."

Of the forty men shot, five were from that SCS. However nobody lingered near the notice. But soon a second and a third notice went up on the board. People got used to them and began reading them and looking for familiar names.

They still kept taking men out, and at first it was possible to find, if not logic, then some sort of crazy system in it: they were taking Trotskyists; repeaters; those returned from abroad; work refusers (that is, those whom the local medical orderly considered to be malingerers), but then they started hauling off ordinary criminals and farm workers and sloggers, and finally came the turn of the really keen camp curs; the detail-commanders, trusties and team-leaders – and oh, the howls, the cursing and swearing, as they knuckled the tears from their eyes while they were being taken past the gates. They even took an old doctor, a Latvian called Dile – a sullen-faced rogue, well known for his love of Latin tags, toadyism and lack of compassion. Evidently some people who were smart enough to know what was what had got themselves involved in this crusade.

Then all of a sudden it all came to an end. The notices were taken down, the last transit batch came back. These spoke of what Prokofiev had kept to himself. The shooting had taken place in the mornings, close by a clay gully – to a tango rhythm. That is, to the sound of two revving tractors – that was to drown the cries (although who would have been bothered by them in a place like that?). They came and called people out, using a list. Was it very frightening? No, not really very frightening. There were some who were positively glad: "Ah, just let me finish off my last ration and then I'm off! And the lot of you can get stuffed! My troubles are over!" They were always taken away after the bread had been given out. Always after, never before. Perhaps this order of events, first bread then the bullet, arose from someone having heard of the condemned man eating a last breakfast.

About a fortnight later, a commission came to visit the camp; they rustled like white angels round the hospital, glanced inside the huts, spent time in the dining hall, checked the contents of the boiler, asked whether the bed linen was changed often, and whether the bathhouse was all right, then vanished like bright visions. After this, there was loud talk that red-chops had been sacked, cashiered and shot. That he had been sacked could not be gainsaid, but few believed all the rest of it. Still, it was pleasant to listen to news of the swine's demise and so everybody did.

That was the first misfortune to strike the camp in the spring of 1937.

The old man recounted his tale with a chill, harsh crispness, without any digressions or explanations. He didn't have time that day to describe the second misfortune. Lights out sounded and the rules were very strict in that regard. For any nocturnal conversation you were taken straight to the punishment cell.

"So what had happened really?" Zybin asked the following morning. The old man's story had disturbed him all night; even the other's tone had irritated him. What sort of a figure was he trying to cut? What was the point of this senseless bravado? The old man meanwhile was once more in a sunny mood. The tea urns were moving along the corridor and he was busy at the table preparing breakfast.

"What happened?" The old man took out a papirosa and slightly crushed the end. "You have no objection? Well, who really knows,

Georgi Nikolaevich? Different things were said at that time about the camp management; for example rumours were set going through the team-leaders, that it was sabotage by the Japanese."

"Wonderful! How was that then?"

"Very simple. The newly appointed camp commandant was on his way by sea from Magadan. Well of course, he was a patriot, a humanist and all the rest of it. A Japanese agent slipped into his cabin and after that it was like a film: he wrung his neck, threw him overboard, dressed up in his uniform, got hold of his papers and came to the appointed place. He began carrying out his duties. That's it. He was exposed by mere chance; the wife came and saw he was the wrong man. That was one version."

"Did people believe it?" Zybin asked sardonically.

"Well some did. I didn't credit it much."

"Well, good heavens, what utter rubbish!" exclaimed Zybin, despairingly.

"Oh no, dear Georgi Nikolaevich, not rubbish. Far from it. Just think: a saboteur has been destroying people for two months while everybody thought it was nothing out of the way. It follows that there's no way at all you can differentiate between the actions of a Japanese agent and one of Stalin's falcons. It means there's no feeling for legality either in the one who's lying or his hearer. That's the appalling meaning of the Japanese legend. And you say it's rubbish!"

"Yes, yes," sighed Zybin, "quite correct! I've heard of that, oh yes. The faculty of useless knowledge. Law is the faculty of useless knowledge. Only socialist expediency exists in the world. That's what my investigator woman kept dinning into me."

"Re-ally?" The old man evinced some surprise. "Well, you must have had a very erudite investigator! Very! A woman with a lucid philosophical mind. But you know, she's just a teeny weeny bit behind the times. Comrade Vyshinsky has arrived and set everything to rights again. Don't worry about the law, he said, we'll get along splendidly with it. We'll just cut a bit out of it. And so he did, to the general applause. After all, ten years ago, back in the '20s, the professors were declaring "away with the law" from the lofty heights of university chairs, no less. And what professors! Luminaries! Thinkers! The brain and conscience of the revolutionary intelligentsia! That's what they said: the law is one of the chains by which the bourgeoisie has fettered the proletariat. But we will free it from this burden. And so they did. There was a whole flock of fine folk like that."

393

"Listen!" Zybin exclaimed. "But one of that flock of fine folk, if I'm not mistaken, turned out to be a member of the Tsar's secret police."

The old man laughed and gestured with his hands. This seemed to tickle him greatly.

"Not proven, not proven! In any case, as they say, that's from quite a different opera. So that was the first variant, the Japanese saboteur. There was also a second – it had been a preventative measure. During the trial of Tukhachevsky it was supposed to have been revealed that this inveterate enemy of the people looked on the camp residents as his recruitment reserve. These were the recruits who were being destroyed. Well, that was something a good deal more plausible. I imagine even Comrade Vyshinsky would have put his name to that. However, I think the business was even simpler. A general decision had been taken about how to resolve the enemies of the people question once and for all. We were proceeding towards communism; that had been proved. Under communism there would be no criminals – that had also been proved. But progress towards this was hampered by these enemies; that was absolutely undeniable. So then, the enemies were to be destroyed and the ordinary criminals, those who had fallen into error, were to be chased away: Go and sin no more! Remember in Mayakovsky: 'A necessary thing – good, come in handy; an unnecessary – to hell with it, the black cross'?"

"You like Mayakovsky?" Zybin asked him.

"The early things? Yes, I liked them a lot. As for the later, well, my investigator at the beginning of the '30s read them to me and said: 'And you, dear so-and-so, are a thing that is not only completely unnecessary in our socialist system, you're objectively pernicious. That's why we're putting a cross on you. And why talk to me of the law? The law helped you to fight us, that's why you clung to it. But we realized long ago how things stood. We have a lot of Speranskys who can build a system of law, but where are we to find even one Razin to destroy it.' Know who said that? I did know, alas!"

"That secret policeman?"

"No, no. His devoted disciple and admirer though. A most honourable communist. Now, it seems he's finished or close to it. They trumpeted all that a bit too loudly: 'Destroy! Destroy!' They shouldn't have done it that way. They needed to have been a bit quieter, more artful. Vyshinsky was right about that. Whereas you're wrong to attack your secret policeman. He's a man of conviction. Really according to any law, he should have been put away for at least five years. He's weaker than Okladsky, of course; he got ten years, whereas our man, legally, by way of this same socialist expediency, had a professorial chair, and honours, a vocation and pupils. And all of that was right, because it was expedient."

"And conscience?"

"Well now, what's conscience, Georgi Nikolaevich? And what sort of a concept is it anyway? It's virtually Pilate's question: 'What is truth?' It's what? 'A witch who makes the moon grow dim, perturbs the graves and sends forth their dead into the world?' Well if so, it's a dreadful thing indeed, not like Pushkin's conscience.

> And with revulsion reading my own life,
> I tremble and curse.

But there is another. 'And have you no conscience?' the carp asked the pike. And the pike opened up its maw and swallowed the carp. That's all the story there is. That's a different sort of conscience, the pikish one. You should read Schedrin, Georgi Nikolaevich, you really should. It would explain a lot about the world to you. You know our leader holds him in high esteem?"

"You mean that luminary has the same sort of conscience? Pikish?"

"Oh no. He's got a professorial one! He would explain to you in layman's terms that conscience is strictly a class concept, historically determined, and therefore conscience as such simply doesn't exist! That's the first thing. After that he would tell you this: 'My dear young friend! I have not touched the really valuable people: I knew who they were and have worked in close contact with history among types who were objectively pernicious – SRs, SDs, Cadets, Mensheviks, Anarchists, Bundists and the other rotten filth and scum of history – that's the second thing. Thirdly, thanks to that essentially minor compromise, I preserved for socialism something of great value, namely my life; the proletariat needs that a hundred times more than those ninnies, whom later on we would have had to let rot in the camps in any case. And just look what a younger generation I've reared. Handsome, strong, progressive. You yourselves pray to them like saints.' That's it! And from his own point of view he'd certainly be right. Ah, Georgi Nikolaevich, Georgi Nikolaevich! Conscience is all very well, of course, but everybody has his own model and believes in it religiously. Especially if he's a scoundrel!"

"Religiously?"

"Certainly! Because he doesn't believe it, he believes in it! However,

'Lord, I believe; help thou mine unbelief' is one thing. God will accept it and not help. There's something else – a demarcation line in our artful and crafty brain. Like if you have erysipelas. It doesn't allow the poison of corruption to pass it. A man isn't pretending, he really is immune to the truth. Not altogether of course, but to some of its aspects. Anything dangerous remains on the far side on the line. And that's not the devil's prompting – no, not at all! It is a mind which doesn't want to die and places a shield between itself and death: 'Go away! Everything is right and correct! Everything is rational! I don't believe the slanderers and alarmists! They're as blind as moles. Everything is fine, good and rational!' "

"And Order number 500?"

"Now that is the sacred truth! If people are shot in accordance with it, that means, sirrah, that it is truth itself! Oh well, let's have done. It's such a hoary old story it doesn't bear repeating. It's what brought me here, when it comes down to it. Yes, my demarcation line let me down."

The misfortune was famine. It had long been stalking the camp. In spring, the camp always went hungry for some reason. Unaccountable interruptions in supply took place: sometimes there was no bread allocation (the oven had collapsed); at other times the meat was replaced by sardines, or there were no groats, just dried potato; gruel made of that was dark and bitter. Sometimes they just got Baikal anyway. At least the parcels kept them going, but now they were cut off all of a sudden. Either the road had been washed away and they couldn't be fetched, or the dispatcher had drunk himself crazy and was in hospital (that had happened more than once). There is nothing more demoralizing than hunger in a camp.

"You see, Georgi Nikolaevich, the terrible thing is: people don't lose their shame, they lose their heads. We, the fifty-eights, don't know how to steal, but we still do it. We get thrashed within an inch of our lives, but we rest up and do it again. And again, and again until we keel over. That's one. Then there are the compromises, any humiliation, any sort of base crawling – nobody more servile than us. It stands to reason: the thieves have everything, we've got nothing. So we are willing, for a quarter pound of bread or a ladle of dishwater, to tell stories all night. We wash their 'stamps' (handkerchiefs) for them, scratch the soles of their feet for them, and perform any kind of obscenity – so how should they not despise us, you will say. I will hang my head in the face of that contempt; they're right, a hundred times over! And then, we're scholars;

we sit and calculate scientifically: half a pound of sugar for two pounds of bread – what's that? Is that a profit or not? How many calories? So there we sit, calculating the calories! The thieves choke with laughing – and with contempt too. The most richly merited contempt. And besides, those awful waste heaps. Oh!" – his face registered anger and disgust. "We collect everything! Sardine heads, potato peelings, all kinds of bones, any vile rubbish! Some things stank half a mile away. You walked round festooned with tin cans, bottles, stinking sacks and enormous pockets like this. You've got a whole tarpaulin sack sown underneath your jacket, crammed full of all kinds of garbage. Or there's this: some intellectual gets a bread ration, say a pound or so. He puts it in a tin of gherkins and boils and boils it till it turns into a sort of brown emulsion, then ceremonially perches on the bedboards and starts shovelling it down with a spoon. Can you imagine it? That means he's poured about a gallon of salt water into himself. Well, you're literally faced with the results. He swells up like a bedbug and develops fluid swellings here, under his eyes. His legs are elephant-size; if you press them you leave a great dent. And this is a professor, maybe even an academician. But in the camp the only name he has is 'waterbread'! You'll find two or three dear little phantoms like that wandering round every site. One professor like that got shut up in a slop tank. He'd gone nosing in there after 'calories' and they lay in wait for him. Good job it was summer, otherwise he'd have had it. As it was, he was half dead when they got him out. What a laugh that was!"

"Laugh?" Zybin asked. The old man's relentless gloating had daunted and disconcerted him. It was strange and rather terrifying: how could one make mock of another human being's needs and weaknesses in that way? All right if you're fireproof yourself, but how are others to blame if they aren't like you? What is the point of their suffering?

"Yes, laugh!" The old man affirmed, pitilessly. "Because it really was funny. You think man isn't strong enough? That he can't help stamping himself into the filth? Not make himself a laughing stock, a tin can tied to a dog's tail? Rubbish, man! A thousand times over. And what is perhaps the vilest thing, that shell of culture, those little words, the pretensions, the erudition, the proud bearing – we hang on to all of those. The crown of creation, indeed . . . 'Could I ask you? . . . Would you be so kind as to . . . the lot, as in the best Philadelphia houses.' He gave a brief guffaw. "You've never heard tell of Sidor Polycarpovich and Fan Fanich? Well, they'll tell you and show you in the camps. We two are culture-vultures and intellectuals! The people

397

who rake over garbage heaps and talk about the knights of the spirit. Why, the . . ." He choked something back. "The criminals thought up a really good sketch about those gents. But it needs a good storyteller. I can't do it. You come across some real actors among the criminals. You won't find better in the Moscow Art Theatre. They'd picture it for you."

"You could tell me anyway," Zybin pressed him. "It's bound to be really interesting."

"Don't you mean terribly interesting! Side-splittingly interesting. But you need a special talent for that." He deliberated. "Something like this. Fan Fanich, that's you, goes off to work and asks Sidor Polycarpovich, that's me, to keep his bit of ration for him till he gets back." The old man pronounced "ration" in a soft, tremulously delicate voice. "I fetch it and say: 'Sidor Polycarpovich, permit me, if you would be so kind, to leave my ration with you.' 'Certainly, certainly, Fan Fanich.' I come back from work: 'Hello, Sidor Polycarpovich, how are you keeping?' 'Thank you, Fan Fanich, splendidly, splendidly . . .' 'Well, praise be, permit me then to request my ration.' 'Well, you see, Fan Fanich, all of a sudden I felt so hungry I ate it.' 'How can that be, Sidor Polycarpovich, that ration was mine.' 'I earnestly beseech your forgiveness.' 'What do I care about your bloody beseeching, can I shove it up my backside or something? (Stronger words used of course). Hand over the ration and have done with it.' 'Kindly refrain from shouting at me, Fan Fanich.' 'I'll put your mouth to good use in a minute (stronger, much stronger of course), Sidor Polycarpovich!' 'Suck it yourself if you're hungry, Fan Fanich.' Well, after that, there's a fight and the fur starts flying." The old man guffawed again, maliciously and as it seemed, vengefully. Something clanged at the door – the guard had come up and peered through the eyehole, raising its iron visor.

"Yes, not allowed. We're laughing," said the old man. "All right, we won't. So then one fine day, your humble servant is sitting with an old friend on a bench, after a mess of rotting cabbage and sardines, saying: 'There is actually a loan outstanding but I don't really know how to set about claiming it.' The loan came about like this. At one time, when Josif Vissarionovich was setting out for Yeniseisk, I loaned him 50 roubles, as I recall, plus a bearskin coat and some superb felt boots of fine white wool with red-patterned trim. He'd been dressed very skimpily and the cold was bound to hit him. I'd known him before that. I'd been instructed to meet him when he went into exile after the Petersburg house of detention. Then we, together with several Caucasian comrades

– spent the whole day together. We even went to the circus. And do you know what? I took a great liking to him then. He told a lot of interesting stories, never exaggerating, never bragging – and was so vivacious, unpretentious, sociable, even – I know it's hard to believe – genuinely witty. At any rate we laughed. That's how I remembered him. And then a few years later, I learned through my cousin who used to go to visit prisoners, that he had been arrested again and was absolutely penniless. He had no travelling clothes. I was living in Moscow at the time, I'd got married and my practice was booming: I'd pulled off one or two big jobs in Baku and Tiflis – a bank, one of them – and had money by me. So, when occasion offered, I sent him money and these things. And also wrote that if he needed anything he wasn't to be shy, but let me know at once. As I recall it now, I got a telegram back: THANKS. NOTHING MORE NEEDED. MOST TOUCHED BY OFFER. YOURS . . . Soon after that he was transported."

Zybin sat and listened, all else forgotten. The story was as miraculous as his constant tormenting dreams about that man, or some terrifying fairy tale. He knew it had indeed all taken place, but picturing Stalin walking about with this old man (though they had been young, then, so young), sitting at the same table, borrowing money from him, thanking him, writing "yours" – it all seemed quite miraculous. And of course it really was a miracle. "Time is the father of miracles," as the Arabs say.

"And you never saw him again?" Zybin asked.

"Oh no, I did see him. On one occasion, he intended giving me something back, but I laughed and said: 'You can give it to me after the revolution, or when I'm in the same position as you were then.' Well, of course, we all had a good laugh and started talking about something else.

"That's what I told my friend. 'Yes,' he said, 'exactly. It wouldn't be a bad idea to call in that debt, but how can it be done? A letter won't get there, will it? It'll get sent back and you'll be put in the punishment cell. You'll have to get somebody to drop it into the box inside the Central Committee HQ in Old Square. Even then there's no guarantee that it'll get through. It never occurred to any of us that the letter could cost anyone his head. There the conversation ended. And then, about two months after that, my son arrived. I should say that everything had altered in the camp over that month. Everything! The way it can only happen in camps. First of all, they arrested the commandant, then that commission descended on us. All debts were wiped out. Everybody got about two kilos of sugar. In a camp that's riches indeed! The drunken old medical orderly went out on his neck. A newly qualified young doctor was appointed. He sent all the sick to hospital straight away. Ashot, who was an Armenian, and myself were the first in the queue. And it was to the hospital that my son came. Before that, I hadn't had a letter from him, never mind a parcel, for some six months. Everything had been sent back to him, it seemed. Despite this he kept up the pressure to have a meeting arranged, but they never even replied to his applications. And then chance took a hand. One of his friends suddenly entered the ranks of the high-ups; he became the chief secretary of a really powerful man. My son complained to him: I want to get married, and follow the ancestral custom by bringing the bride to my father. I've written times without number but the bastards haven't once replied. 'We'll sort that out sharpish,' said his friend, and permission arrived in three days. So they came. And brought me, well, what didn't they bring me? The authorities turned a blind eye to that. In camp, that's always the way; either they're on your bones, or they see nothing and don't want to see. Right. I met my son. I keep looking, listening and looking at him, thinking: I must have a try. I have to, I just have to! You never know. There's no politics involved. A personal debt, that's all. And so before he left, lights out already sounded, I asked my pal – we were always next to one another in the hut: 'Ashot, you remember what we said about the loan?' 'I do,' he says, 'but I thought you'd changed your mind.' 'On the contrary,' I reply, 'it's all I think about.' 'So that's it!' he says. 'Well think away then.' And turned to the wall. All right! Now there can be no turning back. And so in the morning I went to the reading room and wrote a note. I know it off by heart:

'Citizen Djugashvili (Stalin). Josif Vissarionovich, being in a difficult material situation, I would remind you that in 1904 at the Yenisei station I handed over to you by way of assistance in the Stolypin carriage 50 roubles in cash, a fur coat worth 120 roubles and Siberian fur boots to the value of 5 roubles. In all 175 roubles. I request you to return the debt at present cash equivalent. I would remind you that the above-mentioned articles were my own property and had no connection with party funds.' Signature. Month. Year.

"That was the little letter. I wrote it, stuck down the thick envelope and asked the cultural worker for some sealing wax, sealed it with an ink bottle top and wrote: 'To a member of the Central Committee, so and so, personal, to be forwarded . . .' and gave it to my son. 'This is very important.' He read the address and his face altered at once. 'Dad, what's this? Another complaint? But why to him? And why personal?' 'It's personal because my son, that envelope contains a very great secret, and if any outsider reads it, it's the end of me.' 'You can't tell me the secret?' 'No, I'm sorry, I can't.' 'Well, how am I going to hand it over? I don't know the big wheel at all.' 'Do it through your friend.' 'What if he won't take it?' 'He will! You just have to swear to him that it's a matter of national importance. But don't let him open it. If anything untoward happens, destroy it.' He turned a little pale. 'All right. I'll do it.' Well, we said our goodbyes, shed a few tears even, and his wife-to-be burst out crying on my shoulder. I took a great liking to her. I tell you Georgi Nikolaevich, a great liking! Tall, she was, slender, beautiful, blonde. You remember Botticelli's 'The Birth of Venus'? Can you picture it now? Well, she was exactly the same type. I think she's absolutely the same in fact. But that of course is just my opinion. We embraced. My son says: 'Keep hanging on, Dad, you're a man of iron.' 'I will, son, I will,' I tell him, 'but how much longer have I to hang on?' Then of course I remembered the Archpriest Avvakum 'Till death itself, Markovna'. We both remembered probably, because he smiled. My son left and I came back to the convalescent hut. Ashot asked me: 'Well, how did it go?' 'We said our goodbyes,' I said. 'I gave it to him!' 'You did? well, now it's a matter of waiting – either a bullet or freedom.' 'Why would it be freedom, then?' 'Because he hasn't forgotten what goodness is.' 'In that case why the bullet?' 'So he wouldn't have to think about his goodness any more.' 'Yes, that's logical.' 'All I'm worried about,' said Ashot, 'is that your son will feel sorry for you and not hand it over.' 'That could happen too,' I replied, though I knew we weren't the compassionate kind. Well, we waited and waited and nothing happened. Meanwhile we were transferred from the hospital to a recuperating zone – something like a camp sanatorium. The only work in the zone was looking after the place, laying out flowerbeds, making sun dials out of little bricks, sweeping out the huts. Half of us were on hospital diet and half on full working rations, not bad either. So no one went hungry. I'll digress a bit from my subject, Georgi Nikolaevich and tell you – the camps only grind the very strongest down, the very toughest, categories HPL and MPL – heavy and medium physical labour – they go timber-felling, coal-hewing, on the wheelbarrows, road-building across the swamps. You can't survive that in the camps whatever ration you're on. Twelve hours on work like that, counting travelling time and assembly – seven till seven – no, nobody can stand that. After all, there are practically no days off, living conditions are poor, clothing rotten and the doctors only release those who are dying. It means you work, work and work till you drop. It's a pretty quick process. I tell you, a strong man will keel over far quicker than some goner, a skeleton in bandages. In the camps a creaking tree really does last for ever. As for those who are no use for work, they don't need to die at all. The blind, the deaf and dumb, the crazy, the armless, the legless, those who have lupus, syphilis – they live on and on. From casualty to out-patients, from there to the hospital, from there to the hospital zone, from there to the camp invalid area and then round the circle again. And there's plenty of them, lots and lots of them! Even with the strictest discipline, there's half the camp not at work. Really, to put it in a nutshell, a camp is a factory for producing deformed beings, a vast plant working on self-digestion. If it doesn't get a fresh supply of humanity in time, it seizes up immediately. But they keep sending in the supplies, and it keeps grinding them down and asking for more. That's how it is, man. Still, I'm getting off the point again. So then, after a couple of months, Ashot and I got ourselves into the convalescent camp. I was the senior hut orderly, i.e. hut leader, old Ashot was a gardener. And how he roared with laughter, as he picked up a box of seedlings: 'Well, at last I'm working at my speciality again.' He had been a professor at the Petrovskaya Academy. And I was getting my parcels regularly, at the beginning and the end of the month. And her influence could be seen in every one, a lavender-scented hand-kerchief, or a shirt with my initials in silk, a list in her own handwriting. Another two months passed. Ashot said: 'Well you can live now, there's nothing to wait for now. Your Georgi has torn up your letter. And he did right. At a time like this . . .'

"And two days after those words, they pulled me out – and how! At night! The head of section came along with the commandant of the SCS – no one had ever been taken like that before. Not even when they were going to be shot. They did the routine check and ordered me to collect my things. On the way, the camp commandant said to me quietly: 'Did you write it?' 'Yes.' 'Well then, you've brought it on your own head.' When I was passing the bunks, the whole hut was silent. Ashot was lying near me, asleep. When they came, he hadn't even opened an eye. It was only when I was bending over him as I left, that he said quietly, still without opening his eyes: 'Goodbye, Georgi! I'm sorry, I was putting my trust in a brute. Never mind, we'll all be going that way soon. Now I'm going to try myself, and stop holding back.' That's how I turned up in your cell. That's the whole story."

He sighed, lay down on his bunk and stretched out.

They took the old man the following day after dinner. He was summoned to interrogation and ten minutes later they came for his things. They took the lot away, even the mattress and blanket. So once more there stood next to Zybin a bare black metal skeleton. He contemplated the metal and thought: "Thus ends the life of a good, kind man – Georgi Matveevich Kalandarashvili. All his life he believed in the law, and what it meant was demonstrated to him in full measure. Let us honour his memory by mentally rising to our feet, because at the moment I don't feel like getting up physically, nor is there any reason to do so. Peace to your ashes, comrade! Ah, why didn't that old Armenian manage to talk you out of it. And the trouble is, isn't it, that death came to you just at the moment when you began to want to live again. Those window panes – green, red, blue – it always comes down to them!"

V

CHAPTER 1

BEYOND WINDOW PANES of mother-of-pearl and gold, a band was playing: trumpet, saxophone and teeny-weeny cymbals. Zybin was walking down the stairs between two guards, and kept lagging behind in spite of all his efforts. His leg had "come on," as Grandpa the carpenter used to say, and every step was painful. He hadn't noticed it in the cell; they hadn't let him out for a walk in a month. "It's not allowed here," the duty man had explained to him. "When they transfer you to the investigation block . . ." What block or corridor had he been in then? The duty man hadn't answered that, but he had begun to notice one or two things himself. For instance, starting from his cell, the corridor was lined with thick grey tarpaulin for some reason. Once, coming back from the toilet, he deliberately jogged against it with his shoulder and felt the taut resistance of an awning. You certainly wouldn't be able to brace your back against a wall like that!

"You touch that and I'll touch you!" the soldier shouted in his ear.

In the morning during changeover, the sentry being relieved said: "I'm warning you: do that again and it's the punishment cell for you."

"Or you go to those cells," added the relief.

"Those cells – what cells?"

They made no reply, simply turned and went out.

Those cells were at the other end of the corridor. It was to them that the tarpaulin corridor led. During the day, the muffled hubbub coming from them indicated a considerable human presence. Evidently, as well as single cells there were communal ones too. Three times a day, round containers and huge copper kettles were pushed along the echoing tiled floor. About three times a week, after lights out, a silent procession went past his cell. Pressed up against his door, he listened hard: three pairs of boots went by and one pair of shoes. Further on, the steps ceased at once on the carpets. A pause. Somewhere, a door clicked. The noise was cut off instantly. Silence. Then the door clicked a second time, and once more silence supervened and lasted till morning. That meant they had called someone out, ordered him to collect his things and then taken him away. Where to and why? Why at night? He soon realized why, where to and what for. On one occasion, something had gone wrong with the plumbing and he was taken to a different toilet. It was situated at the opposite end – a huge, cemented place, rather like a bathhouse, with shower partitions fixed into the ceiling and wooden latticed blocks in the floor. A metal door fitted with bolts had been cut into the wall, and an icy draught blew from underneath. So that was where they took those people! He was puzzled though, by the fact that he had never heard any outcry – a man could be compelled to go to his death, it seemed, just as to the lavatory. Or simply equate death with the relief of bodily needs. He speculated that this was all too possible, but he didn't understand what could bring it about. Then one day he found out. On this occasion, he had been taken into the cell next door for some reason (those to left and right of him were always unaccountably empty). He entered and felt everything abruptly shut off. Though it was morning outside, in this cell it was a rarefied dank twilight. Instead of a window, a latticed brick-sized strip of light glowed dimly yellow near the ceiling. A wooden bedstead had legs sunk into the cement. The slop tank was on a lock and chain. The table was a plank sticking out from the wall. A massive brick projection the size of a Russian stove, took up a quarter of the cell. There was no room to walk. He sat down on the bed, and brought his hand to his face without being able to make out the palm. An hour later, it seemed to him that he had spent many hours there; an hour after that he had lost all track of time. By the time they finally took him back in the evening to his original cell, with the books, the bowl, the mug and spoon, he looked at them and almost wept from quiet joy. Yes, he realized now, spend a month in a box like that and you'd go to your death whistling. Some bright noddle had put thought into that.

. . . The trumpet beyond the golden window suddenly snarled and went mute, as the cymbals began a nasty tinkling.

"Tilly-tilly-tilly-bom, they've set fire to the house of the ginger tom!" He sang along and then stopped to draw breath. "What's the matter?"

"No talking!" the guard cried out and even clanked his keys together. But he at once evinced sympathy. "You should see the doctor! How come you're like this? You can hardly walk, can you?"

"I'm all right!" He returned. "It's passed off already. Let's get on!" They got on.

"There's a fête going on," said the soldier sheepishly. "A dance competition."

They had reached the landing and come out into the corridor. There was repair work going on. Buckets and tins were standing about. There was a smell of damp limestone and drying oil. The board with the wall gazette *Salvo* was propped against one wall. "Hands behind back," hissed the guard and knocked on the leather door.

"Come in," came the reply.

They entered. The guard behind him stayed where he was. Evidently, this was to be a short visit.

Neiman, as he had been a month before, florid, civilized, clean-shaven, was sitting at the desk, regarding him.

"Good day," said Neiman. "Please, over here." He indicated a chair in the corner.

He signed the pass, dismissed the soldier and raised his round blue eyes to Zybin. Once again the latter detected in them that expression of deeply concealed fear and anxiety, though the face itself was calm and untroubled.

"How are you feeling?" he asked.

"All right, thank you."

"Thanks are not called for. But you have been able to relax and get your strength back? We've deliberately let you alone for a long time and transferred you to our quietest corner. And we've also changed your investigator. So that now you'll have . . . yes! Come in."

The tall, beautiful, dark-haired girl whom Zybin had already seen in Khripushin's office now entered. Without looking at the prisoner, she approached the desk and placed a thin blue folder in front of Neiman. He opened it, took a glance, remarked jubilantly, "Well, that's splendid," and rose to his feet. "I'll be in my office," he said as he went out. "I'll call you."

The secretary waited until the door had closed, then pulled the armchair out and sat down. "She's taking liberties, the bitch!" thought Zybin. "Of course she's not Neiman's. Somebody higher up. Neiman hasn't risen to perks like that. No doubt some deputy from Moscow brought her along. But she's a looker! By hell she is! Or am I so unaccustomed by now that I think they're all beautiful? It could well be that. Dirty devil!"

The dark-haired one sat poker-backed, silently smiling and letting herself be scrutinized from all angles. She was worth it too, of course. Everything about her was neat, smart and tidy; the jacket in large brown check, waist, cuffs, hairdo, tight wristlet watch. Not Russian, apparently, but not really like a Jewess either. Pink nail polish. The face rather dusky, almost cream-coloured, with a certain elusive, lustreless violet tint about the eyes. Brows plucked and sharply etched. Dark blue dipping lashes, giving her glance a kind of fringed effect. The mouth, however, was standard – cut out raspberry celluloid, they could be seen in any halfway decent hairdressers. All in all, an excellent model, age twenty-three – but lots of polish. Interesting to shoot off with her up into the mountains. Although no, girls like her don't go for me. I never get anywhere with them. Kornilov, now, he could take her apart straight away, brick by brick. At the moment he's giving Lina a working-over no doubt. Hells bells!"

"Good day, Georgi Nikolaevich!" said the secretary all of a sudden, softly but very distinctly; he was confused, however, thinking of Lina and replied at random: "Good day, Miss."

She smiled.

"Oh, I'm not a Miss, Georgi Nikolaevich."

"She can't be allowed to do this sort of thing, surely?! Oh Neiman, you dummy! You'll come a cropper over this one." He marvelled and said formally: "Forgive me, I'm not experienced enough to . . ."

"I'm your investigator, Georgi Nikolaevich," she said softly.

"Well here's a novelty act." He was dumbfounded. "Hold on to your hat, boy, here's where it starts. First the psychology. For the highly strung. She'll start effing and blinding in a minute, but she'll be no match for that Moscow one."

He'd heard about that one, the Moscow one, some four years before. People said that she was either the head of the SPD – the secret police department – or its deputy head; not a plain investigator at any rate. It was said too that she came of an old liberal intelligentsia family. Beautiful, cultivated, refined, she could talk about Proust and quote Selvinsky. And her flights of fancy, great and small, really shook the young thieves. They squealed with delight as they quoted her words. He himself, as he listened to them, did not share their delight, not even smiling; he simply believed that she was actually the sister of a certain well-known, talented Soviet authoress, specializing in tales of vigilance, the wife of another literary man, almost a classic (he's on the middle-school curriculum) – and the sister-in-law of the general secretary of the Writers' Union.

"I'm simply beside myself with joy," he said, "to see within these grim walls, such a charming woman, and hear her voice! Speak with her! Oh!"

"Yes I can see that, Georgi Nikolaevich, indeed I do," she smiled, almost good-naturedly. "I see your joy and realize what prompts it. Very well, I also think we can find a common language. I'm not a demanding person and there's not a great deal I want from you."

"I shall be glad to serve, if I can," he said.

"You can, Georgi Nikolaevich, you certainly can. I don't want anything supernatural from you. I shan't touch upon your intimate affairs. If things go well between us, I can even arrange a meeting in my office. All you have to do is tell me about your trip to the Ili. That's all. Are we agreed?"

"I shall be glad . . ."

"Well, perhaps you won't be all that glad, but it has to be done. You know why? Because I'm not going to indulge in a swearing match with you: in the first place I've never learned how, and secondly, as I understand the matter, it doesn't work too well on you. Right?"

"The holy truth, citizeness investigator, your words are sacred! I . . . forgive me, I don't know your name and patronymic."

"Yes, yes! Let's be introduced," she smiled. "Investigator Dolidze. So then, Georgi Nikolaevich . . ."

"Excuse me, but your first names?"

"You don't really need that, do you, my first names? In our dealings it's only my surname that will figure, Lieutenant Dolidze. That's quite sufficient. So then, Georgi Nikolaevich, telling the truth is something you have to do in any case. Because if I see that you're lying or being evasive, I shall, without swearing or getting worked up, quietly and calmly send you to the punishment cell, understand?"

He smiled a smile of gentle indulgence.

"I understand perfectly, citizeness investigator, Lieutenant Dolidze. What sort of an investigation would it be without the punishment cell? Am I visiting my mother-in-law, or something?"

She laughed good naturedly.

"I know what you're capable of, I know. But there's no need for the moment. With Khripushin it was all right, but with me it's pointless . . ."

"I hear and obey, Lieutenant . . . No, say what you like, but it's impossible. You call me by my first and middle names, like a sweet and cultured woman, and I have to address you, like some ill-mannered oaf, by your surname and rank! That's bad. I'm a refined individual, it wounds me. I'm embarrassed."

"Well, all right," she gave in. "It's Tamara Georgievna."

"Now that's a different matter. A lovely first, and especially middle name, Tamara Georgievna. We Georgis aren't just anybody. If I'd had a daughter, she'd have been Georgievna. You see I've already been in the punishment cell. I spent ten days in there. I thought over my whole life while I was there. When I get out I'll write a novel."

She shook her head.

"No, no, Georgi Nikolaevich, you haven't been in one like this before. I'd send you to one that's dark and cold. With a damp floor, where you can't sit or lie down. And there's a draught! People aren't held in there beyond five days. Then I'll call you in after five days and ask you: 'Well then, are we going to tell the truth?' Then one of two things will happen: either you say 'no' – in which case I'll send you back for another five days, and you'll either make it there, as they say, or you'll say 'yes' and we'll start talking business. In that event, what would have been the point of the five days? They'd be just a tax on stupidity."

"Well, if you give in now," he said to himself (over the last month he had learned how to do that), "if you make a face or cringe, I'll smash you against the wall like a pot, you stupid head! And that'll be the end of you! I mean it, hear me?" "I hear you," responded his stupid head, "don't worry, I shan't let you down. Everything will done properly."

"Well now," he said, "I'll be thinking of your beautiful dark eyes all those five days and recalling our great poet: 'Beauteous as an angel celestial, as a demon so crafty and cruel.' She was your namesake and fellow-countrywoman."

She frowned.

"All historical parallels are risky. Georgi Nikolaevich, the given parallel is simply senseless, you know whose words they are? Tamara was a feudal princess, I am a Soviet investigator; she rid herself of lovers, I am enquiring into the case of a criminal; she was moved by lust, I by duty. So you see, we have nothing in common."

Her curt, matter-of-fact tone puzzled him and for the first time, he found himself at a loss.

She regarded him and picked up the receiver.

"Yes, that's it. To room 350 for prisoner Zybin! Well at least we've got acquainted now. It'll be better for both of us if we sort things out. In any case remember: I'm neither cruel nor crafty. And if I promise something I do it. I've been given your case – and I'll finish it. I give you my word of honour on that, Georgi Nikolaevich!"

CHAPTER 2

I T WAS NINE OR TEN in the evening. It was raining slightly, a fine, grey, nagging drizzle. Long streamlets ran down the window. It was windy too; leaves were flying across the yard into the light of the big yellow street lamp. Her uncle had been away on a trip for about three days now. Old Nilovna was cleaning the kitchen floor and crooning something slow and churchy under her breath. For her part, she was imagining herself to be a schoolgirl again and had got into her light blue student dressing gown and kept it on till evening. She sat with her legs on the settee, gnawing at a huge red apple and thinking: Gulyaev, during their first serious one to one conversation, had heard her out and asked her to give him a report and set down all her conclusions.

"You realize," Gulyaev had said, "that what you and your uncle propose, amounts essentially to altering the whole format of the accusation. The question arises at this point: Why? Hold on, hold on! There's a new instruction that all cases of this nature, if they take longer than six weeks are to be referred to Moscow. Khripushin will undoubtedly take advantage of that and send in a report about you. What I'm considering, dear Tamara Georgievna, is whether or not we've both been getting involved right from the start in something we shouldn't, eh? Because I'm very keen that our first effort shouldn't turn out to be a flop. In that event we would greatly distress all our well-wishers. That doesn't worry you, eh?"

He was talking to her with respect, gazing affectionately into her eyes and she answered in similar fashion.

"No, Pyotr Ilich. You've just said 'cases of this nature'. But this is a case of quite a different nature. There's obviously a second dimension to it."

He frowned.

"Oh these grounds and dimensions – second, third and fourth. I always dread those! It's not a theatre you know. ("That means he knows that I spent two years studying at GITIS," she decided swiftly). We have the investigative process, I mean arrests, prisons, transit points but not ... Take a look at this." He slapped his palm lightly on a folder

413

which lay in front of him. "The operational file on the charge against Zybin G. N., in accordance with article 58.10, part one, of the Criminal Code of the RSFSR. Ninety-six pages. All finished and correct. But the investigation has to be included too, hasn't it? According to that and our special note, this same socially dangerous and unreliable citizen Zybin, would certainly get his well-deserved eight years. After that, we'll see. Major Khripushin has been conducting the case. Conducting it without notable brilliance certainly; that's why we've taken it from him and handed it over to you. Now: how are you going to rejoice our hearts? Just hold on, hold on a moment! Everything you've said is really just general ideas, what I would like to know is how you're going to conduct the investigation itself? Where are you going to start?"

"By putting to this socially dangerous and unreliable citizen Zybin just one question, and listen to how he answers it: 'Why did you have to go to the River Ili in such a hurry?' "

"Oh, he'll make some insolent remark; that won't cause him any bother. 'Oh I didn't have to go there specially. I just bought some vodka, picked up a girl and off we went. The vodka to drink and the girl . . .' " He started to laugh, but then began coughing. He coughed long and agonizingly. "Well, what are you going to say to him?" he said, catching his breath and mopping his mouth and face. "It actually isn't a frontier zone, not a test area, no secret installations. Maybe half the town goes there for the same reason."

She made as if to object.

"Wait a moment. I do understand you: it's all very suspicious. He shot off all of a sudden, loaded up with vodka, picked up the girl for some reason, and all this took place on the day his raving beauty arrived, and the gold had slipped through his fingers as well – of course there's something fishy there. But all that will only amount to something on one indispensable condition: if you have a single incontrovertible trump card. So you seek it out. Look through the whole case again; check all the documents, reread all the reports, get him in; get a good idea of what makes him tick, then let fly with your trump card. Don't allow the fact that Khripushin didn't get anywhere put you off. Everybody knows, a poor dancer always . . . well, let's put it diplomatically, that his heels get in the way?" He laughed and again coughed his protracted, dry, agonizing cough. "And pay no attention to your uncle!" he cried piteously in the intervals. "Do your own thinking! Your own!" He took out a handkerchief, wiped his eyes – his fingers were trembling – and sat like that for some time, lying back in his chair. His face was completely dark and empty. She gazed at him in alarm. At length he sighed, gave a smile, tugged out a desk drawer and retrieved a small red paper packet. He tore it across and placed two white pills in his mouth. Then he pushed the packet towards her.

"Try them. Mint dragees. Specially for non-smokers."

She shook her head.

"I do smoke."

He frowned severely.

"Girl! Learned at college, I suppose."

"No, in the fourth form."

He rummaged in his desk again and found a box of Osman papirosi. "Be my guest." She shook her head. "No-no, go on smoke!" He took a lighter from his pocket and flicked it alight. I keep it specially for smokers – they always seem to be out of matches."

She had perforce to light up. Gulyaev sat there smiling as his tongue rolled the dragee round his cheek.

"Have you been to see the doctor, then?" she asked.

"A-ah!" he dismissed this, quietly hopeless.

At this she began to feel very sorry for him and said: "Anyway you look fine."

"Really?" He swallowed his dragee, and with a caustic smile, got up from behind the desk and went over to the cupboard. He beckoned to her.

She came over and he lightly embraced her with one arm, or rather, touched her shoulder lightly with three fingers – and opened the door wide with the other. A blue mirror flashed obliquely and subsided.

"Look at that," he said.

They stood together.

A beautiful young woman – dark, supple, long-legged, long arms, a shock of hair – and next to her, at shoulder level, a puny creature in a field shirt. He seemed almost black from the deep depressions at his temple, and the deathly grey of his skin, the colour of hospital oilcloth. His feeble paw, lying on that splendid shoulder seemed especially pitiful.

"Well then," he said. "How do I look? A sight for sore eyes?"

She found herself at a loss, as they both stayed standing there. Then he took his hand from her shoulder, closed the cupboard, returned to his desk and sat down.

"All right," he said, "another ten years will be enough for me.

Probably not wanted on voyage after that. By that time communism will have been built and we'll all be converted into firemen. We'll ride round town in gold helmets. What's wrong with that?"

"Have you been like this long?"

He considered.

"Well, you know, probably since I was a boy, but then I just . . . had a bit of a cough. Hard to avoid that! For you 'the bad old days' is just the lead-in to some story, but I had my bellyful of them. My father was a cold cobbler, that is, one without a sign. He used to bang on soles and heels. We lived in the traditional cellar. A big room for five people. The sixth was my mother's sister from the country with a sick baby. How the thing yelled and yelled! It was always dark, as you'd expect. Cellar windows are tiny and you can't wash them properly, and secondly, the sills were choc-a-bloc with all kinds of balm stuff: my mother had been left them by an old general's wife – she used to scrub her floors. So mother wouldn't let anybody touch them: 'They're the best cure for a fever – you breathe in the medicinal air from them.' And actually we never did get fevers. I got this bronchial asthma after pleurisy. I picked it up in Sochi, in a government sanatorium. Now there's a joke for you."

"Well, people don't die of bronchial asthma," she said.

"Hmm! So sure of herself! All right, people don't die of it, but they die with it, my they do! All right, let's give it a rest as they say. So, my girl, take the case and move it on with all your youthful vigour. But don't listen to anybody. Tell all these advisers to go to . . ." he made a gesture. "But let me have a report with a detailed basis, a plan of investigation, so that I have a document."

And so here she was sitting, reading through her jottings, gnawing her apple and thinking. On her pad was written: Lay before Zybin the whole plan of investigation. I shan't use foul language, punishment cell. Then answer:

1. Why the hurry?
   a) That day in particular?
   b) With Clara? Lina had arrived after all;
   c) Why so much vodka – four pint bottles. Enough for four strong men. Who were they then?
2. What are his thoughts on the missing gold? (his police parole).
3. "The trump card".

A great many question marks followed that "trump card" – probably as many as her hand had thought to write, followed by one big exclamation mark.

The telephone rang. She picked it up. "Yes," she said. Silence. "Yes!" she repeated. Silence and breathing. "Well, ring when you've made up your mind," she said and tossed the receiver down.

Nilovna came in, a wizened, white-haired old woman with yellow cotton wool in her ear: she had a permanent shooting pain in her temple.

"Did you call?"

"Nilovna, just look, aren't they beautiful? Feel them." She deftly tossed a couple of apples to the old woman.

"Thank you, but I don't eat them! Or only in tea for the smell. See," she bared a lilac-coloured gum with her finger and displayed her brown rotten teeth – only molars left! Why did you want me, then?"

"No, it was the phone ringing."

"Aa-h! That happens here. The exchange gets it wrong. Are you going to eat here or the canteen?"

"Oh, I'm full up to here," she replied. "What about you – have you eaten?"

"Well, you don't think I'm going to sit and starve, do you?" Nilovna grinned. "They've been ringing you from the library; they asked you to bring some book, something about France, if you didn't need it any more. They said you would know."

"Thank you, Nilovna, I know."

She went over to the shelves – she still needed to lean on her stick, her leg ached – and took down *The Life of Joan of Arc* by Anatole France, made her way back to the sofa again, opened it at the bookmark and wrote on her pad:

3. Trump card??

"The prosecutors were risking more than other citizens, and more than one, no doubt, as he passed through the execution yard, reflected that before a year had passed, he too would be judged on that spot." (A. France. *J. A.* p 177) – in the margins was written in indelible pencil. "But our idiots don't reflect at all, and aren't frightened of anything – they're wrong! There won't be enough lampposts to go round!"

She had stumbled on these marked lines and the marginal comment, after the book had arrived by messenger and she had started to look through it. She had shown it to Yakov Abramovich; he had read it and

417

said sadly: "The handwriting isn't his though. Keep hold of it anyway, it's a very interesting point. He also used that library." "Does it amount to anything, then?" she had asked. He had looked at her in surprise and exclaimed softly: "Clever girl! It's an open and shut eight years, isn't it?" So she had kept the book.

The telephone rang again. This time it was a confident female voice asking for Yakov Abramovich. She replied that he wasn't there. There was a silence, then the voice asked if he would be long – the voice was young, lilting and somewhat drunk as it seemed to her.

"I don't know," she answered and suggested she leave a number. Another silence ensued. "I'm his niece," she added. The receiver was removed from the caller's ear at this, because she heard the tinkling of glass, voices and the half sentence: ". . . I prefer whatever you like." The voice was rough and masculine; obviously there was drinking going on.

"No, no, it's nothing special," said the receiver. "It's just a friend of his calling."

"A-ah," she said.

"From the Medeo," the receiver added with an embarrassed laugh. "I just wanted to invite Yakov Abramovich to my name-day party."

"Ah, I see," she said. "Well, thank you. Let me congratulate you as well, then. I'll certainly pass the message on. I'm his niece."

"You live there?"

"No, no," she answered garrulously. "I only got here recently from Moscow. I came here to relax after graduating, but who knows? I may be working here."

"There's a lot of work to do here," the receiver assured her. "Do you work in your uncle's field?"

"Yes," she replied cheerfully. She was greatly enjoying chatting to this unknown woman.

"There's a great demand for geologists here," said the caller earnestly. "Both you and your uncle are welcome to come. I'm not in the Medeo at the moment, actually, but I'll give him a ring later and explain personally. My name is Marietta Ivanovna."

"Thank you, Marietta Ivanovna. I'll come over. Medeo – that's in the mountains, isn't it?"

"Yes, right up in the mountains. In the ravine. Only at the moment I'm . . . not actually there – well, anyway, I'll ring later. We'll be having a party." The noise in the receiver had wholly subsided; there was only a low hum of voices. No doubt they were already starting on the drinks.

"Thank you, thank you, Marietta Ivanovna. I'll certainly try to come."

She put the receiver down and seated herself on the stool next to the old woman.

"There now, Marietta Ivanovna of Medeo has invited us over," she said. "Is it far?"

Nilovna put down her knife.

"The buses go from the Green market. Get on there and it's the last stop. They don't go any farther. Who's this Marietta, I've never heard tell of her. It's not the one who brought the book?"

"Yes, yes, that's the one!" (Ah, Yakov Abramovich! You artful geologist, you!)

"Well, off you go then, the mountains are wonderful up there! Shaggy Hill," said Nilovna. "You can have a bite to eat, relax, and spend the night. There's accommodation. Before you've gone three stops, there's a rest home. Marina Savishna took me up there once. Somebody was arriving; the floors had to be scrubbed, the dishes washed . . ."

"Does my uncle often stay there?" she enquired.

"No, you wouldn't drag him over there with a lasso. It's the Volga they like, they fly over there as if it was the seaside. But they don't go up there. 'What have they got I haven't seen? I look at those hills every day through my window. I'm sick of them!' That's all you hear him say."

"So then, that's marvellous," she said, moving away from Nilovna. "I've got you in my pocket, Yakov Abramovich! My, my! No doubt young and shy! Yakov Abramovich, you're done for!"

"Now who can the Lord be sending at this time of night?" grumbled Nilovna and went out into the hall.

She herself swiftly retired to her own room. It was late for visitors of course, but it wasn't her uncle. He had a key.

There came a clicking of the lock and a jingling of the chain. A mellow, youthful bass she recognized as Myachin's announced: "And here is our housekeeper! Maria Nilovna, our pious old lady! Here's a welcome visitor! This is Yakov Abramovich's brother, Roman Lvovich – our very very top man!"

"Now now, don't go frightening the housekeeper!" said the visitor. "And where's our beautiful and charming young relative? Asleep or out visiting?"

She quietly put the hook on the door and tiptoed over to the wardrobe. She opened it soundlessly, looked around and took out an evening dress, but after some deliberation, put it back. She pulled out a severe check suit.

It was Shtern, a distant relative, her uncle at three or four removes. He had scarcely been mentioned at home, but as soon as she got to college, she was to hear his name virtually every day. It was said that he was kindly, charming and rather terrifying. A great master of his craft. A wit! A savant! She had dreamed of meeting him for ages.

In the morning, there came a loud knocking at her door, followed by a jovial bass, half singing, half declaiming:

> I have come to you at dawning
> Just to say the sun has risen,
> And that he . . .

"It's with greetings, not at dawning," she amended through the door as she lay on the settee.

"I don't care. And that he ta-ta-ta the morning, ta-ta begins to glisten! Out of bed, sleepy head! Come and see what's going on outside!"

She opened her eyes and at once closed them tight. The whole room was flooded with sunlight.

"What's the time?"

"Well might you ask! Ten already. Up you get, up you get! I've already made the coffee."

"I'm getting up," she said. "I'll be ready in ten minutes."

"Ten minutes indeed! This very minute! An investigator too. An investigator should be . . . You know what he should be? Ooh! All right, get up and I'll tell you what he should be."

But she did not appear in the dining room straight away. First, she trimmed her eyebrows with a razor – they always had a tendency to grow together. Then she went through into the bathroom and spent a calculatedly long time in there. She came out fresh and sparkling, her hair still damp. Roman Lvovich, plumply good-humoured and in good form, greeted her in a loud suit, as he presided over the coffeepot. She offered him her hand and he kissed it respectfully.

"Strong for you?" he enquired.

She always drank tea, not coffee, but said yes, as strong as possible and no milk.

"Ah, yes, that's our style," he approved. "You know, Catherine the Great once offered a cup of coffee to a courier. He had just galloped up with a packet for her and she was partial to handsome young men. So then, after he'd drunk her coffee, he went completely giddy. That's the sort of coffee they used to make in the old days!"

420

Roman Lvovich though not a tall man, was broad and powerfully-built. Like Yakov Abramovich, a chubby full-faced infant, his mother's pride and joy – how amoretti used to be painted in days of yore, or the way the four winds on old maps were depicted with inflated cheeks. "He may not be the cleverest of men, but he is the vilest," she recalled someone saying of him in their house.

"Come, my dear, at least let me look at you in daylight," said Shtern. "I hardly managed to get a glimpse of you yesterday. Why did you vanish so suddenly?"

"Well, you had business of your own to discuss," she said with a hint of venom.

"Business? With the prosecutor?" He seemed astonished. "No, no, what business? What could that be? Yes, you have your dad's brows and eyes. I haven't seen Georgi for ages and ages, how is he?"

She gave a slight shrug.

"Fine."

"More specifically?"

"He's alive, well and working."

"And still running up to the fourth floor?" He sighed. "That's what being born in the Caucasus does for you, rather than Smolensk or the Arbat. Tell him, when I'm in a really bad way, I'll crawl to his office and collapse in there, because there's no one else I trust. And I know he'd do anything for me."

She smiled faintly. Yes, that was the trouble. For him, an outsider, her father really would do anything. Georgi Dolidze was a celebrated heart specialist – ardent, passionate, explosive, a sportsman, mountain climber, hunter and excellent companion, regarded by one and all as a caring family man, one of those who couldn't bear to see his family lack for anything. But at the same time – and this was something almost no one knew – he was absolutely indifferent to that family, and that included his daughter. It was because of that indifference, or rather benevolent lack of concern, that he had taken no interest in which law college she went to, once she had abandoned GITIS, or that it had been a wrench to give it up in her fourth year. Georgi Dolidze couldn't abide the relations on his mother's side, although he seldom spoke of this, and the words about "cleverest and vilest" had not been uttered by him – he didn't even regard Shtern as being especially bright.

"Yes, it's been ages and ages since we set eyes on one another," said Roman Lvovich. "When was the last time I came to see you? Yes, it would be the summer of 1928. That was when I fetched you that box of "Ladies Fingers" from Tbilisi. That was when I saw you for the first time. You were playing at Indians out in the garden. So I remember you with a bow in your hand! You were a dashing Indian, my word! Hair over your face, all stuck with white feathers. Remember, eh?" He laughed.

She didn't remember of course, but exclaimed: "Of course!" And so sincerely, she even surprised herself. (Those wretched Indians again! Damned bows and arrows. The grown-ups had decided for her that she definitely must read Mayne Reid and fantasize about Indians, scalps, bison, tomahawk and she, so as not to let them down, would career about the garden with warlike cries, collect goose feathers, and daub weird smudges under her eyes. She wasn't allowed to soil her clothes.)

"Yes! And now I find ever such an enchanting grown-up niece. That, of course, is the nicest thing of all. I hear you're going to do your probation here."

"I'll be working here, Roman Lvovich," she said. "I'm to be taken on for experience. I'm also thinking of collecting material for a thesis."

"What subject would that be?" he asked.

"The tactical bases of preliminary investigation in cases of counter-revolutionary agitation." She had rapped this out swiftly and without thinking, because it had been suggested and formulated by her tutor, with whom she had long been hopelessly, as it seemed, in love. That same law specialist who had been invited once to GITIS as a consultant on their course curriculum. That's when they had started meeting.

"O-oh," said Shtern deferentially, and suddenly became very serious. "A splendid subject. But a very difficult one. In the first place, it's wholly bound up with Comrade Vyshinsky's latest doctrine concerning criminal complicity and association, you know of it? You've heard of it? A chain, not a cluster. And secondly with the new Soviet theory of circumstantial evidence. We Soviet jurists, for the first time . . . Sugar, sugar!" he cried and pushed the bowl towards her. "Two lumps to a cup. And sip it gently. And what about GITIS then?"

She shrugged slightly. (Whatever the rights and wrongs of that, she couldn't start all over again now, and this was a far warmer place in the sun). He put a fatherly hand on her shoulder. "Never mind," he said. "You won't regret it. I trained to be a writer as well, you know!"

"But you are a major writer!" she said.

He waved this away as an expression of pain flitted swiftly across his face and vanished, probably assumed deliberately.

"A-a, there's no getting away from it. I'm a prosecutor. Prosecutor prosecutovich, supervisory staff, the genuine article! And that's it."

"There you are you see, and at first you went to Bryusov College. I'm answering your question."

"I understand. I'm sorry. With me it was as simple as could be. They just slipped me a Komsomol pass in committee and said: 'From tomorrow you won't be coming here, you'll be going there.' That's all there was to it. From then on I didn't go here, I went elsewhere. That's where I've been going ever since."

"And no regrets?"

"Why ever not? I had regrets aplenty. I couldn't sleep. I wanted to run away, hand in my Komsomol card. I should just think so! Here I'd been dreaming of noble deeds, heroic feats, glory, and now I had to mug up legal statistics, do my stint in the department, write an examination report on the scene of a road traffic accident. They even dragged me off to an autopsy. And the people! My pals were policemen, agents, informers, pathologists: the other side were abortionists, gangsters molls, pickpockets, murderers – foo! Spend all my life with them?! In the other life, I'd left literature, the Art Theatre, Blok and Chekhov, Pushkin and Shakespeare – that's what I thought then."

"And the upshot was that a few years later you had become a very famous writer," she flattered him. "Your 'Single Combat' in *Izvestiya* went from lecture to lecture for a whole week in our college."

He frowned slightly.

"Oh, that was a one-day wonder, enchantress (he really did select the appropriate little phrases). One read and into the wastepaper bin. You don't find things like that on peoples' shelves. No, my love, I'll write something genuine, if I still have the strength, in ten or fifteen years' time, when I retire, but it's all milestones, milestones! Stages on a great journey. No, I didn't get to be a writer. But," here he scowled severely, "that I chose this precise road I don't regret now. No, a thousand times no! And you know why? Because I soon realized that I had not left Chekhov and Shakespeare behind at all. They were all with me in my office." She made to say something but he cut her off. "Wait a moment, listen. Now a man comes to me. Well, seeing as we've already mentioned it, the hero of 'Single Combat', that doctor, the forensic expert, who murdered his wife in their apartment, then chopped her up into little bits and came to me at the prosecutor's office in search of her. We say our hellos. I sit him down, and courteously enquire as to his health and how he feels. He smiles sorrowfully: 'How can I feel with this misery!' 'I understand, I really do. We're looking for her, we're taking steps. Perhaps we'll find her.' So we sit there smoking, before getting to the point. Still the light touch. I shift a witness interrogation form towards me. Nothing out of the way. Question, answer, question, answer. I note it all down without demur. He's at ease. Then all of a sudden I disclose one corner of my joker: 'But tell me, dear colleague, if, as you surmise, your wife has gone off with someone else, why has she left behind her favourite silver powder compact? Women don't like parting with such things.' He looks at me. I look at him. He got the picture at once bright lad, and quickly parried: 'It was my present to her on our wedding day; she probably didn't want to take it.' So, a matter of fact reply – but that was it. Something clicked inside me and the man sitting before me gets fainter and fainter, and quite a different face emerges – the face of a criminal, a murderer, not as he is now, but what he was then, when he killed his wife and dismembered her body; and I can clearly picture him doing it, what he was thinking when he did it, how he erased the traces. And he too realizes I've run him through and starts to panic, getting mixed up, letting things slip and talking through his hat. Fear had confused and disoriented him. Up till then he'd been living a solitary existence, fenced off from everyone else, thinking no one could find a way through to him. Then all of a sudden the door is flung open and I am standing there on the threshold. The end! Resistance is over and he gives in."

"Like that doctor?" she asked.

Roman Lvovich threw her a swift, piercing glance, then got up and went towards the window. Beyond the glass lay the peaceful, normal yard, acacias, the sultry heat, dusty hollyhocks, listless hens in their dust-holes, glaring sunlight and pink and blue vests on the wire. He stood for a moment, watching, then went back to the table, sat down and asked: "Well, more coffee?"

This doctor business had ended in a mysterious but spectacular fiasco. After the passing of the death sentence on the murderer (and he was condemned as a terrorist. Well, stands to reason. Soviet people don't commit murder, do they? Therefore the murderer was an anti-Soviet individual).

So then, for what reason does an anti-Soviet murder a Soviet person – his wife? Only because his wife, like a good Soviet, was intending to expose him. That meant it wasn't murder, pure and simple; it had a political motive (i.e. terrorism). So, after the passing of the death sentence, all of a sudden the murdered woman turned up in court! The fact of the matter was that Roman Lvovich had overreached himself.

He had broadcast the story of the doctor-murderer too widely. The issue of *Izvestiya* carrying his "Single Combat" had reached the murdered woman's neighbours. At that time, she had been living perfectly happily for over two years with her new husband in the Far East. But there are always those who want more than others. Rows broke out. A policeman arrived and wrote a report. She had perforce to make an urgent trip to Moscow and appear in person. No one else but Roman Lvovich would have got away with it unscathed – but how could one hurt such a pure, fine, naïve and honourable man. Nobody in authority would have considered such a thing! Just chuckled and prodded him a little: 'There you are! Don't go thinking you're God!' And they would put an article in some restricted bulletins under the heading "From legal practice".

"Yes," Roman Lvovich went on, pushing away his cup, "the criminal has to be opened up like a safe and you go steadily through the keys, one two, three. Don't get anxious, whatever you do! That will only show how helpless you are. No, stay calm, smile and activate your keys: psychological, logical, emotional and ultimately – regrettably – when really necessary, the big, rough, key of physical coercion. Let it be the very last, but it is the most reliable. Understand? The most reliable!"

"Not quite," she said. "What do you mean ... beating? Verbal abuse?"

He frowned.

"Come, comrade investigator, you're the last person I would expect such questions from! Love of my heart," he cried. "Would you really be able to administer a beating or verbally abuse someone? So why ask? No beating, no abuse, it's simply a matter of writing a report – you were taught how to do that at college, weren't you? So then, a report to the chief; he has punishment cells to suit all tastes: cold ones, hot ones, ones where you have to stand up; dark ones, ones with searchlights, and simple cubicles. And for the most obstreperous, damp shirts made from nice rough canvas. A dose of that and people become wonderfully biddable! But it has to be done at the right time; not too soon, not too late, but at a certain definite moment. And I may tell you at this point that your time at GITIS will stand you in good stead. It's a grand education for an investigator. Everything depends on your ability to assume an image, to be reincarnated. In that process, the writer, the investigator and the actor are all united. Because, if the investigator lacks this ability, he's not worth a light! He's a broken man. If he does not sense the tragic nature of thought ... very few even of our greatest understood what that meant. Dostoevsky – yes. He did. I often think what a wonderful investigator he would have turned out! He's the one I would have liked to work with. He knew where crime is concealed. In the mind. Thought is criminal. That's what he knew. Thought itself. That's been totally lost sight of since his time. That's the starting point for everything – nip it in the bud and there will be no crime committed. So then, if an investigator isn't capable of understanding all that, he has no future with us. Let him join the police. They always need honest and industrious folk. But we need creative spirits."

"So then, an investigator is a creative artist?" she asked.

Next day was a rest day. By four she had finished her report notes and typed them up on her uncle's old Underwood. Just then, Roman Lvovich knocked on the door.

He had just come back from the people's commissariat and was glowing and radiant.

"Now, niece!" he said as he came in. "What a clever girl! You have captivated our most revered homunculus. After a businesslike talk – I'm arranging something most amusing there which I'll tell you about later – he suddenly comes out and says: 'Well what do you think to your niece becoming our colleague.' And put on that crafty-crafty look. 'Well, I'm very pleased and proud.' 'Yes,' he says, 'that's a really smart girl you've got.' 'There's never been any idiots in our family, dear Pyotr Ilich – I'm the stupidest one there's been!' " He laughed complacently. "You pay heed to him. He's got a head on him, and strangely enough, he's not such a bad chap at all. He can always come up with some useful suggestion. Let's have some coffee."

In the dining room he resumed: "And I found out from him that he'd taken Zybin's case out of Khripushin's hands and given it to you. I knew this Georgi Nikolaevich once upon a time."

"Really?" she exclaimed in a low voice.

"Yes, really! We met in Anapa." He poured the coffee. Yakov Abramovich's tiny cups were special ones – pink and paper-thin, almost transparent. "Even went drinking with him once. Yes, it really happened. Still, that was three years ago. He'll have changed by now."

"And what was he like then?"

He laughed.

"That type! Very sure of himself. Slippery. Shifty. Wanted to be the life and soul. Went about with some girl there and called on everybody to join them. They picked me up as well. Straight off the beach. I was dreadfully bored, so I tagged along. We went on some excursion, did

426

some drinking, singing; she read something. Incidentally, she's flown into town as well. You'll probably have to bring her in, though I strongly doubt it'll do any good: she's a sly creature!"

"I've just made Zybin's acquaintance actually," she smiled.

"Well, what was your impression?"

"Oh, just the same as yours I suppose. Artful and secretive. Keeps trying to feel out the weak spots. Not averse to provoking a bit of shouting and swearing. But I warned him I wouldn't descend to abuse."

"Correct," he said. "Smart girl."

"Or coax him either."

"Correct."

"But if he sabotaged the investigation, or started playing blind man's buff with me, I'd simply send him to the punishment cell."

"Now that, perhaps, was not the right thing to do, or rather, it's the right thing but too soon. The prisoner should know nothing of your plans. That's one of the immutable rules. In the given situation, it's not all that important, let's say, but in general, every twist in the course of an investigation should come as a complete surprise. Especially with somebody like Zybin – he's a cool customer, that he is! I've seen him and this little lady working someone over – true, he turned out to be too fly for them, but they made use of everything, boat, vodka, guitar, moonlight! And what was his attitude, tell me?"

"Very free and easy! As if he was visiting friends! I've been looking over Khripushin's records. An awful lot of slip-ups there. Obviously they'll all have to be destroyed: there's nothing of any substance. And the investigator is an experienced man, it seems, so it's grim."

Shtern regarded her and grinned.

"And Gulyaev didn't explain anything to you?" He shook his head. "Or Yakov Abramovich? . . . Well, that's understandable! Nobody wants to show themselves up. It's not a matter of stupidity here, it's political immaturity. They are mooncalves, god forgive me for talking about my dear brother like that. The mooncalves wanted to fix up a grand mass trial here in Alma-Ata: sabotage throughout the fields of literature, science and art in Kazakhstan. This wretched Zybin – this dubious, crafty character – was to have been the chief defendant. His testimony was to have set the ball rolling. They had a good dozen more defendants lined up. Anyway, just like Moscow; columns in the papers, prosecution speeches, news footage and all the rest of it. They got slapped down by Moscow. What sort of a national cultural centre do you think Alma-Ata is? Why have all the wreckers gone crawling over there – what don't

427

they like about Moscow? Secondly, if you're so keen on organizing a trial, your first job is to give the Alashordin nationalists a shaking, and filth of that sort; there's plenty of them, why pick on the Russians? That's being politically illiterate. In Russia it's Russians who do the wrecking, in Kazakhstan it's Kazakhs! Why on earth go complicating everything and obscure the nationalist threat? The provincial court will do for Zybin, or the Special Board if it comes to the push. Nobody told you anything about all that?"

"No."

"Well, stands to reason! A good job the prisoner didn't give in straight away. He obviously smelt something fishy, otherwise he'd have come out with name after name and caused us an enormous amount of trouble. Things like that are done only on direct orders from Moscow – and they wanted to give Moscow a surprise. Afterwards all hell was let loose. Somehow, wind of all this reached the ears of the museum director: that this was what they were trying to rig up. Anyway, someone tipped him off. Not being a fool, he upped and went to Moscow. Got an audience and put it all to them. He's a smart man, articulate, chest full of medals; he put the thing in the right way. The upshot was they got a flea in their ear. And now what's to be done with Zybin? The investigation's a wash out. Letting it go as a straightforward 58.10 goes against the grain, but betrayal of his country won't wash. Here they've dreamed up some missing two-thousand-year-old gold! A fairy tale! Opera! Why are you shaking your head?"

"They didn't dream up the gold," she said. "It did actually exist. Listen . . ."

And then she began to tell the story. He heard her out to the end without interrupting and said gravely: "Yes, if matters really do stand the way you've put them, then yes, it's worth pursuing. Mysterious loss, visiting the shopkeeper, mystery trip, vodka for four people . . . none of them known. Oh, why didn't the idiots let Zybin finish what he was up to? We'd have had it all in our hands by now! The idiots! You've got a plan of interrogation? Let's have a look at it." He read it through to the end, then said: "That's my girl! Clever lass! Go ahead. I'd just make a few tiny changes in the form of the questions. Let's go to your room and sort it out."

She called Grandpa Sereda in for questioning. The central museum carpenter was broad-boned, tall and husky. He wore a canvas cape, the kind cabbies wear, rigidly stiff and fireproof and strong leather boots splashed with cement. He declined to remove the jacket, said he had come straight from his workshop and didn't want to spoil expensive furniture with paint, glue, sawdust and wood shavings. She didn't insist. So he sat opposite her – massive, grey-yellow, stony, rounded knees apart, twisting a brown handkerchief in his hands.

Though he was dark about the face, he was cleanly shaved and his moustache was trimmed. His nose was like that of all boozy old men, livid and veined.

To begin with, she tried to engage him in conversation, but he replied in tense monosyllables, with the occasional ingratiating laugh. She realized this was leading nowhere, and moved on to the questionnaire. Here things went very smoothly. The old man answered every question in precise detail.

When she had finished writing, she laid aside her German fountain pen with its gold nib and asked Sereda what Zybin had called him. The old man failed to comprehend. She explained: Was it by his first name, first and middle, surname or what?

"Grandpa," the old man snapped firmly.

She shook her head.

"How could he park you among the ranks of the old men straight away? You're not old at all, are you?"

He spread his fingers slightly.

"That's what he called me."

"And how did you address him?"

The old man again failed to grasp this. She explained: Well, was it by name, patronymic, surname – how?

"I called him by his first name, mostly, the middle one sometimes, but in front of outsiders it was always comrade; comrade Zybin."

"So you were on fairly close terms, yes? Well, what sort of an impression did he make on you?"

The old man pulled out his handkerchief and began rubbing his chin. "Well, was he abrupt, rude, or the opposite – courteous, mannerly; did he have the common touch, as they say?"

The old man withdrew the handkerchief from his face,

"I never saw him do anything bad."

"What about other people?"

"I don't know about them."

"Now how can that be? He called you Grandpa, you used his patronymic, therefore you were on friendly terms. So how don't you know?"

"Hmm!" grinned the old man. "What sort of friendship could we have had? He was on the staff, a scholar. I'm a carpenter, a plain working man; I can hardly scrawl my own name here. What friendship could there have been? He could be my grandson."

"So what follows from that?"

"What do you mean, what follows? A lot follows. The ideas he gets when he's off duty, they're not the same as mine at all."

"What are they then?"

"What are they? They're daft! Getting to know or meet some woman, go off somewhere with a crowd of folks, take a gramophone with him, get hold of some records – that's what he thinks about. What has friendship got to do with it? I'm surprised you ask!"

"So you played no part in any of that?"

"What part could I have played. What in? In his company? Over yonder's where all my company is, in the cemetery!" She laughed out loud. "You're still a gay dog yet! My grandad married a girl of twenty when he was eighty years old."

The old man silently examined his brown thumbnail.

"Well, did you ever have a drink with him."

"I did," responded Grandpa.

"You did. How often?"

"I didn't keep count of course, but if he brought it, how could I refuse?"

"No, no, naturally you couldn't refuse. So you drank and you talked, yes?"

Grandpa deliberated before replying: "Well we didn't sit and say nothing."

"What did you talk about then?"

"Different things."

"Well, for example."

"Well, for example: This year there'll be a bumper crop of apples – it happens every other year. I'll have to send a parcel off. Make me some boxes, Grandpa, with holes in so the apples can breathe. Or: Why are they digging in front of the museum? They're surely not thinking of putting a fountain there? Or: I don't care for kumiss at all; it roils my stomach. There you are!" Grandpa smiled.

"Did he not tell you anything about himself? What he did before, why he came here? Whether he'd be here long?"

"No, he didn't like to do that. He preferred joking about things. He used to laugh."

"What about Grandpa?"

Grandpa sat thinking, then grimly: "Never about the authorities."

"What about then?"

"Different things. He didn't care for our Massovichka; he made fun of her."

"Who else?"

"Well, who else? I didn't pay any attention at the time. Well then, there was the chief secretary at the science library. They didn't get on. He was very annoyed at her."

"Because they didn't get on?"

"No, because of her stepdaughter."

She moved the record towards her.

"What about her? Did he do anything . . ."

"No," Grandpa shook his head sharply. "The father, a doctor, was pulled in, but the secretary took all his things over. She stopped looking after the daughter: 'You're no daughter of mine, go where you like.' So she went round sleeping at other peoples' houses. He was very sorry for her. He asked her whether we could take her on as a relief ticket girl. I said: 'Have a word with the director.' 'I will.' But he didn't have time to do that."

The old man lapsed into silence and fell to examining his thumb again.

"What have you done to it?" she enquired solicitously.

"I just banged it with a hammer. The nail will come off now."

Silence.

"Are you sorry for him?"

He lifted his head and stared at her.

"I'm sorry for nobody! What's he to me, my brother-in-law, my brother? You can't break your heart over every mother's son," he said testily.

"Well, all right," she said, "but this gold of yours has gone missing." The old man did not reply. "So how did it vanish, then? Right out of the museum itself. Why didn't he keep an eye on it? What do you think? Was he to blame?"

"Not his fault. He was away up in the mountains. We sent for him to come back. If he'd been here, he'd have seen through those jokers on the spot."

"What was there for him to see through? He knew them very well, didn't he?" She feigned surprise as she stared at the old man. "Now what are you saying, grandfather? He knew them perfectly well. Perfectly well! No, no, you don't have to . . ."

431

The old man said nothing.

"And he told you himself that he knew them?" The old man remained silent. "Come now, speak up!"

"Not nohow," replied the old man stoutly. "He never said that."

"Well, how can that be?" She even made a slight gesture of throwing up her hands. "How could he not say it when he did? He doesn't even try to conceal it even now." The old man said nothing. "And they told you as well, when you were sitting with them in that, . . . what's its name? Glasshouse is it?"

"Glasshouse, just so!" The old man answered in stern, soldierly fashion, even adding the "sir", to keep it official.

She glanced at him and realized she would get no further. She went on: "Well, all right, we'll leave that for the moment. But what was his way of life. You did spend time in his room, didn't you?"

"Well, he lived the way everybody does. On his beam-ends. Nothing in his room apart from a bed and a few chairs. And books. Some pots and pans. That's about all."

"What was people's attitude to him?"

"Depends. Nobody saw him do anything bad. If a workman asked him for beer money he never refused. He used to give boiled sweets to the boys. As soon as they saw him they would come running."

"Who else lived with him?"

"Who else? The cat. It was a wild one. Kasya! He found it as a kitten among the reeds up in the mountains somewhere. He used to feed it with his finger. If you called on him early, they were always sleeping together. Him curled up, the cat stretched out. He called it Kasya. He'd stick his head out of the window: 'Kasya, Kasya, where are you?' And she'd run to him in a flash. The length of the yard. Like an arrow. A cat and a half!"

"And now it's where?"

"Somebody's taken it in. But it still goes over to his place, to the window. The door's sealed, so it goes to the window. It miaows away, and pushes its nose against the glass and knocks with its paws. Then somebody comes out and tells it: 'Now what are you after, Kasya? He's not here.' And she disappears as if by magic."

"And the same next morning?"

"Without fail. Again! Yesterday now, I was walking in the park. I hear her miaowing behind me. I stop. There she is standing there, staring straight at me, all eyes.

"He's been pulled in, Kasya, I say; he won't be here any more, so don't wait for him. And she looks at me just like a human being would and there were tears in her eyes. I felt really terrified. I wanted to stroke her, but she flashed away out of sight."

"So it's a stray now?" For some reason, she felt very sorry for the wild cat. They loved cats in her house.

"No, no, she's house-trained! No, someone's taking care of her."

"So he likes cats as well, does he?"

"He liked all living creatures the same way. The boys brought him a falcon chick once, fallen from the nest. He reared that as well. His hands were a mass of bites, but it grew up big and handsome. 'Yasha,' he called it. 'Yasha, Yasha,' and it would fly straight from the beam down onto his shoulder and look him right in the eyes. It was wonderful to see them."

"And it got on with the cat?"

"Why not? He was up above in the rafters. She was down below on the bed or mousing round the yard. In the evenings he'd come back from work bringing some sliced meat and feed them both together. It was very funny to watch them. The boys used to come running from all the yards round about."

"This, incidentally," she reminded him, opening the case folder, "is what you told the investigator on 11 September. I'll read your statement out. Listen carefully.

"Question: 'In what way do you know the scientific assistant at the Kazakhstan central museum, Georgi Nikolaevich Zybin?'"

She glanced at Grandpa.

"Answer: 'I know Georgi Nikolaevich Zybin as a corrupt individual. He was always arranging drunken parties with casual women and suspicious women. Even the boys were indignant at his orgies.' That's the way you put it, 'orgies'." She smiled derisively. "Grandfather, what's an orgy?"

Grandpa grinned.

"Well, when they're drinking and shouting."

"I see! If they shout it's an orgy. But what are these children doing there late at night? Or is he at it during the day as well? And what about the director in that case? 'When the son of a colleague asked him to stop his disgraceful behaviour, he swore at him using obscene language, offending his mother. She was outraged and told me about it.' Why is there no name here? Who was she?"

"It was Smirnova, that's who! Zoya Nikolaevna, she is!"

Grandpa grimaced painfully.

433

"A-ah. (It all made sense to her at once: in Smirnova's record there was written: 'hostile relations'.) So why were they on bad terms? Because of these drinking parties?"

"No, no. They don't live in that house. It was over the portraits. We had portraits of toilers of the land hung up. Zoya Nikolaevna says: Get them down! A year ago they were toilers of the land, but now they could easily be wreckers. Get a stepladder and take them down. But he wouldn't. 'Do you mistrust the entire population? You can't do that.' So they fell out. I said all that at the time, but the investigator didn't bother to write it down."

"And how did the boy come into it?"

"I saw the boy business with my own eyes. Her lad comes running up to Zybin, crosses his eyes, the piglet, and asks: 'Uncle Zho-ora, why is it all these women come walking in to see you, eh?' " Grandpa portrayed the piglet to the life, using eyes and voice. "But Georgi Nikolaevich just grinned at him and said: 'Tell your mother that women are human beings as well, that's why they walk. Got that? Tell her those exact words.' "

"I see. '. . . He made sharp attacks on the Soviet system, told anti-Soviet jokes, slandered measures taken by the party and government.' Did that happen?"

Grandpa harrumphed.

"Did that take place, Grandfather, or not?"

"If it's written down there, it must have happened."

She looked at him sternly.

"What do you mean, 'If it's written down there?' Come off it. What's written here is only what you said. So let's have no more of that."

Grandpa made no reply. She gave him the record.

"Is that your signature? We don't need expert witnesses? You don't repudiate it?"

"That's right. No I don't," Grandpa brought out.

"Or what's written here? So then we'll arrange a confrontation with Zybin and you can repeat it all to him." The old man shrugged and turned away. "What's the matter now? Wouldn't you like a personal confrontation?"

The old man grinned.

"You talk as if it was some tea party. Honestly! 'Would you like, wouldn't you like'! What choice have I got in all this? I've got no say in it, it's all yours. If I have to, then okay!"

"But you yourself don't want to see him?"

"Why should I? What pleasure will it give me to look at a man under arrest? What use am I to him? Just to make sure he sinks? He won't get out of this whether I put my oar in or not. Look at those walls! Grand workmanship! Only monasteries have as good work as that!"

Here she suddenly realized that on his way up here, he'd had quite a few and it was now going to his head. She quickly signed a pass and said gently: "Off you go. I'll see you out."

Grandpa made to rise clumsily from his chair, but took his time about it, fussing with something. Then she glimpsed a tightly swathed bundle standing on the chair, wrapped in a red spotted handkerchief.

"What's that?" she asked.

Grandpa snuffled and spread his brown hands.

"They're just apples," he said awkwardly. "Might be allowed. The boys slipped them to me on my way here. They said they were from the place where he was digging. Maybe you can pass them on, eh?"

But how had the old devil contrived to get a big bundle like that through? Although in that waterproof . . . So that's why he didn't want to take it off! Oh, Grandad!

"Dear me, Grandfather Sereda!" she said. "Now what did you do that for?"

Her voice was edged with uncertainty. Something seemed to have turned the wrong way inside her. She could take the bundle and pass it on to Zybin. Perfectly easily! It was perhaps worth dilating on this theme in her dissertation on investigative procedure: the abrupt emotional change, a positive emotion, stemming from the investigator, and by its very unexpectedness subverting the prisoner's normal, stereotyped behaviour. All that was so. And yet . . . and yet. She had an odd feeling that this handing over held a good deal more than met the eye. It had a peculiar significance, a hint of some special relationship; it would disconcert not just the arrested man but the investigator too. She did not yet understand, in what way this bundle was dangerous – the old man had hastily uncovered one end of the handkerchief to reveal the fiery, sparkling, sheer-sided apples, patterned with crimson and green whorls – but she had a perfectly clear intuition that these apples were incompatible with the investigation. At this point, it seemed she was considering for the first time what this investigation really was. At the heart of this investigation into these particular matters, in an office like this and with these investigators, there was a cheerful boorish insolence and lack of integrity. But it was a lack of integrity that had been

435

legitimized and established by theory and practice. One could do anything here, appropriate money during searches, use foul language, manhandle the prisoner, use blackmail, wear people down with lack of sleep, punishment cells, hunger, swear on one's honour or party card, forge signatures, documents, records, snigger when reminded of the constitution ("And you still believe in that, idiot?" That had acted like a blow to the jaw.) – all that was within the rules of this house: only one thing was strictly forbidden – yielding to the truth by so much as an iota; the old man had been forced to lie (why lie, though?). They'd simply given him forms of words to sign which had been worked out once and for all. Thus the police always write in their reports "used obscene language" – and that was in order; that she had picked up the baton of this lie in her turn, or rather this conditional truth, and proposed to consolidate and legitimate it with a personal confrontation, that was in order too (it was an operation after all and in an operation there were no holds barred); that because of this lie or conditional truth, Zybin would receive a sentence and of course leave his bones there, that was simple socialist legality – all true. But in all this elegant, strictly regulated system, there was no room for the bundle of apples. She sensed this without fully understanding it, that was the trouble.

And therefore said the first thought that came into her head: "Dear me, Grandfather! Now what did you do that for? You don't know, he might have said such things about you . . ."

"Yes, I know, I know," the old man scowled. "I know all about that! They read it out to me. A loafer, a drunk, a dispossessed kulak! I'm never a dispossessed kulak, I've lived in town for donkeys' years ("Now that's great! Bravo Khripushin! Bravo you swine! What a thing to dream up", she thought with disgusted respect). I'm telling you this. When I was going home from here, I kept thinking. You've seen a dog-catcher at work around the town. They catch them in nets round all the streets. They fill the cages with them and cart them off. So when the cartwheel catches in something and lurches, they all land on one another in a heap. See the fur fly! They even forget about the cage. The dog-catcher says: "Whisht, damn you!" and goes round the cage with a rope's end but they couldn't care less! The squabbling and fighting! And the cart rolls on and on, carrying them all to the flaying-house. There they rip their hides off with steel pincers. That's what we're like. So why should we be angry at one another? He at me, I at him, and the cart goes rolling on its way. And the same fate awaits us all. So all this means nothing."

"But you did testify the truth?" she asked. There was no point in arguing with a drunken Grandpa.

"What? The truth?" Grandpa sighed and grinned. "Truth or lies, it's all one to him now. Once he's been pulled in, that's it! They don't bring dead men back from the cemetery. No use in that, they've already started stinking. But take the apples and give them to him. There's nothing behind it. We put them on graves at Transfiguration time. Near the crosses. So the dead can break their fast too. Take them, they're his favourites! He'll be pleased. Let him eat them, go on!"

And she took them.

A second meeting, no less noteworthy in her life, took place on the same day. She was already getting ready to leave and was standing in her raincoat locking the cupboards, when there came a knock at the door. Shtern had come to visit. He was positively beaming.

"I know," he said in the doorway. "I possess the most comprehensive information. Today a certain old alcoholic brought to a certain citizen investigator under his coat a whole sack of apples for the prisoners and the citizen investigator without hesitation accepted it. Did it happen or not?"

"It did," she replied," but I'm amazed at your . . ."

"Everything amazes her! I got a telling-off on your account. Now was that any way for me to bring up a young relative . . . What could I say? I told them she's not with me, she's with Uncle Yasha, Uncle Yasha . . . Address your enquiries to him! No, I'm joking, just joking. They only laughed. They all have the highest regard for you there. But bear in mind for the future: your superiors have to know everything. Especially what you hide from them. There's the phone, make the call. Here, show me that sidor. What, you don't know what a sidor is? There's an investigator for you. It's a sack, a bag! Oh, what beauties! Any serpent could beguile any Eve with apples like these. They picked them out specially, the sods! Hand them over to him. You must do that. Then put in a report! Here in this office, as if you were breaking all the rules, hand them over to him. And when he starts to undo the sidor, you pretend to look slightly gloomy and sigh: 'Oh dear, Georgi Nikolaevich, how could you, eh?' GITIS couldn't teach you that sort of thing!"

"It certainly couldn't," she picked up her glove and thought: "It's all so easy, after all, and I, like a fool . . .

"During unexpected emotional twists, carefully planned by the investigator," she said sternly, "the prisoner's behaviour stereotype is broken and he is unable to adopt his former attitude immediately.' That's from my thesis, will it do?"

"Clever girl!" laughed Shtern. " 'Behaviour stereotype'. Clever girl! Splendidly put."

"And therefore," she went on, "in accepting that bundle, I decided: right, first he gets the apples, then a confrontation with the sender."

"Clever once again. The right decision. Just one thing more: when you start asking him about the gold, he might, especially after the confrontation, simply clam up. Don't let him do that. Use any means to draw him into conversation. About anything. A long way off the matter in hand maybe – as long as he doesn't dry up. If somebody talks, he will certainly give himself away. Take these apples, for instance! Where do they come from in Alma-Ata? You don't find them like that anywhere. Are they hard to get? Where? In the mountains? Ah, where you were digging? Well, and so forth. What else does he like?"

All this had suddenly become very distasteful to her and she snapped: "Cats, he likes, wild life, other peoples' children."

"There you are, there you are! Be sure to take an interest in wild animals. Remind him of O. Henry's story. 'You lover of animals and tormentor of women, I arrest you for the murder of your wife.' Yakov has an O. Henry, read it. And that can be a lead into the women's complaints against him. Incidentally they found a woman's skull among the gold ornaments. There's a second lead into the gold. Have a think and work on it. All right? Your working day's done. You can ring about the apples in the morning. Right then, come along with me. I want to show you a remarkable old chap. A genuine excellency, an aristocrat of the spirit. A boyhood friend of comrade Stalin."

"How did he turn up here?"

"The same way as everyone else! By reason of his heinous sins, of course. He spent ten years behind the wire and has now been freed by personal order of the Leader. I have been entrusted with the pleasant duty of welcoming him, releasing him and delivering him to Moscow, where his son's going to meet him. That's life isn't it; an hour ago he was sitting and wondering why he'd been pulled out: to be killed or pardoned. Isn't that great?"

"Great," she blurted. Despite having schooled herself for nearly four years, getting used to the idea of working in this place and everything connected with it; despite having done her practical, attended interrogations and conducted them herself, even managing to break that crazy old girl straight away; despite all that, what she had glimpsed over the last two days had overwhelmed her with its fantastic improbability, its flavour of nightmare.

"It certainly is," stressed Shtern. "And you know why? The old man is a long way from being sugar and spice. I've seen his case file. The poor investigator couldn't stand it, and because of his vile temper and cunning pinned a TA, Trotskyist activity, as well as the SE, suspected espionage, on him. You realize? To survive with letters like that, you have to be born under a special star. So you see, he must have been and he's being let out."

"So why do you need me?"

"This is why, my dear. Shortly he will be brought to us washed, shaved, hair cut and in a new suit and tie, and we're going to take him out for a meal." He laughed. "Really, God alone knows where else it could happen. Only here! They're right to call this 'the land of miracles'. And he's been inside with this Zybin of yours. And going by the report of the guards, they talked incessantly, round the clock, day and night. Touching on, of course, the gold."

"So?" she asked.

He shrugged.

"That's it, unfortunately, nothing. The operations side didn't go into action. They say they had no instructions. I didn't know anything either. The prison people didn't have a notion why he'd been brought in. A slip-up, as you put it, took place. So then, you are being presented with a golden opportunity on an unofficial basis, in a personal conversation on this and that, after a glass of good wine, in armchairs . . . We won't hide the fact that you're an investigator, but you're . . . a kind investigator. They all have this legend of the kind investigator, a magical tale, that somewhere there is one honest, decent, humane investigator. And the old man, it seems, hasn't set eyes on a female face all these years; it'll be nice for him . . . So you have no objection?"

She shrugged her shoulders.

"Do as you think necessary, of course. I'm as much a visitor as he is. If it's necessary . . ."

"Oh it is, my dear! Necessary! So up you get and let's go. It's on the next floor up. In the deputy people's commissar's office. He's just come back, incidentally, and hasn't seen you before. Off we go."

What had happened a week before was this. About seventeen miles from the capital of our homeland, Moscow, the evening had been still warm, bright, indeed sunny, though the sky had been dotted with fluffy, white cloudlets since morning.

439

Comrade Stalin was working in the garden. Papers lay before him on the table, some pinned together, some loose. He had managed to get through them all and was now simply sitting, reclining in his willow chair, observing the clouds and the tree tops as he relaxed. "The sun's got out," he mused. "That's nice! The breeze is rustling among the birches, that's very nice as well! Might even be a drop of rain tonight, good for the mushrooms. There don't seem to be any at all this year – and what's summer without mushrooms?"

He had already spoken to the gardener – couldn't something be done so that cèpes and birch mushrooms would grow here. "No," the gardener had answered firmly. "There's nothing you can do about it; champignons, yes, they'll grow where you want, but cèpes, birch, aspen, even stickies – they were fancy-free, clean, forest mushrooms; they grew where they had a mind to."

"Why so fancy-free?" he asked, much tickled. The gardener had spoken so respectfully of the stickies. "Grow where they have a mind to, do they? That's disorderly conduct isn't it?" and laughed. And the gardener had also laughed a little, but in a very measured fashion. He laughed but didn't look the boss in the eye; he looked no higher than his chin. The boss hated it when people looked him in the eye. But he would notice an averted glance too, and draw his own conclusions: "Not a well-disposed individual, insincere, talks but doesn't look you in the eye. His conscience can't be clear." And he was recalling that conversation with the gardener now, and once again he laughed. "The fancy-free cèpe!" He said pleasurably. "It grows where it has a mind to. My, my . . ."

And at this point, the strong, diffused sunlight fell directly onto the white willow chair, and the dazzling glow began to bother him; comrade Stalin remained there for a few minutes, closing his eyes and drinking it in. But then a cloudlet flitted across the sun, dowsing everything. He sat up abruptly, took a large-format book from the table, and opened it at the bookmark. It was a typed copy, bound as a booklet, "Circular of Home Affairs Ministry, police department, special branch, dated 1 May 1904, no. 5500."

He grinned. 1 May 1904 was a day he remembered particularly. He had spent it in Tiflis, out of town, at an illegal May Day meeting, among rocks and trees. It was a scene of sunny, relaxed gaiety. Many were the speeches, many the toasts proposed. First they drank to the revolution, to the working class, the party, to the destruction of its enemies, then to all present, then to all those absent, then to those who were languishing in exile or prison (there were no members of the RSDRP, the party of the majority, in jail; the police department at that time considered it of small importance). Then they drank to those who had escaped and were here present, then to what, if they had to perish . . .

Altogether, it was very pleasant, warm and easy-going, and he was able to forget Siberia, the dark and cold half-hut he had rented from the solitary old-believer woman with the swarthy face, severe and taciturn, to forget his escape and anything connected with it. And although there was mention of all that at the meeting, it was in very broad and general terms, with no detail. Just this: and among us there are courageous and unbending fighters for freedom of the working class, who . . . and so on to the end.

And not many of all those present, perhaps only two or three, knew that this referred to him; and toasts were also proposed to him. They were indeed the first toasts to him and the first speeches about him. Therefore he remembered them.

Yes, yes, he had thought then. If he had to perish in exile or some damp jail, he wouldn't sell his life cheaply. He was completely suffused with that lofty sense of soaring release from everything personal and petty.

Thus are heroes born; thus are heroic deeds done, bombs thrown into moving coaches, men going to their death.

But he was not called upon to perish. The arm of the police department at that time did not stretch so far. But this circular found its way round the country, passing from hand to hand, spawning new circulars and police documents. Perhaps something of the sort was nestling in the pocket of one of those present. But he was not daunted. He could not have known of the circular of course, but that they were looking for him and had possibly nosed out his present whereabouts, he knew for a fact. That was why he was like a primed trigger – he drank, but didn't get drunk, he joked but didn't allow himself to relax totally, he was carefree, but on the alert. He was ready for anything at any second – just as he was now, thirty years on.

This sense of perpetual watchfulness gave him total freedom of choice, the right to take any decision personally and with lightning speed, see enemies anywhere, wherever they might be concealed and whatever guise they might have assumed. It was no longer even a sense; it was something more profound and subconscious, something that had seeped into his very blood and skin.

"To the gentlemen provincial governors, town governors, police chiefs, militia heads, provincial and railway police authorities, heads of secret police departments and all frontier posts . . ."

Yes, the thing had been solidly put together. A lot of work had gone into the binding. How many booklets like this had been sent out? Couldn't have been fewer than a thousand. To all frontier posts! Every railway authority! All secret police departments! No, of course not, a lot more than a thousand.

"The police department has the honour to forward herewith for the appropriate instructions . . ."

He had always liked that sort of language – precise, impersonal, liturgical, tightly buttoned. He had a perfect appreciation of its solemn brass, flowing mightily over town and country, its austere contours resembling the cut of a military uniform. In a nutshell, he loved its aura of high state. People didn't converse in that kind of language, they entered into relationships. And not people either, but uniforms and their posts of duty. In a language like that it was impossible to quibble, evade, answer vaguely or ambiguously. What a pity that nowadays nothing of the sort had been introduced into state affairs. It should be! It should! A subordinate should simply be deafened if he got anything like that from his superiors.

No, style was a great thing. In days gone by, people understood that. Being an old man himself, he understood it too.

And so: "The list of persons wanted for political reasons, the list of persons for whom search should be called off and the list of persons being sought in accordance with previous circulars, with regard to whom, on their location, it appears necessary to take appropriate measures, are indicated below."

Good. But under the booklet lay another list: "I am sending for confirmation four lists – being dealt with under the jurisdiction of the military tribunal. List number one. General. List number two. (Former military personnel). List number three. (Former NKVD staff). List number four (Wives of enemies of the people). I request sanction to condemn all of them according to the first category. Yezhov."

He had already received hundreds of such lists. Each contained thousands of names. First category was a bullet in the back of the neck. Men and women, young and old, a horrible business! But picking the lists up wasn't horrible, not the least bit. And not because he was used to it, but because: "I send for confirmation", "I request sanction", and not death, but "first category". Words, words, the language of bureaucracy!

Well, in this case, let's say, the fewer words the better. Only two or three people would read it. The others, the typist, the prison governor, the executants, they didn't count. There would be a special list for them when their time came.

But the verdicts would also be written and those would be read out at meetings like prayers. "Being an irreconcilable enemy of the Soviet system, so and so, on the instructions of the intelligence service of hostile states . . ."

That's the way it was written these days. "Being!" A newspaper editorial, one of Zaslavsky's columns! Koltsov couldn't write it that way. No, not just "irreconcilable enemies of the Soviet system", but "now unmasked as enemies of the people", that's what they should be called! Villainous murderers! Traitors to their country! Judas! So that these words were driven into their heads like nails, so that what blurted out of peoples' throats was not, say, Trotsky, but inevitably "enemy of the people. Judas Trotsky!" Not the opposition, but "a gang of political murderers!" Everyone could understand words like that.

And so: "List no 1, Persons wanted for political reasons, page 20, no 52 Djugashvili, Josif Vissarionov. (There was that language again). Not Vissarionovich, Vissarionov, the old fashioned way, as under serfdom, peasant of the village of Didi-Lilo, born 1881." Incorrect, incorrect; it was two years earlier at least, excellencies, maybe even more. They had written it down like that, to delay his conscription into the army. Still you were well aware of that. But a form is a form.

"Studied at Gori Theological Seminary." Correct. They had forgotten to add that he had been expelled in 1899 for revolutionary activity. "Bachelor". Correct. That wasn't the time to go courting! "Father Vissarion Ivanovich", by profession shoemaker, present whereabouts unknown. Correct. Whereabouts unknown to you! And to me to this day. Only mother knows where he is and try getting anything out of her! Here she is: "Mother Yekaterina, lives in the town of Gori, Tiflis province." All correct.

He got up and walked about the garden. There was a powerful scent of fading autumn grasses and fallen leaves. The smell was acrid and somehow all-pervasive. It permeated everything and was a constituent of everything – this garden, the evening sky, the grass and even himself, Josif Vissarionov Djugashvili, as had been written on the wanted notice. Because, for a brief interval, it seemed he had actually become that same wanted Djugashvili of the circular of 1 May 1904 . . .

Josif Djugashvili picked up a yellow leaf and crumbled it between his

443

fingers. When it had happened to his father, it had also been autumn. He had already been nodding off and was awoken by the low anxious calling of his mother; at once, from behind the closed door there came the rustling and whispering of many people, at first loud and excited, but nevertheless suppressed and later on quieter and quieter. He got up and wanted to go out but his mother came in quickly with a paraffin lamp in her hand. Her eyes were dry and red. She lightly pressed her hand to his forehead and said: "Sleep." Meanwhile, the people beyond the door spoke in even lower tones; then all at once something else happened. Somebody came in, or went out, and they all went out after him, mother too. In the morning, when he awoke, his father wasn't there. All his simple shoemaking gear was still there: stool, a box instead of a table, lasts, needles, waxed thread and a lump of cobbler's wax – but he wasn't there. In the morning, mother said: "There's just the two of us now. Father's gone away." "Where to?" he had asked. "Baku," she replied, "and maybe a bit further on after that." "When's he coming back?" he had asked. "When he can, he will," his mother had snapped. "In the meantime there's just you and me . . . But don't tell anyone." "Why?" he had asked. She wanted to say something but suddenly slapped him lightly across the back of the neck. Not a blow, she simply drew her hand swiftly down across his hair. "I told you, no talking about it." He said nothing and looked at her. "Well, last night there was a big fight," she explained reluctantly. "Somebody stabbed another man with a knife. Who did it isn't known. Your father was on bad terms with the dead man and had threatened to kill him. Well, so that man was killed and your father has to run away, otherwise he'll be killed as well. And our house will be sealed by the police and we'll be thrown out into the street . . . You understand, yes?" He understood. When they talked like that to him at home, he understood. He had realized something else of late – something was certainly going to happen to his father. In recent days something dark, heavy and unspoken had been looming almost tangibly in their house, something unpronounceable in front of him. Up till then they had lived like anyone else, now there was either shouting or they spoke in whispers, or said nothing at all. Up till then his father had often come home merry, and mother had poked him in the face with a bottle: "Go on, eat that! It's what you love best of all!" But now he came home once absolutely sober and as soon as mother opened the door for him, he hit her across the face. Then he snatched up a curved cobbler's knife and advanced on her brandishing it about. "Now," he said, "remember there's never been a case in our family yet . . ." But mother had shouted out and rushed into the house, and he went away. He only came back, drunk, when it was nearly morning. Mother hadn't scolded him. A period of silence ensued. Nobody spoke to anyone else. Mother got him his breakfast, replied to one or two questions and stared at him calmly and rather grimly. After that things went their usual course. But he knew by now that something was bound to happen to father soon. Since that time, a secret had descended on their house. That is, a silence. He sensed this secret almost physically. It prevented him from breathing freely, taking an interest in things going on around him, sitting at the same desk as his pals, running out at break time. At first, all this oppressed him dreadfully: nothing said about himself or his parents, nobody invited to the house, and going nowhere out of it. His pals, too, regarded him rather oddly and he thought they were whispering among themselves. There was one lanky individual who used to grin as he passed, and there was even a fight between them once; at that however, the religious master, the tall young David Egnatoshvili, who taught homiletics, stepped in and although it was he who had struck the first blow, the teacher, without making any enquiries, went straight to the tall lad and taking him by the shoulder, shook him back and forth before leading him away. Afterwards he came back and said quietly: "Djugashvili." In the room to which he was taken, two teachers were sitting. The elder one said kindly to him: "Now surely you can't believe what a fool like that tells you? You never know what he's going to blurt out! You're a good student, go and get on with your work, if anyone starts getting at you again, tell me. Is that understood?" "They won't get on to him," replied David on his behalf, and smiled meaningly. And in fact, ever since then, no one did get at him. As time went by, the secret grew lighter, almost weightless. At the seminary, he so grew to live with it, so domesticated it that he soon created his own special world, one belonging only to him. His behaviour was almost the same to others, but there in his own world, everything obeyed him and him alone; there he was the one who mattered, handsome, successful, adroit and clever. He already knew the Russian word "wise" but was not aware of its nuances; for him, a sage was always an old man. He was never handsome. And when he was passing from this world to that, to his mother, the college, his pals, he was aware of it, in a perfectly calm, commonsense fashion. No, never a pretty boy, never a fancy rider, but he had no need to be. And so the secret not only began to fence him off from the world and its annoyances, but to raise him above them. He was unique and realized it. "Mother Yekaterina lives in the town of Gori." Yes, even afterwards she wouldn't move for anything. But at that time, thirty-three years ago, she had still been young and good looking. The last time they had met had been a month prior to his arrest. Later, after the bank robbery, she had been visited and questioned, on the assumption that he might be hiding out with relatives or neighbours. They had asked her about that and she had answered in the proper way; that is, she told them nothing. So they left empty-handed. He had heard about that from other people. Bravo mother! Flint and steel! What a good thing it was that he turned out like her and not his father. He'd have perished like his father and that would have been that.

"On the basis of the highest instruction, 9 May 1903, for state crime exiled to Eastern Siberia, under the open surveillance of the police and settled in Balagansky district, Irkutsk province, from which he disappeared on 5 January 1904." All true, all absolutely accurate. Actually he had fled on New Year's Day, when all the men in charge were lying flat out: he collected a hunk of bread, some salt, a knife, a lump of fat bacon in a clean cloth, put them all in a bag and walked as far as the last graveyard to find a sleigh waiting for him. That was all there was to it.

"Distinguishing marks: height 5 feet 4 inches, gives the impression of an ordinary man. (Terrific! that was when the police realized that he was a special individual and only "gave the impression" of an ordinary man). Hair on the head dark chestnut, moustache and beard chestnut." Yes it had darkened over the years. Darker. His mother, now, had been a real redhead. "The hair appears straight (a scholar – it was clear at once that this had been written by a fusspot of a clerk) without parting, eyes dark hazel, set of the head normal, forehead straight, not high, nose straight, long, face long, swarthy, pockmarked from smallpox." (Here he smiled, recalling Gorky's flat where the Leader had famously met the literary men; one old fool had been deeply moved and began wailing to him: 'We're really under the thumb of Glavlit and the editors. You have pockmarks on your face, Josif Vissarionovich, but we mustn't write about them, must we?' the old idiot had bleated.)

"On the right side of the lower jaw there is a missing molar. The mouth is average, the chin pointed, voice quiet, ears of medium size; on the left foot, the second and third toes have grown together." Correct. All true. They really had grown together. "The mark of Antichrist," as somebody in the seminary had told him. This had appealed to him at the time. But now it couldn't be said; now it was slander, a lie; he was perfect in all things – no pockmarks, no missing teeth or grown-together toes.

446

All in all a pleasing document. He would take it over to his daughter today. Let her know there had been a time when her father had been the most ordinary of Georgians. With pockmarks and a front tooth missing, and that he had been chestnut, almost fair.

Now he noticed an adviser coming towards him on state security matters, together with a guide. He rose, gathering up his papers, and went to meet them. And the adviser saw the boss also. Jolly, kindly, smiling. He looked at the guide and that individual melted into the air.

They went over to the house, where the boss went quickly on ahead and sat down at a desk in a small office adjoining the terrace.

From time to time the Leader enjoyed moving into rooms such as this, small, cosy, opening onto the outside, with big soft settees and narrow desks (only his real office had a wide desk).

"Well now, what's he up to?" he asked, seating himself. "Incidentally, are we talking about the same one? There was a whole family of them, you know."

"I've got hold of a photo taken at the time," replied the adviser, opening the folder.

"The son gave it to you?" asked the boss, taking the photo and scanning it.

"Yes."

The son hadn't given him the photo of course, it had been taken away with other materials and should have been burnt as being of no further use, but had been preserved by some miracle. The boss was looking at it and smiling. He liked holding fragments of the world he had smashed to smithereens. The photo was, of course, one such fragment. On the wide ashen-blue passe-partout, edged with silver, two people stood and stared fixedly at the Leader of the people – a handsome young Georgian with pointed moustaches and a fabulous, delicate beauty. Behind them was jumbled the unsophisticated universe of the photographer by appointment to his imperial majesty, his name and title scrolling beneath the passe-partout, all these mirrors, potted palms, papier-mâché tree stumps, and finally a dense forest painted on canvas, with the moon above jagged heights. The young people stood absolutely rigid. The hand of the bride, holding a bouquet of lilies of the valley drooped downwards. The young man regarded the Leader with an expression of mingled savagery and helplessness. The sharp tails of his frock coat fairly assaulted the eye of the beholder. It all produced a vaguely worrying impression, at any rate not in the least appropriate to a wedding.

447

"He might be the court photographer but he was a fool," said the boss crisply. "Why all those mirrors and palms? Is it supposed to be a restaurant? Caravanserai? Brothel? Countess Panina's public assembly rooms?" He put down the photo. "Was she Russian?"

"Princess Golitsina," replied the adviser.

"Well that caps it all!" He wagged his head. "So much for our Caucasian democracy! No wonder he left the party soon after. This son is hers, is he? Yes," he repeated, deliberating. "Yes, yes, he was a handsome man. Handsome."

He knew that apart from this semi-official portrait, there would certainly be lying in the adviser's folder another snapshot, stuck onto a prison identity card; the same man would be depicted, thirty years older. Better not look at that one.

He put the portrait aside.

"Make your report," he told the adviser.

"No camp violations recorded," said the adviser. "He wasn't in the intensive regime huts. Three years ago he was medically excused on account of his heart. Last in hospital three months ago; works in the convalescent hut as senior orderly."

"Will he last the course?" enquired the Leader.

"It's not that he's all that old," responded the adviser.

The boss sat for a moment, knocking out his pipe, then said: "We recently discussed the timber and coal industries. Afterwards I called in both commissars and asked them: 'Why is your work so poor, comrades?' And they answered: 'Because we haven't got the workmen. We're stuck with this agreement with the Gulag and since they've been sending us their zeks, we've gone right down the drain; forgeries, fiddling, plain sabotage – and you can't find the culprits.' Why is it that the Gulag supplies such unsuitable material. What do you think?"

The adviser had been prepared for this conversation too.

"Well, there are a number of factors involved," he said gravely. "Firstly . . ."

"Aha, firstly!" the boss was delighted. "So to begin with it'll be firstly, then secondly, then follows thirdly, and to round it off, perhaps fourthly. But I'll say plainly, the prisoners work like prisoners, right?"

"Right," responded the adviser (so far all according to plan).

"So that must be kept in mind," Stalin raised his voice slightly and brandished his pipe. "Food, clothing, footwear, medical care, promotions. In special cases even release, so that everybody knows about it. Put notices up round all the camps, with names. He was a good worker and has been released early." He considered, then stared hard at the adviser. "In Tsarist times the official norm was three pounds of bread a day – how much do they get now?"

"We allow more nowadays," said the adviser. "For work underground, we allow meat, milk, rice even."

"Rice?" The boss was astonished. "Well, well! No," he said sadly, "we weren't given rice; at that time it was regarded as a foreign product, colonial, as they used to say then, but we didn't go hungry. You say he's old and ill? So he won't last out."

It had been explained to the adviser that the boss evidently wanted to free the old man – his close acquaintance, the witness of his role in the struggle, but along with all that, one had to be very cautious: it was forbidden to probe the thoughts of the Leader. No suggestions, no jumping to conclusions, one had to be disinterested and let it all happen of its own accord.

"Well then, what's his case about."

The adviser took a paper from his folder and held it out to the boss, but the latter merely glanced at it before handing it back.

"Agitation! So how are we going to decide though?"

Here the adviser realized that the boss wanted to release the old man, but the decision was to be foisted onto him, i.e. the Russian people. What would the people say? That was his constant position. The Leader punished nobody after all; his business was to contend for the happiness of the people, responsibility for all the rest was devolved by the party and the government to others: let them decide everything, they would be responsible for it. "The party," he would say to the workers of the State Security Directorate, "has entrusted you with the brunt of the work and done everything to help you to carry it out. If there is anything else you need, ask and we shall give it. But work! Spare neither brain nor strength!" All of this was repeated hundreds of times and only a handful of people in the Central Committee or the very highest reaches of the people's commissariat knew how specific, precise and definite all the Leader's instructions were: take, isolate, destroy or, as he would write in his resolutions, "act according to the law". Simple lists of those condemned to death, signed by three politburo members were sent round; these were called "first category sentences". And of course, not a single scream, not one letter from the internal prisons or death cells reached the Leader. The fact that Beria had given the Leader one such letter the day before had been an absolutely extraordinary event. This the adviser understood.

"He confessed his guilt in full," said the adviser.

"I'm not talking about that," scowled the boss. "Guilt, guilt! He's a Menshevik, that's what he's guilty of. But what do the GPU think (he always referred to the security organs this way) – can he be released or not? Can we, for example, can we solicit the presidium of the VTsIK regarding a pardon? What do you reckon?"

"Certainly!"

The Leader was silent.

"Do you give instruction that such a petition be prepared, comrade Stalin?"

The Leader was silent.

"Yes," he brought out at length. "Prepare a petition then. But how are we, I for example, to apply to the VTsIK? On what legal basis? I'm not an autocrat after all, not emperor of all Russia; he could execute, pardon, anything he liked – I can't. Above me stands the law! What does it matter that this Kalandarashvili is a good man? To the Soviet system he's bad! That's what matters!"

The adviser said nothing. He realized he had spoiled everything; he hadn't even had time to be terrified, he simply felt his nose contract.

"Our comrades," the Leader went on methodically, eyeing the adviser didactically, "acknowledged him to be socially dangerous. I have no right to disbelieve them. The decision to isolate socially dangerous elements temporarily was taken by the politburo and confirmed by the VTsIK. So on what grounds are we to alter it?"

"The old man's had it now, and so have I, damned fool," the adviser decided. "And his son, and the camp commandant and the operations chief, all goners, the lot!"

The leader rose, paced about the room, went over to the wall and adjusted something before returning to his desk.

"On what grounds?" he asked. "I simply don't see any grounds at all?" He spread his palms briefly.

The adviser said nothing. The Leader hemmed and shook his head.

"But there again, he's ill, if he dies in jail, his sons will be angry," said the Leader, seeming to pursue this idea. "Why, his sons will say, did the Soviet system hold a sick man in prison; surely a sick man isn't an enemy? He's just a cripple. So what are we going to do, eh?" He stared hard at the adviser. "Well think, man, think!" that stare said. "Get the brain cells moving, well, well?"

The cells in the adviser's brain were spinning frantically at more than light speed. Everything around him hummed and whistled. The Leader

450

watched and waited, but nothing occurred to him. Then suddenly the Leader smiled craftily, winked slightly and lightly stroked the left side of his field shirt. Then a blinding light dawned on the adviser.

"It's possible to get by without the VTsIK," he said.

"And just how can that be done?" The Leader raised his eyebrows. "Just leave them out? Is that it?"

But the adviser had his fire-bird firmly by the tail and had no intention of letting it go. He ran his tongue round his parched gums.

"Very simply," he said methodically, quite unhurried. "According to the UPK, a sick man who cannot be cured in detention, may be released from his sentence according to article 458. Here!" He commenced rummaging in the folder.

"Don't bother," the boss raised a gracious hand. "I believe you. Yes, yes, I've remembered, we do have an article like that. And a very good thing too." He got to his feet, approached the adviser and touched him amiably on the shoulder. "You see how it can come in useful. So then, we must release Georgi Matveevich Kalandarashvili, as the humane Soviet law demands. Let's go and have a wander round the garden. Isn't it lovely and sunny!"

The office was vast and bright, with pink curtains the colour of the dawn, potted palms and leather-covered furniture. When she entered, there were already a number of people assembled. The deputy peoples' commissar himself was sitting at the desk; a rounded, swarthy-faced man of indeterminate years, wearing horn-rimmed glasses. Perhaps it was something about his powerful sparkling teeth and smile that reminded one of a Japanese. Some distance away, at two other tables at an angle, sat a woman in military uniform, with a red folder next to her, and a tall clear-eyed young man with a handsome long aristocratic face, and fair hair brushed back. He looked like a poet or a philosopher. His briefcase, packed and bulging, lay on a separate table.

The deputy commissar was smiling as he talked to someone on the telephone. On seeing them come in, he said something quickly and hung up the receiver.

"What's keeping them so long then?" asked Shtern, displeased. "Two hours gone already, and he's supposed to ring."

"They've finished sorting him out, but they ring to say they can't find a proper suit. I told them to put Schneider on the job."

"Yes, the suit has to fit well," Shtern put in gravely. "He might be seen personally."

"I have that in mind," nodded the deputy commissar. "Still it's all right, Schneider will see it through. He's a wizard, that man. Right! And this, if I mistake me not, is our new colleague . . . the niece of our dear . . ."

"And mine too," pointed out Shtern, unsmiling, just as seriously. "Mine just as much as his."

"Well, very pleased to meet you." The deputy got up from the desk and respectfully introduced himself, pressing her hand.

"Very pleased," he repeated. "I can tell you in all honesty that this is a good place to work. We're straightforward friendly folk. Staff morale is strong, lots of young people, sportsmen, climbers; there's a school of western dancing. And it seems you," he glanced at Shtern, "trained to be an actress?"

"Graduated," Shtern answered for her.

"Listen, you're a treasure for us! A real find!" The deputy commissar seemed somewhat surprised. "My wife has been working in the drama group for over two years. You know? We got second prize in the republic competition.

"Only second! So you've missed out on going to Moscow again," Shtern laughed.

There was a timid knock at the door.

"Try the handle," said the deputy commissar.

A very young and beautiful woman, almost a girl, came in, carrying a black box. She was wearing a white overall and resembled one of Levitan's autumn birch trees. The young man stood up and swiftly went over to her.

"Thank you," he said, taking the box. "I'll be back shortly, Shura. Have you finished? Go straight home then."

The birch tree gave a covert nod in the direction of his briefcase. He returned the nod. She smiled and went out.

"What's this then?" Shtern asked, indicating the box.

"It's an instrument bought with foreign currency," replied the young man. "It measures blood pressure."

"Why?"

"So I know in advance whether you're going to have a heart attack or not."

"I will! I most certainly will," sighed Shtern gravely. "Another year or two of this work . . ."

"I have to have a little talk with you, Roman Lvovich," said the young man gently. "The fact is, my wife is a haematologist . . . and she has a suggestion . . ." He went over to the briefcase.

452

"No, I'm not taking anything," Shtern cut him off harshly. "I'm not even supposed to be taking anything at the moment. I'm going to Moscow tomorrow."

But the young man appeared not to have heard him. He went over to the table, opened the briefcase and took out a substantial bound manuscript. He extracted a beautifully typed sheet of some dozen lines, which was lying separately on the top.

"Just have a glance at that," he said, with gentle insistence.

Shtern peevishly took the sheet from his hand, read something, then glanced at the young man, grinned sarcastically and gave the sheet to Tamara.

"Open my briefcase and stick it in there," he said and once again glanced at the young man – this time in rather a different fashion.

"All right. I'll take it. Apparently you . . ."

There came another knock at the door.

The old man was brought in.

He was tall and very thin, but the commissariat tailor, Schneider, had indeed proved a wonder-working wizard: the suit was an excellent fit and the tie was also an excellent match – bright and floral, as the taste was in those days. The collar too, lilac-fresh, and the cuffs with the malachite studs – everything was all of a piece. The deputy commissar advanced and offered the old man his hand. Shtern hung back.

"Sit down, please, Georgi Matveevich," said the deputy commissar, with grave cordiality. "I'm glad to meet you. We are always pleased when someone is released, but in this case . . ."

"Thank you," replied the old man, sinking into a chair, and bowing his head briefly.

She, Tamara Georgievna Dolidze, investigator of the first secret political department (ideological diversion), stared fixedly at the old man. These were probably the first steps he had taken without a guard in many a long year. And he had just come in, sat down, as he was sitting now, his hands on the chair arms. He was very bony. His bones were broad. There were dark depressions at his temples and his face was dark too. After a while, she noticed that he was stoop-shouldered, and when he half rose, she observed that he looked like a dark skinny camel with one hump – the sort she had seen once from a train crossing the Hungry Steppe.

"How are you feeling?" asked the deputy commissar. "Well, that's fine! That suit fits you like a glove. At this point we have to go through certain formalities, Georgi Matveevich. You'll get your identity card for a start, after all, you're going to Moscow. Here you see the people dealing with that; our doctor and our head of statistical accounts, comrade Yakusheva. To be honest, I'm a spare man here, just here by accident really. Roman Lvovich now . . ."

But Shtern had already advanced with cat-like tread, gentle, kindly-disposed, rounded, utterly transparent.

"Do check all the particulars, Georgi Matveevich," he said with earnest benevolence. "It's all taken from your official file right enough, so on the face of it there shouldn't be any mistakes, still . . ."

But the old man just flicked through the document, stuck it in his pocket and signed the form.

"Thank you," he said. "It's all correct, thank you."

Shtern looked at the doctor with a meaningful smile.

"Now doctor, it's all yours," he said. "Is Georgi Matveevich fit enough to take the plane to Moscow . . . ?"

The young man approached, placed his case close at hand on the desk, and opened it up saying: "I would ask you to undo your cuffs."

Then he felt the pulse, listened to his heart and lungs. The examination went on for about five minutes, then the young man said "thank you", went over to the other desk and sat down to write.

"Well then?" Shtern asked, coming over and staring intently into his face. "Can we fly tomorrow?"

"Yes, of course," replied the young man, countering Shtern's suddenly lowering gaze with his own clear and flashing eyes. "But for now I would recommend Georgi Matveevich to take things easy. Just go and lie down. And try to sleep."

"Why's that?" enquired Shtern, without altering his look or voice. "Something to worry about?"

"No, no, the moderate noises in heart and lungs, that's just age; then the blood pressure is rather on the low side – hence the feeling of weakness, but otherwise . . ."

"Otherwise what?" Shtern asked.

"He'll have to see the doctor when he gets there of course. He would recommend a sanatorium of some kind, most likely."

"Blood transfusion not required?" Shtern stressed this.

"No, not required," the doctor smiled.

"But if it should be, there's a suitable group standing by? We have supplies?"

Shtern kept his eyes fixed on him, while the other fastened his briefcase imperturbably.

"Of course," came the simple reply.

"Good. You may go," nodded Shtern.

The doctor gathered up his box and briefcase, then bowed and left the room.

"Why did you press him like that?" asked the deputy commissar. His eyes had been on them from the start.

"That Shura who came in, was that his wife?" Shtern indicated the door.

"Yes. A nice woman, isn't she?"

"Where does she work here?"

"In the hospital. Surgical department. The patients adore her. She's so gentle, caring and kind."

"She's working on blood transfusion? Writing a thesis about it?" He swallowed some remark and turned to Kalandarashvili. "Now. dear Georgi Matveevich, you are as free as the winds that blow. Permit me to . . ."

The old man suddenly got up from his chair. He must have been extremely agitated to have interrupted the citizen chief in mid-sentence.

"I wished to make one request," he said softly, lightly pressing his hands to his chest.

"Ten if you like," Shtern granted magnanimously.

"With the greatest of pleasure, if it lies within our competence," said the deputy commissar with a faint shrug.

"I left a bag of groceries here in the commandant's office," said the old man. "I brought them from the camp. I would like to ask if they could be given to my cell-mate."

"Well, as for that," said the deputy with a slight frown, "we'll have to ask the investigator. If he has nothing . . ."

"We'll find out, we'll find out, we'll have a talk, I'll do it myself. So let me introduce you. This is my niece Tamara Georgievna. For us old men, just Tamara. Our young colleague. Graduated from the college law faculty not long ago. Yes we have people like that now, Georgi Matveevich! People like that!"

The old man bowed. Tamara offered him her hand. He brushed it with his cold, soft lips.

"Well now!" declared Shtern breezily. "Keep well, colonel. Let's go."

The old man shot a sudden glance at her. And at that moment something happened; something that had occurred before when she had had malaria. Everything shimmered and dissolved. As if someone was playing with her – playing and watching from above to see what the outcome would be. She had a strong sense of the unreality of everything that was taking place, as if she were taking part in some great performance. Everything seemed insubstantial and unreal, it all trembled and pulsated, like a sort of rainbow film, a tulle curtain or the last fretful dream before waking. And there seemed to be something else: she had only to flex herself and this flimsiest of films would tear and the real world would break through. It was only later that she realized her heart had been playing up.

"I will be grateful to you till my dying day," said the old man deferentially, addressing her too, "if you fulfil my respectful and most humble request.

"We'll help," she said. "We'll help of course."

"Well, how are you feeling?" The investigator glanced fleetingly at the zek before bending once more over the interrogation form.

Zybin sat on his usual chair by the wall and regarded her. These chairs – flat, low and narrow – were made in some camp specially for prison and investigation purposes. You could only sit on them stretched out, or with your legs drawn up. So he sat, upright and stiff, buttons cut off, but all the same he had a mettlesome look. He had even crossed his legs and was gently swinging his laceless shoe. "Just wait, hero, just wait," she thought, as she asked: "So you've thought over carefully what we talked about last time?"

"But of course!" he exclaimed.

"Splendid! We can get to work." She swiftly filled in the form and laid aside her pen. "And afterwards I will give you a pleasant little surprise."

"Is that from the citizen prosecutor?" He grinned sarcastically. "If so why wait till the end, beat me up now. A makeweight to the old charge – drank, womanized, used foul language, made vulgar remarks about the Soviet system, something out of that opera, is that it?"

"Well I think there's enough of that without me taking a hand. Enough to fill a book," she fingered the case folder. "No, it was just that I had to have a talk with your friend, Grandpa Sereda. I took a great liking to him."

"Grandpa is a treasure," Zybin assented readily. "Manufactured, as he puts it, in 1870. So he's the same age as someone else we know! So what did he testify about me?"

"Well, what he testified we'll leave for the proper time. But he brought a bundle of oportos and lemons for you. And who you drank, womanized or used foul language with, Georgi Nikolaevich, is the least of my concerns. Just explain something else to me, please. On the day of your arrest, suddenly, at seven in the morning, you set off for the Ili, where you were pulled in. What was the purpose of your trip? What were you after on the Ili?"

He shrugged slightly.

"Oh, nothing special," he answered lightly. "I went to get a bit of air, swim and laze about in the sun."

She smiled.

"Oh yes, sand! I've been there, Georgi Nikolaevich, and seen it. There's nowhere to swim or laze in the sun, there's nothing but flints and sharp stones. The banks look as if they'd been hacked out of the rock. So no, you couldn't have lain about."

"You wouldn't, Tamara Georgievna, but I . . ." he answered sweetly.

"Nor would you. Very well. I'm writing the question down: Explain to the investigation, to what end did you travel to the Ili on the day of your arrest."

"Well what about it, is it a crime to go to the Ili on my day off?" He frowned. "If you're so well-informed about everything, then you know who I went with. Write it down: Wanted to relax, have a pleasant time. I was fed up to here with museum affairs, so I arranged things with a young colleague and went away with her on my day off. Does that suit you?"

"I'm writing it down!" She wrote out his reply and then put down her pen. "It would all suit us except for one thing. It was just the wrong time for you to decide to have a pleasant time, as you put it. Excuse me, but at this point I have to touch upon matters of an intimate nature, but . . . All that day you had been rushing about, ringing up every ten minutes, you were summoned to the CID about the missing gold; you kicked up a fuss there because you were being delayed, missing meeting someone; you finally got out of there, rushed off to the park and telephoned, and didn't get through! You came home to find your Lina with that colleague of yours. An hour later they left, you saw them home, came back and went to bed. That was that. Then suddenly, the next morning, you tear off, arrange to meet this girl Clara by telephone, tell

457

her some kind of tale and race away to the Ili. How can you explain all that?" He made no reply. "Well, I'm waiting. Say on."

He suddenly smiled mischievously, even seeming to wink at her.

"Well what's there to say? No doubt you've guessed it all for yourself! Man is sinful."

"This is no time for jokes," she said sternly, rejecting his smile. "Speak and I'll write it down. Of what do you confess yourself guilty?"

"Of wanting to get away with it on the quiet. Stands to reason. My loved one had arrived. And the little girl's eyes are red, her nose all swollen. What could I do? There would be a row. So I thought and decided: the next day, before I saw Lina again. I would take the girl away to the Ili on whatever pretext and have a heart to heart talk with her. At least I would find out what was on her mind and what I could expect her to do. In town she could have run off and done something silly and made a big song and dance about it. Out there, what can you do and where can you run off to? It's desert country. So I told her that there was an official job on, named the time of departure, she agreed and we went."

"Logical," she thought. "There goes your trump card!" The thing was, there was no budging him from this tale. What a fool she'd been! She'd made a good start on this tack, then made a mess of the whole thing! Well, she still had one winning card and she tossed it onto the table at once.

"Well then, let's say I believe you," she said. "We'll leave the women in peace. But again there's something odd. First of all you appeared at the farm office and started asking for various people. What people? Why? Then there's the personal search record: four bottles of point five Russian vodka, a bottle of Riesling, an 850-gram sausage, a loaf of bread 700 grams, a couple of tins of bullheads in tomato juice – a decent spread, eh? How do you explain that? Surely you didn't need all that to have it out with a girl? That's for a very nice little party of five or six men. What have you got to say to that?" He made no reply. "You see, you're caught whichever way you look."

A silence ensued. He sat, head drooping, brooding over something. ("They know nothing and don't suspect anything and haven't found anybody either of course. That's good, stick it out, boy! They don't seem to have anything left up their sleeve either. But we'll find out in a minute.")

"Yes," he said heavily, "indeed I will have to talk. Have to!"

She got up and moved towards him.

458

"You must, you must," she said, urging him in plain friendly fashion, even touching his shoulder. "You'll see, it'll be better, believe me."

He spread his hands.

"Well, I suppose I'll have to believe you. Nothing for it. Yes, of course you're not Khripushin! Well, you have the right of it. I did contemplate it!" He stopped, raised his head and declared: "I contemplated a grave crime against socialist property. The decree of 7 August – state and public property is sacred and inviolate. I wanted to incite the collective farmers to steal state property. Not in the books, not even identified, but all the same it's ten years without amnesty – devil that you are!"

He fell silent again and hung his head.

"Yes, go on, go on!" She raised her voice. "You wanted to grab the gold and . . . go on then!"

He knit his brows.

"No, no, what the hell gold are you talking about? Where does that come into it? I wanted to buy marinka on the sly from the fishermen – about five kilos, that was it!"

"What marinka is this?" She was outraged. "You're pulling my leg!"

"I'm not pulling your leg! Ordinary marinka. They catch it there and smoke it. It only breeds in the Ili. I wanted to exchange some of it for the vodka. I dropped into the office, tried to find out where things were and got nowhere. There was a woman sat there like a lump of wood. So what will it be? An attempt is it, or preparation for one? Is it a 19 or a 17? There's a big difference in length of sentence."

"Wait a minute," she said. Something ludicrous was going on here, but she couldn't quite put her finger on it. Had he confessed or was he wriggling out of it again? "Marinka? What did you want marinka for? On the day of the arrival . . ."

"The day of the arrival, exactly! Exactly!" he exclaimed. "It was to be a lovely, touching present, so to speak, not only from the heart but the memory as well. Oh the memory of the heart! Lina and I used to go fishing together, you see. We bought an extraordinary crab from a fisherman. I don't know whether that would be regarded as state property, but there was no such decree in force then I believe. So I intended to get the fishermen drunk and grab the fish. Property of the state. I have revealed a criminal design. Write it down, I confess. Ten years of strict isolation with confiscation of property, and without amnesty! Oh yes, I ate a fish on the Ili and shared it with others! Write it down."

*   *   *

Gulyaev read the interrogation record, pushed it to one side and said: "Yes!" Then again, "Ye-es!" Then he smiled and asked: "Why aren't you smoking then? Please do, go on. There's an ashtray, go ahead."

"No, no, I . . ." she was somewhat flustered. "There's only one question and answer. He asked me to cut short the interrogation. He found it hard to speak. He was almost in tears."

"Bad as that? Go ahead, do smoke." She took out her papirosi, because he was already holding his lighter. "Well then, as he's confessed, we can send the case to court."

"You think we can send it straight to court?"

"Well naturally. If we have a confession, we send it to the district people's court of the place of residence."

"People's court?" She thought Gulyaev had made a slip of the tongue. Within these walls, in this office, with this man, the words "people's court" was almost a joke, like a quotation from the works of Mikhail Zoshchenko, where it occurred alongside other similarly amusing words: "policeman", "moonshiner", "department", "pickpocket", "cut off his pocket-watch", "my dear citizens". She looked so upset that Gulyaev shot a glance at her and burst out laughing.

"Now what are you looking like that for? Where else can we send a case about marinka fish? It wouldn't get to a provincial court. The material is on the trivial side. I mean it isn't the theft itself, is it, or even an attempt at theft, it was the int-en-tion! That's how you have it: 'the exposure of a design'. In connection with other crimes it isn't punishable. It's another thing altogether here of course – the 7 August decree, one, the personality of the prisoner, two – so they'll try him, and that's in the lap of the gods."

"And the SB?" she asked, despairing.

"The SB! Come now, the SB has nothing to do with this at all. It doesn't deal with larceny. You can't attach a package to this."

"Why not?" It was almost a shout.

"How can it be done? Attach to what? Inside the package is a memorandum, but 7 August is an open crime, an economic crime. There can't be any secret about that. Therefore the official in Moscow wouldn't unseal our package at all. He'd glance at the heading and return it 'we do not deal with such matters. Send it to the court'. And that would be it."

"And that would be it," she repeated inanely.

"Down to the last kopeck, Tamara Georgievna. And you know what would happen? Zybin would get away from us! Like the round loaf in the fairy tale. Such cases are the province either of the prosecutor's office or, at a very great pinch, the economic-counter-revolutionary department – ECD, and we are the SPD, the secret-political. They say truly that politics and economics are indivisible, but that doesn't apply to us." He smiled, and ran his thin little hand first across his pinched, but sharp marmoset's face, then through his beautiful, swept-back raven hair. "So the case goes to the district court, and he goes to Tashkent Avenue to the common prison. That's clearly the limit of his ambition now."

"And the court?"

"The court will try him according to the criminal code. You've been to district courts? Well, did you enjoy it? Total democracy. The hearings are public, with both sides represented. The lawyer speaks and calls witnesses. So he'll call them: the director, Grandpa, Kornilov, that little creature he went to get the fish with; the court will summon them all. And what will be the upshot? He's on top of his work, no squandering or theft. On the contrary, he has a diploma for the conduct of the inventory as well as for bringing to light and identifying valuable arte-facts. There was something about it in *Kazakhstan Pravda*. He'll put all that on the table of course and the witnesses will testify accordingly – they won't be intimidated there, different atmosphere altogether! So what's left? Intention. The intention of unlawfully obtaining fish from fishermen. And he'll say: "No, I was going to get them through the farm office and went over there to find out if there was any fish available in the first place. From whom, individually, did I intend to acquire the fish? Where are these people? I've never set eyes on them. They don't even exist. You, he'll say, have questioned the shopkeeper, whom I saw. She says I mentioned certain names but she can't remember them. Citizen judges, if those people had actually been members of the collec-tive, why couldn't she have remembered them? Is that not logical? Of course she would recall them. I rest my case."

"They wouldn't find him innocent would they?"

"Not impossible! We'll be trying to get them to slip him five years or so in any case, but it's not beyond the bounds of possibility that they'll find him innocent. Because of the absence of a *corpus delicti*. Or they might send it for further enquiries, and he'll walk out of there. All right, suppose they don't find him innocent, and stick five years on him. He'll start writing from the colony, his relations will start running about – it's a public case after all – and in a couple of years he'll be free, and might easily meet and hail you in the street. Why the surprise? We are the only irrefutable people, all the rest . . . Democracy, you know!" he waved a hand and laughed. "So he could quite easily say hello. They say he's a courteous chap, is that right?"

"That's not going to happen!" She jumped up from her chair. "I swear by my head and honour, it will never be! May I go?"

"No!" He smiled, rose and coming over to her, hugged her lightly as of old. "Dear me! Worked up and seething already, there's Caucasian blood for you. Sit down, sit down, I tell you." He pressed a button to call his secretary and ordered two glasses of tea. "He's a crafty animal, this Zybin! Either there's nothing in this, or he's . . . I don't know, don't know."

"You think there might be nothing in it?"

He shot her a swift, stern glance.

"I might think there's nothing in it, but you don't have that right. If I've handed him over to you, it means that he's certainly guilty. That's the way you have to think. And another thing: whoever's sat in our chair will never sit on any other, that's two. And thirdly, since you're working here, you can't allow yourself to think a mistake possible."

"And you can allow yourself that idea?"

"Certainly," he smiled, kindly and straightforward. "How could it be otherwise? How otherwise can I check your work, girl? How will I know what any one of you is worth to me? Or move people about? If I didn't have doubts, I couldn't move a step. I have to know everything. Everything as it really is of course."

"Everything?" she queried. And it suddenly occurred to her that Gulyaev was drunk. "Really?" she wondered, peering at his clear, bright eyes. He caught her glance and laughed.

"Everything, girl, all and everything!" he said with breezy swiftness. "That's why I'm the chief. The authorities know everything, don't they. And here's the tea. Take your glass and let's sit and chat and have a think. You finished up with his confession. You know what, let's try it this way . . ."

"So then," she said. "We finished with your confession. Decree of 7 August. Ten years without amnesty." He stared at her mutely. "Right? Watch." She took the record out of the folder, folded it neatly in two, then four and slowly and delicately (he watched) tore it up over the ashtray. "And now I'm going to ask you," she went on, "whether or not we've had enough of all this? Enough of thinking you're the only

462

intelligent person here and all the rest are idiots, right? Otherwise I'll send you to the punishment cell as I promised. For obstructing the investigation. This minute. How does that strike you?"

"This minute?" he asked.

"Yes, straight off, direct from this chair. For five days."

"Five days?" he queried again. "Well, so be it. At least I'll get my sleep out there."

"For five days will you? Of course you'll sleep and do a bit of thinking; and if you don't come up with anything, we'll continue with another five, and another."

"That makes fifteen," he summed up. "Half a month. Yes that's impressive. Will you permit one question? I'll go to the punishment cell, but where will you go?"

"What do you mean?" she asked, astonished. "I'll remain here."

"Here in this very office? That can hardly be. What on earth will you do here? Read books? This is the situation: each of you has only got one zek. Just one! There aren't enough of you for more. You and he are practically one creature. You sit on his bones and squeeze out his soul drop by drop. A month, two, three! And you can't possibly take on two. That would be half a horse power's work. And you can't haul two horses through on your conveyor. The machine can't cope. We'll suppose the first five days go easily. The boss signs everything for you, but come the next five, he's going to call you in and say sweetly: "Now then, girl, have you come here to enjoy yourself or what? The zek's in the punishment cell and you're sitting reading a clutch of novels. Why did we get rid of Khripushin then? At least he worked, but what about you? And that will be the finish of your career as an investigator, Lieutenant Dolidze."

"That's some imagination you have," she shook her head. "Where does it all come from? I shall just take up some minor matter, some moonshiner, and finish him off in excellent style in half a month."

"You don't have any minor matters! You haven't! No vodka distillers either. All you have is us, enemies of the people, rabid dogs of the bourgeoisie. And there are so many of us that we'll soon be squatting on top of one another in here. The priests say that's how sinners sit in hell. So they're not going to let you put your feet up. I'll simply come along and pepper you with foul language while your supervisor's standing there. Well, and what will you do? I of course will get a booting right away – your gallant knights are always at hand . . . but you'll be sent along to accounts/statistics, to Major Sofochka Yakusheva to fill

463

in cards. I used to know old Sofochka, I was at school with her once; very prim and proper girl, squeaky clean, a mother's girl. Or they'll put you on operations, which means you'll go on students' picnics, write reports, why not? You look the part – attractive, intelligent recruits are in great demand over there! They've been taking on lorry drivers and farm girls. That's what'll happen to us. We'll give it a try if you like."

His voice was measured and composed. It was evident that all this had been thought through long ago. "I was wrong to get mixed up in this, maybe I should go off sick?" flashed across her mind, but it was only a passing thought, she couldn't really have refused. But nor was she able to flare up, get angry and feel she was mistress of the situation either. Something quite other came to her instead – a cold, vexed irritation at herself. After all, if this rascal had the spirit to do what he promised . . .

"Surely it hasn't slipped your memory," she said provocatively, "that people don't get out of this place. I'm only a small cog in here, if I wasn't here it would be someone else. I can neither help nor harm you. You should realize that at least."

"I should, I should," he assented, "and of course I do realize it. Thank you for being open and truthful about that at least. It's just that I don't want to accept this truth of yours, no, not in any way. That is the point, Lieutenant Dolidze!"

"Truth?" It was here that she became really aroused at last. But it wasn't animosity against him, it was a sense of profound contempt for herself, for the role she was being compelled to play. Had she been given to him as a plaything, or what? Would she have said a single word to him of her own free will, or even gone near him? She wouldn't have had the slightest need of him. But now she did need him, oh how she needed him! More than anyone in the world! He was indeed a part of her. She thought of him all the time, trying to penetrate his mind, his character, his attitudes. She had never thought about anyone she loved, not even HIM, so much as about this jaunty ragamuffin.

"And just what do you know about our truth?" she asked. "Or any truth, come to that, if it doesn't affect your own hide? What do you know? A man like you."

"And what am I like, then?" he asked, very coolly. "A spy? Saboteur? Come with a mission to blow up this sweet set-up of yours. Kill the iron chekist Khripushin?"

She frowned. Things were getting back to normal bit by bit. Terrorist indeed!

464

"No, no," she said. "Hardly a terrorist. That demands scale, courage. You're just an alcoholic, or as the criminal classes say, a yob, all mouth. An intellectual yob of course. With the simple folk, it's easier, they're more honest; you're just slippery, a nasty little smarty-pants. A slob. Your trousers keep falling down, you pull them up and they slip down again . . . I know, I know – the buttons have been cut off? . . . They do that to everybody, but it's only you who go to interrogation looking like that. And your ridiculous excavations, booze-ups, bottles, girls, little jokes and funny stories, marinka! How disgusting it all is. During the Civil War people like you were put up against a wall, but now we have to mess about writing this, filling out that, as you rightly say, playing the fool . . ." She was trying to speak dispassionately, but inside everything was jangling, and her voice trembled also. She took a papirosa and lit up.

"There's just one thing I don't understand," she went on in a light conversational tone. "Why do you have to play the fool now? You really will turn up your toes. All right, say you get your way and I'm taken off the case. What happens next? There are six floors in this building. We're on the third; this is room 325. There are two people in every room like this. Does that tell you anything?"

"Yes," he replied thoughtfully, almost sadly. "Yes, six floors, room 325 . . . It says a lot, a very great deal, Lieutenant Dolidze! Last year there were five floors, the year before four, and when I came there was just a long grey two-storey building standing here. You're inflating like drowned bodies. In three years or so, they'll have to build a skyscraper. You're a wonderful institution, aren't you. You work on yourselves and for yourselves. The more you do, the more remains to be done." He grinned. "There's an old folk tale about how the heroes departed from Holy Rus. You've no doubt seen Vasnetsov's *The Heroes Set Forth*. Well, the trio of knights ride out into the steppe. They ride along, whistling, swaying a little in the saddle. Coming in their direction along the road, the verge, comes a little old man, hobbling, hobbling along – a wandering cripple, old and grey, in bast shoes; he's got this bag over his shoulder, and goes along carefully, testing out the road with his staff. How that knightly power rushed upon him! Alyosha Popovich chopped him and clove him to the brisket. And then there were two old men. Ah, you would, would you? You werewolf! Take that, and that! And then there were four old men! Then twice four, then four times four! Then all the knightly power waded in. They struck, chopped, hewed, covered in blood from head to foot, and the number of old men grew and grew.

465

And at length they closed ranks, that numberless host! How they roared! And moved forward – and the knights fled. And those others, hacked, headless, stricken and trampled, chased after them, whooping, lashing, crushing! And drove them to the Black Sea itself and the knights were turned into rocks. Do you see the point of that story? Only you won't turn into rocks, you'll be scattered like sand, dried-out dung, a handful of dust."

"You hate us then?" she asked. It was the only thing it occurred to her to say.

"You personally, you mean, Lieutenant Dolidze?" he spread his hands slightly.

She had noticed that gesture long ago. He did it when he was seeking some word he wanted and it didn't at once come. "No, I'm actually sorry for you. Yes, definitely sorry. As regards the others . . . what is there to hate, really? They're not even existence, they're a kind of non-life. They don't know what they're doing themselves. And evil spreads from them in circles across the entire world. It's they who nurtured Hitler."

"That's a new one!" she cried. "How is that then?"

"Very simple. While Lenin was alive, Hitler would have been impossible. At that time he was in jail writing his memoirs . . . While Lenin was alive, only that buffoon Mussolini could appear. But as soon as you appeared, archangels, cherubim and seraphim, as the song goes – with steel arms for wings and a throbbing engine instead of a heart – and began to hew and burn – then the western man in the street took hysterical fright and fenced himself off with a similar steel Führer. Of course, the workers' parties could still have restrained him. But you had also set them at one another's throats and such a dogfight had broken out between them that they welcomed Hitler like Jesus Christ. And when he came, war came. And now war is on our doorstep, knocking on the door, and what do we have: now you and I are sitting at different ends of this office, but when Hitler comes we'll be side by side against the wall. If you haven't deserted to the enemy by that time. But oh yes! Of course you're the sort who will. And be in charge of shooting us."

"How dare you!" she exclaimed.

"No dare about it!" he shrugged his shoulders imperturbably. "Who are you anyway? Who are your leaders? What end are you serving? I'll go up to Hitler and ask him: 'Adolf, why do you annihilate people? You organize pogroms, beat up yids, promise to wipe out half mankind; you've invented a list of clean and unclean.' And he'll answer: 'You've read my book *Mein Kampf*? It is what I promised the people, when I was a prisoner, and not yet the Führer; with that I came into the world.' And what will I say to that? Just one thing: 'How consistent you are, Führer!' 'Yes,' he'll say 'that's why I am Führer. And you're *scheisse*, a shit, go from me, shit, and don't try to stop me re-making the world the way I want to.' Very well, nothing for it. I'll go, he's right. And now I'll ask you: Comrade Stalin looms over you; does he know what you're doing here with his boots or not? Or have you perhaps got some special instruction from him? Perhaps he's ordered you to work this way himself. Perhaps he thinks it's the Stalinist road to socialism! If you say yes, I'll believe you!"

"Quiet!" she shouted and jumped up from her chair. "Be quiet immediately, otherwise . . ." She was genuinely terrified.

He smiled.

"Feeble, feeble! Short on bad language! Now Khripushin would have found a reply. But on the whole it proves my point. You can't answer one way or the other, yes or no. You know the old game: 'The lady has sent you a hundred roubles, you can buy whatever you wish, "yes" and "no" you mustn't say, black with white not take away: what will you buy?' That's what you and I are playing at the moment. We don't say yes or no, we're afraid. So as far as Hitler's concerned everything's clear and honest – he grows out of his cannibalistic theory, but where on earth have you sprung from? Who are your teachers? Anybody you care to name will shrink away from you: 'No,' he'll say, 'leave me out, I didn't spawn people like you.' So, once again, who are you? Plankton, slime on the surface of the ocean? Well, historically speaking, that's it, slime! But personally, as people, who are you? A den of thieves? A gang of criminals? Just gangsters? Fascist hirelings? Take you, for example, you certainly didn't come in here off the street; you graduated from some special law college. Of course the best in the country. Everything about you is the best. And obviously you were taught by the best teachers, professors, doctors of philosophy; that means that you spent four or five years having the study of law and the truth dinned into you, and the ways of reaching the truth. And it's very ancient, that study. It's been elaborated, tested and honed in the course of millennia. No doubt you wrote various course essays on the subject of 'The Theory of Proofs'. And so, having learned, understood and absorbed it all, you come here, sit at that desk and shout: 'If you don't sign this and that incriminating yourself immediately, I'll turn you into a frog!' That's just you. As for your redoubtable predecessor, he would have been straight into foul language and the fist on the desk: 'Tell us, prostitute, before I turn you into a cake of dogshit! Think you're on a visit to your mother-in-law do you, whore!' But the learning, where's your learning gone to? What they spent five years putting into your head? You don't need it, then – what you need is swearing and fists! So then, you and learning are incompatible. So who are you then really? Or is that a lie again, slander?"

He was noticeably emotional (she had never seen him like this), and passed a swift hand across his brow, then furtively wiped the hand on his jacket. Suddenly this touched her, for some reason.

"Would you like some water?" she asked.

He shook his head.

"Drink it, drink it." She poured him a full glass, came out from behind the desk and put the glass to his lips. His lips were dry and parched. He took the glass, fingers trembling, and drained it in one draught. She shook her head, poured another and fetched it to him. He turned her hand away and she hesitated before placing the glass on the floor next to his chair. "Now what on earth are you doing to yourself?" she said. "Why? Should I send you back to your cell?" She shook her head once more.

"No, no, I feel fine. We'll talk a bit more," he said cheerily. "You say that we are isolating socially dangerous elements. Tell me, as a girl, did you like playing with pebbles by the sea?"

"What pebbles?" she asked, irritated.

"Just ordinary ones: white, black, grey, red. Collecting, selecting, sorting them out? Some in one pile, some in another?"

She shrugged.

"Well, what of it?" she asked, lost.

"Just this; if some kind gentleman came up to you and said: 'Little girl, little girl could you give me just the light-coloured stones?' 'That's easy!' you say and you go and choose just the light stones, and throw the dark ones in the sea. 'There you are!' And the kind gentleman would say to you: 'Clever girl!' That's what you're doing now, selecting people, not pebbles. A stone doesn't change colour, though, but a man, now he's a swine, cunning, fickle. Today he's light but tomorrow he's darker than an autumn night. And the little bright-coloured ones you've got in your hand turn grey, greyer and in a couple of months they turn completely black. But that's inside, on the outside their colour stays the same. I wouldn't mind betting they get even lighter. Just remember how witnesses answer you. Whatever you ask them, they'll confirm it; whatever you ask of them, they'll oblige: someone else's life, their honour, so be it ... With supreme pleasure, even! Out of sheer devotion and eagerness to please, the sweat fairly drips off their nose! Baseness flows through every vein. Their heads are throbbing. Anything to get out of this house of death! He's out! Heavens, what happiness! I'm alive, alive! Free, free! People walking about; sun shining, wind blowing and I'm free and going home! And the fact that I've sold my best friend – well who's to blame? The state required it, so I sold him. All this is so, but why then should not he, when your turn comes, not sell you, O unrighteous and shameless judges? Oh yes, he will sell you to whomever he wishes with the very greatest of pleasure. He gave me up, like his own soul, only in the face of great terror and bitter necessity, but you he will give up with relief and rejoicing. There is a God after all, you bastards! You'll get what's coming to you! In a certain Roman tragedy a husband asks his wife: 'What crimes do you find me guilty of?' And his wife replies: 'All those I have committed for you!' It is for these crimes of yours that you'll be sold. And you'll be imprisoned and shot like lousy dogs! And it won't be just anybody doing it; it'll be your own colleagues! That hour will strike for you! It will certainly toll for you! And then you will see the face of your brother. Your brother Cain! And you will learn how many such brothers shared a table with you. And were only waiting their hour. But it will be too late. Both for you and for Cain. Yes! For Cain it will also be too late! That's the real trouble. You're defending the country? That's what you think! You're bringing forth Cains, that's what you're doing!"

"And you're not my brother Cain?"

"No, no," he replied simply. "I'm not your brother at all, so I can't be Cain. All right. I don't care about the rest, it's you I feel most sorry for."

"Us?" she asked quietly.

"No, no, to hell with the others! It's you alone I mean. Just you, Tamara Georgievna." He lifted the glass from the floor and calmly drank it all down. "Very well, I'll amuse you with a little fairy tale. The Persian emperor Cambyses had an unrighteous judge. So the emperor ordered him to be executed, flayed, the skin tanned and used to upholster the judge's chair. Then he sat the son of the executed judge on that chair and commanded him to judge. They say he did his work in exemplary fashion. Find out sometime how many skins went into that armchair of yours. After all, the normal span of an investigator of your intelligence is five years; after that it's the knacker's yard. Well what else can they do with a criminal investigator when he's done his stint?

Off with his skin and into the pit. And your commissar's there and all his henchmen. And all the department heads – all of them, every one, lying peacefully there side by side. And you're on the high road to that. And I'm sorry for you, and your youth and freshness, perhaps your soul even – everything, I'm sorry for it all! Your soul's not as vile as you've convinced yourself, Lieutenant Dolidze! It looks quite differently from what you think. It's whimsical and silly, that's the trouble! Even now you're playing a part, not conducting an investigation. You should have been an actress, not an investigator. My, my, girl! What have you got yourself into? Why? Who will weep for you? Is your father still alive?"

"But how did he find out about GITIS," she wondered, with a fleeting pang of despair, "how did he find out? But he has, so that means . . ."

She sighed and lifted the receiver to call the guard, while Zybin looked at her, wanting to say more, then suddenly saw that she was no longer there, just as there was no desk, or room with grey-yellow curtains; there was only a murky film, something smooth, lifted with a light rippling, green and black. It wavered slightly, falling and rising – white blotches flickered above him, seagulls perhaps?

"As long as I'm not sick," he thought. "There's a spittoon in the corner, have to . . ."

. . .When the zek was pierced and stricken, and went green, grisly and dead, jaw slack and limbs somehow too twisted, she abandoned the phone and rushed over to him. At this he rose, stood for a moment very steadily, then crumpled full length to the floor, absolutely rigid. A little table stood there and his temple caught it right on the corner. She cried out.

He lay motionless, a red weal swelling on his forehead. She sank to her knees and cautiously raised his head. Under her fingers one stubborn fine vein went on beating cicada-like. Her fingers at once became sticky.

In the Big House silence reigned as before; it was the night shift; there was no one on this floor besides the two of them, and she was kneeling in front of him, holding his head and repeating, softly at first, then loudly and inanely: "Oh what have I done . . . Oh what have I done . . . what have I gone and done . . ." And the receiver hung, dangling, as voices became audible within.

That was how the guard found them.

*   *   *

"And you've never once been ill?" asked Shtern. "Well, a miracle! It's a miracle that's all. Ever been in hospital even once?"

"No, no, never was," responded Kalandarashvili, then suddenly smiled as he raised his eyes to look straight at Shtern. Tamara understood the smile: "You're playing some sort of game with me, but I'm not playing with you."

They were sitting in a private room off the NKVD restaurant. This restaurant was located in the Big House itself, on the ground floor so that the windows looked out into the yard – at the long, squat building of the internal prison. At the moment, however, the prison was not visible. It was shut off by the soft gold of the curtains. This gave the office a soft quiet semi-darkness, and made everything look cosy, white and serene: tablecloth, glasses, porcelain, silver.

"Yes, but then you're a real iron man," sighed Shtern. "Not like us, Sovofficials, men of the age of Moscow Garments. It's always one thing or another with us; gastritis, colitis, bronchitis and God knows what else. But I'll tell you one thing: your camp was something special; a northern sanatorium, not a camp at all! Well, whatever it was like there – here's to you! To your courage, fortitude and buoyancy, Georgi Matveevich, to the fact that you're with us. Tamara, what about you?"

"I won't," she replied quietly.

"Nor should you, dear. No more should you! A beautiful woman shouldn't drink. But we will to you . . . Ah, that's good. Haven't had cognac like that for a long time. Still, Georgi Matveevich, what sort of a camp was it? Some sort of invalid establishment perhaps?"

"No, no," the visitor shrugged. "Why should it be? It was a camp like any other. Like all concentration camps in the Soviet Union – a compound, hut, barbed wire, fence, watchtower, sentry on it, beyond it the work area, searchlights at night. Up at seven, finish at seven. You go out in the dark and come back in the dark. Working ration, 700 grams, invalid 500, punishment, 300. That's all really. If one doesn't mention the excesses."

"And if one does?"

The old man lifted his goblet made of smoked-ruby glass with a heraldic leopard in a medallion and regarded it against the light. Then he lightly flicked the rim. The sound was gentle, mournful, a dying fall.

"It's a family piece," sighed the old man. "Venetian glass. Should be in a museum. If we are to mention excesses, Roman Lvovich, life there was extremely hard. There were mornings when you didn't know

471

if you would survive till evening. Still, you know yourself how it was."

Shtern's face at once became grim.

"Not only do I know, but this hand that raises a goblet to you, signed the indictment. All those scoundrels went before the military tribunal. So the greater part of them . . ." he lightly tapped his temple.

"Really?" The old man glanced at him. "Good."

"No doubt the camp prisoners know nothing about that," grinned Shtern. "They think they're running rest-homes now. Right?"

The old man grinned at him.

"No, no, not quite. They believe they were shot."

"And what do they say about that?"

"Oh different things. Some say they were Japanese spies, and that's why they were shot . . ."

"Terrific! Very bright! And the others?"

"The others say that they were Soviets, and they were shot for that."

Tamara couldn't resist a smothered laugh.

"Yes," agreed Shtern, also smiling. "Laughable of course ("laughable" affirmed the old man), but sad too, really, Georgi Matveevich. Surely it must have occurred to sensible mature people that the very simple reason for all those shootings was that it was an enemy diversion, not by the Japanese of course, that's silly! – but by Trotskyist gangsters, Yagoda men, Blyumkins – people who were up to their elbows in blood? Surely it must!"

"No," the old man shook his head. "That never entered anybody's head." He grinned suddenly. "Anyway, how could it? We were all diversionaries weren't we; we'd be on their side. So diversionaries had penetrated the camp to destroy their own recruits? Why? It didn't make sense."

"To stir up the people," interjected Tamara.

The old man turned to her.

"Yes, the Soviet people really needed us saboteurs. During the investigation, it was made clear to us that the people knew everything and detested us as rabid dogs and lackeys of capitalism. That was why, they said, children rejected their fathers, and wives consigned their husbands to jail. And no doubt you yourselves tell your prisoners that if it wasn't for the security organs, the people would tear them in pieces ("A good thing I didn't have time to say that," thought Tamara), no that was a puzzle! Very puzzling that was, Roman Lvovich. Our primitive zek brains just couldn't make sense of a complicated strategy like that."

"But that the authorities could lawlessly wipe out its own citizens –

that was easy to take in, was it?" Roman Lvovich shook his head bitterly. "Ah, people, people! Citizens of a great country, the creators of the five-year plan! And how gullible you are, and weak, and faint-hearted, and as soon as you get your finger jammed in a door, you're ready . . . Well, there's no denying it, I'm a man myself, I'd likely do the same!"

"Those same authorities are allowed to beat people," the old man interrupted harshly, "but are they allowed to collapse someone's lungs during investigation? Imprison a father because of his son? 'Heard-resolved' – what's that? We are lawyers, Roman Lvovich, so tell me – just what's that supposed to be? Eh?"

Shtern shrugged.

And through the office just for an instant, there passed like a ghost, a short stifling silence, filled with tension. Tamara half rose, half-filled her goblet and drank it down. Silently; swiftly precise.

"You were beaten?" asked Shtern tetchily. His favourite aria had been spoiled, before he'd even finished singing it.

"Not me," the old man shook his head with what seemed a hint of regret. "No they didn't beat me for some reason. Look, Roman Lvovich, I'm perfectly well aware that it was not the work of the Soviet system."

"Who did it then?"

"I don't know. The devil! Satan! Some madman! But one with all his wits about him. One that knows exactly what he's about. After all, what happened? There arrived . . ."

"Georgi Matveevich, my dear fellow!" Shtern implored him, placing both his fat hairy arms with the gold cufflinks to his chest. "Do we have to go through all this again? Rations, shootings, punishment cells! What's the point? There's the decanter and the food. It's my fault for starting all this nonsense. The lady here's bored stiff and has started without us. Let's both . . ."

"No, I beg you, do go on," said Tamara in tones of steel. "There arrived . . ."

The old man looked at Shtern, who sighed.

"Yes, we've forced the lady to wait, indeed we have! Here she's . . . Well, it's not very polite."

"There arrived . . ." repeated Tamara, keeping her eyes fixed on Kalandarashvili.

"Well, if you must have it . . ." the old man shrugged slightly. "A new commandant arrives at the work site. Five cars, bodyguard, retinue, women in white, civilian clothes. They've been waiting for him for a

473

week. They are working flat out. The duckboards groan as the wheel-barrows fly across them. The team-leader walks about, checking, shouting. Just as if nobody had been expecting a visit. A normal, cheery camp day. Then all at once – "Attention!" Everybody freezes. Five cars. The chief commandant climbs out of the first car and goes up to the team-leader. Greets him. Receives his report. "All right, put your cap back on! All these your eagles? Ri-ight! And how comes it, team-leader, that with eagles like these you can't fulfil the plan? Not supplying the country with timber? You're on my list of backsliders. Eh?' 'Yes, citizen commandant, I would . . . But you see . . . so on and so forth . . .' 'Ri-ight! You mean objective reasons? You're working the best you can? Who's your chief slacker.' 'There's no slackers, but that one does lag behind, it's true.' 'Really? You, what's your name, come here.' He comes up. 'You're a right one, aren't you? I've heard about you, indeed I have. What was the charge? SB? CRTA? Ah, a Trostkyist, then? Former party worker? How comes it that a former party-man neglects his duties? The authorities have given you a full opportunity to wipe out your guilt before the people; still peddling your line are you? Eh? Eh?' 'I'm ill, citizen commandant. I've a bad heart and my legs are covered in ulcers – look, see!' 'Cover them up! This isn't a museum. That's what doctors are for, looking at that. Doctor, come over here. What are you doing forcing a sick man out to work? Here he is saying he can hardly walk and you're chasing him out to work. How can that be?' And the doctor is a prisoner himself. His teeth are chattering with terror. He yelled out at once. 'He's no sick man, citizen commandant! He's a slacker! He mutilated his own legs!' "

"Yes, that's the way they damn each other," sighed Shtern gravely. "It's true, so true."

"No, no, the doctor isn't to blame either! He's got a norm to fulfil! No more than two percent off sick. That quota all goes on the criminals. They come up to him on sick parade with an axe in their hand! 'So then, you say he's a slacker. He was an enemy and still is? Yes? That's bad! All right! We'll have a word with him and convince him! Put him in the car.' And that's it. They came. They went away. A week later comes the order to all SCSs: 'So and so, previously condemned to eight years in the camps for counter-revolutionary Trotskyist activity, has been shot for sabotage.' And that's that. It can be even simpler. Two sloggers were dragging a log, and one of them strayed outside the compound by a whisker; that is, he crossed the line drawn in the earth. The guard took aim and killed him. In a flash! They're snipers! The

474

guard went on leave for two weeks; the slogger went for good. So what is that then, an order? A law? Part of the guard's instructions? Or did some madman escape from his straitjacket and start laying about him right and left? I don't know and I don't want to know. All I know is such things cannot be and yet they exist. So it must be delirium, the DTs. Not just one man though. Maybe the whole of mankind. Maybe. I don't know."

He had been speaking composedly and it was only towards the end that he became somewhat emotional. Even so, he didn't raise his voice; just his fingers betrayed a tremor. Meanwhile he himself began smiling a rigid and terrible smile.

"How on earth can he be released?" wondered Tamara. "He'll go round telling everybody, won't he? An undertaking not to talk would be pointless here."

She couldn't stay seated, and so rose, but Shtern gripped her wrist painfully and she resumed her seat.

"Of course all that's appalling," he said, "and I understand what happens to the mental state of prisoners, but . . ." The old man suddenly laughed, gently and good-naturedly.

"Allah be with them, the prisoners," he said simply. "They're enemies of the people and get what's coming to them. Do you know," he suddenly addressed Tamara, "there's probably more suicides among the civilian volunteers and the army reservists in the camps, than anywhere. And all of them are somehow motiveless, crazy."

"How do you mean motiveless?" Shtern grinned unpleasantly. "Their conscience torments them so they shoot or hang themselves. Isn't that what you want to say to us, Georgi Matveevich? Conscience!" He laughed. "You take a look at their bellies and you'll see what sort of a conscience they have! You know how much they rake in out there? Here it's not every commissar who gets in a year as much as some head of department can pull down in one summer! And you go on about conscience! You're an idealist, Georgi Matveevich, that's all I can say to you."

"No, no, I don't say it's conscience," the old man frowned slightly. "That is, no, no! It's conscience of course, but not human, some sort of wolf's conscience perhaps." He paused, getting his ideas straight. "What do you have?" he resumed. "An SCS, separate camp site. It really is isolated from everywhere else. Around it there's only forest and steppe. It's like an island in the ocean. Free people don't live there and aren't seen there, so you get two zones, one outside, the guards, one

475

internal, the zeks. Two circles of earth. Each circle has its own laws. The zeks work all day and sleep at night. Their whole existence is mapped out, get up, work, dismiss, supper, lights out, sleep, get up. That's all there is. But to live according to that timetable you have to calculate as well. Every hour, every minute, for the entire duration of your term, calculations. Because if you don't you're done for. Zagib Ivanovich will come for you, and that's the end of it! There death is masculine gender and he's called by his first name and patronymic, like a squad-leader. There's no time to be depressed, reflect, have sad thoughts or memories. That's in the inner circle. In the outer circle, though, it's a different matter – there's life there. And that also has to be worked out ten years in advance. And they do – and they work. And the work is five hundred or a thousand living corpses: where they're dragged, they have to tag along too. But these are very cunning corpses – they're vampires – they pretend to be alive; but there's a smell of dead flesh emanating from them, and on free, proud, independent Soviet citizens, a certain ptomaine poisoning begins to manifest itself. It's a very gentle, sluggish, insidious sort of poison; you hardly feel it at first – a slight nausea, giddiness, a bit dazed, a feeling of weakness, but basically everything's all right. The work – let sleeping dogs lie, there are enough women; they call them 'cheapies' almost officially, so that if you get bored, they'll console you. There's plenty of cash. For a block of tea you can get any suit in the zone. The rations are army standard, the drink's your own, drink till you burst. So they do. First in tots, then glasses, then pints. Fights every evening. They fight in silence, just snuffling; they hit each other horribly, boots in the ribs, stampings into the snow. And then on one dark night, it usually happens in the autumn or winter – emergency! A sentry has shot himself. Right on top of the tower. Took his boot off and pulled the trigger with his big toe. Skull blown to smithereens of course. Brains all over the ceiling. Motive unknown. In the morning, an assembly in the reading room. Commission of enquiry, reprimands, speeches, admissions. Didn't foresee. Didn't take into account. Didn't display vigilance. Resolved, condemned, promises made. Then a week later another emergency, this time a bit more serious. A senior lieutenant has put a bullet through his temple and left such a note on his desk that they put a match to it straight away. Another commission. A Moscow one this time – a senior lieutenant, after all! They're called in one by one, questioned and once again they're all in the dark. He was an ordinary chap, worked conscientiously, Soviet-like. Had commendations, been saving his money, showed his bankbook. Carried a photo in his wallet. Little white house on the Black Sea. He'd got that in mind. His tour of duty was coming to an end. Drank? Well who didn't? Not a lot, though. So then, there was no obvious motive. Hidden ones – well, the human heart is a dark mystery. So it was in that darkness that he had lost his way, become depressed and sought a way out. And found it. That's how it happens. Incomprehensible? That's right, of course. But as I said – it's delirium! DTs! Ptomaine poisoning!"

Tamara sat twisting the end of the tablecloth round her finger; one tug and everything would go on the floor.

"Yes!" Shtern grunted and rose from his chair. "I'll go and chase up the waiter. They want to starve us, I can see."

He left and as he passed, swiftly bent over Kalandarashvili.

"Thank you for that, Georgi Matveevich! Thank you very much! You speak most graphically. Yes indeed. Got lost in his own soul. That's good. Our writers could do with images like that. I pity our soldiers. I really do, poor souls. Thank you for your cruel humane truth. But don't let things like that trouble you any more. We'll think about them. But you're a free man! Tamara, my dear, you've gone all gloomy! Come now, pour us another full one. That's it, that's it. Cheers, Georgi Matveevich!" He set off again, but once more stayed his steps. "But don't vex your son with such questions, all right? Why do that? We're at fault, we'll answer for it. We'll deal with it ourselves. But for your truth-telling, thank you, thank you very much. That's the sort of thing we need! Right, I'm off to find the waiter."*

Neiman returned from his trip the following day in a car going his way. Prompted by obscure forebodings, he went straight to the Big House, without calling in at home. And it was as well he did so; the commissar had paid him a sudden visit. Apparently such a thing was unprecedented. The commissar never came below the fifth floor, where his secretariat was located; if the need arose, he would summon people to seventh heaven, as the staff called the penthouse where his personal office and tiny assembly hall were situated.

It was a fine autumnal evening. The commissar knocked, came in and greeted him. He was quietly good-humoured in his purple suit and bright tie.

---

* His real name was Baron Bibineishvili. He died some days after his release. (The writer Chubuk Amiradzhibi tells the story.) [Yu. D.]

"Don't get up, don't get up," he graciously insisted, "I'll just . . ." He went over to the half-open window, flung it wide and inhaled deeply. "Heavenly," he said. "No, I'll simply have to move in with you here, it's so steamy up on top there." He breathed in again. "That's good! Smells of the sea. The pines, the pines!" He stood for a moment, looking at the trees, at the looped light bulbs, red, green and dark blue along the avenues, listening to the children shouting and the creak of the merry-go-rounds. He came over and sat sideways-on to the desk. "What's that you're signing? A-a! All this blasted paperwork. More trouble than it's worth!"

These were enquiries of the second secret-political department. Camp operational chiefs were obliged by these documents to bring in a zek under their supervision and take his evidence as a witness. Most often the man they were enquiring about was still at liberty and was not only known to the one being questioned, but was either his enemy, or the friend who had given "incriminating" evidence in court or at a confrontation. It was therefore assumed that now, when the zek at last got his chance, he would be keen to settle accounts with his friend or enemy. (In this context and within these walls, both friend and enemy sounded approximately the same).

"Right," said the commissar, having listened to Neiman complaining that though lots of these enquiries were sent out, the recipients were dilatory and slipshod about filling them in. "But I see that here you've got a downright refusal. There's even a hint of malice, I would say, 'I know him as a Soviet man and a patriot'. And who took the evidence? Lieutenant Lapshin! Well, he's a fool, our lieutenant. Probably one of those just called up. Do you often get notes like this?"

Neiman shrugged.

"It does happen."

"It shouldn't happen. Have you thought why replies like this arrive? In this case for instance? Why the prisoner answered in that way? Or did the other one not give evidence against him in the first place? If so, it's not worth asking for him."

"What's eating him?" wondered Neiman. "It's a routine matter. Formalities! The man in question would go inside in any event! Why had he come at all? In civilian clothes. Yellow shoes. A tie. He always went about in uniform. Had a row with his wife, maybe?"

"No, no, he did indeed testify," he answered. "True, he didn't say anything vital, nor could he do any damage by that time. But in general you're right, comrade commissar. This witness is a repeater, a brazen, cunning type. He's been in the punishment cell twice; might have known what his answer would be."

"So it's all down to character," grinned the commissar, shifting his chair slightly. "No, stay where you are, stay where you are! One has to take character into account of course, but that's not the main thing. What matters is who does the questioning. You follow me? No? You should! Here's your enquiry to this recently called up Lapshin. He calls the zek in. Sits him down, then writes down word for word what he says. That's the form isn't it?"

Neiman gave a faint shrug. He still didn't realize what was required of him.

"Right? How else could it be? In the first place, there in the camp, Lapshin knows nothing about the case, and secondly, what the hell does it mean to him in all honesty? Now you're a directorate investigator; you live in the capital, get a decent salary, beautiful apartment, but what about him? He doesn't have any of that. And his job's different – rotten, and his pay's different, whence derives the psychology of: 'Why don't you all go to . . .' No, I have no confidence in these second-hand papers at all." He got up. "There's only one way to do it: if anything needs doing, go yourself. Arrive at the camp office, sit down in the office, demand to see the prisoner, special guard obligatory; hold him for a day on his own, let him sit there thinking it all over, then call him in. Sit him on the edge of the chair, over by the wall, and then grill him. Our style, with a bit of drive behind it, not like them out there. 'I know him as a Soviet man and a patriot'. Good lord . . . If we weren't so overloaded at the moment, I would have put a stop to all this paper-pushing long ago."

"Yes," Neiman sighed gravely, "our workload is appalling. Us old hands are bearing up all right but the young ones . . . We've already sent two off to the nerve clinic, one of them was a first-aid case right in the office."

"There you are, there you are! They're carrying our people out on stretchers, while those fellows sit out there thinking we're metropolitan loafers, filling in forms. And everything's to hand. Theatres. First screenings, apartments, showers, dachas, restaurants! While we sit out here on the steppe with the prisoners and the dogs and swill hard liquor!" He intercepted Neiman's look and concluded, scowling, "So it's us here who get all the pleasure, and they're delighted to play these dirty tricks on us. Well not all of them of course. A tiny minority, but still . . ."

"No, something's definitely happened to him," Neiman decided. "But what?"

The commissar was a metropolitan creature; he was one of the retainers, loaded down with favours, adorned with various chekist decorations and orders. He was welcome in the Kremlin, visited Kuntsevo, had been to the "near" and "far" residences, and the fact that he now found himself all of a sudden in Alma-Ata had prompted various speculations. Formally, the fact that as head of the provincial directorate he had become people's commissar of a large republic, indeed looked like a promotion, but people of course were aware that real high-flyers like him didn't swap Moscow for Alma-Ata. That meant there was something in the wind. Still, there were other opinions. It was just a case of a new broom being sent out from the capital – our work's been sub-standard so a new "iron fist" had arrived. And if this "iron fist" had started demoting people, or sacking and transferring them, all would have been plain and simple. But that was the point, he had left everything as it was, and even his speech from the throne at the general assembly had not been over-menacing.

Then they started gossiping about the commissar's wife, a cow-eyed, stout and ageing lady of eastern type. She was the younger sister of the one who had either died suddenly, or (but shh! Just you! And don't you tell anyone else, please!) had shot herself. (Shot! Of course she was shot!) So then, perhaps, in order not to prompt inconvenient associations, it was decided to send him here from Moscow?! Who knows? Perhaps that really was so. The commissar's wife, however, began making her presence felt from the outset. For a start, she drove all the EGs out of the entrance hall and into their sentry-boxes on the street. The rosy, full-cheeked lads of course set up a wail. Attempts were made to prove to her that this was unwise, against the rules. But she asked very curtly what actually EG meant? External guard? Very well then, let them guard from outside.

And so the EGs sat in their boxes, behind their little windows, while the commissar's wife, accompanied by the girl Dasha and a bearded Mordvin gardener strolled about, pruning the roses and planting out tulips. She was detested above all on account of those tulips. And especially by those nobodies who didn't even dare dream of the commissar's entrance-hall. Goodness gracious, should a progressive Soviet woman be acting in this way, the wife of a commissar who was a member of the most democratic government in the world? The example, think of the example!

480

But soon everybody calmed down. It suddenly transpired that along with the new commissar, a whole swarm of houris had fluttered into the Big House – personal secretaries (they were called sextitutes and feared like the plague), secret typists, buffet maids, waitresses in headbands and white wings at their shoulders. In a word, such valkyries and maids of the mountains fluttered throughout all seven stories that one glance was sufficient for the soldiers and young investigators to feel their trousers were on the tight side. And up in the seventh heaven, in the little tower, where eternal twilight reigned (golden curtains were hung) a new counter was installed and a blue rest-room. The commissar's wife never showed herself there and this consoled everyone mightily. She could keep her tulips! But again, people who have been dismissed don't allow themselves such things. They get hysterical, they yell blue murder, they thunder away at meetings, the screws are put on so tight, their heads are worn smooth. In a word, around the commissar, a heavily built and broad-shouldered man with coarse, straight dark hair and a strong blue-grey beard, there hovered a perpetual cloud of innuendo and puzzlement.

His work however was quick and precise. He read everything himself, and every week heard the reports of his heads of department. "Leave your paper behind," he would say after the report. "I'll have a look at it." This he actually did, as he returned them with added comments. He was highly regarded in Moscow. Swiftly, and without any additional explanations, he approved the estimates for increasing staff and the SB stopped sending cases back for further enquiries. The new commissar did not visit the provincial special prosecutors and made it hard for them to see him, fitting them in as and when. However he liked the republic prosecutor, a tall, pockmarked, easy-going alcoholic, and every season went with him to the Lake Balkhash reedbeds to hunt wild boar. Exactly like all his predecessors, the new commissar neither knew nor understood what mercy was, nor indeed plain justice; he had never gone into the matter in any depth. At one conference he had even gone on record as saying that there was an everyday sort of truth and a higher truth, an ideological one, an investigative one in the given context. This latter was the only one which was strictly binding as far as security organ staff were concerned. On the other hand, he was not fond of unnecessary twists and complications, and when, for example, Neiman had thought of setting up a big political trial with speeches, lawyers and confessions, it could have ended up quite nastily for him. His brother's timely intervention had assisted him, however, and smoothed everything over.

Nevertheless, the head of second SPD felt ill at ease. And now this abrupt friendly visit.

"Give me the case of this museum man," the commissar demanded abruptly. "Incidentally, your niece is conducting that? So how come he's got that great bump on his forehead?" ("That's all I needed! That means he's been in the prison as well," thought Neiman, aghast).

"I don't know," he responded hastily. "I haven't called in at home yet. But you must believe my niece had nothing to do with that. He'd been on a ten-day hunger strike, after all. I expect he fell and struck against the wall somehow . . ."

"Ah! Maybe that was it," the commissar acquiesced. "Right then, I've been looking through the material on this gold. It's all very mysterious, you see. This trip of Zybin's to the Ili. He called in at the farm office, talked to the shopkeeper and mentioned some names. What names? Don't we know? The shopkeeper hasn't even been called in. Why not? The girl from the museum knows absolutely nothing (oh, he's got to the girl as well, my but things are moving!). How does all this come about?"

"The shopkeeper doesn't recall the names," Neiman answered glumly. "I talked to her myself."

"Ah, doesn't remember," frowned the commissar. A straight leonine crease cut across his forehead all of a sudden. "Into a cell with her then, without any chat, let her stay there for a while, she'll remember. Go over there tomorrow and get the business finished with. Report to me personally! It's shameful, a disgrace! Doesn't remember!"

"Very good, comrade commissar." Neiman slightly inclined his head.

Now the commissar was speaking with harsh asperity, his eyes fairly blazed, like a spitting cat.

"Never mind that, just do it!" He raised his voice. "Instead of dreaming up fantasies you'd be better employed . . . We still haven't got a Hall of Soviets built yet for the sort of spectacle you propose, dear comrade chief of second SPD! We haven't got a Hall of Columns! . . . Nowhere for the criminal to confess – that's the trouble!" He brandished an arm, walked over to the window and stood with his back turned ("What on earth's got into him?" wondered Neiman). Then Neiman heard the commissar mutter a swift "bad, bad", and give out a queer sound, quite unlike anything he'd ever heard – the commissar was grinding his teeth. He stayed standing there for several seconds, grimly erect, with fists clenched, back also grimly rigid. Then he gave an abrupt sigh and subsided like a pricked balloon.

"Go over there then, go," he said, gently now, sighing as he left the window. "Put the heat on that blasted shopkeeper. Those old bags have got a devil of a memory. I was short of five kopecks once, in the tsarist time, and she reminded me after the revolution. Doesn't remember the names . . . She will!"

The phone rang. The commissar's personal secretary was looking for him through all the offices. Urgent call from Moscow. From the personal secretariat of Nikolay Ivanovich. The commissar hung up the receiver carefully and gave Neiman a very simple, almost meek glance. And at the same time, something momentous flickered for a moment in his eyes. He was about to say something, but instead turned sharply and went out.

"Goodbye, comrade commissar," Neiman shouted belatedly after him.

"Yes, yes!" returned the commissar from the doorway. "Yes, yes, au revoir! Go over to the Ili and ask, that's best. They've got a memory like . . ."

Neiman came home tired and worn out and had just set foot in the door when Nilovna came fluttering noiselessly out of the kitchen.

"Goo . . ." he began, but she pressed her hand to her lips, nodded towards Tamara's room and led him off to the kitchen.

"It's our Tamara," she whispered. "Kept talking to herself at first; I kept hearing her and thought she was on the phone, but no, she was talking to herself! And before that she'd been with Roman Lvovich in a restaurant. When she came back . . . she was swaying. He was supporting her elbow."

"Ri-ight!" Neiman quickly threw off his raincoat, picked up a comb from beneath the mirror and ran it through his hair. He had thick, wavy hair and was proud of the fact. "So then, with me out of the way they've been living it up. Very well!" He went over to her door and paused to listen. She was indeed talking about something, but he couldn't make out the words. Then he knocked and asked: "May I?"

"It's you, uncle?" she responded. "Come in, come in, you've come just at the right time, hello. There's a letter for you here from Roman Lvovich."

She got up from the ottoman, took a folder from the table, opened it and drew out a large sheet-sized envelope and held it out to Neiman. On it was written: "R. L. Shtern. Personal."

"How did you get hold of this?" Neiman was surprised and apprehensive. "Did Roman forget it? Why have you broken the seal on it then?"

"It wasn't sealed," she grinned, "it was lying in full view on your desk. So have a look."

"But why me?" Neiman exclaimed. "I'm not the least bit interested in Roman's affairs."

"Then take an interest, do," she went on in the same tone, half mocking, half contemptuous. "There's a sheet lying on the top, take a look at it . . . Oh, let me read it to you.

" '. . . The method for transfusing corpse blood is a dazzling triumph for Soviet medicine. It was first applied in the Sklifovsky Institute in 1932, and in 1937 it was permitted throughout the whole territory of the Soviet Union. Corpse blood has the following advantages as against donated blood: firstly,' – listen uncle! – 'the blood of someone who dies suddenly (she repeated: suddenly) thanks to the phenomenon of fibrogenesis, remains liquid and does not require the addition of a stabilizer.' She glanced at Neiman. He was standing listening. 'Secondly, one can obtain on average up to three litres of blood from a corpse, which permits, should the need arise, one recipient to have massive transfusions, without mixing the blood of various donors. Thirdly, as a rule, blood can only be assessed as being suitable after a post mortem. Because of changes in lungs, stomach, pancreas and liver, the blood is then rejected as unusable. Up to now, therefore, procuring this most valuable product has been a chance business and therefore it is the blood of road accident victims which has been employed for the most part. Now however, we, the directorate medical section, bearing in mind the present circumstances and the ease with which fresh corpse blood may be obtained, put forward the rationalizing proposition . . .' "

"Oh give over!" Neiman interrupted her and banged his fist on the table. "Give me that muck over here." He seized the packet and threw it onto the settee. "Good lord, the mad little fool," he swore. "Birch trees, Botticelli! What a thing to dream up, the bastards!"

"Who are you talking about?" asked Tamara.

"Well not about you, anyway," he bit back his words. "And that creeping Jesus as well . . . Ah, what wouldn't I . . . ! Give over thinking about that, otherwise you'll . . . ! Oh she's an idiot, a psychopath!! That's what she is! And Roman's a fine one, giving you a thing like that. Listen, he's not a good man, that Roman, not at all! Of course he's a brother to me and I love him, but all the same . . . he's not a good man. Hell knows what he's got in that head of his. Making himself out to be something . . . You see, in spite of everything that he has –

484

and he's accumulated plenty – he wants to stay honourable and good. He wants to be whiter than white. And what's being honourable? *The Great Soviet Encyclopaedia* hasn't reached that letter yet . . ."

"Isn't everybody like that?"

Neiman regarded her closely, then abruptly came over and took her hand.

"You know what I should do? Ring my sister for her to come out at once and take you away?" She said nothing. "Speak up then: shall I? I'll ring her right now! You know where things like this end up? In the stove. Investigator! And I like an idiot believed you could do it. The first alcoholic shit you come across and you go to pieces. You shouldn't have dropped GITIS back then. You'd be singing in operetta by now. And I was proud of you, it was me who said it: so intelligent, so intuitive! All right, you've shown your intelligence. My God," he implored suddenly. "God of Abraham, Isaac and Jacob, as my father used to say. How little it takes for people now. One push and you're down! If we were like you, where would the Soviet system be? Would you have graduated in law? You'd just have got married to some Georgian princeling, or dragged around with somebody like this Zybin: he would read you poetry and you'd applaud . . . That's more likely." He was pacing the room as he talked. Nilovna was sighing out in the corridor.

"What on earth are you saying?" cried Tamara.

"What's the matter? You don't like it? Do you think I like seeing you like this? I've got to go off again, so how on earth can I leave you in this state?"

"Go off where?"

"To whereabouts mountain to check whether the cranes have laid their eggs yet. I'm going on business. That same idiotic case. Well, how can I leave you? You're conducting the investigation, aren't you? Investigating a real enemy. It's obvious already from everything we've got that he's an enemy, but you . . . Honestly, I don't know what to do. Already the commissar's got wind of something! Good lord . . ."

She suddenly came over and hugged him, rubbing her chin along his shoulder like she used to do when she was a child.

"Now, now," she said with humble contrition, "don't be like that! Everything will be all right. It's just that the rogue goaded me to the limit."

"How, though, how?" It was a cry of despair. "Good God, how specifically could he drive you up the wall, a clever, educated woman like you. How?"

"I don't know. It wasn't so much him driving as me cracking up. In our family we're all a bit," she twisted her finger at her temple.

"Even your dad?" He grinned.

Tamara relaxed and sat down at the table again.

"Well, if he let me out of GITIS into your law college," she smiled as she furtively brushed away a tear, "it means . . ."

She approached the mirror, glanced at herself and as she walked away, instantly forgot her face.

The commandant of the SCS was being shaken by his wife, but he merely moaned and fended her off. He had taken a good deal on board at a wedding the day before, then collapsed on the hosts' bed and had to be dragged home with considerable difficulty.

"Misha. Mishenka, get up, get up!" implored his wife. "The prosecutor's arrived. He'll be here in a minute. Misha, Mishenka, it's embarrassing!"

Misha just moaned and buried his face in the pillow. Neiman came in and, gently pushing the wife aside, enquired: "Your head hurting, Misha?"

"Aha," responded Misha, without turning round.

"You want to sober up? Here, this'll do the trick."

"Well?" said Misha, stretching out a hand without turning round.

"Here, take it. Look, turn round, turn round! Come on, come on!"

"Come on, come on? you know what that choked on in Moscow?" Misha asked breezily all of a sudden. "Who are you?"

The wife came in and poured a jug of water over the commandant. He jerked up at once, roaring: "I'll murder you, bitch!" But then he saw Neiman with a glass in his hand.

"Give it here," he commanded.

The other held it away from him.

"Just one second! The shopkeeper Glafira works for you?"

"I'm going to kill her too, the bitch," said the commandant calmly, and sat up in bed. His eyes were red, like a rabbit. "She sells vodka to the prisoners. Not having that. I'll kill her and won't answer for it. What are you displaying that for like . . . give it here!"

He thrust out his hand again but Neiman again withdrew the glass, before asking: "Is it her shift today?"

"She'll be here shortly," said the wife. "She's delivering."

The commandant was still sitting looking at Neiman, then something dawned on him. He suddenly got to his feet, wrapped a blanket round him and left the room in silence. His walk was almost sober.

"Excuse me," he called out from the corridor.

An awkward pause ensued. The wife pulled a chair to her and sat down. She looked at the floor, then at Neiman. He too got a chair and sat. And so they sat opposite one another. "Just as if he had mounted a guard on me, the sod," thought Neiman and said: "May I ask you for a glass of water?"

"Yes," she replied, but made no move.

"You bitch!" thought Neiman again. "There's a glass of vodka there, should I drink that?"

"It's so hot out here," he said. "So much dust in the car, it gets in your teeth."

She looked at the floor, then at him, and said nothing.

The commandant entered, by now in uniform.

"Excuse me," he said harshly. "I got to bed late last night. Work. Are you here on business?"

"Not a social call, of course," replied Neiman. "I have to interrogate a witness."

"Your papers?" scowled the commandant.

"So, it's documents straight away is it?" Neiman smiled, handing over his official identification. The commandant gave them a glance and returned them.

"I'm sorry," he said morosely. "Yesterday we had a bit of . . ."

"A domestic matter," Neiman waved this graciously away. "My business is with the shopkeeper."

"We've got three of them. Oh yes, you want Glafira; I'll call her in directly."

"Have you got a free room anywhere?"

"As many as you like," smiled the commandant. "We'll invite her in," and reached for the telephone.

Everything turned out predictably. The shopkeeper, Glafira Ivanovna, a plump, white-faced woman of about thirty-five, very reminiscent of Kustodiev's merchant wives, looked at him in alarm, gesturing helplessly, as she whimpered and even tried to cry, but she couldn't remember anything. "You could have lied at least, stupid," he thought towards the end. "Blurted out the first names to come into your head; I'd have noted them and gone away. There'd have been trouble later of course, but I'd have wriggled out of it somehow. She just doesn't realize, the idiot." And the idiot really didn't realize; she just goggled at him with her bright, tearful eyes, now blank with terror and stupidity; she either said nothing or came out with rubbish. At that point there came a knock at the door and it was with enormous relief that he shouted: "Yes!" The commandant wanted him. When he entered the office, he saw him sitting at the desk, dishevelled, angry, and with a miserable tormented face; he nodded scowlingly at the receiver lying on the desk: "You."

It was Tamara. At her first words, Neiman sat down and remained sitting till the end of the conversation.

"Richard Germanovich has been summoned to Moscow. He's gone by plane, and they say he won't be coming back," said Tamara. "Gulyaev has twice sent for you, asking where you were. I said I didn't know."

"Right," drawled Neiman, and found himself unable to add anything. "So then." The commissar's name had been Richard Germanovich.

"After that, the deputy commissar phoned and asked where you were. I said I didn't know. He instructed me to tell you, if you rang in, that you should come back at once. Three people from your department have been arrested."

"Right," he said. "All right then, 'bye."

When he came back, the shopkeeper was sitting weeping. Dissolved in floods of tears. Good god, the cow makes a row. What do I want with you and your names now?

"All right," he said angrily. "Off you go." She leapt up and stared at him. It was then he remembered where he had seen her before. In Medeo, at Marietta's. She had been her relief. That's where he should have gone! To Marietta! Grab three bottles of cognac here, some sweets and away! That was the thing."

"Well what are you staring at? Go on!" he said with good-natured roughness.

"But . . ." she began.

He got to his feet, opened the door and ordered sternly: "Quickly! Go on!" Then he stood for a moment, thinking. He sighed and then knocked resolutely on the commandant's door. He was sitting at his desk staring dismally out of the window. He had unbuttoned his collar. When Neiman came in, he stared at him with hot eyes.

"Where's your vodka?" asked Neiman sternly.

"What?"

"Vodka. Where is it?" Neiman half-shouted. "In the desk? Let's have it! My head's splitting from yesterday as well."

"Hmm!" said the commandant with respect, his face at once brightening.

"What do you mean, hmm? Do you know Buddo, Alexander Ivanovich? Is he still working in your fuel store? No, no, let him work. All creatures have to look out for themselves. So where's the vodka then? Aha! Let's have it over here! Glass? Only one? Never mind, we'll use the one. We aren't infectious."

They sat next to one another and drank. Now the commandant of the SCS, Mikhail Ivanovich Shevchenko, seemed quite a different man to Neiman: he was unhurried and placid, speaking with a broad Volga "o" and his plain, simple face with its Russian snub nose, freckles, and yellow hair, did not go with the stern military uniform and badges at all. Among these emblems was the chekist badge of merit and the Voroshilov Marksman, and even something white and blue denoting a climber. So that now he seemed not only serious and experienced, but someone with services to his credit. He was the first person Neiman told about the commissar – he had been summoned to Moscow and would hardly be likely to return. He shouldn't have said that of course, but there it was, he was carrying too great a weight of misery. He felt like sharing it with somebody at least.

"Yes," said Mikhail Ivanovich indifferently. "He didn't last long, did he, although what am I saying? Two years! That's quite a stretch!"

"Of course he may come back, Allah alone knows," thought Neiman aloud.

"He may come back," concurred Shevchenko. "Yes, we're on the job now! But just think how neatly they had it all planned out – they'd got it all sewn up, every seam! Somebody in every niche! Stands to reason, they'd got people in the top jobs. They controlled it all! What if they'd got together in time and gone into action, eh?"

Neiman frowned. He didn't like this sort of talk: it always had a dubious whiff about it. Add a word here, subtract one there, and you had a ready-made case.

"The brilliance of it, destabilizing that whole hellish machine by pulling out one little man at a time," Shevchenko went on pensively. "Little men at first of course, then a bit bigger, then bigger still! And the president of the Soviet people's commissariat gets his collar felt. Our wise man devised it so cleverly, so precisely, that none of the swine so much as budged. They all sat and waited like rabbits. That's what it means to work under a single leadership."

Neiman scowled. It wasn't that Shevchenko was spouting rubbish, no, but in general it wasn't done to talk about things like that. Read the papers. It was all written there.

"We've never feared the enemies and never reckoned up how many there were," he replied stiffly, to break off the conversation at once. "They were only a tiny minority."

"Yes, that's true, a tiny few," agreed Mikhail Ivanovich listlessly. "What are we to say when the government and the party have said their say, but they're cunning, they're extraordinarily cunning, they can crawl into any opening, but when their hour comes, they don't budge. Their own people give them away, don't they? He paused, grinned at something, clinked glasses with Neiman and resumed. "We had something happen here once. We were sent a new head of accounts/supplies. He was such a foul devil you couldn't find a clean place to put the brand; young, smart, creaking about all in leather, but he set about pleasing the prisoners: no substitutions, meat was meat, fat was fat, every gram exact. His brother was a big wheel in camp administration. So he was afraid of nothing! He drank with the prisoners, not all of them of course, his own trusties. Then his brother got raked in. Well of course, they were bound to come for him. He found out before anybody else and with his closest pals, unguarded, he went off to the station. His friends were all reliable, trusty types, the ones who die before they give you away, well it stood to reason! He used to bring women in for them as well, fix their work records, even put money in savings accounts for them – stolen money, of course! But when they had got out onto the steppe, these pals said to him: 'Now, chief, let's have a proper talk, camp-style!' And they had a pro-per talk! And they talked! Didn't they just! By using boots on his face. When they took him to sick bay, I came out: I couldn't look. There was no face left! They beat him and beat him and handed him in to the railway section. We've caught this one, they said. He was trying to run away. No, there's no running away for the likes of us. They turn you in. Criminals, oh yes, they've got friends, women, identity cards, safe houses, but what have we got? That's how it is." He sighed and raised his glass. "Well, let's drink a last one, time for bed! You won't be going back tonight, will you. I'll have a bed made up for you in my office. Your health. Maria Nikolaevna, come in here please! He's staying with us, see how late it is. Can't go now, can he?"

"Yes, he's not telling me all this for nothing," thought Neiman, and felt himself getting heated, like before a visit to the baths. "So then, he imagines I'm done for – the commissar's been pulled in and I'm headed the same way! That's why he's keeping me here, so he can hand me over nice and easy. He'll be on the phone directly!"

"I shan't have a drink," he said. "I'm going out for a breath of air!"

That's the most appalling thing in the world – a secret typist. Some especially trustworthy trash with a personal salary and rationbook! That bitch is sitting somewhere now and typing out a document about me! Just like that Ifarova. No one dared enter her room; the commissar's chauffeur used to drive her home if she had been kept late. She worked only for the commissar and his deputies. Then afterwards of course, she worked on the case of the commissar and his deputies. She had outlasted four commissars before someone informed on her. Her father had a capitalist enterprise here in the town of Verny: something between a cafeteria and a brothel. Anyway, they flung her out, damn her, out of our saintly portals. She's in the Writers' Union at the moment, producing interlinears. Never mind, she doesn't bear a grudge. Previously she used to type out writers' denunciations of one another; now she rattles out their poems and novels dedicated to one another. I met her once, walking along, contented and smiling. "Well how are you getting on there? Treating you well?" "But of course! Very cultured people! Quite a different atmosphere! I enjoy peace of mind." Damn her, the bitch! And she looks green and viperish, and her neck's withered like a rattlesnake! Someone once nicknamed her Madam Death. Somebody like her's typing about me now. I was sent a little drawing once. There was I, sitting writing something at my desk, and death is whisking a scythe over me! Ah, my dears, surely death doesn't have a scythe now!? She's got an Underwood and a folder "For signature" and you give me this mediaeval stuff: scythe, skeleton. All that's "pshaw" as dad used to say. So it's perfectly possible I shall run across Zybin at some transit point. And he'll repeat to me what he told that nitwit Khripushin. He had started talking to Zybin about the Homeland, the Fatherland, and he replied: "Homeland, Fatherland! What are you talking about them to me for? You never had a Homeland or a Fatherland, nor can you have one. Remember, Pushkin wrote about Mazeppa, that he was ready to shed his blood like water, that he despised freedom and there was no fatherland for him. Because a fatherland without freedom is the same as a prison or an investigation block." Surely Pushkin didn't really write: Fatherland and freedom? No, no, that couldn't be. He'd made that up himself, on his own. And he was rightly put in jail. In the profoundest sense. Guilty or not, whether he purloined the gold or not – that's another matter. But if I, my brother Roman Shtern the playwright, Tamara and that slippery, hysterical scoundrel Kornilov have to exist, then he has to cease to be! Or should it be the other way about? Anyway, to hell with him. My business at the moment only concerns that bitch on the fifth floor, sitting and typing her sheet of paper. The paper that means my head. No wait a minute, that's not it . . . She's sitting typing a sheet of paper . . . her sheet of paper . . .

He came to a halt and ran his palm across his brow – an extremely sweaty forehead. The steppe, the wind blowing, and I'm sweating like a pig. In the heat. I'm walking about talking to myself. It's already night too, can't see your hand in front of your face. Over there though, on the edge of the gully, it looks as if there's a light shining. I can see rocks, bushes; now I can see every branch plain as day. Ah, they've got a bonfire going. Not fishermen sitting by the fire is it? At night? Whatever for? They should have been asleep long ago. Maybe they're runaways, no identity cards. There's a lot of them about here, runaways. They say there's a whole gang of them now. I've got my Browning, maybe I could go over there and check? Phew, hell, I'm rambling again. I need my Browning for myself, to leave those swine with egg on their faces. They won't institute proceedings in that case – they'll be afraid because they let their man slip, didn't show timely vigilance. They'll write it down as something like "nervous exhaustion". And it might actually . . . After all, years of torment, illness, hunger, humiliation, and now a couple of seconds and it would all be over! Account rendered to the last kopeck, the last copper. And you wouldn't regret it ever, no repenting afterwards. Because there simply wouldn't be any afterwards.

He felt for his Browning, its grim, heavy, rough grip. He tugged it out halfway then thrust it back: what's simple about it? What's simple for you, idiot? You've simply gone off your head. It's not delirium either, it's madness. Madness that's all!

He had approached the edge of the gully. Down below, the fire burned and someone was sitting at it. A pot was hanging from two sticks. "Fish soup!" he thought. "They're boiling up some marinka." Why not go down to them? Taste marinka at least once in my life. Somehow he'd never had occasion to before. On this bank they catch and smoke it. There's none anywhere else in the world, so they say. Wait! Wasn't there something connected with that word?

He stood for a moment, thinking. A great deal was flitting through his head, but it was all vague, confused and scrappy; he couldn't lay hold of it. "Lord, I shouldn't have drunk so much," he thought and began a cautious descent from the steeply sloping bank.

There were two men on the bank. One was sitting by the river with his back to the fire. One was boiling something up in a blackened army pot. The fire burned with a tall white flame – dry reeds burn like that on the lakes. Neiman emerged from the darkness and made his way towards the fire.

"I wish you good health," he said.

The man by the fire raised his head, glanced at him, then once more bent over the pot, carefully removing a speck of dirt from the broth with his spoon. With a short powerful movement, he flicked the spoon. Only then did he reply.

"Health to one and all."

He was a short individual, with broad shoulders and a large head. Neiman came close up to the fire and hunched his shoulders.

"Can I have a warm?" he asked "It's cold!"

A mist had begun to rise; from the river drifted the smell of great flowing waters and wet clay.

"There's room enough for you," responded Big-head. "Please sit down. From the town?"

"Yes," he answered.

Big-head bent down and picked up a grey hessian bag, took out a cloth and wiped the spoon dry before sticking it back in the bag.

"You haven't got the time have you?" he asked abruptly.

Neiman looked at his wrist.

"Soon be ten," he replied.

"I'm going to town tomorrow myself," said Big-head. "I have to buy some rubber boots, just look at these: been here a week and no boots."

His boots were army issue, indestructible, with mighty projecting seams.

"You don't know if there's any decent leather boots to be had?"

"Any amount," replied Neiman. "Go straight to the Dynamo shop on Gogol Prospect, know it?"

"Yes, I've been there." He sighed. "Got to buy blocks of tea as well. We get through a lot of tea, comrade. We live a salty life. On fish! Well now, you wouldn't like a taste of fish broth would you?"

He swiftly seized the pot and took it off the fire.

"That's it, there now, there now!" he kept repeating quickly as he settled it in the earth. "Ah! Fishy soup! With onion, pepper, carrots! Father, hey, Father!" he turned towards the river.

493

"Just look at that!" answered the other without turning round. "I won't just now. I'll just . . ." He stood up and went over to something dark and lengthy, lying on the ground, covered with tarpaulin, and leaned over it.

"A fish?" asked Neiman.

"Drowned woman," Big-head answered reluctantly. "We've been on watch since this morning. Join us, please. There's bread, a spoon, there you are!

"What about him?" Neiman asked.

"He can't; strictly forbidden. He'll have some later."

"Yes, I'll have some later," confirmed the one by the river, who then turned abruptly to stare at Neiman. "You're not a medical orderly from the camp?" he asked.

It was then that Neiman glimpsed his face. It was still a young face, but the features were small, giving it an animal-like sharpness, narrow and watchful; the man resembled a fox. In Neiman's world, such faces were never trusted. He was fearfully thin: his cheeks showed as dark patches in the light of the fire. His hair however was fair and coarse, like a forest animal.

"No, I'm not from the camp, not a medical orderly," Neiman told him.

"Why aren't you eating?" asked Big-head. "You should have a good bite now, otherwise you'll freeze. The wind's like a knife out there. Ah, still looking at the drowned one. What's the point of that, then? That's what we have a river for, to drown in. Eat up! People eat at wakes as well!"

"But how did she drown," asked Neiman. "Was she carried away, maybe?"

He recalled talk about the River Ili being a very treacherous, unreliable river – seeming to flow quietly and steadily, but having eddies and whirlpools that would lay hold of you, spin you round and drag you down. There were plenty of drownings.

"Might have been," assented Big-head. "Maybe somebody drowned her, the river's quite safe here. There are places like that. Never mind, the police will come and sort it all out . . ."

"Raped and dumped," said Neiman.

"You just get a bite to eat," reiterated Big-head.

He had the appearance of being clumsy and slow-moving, yet everything he did was deft and nimble; using his discarded mittens, he lightly raised the boiling pot, took it from the fire and settled it firmly and securely among the stones; then with swift neatness, he cut large equal slices of bread and laid them out on a kind of plywood board; it was as if he had not only made fish soup, he had laid the table as well.

"Are you from the local collective farm?" Neiman enquired.

"Foreman of fishing team number six," responded Big-head. "Those are our huts over there," he nodded into the darkness down by the river.

"The dress doesn't signify anything," said the one with the foxy features. "We had one once: she dolled herself up in brand new clothes, never been worn, and jumped off the bridge. They never did find the body. Just her patent leather shoes on the bridge. Could have happened with this one."

Something silly and unseemly came over Neiman all of a sudden. He blurted:

"How I suffered, suffered badly,
From the bridge I jumped off sadly.
Through that devilment of yours
I was swimming three whole hours."

"No, it wasn't like that," Foxy-features took issue. "They'd all been given twenty-four hours to leave, and her wedding had already been announced. The groom intended to go with her but he was in good standing; she thought about it and she . . ."

"Was a fool," said Big-head firmly. "A great fool at that. What are we supposed to do then? At that rate the whole village should lie down on the railway track? That's all we've got left. I had three little ones, brought them here – in two years not one was left. They all die of the bellyache. So what am I supposed to do now, eh?"

"What's all the shouting about, Lukich? The whole river can hear you."

Out of the darkness came an old man, tall, wiry, hair grizzled, only his little beard was yellow-white as if from smoking. His face was brown and fissured, not by wrinkles it seemed, but scarring. Only the eyes remained merry, sharp and youthful.

"Well, how are things with you?"

"There's this," said Big-head, indicating the drowned woman. "Doesn't want to get up; we've been waiting and waiting, keeping an eye on her, but she's still lying there."

"Really?" The bearded one wagged his head. "Thing aren't so good then. The citizen chief isn't here yet?"

495

"He's having his third sleep, is the citizen chief," grinned Big-head. "He'll probably be here towards morning. He can rely on us, we won't let her run away, or conceal her identity."

"That's so, of course," the bearded one sighed. Then he appeared to notice Neiman for the first time, though he had been staring at him since he arrived on the scene. "Good health to you," he said respectfully. Neiman nodded to him. "Not from the office?"

"No, I'm here . . ." Neiman began rather awkwardly.

"And I thought you were one of the bosses. Well you go, you go, Lukich," said the old man, peering into the murk, as if only now glimpsing Foxy-features for the first time. "Ah, you here too, Yasha, man of God, leather-shod," he said. "So all together in one big happy family. No chance of getting bored. When you go, tell my old woman to wake Mishka up in two hours time. Otherwise, you see, as we aren't visible from the town, they might come tomorrow at dinner-time."

"Well, good luck." Big-head got up, gathered up his sack and set off.

"Is that fish soup you're boiling up? That's good," said the old man.

At this there came a sharp gust of wind. The flames guttered and lit up the hunched grey tarpaulin and a thin female hand next to it on the stones. The hand was white with fingers spread. The fingers seemed to move as the fire leapt.

"She was clutching," sighed the old man. "Drowning people always do that. I was dragging one little lad out of the Volga once and he nearly did for me as well."

He got to his feet and went over to tuck the hand back under the tarpaulin, but it crept stubbornly out again. At this, he rolled the tarpaulin back completely and Neiman glimpsed a red dress, a necklace, a head flung back with loose-flowing hair and half-open mouth. The eyes were also open. The flames and the shadows played about the face and it seemed the drowned woman was pursing her lips and narrowing her eyes.

"As if she'd fallen asleep," said the old man. "Ah, lassie, lassie, what have you gone and done to yourself?"

The flames went on leaping and flickering on the drowned woman's face; she lay absolutely still and straight as if she really had fallen asleep or was dissembling; this and the fact that he could see her strong even teeth, and especially that the eyes were open and were filled with the dark milky cloudiness of death – something Neiman had noted as being always present in the eyes of the dead – all of this caused him to shudder in a most peculiar way. It wasn't from fear, and not even the grim and aching sense of mystery which always surrounds a coffin or grave; it was something other – lofty and ineffable.

"Why on earth didn't they try artificial respiration?" asked Neiman. "They tried everything for four hours," responded the grizzled figure. "The medical orderly was here and the doctor – the lot of them. They shook her so hard once, blood came, and they were glad, thinking she was alive. The dead, so they said, don't bleed. No, not a bit of it!"

"The bastard!" Neiman suddenly said aloud. "Birch tree! 'Blood from corpses' . . . she'd got it all worked out scientifically, the bitch! You . . ." he recovered himself instantly and bit his lip. But the relief man was standing holding the tarpaulin in silence.

"Well, may she rest with the saints," he said and covered the drowned woman gently, as if she were sleeping. The head he left exposed. "Best if she knows everything! She came from a long way off, it seems, specially." He stood for a while, thinking. "Yesterday at this time she was still alive," he said. "Eating, drinking, walking about . . ."

Just then an odd voice came from behind them. Neiman looked round. Yasha was standing near the corpse and looking at them with artful glee. "Come and give the dead one her last kiss, brothers," he invited with plain matter-of-factness. Then he paused and said: "Such parting, O brothers, such weeping, such lamentation is now upon us." He placed his hands across his chest and bowed to the deceased. "Come hither to kiss one who, being with us but a little time," he said, "and is conveyed into the coffin, covered with a stone, consigned to the dark, buried with the dead, and parts now from all friends and kin."

"Being with us but a little time," sighed the old man. "The ancients knew how to speak. Every word is like a stone. He crossed himself and glanced at Neiman. And Neiman too bowed his head devoutly, and was actually about to raise his hand, but he recollected himself instantly. "Hell's bells!" he reflected. "It really is the faculty of useless knowledge! Drunken fool!"

And the same voice, now sorrowful, unaffected, musing, almost sang rather than spoke: "Weep over me, brothers and friends, kinfolk and acquaintance: yesterday I talked with you and suddenly the dread hour of death found me. Come hither all who loved me and give me the last kiss." He made a vague gesture of invitation, and both of them, the old man and Neiman moved towards the body as if at a command. Yasha was already kneeling at the head holding a short, stumpy church candle. It flickered and wavered, burning with yellow and blue flame. When they came up, he moved to the very forehead of the dead woman. And now she lay revealed to Neiman in such pure deathly beauty, such serene clarity of life overcome, along with all its insubstantial envelope, that he sensed a cold tremor running through and disturbing his hair. And he realized that at this moment, this very second, he was going to do something incredibly momentous, something that would erase his past life completely. Now, this instant! But he did nothing, because he could not do anything, he simply did not have anything within that he could drag into the light. He merely bowed and touched his lips to the forehead of the deceased. It was smooth, cold, polished smooth as a tombstone by death. The voice broke off as he kissed it and then rose up again. He did not hear the words, or didn't understand them, but he was aware that they explained all that was taking place before him. But by now he no longer cared. Nothing of himself remained any longer. He went aside and squatted down by the fire. A minute later, the old man came over too. "Who's that?" asked Neiman.

The man was still singing and bowing towards the deceased. The candle burned. The dead woman's forehead was high and pure ... The eyes were open.

"Nowadays they are called declassed elements," grinned the old man. "He works with us in the co-operative, he's the man of God, Yasha. They say he was driven out of a seminary by the revolution. Then he was imprisoned. He was in the North. He had his fingers caught in a circular saw. He's waiting for some papers from Moscow, so he can go to his relatives."

"Does he always read over the dead like that?"

"If he's invited, always."

They were seated round the fire again. But Yasha had joined them this time. He sat in silence, pulling the pot towards him, as a reward earned.

"Nowadays they're allowed to do it," the old man explained. "Once he's sung his liturgy, he's allowed to have a bite to eat, he was strictly forbidden to do that before. It's a priestly law. Eat up, eat up, Yakov Nikolaevich! It's got a bit of body in it, millet."

The nostrils of Yasha, the man of God, were still quivering, and his lips were twisted as he wiped them with the back of his hand and silently thrust his spoon into the pot.

"Bread?" The old man asked him.

Yasha accepted a slice, bit into it, and set to work with his spoon. He gulped avidly, without chewing, and burnt himself.

The old man stood above him, repeating: "Eat, eat. Eat, Godly man that you are. You read very well today, heartfelt. Yes, all is vanity! You spoke truly. I had riches once: two cows, two horses, sheep, pigs, so many . . ."

"All is human vanity that does not outlast death," Yasha interrupted him harshly and explained: "Wealth does not abide, glory does not exist. All is dust, ashes and shadow."

"Yes, yes," agreed the relief and shook his head. "That's so! All shadow. And we are but shadow. From earth to earth. Wise men thought of that! It's the truth. Take her now, there she lies, beautiful and comely as if she slept. And those others will come rolling up on their motorcycles, crash about and take her over, put her on a table and start disembowelling her. They'll cut the skin open all over her head, bind it up with a red stocking, thrown on her face, I've seen them do it. They'll start digging into the brain, to see what was wrong with her, what brought her to this. Was she in her right mind or not."

Yasha's face was painfully distorted. He said nothing.

Neiman loosened his jacket, retrieved a bottle from his pocket and offered it to the old man.

"Ah, just what we need!" The old man was delighted. "There's a mug somewhere round here. I tucked it among the stones somewhere.

But the Godly man Yasha was already stretching the aluminium mug across the fire towards him.

"Aha! Now this is the real orthodox way. A wake! Then Yasha shall have the first taste. I'll pour him out a full one. Drink up, Yasha."

And Yasha, the man of God, took the mug and silently downed the lot. He then wiped his face with his hand again, rounded his lips and gave vent to a powerful rounded sigh.

"Her soul is still here, walking near us; it keeps watch over the body for forty days," he said.

"And sees us?" asked Neiman.

"Certainly," grinned Yasha. "It can see everything. If we cry, it cries with us; we for her and she for us. It's just that our tears are sour and earthly, and hers are sweet, celestial, light."

"What is she weeping for then?" Neiman asked.

"For us. From affection and pity she weeps," responded Yasha. "Ah, my nearest and dearest, my kinfolk. Why weep so for me, why these floods of tears? All is well with me now, I want for nothing from anyone. Now all that is earthly – death, the love of the flesh, sorrow, persecution – all that is left for you. I am now light, white, radiant through and through. I have discarded all earthly things like a cloth, and donned the robes of eternity. It is now mine for ever and ever, there is no power to take it from me! Yes please, we thank you!" And he held out the empty mug to the old man.

"That's if she's a lamb," said the old man with a stern glance at Yasha. "But what if she's a wolf instead? What then?" he poured himself a mug and drank it down unhurriedly; poured one for Neiman and waited till he had finished it, then resumed. "Then she will be filled with terror: 'Oh, what will become of me now! Where will I find my peace? It's only now that my torments begin, and there is no end of them to be seen. That's how it is!"

"Permit me a little more?" requested the Godly man and positioned the mug. "I thank you." He calmly drained it dry. ("There you are!" the old man grunted). "This we cannot know, Tikhonovich, it is hidden from us, but hints," here he raised his voice, "but hints we do have! Remember the robber who was crucified with Christ? He suffered deservedly, did he not. And what did Christ say to him? 'Today thou shalt be with me in paradise.' How could he say such a thing? To a robber, eh? A man who had killed, orphaned plundered . . . ?"

"He had repented, hadn't he," the old man replied, displeased. He said, didn't he: "Remember me Lord, in thy kingdom."

"Aha! He said that! That's another matter!" Yasha agreed. "You've gone to the heart of it there. In the hour of death, the robber lifted up his voice: "Save me!" and was saved. That is like us. If we lift up our voices from the heart, then it shall be given unto us. But there must be no tricks. For we're very skilled in that. They made me do it, we say! I suffered as I did it! Or: The children! I forwent my conscience for their sake! We're very sharp over little tricks like that! No, that will not be accepted. There they know: it's just the same old devil inside you, working away. No, you must understand something else: there is no forgiveness for you from other people! That is why they are people, that they may punish, not forgive. You have had pity on nobody and no one will pity you. There, it is different. There, your innermost essence is what is wanted. That is what you have to reach. Even in your final hour, you must! It is not of this earth, it is given to us from heaven. Our essence!

"Well and what happens then?" The relief shook his head. "Do they give you another hide or what? Here, Yasha, they'll say, here's you're new skin – go away and earn it. You were Yasha, now you're Masha. So off you go, Masha, earn paradise for Yasha. No, I somehow don't see the point of all that. You sin away for all that time, then all of a sudden . . ."

"No! That's what you have to comprehend: essence!" Yasha cried, so agitated that he sprang to his feet. "Time and your actions aren't relevant. A minute there can last millions of years. It's all one. In the Old Testament that wasn't so; time existed there. But for Christ, time does not exist! Your essence is what's important to him, so that even at the very last moment you comprehend everything. He can squeeze your whole life into that instant, For that one second he will give it to you to live over again. That is why he is the Saviour."

"So it works out well," scoffed the old man. "We used to have a certain Mishka Krasnov, a priest's little boy. A real swine he was! A stinker! The reds shot his father, and he stood there with a red ribbon, cried into his hankie and preached to him: "It's your own fault, Daddy, I warned you!" He sniffed around with the whites, the reds, the greens and some yellow lot – everybody, the bastard. Then he went off to town. To study. Came back as a commissar. All in black leather, shiny new boots, right up to here . . . Goes about, all shiny. Nagant on his hip. Tsar and God. In the next village there were five dwelling houses left. Some had fled, some been shot, some died of hunger. He couldn't let a wench go by. He'd meet some pretty lass and it was: 'Come with me, Marya, I want to ask you some questions.' And he spent all night at it. And he overdid it. The 'dizzy with success' letter came round. And then the order to detain Mishka, the priest's son. They came to get him and he, the louse, goes down on his knees in the empty deacon's hut and bows his head to the ground. Raised a bump this size. He howls. 'Lord!' he wails. 'Forgive me all my great sins! Lord, have mercy! My father, innocent martyr, pray to the Lord for me!' And bangs his nut one! two! on the floor. In an empty hut! Where he'd driven out the whole family. The cur! Cholera of 1930! You say the robber repented on the cross. This one repented before that! And how! His eloquence at the meetings improved no end. You should have heard him!"

"It has to be from a pure heart. You!" shouted Yasha.

"Ah, a pure heart! His heart couldn't have been purer! I ask you: yelped and yelped, wrung his hands! All those orders and mansions he'd been earning, and now he'd earned himself the chop! Well of course, he clutched his noddle! 'Ah what a fool I am! Ah what a so and so I am! And so on. Where were my eyes? What did I sell my conscience and my father for? A man reaps what he has sown.' And that's as pure a repentance as you'll get!"

501

"Yes, that's a hard one to fathom," pondered Neiman. "Obviously you just have to believe. Do I believe in anything? Here my end has come, and what am I left with? I can't even shout 'Lord! Lord!' to anybody!"

It was almost dawn when Neiman rose and left the fire. Yasha, the Godly man, slept curled up like a child. His narrow yellow face, creased with crafty wrinkles, the face of a holy fool or a genius, or simply a cunning and adroit rogue, was calm and untroubled.

The relief man led Neiman onto the high bank into the steppe and said: "You see the lamp? Head straight for that. That's the office on the hill. There's bound to be somebody there. Either the night watchman or the cleaner."

"Thanks," said Neiman, with a curt nod. "I'll ring town straight away from there and tell them to send somebody out to you."

When he went out onto the steppe, the sky in the east was already quite light. In that direction, into the clear cold yellow, black birds were flying, in a skein rather than a flock, dots, rising and sinking. It was the first time he had seen the vast dawn sky of the steppe. And therefore stood and gazed at it until the birds had disappeared. There was a light cross breeze. The earth lay, grey and cracked, and from it grew a long thin grass that looked like horsehair. He saw a large white bush and threw a lighted match into it. The bush at once burst into a transparent hydrogen flame, until the conflagration subsided and petered out on the soil, unyielding as an earthenware pot.

The house on the hill was dark and silent, but he cunningly circled it and as he came in via the yard, saw that the light was on in the rear window behind the white curtain. He knocked but received no answer. He knocked again – a cream-coloured shadow fluttered and began to peer out. Then he knocked a third time, hard, sharp, crisp. The curtain trembled a fraction and a woman's voice asked: "Who's there?"

"Open up," he said. "Investigator." And inwardly smiled wryly at himself and added: "Come to give myself up."

As he entered he stood stock still in the doorway. Before him, in the dim yellow light, clutching the lapel of her dressing-gown stood Marietta Ivanovna.

"Lord," she said, relieved, recognizing him as she fell back on the stool. "And here was I . . . where've you been?"

"B-But . . ." he began, but that was as far as he got: nothing else would come out. There was another stool standing there and he collapsed onto that.

"What about you?" he asked hopelessly.

"I've been here over a month!" she replied. "Lord, how scared I was: investigator," she laughed. "I don't need that! They transferred me here to sit in for the manageress while she was on holiday, so here I sit. I did ring you and ask you to my name-day party! Your niece answered the phone."

"Yes, yes, yes."

He ran his hand across his head. It wasn't his head that ached, it was his whole skin, his hide, his hair.

"What about Glafira?" he asked. "I mean she's ..."

"She's my relief. Lives at the station. But yesterday she ... wait!" Her eyes opened wide all of a sudden and paled in fright. "Investigator?"

"Yes, this is a fine mess and no mistake. Bloody hell." he thought. "This would have to happen! All my pretending gone for nothing! Never mind. I'm drunk – I don't remember anything, I don't know anything and I don't want to know!"

He got up and went over to Marietta; he placed a hand on her shoulder.

"No, no," he said. "Investigator, a likely story! That was just a joke. Fool that I was, I wanted to put a bit of a scare into you. What the hell sort of an investigator would I make, now?"

"Oy, you're all hot!" she exclaimed. "Well, of course, out on the steppe all night in just your raincoat – it gets really cold here by morning! Now then, you lie down. I'll rustle up a bed for you directly. Why, you're soaked in sweat!"

"What about you?" he asked, catching her by the shoulders.

"I'll be back, I'll be back! I have to see to the deliveries. They bring them in on the night train. There they are, hooting already. That's the signal to me. Lie down, lie down. I'll be free in two shakes. Good lord, I could wring you out. Drinking with those geologists I expect? Oh yes, there's a whole group of them working here. Oy, Yakov Abramovich, they're all youngsters but you ..."

"That's who I was drinking with! Near the drowned woman we sat and drank."

"Now, now," she said, "come along. Lie down, I'll help you get undressed. Drowned women! Don't mention such awful things! Oy, don't touch that cannon of yours, why do you keep grabbing at it? Put it under the mattress. It'll be safe there."

His penultimate thought, as she undressed him, repeating something gentle, was: "How did I get here anyway? I can hardly stand up." And the very last was: "And she won't give me up, so there, my little camp commandant, she won't give me up."

He woke for a second towards evening and saw that the room was empty. There was an abacus on the table, a white apron hanging on a chair; he turned on his side and fell asleep again.

The second time, he awoke because someone was gently tugging his shoulder. He sat up at once. A quiet green lamp glowed on the white tablecloth, the crockery was set out and the samovar was hissing. Marietta was bending over it.

"You were groaning a bit so I woke you up," she said. "Were you having a nightmare?"

He stuck his hand under the mattress and checked that the Browning was there.

"No, no, I had a really good sleep," he returned. "Thank you. What a mattress you've got, once you lie down you can never get up."

She laughed.

"Do you want to lie on for a bit. Otherwise you can get up, eh? It's late. I've done my trading. Time for supper."

He glanced at his watch: it had stopped.

"How many hours did I sleep then?" he asked.

"They were all yours," she laughed. "Well, if you aren't going to sleep any more, get up. I'll set the table directly."

He threw a blanket over himself and sat there for a while, saying nothing. Then he suddenly remembered the main thing.

"That woman," he asked. "The drowned one. What about her?"

"Oh, they've taken her away," replied Marietta carelessly. "They came for her this morning. They asked all of us about her. What was there to ask? I'd never seen her in my life. Are you going to sober up?"

"Sober up?"

His head didn't so much hurt as feel somehow completely vacant, resonant. He threw off his blanket and got dressed. Marietta gave him his shoes. He asked where the toilet and washbasin were; he went in and proceeded to get himself tidied up. When he returned, a bottle and glasses had already appeared on the table. His former clarity and precision were returning to him and he decided that he ought to appear in the people's commissariat the following day. Of course, there was little for his comfort there. That is, the fact of the commissar's removal need not affect him at all, but the fact that three of his colleagues had been pulled in immediately afterwards was a very bad sign indeed. They hadn't even waited for his return; only Moscow acted in that fashion.

Of course, he might derive consolation from not being conscious of having done anything wrong, but, like every other citizen of the Soviet Union, he knew perfectly well that whatever he felt was of no significance whatever. But even that did not alarm him unduly. If that was the case, so be it. Up to now he had been lucky. He had honestly and punctiliously carried out the orders of the boss. He had not tried to be too clever and hadn't poked his nose into anything. But now the boss was demanding a rendering of accounts, for what – that was something known only to him. Well, it was all up then. There was no one he could run to. No way he could vindicate himself, even, as the biblical robber had done, by crying: "Lord! Lord!" Even that was denied him. That direction was as blank as everywhere else. At least for him.

He sat and regarded Marietta, big, warm, soft, noiselessly moving about behind him, going out somewhere, coming back in, getting things from somewhere, bringing them in and placing them all on the table. At length her openness and submissiveness reached through to him.

"Come closer," he said. "Well, shall we drink?"

"Let's," she replied and tossed her head diffidently.

"Then go to bed," he commanded.

"And then what?" she grinned.

. . . The following morning – and here, just as in town, cocks crowed and dogs barked – he was sitting at the table, stern, clean-shaven, drinking tea. Just strong tea, nothing else. Marietta was rummaging in the night-table then came over to him, saying: "Now I want to ask you . . ." and placed in front of him a light-blue tin box; in Tsarist times fruit lozenges used to be sold in them.

"Landrin?" he asked. " 'George Borman, the noseless poor man'? What, you keep buttons in it?"

"Yes," she replied and shook the box out onto the cushion.

It was gold. That same cunning, ancient, patterned gold which had brought him here. But it was also a miracle he had not dared to hope for. And it had happened, like all miracles, unexpectedly and simply, according to that inherent logic, through which everything extraordinary happens: a box had been opened and gold had poured from it onto a table. That was all.

"Where did you get it?" he asked without expression.

"Ah, the fishermen brought it? Aha! And they're here? A long way off? So then."

He got up, stowed the box in his mapcase and said: "Well now, up you get, we have to be off."

"Where?" she said, stiff with terror.

"What do you mean, where? To those fishermen."

She flushed in alarm.

"But why?" she whispered.

"Well, we'll go and see them and have a talk. Pleasant sort of people, are they? Well then, we'll have a chat." He pulled out his Browning, examined it, and stuck it back in its holster. "No, no, I'm not going to do anything with it. Just ask a few questions. Let's go, let's go."

"You mean it's really gold? I thought . . ."

"We'll find out when we get there what it is and where it's from. Let's go."

CHAPTER 3

A FTER ZYBIN HAD BEEN taken from that interrogation and dragged back to his cell, time for him disappeared entirely. He would close his eyes and night descended; the electric light burned with a steady glow, it was quiet in the corridors, in the thin, brittle air beyond the window came the sound of locomotive hooters, loud and gentle. Dogs barked. He would open his eyes and it would already be morning; the guard would be doing the round of the cells, knocking on the metal plating with his key: "Up you get! Up you get!" The tea urns rattled along the floor, food slots opened; women in grey aprons noiselessly placed bread and hot water on the folding windows. Sparrows chirped. Then the duty men came round – one handing out, the other collecting in, asking whether there were any complaints or statements. What statements or complaints could he possibly have? He never had anything! He floated in a bright, limpid void, merged with it, and himself became a part of that void. The sea came no more into his cell. Or that woman either. And that was good too. He didn't need her just now. Only the calls of the body made him get up listlessly and without pain and go into the corner. He drank the water and ate the bread, so it wasn't a hunger strike and he was left in peace. Having done what was required, he would lie back on his bunk and gaze at the light ceiling, at the ever-burning bulb, and range about the prison, the city, the world. Zybin now ceased to be; there was a bright vacancy. That lasted for some time, perhaps two days, perhaps a month. Once, a number of people came into his cell: the prison governor, the overseer, prosecutor Myachin and a fair-haired young man of intellectual aspect, reminiscent of the young Khomyakov. The prosecutor asked him how he felt.

"All right, thank you."

"You can walk?"

"Perfectly well."

"Sit up on the bed."

He raised himself and sat up.

"He's a good man," smiled the doctor, who looked like Khomyakov.

"We'll prescribe him a richer diet, including glucose and he'll soon be on his feet."

"What's the matter with him?" asked the prosecutor. "Georgi Nikola-evich, what's the matter?"

"Nothing," he replied.

"What do you mean, nothing? Why are you lying down? Are you unwell."

"No, no," he answered.

"Well, what's the matter then?" asked the prosecutor.

"Nothing, I'm just dying that's all." He knew that for a fact; he wasn't ill, he was just dying. And they couldn't ask one damn thing of him now. He owed none of them anything.

A short silence ensued.

"Well, let's just say that's nonsense," said the prosecutor. "You'll survive. You're young! All your life ahead of you! You have to get better, Georgi Nikolaevich. That's what! Get on your feet again. It's high time, high time."

And everything floated off into the mist again as he closed his eyes.

They came for him on the following morning. Two overseers took him carefully under the arms and led him off. There in the corridor, consciousness returned to him and he asked: "Is it to that end?" "Yes, that end," came the answer and he relaxed and nodded. Everything was proceeding as it should. Now the handsome young doctor would appear.

But they didn't take him to the end where people were shot, but to a large light-filled room. A bed stood against the wall, made up hotel-style, like an envelope. A water decanter glistened on a white table cloth. The cream-curtained windows were drawn.

"If you get under the blanket be sure to undress," said the overseer. "And hang your things on the back of the chair."

And indeed, a soft chair, not a stool, stood by the bed.

He lay down, stretched out and closed his eyes. His former state did not return to him. There was none of that warm, serene, ooze that softly sucked him in. Everything had precise outlines, an unpleasantly sharp sensibility. His heart throbbed in his temples and a red mote leapt in front of him on the white wall.

He lay there for about an hour, then something pushed him steadily and he opened his eyes.

A vision in white was bending over him.

Behind him, near the door, stood another woman, a kindly broad-nosed old girl, holding a nickel-plated tray. A hypodermic needle lay on the tray and a spirit lamp glowed. He glanced at the white vision and glimpsed her face, so clear and pure, she seemed to give off a glow. "The bloodsuckers," he thought, and was at once flooded with grim hostility – "Up to their tricks again! Dolidze wasn't enough, now we've got this Ophelia."

"Hell's flames!" he swore.

"What's the matter?" said the white vision, very simply and cheerfully.

"This isn't a prison, it's some guesthouse or a soldiers' brothel. What do you all want of me, eh? What then? I've had it, get that! Utterly and completely!" he roared out suddenly.

She did not take offence and did not step back.

"Now why take that tone?" she said, seating herself on the edge of the bed. "I'm a doctor and this is our surgical sister. We're going to make you well. Shortly I'm going to take a blood sample for analysis, to see what's wrong. It's not the slightest bit painful. Then we'll give you an infusion, that doesn't hurt either. Now why the scowl? You're a man. Just fancy – an injection!"

"I'm a man, yes," he scowled, "but what are you, then? You're . . ."

He choked back what he was going to say. She was still smiling.

"He's in a temper!" said the old girl at the door. "You could fry eggs on a temper like that. Fancy saying such things! Here, give me your hand, do, professor. You're . . . And what are you, then? Now lie still!"

Zybin looked at her and began to laugh.

And so several days passed. The injections began to do their work. Towards the end of the second day, he started getting out of bed and they brought him a whole pile of books. Along with Grillparzer's plays, he got a stout volume of *Bee-Keeping* for 1913. Both books had identical binding.

"Probably that old man," Zybin mused. "Went off somewhere and took up bee-keeping. That's where they picked him up. There's nowhere to hide."

"The birch tree" – as he mentally christened the lady doctor, came to see him two or three times a day. She had limpid blue eyes and white, close-cropped hair. She was straightforward and unassuming, never mentioning any outside matter, but when she bent over him to listen to him or tap him, he sensed her warmth upon him. On one occasion, she suggested a blood transfusion. He asked what he would get out of it.

"What a question," she marvelled. "Just everything." And her eyes took on a frighteningly deeper tint of blue, as if she were speaking of the thing most dear to her heart. "Well Blood," she pronounced the word with a capital letter, "Blood! It's the river of life. When it dries up, life comes to an end. If we always had a sufficient supply of good quality fresh blood in all groups ready to hand ... what wouldn't we do then. We could raise the dead!"

"You mean you don't have that?" he asked.

"Where can we get it from?" She clapped her translucent palms together in distress. "We ask for it, but never get it. Even if we do get it, it's no great joy. Untested blood that isn't fresh is death, but sometimes we even get sent that."

"So how do you manage?"

"We get hold of our own," she answered simply.

"My, my, what a treasure you are," he thought. "She shares her blood with prisoners. And how did a little sunbeam like this get here? Though Doctor Gaaz now ... The saintly doctor. Chief medical officer of the prison inspectorate. He fell on his knees before the Tsar in the jail : 'Sire, have mercy on an old man.' And the Tsar pardoned him."

On one occasion, when she was listening to him, the tall, fair-haired, pale-eyed, intellectual young doctor came in, the one who looked like Christ or the young Khomyakov and who had been in his cell with the prosecutor the week before. He had greeted him, beckoned the birch tree and taken her over to the window. They talked quietly about something and he heard the name "Shtern", then after a while, "Neiman" several times and stiffened in helpless rage. So, those monkey paws had reached as far as her, had they?

"I don't know what he's going to think up next," said the doctor, "but there's a row going on." He swiftly left the room. And she was left by the window in a kind of stupor.

"Ah, you poor thing," he thought. "So who do you have to tangle with: Neiman or Shtern, that bastard. And the other one as well, the top man – comes in, telling people off, dishing out threats! And my presence didn't put him off. Good God almighty!"

He wanted to say something to her, but she had said her farewells quickly, then gone out and he hadn't seen her since.

A week later, the corridor guard arrived and summoned him to a talk with the prosecutor.

He got up and got dressed. He was sorry she hadn't been in that day and he had no one to say goodbye to. He knew he was being summoned to the end of the corridor where the sentence would be carried out.

*   *   *

Four of them had gathered in the small office. Two he already knew, the prosecutor Myachin and Gulyaev. The other two were in civilian clothes and sat by the wall. He had never seen them before. Gulyaev, small, puny, sallow-dark, with his splendid, shiny swept-back hair, was sitting at the desk. In front of him lay the blue tin box "Georges Borman". Myachin was standing near the window. When Zybin was led in, Gulyaev stared in astonishment at the prosecutor and spread his hands: "What was that you were telling me about Georgi Nikolaevich not getting up. He's quite a young chap," he said. "Sit down, Georgi Nikolaevich, we have things to talk about. Firstly, how do you feel?"

"Quite well, thank you," replied Zybin.

"Well, that's splendid. No, not on the chair, sit up to the desk. Well now, I've been telling you that archaeologist Zybin can go through fire without getting burnt and water without getting drowned. So then, Georgi Nikolaevich, I can give you glad tidings. Your case has been concluded; we are parting, therefore ... but above all, do you recognize ... ?"

He opened the blue box.

It was gold; fragments of something, scales of some sort, edging, platelets, pale yellow, dull, lacklustre. It was genuine dead gold, the sort that spills from the eye sockets when a brown skull is ripped from the clinging earth, the short that glimmers between the ribs, and settles in the grave. In short it was unmistakably archaeological gold. Zybin, instantly oblivious to all else, stared at the roundels and platelets, earrings, tiny hooks, little spirals and figures of people, horses and wild animals.

It was quiet in the office. Gulyaev glanced significantly at Myachin.

"Where did all this come from?" Zybin asked.

"There's this too," smiled Gulyaev, pulling out a desk drawer and taking out another box, a long cardboard one this time with the gold inscription "Liqueur Cherries". On the cotton wool in this one, lay a fragment of figured gold plate, precisely that central and largest part, without which the diadem would have been merely two fragments and not a diadem at all.

Zybin picked it up, looked at it and said: "Yes, now it's complete. And here was I thinking the lot had gone."

"Well it's been found," smiled Gulyaev.

"But it could have been lost," said the prosecutor reproachfully. "If we had still been dilly-dallying and hadn't taken vigorous measures, it would have been lost. For a month you've been leading us round in circles."

"A month?" Zybin asked. "Not more than that? Surely more than a month has passed?"

He raised his eyes to the prosecutor.

"Well, what about it?" he asked point blank.

And the prosecutor at once subsided at his tone.

"Let's not reckon up, Georgi Nikolaevich," he said swiftly. "All's well that ends well. It's all here. And I have just one question for you: did you know where it all was?"

"Did you?" asked Zybin.

"Georgi Nikolaevich," laughed Myachin, "up to your old ways again? No, you answer me, otherwise we'll get totally confused. To wind up the case we need one more record, but it must be precise, clear and brief. You follow me? Wait a moment." Gulyaev closed both boxes. "Not like that. We, Georgi Nikolaevich, understand now why you went to the river Ili. But why on earth didn't you tell us that straight away?"

"And what should I have told you?" asked Zybin.

"Well, essentially just one thing: where these things were actually found."

"And where were they actually found?" asked Zybin.

"Well on the Ili of course."

"Right. And what was there on the Karagalinka at that time?" Zybin asked again.

"It's like an examination, honestly! There was absolutely nothing on the Karagalinka – no boulder, no gold. It was on the Ili in a robbed tumulus. And you realized that immediately. But give you your due, you fooled us brilliantly. We looked at all your extracts from the *Tomsk University Transactions* for 1889 which has a list of all the Ili tumuli, but still didn't understand why you wanted it and why it was in the Diadem folder."

Zybin paused before asking.

"So why did those people come to the museum?"

"That's something else you realized perfectly well. They came because they didn't know what it was they'd found, genuine gold or copper, they wanted it checked and an answer given. But there was no one to give them that answer. You were away in the mountains, and without you they could twist the director round their finger like a child. And that's what actually happened."

"Yes, we've certainly landed up with a military mind in the museum. He does his directing with weapons glinting in the sun," Myachin grinned.

"The director has nothing to do with this," said Zybin swiftly and looked angrily at the prosecutor.

Myachin shot a glance at Gulyaev and both burst out laughing.

"All right now, don't frighten him," Gulyaev waved a hand. "It's not our business to check directors. But he's not a practical man, no doubt about that! That's something he admits himself. Aha! Still that's not the point. But why did you have to do all this. You could have told us all about it at the start."

"And what would have happened?" grinned Zybin.

"How do you mean?"

"I'll tell you what; the gold would have gone missing. Neiman would have come to the museum, picked up the gold and put it into some State Fund or State Bank at weight value to be melted down. The bits would have gone into various pockets. And I'd still have been in jail, just as I am now."

"Excuse me, which pockets are these," Myachin flared up at once.

"Well whose? Khripushin's, Neiman's, yours, there's plenty to choose from. The woman who interrogated me, a bit for her, the bitch, for earrings or a ring. It could be broken up for that."

"Have you gone mad?" cried the prosecutor, aghast.

Zybin, grinned at him.

"Really," he jibed. "Haven't you seen records – 'ring of white metal with glass inset'. And a platinum ring with an emerald in it goes for a rouble. Seen them?"

"Just a moment. Did something stick to my fingers too?" Gulyaev enquired.

"I've heard nothing about you."

"Well, thanks for that at least. Yes, there were such people of course, Georgi Nikolaevich, but they were cleared out of the security organs long ago. Some were shot even. As for Neiman . . ."

"He's no longer with us," said the prosecutor.

"Phew," Zybin whistled. "You mean he's already, you know . . . ? Been playing the white metal and glass game? You got all this out of him? Neat!"

"Well, we can talk about that later."

"And now to business," Gulyaev broke in imperiously. "There's no Neiman and we have to wind up the case. The bright lads who brought the diadem in levelled the burial mound with a bulldozer. Whether someone taught them to do it, or it was an accident, we don't know yet. We do have the interment inventory. True, there's talk of another lateral chamber perhaps being there. The experts are coming in today or tomorrow and it'll be finally cleared up. The cashier will be bringing you your money and belongings shortly. Take them and go home. Everything's in order there. Here's the key. I'd advise you to lie down and not go anywhere else, have a rest."

He emerged from behind the desk and walked over to Zybin.

"Well, goodbye, Georgi Nikolaevich," he said, in good-natured fashion, almost friendly. "We led one another a dance, eh?"

"Well, speaking for myself . . ." Zybin began stiffly, "I . . ."

"All right, all right," smiled Gulyaev. "Don't start a quarrel, and don't be too hard on Neiman either, he did bring all this in to us. He arrested those treasure-hunters as well, and took them into the Ili police station at gunpoint. If it wasn't for him, we'd still be floundering about in the dark."

"But how could that be?" Zybin marvelled, his voice fairly trembling. "Why, in that case . . ."

"Never mind, later, later . . ."

An hour later he emerged from the low, narrow, metal doors and walked along the street. It was absolutely deserted, but the whole of this side of it was occupied by the Big House, with its hundreds of windows and curtains. Behind every curtain, of course, there were people. He walked slowly, without looking back, past hundreds of hidden eyes. He walked to the end of the street, crossed it, went up through a tiny square, with a monument in a greatcoat, and turned into the park of pines. There was nobody in the park either, just a watchman shuffling along with his broom near the figured wooden gates, sweeping up seeds and sweet papers. The cool silence of the forest lapped about him as soon as he stepped into the avenue. There was a smell of resin and hot sand. In the playground, the wind rocked painted wooden dragon-horses, all daubed and garlanded with red and black apples. In the middle of the playground, someone was snoring in the pavilion. Heavens, how quiet and serene the world was! He sought out a bench some distance away, sat down, leaned back and sensed a thin mosquito-like buzzing in his head. "All I need now is to fall ill," he thought, and all of a sudden, realized how deadly tired he was, and that he might be all his life.

Two little boys in pioneer scarves and carrying catapults, went racing past. They stopped, looked back at him and started whispering. Evidently there was something about him which had attracted their avid boyish curiosity. No one in the world was more observant! But even little boys got on his nerves at that moment.

"Boo!" he said, and made a face.

They snorted and ran off. He sat for a while, smiled a little, frowned a little, then got up and walked on.

And emerged in the middle of the park. He knew this place well. In the evenings a band used to thump away, and there was a wooden stage. Conjurors performed their hocus-pocus there and the pioneer choir sang. People always arranged to meet here. There were fights and dances. But now it was peaceful and deserted. He looked at the soft sand and thought: "Ah, how nice it would be to walk barefoot across the sand and stones and pine needles – wonderful." Suddenly he saw a telephone box in front of him. Good lord, how could he have forgotten! He leapt into the booth, slipped in the coin and dialled Lina's number. He was put through, but the number did not respond. He stood for a while, thinking, yes, he'd chosen an awkward time of day; she'd be at work. He didn't know her work number, so he would have to wait till four o'clock! What could he do till then? Then suddenly there came a piping childish voice "Allo".

"Could you please get Polina Yurevna?" he requested.

"But she's gone away," came the cheerful reply.

"What?" He'd expected anything but that. "When?"

"Two weeks ago, we don't know the address," replied the child in a prepared statement, and rang off. He stood there for another minute, trying to grasp what he ought to do next. Then he quietly replaced the receiver, turned and went out. And saw Neiman standing in front of him. And went forward to meet him.

"Well, my compliments!" he said rather brusquely.

"Good morning, Georgi Nikolaevich," Neiman replied. "Been phoning?"

"As you see."

"She's gone, our Polina Yurevna, gone."

"When?" Zybin clutched his arm.

"Oh, after our second summons she went."

"You mean you questioned her as well?"

"Well of course! She did very well. Spoke very highly of you."

"So then," Zybin sighed noisily. "And what are you doing here? Having a walk round as well?"

"Yes, I was waiting for you."

"And why would that be?"

Zybin was trying to speak calmly, almost smilingly, but inside, all was tremor and turmoil. His spine ached so much that without noticing, he was bent over, as if in pain.

515

"Why?" Neiman repeated pensively. "Yes, why? That's what I'm thinking. I wanted to tell you about Polina Yurevna. Congratulate you on your release. Take you home if necessary, drop into a shop. Did they give you your money?"

"Aha," Zybin inclined his head slightly. "Well, thanks."

Now, when he was standing in front of him, rather than behind a huge, potent desk, ringed with telephones and inkstands, Zybin could see what a poor figure he cut. A miserable sparrow, a small-town Jew, a Chekhov character. Rothschild with a fiddle.

"They told me you'd been arrested, you know," he grinned.

"Really?" Neiman was curious, though not overly so. "Who said that, the prosecutor? Aha! And was Gulyaev present?"

They were walking along the avenue now.

"So what exactly did happen to you?"

He simply couldn't make out what all this signified. What was Neiman doing here? What was this about Lina? Was she here or not? Was she at liberty or not? But what particularly struck him was Neiman's face, his eyes. Now they were humanly and straightforwardly sad. But they held none of that covert terror which Zybin had observed in the first moments of their conversation a month before.

"What happened to me?" Neiman repeated, deliberating. "Well to tell the truth almost nothing. By present-day standards, nothing whatever. I've just been dismissed, no more than that." He paused. "The situation is absurd of course: everybody who worked with me has been pulled in, but in my case they've held back. Why? A mystery. Ah well, I'll go and be an administrator in a film studio. Of course, they can still change their minds a hundred times and take me in. I shouldn't be the least bit surprised." He shot a sudden glance at Zybin and broke into a laugh.

"What's the matter?" Zybin was surprised.

"Oh nothing. I was just recalling what you blurted out to your investigator: you're naked, naked! You've got nothing on you or by you – no profession, no specialist knowledge, just one bit of paper to cover up your shame." He laughed. "Well, we could say that she still has something by her: she is young and beautiful, whereas I really am a naked old Jew-boy! They never even gave me a bit of paper. Just go and wait and see what happens."

"You're getting something mixed up," Zybin scowled. "I never said that to the investigator."

"What do you mean, you didn't say it? She wouldn't have made it up. Well if she did, she's a good girl. She's in Moscow at the moment."

"Oho, you're drunk, man," it suddenly dawned on Zybin. "You've been chucked out on your ear and started hitting the bottle. The usual story with you people!"

"What about the gold?" he asked out loud. "Did you really bring it in or . . . is that another tale, like you being arrested."

Neiman smiled.

"Ah, so Gulyaev did tell you something? No, I really did bring the gold in for them. The shopkeeper gave it to me. Got frightened evidently, or thought I knew all about it already. Well, I went straight to these lads and caught them all nice and cosy. They didn't try to get out of it, they showed me everything straight away and handed it over."

"And so then they released me. It fits, but look, somehow I can't really believe it was because of that. No there was something else involved. Gold is gold of course, but . . ."

"Oh there certainly was something else! The commissar had been nabbed and the whole department was scoured out. Only three of us were left. And they released one or two people."

"Right, right," Zybin nodded. "The cabinet falls, and the monarch shows clemency. Were many let out?"

"Many! What a maximalist you are! Be thankful there were two or three!"

"Good! Like Holy Russia at Annunciation," Zybin smiled sarcastically. "Remember 'Yesterday I opened the dungeon for my airy prisoner'. So then, Annunciation came and they let out Zybin the little arrested bluebird. Terrific!" he looked at Neiman and roared with laughter. "Listen, isn't there somewhere we could go?"

Neiman joined in the laughter.

"Of course, of course there is! Over there, our Markovna's stall. Don't let the stall worry you, there's a special room at the back for decent customers. We were the ones who organized it. Your colleague Kornilov sometimes pops in as well. He might drop in today. I've seen him, wandering round the park."

"And they let him in here?" Zybin marvelled. He had just remembered there was such a man as Kornilov. "What service has he done to deserve that?"

"Well, there must have been services of some sort if they let him in." Neiman looked at him. "But as regards dropping in, that's a good idea. I wanted to suggest it myself, but was afraid you'd tell me where to go . . . No, you don't have to send me anywhere now, I'm – a good boy. Let's go and drink to the Annunciation! Let's drink to justice. Who doesn't want that, eh, Georgi Nikolaevich? I've never seen that man. We all love the truth! All of us! Now I remember . . ." He knocked on the door. "Open up Markovna! Nice visitors have come. Put my special out for us! You know the one! Careful, Georgi Nikolaevich, it's dark in here, crates of bottles; give me your arm. I remember coming across a former student at the college – we'd expelled him for bad attitude and incompetence. He meets me on the street and ve-ery enthusiastically grabs my arm: 'What's up? What's the matter?' 'Victory, Yakov Abramovich Yagoda's been sacked and Nikolay Ivanovich Yezhov is in! Justice has triumphed!' So then, to dear old justice! May it ever triumph! To the little bluebirds! To the Annunciation! Markovna, let's have some champagne and cognac. There's a third guest arriving. He's an Annunciation bird too. Only he was never in the cage: they just caught him and let him go. That can happen in our country as well! To each his own, Georgi Nikolaevich, isn't that so? Well, here's to all of us!"

Two hours later, Zybin left the stall and went straight to the telephone box. It was occupied, however, and he sat down on a bench some distance away. It was still baking hot, but the first evening couples had appeared in the avenue and a drum was thumping roundly somewhere beyond the firs. A patrol of pioneers in scarves marched briskly to the gates and a bugle sounded. The bar had opened.

In the middle of the playground between two dragon-horses stood an artist with an easel. The little boys, old men and drunks had already gathered round, but he ignored them and worked swiftly and urgently. He plucked first one thing then another out of the air and hurled it all onto the cardboard. His face was intent and his brows stern. He was in a great hurry. He was late today and he had to get the thing finished by sundown. And although basically it was completed, he still sensed that something was lacking. Then the artist turned and looked along the avenue.

And saw Zybin.

Zybin was sitting, hunched up on the bench, arms dangling. It was just what was wanted. The dark bent figure against the background of the white shining booth, the blue pine trees and the fading glimmer of yellow sand. The artist remembered that this was somebody from the museum; they had even been introduced once; he shouted out, when Zybin wanted to get up: "Don't move, please! Sit like that for a couple of minutes!" And he did as he was told.

At that moment, two other people came up to him. They started

518

talking and sat down beside him. The artist frowned but painted them in too.

So for ever and ever those three remain on a square of cardboard: the sacked investigator, the drunken informer codenamed "Gadfly" (all epochs need their Gadfly evidently) and that third, without whom the other two could not exist.

The sun was setting. The artist was in a hurry. He wore a flame-coloured beret, striped blue trousers and a green mantilla with ribbons. A tambourine hung at his side, embroidered with smoke and flame. He dressed like that to please himself, for other people and for the universe, Mars, Mercury, for he was indeed "Genius of the first rank, Earth and Galaxy, stage designer and performer at the Abai ballet, Sergey Ivano-vich Kalmykov", as he called himself.

And the sage Martians observing us through their super-powerful instruments, were amazed and at a loss to understand how such a unique gaudy miracle had flared up amid the uniformly grey and monochrome human plasma. Only the most learned among them knew that the name of this miracle was imagination. And that it blossoms with a particular intensity when the earth, on its planetary path, enters the black obscuring areas of the crab or the scorpion, and existence within the cloud of these poisonous radiations becomes absolutely intolerable.

This whole grim tale took place in the summer of the fifty-eighth year of Josif Vissarionovich Stalin, the Leader of the peoples, and from the birth of Christ, one thousand nine hundred and thirty-seven, that hot, evil year, pregnant with a fearful future.

10 December 1964–5 March 1975
Moscow

TRANSLATOR'S AFTERWORD

A striking feature of *The Faculty of Useless Knowledge* is a preoccupation with historical time. Apart from the poignant use of flashback, events and personalities are constantly illuminated by reference to history. This serves both to underline and to universalize the novel's fundamental moral stance.

The gold diadem, for example, whose loss is an important element of the plot, and which, for Zybin and Kornilov, represents both beauty and a key to the past, is seen by the authorities purely in terms of monetary value. Throughout the novel's subtle and complex narrative, it is this reductive philistine doctrine of material expediency which is constantly deployed against the "useless knowledge" of the title, the humane values and disinterested scholarship which Zybin upholds with savage tenacity and mordant wit.

Very occasionally, Dombrovsky also slips into the "present" i.e. the novel's future, as in Zybin's remarks on the painter Kalmykov, for example, or his bitter references to the eventual fate of his persecutors. The very last sentence of the book points to a future which is known to the author, but not the characters.

Nevertheless, *The Faculty of Useless Knowledge* is not an historical document, concerned to establish chapter and verse in the name of truth. It is an artistic re-ordering of life enabling even the grimmest experience to be transmuted into a richly textured work of literature. A great deal in this regard depends on the character of Zybin, through whom Dombrovsky speaks, but even here all is not as it seems. It is the traitor, Kornilov, who is given Dombrovsky's own physical appearance.

Dombrovsky does not, as a rule, use his characters as historical pegs on which to hang a thesis. They are all humanly unpredictable. Prosecutors and interrogators like Myachin and Gulyaev have a pleasant line in banter, small endearing vanities and interpersonal rivalry; the formidable Shtern contrives to enlist our understanding, if not sympathy, in the tour-de-force chapter where he opens his heart to Neiman, revealing the fierce dissatisfactions that gnaw at him. Neiman himself becomes almost sympathetic as we are made aware of his childhood, and particularly towards the end of the novel, as his status declines towards desperation.

The author, however, is ironically aware of the problems this poses for historians, who may be disinclined to read the book solely as a human document. Writing elsewhere, he says that for their benefit he has allowed characters like Buddo, Khripushin and Smotryaev to keep their real names. Some historical figures certainly appear as themselves, or are very faintly disguised. The well-known interrogator and popular writer, Lev Sheinin, is embodied in the gruesome Shtern, while Stalin, who, for Dombrovsky, personifies the effectively lawless state of Russian society in 1937, is a memorable portrait. Oblique references to him and his henchman Yezhov are scattered throughout the novel. Happily, we know also that Dombrovsky eventually married Clara Fazulaevna, who is at the time of writing, still living in Moscow.

Dombrovsky was born in 1909, the son of a lawyer. He fell foul of the authorities as early as 1932, for his part in the student suicide case described in the novel. In that episode he had upheld the independence of the legal process, a theme of great importance in *Faculty*. He was not just released, however, as is stated in the novel; he was exiled to Alma-Ata in Kazakhstan, on the Chinese border. While establishing himself as a teacher there, momentous events were taking place in European Russia, some implications of which are described in *The Keeper of Antiquities*, Dombrovsky's first novel set in Alma-Ata.

Sergey Kirov, who is believed to have led the opposition within the Central Committee to Stalin's personal rule after the 17th party congress, was assassinated in puzzling circumstances in December 1934. This began Stalin's wave of terror which developed into the great purge of 1936–38. (In Dombrovsky's novel, the stool pigeon Buddo has supposedly been re-arrested for taking the wrong line in the Kirov affair.)

The Soviet security organs under their various names, originally the Cheka, and at this period the NKVD, had never been inactive since the Revolution in 1917. There had been the "Shakhty" trial in 1928, and a show trial in 1930 of the so-called Industrial Party, led by Professor Ramzin (mentioned in the novel). Kirov's death, however, was used by Stalin as an excuse to deal with all oppositionists. By 1936, this had broadened into a programme of almost arbitrary arrest. Numerous holders of high political office, including many of Stalin's old comrades, were accused of sabotage, espionage and so on, the sole proof of their guilt being confessions extracted by threats or ill-treatment. A number of show trials were arranged for the most prominent prisoners like Bukharin, Pyatakov and Zinoviev, but the rest, numbered in millions, perished obscurely, either shot or deported to labour camps for long, renewable terms. Dombrovsky states in the novel that it is only Neiman's insistence on trying to arrange an elaborate "confessional" show trial of his own in Alma-Ata which enables Zybin to survive long enough to be released.

Dombrovsky, meanwhile, had been working as a teacher in Alma-Ata, and his articles on literary criticism began to appear in *Kazakhstan Pravda* in 1937. It was in that year that he was arrested for the second time. He was under investigation for a mere seven months at the height of the "Yezhovschina" – a miracle indeed. The final words of *Faculty*, however, seem to run counter to the generally expressed view that 1937 marked the height of the Terror. Dombrovsky himself said later that he had been lucky in being arrested during the partial hiatus marking the end of Yezhov as the head of the NKVD and the beginning of Beria's tenure of office. Nevertheless, the words in the novel are quite deliberate and poignantly prophetic.

Between 1938 and 1939, Dombrovsky was working at the Lycée in Alma-Ata, and in 1938 his first novel *Derzhavin* appeared. He was accepted into the USSR Writers' Union in 1939, but in that year he was again arrested, and this time sent to the Kolyma camps in north-east Siberia, of which we are given brief but chilling glimpses in *The Faculty of Useless Knowledge*.

Dombrovsky served a reduced sentence, owing to ill health and paralysis of the legs. He was in effect dumped out of the camps in 1943 like ballast, as Clara Fazulaevna remarks elsewhere. Between 1943 and 1949, Dombrovsky lived in Alma-Ata, teaching foreign literature. There he wrote *The Monkey Comes for His Skull* and *The Dark Lady*.

In 1949 he was again arrested, this time in connection with the campaign against foreign influences and cosmopolitanism. He received a ten-year sentence to be served in the Siberian areas of Taishet and Osetrovo. We are no doubt right to see some of this grim post-1939 experience reflected in the narratives of Father Andrey and Kalandarashvili. Dombrovsky was released in 1955, and in 1956 fully rehabilitated on all counts.

Until his death in 1978, Dombrovsky lived with Clara in Moscow, with periodic visits to Alma-Ata. Though this last period saw his works published in the USSR and translated abroad, it was a slow and frustrating business. Not one of Dombrovsky's books was re-issued in the USSR in his lifetime. *The Faculty of Useless Knowledge*, begun in the 1960s, took eleven years to write; happily Dombrovsky had the satisfaction of seeing it in book form before he died.

Dombrovsky's novel mirrors not only the periods of savage hardship he endured, but also the inconceivable nervous tension and insecurity that existed at all levels of Soviet society under Stalinism. This sense of fundamental dislocation is subtly underlined in the novel by the fact that all the main characters are displaced, in that they are doing jobs they did not originally choose for themselves. As Dombrovsky points out, the public face of the USSR in the '30s was one of music, dancing and open-air merrymaking. Nevertheless, people go missing amid the genteel small talk at film shows, and Dombrovsky makes telling use of the heart-wrenching contrast between the interrogation rooms and the childrens' park outside. Dainty secretaries gossip and work their office hours as they copy out death warrants. This domestication of horror is, if anything, more chilling than the explicit recital of atrocities.

Since Zybin's preoccupation is with humane secular behaviour, symbolized in its public form by the rule of law, it is curious to reflect that though Dombrovsky draws on a range of literary sources, including the Bible, Russian folk tales, Tacitus, Goethe and Anatole France to illustrate his theses and sanction his prophecies, he does not quote from the most revered of Russian writers, Pushkin. In his popular prose tale "The Captain's Daughter", the young hero is horrified at seeing the results of torture carried out long before, and is grateful to be living in a milder age:

> In the old days . . . it was thought that the accused's own confession was essential for the full exposure of his guilt, an idea not only without foundation but positively against common juridical sense: for if a denial by the accused is not acceptable as proof of innocence, his confession is even less a proof of guilt.

A. G. MYERS, May 1995

NOTES

Page

46 *Matryoshki*: The Russian wooden dolls which contain dolls of diminishing size.

47 *How the Steel Was Tempered* (1932–34): A celebrated Soviet novel by Nikolay Ostrovsky (1904–36), which sold more than 5 million copies in the USSR. The novel features an idealized communist hero, Pavel Korchagin, partly based on the author's own career.

50 *Chapaev, Vasily Ivanovich* (1887–1919): A Red Army hero in the civil war. His fame rests on the 1923 book about him written by his political commissar D. Furmanov and the eponymous film of 1934.

57 *Grin, Aleksandr Stepanovich* (pseud. Grinevsky) (1880–1932): A Romantic storyteller and novelist whose books include *Scarlet Sails* (1923) and *The Road to Nowhere* (1930).

65 *Browning pistol*: A well-known weapon named after John M. Browning (1855–1926) the American firearm designer, which for Russians had an almost mythical reputation for accuracy and ruthlessness approximately comparable to that of the Luger for the British and Americans in the Second World War. Less usual than the Russian Nagant (qv p. 501).

71 *Chernomor*: The evil sorcerer who abducts Ludmila at the wedding feast in Pushkin's poem *Ruslan and Ludmila*.

78 *Khabarov*: A seventeenth-century explorer of Siberia and the River Amur in 1649–53. Khabarovsk, on the Amur, is named after him.

78 *Kutuzov, Mikhail Ilarionovich* (1745–1813): Commander of the Russian forces in the war against Napoleon, 1812–13.

78 *Suvorov, Alexander Vasilievich* (1730–1800): Regarded as Russia's greatest soldier. Defeated the French in Italy in 1798 and extricated his army from Switzerland in one of the most daring feats in military history.

85 *"I have studied the science of parting..."*: the first line of Mandelstam's poem, "Tristia".

85 *Derzhavin, Gavrila Romanovich* (1743–1816): A controversial statesman and soldier, who was the greatest poet of Catherine the Great's reign and the subject of Dombrovsky's first novel.

94 *Kuteikin*: A character in a Pushkin epigram, probably addressed to his persecutor, the journalist Faddei Bulgarin. The implication is "petty wheeling and dealing, small-scale cunning".

Page
95 *Grumble-Rumble*: Apparently a character in the satires of Saltykov-Schedrin (1826–89).

95 *Thiers, Louis Adolphe* (1797–1877): A French statesman and historian who, after the Franco-Prussian War, suppressed the Paris Commune and became President of the Third Republic (1871–75).

100 *Zenkov, Andrey Pavlovich*: The architect who designed many of Alma Ata's buildings. Dombrovsky writes of him at length in the first chapter of *The Keeper of Antiquities*.

101 *The hut on chickens' legs*: The residence of the witch, Baba-Yaga in Russian fairy tales.

101 *Koschei's hoard*: Koschei was an evil being in Russian folklore.

112 *Kozma Prutkov*: A fictitious writer of the mid-nineteenth century (the creation of two talented poets) whose comically pompous sayings became part of the Russian language, and whose satirical verses and plays attacked the bureaucratic and mundane aspects of Russian life.

112 *Dzerzhinsky, Felix Edmundovich* (1877–1926): The first head of the Cheka.

116 *Saksaul*: Steppe vegetation used as fuel in central Asia.

116 *Kirov, Sergey Mironovich* (1886–1934): See Translator's Afterword, p. 591.

116 *Nikolaev*: Kirov's assassin.

116 *OGPU*: Cheka (until 1922), GPU (1922–23), OGPU (1923–34), NKVD (1934–43), NKGB (1943–46), MGB (1946–53) and KGB (1953–91) are the names by which the Soviet security organs were successively known.

117 *Smolny*: A famous girls' educational establishment in Petersburg before the revolution. Subsequently the headquarters of Lenin during the revolution and of the Leningrad party organization after it.

119 *Ramzin, Leonid Konstantinovich* (1887–1948): A prominent engineer. The chief defendant at the trial in 1930, where he confessed to having led the so-called Industrial Party, a group of technocratically minded engineers. His death sentence was commuted to ten years, but he was amnestied a few years after his sentence and repentance. During his imprisonment, he was allowed to act as a consultant and to go on with his design work on a new water-tube boiler. He won a Stalin prize in 1943 and held high academic appointments.

119 *Boyarschinov*: Having repented and reformed after being sentenced at the Shakhty Trial (see Translator's Afterword) Boyarschinov was murdered. This killing was brought up at the Piatakov trial in January 1937, when the conspirators were alleged to have disposed of Boyarschinov because he had been about to expose their activities.

119 *Yezhov, Nikolay Ivanovich* (1895–1939?): Head of the NKVD 1936–38, when the great Stalinist purge was at its height. He was then made a scapegoat for its "excesses", and succeeded by Beria in 1938. He was probably shot in 1939.

119 *Vyshinsky, Andrey Yanuarievich* (1883–1954): Appointed Prosecutor General in 1935 and thus was the chief accuser of the Old Bolsheviks during the Moscow show trials. He replaced Molotov as Foreign Minister in 1949.

124 *Resurrection*: A novel by Tolstoy.

125 *Young Guard*: The journal *Molodaya gvardiya*.

125 *OGIZ*: The State Publishing House; later this became GIZ.

129 *GPU*: See note 116.

130 *Balmont, Konstantin Dmitrievich* (1867–1943): A poet whose opulent sound effects made him hugely popular at the turn of the century. He emigrated after the revolution and died in Paris.

131 *Belikov*: The comic schoolmaster in Chekhov's story "The Man in the Case".

131 *Peredonov*: The paranoid schoolmaster in F. Sologub's story "Petty Demon".

131 *Pavlik (Pavel Trofimovich) Morozov* (1918–32): A member of the Young Pioneer organization murdered by his relatives because he betrayed his parents to the authorities for assisting banished kulaks during the forced collectivization period. He was held up as an example by official propaganda.

131 *Du armes Kind . . .*: Poor child, what have they done to you?

141 *Crocodile*: A satirical magazine.

154 *Thälmann, Ernst*: The Communist candidate for the Germany presidency in 1932. He was later sent to a concentration camp by Hitler and was probably executed in Buchenwald in 1944.

Page

154 *Kamenev, Zinoviev and Rykov*: Prominent Bolsheviks, eliminated as oppositionists by Stalin during the great purges.

172 *Lieutenant Kizhe*: The eponymous hero of a novella by Yury Tynyanov who, by a slip of bureaucratic pen, ceases to have an official existence.

185 *Muzhik*: Russian peasant (male).

192 *Karakozov, Dmitry Vladimirovich* (1840–66): An ex-student who made an attempt on Tsar Alexander II's life in 1866.

196 *Fadeev (Bulyga), Alexander Alexandrovich* (1901–56): A novelist and secretary of the Union of Soviet Writers 1946–53. He committed suicide in 1956.

202 *OSOVIAKHIM*: A voluntary civil defence association which had 12 million members by 1939.

206 *Stankevich, Nikolay Vladimirovich* (1813–40): An extremely influential philosopher who dominated the rising generation of the 1830s.

206 *Khomyakov, Alexey Stepanovich* (1804–60): A poet, philosopher and theologian. One of the leaders of the Slavophiles.

215 *Bestuzhev Institute*: A celebrated centre of women's education in Tsarist Russia.

215 *Severyanin (Lotarev), Igor Vasilievich* (1887–1941): A poet, noted for flamboyance and verbal extravagance. Leader of the Ego-Futurists.

215 *Böcklin, Arnold* (1827–1901): A Swiss artist famous for his painting, *The Island of the Dead*.

215 *Brehme, Alfred Edmund* (1829–84): A much-travelled German naturalist. His great work is the *Illustriertes Thierleben*, on which many other natural histories have been based.

215 *Yesenin, Sergey Alexandrovich* (1895–1925): Leading Russian poet of the early 20th century and probably the most widely read. He committed suicide in 1925.

215 *Antokolsky, Pavel* (1896–1978): A highly regarded Russian poet.

Page

229 *Yagoda, Genrikh Grigorievich* (1891–1938): Head of the NKVD from 1934. Dismissed and succeeded by Yezhov in 1936. Arrested and executed together with Bukharin and others in 1937.

231 *ROSTA*: An early revolutionary telegraph agency (a forerunner of TASS), which issued news bulletins.

231 *Wrangel, Pyotr Nikolaevich* (1878–1928): Leader of the anti-Bolshevik forces in the South in 1920. He evacuated his forces from Sevastopol in that year, and thereafter lived in Belgium.

253 *"Sow what is great and good"*: A misquotation from the nineteenth-century poet Nekrasov's "To the Sowers" (1876).

266 *Katyusha Maslova*: A character in Tolstoy's novel *Resurrection*.

266 *Dmitri Karamazov*: From Dostoevsky's great novel *The Karamazov Brothers*. Dmitri is condemned for the murder of his father and though he did not actually commit the crime, he had desired it, and accepts his punishment as the path to salvation.

268 *The Tur Brothers or Sheinin's Confrontation*: Lev Romanovich Sheinin (1906–1967) was a Soviet prosecutor and investigator, as well as a successful writer, turning to spy fiction after 1950. Dombrovsky bases the character of Lev Romanovich Shtern on Sheinin. The brothers Tur were also active in the same genre, showing the authorities in a favourable light, being vigilant, unmasking spies and the like. They collaborated with Sheinin, and this play, *Confrontation*, was put on in 1937.

268 *Izvestiya* (lit. News): Leading Russian newspaper.

272 *The farm Gazik*: Ubiquitous small lorry produced by the Gorky Motor Vehicle Works.

276 *Fatherland Notes*: The nineteenth-century journal, *Otechestvennyye zapiski*.

276 *Chernyshevsky, Nikolay Gavrilovich* (1828–79): A radical journalist and novelist, author of the famous novel *What is to Be Done?* (1863).

276 *Olga Socratovna*: Wife of Nikolay Gavrilovich Chernyshevsky.

276 *Berthold Schwartz*: A semi-legendary German monk, who was supposed to have brought gunpowder into general use in the fourteenth century.

286 *The Social Wars*: Fought between 90–88 BC over the issue of extending the Roman franchise to all Italians.

Page

326 *Sogdian motifs*: Sogd or Sogdiana is the ancient name of the region in Central Asia whose chief centre is Samarkand in Uzbekistan. It was one of the earliest centres of civilization in Central Asia.

329 *Beria, Lavrenti Pavlovich* (1899–1953): Became close associate of Stalin in 1938 when he succeeded Yezhov as head of the security organs.

330 *Bolshevik*: A Communist Party journal.

330 *Molotov (Scriabin), Viacheslav Mikhailovich* (1890–1986): Soviet Foreign Minister 1939–56. He was staunchly loyal to Stalin and had a reputation for obduracy abroad. He was removed from power by Khruschev in 1957.

331 *Ordzhonikidze, Sergo*: Old Bolshevik, a Georgian and close comrade of Stalin, whom he came to oppose over the purges. It was given out that he had died of a heart attack early in 1937, but in fact he committed suicide, it is thought at Stalin's instigation.

331 *Kaganovich, Lazar*: A loyal supporter of Stalin throughout his career, he survived the 1930s and lived to a ripe old age.

331 *Mikoyan, Anastas* (1895–1978): Armenian Communist who survived the 1930s purges of the Politburo and was deputy prime minister after 1937. After Stalin's death, he was a consistent supporter of Khruschev and enjoyed great influence.

331 *Yenukidze, Abel*: A prominent member of Stalin's entourage. Shot in 1937.

333 *Zk*: Abbreviation of *Zaklyuchonny*, meaning prisoner. Zek is a phonetic rendition of this abbreviation.

333 *Lunacharsky, Anatoli Vasilievich* (1873–1933): A literary critic and politician. From 1917–29 he was Peoples' Commissar for Education, in which field he supported progressive experiments. He also presided over the relatively liberal and non-interventionist policies pursued by the party with regard to literature at this period.

335 *one higher*: i.e. Stalin.

337 *Aivazovsky*: Popular Russian artist at the turn of the century, noted for his marine paintings.

362 *One for the stake . . .*: referring to the three stages of throat sensation when drinking vodka.

Page

364 *Novels like* Sanin, The Pit *and* The Notes of Wanda Sacher-Masoch: *Sanin* (1907) was written by Mikhail Petrovich Artsybashev (1878–1927) and, dealt with sex and free love, topics much in the air at the time. *The Pit* (1909–15) was a notorious journalistic study of life in an Odessa brothel by Alexander Ivanovich Kuprin (1870–1938), a considerable writer.

365 *Nick Carter and Nat Pinkerton*: American private eye novels had a wide readership in the early Soviet period and there was even a move, notably by Marietta Shaginyan, to imitate Anglo-American products, and initiate a "red detective" genre.

369 *Baba-Yaga*: The witch in Russian fairy tales (see note to p. 101).

370 *Fedin, Konstantin Aleksandrovich* (1892–1977): Initially a member of the Serapion Brethren, a leading Fellow-Traveller and novelist whose books include *Cities and Years* (1924). He was later a veteran Soviet Secretary General of the Union of Soviet Writers (1959–71).

372 *Bunin, Ivan Alexeevich* (1870–1953): A distinguished writer in the Russian realist tradition. He emigrated to Paris in 1920 and was awarded the Nobel Prize in 1933.

377 *Papanin, Ivan Dmitrievich*: A much publicized polar explorer of the time.

378 *Nikolay Ivanovich*: Nikolay Ivanovich Bukharin (1888–1938), next to Stalin and Trotsky, was the most prominent Bolshevik of the '20s and '30s. He was expelled from the Party and arrested in 1937. He was the principal figure in the last great Moscow show trial in 1938, at which he was sentenced to be shot.

386 *Vanka-vstankas*: Self-righting "knock-me-down" doll, literally "Johnny, stand up now!".

394 *Tukhachevsky, Mikhail Nikolaevich* (1893–1937): The Commander-in-Chief of the Red Army, who was executed – along with many other military leaders – on trumped-up charges in Stalin's 1937 purge of the army.

394 *Speransky, Mikhail Mikhailovich* (1772–1839): A progressive minister under Tsar Alexander I. He proposed reforms in the state legislative and administrative system. Between 1826 and 1833, he codified the existing Russian laws.

394 *Mayakovsky, Vladimir Vladimirovich* (1895–1930): An important futurist poet before 1917 and the most prominent revolutionary poet afterwards. He committed suicide in 1930.

Page

394 *Razin, Stenka (Stepan)* (d. 1671): Don Cossack who led a revolt in 1670 and had great success in the Volga region. He was broken on the wheel in Moscow, but remains a popular figure in Russian folk tales.

395 *Saltykov-Schedrin, Mikhail Yevgrafovich* (1826–89): A leading Russian nineteenth-century satirist. He was co-editor with Nekrasov of the journal *Fatherland Notes* until it was suppressed in 1884.

396 *Groats*: The hulled and crushed edible grains of oats, and occasionally other cereals. Similar to American hominy grits made from maize.

401 *Archpriest Avvakum* (c. 1621–82): A leader of the Old Believer religious sect, distinguished for his zeal and strictness. He was exiled in 1653 to Siberia and was later defrocked and imprisoned. He wrote of his life of suffering, and produced other powerful inspirational works from his underground cell. He was eventually burned at the stake.

413 *GITIS*: State Institute of Dramatic Art.

422 *"Ladies Fingers"*: A type of white grape grown in Georgia.

430 *Kumiss*: Fermented mare's milk.

443 *Zaslavsky, David Iosifovich* (1880–1965): A journalist and a notorious apologist for Stalinism, who made a vicious attack on Mandelstam (for alleged plagiarism) in 1928 and another on Pasternak after the award of the Nobel Prize in 1958.

443 *Koltsov, Mikhail Yefimovich* (1898–1942): A Soviet journalist and editor of *Pravda*, famous for his reportage from Spain during the Civil War. He was arrested in 1938 and presumed dead in the camps.

447 *Glavlit*: Chief Department for Literary Affairs. This was a body set up to direct and co-ordinate censorship.

450 *VTsIK*: All-Union Central Executive Committee (of the RSFSR).

452 *Levitan, Isaak Ilich* (1860–1900): A landscape painter famous for his lyrically expressive paintings of central Russia.

460 *Zoshchenko, Mikhail Mikhailovich* (1895–1958): A popular satirical writer and member of the Serapian Brethren, who with Akhmatova was attacked in 1946 for his "vulgar parody" of Soviet life and expelled from the Writers' Union.

532

Page

471 *Moscow Garments*: A well-known Moscow enterprise producing ready-made clothing (this is a reference to a line of Mandelstam).

489 *Voroshilov Marksman*: A sniper's badge, named after Marshal Voroshilov (1881–1969), friend of Stalin and responsible for Soviet defence 1925–40.

491 *Personal salary and ration book*: In the early days of the USSR, pay and ration scales were linked to one's job; these secretaries were privileged and enjoyed a personal salary and ration outside the system.

491 *Interlinears*: Literal translations of poems, line by line, for use by more accomplished translators as the basis of their version.

501 *Nagant*: A make of revolver generally used by revolutionaries and government officials in the early Soviet period. The name comes from the Nagant arms firm in Belgium.

505 *George Borman*: A well-known confectionary firm with branches in Petersburg, Moscow, Kharkov and the Nizhni-Novgorod Fair. Suppliers to the Imperial Court.

509 *Grillparzer, Franz* (1791–1872): Austrian dramatic poet. As well as plays like *Sappho* and *Medea*, he wrote lyric poetry and the fine novel *Der arme Spielmann*.